The Search for Claire Holowitz

A story of friendship, love, and having the courage to risk loving again ...

BY HELEN HANSEN
for Sarah Patricia Hansen

Copyright © Helen Hansen All rights reserved.

No part of this publication may be reproduced or transmitted in any form or by any means, including photography, recording, or any information storage or retrieval system, without the permission of the author. The book is sold subject to the condition that it shall not, by way of trade or otherwise, be lent, resold or otherwise circulated without the author's prior consent in any form of binding or cover other than that in which is published and without a similar condition, including this condition, being imposed on the subsequent purchaser.

This is a work of fiction. Names, characters, and incidents are products of the author's imagination or are used fictitiously. Any resemblance to actual events or person(s) living or dead is purely and entirely coincidental. The author accepts no responsibility for inferences made.

ISBN-10: 1480119660
EAN-13: 9781480119666

To Catherine Dunne and Carmen Wood. Without the two of you, I never would have taken the chance.

To my sister Linda Buschmann for all the times you've listened to my stories and told me not to quit ... thank you.

To my sisters Joan Augustino and Marion Grobb Finkelstein ... thank you for your support.

For Allina,
Hope you enjoy the novel & recommend it to your friends. Trust me when I say, Carmen's editing skills helped very much to make this story possible!
All the best,
HP (Helen Hanson)

Acknowledgements

The *Search for Claire Holowitz* has taken a long time to write but finally is ready for print. It is the first of seven novels, yet to be published.

None of my novels would have come to completion without the mentorship of Catherine Dunne and the careful editing of Carmen Wood and Cathie Carriveau.

I owe much to the patience, encouragement and kindness of friends. If by some act of omission, I have not listed a name of someone who has helped me along the way, it is not intentional and I promise to make up for that in future novels.

Huge thanks to Marian McCaffrey for introducing me to Irish novelist, Catherine Dunne. Catherine reached across the Atlantic to a complete stranger and helped me learn to write ... and to once again, hope.

Much appreciation to Anne Marie Cicalo, Tammy Dupuis, Dr. Joanne Lafrenière, James Jeffcott, Pat and Neil Card, Dr. S. Nagpal, Dr. C. Skinner, Lorraine Cantlie, Kate and Rick Seniuk, Tamara Kygier-Baum, Ann Louise Revells, Julie Prak, and Mia Overduin.

To Margaret Wood for being one of the first to read early drafts of this and subsequent novels and to John Wood.

To Fergus Murray, my friend.

I also wish to mention the support and inspiration given by Irish authors Ivy Bannister, Celia de Fréine, Lia Mills, and Rosemary Callaghan.

Gratitude to Sue Raybould and Trevor Stewart.

Author's Note

The Search for Claire Holowitz is my debut novel. The idea for the story came as most ideas do, from a series of events that crystallized into a story. Friendship has been a mainstay in my life and has helped me get through some very difficult life moments. I wanted to pay tribute to the importance of friendship.

I hope you will enjoy *The Search for Claire Holowitz*, as much as I have in writing it.

Soon to be published
by Helen Hansen are:

Prophesy of the Six Trilogy:

Origin of the New Dawn (Book One) Winter, 2012-2013
The Dark Side of the Son (Book Two) Spring, 2013
Echoes of the Moon (Book Three) Fantasy/Paranormal Fall, 2013
Stroke of Luck, Memoire
Jeremy's Ring (Romance)
Invisible Burka (Literary Fiction)

Table of Contents

Prologue xv

Chapter One   Sixteen months earlier 1

Chapter Two 19

Chapter Three 27

Chapter Four 45

Chapter Five 59

Chapter Six 77

Chapter Seven 83

Chapter Eight 99

Chapter Nine 113

Chapter Ten 125

Chapter Eleven 137

Chapter Twelve. 151

Chapter Thirteen 177

Chapter Fourteen 197

Chapter Fifteen. 207

Chapter Sixteen 237

Chapter Seventeen 245

Chapter Eighteen 259

Chapter Nineteen 265

Chapter Twenty 279

Chapter Twenty-one 285

Chapter Twenty-two. 293

Chapter Twenty-three. 303

Chapter Twenty-four 323

Chapter Twenty-five. 335

Chapter Twenty-six 351

Chapter Twenty-seven 359

Chapter Twenty-eight. 369

Chapter Twenty-nine 375

Chapter Thirty 387

Chapter Thirty-one 391

Chapter Thirty-two 401

Chapter Thirty-three 411

Chapter Thirty-four 427

Chapter Thirty-five 435

Chapter Thirty-six 449

Chapter Thirty-seven 463

Chapter Thirty-eight 487

Chapter Thirty-nine 495

Epilogue 497

Afterword 499

Prologue

In life Claire Holowitz had been a relaxed Catholic.

In death, she honoured her grandmother's Hebrew faith by stipulating in her will that her tombstone be unveiled one year after her burial.

Today, I understand Claire's choice.

There is wisdom to waiting for one year after death before unveiling a tombstone. In as much as Claire's funeral had been marked by sorrow, the unveiling of her tombstone symbolizes a celebration of life.

Today is what Claire would have called a 'perfect day'. The sky is crystal blue. The trees are vibrant with spring colours and the sun is warm. The air is what Claire called 'spring crisp'; cool enough to warrant a jacket or coat but warm enough to anticipate the first whispers of a summer breeze on our faces."

Ah Claire… what must you be thinking of us today? You believed so much in the 'legacy of life beyond death'. I truly hope you know that you were and are loved. We are all here; Becky, Sarah, Amy and me. When I look back on the past sixteen months I realize how much you changed my life. There will always be a part of you with me. I am a stronger, better, wiser person because of you. Who would have thought that what began as my search for you – the public Claire, celebrated author and recluse – would change my life?

Chapter One

Sixteen months earlier

Leen

    Casting a fleeting glance in the hallway mirror I grab my car keys, hurry to lock my condo door, and rush down the hallway to the elevator. I poke the garage level button and, caring not in the least for the stares my dark mood generates from the elevator's other occupants, check my watch and mentally rail at my boss, Don Harris, *Just couldn't leave me alone for one day, could you?* A day off to spend with my three best friends is a rare luxury. Until his damned phone call I'd been in an excellent mood.
    Amy is a Professor, Sarah a successful lawyer, Becky a psychiatrist, and I'm an executive in the corporate world of media and advertising.
    I've never been married nor have I particularly wanted to marry. Early on in my career I learned that while most men think nothing of it when their careers demand frequent absences from home and long hours, they balk when the shoe is on the female foot. Sarah insists that somewhere out there, there is a man who will not be intimidated by my passion for my career. I don't think such a man exists, but Sarah is an eternal optimist. She and Joe will celebrate their twenty-fifth anniversary next year. Both Amy and Becky have been divorced but unlike me,

they don't necessarily view the concept of wedded bliss with a jaundiced eye; just a cautious one.

As soon as the elevator doors open, I sprint for my BMW. Henry, the security officer, calls out, "Ms MacLeen, you'll have to use Elgin Street this morning. The City Works department is working on your usual exit."

Gripping the car door handle, I suppress my annoyance at the news of the detour. "Thanks Henry. Best be on my way."

⸙

Amy

Tired, hot, sweaty, and frustrated, I crouch to slit open another box. The raspy voice of a heavy smoker interrupts my unpacking. Leonard, sweat-smudged t-shirt stretching across a protruding gut, is leaning against the doorframe with a surly expression. Rising, I wipe my brow and mentally dub him, *Buddha Belly*.

"Where do you want the couch?"

"Let's take a look, shall we?" Grudgingly, he follows me to the living room where ignoring his sour mood, I point to where sunlight filters in through the floor to ceiling windows. "How about against that wall?"

Rubbing the stubble on his chin, Buddha Belly grunts, "It's your call".

From the front door I watch as he and his partner strain to lift the couch. Unlike Leonard, Steve's flat stomach and well-toned biceps are glowing advertisements for the benefits of regular workouts. Observing beads of sweat on their faces as they inch their way to the living room, I impulsively ask, "Want some lemonade?"

Wiping his brow with his forearm, Steve answers, "That would be very welcome, Ma'am."

Buddha Belly grunts, "Where do you want the chairs?"

Shrugging, I think, *Damned if I know!* But I answer, "For now, just place them anywhere. After our lemonade, I'll decide where to place the furniture." Ignoring Buddha Belly's exasperated expression, I joke, "Indecision seems to be my strong suit today."

"No problem," replies Steve, with his charming boyish smile. "My mother rearranges furniture with every season. It drives my Dad nuts."

"It's your dime ..." huffs Buddha Belly. "We're paid by the hour."

Biting back the sarcastic comment that flashes in my mind, I reply drily, "Yes, indeed you are." Fixing him with my *get real* stare, I add, "If you prefer not to have lemonade, don't feel obliged to take a break."

Steve quickly interjects, "Lemonade will be great." Leonard stalks outside to collect the lamps and chairs earmarked for the living room, but Steve hesitates for a second. "Leonard's not a bad guy. He's just got a lot on his plate these days."

"I'll take your word for it," I answer. He can't be over twenty-five and yet, he has compassion for Leonard who has the personality of a surly bear. I smile. "So, should I bring a glass for him?"

Steve's face breaks into a wide grin. "That'd be great. Like I said, he's just dealing with stuff."

"Aren't we all," I reply, but say it so that Steve knows that I have no hard feelings over Leonard's dour manner.

Back in the kitchen, I congratulate myself again for having had the major appliances installed earlier in the week. Just as I reach into the cupboard for the sugar, a familiar voice laced with undisguised mirth quips, "It's hotter than hell out there! With your doors open, the air conditioning isn't worth spit."

Smiling, I answer, "That's why the AC isn't on."

Sidestepping to avoid the maze of boxes to cross over to my side of the kitchen, Leen replies, "Sorry I'm late. Blame Don. The egocentric twit called just as I was leaving."

Hugging her, I say, "Becky and Sarah are still missing in action but I expect they'll be here soon." Glancing at Leen's khaki shorts and white t-shirt cinched with a stylish brown belt, I groan, "Must you always look like a model for a clothing ad?"

Leen scoffs, "We'll see how much of a poster child I'll be after working in this mess."

"Knowing you, you'll have one or two hairs out of place and I'll still look like something hit by a tornado." Handing over a paring knife, I say, "Use this to open the boxes."

Deflecting my compliment with a roll of her eyes, Leen replies, "You make it sound like this is a *natural* look." Slitting open a taped box, she adds, "It comes with a lot of work. Speaking of work ... why exactly are Becky and Sarah late? I'm usually the one with that distinction."

I pick up a fresh lemon and using it like a pointing finger, I say, "No idea, but I'm sure we'll soon find out."

Crock-pot in hand, she asks, "Where do you want this?"

I point to the cupboards on the far side of the kitchen. "Bottom shelf, middle cupboard. New sandals?"

"Not new ..." answers Leen, opening another box and lifting out a toaster oven, "...picked them up a month ago in California. My old ones had seen better days."

"Looks like we're here in time," Becky cracks, as she and Sarah saunter into the kitchen.

"According to my watch you're late," teases Leen.

"Is that anyway to treat people bringing doughnuts?" counters Sarah. Pulling an injured look she laments theatrically, "And to think, Becky, we made a point of buying Boston Cream *just* for Leen."

"That's what we get for being nice ..." replies Becky, "Leen berating us when in reality we were scouring the city to find fresh doughnuts."

Jerking my thumb in Leen's direction I say, "This one's been humming that chain gang song."

"Be careful." warns Leen, lowering her voice to a stage whisper, "She's a slave driver."

Sarah looks at the stack of lemons waiting to be cut and squeezed. "Lemonade?"

Becky asks, "Where do you want us to start?"

I point to the patio doors. "Start with those boxes over there?"

Handing over two paring knives, I tell Sarah, "Use these to slit open the boxes. I'll finish up here and we can take a quick break. Trust me, every room is stacked."

Leen mutters, "We noticed."

Slitting open a box, Becky says, "Seriously, I'm sorry about being late. I had to take a call from the hospital."

"Yeah, and since she was picking me up," pipes up Sarah, "I was late."

"One of your patients?" asks Leen, pushing back fallen strands of wheat coloured hair.

"Yeah," Becky answers, "a sixteen-year-old who overdosed."

Sarah shakes her head and says, "So young."

Becky frowns. "Never a good age for an overdose. But you're right it's hard to deal with when it's a kid."

"Keep your prescription pad handy," I joke, hoping to lighten the talk. "I might be a candidate for sedation before the day is done."

༄

Amy

"Hey you over there? You seem lost in your own private world." Leen tosses an empty box to the side and walks over to the counter. "What are you thinking about?"

"Do you ever think how much we have changed since university?"

Surprise flickers across Leen's face. "What on earth makes you think of that now?"

"I'm not sure," I reply honestly. "Maybe it's the move, but this morning I unpacked photos that I've not seen in years." Grinning, I add, "The four of us in that apartment we shared while doing our undergraduate degrees, Sarah pregnant with the twins, her wedding, my wedding, Becky's wedding … you and me in California when I went to live with you while doing my PhD. They made me think of how much we've all done together."

"Ah," replies Leen, her grey blue eyes shimmering with curiosity. "Taking a little trip down memory lane are you?"

I don't answer immediately, thinking that perhaps she's right. After obtaining our undergraduate degrees, Leen went to California to complete an MBA; Sarah and I went to Western University where she attended Law School and I earned my Masters' degree in modern literature, and Becky remained in Ottawa to attend U of O for her medical degree. Then, I went to California and stayed with Leen while I completed my PhD. Either by design or fate – perhaps both – we all ended up back in Ottawa.

Shrugging, I say, "We've all seen and done a lot together; covered a lot of territory."

Leen jokes, "And despite the years, look how good you and I still look."

"Hey, what about us?" protests Sarah. "Becky and I *look* good."

"Don't mind her," retorts Leen, winking at me. "She's obviously in need of one of Becky's self-esteem sessions."

Ignoring the jibe, Becky rests a hand on her hip and pointedly stares. "I happen to agree with Sarah. What *about* us?"

"Would you settle for we *all* look good."

Straight-faced, Sarah answers, "I can accept that."

"Always the lawyer," says Becky. "This is not a negotiation. We *do* look good." Posturing like a model, she smiles coyly. "According to Josh I look great."

Immediately interested, Leen demands, "And, how is the master chef? Tell the truth; is he as *good* in bed as he is in the kitchen?"

"Very fine," Becky purrs in a sultry voice. "Yes, indeed, very fine."

"Details, details," prods Sarah.

Making an innocent face, Becky says, "I wouldn't want to distract Amy from getting the lemonade made."

"No seriously …" I interject, smiling at the banter, "who would have thought all those years ago that we'd be standing in the kitchen of my new house unpacking boxes?"

Leen's eyes narrow just a smidgen as she gently squeezes my shoulder. "What's with the trip down memory lane?"

"No real reason. Guess I'm just in a nostalgic mood. Remember California?"

"Lazy beach days, sitting in quiet off-the-road bars sipping cool coronas, munching nachos. Who could forget? Come on Amy, focus on the lemonade."

Returning to my task, I think about how upon receipt of her MBA, Leen took to the media world armed with brains, youthful optimism, and drive. Through a series of campaigns and innate savvy she carved out her success. Clients actively sought her out and with the increase in revenue brought into the business, she attracted the attention of CEO's and corporations. Seemingly endless days increased her profile, bank account, and responsibilities. Business suits replaced the once well-worn casual skirts, jeans, and blouses – every outfit coordinated to compliment her natural curves and accentuate a growing, quiet confidence. By the time I completed my doctorate and accepted a teaching post at our undergraduate Alma Mater, Leen was commanding a staggering salary and had a corner office with a resplendent view.

Adding ice cubes to the pitcher, I say, "Remember how ten months after I returned here to teach you managed to get transferred to Scenes' office here in Ottawa?"

"It wasn't a question of me *managing* anything. It was simply time to come home. I had become so immersed in Spanish and the American way of life I was losing my Canadian identity." Leen grins impishly. "It was easier to deal with linguistic conflicts in my own country than elsewhere."

"Linguistic adeptness has always been one of your strengths."

"Admit it, Leen," interrupts Becky, "you're as comfortable conversing in French or Spanish as you are when ordering in Italian or Mandarin restaurants."

"Languages just come easily to me."

"Come off it, Leen!" scoffs Sarah. "Your repertoire of *creative linguistic expressions* camouflages expletives in various languages."

Taking a theatrical bow, Leen answers, "It's a talent; a linguistic gift from the celestial powers of the universe. What else can I say?" Expression serious, she admits, "Amy's nostalgia has got me thinking. We *have* covered a lot of ground over the years."

"No kidding," I reply. "The photos brought back a lot of memories ... Ice Sculptures, Winterlude, skating on the Rideau Canal, shopping in the By-ward Market, the Tulip Festival, and drinking hot chocolate on a cold winter day."

Leen grimaces. "Do you also remember that while we were skating, dauntingly joining hundreds of others thumbing their noses at winter, we were freezing our hands, feet, and butts off?" Speaking of which," expression puckering into a comic pout she says, "We missed Winterlude skating this year but Beaver Tails are one thing I refuse to give up."

Sarah, Becky and I exchange amused glances. Leen's sweet tooth is legendary and she loves the deep fried, sugarcoated pastries shaped like beaver tails.

"You can pack those things away and never gain an ounce. I, on the other hand," groans Becky patting her waistline, "just have to look at one to gain weight."

Sarah says, "I forget. Why did we miss Winterlude this year?"

"Leen was in Toronto and I was in London for a conference," I answer.

"Jobs have a way of interrupting social events," grins Leen, "but they do pay the bills."

"Of all of us, you're the one with the cosmopolitan career," comments Sarah.

Leen counters, "Look who's talking. Your careers haven't exactly been insular ones. Or was that someone who *looked* like Amy guest lecturing at Oxford and Harvard last year? And how about you Sarah? You're recognized as a leading advocate for abuse victims. And then there's the good doctor who has an interesting career as a psychiatrist and who has been published in numerous medical journals."

Leaning against the counter, arms folded across my chest, I ask in what I hope is a casual tone, "Speaking of Winterlude, remember when I met Dick?"

"Dick was a prick of the first degree," grimaces Leen. "Enough with memory lane."

Eying the lemonade pitcher, Becky asks, "You done yet?"

Using a teaspoon, I do a taste test. "Needs more sugar."

"Get two more," I say, as Leen withdraws glasses from the cupboard. "I told the movers that I'd give them some."

Leen places the glasses on a tray and calling over her shoulder as she strides to the living room, says, "Come on ladies, let's see where we're going to place Amy's furniture."

Leen places the tray on the coffee table and then plops down on one of the two leather couches. Sarah quickly joins her and Becky sinks onto a chair; both following Leen's example of feigning exaggerated relief. I smile at their comic poses and mutter, "Everyone's a comic."

I, Leonard, and Steve pull over dining room chairs and sit down. Rivulets of sweat streak their faces and I feel a twinge of empathy for the hard work they are doing. Pouring the lemonade, I tease Leen, "Comfortable?"

Stretching out her long, tanned legs, she answers, "I might just supervise from the comfort of this couch."

Steve's eyes wander over the rim of his glass. Amused, I signal with a glance for Becky and Sarah to watch Steve's reaction to Leen's legs. Right on cue and without thinking, he blurts, "Wow!" Immediately he realizes his mistake. Flustered, he tries to cover up with, "This is really good lemonade."

I suppress a smile. Leen has that effect on men. Without even trying, she oozes pure sex.

Ignoring Becky and Sarah's grins, I reply dryly, "Glad you like it." I rescue him from further discomfort by suggesting, "Why don't you, I, and Leonard tackle where to place the upstairs furniture?"

Groaning with mock reluctance, Leen picks up the empty pitcher and glasses. "Guess we're done here. Come on Sarah and Becky, boxes await us."

Half an hour later I hear the doorbell ring. I holler down from upstairs, "Answer that will you Leen?"

∾

Leen

Standing on the front step, with an engaging smile, is an older petite woman with short grey hair capping her ears. Pointing to the house on the left, she says, "My name is Anna Wright and I'm your neighbour. Just thought I'd drop by to say that if you need anything like the use of a phone until yours is connected, feel free to ask."

Accustomed to the aloofness of city living I'm taken aback by this seemingly Norman Rockwell moment; half-expecting Anna to proffer a freshly baked pie. The thought crosses my mind that other than occasional nods on the elevator I and my condo neighbours are like silent strangers, all abiding to an unspoken agreement to remain anonymous. By contrast, Anna stands at Amy's front doorstep with the grace and charm of a time past, as if welcoming a new neighbour is the most natural thing in the world.

I return her smile. "Amy Keiffers is your new neighbour. I'm Adrienne MacLeen." For reasons I can't understand and completely out of character, I find myself wanting to engage in a casual conversation with this woman. I point to the foyer's newly restored hardwood floors. "This is a beautiful old place. Amy is already working to restore it to its former style."

Anna's brow furrows slightly. "Well," she says thoughtfully, "some things fell by the wayside after Gary's heart attack and Kate started having blood pressure problems. They finally decided the house was too big for their needs and bought a condo in Florida. They spend the winter months there and have a bungalow near their daughter's place in the Niagara area. When you get older, house maintenance is no longer a priority." Eyes twinkling, she adds, "It's more a question of what fibre to eat and how regular you are."

Not certain how to respond to her earthy comment, I reply, "Well, I guess you're right about that." Charmed by Anna's direct approach, I say, "I'll be sure to tell Amy that you dropped by. Perhaps once she's settled in, you could come by and see what she's done with the house?"

"Please tell your friend that if I can do anything to help, just let me know." With a pleasant smile, Anna turns and walks across the adjoining front yards, leaving me with the sense that somehow during our brief encounter that small dynamo of a woman has taken my measure.

Amused, I step back from the doorway just as Amy comes down the stairs. Wiping her hands on her shorts she asks, "Who was at the door?"

"Anna and I quote, *'your new neighbour to the left.'* Looks to be about mid-seventies."

"Nice of her to stop by." Heading towards the kitchen she asks, "Or was she snooping?"

"Who's snooping?" asks Becky, poking her head out from the hallway bathroom where she's been installing toilet paper, hand lotion, and soap. "Who was at the door?" She shouts out to Sarah who is working in the dining room, "Sarah, stop what you're doing. There's gossip to be shared in the kitchen."

Grimacing in response to the nagging ache of my muscles, I answer Amy. "No, I don't think so." I make quotation marks with my fingers as I add, "Seems like a real character; kind of quaint in her own way." I glance at Becky. "She'd be a real study for you; characterization and all that sort of thing."

The sound of footsteps interrupts us and we turn to see Buddha Belly. Handing an invoice to Amy, he mutters, "Well that's it. Everything has been placed where you wanted it." Working on a wad of gum, he moves his jaw in quick motions while Amy writes out a cheque.

After he and Steve leave, Amy asks, "What do you think?" Not waiting for an answer she strides to the centre of the living room and pushing a hand through her auburn curls she muses, "An apartment would have been so much easier."

"You're just tired. Once you have a chance to settle in you'll be pleased with your investment." I walk to the stairway. "How about a tour of the upstairs?"

"It's not exactly how I want it but the overall effect isn't bad for the first day."

"Lead the way."

"Wow!" gushes Sarah, "I love the skylight! The computer nook overlooking the living room and front hallway is marvellous."

Pleased, Amy replies, "I wanted a change from a traditional office area. This nook allows me to feel less confined."

I sit behind the sleek cherry wood desk and pretend to speak into a hand held microphone. "From this desk will come the next great academic book by Dr. Amy Keiffers."

"Don't know about it being *great*."

Needling for a clue, I purposely take on a plaintive whine. "Any hints?"

"It's in the final editing stages. Pretty boring academic stuff."

Grimacing, I ask, "What do you do for light reading?"

She runs her left hand over the banister, trying for a casual pose before answering, "Kidding aside, I've started to draft a novel."

My curiosity is piqued. "A novel? Well, well, this is interesting, Professor. Do tell all!"

"It's just in the beginning stages; I'm not sure how it'll develop."

Spurred on by encouraging looks from Sarah and Becky, I cajole, "Just a hint?"

"I've got a long way to go before I start talking about it and then, I'll have to deal with the problem of trying to find an agent to pitch it to a publisher."

Becky says, "One step at a time!"

"Good for you," says Sarah.

"What made you want to try your hand at writing a fiction novel," asks Becky.

Amy shrugs. "I'm just tired of writing for academic journals. I want to try something different."

"Move over Dan Brown and Danielle Steele," I joke. "Make room for Amy Keiffers! I assume your *trusted* friend will get first dibs on the media campaign and all movie promotions."

"But of course!" Playing along, Amy asks, "Who else?"

Rubbing my hands with devilish delight, I say, "I'm going to love watching Don's reaction when he learns that the next great author to burst upon the public scene is none other than one of my best friends. He'll pee his pants in sheer expectation of the money that will roll into the firm."

Laughing, Amy answers, "Sometimes, I honestly wonder how you manage to elude the trouble that some of your comments can create. Have you ever heard of social niceties or political correctness?"

Tapping my temple with my index finger, I drawl, "I know when to shut my mouth and retreat into my *'mental mind fuck'* mode."

Guffawing, Becky quips, "I might use that one with my patients. Can you imagine their reaction when I say, 'Today we're going to explore a new type of therapy. It's called the mental mind fuck mode.'"

"You can think what you want; you just can't always say it," I reply. "You're the shrink, Becky. You know it's good to have stress reducing techniques."

"Speaking of stress levels," comments Amy, leading us through French doors to the master bedroom, "you weren't too happy with Don this morning. What was that all about?"

Groaning, I get serious. "Scenes' has been approached by a consortium of interested patrons of the Arts, directors, and theatre financiers to sponsor a Gala in New York. His puny, mercenary heart was all a flutter with the promise of the million-dollar retainer. He was going to get more details today, but he did say it has to do with Claire Holowitz. The purpose of this morning's call was to let me know that I'm *not* there and he's the king of the fucking universe."

"*The* Claire Holowitz!" Becky rivets her attention on me. "I saw *Whispering Hope* in Toronto last spring. The critics hailed it as one of the best plays she's ever written." She flashes a sympathetic smile. "She's not been seen in public or talked to anyone from the media in close to forty years."

"Missing, but not absent," replies Amy. "Don't forget she's published some very successful plays, novels, and is a recognized photographer. In fact, I have two of her novels and one play listed on the syllabus for my third year students. When I attended the Paris symposium last summer I went to see her latest photo exhibit, *Images of Reflections*. It was amazing! She used shots of people of all ages, with backdrops of windows, mirrors, and even pond reflections." Folding her arms across her chest, she asks, "Why would anything having to do with Claire Holowitz get you so upset?"

"I'm not upset with her ..." I reply, more defensively than I intend, "but if I read Don correctly this morning, he wants us – more specifically *me* – to find and persuade her to come to the Gala. When I can't achieve that, he'll use it to discredit me in the firm."

Becky commiserates, "She's infamous for eluding media coverage."

Plopping down on the bed, I moan, "Don's such an incredible idiot. He'll do his best to garner all the glory and to dump the blame for Holowitz not being there on me."

"How can he do that?" demands Sarah, instinctively using what her twin sons, Jeremy and Jake, call her *courtroom* voice. "It's an established fact she shuns public appearances."

"He's Don, is how!" I snort contemptuously, "A supreme ass of the first order."

Taking their cues from the finality in my tone, Sarah and Becky turn their attention to Sarah's bedroom furniture.

"Don't let Joe see this," says Sarah, pointing to the surround sound system. "If he does, I'll be falling asleep to the sound of NHL games." Her comment makes us laugh. It's no secret that her husband and sons are avid sports enthusiasts. She often jokes that if she wants attention during the Stanley Cup playoffs, she has to make a pitch for it during commercials.

"No hockey here," replies Amy, "strictly music and videos. I put in this new LCD flat panel television, so I can just lounge around if I want to."

"Creative lounging. Now that's something I can identify with!" Speaking in suggestive undertones, I tease, "Just settle back in bed, with a bowl of buttered popcorn, a video, and imagine the possibilities with a certain Mr. Someone." I bat my eyelashes. "Play Date time at its very best."

"Tell you what, Leen," retorts Amy, impishly, "I'll get a *Play Date* when you do. You're all talk and no action. We can double-date just like teenagers?"

"There'll be no teenager sneaking around or back seat rendezvous' for this girl," I tease back. It'll be the Chateau Laurier complete with dinner and a very luxurious room afterwards. After all," I add, affecting my best sultry tone and patting the pillow, "comfort is important."

"You're incorrigible!" groans Sarah, checking her watch. "Let's call it a day and have something to eat."

"How about pizza from Rocco's?" Pulling my cell phone out of my pocket, I google for the phone number.

Thirty minutes later we carry a hot pizza loaded with extra pepperoni, bacon, onions, and thick gooey mozzarella cheese along with two bottles of good red wine, out to the patio. Using an overturned crate as a table we sit on Adirondack chairs and chat amicably. By the middle of the second bottle of wine we're all yawning.

"We really should get some sleep," says Amy, starting to rise from her chair. I put a restraining hand on her wrist and she sits back down.

"Are you kidding me?" Reaching for the bottle, I say, "There's more wine left. We're going to do it justice." Not waiting for agreement, I pour refills. "No one's leaving until Becky fills us in about talk-of-the-town, Chef Josh Sinclair."

Feigning frustration, Amy picks up her glass, "To friends getting pleasantly drunk. What will my new neighbours think?"

Arching an eyebrow, I reply, "Hopefully the neighbourly thing."

"And that would be?"

"Invite us over for some wine." Shrugging at her incredulous look, I say, "You asked, I answered."

"You almost made me lose my wine," accuses Sarah, wiping the corners of her mouth. "If you ever lose your job at Scenes, you might want to consider a career as a stand-up comic."

"I make more at Scenes. Besides, I save my good lines for you three." Turning my attention to Becky, I demand, "Okay Becky, give with the details."

"Not much to say," answers Becky coyly. "At least nothing I want to share in public."

Leaning forward, Sarah uses a stage whisper. "I love it when she alludes to sex."

"No one said anything about sex."

"If it wasn't about sex, you wouldn't be concerned about talking *in public*," says Amy. "You like him a lot, don't you?"

Running a hand through her tussled hair, Becky answers quietly, "I enjoy his company."

"Well I'm glad for you," replies Amy, her brow pulling thoughtfully. "Do I detect that things are starting to get serious?"

"Who would have thought I'd fall this hard?"

"It happens," says Sarah. "It's been ten years since your divorce. The person is right. You're ready. Go for it!"

Stifling a yawn, I throw in my two bits, "You and Joe have had a good run of it."

"True enough," answers Sarah. "Next month we'll be married twenty-five years. With the twins off to university in the fall we'll be rambling around the house wondering where the time has gone."

"You're not ready for green pastures yet," counters Becky. "You and Joe will have some readjustments to deal with, but you'll do just fine."

"Is that the shrink talking or the friend?"

"Both," grins Becky. "Of all of us, you're the one with the fairy tale marriage." Patting Sarah's knee she adds, "There's no way that Joe will go looking for another woman to tease his imagination when he comes face-to-face with the male version of the empty nest syndrome. You're simply not the type to play adulteress to a man's wet dreams and longing for recaptured youth. Nope, *this* shrink doesn't see any mid-life marriage crisis on your horizon. You've been smitten with Joe for years and he with you. Nothing's going to change that." She sips her wine. "Yep, yours is definitely one of the fairy tale marriages."

"Maybe not fairy tale, but good," agrees Sarah, truthfully. "We've had our challenges and disagreements but at the end of the day, I can't imagine a life without him."

"Spoken like a true wife," I say.

"You know Leen one of these days you're going to stop being so career driven and *actually* make time for a social life." Ignoring my sceptical groan, Sarah adds, "When you least expect it; you'll fall hard."

Dismissing the jibe about my lack of a social life, I address Amy. "You sure were tripping down memory lane earlier today."

She hesitates. "Remember when we met Dick?"

I glare at the three empty wine bottles we've consumed while sitting outside and gripe, "I can't believe I've just resurrected that can of worms." I puff out an exasperated breath and rise. "Look, if you really want to do this, I'm definitely going to need another glass of wine." Glancing at Becky, I warn, "And there'll be no side-line comments from the shrink."

Becky grins and motions as if she is zipping her mouth shut.

I say, "Becky, you're the shrink. Tell her she's better off without Dick the Prick."

"She knows that," replies Becky. "Purchasing the house has just triggered old memories." Expression serious, she asks, "Right, Amy?"

Staring into her glass as if it's the well of truth, Amy answers, "I can't deny my past."

Seeing that Becky and Sarah are settling in, I set off to the kitchen to fetch another bottle.

Through the screen door I hear Amy say, "Leen hates Dick for what he did to me."

"It was high time for you to get out of that condo," answers Becky softly, "too many memories lingering there. Learning to trust a second time is, in my humble opinion, more difficult than the first because you know that love can hurt deeply when it's one-sided. You're moving on. Wait and see. You'll meet someone."

"Like you did with Josh," pipes Sarah. "Leen, not Amy, is the one who has the anger issues with Dick."

Returning, I start to pour refills but Becky, covering the rim of her glass with a hand, says, "No more for me. I'm driving."

"Well, I'm not," grins Sarah, sliding her glass over.

Pouring wine for Amy and myself, I huff, "I heard that crack about me having anger issues. Damn right I do when they're about Dick the Prick." I glance at Amy. "You've been thinking with your heart again."

"I guess so," admits Amy, "but the pictures did resurrect memories – like the day we met him when we were skating on the canal during Winterlude?" A fleeting smile creases her mouth. "We looked so young and cold."

"We *were* young and we *were* cold." Suppressing a yawn, I see the look of consternation registering on Amy's face and reassure her that she has my attention. "The wine is starting to hit me. I'm still listening."

"He spilled coffee on my jacket."

"I remember. We were standing in line waiting to buy beaver tails."

A small sigh escapes as her expression becomes pensive. "Looking back, I should have turned and ran instead of letting him buy us coffees and beaver tails."

"Hindsight is always twenty, twenty," I answer, lifting my glass to toast her comment.

Amy doesn't argue. She knows I've spoken the truth. Six months later, on a hot muggy Saturday afternoon in July I stood smiling, dressed in a soft moss green silk gown, holding orchids as the photographer's flashes went off. I was also the one whom Amy called sobbing her heart out seven years later, when he left her for Andrea. That was the night I officially dubbed Richard, 'Dick the Prick' and although I have used a variety of names for Andrea, my preferred nickname has always been 'Office Tramp'.

"Say what you want," Amy says, sipping her wine, "but there *were* good times."

"People move on. You caught a lucky break when *Dick the Prick* took up with *Office Tramp*." Resting my head against the back of the chair and staring up at the stars, I think for a moment before adding softly, "It wouldn't have mattered what you did, Amy."

"Buying this house was a step forward," reaffirms Becky, "you've been living with memories for too long. Keep what was good and remember those memories but it's definitely time to let go."

A whimsical smile creases Amy's face. "Thanks for listening. I know it's been ten years but I can't help thinking about him sometimes and just wishing we could at least have been friends. He had so much of my youth."

There's a brief moment of awkward silence as Becky, Sarah, and I try to decide what our responses should be.

Sarah raises her glass. "To Amy's new house."

Tension broken, I squeeze Amy's shoulder and say, "It's good that you bought this place. Glancing around our circle, I grin and say, "So we're all agreed that always and forever Amy has officially let go and that Dick will continue to be known as *Dick the Prick*."

"Done!" To seal the deal, we clink our wine glasses ceremoniously.

Using the chair's armrests to push upwards, Becky says, "Come on, Sarah, it's time for us to leave. I have early rounds at the hospital tomorrow with a new rotation of med students."

Sarah answers, "Becky, I vote we call for a taxi. You can spend the night in my guest room. Joe will drive you here in the morning to pick up your car."

After they leave, Amy and I go upstairs and dig out some towels and bed linen. "You got a new toothbrush in any of those boxes? I hadn't planned on spending the night."

"You're in luck," answers Amy. "I unpacked bathroom articles earlier this morning. You can use the guest bathroom."

We make up the bed in the guest room first before fixing up Amy's. Opening the bottom drawer of her dresser, she tosses over some jogging shorts and a t-shirt. "Big day tomorrow?"

Wishing that I hadn't been so liberal with the wine, I answer, "Yeah, back to the grind and dealing with that slime ball Don."

Yawning, Amy replies, "Don't let him get to you."

"It's hard not to," I answer. "He's such a jerk."

"Try to get some sleep, Leen," says Amy, crawling into her bed.

"See you in the morning," I reply and head off to the guest room.

Chapter Two

Leen

Three weeks later we're all back at Amy's for a barbecue and par for the course, I'm running late. By the time I get there, the preparations for the meal are just about finished. Sarah is brushing Amy's bourbon sauce recipe on the ribs and Becky's cutting up the romaine for the salad. Both have glasses of wine on the go and are kibitzing. Placing a fresh baguette on the counter I apologize, "Sorry, I'm late."

Handing me a glass of wine, Sarah asks, "Long day?"

"Don's been at his finest." I suck in a breath and exhale slowly before taking a sip of wine. The tension in my shoulders starts to ease. Sitting on a kitchen chair, I think of how much I enjoy our third Friday of every month get-togethers. They serve the dual purpose of just relaxing with friends and therapeutic, venting sessions. Having our own in-house psychiatrist is a bonus. Becky likes to hand out a plate and joke about us leaving tips.

Lifting the platter of vegetables lightly seasoned with olive oil and garlic, Amy asks, "Are the ribs ready?"

With a dramatic final brush stroke, Sarah proudly declares, "There you go, oh great Chef!" Picking up the rib platter and mimicking a servant's pose, she follows Amy out to the patio.

"I'll wait to toss the salad until we're actually ready to eat," says Becky, wiping the counter. Casually, she asks, "Aren't you going outside?"

"In a minute. I just want to sit still for a while."

"Take your time," answers Becky.

Practically cooing with relief the second I slip off my high heels and wiggle my toes playfully on the cool terra cotta floor tiles. "There's something so satisfying about freeing my feet from the confines of shoes."

"Has to do with shedding off the remnants of a long day," answers Becky. Grinning she adds, "Why not slip off the pantyhose."

"That's why you're a good shrink; you spot the patient's needs without the patient having to ask for help. Be right back." I go down the hallway and use the small guest bathroom.

Returning to the kitchen, I stuff my pantyhose into the pocket of my taupe jacket and sling the jacket over the chair's back. Grinning, I say, "Feels better."

The patio door slides open and Amy heads for the built in wine rack underneath the kitchen island counter. She pulls out a bottle, checks its label, and grins approvingly. Glancing in my direction, she remarks, "You look a little tired today."

Swirling the wine in my glass, I grumble, "Don's such an incredible ass."

"Come outside and entertain us with what he's done this time," grins Amy, "as I grill the ribs."

Becky carries out the salad and I bring the pickles and garlic bread. Once we're seated, Becky cheerfully commands, "Spit it out. What's happened in that corporate world of yours?"

Not ready to talk about Don, I get up and walk to the grill. Brushing barbecue sauce over the ribs, I say, "Maybe after supper we can talk about him. Right now, I just need to relax."

"Should be done in about two minutes," says Amy.

Ten minutes later I'm wiping barbecue sauce from my lips and complaining, "I'll have to diet for the next week, but these ribs are fantastic."

"It's the brown sugar sauce laced with bourbon," replies Amy, licking two fingertips.

"So, Leen ..." says Becky, finishing off a rib, "are you ready to tell us what had you so riled up when you came in?"

Becky winks. "Come on Leen, spit it out. The doctor's in session."

Sarah and Amy smile their encouragement, giving me permission to vent. "You all know what an anal jerk, hard ass, Don can be?"

"Tell us how you *really* feel Leen," jokes Amy.

"*Don Stories* are like following a comedy sitcom detailing how stupid one's boss can be," enthuses Sarah. "Sometimes I entertain myself thinking about the fun I'll have when you decide to sue him for work place harassment."

"You deal with Family Law not Employment Law," points out Becky.

Squinting, Sarah speaks with deliberate emphasis. "For Leen, I'll make the exception and take this one pro bono. Just for the sheer pleasure of watching the fool squirm."

"One of these days Don will get his, but in the meantime, I have to put up and shut up." Seeing that Sarah is poised to challenge what I've said, I quickly clarify, "There's no point in rocking my boat until I'm sure that I have him trapped like the snake that he is. Until then, I'll continue to collect a nice salary for my pains."

"Duly noted. But, the offer is there; I'm ready and waiting to take him on."

Amy coaxes, "What did the infamous Don do this time?"

"Do you remember me telling you on the day that I took off to help you with your move that he'd called all pissed off that I wasn't at work?"

At her nod, I continue, "Do you also remember me telling you that he'd babbled on about Scenes handling the Claire Holowitz Gala in New York?" She nods again. "Well, today he announced that we're not only going ahead with the media aspect for the Gala but we're, also, going to handle all the arrangements; right down to the hors d'oeuvres. It seems that the forty-fifth anniversary of her first publication *When Angels Weep* is coming up in March. March 27th to be exact."

Snatching the last morsel of Caesar salad, Sarah plops it in her mouth, licks the dressing off her fingers, and asks, "Point being?"

"The *point being*, no one has heard from Claire Holowitz for over forty years. Her works command top dollar. Auction an original Holowitz photo and watch the money roll. Decide to produce a Holowitz play and people line up for tickets. She's *that* marketable." I rub my fingertips against my eyelids to ease the tension. "Holowitz's team of lawyers throw up barricades that the FBI, RCMP, and CIA couldn't penetrate."

Becky idly swats at a mosquito that has landed on her right forearm. "I remember reading about her public withdrawal in a psychological journal. She was cited as the classic case of a person who withdraws from life in order to survive it." Brow furrowed in thought, she takes a moment to reflect. "Most people withdraw into themselves, from time-to-time, in order to get on with life..."

Sarah interjects dryly, "Forty-five years strikes me as being excessive." She rises and moves towards the patio door. "Can I get anyone some water or something else to drink?"

Calling out after her, Becky says, "That's why her case is so interesting." Addressing me and Amy, she explains, "Holowitz's self-imposed seclusion gave a whole new definition to the meaning and action of withdrawal. The remarkable thing about her withdrawal was that the same society from which she withdrew became the source of her identity and self-expression. She just removed the public personae of Claire Holowitz from having to endure any face-to-face exchanges."

"Yeah, well, that *withdrawn* Claire Horowitz is the focus of this campaign. Don wants her found and in attendance at the Gala." Mimicking his annoying nasal twang I say, "We're not only going to make this the most impressive Gala in a very long time, Leen; we're going to find Claire Holowitz. Make that your priority. This will be a major coup for the industry." I twirl a carrot stick in some onion dip and wiggle it like a pointer before taking a bite. "It was almost comical to watch. Honestly, I thought he was going to have an orgasm. He was practically salivating at the thought of the retainer."

The image of Don in orgasmic throws and salivating causes Becky and Amy to laugh. "Honestly, Leen, where do you get these expressions?" quips Becky.

"A God-given talent. Part of my genius."

Returning, Sarah asks, "What's part of your genius?"

"Leen's regaling us with descriptions of Don in the throws of orgasmic delight and salivating."

"That'd be quite the sight," agrees Sarah. "Must have been hard for you to keep a straight face, Leen."

Puzzled, Amy asks, "But if other people can't find her, how do you expect to?"

Reaching for one of her homemade kosher pickles, Becky jabs at the air with comic flare and says, "I'd say you've got yourself one *pickle* of an assignment."

⁂

None of us pay attention to the slow, squeaking sounds of a swing coming from the backyard of Amy's neighbour as we regale one another with work stories and listen to the latest antics of Sarah's teenage twins, Jeremy and Jake.

Voicing concern that interests in girls are sidelining the academic diligence necessary to gain admission to the universities of their choice, Sarah says, "It's not that they're not nice girls; it's just that the boys need to focus on their studies."

Pragmatically, Becky answers, "You'd be worried if they didn't have a social life. Relax. It's all about balance. And, face it; you're not going to see what they do or don't do when they go off to university." In response to Sarah's expression, she adds, "That's the *doctor* talking, not the friend. You've got nothing to worry about."

Doubtfully, Sarah murmurs, "I hope you're right."

Shifting the discussion from Jeremy and Jake, Amy leads the charge of questions aimed at Becky. "So," she demands, "what's been happening with Josh?"

"Friar Will's been open for a year now," answers Becky, her pride evident, "and already Josh has made back his initial investment. Buying the Brown House and renaming it Friar Will's was a gutsy move."

Prodded to respond Becky relents and entertains us with vivid descriptions of the gourmet meals Josh has prepared especially for her, ending with a smug, "All that just for little old me."

In response our bantering for more details, she laughingly retorts, "Privileged information, my dears ... Just let it suffice," she adds mischievously, "that between the pleasing of the taste buds and the pleasing between the sheets, this shrink is currently in a very mellow state."

"Ah," remarks Sarah, "now we're getting somewhere. The wine has loosened the lips." To which, Becky mimics zipping her mouth shut.

As we clear away the leftovers, Sarah asks, "What's that noise?"

Silent, we listen to the creaking sounds of a swing moving back and forth.

Amy says, "That's Anna. She often sits out there, rocking away the time and enjoying the fresh air."

"Have you met her since she came over to introduce herself?" I ask, slipping on my jacket and reaching for my discarded shoes.

"Briefly. About a week ago. She was getting out of a cab with two bags of groceries as I pulled into my driveway. Seems like a pretty independent little thing."

"What's she like?" asks Sarah.

Looking at me, Amy says, "You're the one who had the long conversation with her when I was moving in."

"Kind of like a small, witty Diane Keaton but feisty like Meryl Streep."

Grinning at my peculiar penchant for comparing people to favourite actors, Amy says, "Yes, I think you're right. There's a similarity between them. Perhaps it's the vitality and innate intelligence that they all project."

"Do you think we were too loud?" asks Becky, staring at the fence.

"No, I think it was okay. It's not like we were throwing a wild party." Impulsively I suggest, "Maybe we should invite her to one of our Friday get-togethers. She might enjoy an evening out."

Shrugging off their surprised expressions I say, "I liked her when I met her. She seemed like quite a character. And ..." I add with a grin, "Amy lives in suburbia. When in suburbia, do like Betty Crocker and Norman Rockwell."

"Next, you'll have Amy signing up for church raffles and summer picnic baskets," teases Becky.

"Maybe, Leen's right," agrees Sarah. "It wouldn't hurt to extend a friendly invitation. After all, she was the one who made the first overture of friendship. But," she qualifies, "we'd have to find some common ground to talk about and," she glances meaningfully at me, "be sure that no off-colour remarks come out of Leen's mouth."

Dripping with fake innocence, I ask, "Who me?"

Poking my arm, Amy retorts, "Yeah, you, Miss Innocent!"

I reward her comment with a middle digit response.

Anna

After my new neighbour and her friends call an end to their evening, I wait until I hear the cars pull away. Within a few minutes, I see the downstairs lights go out and look upwards to the second level. I hear the sound of a bedroom window opening to let in the night air and watch as the curtains are pulled. Slowly, I get up from my swing and enter my own home. I hadn't intended to eavesdrop but their voices had carried and as such, I had learned much about my new neighbour and her friends.

When I wake in the morning, I move about my kitchen methodically as I ponder what my course of action will be. Waiting for the coffee to brew, I busy myself making toast and peel a tangerine. Placing the toast and the tangerine wedges onto a small plate, I add milk to my coffee.

This morning I'm tired. I'd tossed and turned the hours away searching for answers to the questions running through my mind. I've found over the years that an event, a memory, a word, or a gesture encountered can dredge up sub-conscious thoughts. Like demons they play on my mind. When that happens I wake up, as I did this morning, feeling like a marathon runner aiming for the finish line but lose my stride and end up gasping for breath.

"It shouldn't be this way," I grumble, nibbling on my toast. My eyes wander, taking notice of the fact that the kitchen walls could use a new coat of paint. Sighing softly, I decide that I've procrastinated long enough. I have work to do. I refill my coffee mug and take it upstairs to the room I use as my work area. I place the mug on the mahogany desk and flip open my laptop. Dispensing with the normal pleasantries, I compose a terse e-mail. Satisfied with my efforts, I hit the send key.

Finished with my tasks I walk down the hallway to draw a bath. I ease myself into the tub and, welcoming how the warm water soothes the tension between my shoulders, I think about the day ahead and wonder what the response to my e-mail will reveal.

Chapter Three

Leen

The first signs of a fall frost dust the roads. Furiously tapping the steering wheel with my third finger, I inwardly swear for having pressed the alarm's snooze button which let me sleep for an extra twenty minutes. The price of my indulgence is my having to deal with traffic congestion. The Queensway is like that. If I get on it ten minutes before the usual morning congestion, I sail through. But, if I make the mistake of being ten minutes behind my normal routine, the result is bumper-to-bumper traffic. As my BMW crawls along, alternating between dead stop and slow, I have plenty of time to think about what I've been doing with the Holowitz file.

The response from many heavily invested people in the Arts' community has been staggering. It's clear that even though Claire Holowitz remains an enigma; her novels, plays, and photo exhibits are held in high esteem. In as much as I have been steadily acquiring information about her, I have not been able to locate anyone who will admit to knowing where she lives or what identity she's using to hide her true self.

Don, ever the media hog, continues to stoke the fires of speculation that Claire will attend the Gala. The clamour centred on his foolish claim is making me uneasy. The more the expectation, the greater will be my fall if I don't succeed in finding her. There is no doubt in my mind that despite his public expressions of confidence that I will find Claire and convince her to attend the Gala; Don is doing everything to ensure that my failure to do so will smack of incompetence. In his interactions with me, away from the scrutiny of the public, he has never made any secret of wanting to remove me as the threat to his job. At Scenes, he has the top portfolio and I hold the second highest. He can't stand the fact that from the first, I have neither grovelled nor bowed to his power. To me, he is the true narcissist; a legend in his own mind. Working one-on-one I've had plenty of experience in dealing with his exaggerated self-importance. On many occasions I have bitten back responses when he's blathered on about the importance of his work at the firm. From the outset I have known him for what he is – a classic bully who gives lip service to equality in the work place but harbours resentment for any woman with brains.

By the time I reach my office, I've worked myself into a foul temper and I am deliberating how to put the brakes on his interference with my search for Claire. Dutifully, I have contacted the legal firm handling her affairs and I am still waiting for a response to my request to meet her. Brushing past my administrative assistant's desk with a nod in her direction I enter my office, fling my black leather jacket over the back of my desk chair and click on my laptop to check my e-mail.

"Safe to come in here?" asks Kathy, standing in the doorway with a cup of coffee in one hand and holding an envelope in the other. "I come bearing a peace offering." Sniffing the coffee appreciatively, she says, "Smell that java."

Smiling, I respond, "Of course it is."

Making a show of carefully tiptoeing across the room, she jokes, "Proceeding with extreme caution."

"Is my foul mood that obvious?"

"Let's just say that you're not going to win any personality awards this morning."

"Damn traffic," I whine, "… what should have taken twenty minutes, took forty-five."

"Got up late this morning?" teases Kathy, hitting the nail on the head.

Rolling my eyes, I groan, "The Queensway is a bitch for traffic during rush hour."

"True enough," she answers reasonably, "... that's why it's important to get on it before the morning congestion starts."

"Okay, okay, so what if I was running late? It's still annoying and I was only twenty minutes later than usual."

"Huh ha," Kathy agrees complacently, passing over the envelope. "Do the crime; make up for it with the time." She eyes the envelope. "That ought to make your day even more special."

"What's this?"

"It was dropped off personally by his *lordship*; about ten minutes before you arrived."

"Oh that's just great!" I sneer. "A personal missive." I read the contents and groan, "This day is getting worse by the minute!"

"What?" demands Kathy.

"Claire Holowitz's lawyer is coming here."

"When?"

"Today," I snap. "This morning."

༺༻

Kathy

Realizing it is futile to respond to Leen's acerbic comments and pissy mood, I wait as her fingers fly over the keyboard. We've worked together for eleven years and knowing her the way I do, I don't take offence when she has an occasional outburst or flare of temper. Her work is demanding and Don is a supreme ass of the first order. Company employees defer to him because of title but our respect for Leen's humour, ethics, and brilliance is genuine. To be honest, I sometimes think I serve the dual purpose of organizing Leen's schedule as well as being her "sounding board". I am Leen's "safe zone" and she is mine.

Leen has been great to me and mine. She's a frequent visitor to our Burnett get-togethers. It's a source of pride that a family photo of me, my husband Tom, and our three children hang on Leen's office wall alongside those of Sarah's twin boys, Jeremy and Jake.

"Ah, here we go," mutters Leen. Eyes focused on the screen and her expression intense, she explains. "One documented file regarding Marc Andre Aumount. He's Claire Holowitz's legal big whig and according to Don, he will be here for a meeting at nine thirty." She hits the print key and waits for the whirl of the printer to sound before turning to face me.

Grimacing, I say, "I don't remember receiving any memo about a meeting this morning."

"That's because Aumount let Don know last night that he *wanted* a meeting," answers Leen, snatching the printed sheets from the tray. "Damn him. He calls me enough on my off hours about stupid things. He should have called to let me know Aumount was coming. And, today of all days, I'm late."

I answer tersely, "Nice of Don to let you know last night."

Grunting with disgust she replies, "He did it deliberately. He's probably sitting in his office gloating that he caught me being late and probably thinking that I'll be so rattled by Aumount's visit that I'll go to the meeting unprepared."

"Ambush would be a better word," I gripe.

"Doesn't matter now," answers Leen, her chin jutting the way it does when she's settled on something. "Don's the one in for the surprise." Waving the papers triumphantly, she adds, "I started this file at the beginning of this project expecting that we would meet sooner than later. He's probably coming in response to my letter informing him of the Gala, the people involved, and their intent to honour Claire Holowitz with a Gala in New York. In that same letter, I also asked if there was any way possible to have a meeting with Claire Holowitz if for no other reason than to get her input as to how she might like to have her works showcased."

"You sent that letter a week ago," I reply. "That's fast for him to be responding."

"Well, not really," rationalizes Leen. "Aumount has probably heard the gossip buzz caused by Don's incessant rumours. He's probably coming to caution us to not speak for his client." Frowning, she leans her hands on the desk. "His office assistant called last week saying that he had received my request and that I would hear from him after he'd talked to Claire Holowitz."

Slipping on her jacket, she groans, "Likely he's coming with her answer which is a big fat no; largely in part due to Don's big mouth."

"Coming in person to deliver her response is more than just a reply."

"Yeah, that part is a bit of a mystery," replies Leen, biting her lower lip – a gesture I've come to know as expressive of her inner worry.

"The firm is very prestigious in the legal world with offices located in Toronto, New York and here in Ottawa. His father, Emile, was a founding partner of the firm. He's retired but continues to oversee the management of a few clients – Claire Holowitz being one. I had expected one of the partners from the Ottawa office to be my contact."

"Why?"

"According to my research, Marc Andre divides his time between the Toronto and New York offices." She looks up from her notes and asks, "By the way, how do I look?"

I give her an approving once over. Black pinstripe jacket and skirt, white silk shirt, black pumps and a simple necklace with a single oval-shaped pearl pendant at the base of her neck. "As usual your clothes are coordinated and you project a very corporate image."

Scanning the file one last time, Leen summarizes. "He was Forbes' magazine poster boy two years ago. Putting it bluntly, he's infamous in the corporate world as a lethal adversary and renowned in social circles as a philanthropist. Although a personal friend of many of the rich and famous, he himself is a very private individual." She slides the file into her briefcase, snaps the lid shut, and offhandedly refers to my comment about her suit. "Thanks. I picked it up at Jones' last week."

"Where do you get that stuff?" I laugh. "How do you do it?"

Puzzled, she asks, "What stuff? What are you talking about? You've lost me."

"I'm referring to your notes on Aumount. It's not the first time that you've pulled out background information on clients or their lawyers and agents, on a moment's notice." I tease, "Ever consider a career with the CIA? Your sleuthing skills are exceptional."

"If I was that good at it, I'd find Claire Holowitz," counters Leen. Her phone rings and looking at the caller ID, she mouths, "Don." Exasperation evident, she flicks on speaker and snaps, "Leen here."

"Good mood today are we?" retorts Don, with an edge of impatience.

I grin as Leen refrains from uttering the string of expletives which no doubt she's mentally reciting. "Got held up in traffic." Checking her watch, she adds, "We've got a good hour to plan for the meeting with Aumount."

"Right. Come up now," barks Don and, not waiting for her response, hangs up.

Grabbing her briefcase, Leen salutes, clicks her heels, and groans, "Off to please the King."

Returning to my desk, I think, *'This might well turn out to be one very interesting day.'*

❦

Leen

The standing joke is that Erma, Don's administrative secretary, is the 'sentinel'. Plump, mid-fifties, and of the opinion that she is indispensable to Scenes' effective management, she epitomizes everything that is obnoxious about one who is inflated with a sense of self-importance. Don is more facetiously referred to as 'the Don'. Known to be petty and possessing what are commonly viewed as characteristics associated with a despot, employees tend to give him wide berth. Stepping out of the elevator, I stride purposefully past Erma's desk. "He's expecting me." Without waiting for permission, I march into Don's office.

By the time the legal legend arrives, my initial annoyance with Don has cooled down and I'm ready and curious to meet Marc Andre Aumount. As introductions are made, I mentally admit that this man is easy to look at. His charcoal Armani suit, slate-grey shirt and silk tie accent intelligent dove-grey eyes. He enters Don's office with the confidence of a man used to being catered to, but shows the common sense to extend polite courtesies, tacitly acknowledging that he was on our turf.

Handing a slim envelope to Don, Aumount loses no time addressing the purpose of his visit.

Frowning at the sealed envelope, Don says, "This is addressed to Adrienne MacLeen".

"True," admits Aumount. "But in deference to your position as Scenes C.E.O., I wanted you to be aware that I am under instructions to deal specifically with Ms MacLeen."

Picking up on a trace of a French-Canadian accent, I purposely avoid Aumount's scrutiny; painfully aware of the slow treacherous blush creeping up my cheeks. When Don hands me the envelope, I walk to the windows at the far side of the office and make pretence of looking at the street below before opening the envelope. In reality, I'm taking time to think, away from the careful gaze of those dove-grey eyes.

Using a conciliatory tone, Aumount says, "I'm pleased, Mr. Harris, that you have shown your personal commitment to the proposed Gala honouring my client, but I must reiterate my position." Pausing, he takes a moment to allow the weight of his authority to settle before his voice takes on a cold edge. "Any negotiations concerning Ms Holowitz are to take place solely with Ms MacLean." Half-turning around, I watch as he casually straightens his tie, leans comfortably back in the brown leather chair, and waits calmly to see what Don's reaction will be.

Fuming at Aumount's ultimatum and pointed dismissal, Don replies, "Your condition is accepted. Having said that, please know that regardless of Ms Holowitz's stipulation that you deal exclusively with Leen – all information and progress pertaining to Scenes' management of the Gala, *will* be reported to me."

I can see the outline of the Parliament buildings and the stained copper roof of the Chateau Laurier Hotel. Cars creep along the street like small ants in a myriad of action. Detecting the underlying venom in Don's voice, I steel myself for Aumount's retort but I'm not entirely surprised that Aumount does not deem Don's comment worthy of a response. I return the letter to Don and wait as he makes the pretence of giving it a cursory read. If Aumount notices my deference to Don, he gives no indication. Instead he waits as if he has all the time in the world.

Don passes the letter back to me as if it's worthless and would be better placed in the garbage. Measuring my words carefully, I face Aumount and say, "I can only surmise, Mr. Aumount, that since you are here in person, we have caught the attention of Claire Holowitz?"

"Your assumption is correct, Ms MacLeen. More germane to this meeting is that *you* have caught Claire Holowitz's attention." The implication of his direct answer, despite his engaging smile, evokes a disturbing thought. *She's sending me a message. If I'm going to seek facts about her life and self-imposed isolation; she's going to put my life under a microscope.*

Don inhales sharply. Previous peevishness gone, his voice bridles with excitement. "Are you saying that Ms Holowitz will meet with Leen?"

Aumount's tense smile suggests ill-concealed impatience with Don's interruption. "There has been no mention that Ms Holowitz will consent to meet with anyone. As I said earlier, Ms MacLeen has caught

The Search for Claire Holowitz

Ms Holowitz's interest. To that end, I'm to learn more about the project, the interested parties and very specifically," he adds, focusing on me, "to learn more about you."

I take the chair opposite him. "Well, then, Mr. Aumount," I say deliberately, "what exactly would Ms Holowitz like to know and why does she need to know about me?"

Even though we both affect casual poses, this meeting has reached a turning point where it has the potential to be explosive. Avoiding Don's piercing gaze, I concentrate on Aumount. Before he can reply, Don interjects, pompously, "We, at Scenes, are always happy to answer a client's questions and cooperate fully. I suggest that you and Leen move to *her* office where you can proceed with your questions."

Aumount's eyelids flicker slightly. I can tell that Don's arrogance is more than he would normally tolerate, but he's here to garner information and I'm his target. Don is merely a pawn in what is turning out to be a much more serious game of corporate chess.

"Certainly," Aumount replies agreeably. "I have all day. I'm here at Ms MacLeen's disposal."

He's actually trying to bait me, I think, forcing myself to not reveal my annoyance.

I manage a smile that I don't feel, rise and say, "Shall we go then?" Not waiting for his response, I head to the door and cast a withering glare at Don indicating my displeasure at being forced into this inquisition. He returns my look with one that clearly implies I'd better not mess up this deal.

Aumount's lips form just a hint of a scowl as we step into the elevator. "Are you always this direct?"

I answer evasively. "I'm not sure I understand the meaning of that question." The elevator stops and we exit.

"Business is business," he replies, "but experience has taught me that sometimes exchange of pleasantries can reduce ambiguity and create a more welcoming environment."

Oh so you're now going to teach me manners? I bite back my angry retort and counter with, "Would you like coffee, water, or juice?"

"Coffee and some bottled water would be most welcome."

Stopping in front of Kathy's desk, I ask, "Would you please arrange to have coffee, bottled water, and bagels with cream cheese brought into my office?" Acknowledging Aumount's presence with a slight wave of my hand, I add, "Mr. Aumount and I will be busy for the better part of the morning. Please hold my calls and re-schedule any appointments."

"Actually, Ms MacLeen," he addresses Kathy with a charming smile, "will be busy most of the day." Looking at me, he adds, "Perhaps you will agree to have a late lunch with me mid-afternoon? That will permit us to tie up any loose ends before I catch my flight."

My shoulders tense in reaction to his commandeering of my schedule. Kathy doesn't help matters by the nod she gives as if it's perfectly natural for me to want to set aside my schedule in order to devote my whole day to work with Aumount. I know her well enough to interpret her silence as her way of waiting to see what will happen next.

If Aumount notices my annoyance, he doesn't let on. Addressing Kathy again, he pleasantly explains, "I have to get this information before my flight back to Toronto for a meeting this evening. My client is expecting to be fully debriefed by tomorrow morning. That's why I'm asking for Ms MacLeen to rearrange her schedule."

The smile she returns in answer to his charm makes me want to shake her but picking up on what he's said, I ask, "Your client is in Toronto?'

"I have several clients in various cities across Canada and the U.S., Ms MacLeen. If you are referring specifically to Ms Holowitz, her whereabouts are not to be divulged. I'm simply pointing out that in addition to completing this request, on Ms Holowitz's behalf; I too have had to rearrange my *own* busy schedule."

Message delivered; slam and dunk. He did notice my annoyance and was clearly not in the least perturbed by it. In fact, he seems to be enjoying it.

Realizing that the verbal sparks flying between us might actually ignite the air, Kathy interjects with a congenial smile, "Is there anything else I can do?" She looks at me as if to say, *"Round one to Aumount!"*

Feeling like I've been sandbagged, I tell her, "Please make arrangements at the Tuscan Valley Grill for a late lunch." Glancing at Aumount, I ask, "Say around two p.m.?"

"The timing would be ideal. It will allow us to have a leisurely meal and give ample time for me to make my six o'clock flight."

Before closing my office door, I direct a deadly look at Kathy who is sitting there with a stupid smirk on her face.

"So Mr. Aumount," I ask, as we sit down at the small round table I use when meeting clients, "what can I say to assure Ms. Holowitz that the intent of the Gala is *not* to invade her privacy but *rather* to celebrate a life-time of literary and artistic achievements?"

Smoothing his silk tie, he replies with cold civility, "Let us agree from the start that this invasion into your privacy has resulted from *your* request to intrude on Ms. Holowitz's privacy. No," he waves his hand dismissively, "Let's not argue about semantics. We both know I wouldn't be here had you not sought to have Claire Holowitz in person for this affair."

"Our firm was *asked* to arrange the Gala," I retort. "We didn't start out to disturb Ms Holowitz or to invade her privacy. Her seclusion from the public eye is a well-established fact."

"So well-established that your firm felt the need to try to bring her out?" He makes no attempt to conceal his sarcasm. "Trust me, if either I or my client felt your involvement with this request was anything but professional responsibility, I would not be here." His overall manner has stiffened and I notice the slight but definite coldness to his grey eyes.

I take what I hope is not too noticeable of a deep breath. The man is exasperating! Nothing seems to rattle his sense of composure and confidence. Realizing that overt hostility is not going to end this interview well, I relent. "We're both professionals…" I pause to let the words hang in the space between us, "what can I tell you that will alleviate Ms Holowitz's concerns and satisfy her curiosity?"

He snaps open his briefcase and withdraws a legal pad and pen. "Mind if I take notes?" It's a rhetorical question so I don't answer.

Business-like, as if he's taking a deposition, he says, "Let's start at the beginning. When and where you were born, early schooling, parents etc. etc."

"Thorold, Ontario. My mother died when I was four and my father raised me. He was a good man." Mentally, I think, *Why did I say that? I don't have to justify anything to him.*

Aumount looks up from his notes. "I'm sure he was. What did he do?"

"He was a mechanic and a tool and dye maker."

"Still living?"

"No, he died four years ago." Kathy knocks lightly before entering. I use the opportunity to release myself from his scrutiny and rise to serve the coffee.

"Will you need anything else?" asks Kathy, not attempting to suppress her open interest and throwing a furtive glance as if to ask, "How's it going in here?"

Not wanting Aumount to pick up on my inner tension, I answer, "No, thank you. This will do very nicely. Did you get a chance to make the reservation?"

"All done, as requested." smiles Kathy, addressing Aumount which only serves to annoy me.

"Thank you for the coffee," says Aumount, holding his cup as if he's toasting her. "You're welcome," she smiles back, ignoring my stifled groan. "I'll be at my desk if you need me."

As I reach for a bagel, I sense Aumount's observation and wonder fleetingly if I've suddenly grown another eye or nose. *This is ridiculous,* I think. *What does it matter what he thinks of me?*

"So," he resumes, "You obtained your undergraduate degree from the University of Ottawa and completed your MBA at the University of California."

"You've done your homework, Mr. Aumount."

Ignoring my obvious dig, he replies, "Please call me Marc or Marc Andre. Let's not be so formal."

Pretending to be flattered I decide to reverse the charm game on him. "Okay Marc, what next?"

"Tell me about your hobbies and friends."

"My hobbies and friends?" The question momentarily takes me off guard.

"Your professional track record is outstanding," he concedes, "and well-published. But little is known about the private Adrienne MacLeen or should I say, "Leen".

"My friends and business associates call me Leen."

"What category would you put me in?"

For a fleeting moment I'm stumped as to how I should answer without sounding rude. "Leen is a nickname but, professionally, I go by Adrienne. Since we will hopefully work together in a spirit of collegial collaboration, I'm comfortable with foregoing the formality of my Christian name."

In slight deference to the point I've made, Aumount inclines his head slightly. With casual indifference he replies, "I will call you Leen."

Marc-Andre

Ignoring her attempt to evade questions about her private life I say, "Your private life is of interest to Ms Holowitz. You both share well-documented public lives. She recognizes the good intentions of the people who have hired Scenes to manage the Gala and understands your request to meet her." I make a point of staring directly at Leen. "She would like an exchange of information. Quid pro quo."

"Okay," she answers. "I get it. Claire Holowitz feels that if her private life is to be invaded by the media then she has the right to know about the invader?"

"That about sums it up." I smile. "Claire Holowitz has a deep sense of right and wrong, fair and unfair. Your profile and reputation has caught her interest."

I can almost hear her mind churning with random questions. *Interested in what? What do I have to do in order to become Holowitz's conduit for re-entry to public life?* Nonetheless, she answers, "Hobby-wise, I enjoy golf and like to read."

"Any good at it? Golf, I mean," I quip back. "Mind if I loosen my tie?"

The flicker of annoyance in her expression tells me that she is suspicious and probably thinking, *Old courtroom trick. Present a relaxed approach to draw the witness into a state of false assurance before pouncing with the revealing question.*

"Fair player," answers Leen, "Some days I golf better than others. Other days, my game leaves a lot to be desired." With a slight shrug, which I can't discern if it's dismissive or modest, she adds, "My putting could do with some improvement but since I never planned on being golf pro, I'm happy to get in the occasional game."

I keep my tone conversational. "Golf is one of the few sports I thoroughly enjoy. The competition is really not with anyone else but, instead, involves testing your own skills and relying solely on yourself to excel." Grinning, I add, "I'll admit to enjoying the 19th hole where my friends and I can enjoy a beer afterwards."

By the time we break to go to the restaurant, I am pleased with the progress we've made. Leen has been frank in answering my questions.

I'm curious as to what Claire will think when I report back to her. I had come here not knowing what to expect but as I follow her out of the office, I realize that she's exceeded any expectation I could possibly have had.

༄

Leen

As I slip my coat on to go to the restaurant I try to compartmentalize my reactions to Aumount's piercing questions. He has done his best to poke and prod into my private life. I've tried to frame my responses to satisfy Claire Holowitz's curiosity without elaborating on details. Aumount has inquired about my friends, commented on Amy's academic publications, Sarah's legal practice, and Becky's speaking circuit regarding psychological trauma.

Rubbing my left lower jaw, I wish that I could just omit going to the restaurant and instead, see if I can get an emergency appointment with my dentist. My molar is throbbing. *Serves me right,* I think, knowing that I've put off making an appointment because I've been swamped with the task of gathering information about Claire Holowitz. Now, of all times, that darned tooth has decided to protest my negligence.

"Sore jaw?"

I lower my hand and smile apologetically, "A reoccurring tooth problem that surfaces at the most inconvenient times."

"I didn't realize there was a convenient time for a toothache," he comments. "Are you sure you're up to going to the restaurant?" I look to see if he is being sarcastic but notice only genuine concern. He's actually giving me an out. Impulsively, I nix the idea of going to my dentist. "I may just have something light such as soup so as not to aggravate it."

Conversation is pleasant as we drive the restaurant. He tells me that he maintains an apartment in Ottawa and although he primarily works between the Toronto and New York offices, Ottawa is where he grew up and will always be *home* to him. "My father lives here," says Aumount, "and I make it a point to come home as often as I can to see him and to stay current with the Ottawa office." Somehow we get onto the topic of tourist attractions in Ottawa and his informality relaxes me so much that I'm astonished to hear myself admitting to a fondness for sugarcoated beavertails.

"Yes," he agrees amiably, "beaver tails are quickly becoming synonymous with a *must-have* experience when in Ottawa. Perhaps on my next visit, we can arrange to have some. It's been a while since I walked down by the Rideau canal and Parliament buildings. There are several excellent restaurants in that area where we can have dinner."

Surprised by his comment, I answer, "I generally conduct business in my office."

"Agreed," he answers, "when handling sensitive matters, it is best to work in an office but once those matters are dealt with, it can be pleasant to discuss the lesser issues over dinner."

Flashing a charming smile, Aumount says, "That's why they're called *business dinners*."

I joke, "Next, you'll be suggesting we discuss business on a golf course."

He replies, "Provided the weather cooperates that, too, is an option to the formality of an office. There is some truth to the saying that many business deals are closed on the golf course."

The hostess leads us to a table and we take a few moments to peruse the menus. After ordering pasta with a sundried tomatoes and sweet basil sauce, he asks, "Would you like some wine?"

"I think I will be taking some pain killers when I go home tonight," I answer, somewhat ruefully. "Can't mix the two." I give the waitress my order for minestrone soup and a glass of water.

"So tell me, Leen MacLeen," he asks, in between bites of warm olive bread, "is Don Harris always so uptight?"

"I'm not sure I understand what you mean?" I reply, evasively.

"Sure you do," he answers.

In spite of knowing that he has placed my life under his personal microscope, I find myself responding to the slight mischievous glint in his eyes. *Careful,* I tell myself, *charm is one of his weapons to lower my guard and garner more information.* I answer, "This campaign means a lot to the firm."

Aumount is not about to be so easily sidetracked. "And you?"

The waitress arrives with our orders and adds the extra parmesan cheese and black pepper to our meals. Aumount picks up his fork and twirls some pasta onto it while I busy myself with my soup.

"So?" he asks, casually, between mouthfuls.

"So?" I counter, pretending not to know what he is asking.

Reaching for his wine, he leans back in the chair and asks, "What does this campaign mean to you?"

I reach for my glass of water, needing a moment to gather my thoughts. Taking a sip, I phrase my response carefully. "Like all campaigns and projects I work on, I want it to be a success. It is not my intention to violate Ms Holowitz's privacy." I meet his intense look with one of my own. "I just can't help wondering why a woman, who is so highly recognized in the Arts' world as well as being known for philanthropic endowments to countless worthy causes, has gone to so much trouble to not be recognized."

I stop the flow of words, suddenly realizing I have done exactly what I had wanted to avoid. He has lured me into a response that, normally, I would not have revealed. I hurry to correct my seeming lack of tact. "I just mean ….look at someone like Geoffrey Hanes. He makes no secret of his philanthropy."

My mention of Hanes brings an amused grin from Aumount. Score one for my side. In my background search on Aumount, I had learned that he and the famous entrepreneur are friends. My reference to Hanes is an intentional reminder to Aumount that he is not the only one who has done his homework.

"To be honest I would like to meet her."

"For the Gala or for her?"

The question was spoken softly, but I glance at him seeking any sign of cynicism or reproach. Seeing none, I answer candidly, "For her but," I smile coyly, "if I could talk her into at least granting a public interview or to actually attend the formal night, it would make for a sensational Gala."

He raises his wine glass in a semi-toast. "Well, that was honest." .But," he puts down the wine glass and returns to his pasta, "I would not count on her making any public appearances. She has her own way of doing things and her own reasons. If you get the privilege of meeting her," he says, holding his fork in mid-air and speaking almost fondly, "You will be meeting a great person."

His reaction has surprised me. I think, *This tender defensiveness is more than just a lawyer's interest in a client. What's the connection?*

"Sounds like you care for her?"

His cell phone rings, interrupting any response. Checking the ID, he says, "I'm sorry, but I have to take this call." He leaves our table and heads to the front entrance."

Glad for the opportunity to be alone, I think about my day with Aumount. He had lured me into conversations about my life, which I would not normally have discussed. For a brief moment, I feel a kinship to Claire Holowitz. *No wonder the rich and famous dislike the media!* With sudden insight, I realize that Aumount's microscopic queries were intended to make me feel exposed and vulnerable.

Aumount returns and after apologizing again for the interruption, he says, "I realize some of my questions may have been intrusive, but I want to thank you for having answered them and," eyes twinkling, he adds, "without overt hostility."

I take a spoonful of soup before asking, "That was the purpose of this meeting wasn't it? To let me know how Claire feels when people want to know about her personal life?"

There's a taut composure about Aumount as he nods silent assent. Then he flashes a bright smile and says, "Guilty as charged."

Without warning, I feel the stirring of a sensual connection. If he notices the hot blush creeping up my cheeks he gives no indication.

"I like you Leen MacLeen. You're astute. Now, I can tell Claire that you have some appreciation of what you are asking her to do." The corners of his mouth turn up into a satisfied smile. "This little exercise has not been in vain." Poker-faced, he asks, "Now tell me is Harris always such a tight-ass?"

Aumount's return to his earlier question about Don is so out of context I burst out laughing, breaking the tension between us. "Yes he is," I chuckle, but try to add fairly, "he still has to be good to be where he is."

"True enough, Ms MacLeen."

He referred to me formally but his tone was gentle, almost as if he was caressing my name. *He must be great in court,* flashes through my mind. *With that voice he could probably lure an innocent person into confessing.*

"But being *good enough* means nothing to Claire Holowitz," continues Aumount. "She is a very humane person. To her, intelligence is only one part of the equation. She likes to see what people do with their intelligence and," he says, with earnest admiration, "she has a deep abiding respect for those who remember the value of human dignity. Money and fame are not determining factors on any of her balance sheets. She uses money and fame to give back to others what she has been given." He pauses and then, adds with a friendly smile, "She will be glad to hear that you, unlike Harris, see her as a person, appreciate her individuality, and respect her privacy."

Over coffee the conversation is relaxed as we discuss the politics of business environments and danger of 'corporate sharks in the water' ready and waiting to attack the weak or naïve. I find myself laughing and enjoying the humorous stories we share. At the end of our meal, Aumount reaches for his cell to call for a taxi. I surprise myself by saying, "Don't bother with a taxi. I'll drive you to the airport."

Aumount lazily extricates himself from the car when I pull up to the departures area. Looking at me through the passenger window, he says. "Thank you for the drive and for the pleasant conversation."

I can't help but appreciate once again the soft dove-grey of his eyes and find it easy to respond graciously to his easy smile. "Assure Ms Holowitz that I respect her right to privacy. Please convey that her personal input as to how she might like to have her work celebrated would be really appreciated."

Aumount's eyelids flicker in acknowledgement of my comment. "I'll tell her." Tapping the door, he adds, "Take care of that tooth." Briefcase clutched in his left hand, he walks towards the terminal and raises his right hand in a parting wave. When he doesn't look back, I'm mildly disappointed that he's not seen my return wave.

Fifty-five minutes later, lounging in a hot bath and sipping on a cold Perrier, I mentally review snippets of our conversations. Without Aumount's support and approval I don't stand a chance in hell of gaining Claire Holowitz' cooperation.

By the time I settle between the cool, doe-coloured silk sheets, I'm reconciled to the fact that despite my initial resentment of Aumount's intrusion into my private life, I had enjoyed his company. Sleepy from the pain medication I've taken for my toothache and relaxed from the hot bath, I snuggle down.

Unbidden, Marc's sharp, chiselled features come to my mind. I fall asleep wondering when I will see him again.

Chapter Four

Leen

Kathy's tone is playful. "So how did it go with the charming Marc Andre Aumount?" She fakes a heartfelt swoon, grasps the edges of the desk for balance and pleads, "Please let me be cross-examined by him!"

Grinning, I say, "Cut it out, Kathy. You missed your calling. You should have been in theatre. It was business, pure and simple; he was here to gather information for his client."

"Nothing wrong with mixing business with pleasure," Kathy observes dryly. "And don't tell me you didn't notice those beautiful grey eyes!"

Exasperated, but not really annoyed, I respond, "Enough, you old matchmaker." Taking a sip of coffee, I sit down at my desk. In response to Kathy's open smirk, I say, "The topic of Marc Andre Aumount and his grey eyes or any other part of his anatomy is closed." I tap the stack of files resting on my desktop. "Now if you don't mind, I have work to do."

"All work and no play make Leen a dull girl," retorts Kathy cheerfully as she exits.

I call out, "Give it a rest, Kathy."

"Give what a rest?"

My head jerks up from the file I've been looking at as Don walks into my office. Kathy leans around her desk and stretches to peer around the door. Behind Don's back, she rolls her eyes in mock exasperation.

"Nothing. We were discussing some files that need to be reviewed." Pointedly I add, "You may recall I was subjected to Aumount's inquisition yesterday?"

Ignoring my sarcasm, he states, "That's why I'm here. You should have been up to see me, first thing."

My response is abrupt. "I was going to come up as soon as I got organized for the day."

"So what did he want to know?" Sitting down, he flicks an imaginary speck from his suit jacket. Calling imperiously to Kathy over his shoulder, he says, "Hold Leen's calls and bring us some coffee. We're going to be a while."

Returning his condescending sneer with a jaw-clenched smile, I call out, "Yes, Kathy, that would be nice." Pointedly I add, "And, thanks."

Throughout our hour-long meeting, I have to make a conscious effort to check my responses. Rising to his baited comments would only prolong his interrogation and my exposure to his arrogance.

"Well, it sounds to me as if he was on a fishing expedition," concludes Don, after I've finished filling him in. "Let's hope Holowitz will permit the interview."

I think, *If Holowitz refuses the interview; I'll be the fall guy. If she permits it, Don will be the hero who orchestrated the meeting.* Refusing to respond to his underlying threat, I shrug noncommittally. Casting him a cold stare I think, *You asshole!*

As Don stands up and straightens his suit jacket, I resist the urge to say something that would wipe that smug look off his face. From his perspective, his little visit has put me in my place and that despite Aumount's dictum that Holowitz only wants to deal with me, Don is in charge. "Keep me apprised of any progress," he orders.

Once he's out of earshot, I mutter angrily, "Narcissistic asshole!"

Kathy waits for about five minutes before she enters. "Well, wasn't his lordship in fine form this morning?"

Her sarcasm is not wasted on me. "That's just the way he is."

"Just the same, his day will come!" Kathy sniffs contemptuously. "And, I want to be there to watch him take the fall."

Wanting her to see the humour of Don's pompousness, I say, "Imagine if you were Erma. Then, you'd get to work with him all day." I widen my eyes and whisper, *"The Sentinel."*

"Oh yeah," Kathy groans. "No wonder she's such a sour puss. He must treat her like dirt!" Her eyes twinkle with genuine amusement. "Then, again, they seem to deserve one another. Someday we should send them a thank you card for all the laughs we've had at their expense."

Kathy winds down her tangent and returns to her desk. For the rest of the morning I work at a gruelling pace. By mid-afternoon, I switch off my computer, massage my neck in an attempt to ease the tension, and decide to call it quits.

"I'm leaving now," I announce, closing the door to my office. "Between yesterday with Aumount, Don this morning, and all those files I've worked through," I roll my eyes, "I've had it! I need some time to think without any distractions."

Surprise registers on Kathy's face. It's extremely rare for me to leave the office early. "While you are thinking about things, don't let a certain lawyer's 'grey eyes' distract you from attending to business."

"You just don't give up, do you?" "No harm in trying to get you to look at the human race as something other than the next business deal or client." Kathy's face clouds with concern. "Look at you. You have dark circles under your eyes. You need to get a life."

Resting my hand on her shoulder, I tease, "Someday, Kathy, I'm going to shock you and announce that I've met *Mr. Wonderful*. But until then, can we please stop with your fascination with Aumount?"

"Okay, let's discuss his broad shoulders and narrow hips." Dismissing me with a wave of her hand, she says, "You need some down time. There should be more to your life then Scenes."

Two hours later, my aimless driving has worked its magic. I find myself on the outskirts of a small village, grumbling noises coming from my stomach. On a whim, I veer my car onto the main street, to the heart of the village.

Within a few minutes I spot, "The Speckled Rooster" and pull into the parking lot. The worn red and black sign causes me to think, *This place is pure cliché.*

Smells of bacon, grease, and strong coffee greet me as I enter. It takes a few seconds for my eyes to adjust to the dim lighting. The room is full of people. Some sipping a coffee or a beer and staring aimlessly at the spaces in front of them; others appearing to be holding animated conversations. Pitchers of draught beer, platters of nachos, and burgers adorn many of the tables. I spot an unoccupied booth at the far back. A middle-aged waitress walks over and I ask if I can sit at the booth. Chomping down on what I assume is a giant wad of gum; she picks up a plastic covered menu from underneath the counter and heads towards the booth with me following close behind.

Sliding into the booth, I ask, "Do you have any specials?"

In a tired voice, she says, "We have an all-day breakfast special. You'll find the breakfasts and entrées listed in the menu. The meatloaf is popular. Want to start with a drink?"

The nametag hanging crookedly above her left breast tells me that her name is Eleanor.

Her face is drawn and her puffed eyelids scream a lack of sleep. Eleanor's manner suggests someone who works hard out of real necessity. I answer, "Coffee would be great."

"Coming up." She wanders over to the next table. "Get you people another round?"

The sounds of the bar drop into the background as I scan the menu. I settle on the meatloaf with mashed potatoes and fresh vegetables.

Eleanor returns with a mug of steaming coffee, creamers, and sugar. "Have you decided yet?" asks Eleanor.

"I'll take the meatloaf special." I smile, attempting to be friendly.

"Good choice. Want extra gravy on your potatoes? No charge."

"Sure, that would be nice."

As Eleanor saunters off to place the order, I try not to be indiscreet as I glance about the room; noticing that the walls are in need of a fresh coat of paint and the windows could do with an old-fashioned vinegar and water scrub. Self-conscious about sitting here in an expensive business suit I think, *Definitely not my normal eating establishment but, hey, it works for me today.* I am surprised to see Amy's neighbour, Anna Wright, sitting alone at the far side, with a mug of coffee in her hands. Anna's direct look shows that she recognizes me too. I get up and walk over to her table.

"Hello Anna. How are you today?"

"Good, thank you." Anna's mouth curves into the hint of a smile. "Come here often?"

Her humour amuses me. "Ah, no," I admit. "This is my first time, but what the heck, the meatloaf sounds good." Realizing that company would be a welcome diversion, I ask, "Would you care to join me for dinner?"

It's just a flicker of Anna's eyelids but for a moment I feel as if my invitation is being judged. I redden slightly, but quickly dismiss my intention to apologize for the intrusion and to walk away when Anna replies, "That would be nice. Your table or mine?" Although she smiles, I can't shake the feeling that she's curious about me and the thought makes me self-conscious.

"How about we share the booth," I answer. "It's been a long day and I could use a little quiet."

"Know what you mean," replies Anna reaching for her coffee cup. "Sometimes it's just nice to sit on the sidelines and let the world do its thing."

Settling into the booth we both instinctively search for a common ground for conversation. Anna is the first to speak. "Your friend seems to have done a lot with the old place. She's spruced up the yard and added a porch. It's looking nice and lived in."

I relax. "Lived in is right. Amy doesn't just live somewhere; she takes it over and makes it her own personal territory."

"Been friends long?"

"Over twenty-five years. We've seen and done a lot together."

"It's good to have that connection with people," Anna replies. "Life is too short to live without the comfort of friends and people one can trust."

I smile. "You're the second person today to tell me that."

Eleanor returns with the plate of meatloaf. Her reaction to Anna's presence is one of pleasure. "Found yourself a friend, Anna?"

"Yes, I did." Anna replies amicably. "This is Leen." Although, under no obligation to explain how she knows me, Anna adds, "She's a friend of my new neighbour." Observing the comfortable by-play between them, it's obvious to me that they share some history.

"Well that's good." Eleanor looks at Anna's half-empty cup of coffee. "I'll get you a refill. Did you change your mind about wanting anything to eat?"

"I'm good, thank you. Coffee will be fine." Anna leans back into the seat and gives Eleanor a warm smile.

"Back in a minute," says Eleanor.

Anna explains sheepishly, "I come here every so often for a coffee. Once in a while I get their all-day breakfast. Two eggs, brown toast, bacon, baked beans, and hash browns – a real Canadian breakfast. Breaks the day up for me."

"Is their breakfast any good?"

"Not bad. It beats having to make it and the drive gets me out of the house." The slight jut to her chin causes me to think, *She's almost defiant ... as if she expects me to make a snide comment about a greasy spoon being the highlight of her social life.*

"It's funny what people will do for a change of scene," I say. "Look at me. Today I had it with work and felt the need to just drive." I shrug my shoulders and attempt to explain. "My father used to say that a drive helps to clear away the cobwebs. On days like today, I think he had it right."

The corners of Anna's mouth turn up in a half smile, making me wonder if she thinks me foolish. Feeling the hot blush creep up my cheeks, I return to the safety of my meatloaf, cut another piece smothered in tomato-based gravy, and swallow. "Mmm, this is really good."

"Meatloaf has always been a comfort food for me. My mother used to make it for my sister and me when we were children." Chuckling, she adds, "Didn't matter if we had a cold, scraped knee, or a stomach upset – she made meatloaf, peas and mashed potatoes. If she really felt the need to offer extra comfort, she would throw in a dessert she called blancmange."

"Blancmange? Never heard of it."

"Wouldn't expect you to," she answers. "It was my mother's private version of a vanilla type custard caramelized with brown sugar. She had a way of making it so that it would melt in your mouth. I've eaten in a lot of restaurants over the years," she continues whimsically, "but I've never been able to taste such a delight as her blancmange."

"It sounds French? Did you get the recipe?"

"Oh sure I did, but it's like the old saying, 'no one makes something better than mother.' Anna's reply gives us both a shared moment of friendly humour. "It's one of those family recipes that seem to get passed down and no one knows the actual origin."

"You mentioned you had a sister. Does she live near here?"

"No." Anna traces the coffee mug's rim with her index finger before picking it up and taking a sip. "My sister died long ago."

"I'm sorry."

"No need to be sorry," Anna replies in a matter of fact tone. "I have dealt with that grief. At my age, I live for the day. For the most part, I've learned how to compartmentalize life's sadness and try to concentrate on remembering the good moments. Helps me to ease my old bones out of bed in the morning and take on life as if I am living not only for myself, but for those whom I have known and loved."

For a few moments we sit in comfortable silence as I ponder Anna's peculiar wisdom. I have the fleeting impression that Anna is a homespun philosopher and for whatever reason, the thought amuses and pleases me.

As if she can read my thoughts, Anna says, "If I've learned one thing in my life it is that sadness, hard times, laughter, love, tears, and friendships make life worthwhile." Gently, she adds, "All of life's experiences help us – well me at least – to appreciate the goodness of others and the wonder of the world in which we live."

"So what are you two ladies talking about so seriously? You look like the rest of the diner doesn't exist." Pouring coffee refills she says, "Been meaning to tell you, Anna, I'm grateful for what you did for Mary Ellen."

"Glad to have helped." Anna returns Eleanor's smile. "Did she do well with her report?"

I try very hard not to appear as if I'm eavesdropping on their conversation but truth of the matter is I'm all ears.

"Better than well," responds Eleanor, proudly. "She aced the project. Her professor said that she had ..." she pauses, searching her memory for the exact words, "a depth of understanding as if she actually knew what the author really meant." Eleanor's well-endowed chest rises with her intake of breath. "Mary Ellen said it was because of your help that she did so well."

Embarrassed by the overt praise, Anna replies, "That's wonderful, Eleanor, but I can't take any credit. I simply helped her organize some thoughts. She'd done the background research. Please say hello for me."

Anna's subtlety in trying to end the conversation is lost on Eleanor. Eleanor looks at me and then, points the coffee pot towards Anna.

The Search for Claire Holowitz

"You ought to get this woman to talk about plays and things." Peering intently, she vigorously affirms, "She knows a lot."

Eleanor's words prompt me to realize that up until this moment I had simply viewed Anna as Amy's quaint, senior neighbour. I'd not even considered that she might once have had a career. *Yet, I think, she resides in a neighbourhood known for its high real estate value which means she has the financial resources to sustain a good lifestyle. She must have inherited the money, had a successful career, or both.*

I look at Anna as if seeing her for the first time. Based on her clothes, I wouldn't peg her as a professor or anyone who would be involved with the arts. She's dressed simply in a blue cotton long-sleeve shirt over a white T-shirt, blue jeans, and has a well-worn leather jacket. *But then, this is a roadside diner.* With a measure of guilt, I realize that I had dismissed Anna's life because of her age.

Curious, I ask, "What was the report about?" Deliberately ignoring the squint of Anna's eyes as she tries overtly to convey that she does not want me to pursue this conversation, I wait for Eleanor's response.

Eleanor proudly answers, "Oh, Mary Ellen is in her first year of university. She's studying theatre arts. Says she wants to be a writer someday." Talking about her daughter seems to have alleviated Eleanor's former fatigue. Animated and openly friendly she says, "That's why I don't mind working here." She looks around at the other booths. "Pays not good but the work is steady and the tips bring in extra money for Mary Ellen's tuition. She works, too, but her studies keep her pretty busy."

I redirect my question. "So what did Anna help her with?"

"A play. It was nothing." Anna speaks quietly but I can detect a hint of curtness in her reply.

Oblivious to the undercurrent of Anna's tone, Eleanor warms to the discussion. "Something about an angel weeping," she says. "Don't know much about it; the play that is. But, Mary Ellen said some famous lady author who lives like a recluse wrote it. She was really taken with that fact. Just imagine," she sighs pensively, "writing all those plays and having so much money, but never having anyone know who you are or where you live. Really strange for a person to live like that."

She pauses to mull over her thoughts. I flash my best smile.

Encouraged by my attentive manner, Eleanor continues, "Mary Ellen said that part of this lady writer's mystery and appeal *is* the fact that she continues to write and *has chosen* not to be known publicly."

"Hey Eleanor," the man three tables away calls out as he waves an empty beer glass and his drinking buddy swirls the empty pitcher over his head, "how about a refill? We're getting dry over here."

Eleanor's animation fades. "Coming right away, boys." She winks and says, "Won't hurt them to wait for a few minutes between drinks." Smiling, she adds, "Coffees are on me, ladies. Not much by way of thanks," she speaks with some embarrassment, "but anytime you're here Anna, coffee's on the house."

Anna inclines her head and smiles warmly at Eleanor, saying, "Thank you Eleanor."

Her gentle and gracious acceptance of Eleanor's gesture makes me think, *They're obviously worlds apart in terms of education and finances and yet, I feel as if I've just been witness to true graciousness on both of their parts.*

Eleanor sniffs slightly. Satisfied that her gift of thanks has not been rejected, she walks over to the men who are clearly on their way to a state of inebriation. I notice that her steps seem less weary and her shoulders appear to be straighter.

I sip my coffee and peer at Anna over the mug's rim. *She's probably embarrassed,* I think. *Maybe she's just shy.* I ask in what I hope is not an intrusive manner, "Were you a teacher?"

"When I was younger I taught high school English. Naturally that encouraged an interest and need to have a working familiarity with literature and the arts," answers Anna. "When Eleanor asked me to help Mary Ellen with her report, I didn't mind. I've known her since she was a little girl, through her mother's stories, and I've met her a few times." She speaks quietly, "It was fun to revisit some of my youth by talking with her about the play."

I wipe my mouth with my napkin and push my plate aside. *Ah, so that's it,* I think. *She's shy. Being the focus of attention makes her uncomfortable.* Just the same, I'm not ready to let the topic go by the wayside. Acting on a suspicion that I already know the answer to my next question, I ask, "Who was the author of the play for the report?"

Anna answers evenly, "Claire Holowitz."

Now, I'm completely stymied. It seems as if my life is becoming inundated with snippets of information about Holowitz. "Are you a fan of Claire Holowitz's work?"

"I wouldn't call myself a fan," answers Anna, "but I am familiar with her work."

I can't help but speculate at the irony of my position. "It's funny – my days are actually being spent searching for Claire Holowitz." I rub my eyes and try to clear my thoughts. "Know what's really strange, Anna? I left the office today because I felt as if I had had it up to here with Holowitz."

Anna smiles as I raise my hand over my head. "Work has a way of following people around. That's just life."

I can see Anna's look of open curiosity as she asks, "What line of work are you in and why are you spending your time looking for a reclusive author? And, more to the point," she adds, leaning forward, "what do you expect to accomplish when or if you actually find her?"

Before I know it, I'm spilling everything about my search for Claire Holowitz. Through it all Anna listens intently. At times, she interrupts to ask me to clarify something but for the most part, she just listens. My litany of complaints about Don makes her laugh and she commiserates saying, "Don't let him bother you too much. Everyone has horror stories of working with someone like him. Egocentric fools in the workplace are not limited to gender or profession. They can make a person's life miserable if and only if, you let them. Sooner or later he'll get his comeuppance."

"Sooner would be nice," I answer. Being able to speak so openly and not feel as if I have to guard my words has helped to restore some balance to my perspective. "Know what else is strange, Anna?" I smile tentatively and plunge ahead. "Normally, I'm only this open with Amy, Becky or Sarah and yet, with you I am comfortable. You must think me a complete fool for dumping so much on you."

"I don't think you're a fool, Leen," she says, gently. "I think you're working under extreme pressure and being asked to do something that nobody has been able to accomplish for forty years." She clears her throat. "Don't be so hard on yourself. Life has a way of working things out. But," she pauses to consider her next words, "you are right to be cautious about revealing your inner thoughts and reactions to workplace circumstances or difficult colleagues. You never know when it can be used against you."

Immediately, I wonder if I've made a mistake but I push that thought aside. Instinctively, I know that Anna is no threat to me. Like a trusted grandmother, she is dispensing well-intentioned advice. I look at her and say, "I can't shake the feeling that we were supposed to meet." I reach to lightly touch the top of her hand resting on the table. "For whatever reason, I trust you. I tend to go with my gut feelings about people."

I lean back in the booth and laugh softly, "From the moment that Claire's legal hauncho walked into Don's office I've felt driven by some force that I can't understand. I've never believed in things like fate or serendipity and yet," I flip my hands indicating my sense of abandonment of reason, "how else can I explain everything that's happening? You here – us talking about Claire Holowitz. It's weird. Just plain weird."

There's a mischievous gleam in Anna's eyes. "I take it from what you've said that your first impression of Claire Holowitz's legal hauncho was favourable?"

"Not at first," I answer. "Initially, I was very guarded. But as the day wore on, I found myself relaxing." Conscious of the warm blush crawling up from neck to cheeks, I admit, "By the time I dropped him off at the airport, I was actually wondering when I'd see him again."

"Good or bad wondering?" asks Anna.

"Both, I guess. Good in that I think in other circumstances I would like to know him. I've not done much in the way of dating. In fact, Amy and the other two tease me about it but my career has demanded most of my attention." I shrug this admission off. "Even my assistant Kathy likes to remind me that I need a social life. They mean no harm. I can't say the same for other people." I meet her intent gaze directly and say somewhat defensively, "If I had been a man, no one would criticize my dedication to my career but since I'm a woman, some people seem to think that I've missed out on life."

Deciding to make light of it, I add, "Besides, I've not yet met a man who holds my interest long enough to make me want to compromise my career. Men don't think twice about following their careers. I shouldn't have to either."

Anna answers, "I agree with you but if the right man came along, you wouldn't have to worry about compromise. He would accept your career as part of who you are." Then, she asks the million-dollar question. "Do I detect a story here? Despite your claims about your career being the reason for your lack of a social life, I get the sense that someone along the way hurt you deeply and you're afraid to experience that again."

I'm not certain how to answer her. The truth is she's hit the nail on the head. I did love someone more than I can ever express but as my career started to rise, his need to dominate me and to make me feel guilty about it overshadowed any chance of our making it.

We order more coffee and some apple pie. Impressed by Anna's depth of knowledge about Claire Holowitz, I remark, "I could use an extra advisor. If you're inclined to take on that role, you could make some extra income."

Despite her amused expression in response to my impulsive suggestion, Anna appears to consider the offer. "I've a lot of free time on my hands," she offers by way of an explanation for not providing an immediate yes or no, "but I have some questions for you."

Her eyes are cool and betray no emotion as she waits for my response. "Shoot."

"First question, why do you want me to work with you? And, second question," she holds up two fingers, "what sort of salary are we talking about?"

I relax. Anna's straightforward approach is refreshing and from her body language and directness, it's clear that she's comfortable with the art of negotiation. In fact, she seems to be enjoying it."

I reply as straightforwardly as I can. "To be honest, Anna, I liked the way in which you asked your questions. It helped me think things through. I want to know Holowitz, inside and out; that is how I do my work. In order to represent people with honesty and ethics, I need to get to know them."

When Anna doesn't respond to my statement, I reiterate, "At the risk of sounding redundant, you helped me to consider some things I hadn't thought of."

Anna doesn't budge. Instead, she returns my gaze with silent stillness.

Plunging ahead with my pitch, I use my fingers to tick off my rationale for my offer of employment. "One, you're obviously well read and familiar with Holowitz's works. Two, it makes sense to have someone with that skill as a resource to tap into. Three, I'm a good businesswoman and I pride myself on knowing when to ask for help. Four, you can obviously fill that need." I lean back into the booth and smile. "If you want it, the job is yours. What do you say to fifty dollars an hour? I have a budget that allows me to dispense fees for contract consultants."

Anna angles her head slightly, as she considers her response. "Okay, but I want to work from home."

"I can arrange for office space at Scenes. I'll even arrange for you to have medical coverage while you're working on the project."

"Let me rephrase it," smiles Anna. "I have excellent medical coverage and I don't want an office. At my age, it's nice to be at home; among the comfort of my own things and not have to worry about dressing up for corporate imaging. I'm willing to work as an advisor to you and *only* you, but I'm not willing to work at Scenes." She shrugs. "I'm too old to travel to and from a downtown office, but having something to do from home interests me."

Eleanor arrives with the bill for my meatloaf special and our desserts. I take out my wallet and realize I only have two fifties so I hand her one. She pulls out a wallet from her uniform pocket and thumbs out the bills and coins for my change. Placing the money on the table she says, "It was good to see you Anna," and with a nod in my direction adds, "Come again. Any friend of Anna's is a friend of mine."

Anna and I both leave a ten-dollar tip. In a spirit of newfound camaraderie, we chuckle at the fact that the tip is bigger than the cost of the meal and her few coffees. Anna winks and I smile as we both say simultaneously, "For Mary Ellen".

On the way out, Anna stops to say good-bye to Eleanor. I overhear her saying, "Mary Ellen will go places if she follows her dreams." Eleanor gives Anna a warm hug. Seeing Anna's tiny frame being amassed in Eleanor's broad arms makes me think, *Anna looks almost frail.* I dismiss my concern thinking, *I guess at her age, I will too.*

We walk out to the parking lot where Anna signals a waiting taxi.

"Please let me drive you home," I offer, feeling a twinge of guilt that I'd not remembered Amy's comment that Anna uses taxis to get her groceries.

"No problem, dear. Driving me home is out of your way."

I begin to protest that it's not a problem but she waves away my repeated offer with a smile. "Whenever I come out here I tell Harry to return around the time that I think I'll leave. He's been driving me around for years and is used to my little wanderings. I enjoy the luxury of indulging myself every now and then." She touches my arm lightly. "I've had a delightful time. Now, you go home and get some rest. Sounds to me as if you have a lot on your mind and much to do." She walks to the waiting taxi, the door being held open by Harry. I watch as the taxi pulls away and return Anna's wave.

Strangely content with how this day has turned out, I make my way to my own car thinking, *Anna will be useful in helping me to put a human face on the lost Claire Holowitz.*

I think about the elements of chance and coincidence. My meeting up with Anna was pure serendipity.

Anxious to get home, I drive towards the on-ramp for the highway. I want to make some notes from Anna's and my discussion while my thoughts are still clear and fresh.

Chapter Five

Leen

Over the next few weeks, following my chance encounter with Anna at the Speckled Rooster, I rush to keep up with my hectic schedule. Using the list that Aumount – true to his promise to cooperate in as much as his client is willing to provide information – I contact art galleries that have held Holowitz photo exhibits. Knowing which gallery to target and who to contact has helped considerably. As a result, I've managed to garner agreement from two collectors, one in New York and one in Toronto, for the use of Holowitz photos for the Gala. Relentlessly, Kathy has tracked down Aumount's sources and they in turn have provided glimpses into Holowitz's work and personality.

I'm now ready to use that information along with the growing file of newspaper clippings about Holowitz's early days – before she became a recluse – to begin a more in-depth profile. Pleased with my organization, I recall a detail needing confirmation. "Kathy," I call out, "any further news on the collector living in Victoria?" I push my reading glasses onto my head and rise to stretch my back.

Standing in the doorway, Kathy answers, "Nothing yet from Victoria. And," she arches an accusatory eyebrow, "before you ask … I placed a trans-Atlantic call to that actor, Marcus Gilles, living in London. Still waiting for a response."

I smile as I once again give silent thanks for Kathy's efficiency. "One step ahead of me, Kathy. Let me know when you hear from him."

"Don't I always? By the way, the Sentinel sent an E-mail asking for the latest expense update for the use of the Holowitz originals that you're planning to have at the Gala."

Groaning, I point my cursor at my laptop's screen to open the business accounts' file and gripe, "Don's got that information. He's still balking at the price I negotiated for the use of those photos and manuscripts. He can't seem to get it into his head that having those articles at the Gala will highlight decades of Claire's work."

"Don't let him get to you. He's just proving once again that he's a control freak."

"Anal control freak," I correct. Frustrated, I hit the send key. "There, I've re-sent the expense spreadsheet along with a terse message asking the Sentinel if she's misplaced the previous one."

"That'll make her happy," replies Kathy, with a wry expression.

"I don't mean to take out my frustration on you, Kathy;" I say, scanning an inter-office memo from Mike, my financial assistant in the advertising department. "It annoys me how Don wants me to put together a champagne affair using a beer budget."

"Understood." Tactfully, she changes topics. "Don't forget that Bill Watkins from Media will be here at noon." She looks at her watch, "That'll give us an hour to review the list for key note speakers."

"Right," I agree, knowing that I've put it off twice already. "If we move quickly, we can get that done before Bill arrives."

At eleven forty-five, Kathy rises to leave. "I'll re-confirm with the speakers the points we've covered just to ensure that we've missed nothing."

I glance at my watch. "I've a few moments to freshen up before Bill arrives. It's going to be a working lunch. Could you please call Rueben's Deli and arrange to have some sandwiches sent up around twelve thirty? Be sure to order something for yourself. After all," I joke, "I'm putting it on Don's expense account, under the heading of business lunch."

"No problem," answers Kathy, picking up her notes. "I'll get them to throw in a few pickles and some apple pie as well." She ambles off towards her desk and hits the speed dial on her phone for Rueben's Deli.

One of the perks of my position at Scenes is a private bathroom and I head towards it. Suddenly hungry, I'm looking forward to lunch. Rueben's Deli has been in the same building since Rueben Flescher founded it some sixty years ago. Samuel, Rueben's grandson, manages it these days. I can't vouch for what it was like sixty years ago but the food is good, the prices are fair, and its location next to the Scenes complex makes it a frequent source of luncheon trays.

I splash my face with cold water and comb my hair. Pleased with what Kathy and I accomplished this morning, I'm looking forward to working with Bill. He's the type of employee that every boss likes to have on the payroll. He's thorough, ethical, and works hard. I'm just finishing up in the bathroom when I hear the low rumble of voices.

As I re-enter my office I overhear Bill, a big man with a tall frame and friendly smile, teasing Kathy, "How's life up here in the Holowitz think tank zone?"

"We're moving slowly but surely," replies Kathy. "Leen had me order sandwiches from Rueben's for lunch. Looks like you're going to be immersed in the think tank for a few hours."

"Hope you ordered some roast beef?" replies Bill.

Kathy laughs. "Any special type of mustard?"

Enjoying their playful repartee, Bill answers, "Well, now that you mention it, I fancy Rueben's house mustard; the one with horseradish."

Leaning against the doorframe, I tease, "If the two of you are through planning the lunch menu, maybe we can get started on the work?"

"Oops," Bill smiles at Kathy, "duty calls. Don't forget the kosher pickles."

Kathy retorts, "Hrmpf. Next time I'll let you place the order."

"So what's new?" asks Bill.

"I met with Joe Scappetti from the Graphics Department yesterday. He left some of the mock-ups for you to look at. Once we decide what we want, he'll put a few people on making it happen."

Bill nods. "I ran into him in the cafeteria yesterday at lunch. He mentioned that he'd left some designs with you. Anything else?"

"No, not really," I answer. "I've had a few conversations with people who have directed her plays, displayed her photos, or acted in one of her plays. The more I learn about her, the more convinced I am that Claire Holowitz is not only elusive but extremely eccentric."

"Eccentric and elusive, maybe," Bill replies with a pensive expression, "but she's also a prolific writer and photographer. She's total box office." Having lost the casual joking demeanour he'd displayed with Kathy, Bill sits down at the conference table and removes his suit jacket. "There's an abundance of information pertaining to her philanthropy ranging from medical research to donations to elementary school breakfast programs."

I sit down and reach for the blue file folder. Each file is colour-coded, depending on the specific facet of Holowitz's life and career that I've narrowed down. "I know," I answer, spreading out photos and newspaper clippings, "but not one of these has a picture of her. There is always someone else ... usually her lead lawyer, Marc Andre Aumount, who represents her at functions." To make my point, I tap a photo of Aumount shaking hands with the Chairperson of a local school board with the caption, 'Claire Holowitz donates $100,000 to breakfast program for local school children.'

Entering with coffee and muffins, Kathy peers at the photo of Aumount. "Hmmm," she says, "isn't that Claire Holowitz's lawyer?"

I roll my eyes. "You know very well it is."

Bill winks at Kathy. He's picked up from my response to Kathy's comment that the mention of Aumount has hit a nerve. Recognizing the opportunity to tease me and to feed Kathy's sense of humour, he makes pretence of looking at a few of the photos and with a straight face, observes, "I see your point Kathy. Guess if we're going to talk about Claire Holowitz, we're going to see a lot of," he taps the photo, "one Marc Andre Aumount."

"Hence the reference to *the* Aumount file," replies Kathy smugly.

"Okay, enough from both of you." I address Bill pointedly, "We have work to do."

Taking my none too subtle hint, Bill asks, "Have you heard from Aumount since his visit?"

"No, but he did fax over a list of contacts which he said Claire Holowitz agreed to and that's helped a great deal. To date, everyone on that list that we've managed to contact has cooperated.

"Which means," Kathy interjects on her way to the door, "that *Aumount* has instructed them to."

After she's out of earshot, Bill says in a casual tone, "Kathy was just kidding, Leen."

I reply, "She has this thing about trying to play match maker."

Bill chuckles. "It's because you react that she keeps it up."

"You're right," I agree. "But Aumount is a reality and we have to deal with him. I just want to keep it professional."

"Okay," says Bill, reaching for his pen. "Let's start to put a spin on the media campaign. What do you know about Holowitz?"

"Little is known about her early life and even less after the car accident which resulted in the death of her husband and daughter." I search through the clippings and pull out a few. "These tell of her last interview given on the day they died. From that point on she became a social recluse."

Bill picks up the article with a photo of Holowitz standing on the hospital steps. "Says here she told the media that if she had not stayed behind to give an interview, she would have been with her husband and daughter." Placing it back down on the table he adds, "There's been a lot of speculation over the years that she blamed herself. Guilt – deserved or not – can be a heavy burden."

"That's my take," I answer. "For reasons, known only to Holowitz, she decided to isolate herself from the media. Still," I trace the photo gently with my finger, thinking aloud, "she continued to write, photograph, and endow various charities."

Bill clears his throat and is about to say something when my desk phone rings. Excusing myself, I walk over to my desk to pick up the receiver. "Leen MacLeen."

"Oh oh," comes the response, "Have I caught you at a bad time?"

Smiling at the sound of Amy's voice, I answer, "Just working on a file with Bill from media. What's up?" Cradling the receiver between my shoulder and ear I move around my desk to study a mock up of the artwork that Bill has laid out on the table. The balance and the colours are good but something is missing. I make a mental note to ask Jean from graphics to revisit her layout.

"My," responds Amy with mock hurt, "how quickly the rich and powerful forget their humble friends."

"What?" I'm momentarily taken aback but quickly recover, realizing what her phone call is about.

"Is tonight the night?" Brushing back some fallen strands of hair from my forehead, I apologize, "I've been so involved with this Holowitz campaign that I forgot. What can I bring?" I flip open my desk calendar. Sure enough, we'd changed the regular scheduled Friday when Sarah announced the twins were having a fall "pre-grad blow-out weekend". She and Joe wanted to be home, as she had put it, "To make sure that our place doesn't become party central."

"How about some fresh bread?"

"What time?" I nod approval to Bill who is holding up a graphic design of a poster for the Gala.

"Six for cocktails. We're having spaghetti."

"Sounds good. I'll be there."

"Great," says Amy. "I know you're busy so I'll let you go but, please," she adds gently,

"try not to be late." I can hear the amusement in her voice as she qualifies her request, "You know how peeved Sarah gets when her salad wilts because she has had to wait for you."

"I'll leave in plenty of time. Tell Sarah not to put the dressing on the salad until I get there."

"Okay. Take care. See you later."

Smiling, I hang up. Amy has always been the more organized. Unlike me, she doesn't' need a blackberry or I-phone to beep reminders of where she has to be. "Sorry about the interruption," I say, returning my focus to Bill.

By four o'clock, we're finished and I'm glad to rise and stretch my legs. Massaging my neck with one hand and tapping the file folder containing notes, follow-ups, and to-do list, I say, "It's starting to take shape, Bill. Thanks."

Bill places the mock-ups into his portfolio case, rolls down his shirt-sleeves, and shrugs back into the suit jacket he'd abandoned earlier. "I take it we'll meet again next week?"

I flick open my cell phone to check my calendar. "How about Tuesday at ten?"

"Works for me," says Bill, confirming his agenda on his blackberry.

"We've done a lot today." I walk him to my office door. "Any plans for the weekend?"

"Nothing special. Beth and I are going to rent a few videos, make some popcorn, maybe share a bottle of wine or two. Carrie and Charlotte want to go to the new marine amusement park tomorrow and Derek has a hockey game on Sunday."

"How old are they now?"

"The twins are six and Derek's eleven," answers Bill. "They keep us busy."

"Sounds like you have it all mapped out." Seeing the dark circles under his eyes, I wonder if I look as tired as he does. I make a mental note to put on some make-up before going to Amy's.

"How about you? Anything special?"

"Getting together with some friends for supper tonight. Speaking of which ..." I say, checking my watch, "if I hurry, I'll have just enough time to pick up some fresh bread and wine."

Bill smiles. "Have a good time Leen."

I leave him to say good-bye to Kathy and head back into my office to collect my jacket, purse and switch off my laptop. As I close the door to my office Kathy says, "Give me a minute and I'll ride the elevator with you."

"You stayed late. I thought the plan was for you to leave early today."

"Had a few things I wanted to finish up before the weekend," answers Kathy. "Beats having to deal with them on Monday morning."

Pushing on the elevator's down button to take us to the parking garage, Kathy says, "I know that you asked me to hold your calls this afternoon but since it was Amy, I put it through."

"Good thing you did," I reply. "I forgot that we were supposed to get together tonight." We walk out to the garage area together.

"You ladies have a good thing going there," remarks Kathy, pulling her car keys out from her jacket's pocket. "Say hi to them for me."

"Thanks, I will."

Kathy smirks, "Any *other* plans for the weekend?" The implied innuendo in her comment is obvious.

Shaking my head, I answer, "Subtlety is definitely not your strong point."

She grins. "Never claimed that it was."

Turning to open my car door, I add, "One of these days, you'll be telling me that my social schedule is overshadowing my work schedule."

"I live for that day," Kathy retorts as she walks towards her car parked three down from mine.

On the way to Amy's, I stop at a little Italian bakery and pick up two fresh loaves of crusty Italian bread and then, take a detour to the liquor store where I select three bottles of Italian wine. Pulling up to

Amy's house, I park my car, grab my purchases, and walk over to Anna's front door. There's no response to my first ring of the doorbell so I push the button again. I'm beginning to wonder if she has gone out when I hear the click of the lock being turned.

Clad in jeans and wearing a stylish red v-neck sweater, Anna beams a smile and says, "Hello Leen."

"Hello Anna. I was on my way to Amy's and thought that I'd drop by."

"Well, this is a surprise!" Anna opens the door wider and I step into the foyer. This is my first visit to Anna's house and I quickly scan my surroundings. Left of the foyer is a living room and on the right, a small sitting room that leads to what appears to be a greenhouse area. Straight ahead, in the centre of the foyer, stands an oak staircase curving its way up to a second floor. Two hallways on each side of the staircase lead to the rooms at the back of the house.

"I was about to have some tea."

Anna's comment draws me back to the moment. Wanting to say something to cover for my less than subtle curiosity about her house, I answer, "This house is bigger than I thought it would be."

"Definitely bigger than I need," she replies, putting me at ease, "but I've been here many years and I just can't seem to part with it."

Admiringly, I say, "It's beautiful."

"Thank you." Smiling, Anna asks, "Have you time for tea?"

I had not intended to stay. Following her to the kitchen, I say, "I'll chat for a few minutes but Amy's expecting me for supper. I thought that since we've not spoken since we met at the Speckled Rooster; I'd pop by to say a quick hello."

The kitchen suggests careful attention had been given to providing for utility and comfort. Admiring the wall colours, ceramic floor tiles, golden honey patina of the cupboards and openness of the kitchen I comment, "This kitchen belongs in '*Beautiful Homes*'."

Opening a cupboard Anna takes out two teacups. "Thank you. I spend a lot of time in my kitchen. I enjoy the lighting and wanted it to be a place of comfort as well as work."

Realizing that she's preparing tea for both of us, I speak up. "I can't stay for tea, Anna. Amy is expecting me." Lamely, I add, "We're having spaghetti."

Returning the teacup to the cupboard, Anna says, "Maybe you can come again when you have more time and we can visit. So tell me …" she smiles, "what brings you here today?"

Placing my parcels on the round oak table I pull out one of the wine bottles and a loaf of bread. "I thought that you might enjoy some fresh bread and wine." Smiling at the look of surprise on Anna's face, I add, "I enjoyed our conversation a few weeks ago. I was wondering if we could get together sometime soon to discuss what I've learned so far about Claire Holowitz."

"I've always loved the smell and taste of freshly baked bread," smiles Anna, "and who can say no to a nice bottle of wine."

Pleased that my little offerings seem to have made Anna happy, I reply, "I'm glad you like them."

Pouring a cup of tea, Anna's expression becomes pensive. "As I've not seen you since the Speckled Rooster, I thought that you might have changed your mind about having me do some work with you. I'm still not certain what I can do to help you out but I'm willing to try."

My response is immediate and I experience a wave of guilt that my workload has prevented me from getting in touch sooner. "No, I've certainly not forgotten but my workload has been hectic and when that happens, I tend to lose time. In fact," I grimace slightly, "had Amy not called me at the office today, I would have forgotten about our supper plans. Lately, every waking moment seems to be consumed with collecting information about Claire Holowitz. I wanted to have something tangible for you to look at before we got together."

Anna's blue eyes twinkle mischievously. "And you have that now?"

Frowning, I answer, "I think so. She's such a mystery woman. Yet, the more I learn about her, the more real she has become. If it's okay with you, I'll put together a file for your reference and drop it off to you Monday, after work."

"She *is* real," answers Anna, smiling at my having stated the obvious. "It's good that you're trying to understand the person, as opposed to the box office version."

"She's not even had one bust or flop."

"At least not one that *is* known about," replies Anna. "I suspect even Claire Holowitz has had some difficult moments that few people know about. Why is it so important for you to understand her as a person?" The directness of Anna's question startles me. Before I can frame an appropriate response, she asks, "Isn't the Gala about her works?"

"Yes of course it is. But to make the Gala unique, I want to represent the human side of Claire Holowitz." Picking up on my train of thought, I add, "You know what I mean. Most people only dream of writing or taking photos that bring fame and success. Few achieve those goals. She has isolated herself from all public acclaim and yet, continues to be some sort of phenomenon. Other than Marc Andre Aumount, no one I've interviewed has actually met her. The people and organizations who have benefited from her philanthropy speak of a woman who has become a living legend." Realizing that I sound like a gushing schoolgirl, I stop talking.

Anna's face is a study of concentration. After a few moments, she says, "I'm still not certain how I can help you."

Hoping that I don't sound condescending, I try to explain. "When we talked you seemed to have an understanding of the context and innuendos in her writing. I want another perspective of Claire Holowitz – different from the ones given by directors of plays, actors, or gallery directors." I try to hide my frustration. "Claire's an enigma; a real contradiction in her life and works. I'm asking you to use your knowledge to help me present her not as a recluse but as a living, breathing woman of passion and insight. If you're willing to take a stab at it, I'd be grateful. I'm one hundred percent convinced that Holowitz, *the person*, must be the focus of the Gala."

Clearly interested, Anna asks, "Contradiction? How so?"

"Well, look at her fame as a writer, photographer, and philanthropist. Most people would seek public recognition, but she hides in anonymity."

"Maybe she doesn't hide," speculates Anna. "Perhaps she has just chosen not to be seen in the public eye." Sipping her tea, she suggests, "Have you considered that perhaps Claire Holowitz is comfortable in being who she is and letting that be?"

"I've thought about it," I answer. "But, she must know that people admire her work and want to know her."

"Knowing what people want and need are two different things," smiles Anna. "At my age you come to realize that as long as needs are satisfied; wants are purely whimsical and self-indulgent. In Claire's case, maybe what she *needs* is her own space – her privacy, if you will."

I let out a short, frustrated sigh. "Just the same, I would like to meet her. The whole world would like to meet her!"

Responding to Anna's amused scepticism to my last comment; I try to defend my claim. "Well, okay, so maybe not the whole world but you know what I mean. For someone to be so acknowledged and, at the same time, so impervious to fame is both frustrating and remarkable." Checking the clock, I realize that I've stayed longer than intended. "I have to get next door or they'll be griping that true to form I'm late."

Laughing, Anna walks me to the front door. "Thank you for the wine and bread, Leen. It was good to see you."

Resting my hand on the door latch, I say, "I'll be back on Monday with the file."

"I'll look forward to it,' replies Anna.

༄

I knock lightly and call out, "I'm here and please note that I'm five minutes early."

Sarah's voice greets me. "By whose watch?"

Rolling my eyes, I enter the kitchen and answer, "Very funny."

"Your car has been parked outside for twenty minutes. Where were you?" asks Sarah.

"We were beginning to think that we should organize a search party," jokes Amy.

"Yes," smiles Becky, as she grates some parmesan. "Not only would there be the ongoing search for Claire Holowitz but there'd be the search for Leen."

"Comics," I retort, placing the bread and wine on the counter. "I was next door at Anna's."

"What were you doing there?" asks Sarah.

"Dropping off some bread and a bottle of wine."

Holding the cheese grater in mid-air, Becky's face registers surprise. "Bread and wine?"

"Sure, why not?"

"Just curious," replies Becky. "I didn't think you knew her other than having met her when Amy moved in."

"I don't," I reply. "I met up with her by accident a few weeks ago at a greasy spoon diner called Speckled Rooster and we got to talking."

Curious, Amy asks, "Speckled Rooster? I've never heard of it. More to the point, what were you doing there?"

I smile. "Trust me, there's a whole other story as to how I ended up there. Short answer is the Speckled Rooster is in a small village – I can't even remember its name – about thirty minutes outside of Ottawa. I'd left work early and just started to drive, wanting to clear my head. I realized I was hungry and pulled off the highway when I saw the sign for the village. I stopped to get something to eat and there was Anna sitting at one of the tables."

"Really?" says Sarah. "What was she doing there?"

"She said that she goes there every once in a while for something to do," I reply. "For her it seems to be an outing. At any rate, the waitress thanked her for helping her daughter with an essay for one of her university classes. Guess what the subject of the essay was?"

Becky says, "Nuclear physics?"

Grinning, I reply, "Hah, hah, very funny."

"Okay, so what was it?" asks Becky.

"Claire Holowitz." I lean back in my chair and enjoy the moment. Their expressions are priceless.

"*Your* Claire Holowitz?" asks Sarah.

I tease, "Do you know of another one?"

"What are the odds of that happening?"

"I asked myself the same question," I reply. "I'm chalking it up to serendipity."

"So you like her?" asks Becky.

"Yes," I reply, surprised at the alacrity of my response. There is certain quaintness to her that–for whatever reason – I find intriguing. Plus, her knowledge about Claire Holowitz seems to be fairly extensive. So much so, I asked her if she'd consider acting as a consultant for the Gala."

"Wow," remarks Amy, "that's quite a leap from being friendly with my neighbour to have her working at Scenes."

"Our agreement was for me to provide her with the necessary files and she'll work from home. As I have not seen her since the Speckled Rooster, I stopped by tonight to see if she was still willing to do it."

"Why not ask her to join us?" suggests Amy. "We have plenty of food and if the two of you are going to be doing some work together, it might be nice for her to get to know all of us." The other two agree immediately.

Surprised, but pleased with the idea, I ask, "So you're all good with this?"

"Absolutely," answers Amy. "Go," she flicks her fingers dismissively, "and ask her. I'll toss the salad while you're gone and we can set another place at the table."

Uncorking a bottle of wine, Becky snorts and we all look to see the source of her amusement. Holding the wine bottle so that the label is visible, she asks, "Stump Jump, what sort of name is this?"

Sarah grins, "Australian. I liked the name so I bought it."

Laughing, I say, "I'll be right back. I'm not certain she'll agree to come."

Amy responds, "You won't know until you ask."

Self-consciously I ring Anna's doorbell, wondering what she'll think about our spur-of-the-moment invitation.

Anna looks surprised to see me again so soon.

"Hello again," I say sheepishly. "I was telling my friends about our meeting up at the Speckled Rooster and they suggested that I ask if you'd like to join us."

For a split second I think she will decline the invitation but, opening the door wider so that I can step into the foyer, she says, "I just happen to have a new bottle of wine that might go well with supper."

"There you go," I answer, smiling, "it's settled."

"It won't take me a moment to get my jacket."

I wait as she grabs a tan jacket from the hallway closet and makes her way back to the kitchen to retrieve the bottle of wine I had given her earlier. Returning, she says, "Wine is best shared in the company of friends. Let's go and enjoy it."

Amy welcomes Anna with a big smile. "We are so pleased you decided to join us, Anna."

Becky extends her hand in greeting. "Welcome, I'm Becky. Can I take your jacket?"

"I'm Sarah," interjects Sarah, shaking hands with her. True to her word, Amy has tossed the salad and set another place at the table.

As we gather around the kitchen table Amy asks Anna, "What do you think about the renovations I've made?"

"The colours are vibrant and delightful," replies Anna. Surveying the kitchen with careful consideration she adds, "This kitchen is absolutely marvellous! It's not only welcoming but it looks to be extremely functional."

"I love the new porch," says Sarah. Teasingly, she adds, "But, now we'll have the dilemma of choosing where to sit – the back deck or the porch – when we want to sit outside and solve our earth-shaking catastrophes."

"I like what you've done to the place," remarks Anna. "When I saw the front porch being added, my first thought was that it added character to the house. It looks as if it's always been part of the house rather than a new addition."

"Joe gets the credit for that," answers Amy. Elaborating for Anna's benefit, she says, "Joe is Sarah's husband. He wouldn't take a cent above his material costs."

Shrugging off the compliment, Sarah says, "He was happy to do it." To Anna, she says, "The four of us are like family."

"We don't disturb you with our talk and laughter when we're outside, do we?" asks Becky, sprinkling some romano cheese on the salad.

Anna chuckles. "Not at all," she reassures Becky. In fact, I find it pleasant to hear the occasional murmur of voices and sounds of laughter. She raises her wine glass in a toast. "It's nice to have the sounds of young life next door."

"Young!" exclaims Sarah. "You've just become my new best friend. I've not thought of myself as being young for a lot of years. I've got two teenage sons.

From my perspective, you *are* young," replies Anna.

The conversation is amicable as we eat our supper and Anna appears to be enjoying the teasing and banter. Twirling pasta onto her fork she remarks, "This meal is fantastic. I love the sauce."

"Thank you," beams Amy. "I learned the recipe when I was growing up from Maria Grifati, a good friend of my mother. She was 'old world Italian'.

"Well, I've never tasted better," says Anna.

"You've just wormed your way into Amy's heart," jokes Sarah. "She loves to cook and she's very proud of her spaghetti." Feigning dismay, she warns, "Don't get her started on her recipes. We'll be here all night."

Amy makes a 'who me' face and addresses Anna, "I'll write out the recipe for you but be warned, making Maria's sauce is an all day affair."

"Well worth it," answers Anna, smiling as she takes another mouthful.

Throughout dinner, Anna proves to be a good listener. Fitting in comfortably, she shows open interest in the conversation and gives sympathetic attention to Becky as she waxes eloquent on some of her favourite medical issues. At the top of Becky's list is the growing number of people facing problems associated with dementia and Alzheimer's and the need for the government to wake up and address the concerns.

"It's projected that as many as 750,000 in this country will be affected with some form of dementia within the next few years," sighs Becky, exasperation evident. We have basic medical care but there's very little assistance for coverage of expenses associated with extra billing of drugs or caregivers. Coupled with those problems is the growing number of cases of elder abuse perpetrated by those who take advantage of the person's inability to function within society."

"One thing I've always been grateful for," replies Anna, thoughtfully, "is that despite how my body has aged, my mind has remained clear."

Embarrassed, Becky says, "I did not mean to imply..."

Anna's reassuring smile alleviates the awkwardness. "Oh please don't even think I thought you were implying that old age necessarily brings with it Alzheimer's. I agree with you wholeheartedly. We live in one of the greatest countries in the world and yet, our government has not addressed the needs of many of its citizens."

Anna's comment sparks a lively discussion about the government's penchant for its members to name call and point the finger of blame as opposed to actually governing the country with a view to serving the electorate.

Sarah pipes up with, "Let me make myself perfectly clear ..." and Becky joins in with, "And, to be perfectly clear ..."

Immediately, we all laugh. Their mimicking of the posturing, for which some elected officials have become famous, is hilarious.

"When the government wants to muddy the waters to avoid giving a direct answer, the pat answer begins with 'Let me be clear,' complains Sarah, the most vocal of our group about politics.

"It sounds cynical," continues Sarah, "but there is a big discrepancy between what politicians promise to do when wanting to get elected and what they actually do."

"Are you *absolutely clear* on that point?" teases Amy.

Sarah reacts by fuelling one of Amy's favourite rants. "How about the federal government's lack of support for the Arts? If a Canadian wants to get recognized in the Arts, it seems that he or she has to leave the country in order to make it big."

"That's why many Canadian artists go south," emphasizes Becky. "Give the Americans their due. They, at least, recognize the Arts as being essential to the fabric of society and *they* support their artists."

I stage whisper to Anna, "They're charged up. Government lack of accountability and the waste of Canadian talent are favourite topics." Grinning, I add, "Never a dull moment."

Sarah makes a face. "How about Claire Holowitz?" demands Amy.

I remove another bottle from Amy's wine rack and, with practiced ease, I twist the corkscrew. "What about her?"

"Talking about Canadian artists made me think of her. Are you any closer to actually meeting her?"

"No," I answer. "I've not heard anything from her lawyer since the meeting I told you all about."

"And that would be the meeting with the gorgeous and easy on the eye Marc Andre Aumount?" teases Sarah.

"What was it you said about him?" asks Amy, picking up on Sarah's reference to Aumount. Scrunching her face, she pretends to search her memory before exclaiming, "Oh, I remember now ... you said he had magnetism about him and his eyes were a ..." she looks at Becky, "what colour did Leen say Aumount's eyes were?

Becky grins. "I do believe she said he had lovely *dove grey eyes.*"

I bite back a sharp retort, knowing that a reply will only encourage them to continue with their teasing.

Anna asks, "Do I detect a little bit of romantic interest on Leen's part for Claire Holowitz's lawyer?"

I try to gloss over their remarks. "It's nothing really. They're making way too much of my having said that he's an attractive man." Narrowing my eyes, I glare at Sarah, Becky, and Amy; trying to warn them that they've said enough.

Not deterred, Amy smugly drives home her point, "Oh, you said more than that! You said he was on the cover of Forbes magazine, is well-respected in the legal world, has excellent taste in clothes, has a trace of a French-Canadian accent, is charming and, that he's ..." she ticks off points with her fingers, "astute, intelligent, and easy to look at."

"Cut it out," I snap.

Ignoring my frustration, Amy points a finger at me and says, "You can't fool us. In spite of his stone-walling you about meeting Claire Holowitz, you *liked* him."

"Adding to his list of credits," interrupts Sarah, "are the facts that he is a partner in one of Canada's most prestigious legal firms, sits on the Bar Review, and is a welcome guest at the Prime Minister's and Governor General's soirees." She grins. "And if that isn't enough of an impressive resume, there is the fact that he is considered to be one of Canada's most eligible bachelors. What's not to like?"

"Okay, so he's impressive," I concede, "but that doesn't mean I'm interested in him. He represents Claire Holowitz, pure and simple. My interest in him lies with the fact that he can open doors for me to gain interviews with people familiar with her work and to hopefully garner her approval for what I'm doing."

"And you're going to do all of this without breaking a forty year period of seclusion?" asks Becky.

"Exactly," I answer, hoping they'll accept my interest in Aumount is professional. It doesn't take long for Becky to dash my hopes.

"How about in the *personal* department?"

I groan. "The three of you think you're such comics."

Out of the blue, Sarah observes, "He has a sexy smile." In response to our open surprise at her comment, she shrugs. "I've seen him a few times around the court house. Just because I'm married doesn't exclude me from looking."

"It's those *dove grey* eyes," oozes Amy. "That does the trick for me."

Throwing my hands up in the air, I whine, "Can we please change the topic?"

Having had their fun at my expense, they relent and stop teasing me. Over dessert, Amy asks Anna, "Did you use to work in the Arts?"

"I've always had an appreciation for the Arts," answers Anna, softly. "I'm not certain how much I can help Leen with her project but I'm grateful that it's led to my having had the benefit of meeting four new friends."

Raising her coffee mug, Becky declares cheerfully, "To Claire Holowitz. She's brought you and Leen together and, because of that shared interest and you being Amy's neighbour, we have a new friend."

I notice that Anna's reaction to Becky's praise is similar to what I had observed at the Speckled Rooster. *Yes,* I think, *Despite her friendliness, she's definitely a woman who shies away from the limelight. She's learned how to relate to people but guards her own privacy.*"

Glancing at her watch, Anna says, "Thank you for inviting me into your home, Amy. I've had a most entertaining evening – one of the best that I've had in a long time."

"I'm glad you had a good time," replies Sarah. "It's just a beginning, Anna. We'll have plenty more."

"And, hopefully, you'll join our bonding sessions." Becky grins, "You can help us solve the problems of the world."

Anna jokes, "I'm not altogether certain the world is ready for the four of you."

The evening ends on a good note and we settle on an Asian menu for our next get together. Anna offers to bring some Cambodian spring rolls.

At the front door, Anna pauses to ask, "You're all sure you want me to come back?"

Becky smiles her reassurance. "Well, of course we do. You've been great and not even balked once at any of our jokes. In fact, you helped make some of them better."

Sarah, Becky, and I see Anna safely to her front door before we head for our cars. We are all soon on our way home, pleased with how our evening turned out.

Chapter Six

Leen

The next two weeks have me hopping between meetings in Ottawa, New York and Toronto. By the end of the second week, I find myself sitting in the Fairmont Hotel, across from Toronto's Union Station. I'd flown in from Ottawa to the Island airport and had spent an informative and productive afternoon with two directors who'd produced Holowitz plays at the Royal Alexandra theatre. Normally, I would have taken the one-hour flight back to Ottawa but Irving Castleman, a behind-the-scenes financier, is only available for a Saturday breakfast at 10 a.m. tomorrow so I made the decision to stay the night in Toronto and enjoy a quiet evening.

Pleased with how things are shaping up for the Gala, I ease my black heels from my tired feet and wiggle my toes.

I spend the next half-hour soaking in a hot bath, letting the courtesy lavender salts work their soothing magic. When the water turns cool, I dry myself and slip into my pyjamas and the thick, terry cloth robe provided by the hotel. Feeling relaxed and content, I call room service and order a bottle of wine along with a plate of cheese, fruit and crackers. I switch on the television, sit back in the upholstered armchair with my legs folded underneath me, and watch the news as I wait for room service to deliver my meal.

The wine comes uncorked. I pour some into the stemmed wine glass and take an appreciative sip before lifting the lid covering the food. Nipping on a fresh strawberry I retrieve my cell phone from my purse and return to my chair. Sipping my wine I use my free hand to press the number pad. Becky answers on the third ring.

"Your timing is good," says Becky. "Another fifteen minutes and I'd be gone. What's up?"

"I've been so busy doing interviews for the Gala that I've not been in touch for the last two weeks. Thought I'd call and get caught up. What are your plans for the weekend?"

"Josh wants to kick off our weekend by trying out the new steak house downtown," answers Becky, "and then tomorrow we'll drive down to Niagara to take a wine tour. He wants to add to the restaurant's wine list."

I laugh. "It always seems funny to me when the two of you go out to other restaurants. You can enjoy gourmet meals whenever you want."

"Staying on top of the competition means keeping tabs on what other restaurants are offering, their prices and service," replies Becky. "Besides, it's nice to get out and let someone else do the cooking. So what's up with you tonight?"

"Nothing much. Like I said, I just wanted to get in touch to find out what's new and exciting in your life. I'm spending the night in Toronto and will fly home tomorrow morning."

"Planning on taking in a play or going out to a fancy restaurant?"

"No, just relaxing with room service and some good wine. If I feel energetic, I might review some of my notes."

"Josh and I have arranged our schedules to take Monday off so we'll be back early Monday evening. It's been a while since we treated ourselves to a long weekend."

"Where's the winery that he's interested in?"

"Virgil, just outside of Niagara on the Lake. I thought it would be fun to visit some of the shops in Niagara-on-the-Lake and perhaps try my luck at the casino. Generally indulge myself and hopefully, raise my weary libido."

"Your libido?" Sputtering, I nearly choke on my wine. "What's that about? I thought you were a convert to Maslow's theory about the benefits to be achieved through sexual release."

"Oh sure, sure," Becky answers, "but it doesn't hurt to look for new ways to stimulate it. Keeping the element of surprise does much to sustain a relationship. Speaking of which," she teases, "when are you going to stop subverting *your* libido to that career of yours? It's simply not healthy. And, that's free advice from your doctor friend since I'm in a very generous mood."

Ignoring Becky's reference to my non-existent sex life, we chat for a few more minutes and then, wishing her a great weekend, I say good-bye.

Feeling relaxed, I decide I've stalled long enough and open my briefcase. Half an hour later I put away my notes and I'm thinking of calling it a night when my cell phone rings.

The first thing I hear is the muffled sound of a sniffle followed by, Amy's voice, "Leen?"

"Amy, what's wrong?" I ask, automatically tensing. Amy's not prone to sniffles or hysterics and yet, from the tone of her voice I know she's crying.

Without preamble, Amy answers, "It's Sarah. Joe just called from the Ottawa General. She's had an aneurism."

Shock registers throughout my body. My throat muscles feel as if they're beginning to spasm. I repeat incredulously, "An aneurism? When? How?"

"In court this afternoon. According to Joe, she dropped in front of the judge's bench. She's still unconscious. They might have to operate."

I suck in a deep breath, forcing myself to exhale slowly. I envision Joe and the boys sitting in an emotionally sterile hospital waiting room, anxious for news. "How are Joe and boys?

"Joe's a mess. One minute he sounds calm and the next he's struggling not to break. They boys are trying to hold it together but it's tough."

I rub my eyes and scramble to organize my thoughts. Sarah has always been the one to deal with any Calder family crisis. It had been Sarah who had dealt with Jeremy's broken arm when he was six and she had been the one to rush Jake to the hospital when he took a hit from a slap shot in a road hockey game. When her father died, Joe had been out of town on business and unable to return for the funeral due to a freak ice storm. Sarah had stood stoically with the boys; not able to lean on Joe for his support. School events, teacher meetings, report cards, and endless car-pooling to hockey, football, soccer, and baseball games had been woven into her busy life as part of her schedule and routine. Joe worked hard and he loved the boys, but the overall running and management of the house fell on Sarah's shoulders. Now, she's the one who needs support.

Amy interrupts my thoughts. "We have to be there for her, Leen."

"Have you called Becky yet? I was talking to her just over an hour ago. She was heading off to supper with Josh. They were planning on travelling to the Niagara area tomorrow."

"I reached her just as they were ordering. She was going to go straight to the General."

"That's good. She'll be able to access Sarah's files and make sense of the medical jargon and interpret it for all of us."

"Leen ..." Amy stops to catch her words. "Joe says the neurologist asked if he would like a priest to be called to give the Sacrament of the Sick."

I swear softly as fear grips my gut. "Oh shit!" I knead my forehead with two knuckles. "Damn it all to hell and back." Memories of grade three and Sister Mary Eva talking about Extreme Unction flash like lightning through my mind. I have enough Catholic left in me to remember that back then it was viewed as the sacrament reserved for the dying. Now, the Church offers it as a comfort for those who are ill. The prayers and anointing are also aimed at relieving a person of sin.

I was never quite sure how the saying of a few prayers and the signing of the cross with oil–allegedly blessed – could do so much but as a child, I knew that it was supposed to be a very big deal. As an adult, I had come to view the whole process as some sort of liturgical clinging to ancient mysticism. Shadow memories of my Catholic upbringing surge forth. In my mind's eye, I can see myself as a four-year-old being led by the hand by Aunt Lydia into my mother's hospital room.

༄

Speaking in hushed tones that brooked no disobedience, Aunt Lydia says, "We must say our prayers for your mommy, Leen. You must be very brave and not let her see you crying."

Aunt Lydia pulls out her rosary and starts to softly recite the Hail Mary. My father's hand weighs briefly on my shoulder as his eyes travel to my mother's face.

The priest clears his throat and says, "In the name of the Father ..." I block out his words and stare at this old man as I edge my body closer to my father's – wanting, needing to be away from him and what his presence represents. His thinning grey hair and gaunt face, offset by his black soutane and stiff white collar, gives him the appearance of a human skeleton.

My gaze returns to my mother – my beautiful, funny mother – who now lies motionless with white sheets pulled up to mid chest, her blue eyes shut, and an I.V. pole dripping clear fluid into her veins. Like a shroud the white sheet has hidden my mother's left arm and I reach underneath It – tentatively – to hold my mother's hand. But her hand is already cool to my touch. The fingers that once would have eagerly enfolded mine do not respond to my grasp.

⁂

"Leen, are you there?" Amy sounds frustrated that I've not answered her.

I blink back tears that I thought had long since dried. Hearing about Sarah's aneurism has resurrected the fear and confusion I experienced as a four-year-old standing at my mother's bedside.

"Yes, of course, I am," I answer, checking my own emotions, "I just needed a moment to think. This is all such a shock. Look," I check my watch, "I'm going to call and see if I can get a flight back tonight. I'll cancel the meeting scheduled for tomorrow and get there as soon as I can."

"Are you sure you can come?" Amy asks, relief evident in her voice. As an afterthought she adds, "Sarah would not want you to jeopardize your job. And right now she won't even know whether you are here or not."

"But I will be," I answer, already planning what I need to do. "I'll cancel tomorrow's meeting and arrange for a flight back tonight. Will you still be up?"

"Yes. I'm going to the hospital. I'll check my cell phone every half hour so leave a message. Becky said she'd meet me there. We'll see what we can do for Joe and the boys. I'll tell them you're coming."

I manage to arrange a ten o'clock flight out from the Island airport and quickly pack my bags, dress in my casual travel clothes, and check out of the Fairmont. I rush into the airport terminal just in time to make the pre-boarding check-in for the flight to Ottawa.

Chapter Seven

Leen

Shortly after midnight, I walk at a quick pace down the corridors of the Ottawa General and take the elevator up to the seventh floor. I had picked up my car at Macdonald Cartier airport parking lot and driven directly to the hospital. Stepping off the elevator I make my way to the nurse's station.

"Are you family?" An overweight nurse, with an expansive chest looks up from the file she has been reading and idly flicks a piece of imaginary lint from her uniform that stretches tightly across her heavy breasts.

"Yes." Not caring about stretching the truth, I pointedly ask, "Perhaps you can tell me where my brother-in-law is?"

The nurse narrows her eyes. It's obvious that she doesn't believe I'm a relative. But since Becky had been in earlier demanding access to the Calder file and had tersely told the nurses to expect two more women to join her, she decides to play along with the ruse. "Mrs. Calder's family are down the hall to the right in the family room. They are waiting there while Dr. Bennett, the neurologist, confers with Dr. Sutherland."

"Leen, you're here!" exclaims a familiar voice.

I spin around. Amy looks dishevelled and has dark, tired circles under her eyes. She glances at the cardboard container with four coffees she's holding and smiles apologetically. "I wasn't sure when you would get here, so I didn't get one for you."

I give her a quick hug. "Any news? Have you talked to Becky? What does Joe say?"

The nurse resumes reading the patient file. We walk away from the station talking in hushed tones.

"Nothing very much. Joe said that Becky came and told him that Sarah was still unconscious. They've done an MRI and there's a team of doctors in there, poking and prodding away."

Walking into the family room, I rush to hug Joe and hold each of the boys in a tight embrace before sitting down in a chair. Amy passes out the coffee. Worry permeates the room, much like stale sweat clings to clothes, accenting the frustration we all feel as we wait for news.

As Joe shares what he knows about Sarah's condition, Jeremy sits with his hands resting on top of his head as if trying to hold in his thoughts. His brother sits with his elbows resting on his knees, head bowed as if in prayer.

"Everything seemed fine this morning when she left for court," Joe repeats for the third time in the five minutes since I've arrived. His quizzical expression and repetition are clear indications to Amy and me that he's struggling to cope with the unexpectedness of this event.

Sensing his need to talk, Amy and I wait for him to go on. He looks exhausted and the strain is showing. Joe, who is normally, well groomed regardless of the situation, looks more like a street person than a wealthy contractor. He had come straight from a construction site. His boots have the residue of dried mud and his denim jeans and white shirt are creased. Jake and Jeremy, wearing jeans and t-shirts, looked fresh compared to him. Their eyes, however, are red and, like their father, they are showing the stress and fatigue of worrying.

"She didn't complain of a headache or anything," says Joe.

Jake blurts, "Yeah, but Aunt Becky said that's what happens with an aneurism. It sometimes just explodes without warning."

Amy and I look at each other. From the time the boys were small, they have called each of us 'aunt'. Sarah's logic had been straightforward. "You're like family to me," she had told us when the boys were born. Not a birthday, Christmas, or celebration, has been missed by any of the aunts over the years, and the boys have been the objects of our affection and attention.

Joe's rehashing of the events gives me time to hear the details. He's telling me about how helpless Sarah looked, when Becky enters the room with a tall, lanky man wearing wire-framed glasses and a blue suit.

Introducing Dr. Sam Bennett, she tells Joe, "He's been kind enough to discuss Sarah's condition with me. Now we need to talk with you."

Shaking hands Joe asks, without preamble, "How is she?"

Dr. Bennett leans against the wall. Although he has had to deliver news like this many times in his career, it's clear that he has never gotten used to being the messenger of bad tidings. With just a hint of a frown, he mulls over his response. "She's sedated," he answers kindly. "She did come to for a while and we were able to determine that she has her faculties. She is a very fortunate woman but her recovery will take time."

"Sarah suffered a bleed to her brain," says Becky as she pulls out a pad and pen from her shoulder bag and quickly sketches a brain for us. "The MRI shows this is where she haemorrhaged. Aside from her apparent speech deficit and weakness on the right side," Becky speaks encouragingly, "she's showing marked progress even at this early stage."

Dr. Bennett nods agreement. "We've started steroids and blood thinners. A speech pathologist and physiotherapist will come to see her in a few days but, for now …" his intelligent eyes scan the concern on our faces as he gently adds, "we want to keep her quiet and as free from pain as possible."

"Is she in a lot of pain?" asks Jeremy.

"She was, Jeremy," answers Becky. Seeing his eyes widen with anxiety, she quickly adds, "That is to be expected. Patients who have had aneurisms often describe it like having been hit with a baseball bat. Intra-cranial pressure from the bleed or bleeds causes the headaches. We're giving her what we can to minimize the pain and that's keeping her sedated." She touches his shoulder. "Had she remained in a coma, things could be much worse."

Dr. Bennett says, "Dr. Sutherland's right. Your mother's overall prognosis is promising." He waits a moment, allowing that positive news to sink in before saying, "We do feel it is necessary to snip the vessel around the primary bleed. Hopefully, that will prevent a secondary bleed."

"When will you be doing that?" asks Joe, the anxiety in his voice evident. He rubs his face in a nervous gesture.

"I've placed a call for Dr. Stittswell, a neurosurgeon. He's on his way to the hospital now. If you sign the consent forms, we can prep her for surgery and he'll be able to operate as soon as he arrives and reviews her status."

Amy asks, "How dangerous is the surgery, Becky?"

༄

Becky

Leen and Amy stand stoically beside the boys, each trying to put on a brave face. I know from their expressions that they are deeply concerned. Amy, the more emotional of the two, looks as if she's on the verge of tears and the colour has drained from Leen's face.

"I want to reiterate what Dr. Bennett has already said," I say, detecting in my tone how I've automatically reverted to my professional voice. Softening my tone, I continue, "This surgery is necessary. John Stittswell is a well-respected surgeon. I would want him to operate on me or *any* member of my family." I squeeze Amy's elbow, "She'll be alright. She has all of us in her corner and we'll help her see this thing through."

Dr. Bennett clears his throat. "I'll have a nurse bring in the forms for you to sign." Anticipating Joe's next question, he says, "I'll let you know when Dr.Stittswell arrives." He looks kindly at Joe, surrounded by his little army of supporters, and smiles, "Try not to worry. She will be in good hands. You're making the right decision." Addressing me, he says, "See you later."

Wearily, I sit down, flanked on each side by Jake and Jeremy. I lightly tousle Jake's blond hair and with my other hand, I gently pat Jeremy's hand. "Okay, boys, do you have any questions that I might be able to answer?"

"Not really," answers Jake, his face taut with emotion. Like his brother, he has been trying hard not to cry. "It's just that she always seems so strong. Was there something I could have done to help her out ..." he hesitates, "you know so that this could have been avoided?"

I can't help thinking how young and vulnerable he looks. I remind myself, "He's just a kid in a young man's body, struggling to do the manly thing." Choosing my words carefully, I answer, "Aneurisms just happen, Jake." This is one of those moments in medicine when I wish there was a better answer. My years as a psychiatrist have taught me the invaluable worth of telling the truth, as best as I can. False hope often jades reality.

Jeremy murmurs, "She wanted me to take out the garbage this morning, but I told her I was going to be late for school and I'd do it later on."

Jake looks at his brother, "She asked me to empty the dishwasher but I begged off saying I had to get to practice."

Sighing, I search for words that might bring some comfort to the boys hoping to absolve them of misplaced feelings of guilt. "Listen guys, taking out the garbage or emptying a dishwasher wouldn't have stopped the aneurism. Sure," I admit frankly, "it would have been nice if you both had just done what she asked, but let's get something perfectly clear, right here and right now. There is no way that any of us could have stopped this from happening. What's important is that, *when it happened*, she was able to receive immediate medical attention. As for helping her out around the house, remember how you feel now the next time that she asks you to do your share."

"But she'll be okay?" Jake asks, trying hard to be positive, but needing my reassurance to bolster his hope.

Desperately wanting to reassure him but not wishing to dismiss Jake's concerns or the gravity of her condition, I answer, "Dr. Stittswell is an excellent neurosurgeon."

Amy smiles weakly and says, "This must be hard for you too."

Leen adds, "Amy's right. You've been dealing with the medical side of things for all of us." She comes over and gives me a quick hug. "Like all of us, you love Sarah, too."

I feel a flood of appreciation that they realize I had to check my emotions and slip into professional mode when discussing Sarah's condition. As a doctor I know that Sarah will have to deal with some difficult and life-altering challenges on her road to recovery. I answer softly, "If the situation was reversed and I needed a good lawyer, Sarah would do the same for me."

A perky, mid-thirties nurse carrying some papers enters the waiting room. "Mr. Calder," she says addressing Joe, "Dr. Bennett has asked me to tell you that Dr. Stittswell has arrived. If you would like to see your wife for a few minutes before we take her to surgery, you can do that."

Handing him the consent form, she waits while he reads it and then asks, "Do you have any questions?"

Joe passes the form to me. "These look okay to you?"

"It's a standard consent form, Joe" I answer, quickly scanning it before returning it to him for his signature. "There's no option, Joe, she needs the surgery."

The nurse hands him a pen and he leans over a small coffee table to sign his consent. Following her out of the room, he glances over his shoulder saying, "I'll tell her that you all send your love."

After Joe's departure, Jake asks, "She won't know that, will she Aunt Becky? You just told us that they're keeping her sedated."

I answer calmly, "She may not be awake now, Jake, but trust me, your mother knows you love her, and" I add with conviction, "she loves you guys very much."

Leen states the obvious. "Well, now, we'll wait." Anxiety makes her restless. She needs to get up and move about; just do anything but sit. "Can I get anyone anything at all? A glass of water, a coke? Have you boys eaten? How about I order a pizza?"

Glancing at his watch, Jake says, "Aunt Leen, it's after midnight. Don't know where we can get a pizza at this hour." He adds weakly, "But thanks for the offer."

Not about to be deterred in her attempt to keep the boys occupied while they keep vigil, Leen suggests, "Well, then, how about we go in search of a vending machine downstairs? We may find one that has some sandwiches or subs."

"That's a good idea," agrees Amy. "These bones need to move and a change of scenery would be welcome."

Their diversion works and the boys stretch their lean frames as they rise.

"Make mine a ham and cheese if you can," I say, digging into my purse and pulling out two twenties and a five. "There's a change machine in the lobby. Use this to help with the sandwiches."

Leen waves away the money. "If we're still here at breakfast time, you can pick up the tab."

"Thanks." Putting the bills back in my wallet, I say, "I'm going to wait here for Joe to return. Once she's out of surgery, I will go to the recovery room to speak with either Dr. Stittswell or Bennett and get the details of the surgery."

"It's like having our own in-house spy," says Amy, reaching to squeeze my hand.

With Leen, Amy, and the boys off in search of food, I'm left with time to collect my thoughts. I've tried not to show it but I'm bone weary and very concerned. The bleed is major. The recovery period will be long, but otherwise Sarah's in good shape. My eyes feel heavy and I close them, employing a trick I learned during my residency in order to take a power nap. I'm just starting to doze off when I hear a familiar voice.

"Thought I might find you here."

Josh is standing in the doorway, holding three brown take-out bags. I feel a surge of love so strong that I literally propel my body off the chair and rush to hug him. The corners of his mouth fold into a lazy smile, as he says, "Thought everyone might like some sandwiches so I stopped at the restaurant before coming over. Where is everyone?"

The immediate comfort I feel as he folds his arms around me acts as a release, granting permission to let go of my own deep emotions. He places the bags on the coffee table and leans his chin on top of my head, nuzzling against my hair. I cry softly into his broad chest.

"It'll be okay, Becky. It'll be okay." He speaks softly, as if I'm a small child needing comfort. "We'll get through this, together. Listen to me Becky, I'm here for you."

Sniffling, knowing that I sound weak and whiny but unable to stop the flood of emotions I'm experiencing, I answer, "I'm a doctor. I'm supposed to be able to deal with things like this."

"You're also a woman with one of her best friends in critical condition and undergoing brain surgery. Lifting my chin with his left hand, he uses his right hand to wipe away my salty tears. "You're allowed to feel, Doctor. You can be human, you know." As Josh brushes his lips against mine, I feel his comfort and strength flooding through my body.

I suddenly ask, "What on earth are you doing here? I thought after you dropped me off that you would go home and get some sleep."

Smiling, Josh answers, "My place is with you. It's as simple as that."

"How on earth did someone as wonderful as you ever come into my life?"

Josh steers us to the couch where we can sit quietly. "I don't know Sarah the way you do," he says, "but I know that I love you. Sarah, Leen, Amy, Joe, and the boys are family to you. I hope that when we're married, they will consider me as part of this big family too."

Not entirely certain that I've heard correctly and too stunned to move, it takes a moment to recover before I ask, "Would you repeat what you just said, please?"

A slow grin plays across his mouth. "You heard perfectly well what I said, Becky."

He cups my chin with his large, tanned hand and even though I feel as if everything is coming to a standstill, I know that this moment in time is altering and shaping my entire future. Josh's grey blue eyes are intensely focused on my face, searching for my response. "In case you missed that, I'm asking you to marry me." A sheepish grin pulls gently on his lips as he teases, "I had it in my mind to ask you at the restaurant but my plans for a romantic proposal were cancelled."

"I don't know what to say," I answer, still reeling with the shock of his proposal.

"I'd like you to say yes."

I'm drifting in a world of surreal. I had started my evening off with every intention of enjoying a wonderful meal and having great sex afterwards. Amy's phone call changed everything.

I love Josh but getting married again is not something I've given thought to. The presence of a divorce decree stuffed in my bedroom dresser drawer testifies to my failure with the marriage scene. As a psychiatrist I realize the telltale indicators of insecurity starting to surface. My mouth feels dry and my fingers twitch against my sweaty palms as I grapple with the need to make a decision. Josh gently covers my hands with his, stilling my movements.

My heart thuds as I form my words, trying not to hurt his feelings. "Josh, I love you, I truly do. I really appreciate you being here tonight to support my friends and me…"

"But?" he asks, breaking my train of thought, stopping me before I can reject his proposal.

"There's no but about my feelings for you Josh." I take a deep breath and whisper, as if I have something for which I should feel shame and wear sackcloth, "I was married. We all know how that ended."

"That was before," he answers in a measured tone, "and this is now. Life is about being with the people who *complete* you, not *divide* you. What you had before was a relationship that ended badly. It wasn't love. It's time to get on with life. Isn't that what you'd say to one of your patients?"

His words are true and make sense. Feeling as if I'm the patient and he the doctor, I allow myself release from years of self-recrimination about my failed marriage. I know the answer to his question. It's time for me to take a chance. Mentally, I tell myself, *Doctor, heal thyself. Don't I constantly tell my patients to live life and not wallow in their pasts?*

Having made my decision, I say, "Yes. I'll marry you." I lean over to kiss his lips but he covers my mouth with his; the force of his kiss letting me know the unbridled passion that he has for me.

A loud, theatrical harrumph startles us and we both jump. Leen, Amy, and the boys stand at the doorway, smiling ear-to-ear, holding armfuls of chips, subs, sandwiches and coffee.

"We raided every vending machine we could find and here's the bounty of our plunder," says Leen briskly, placing vending machine loot down on the table alongside the waiting brown paper bags that Josh brought. The others do the same.

"Are we interrupting?" Amy asks, clearly amused by our embarrassment.

In an attempt to explain my loss of composure and awkwardness at having been caught in the middle of a passionate kiss with Josh, I gush, "Josh just asked me to marry him."

Jake's the first to respond. "Aunt Becky, that's great! Did you say yes?" Standing there with tussled hair and his shirt hanging out over his low slung jeans, he looks more like he did when he was five years old than a young man of eighteen.

"What do you think she said, moron?" retorts Jeremy, grinning. "Didn't you see that kiss as we were walking in?"

Facing me with a comical expression, Jeremy flicks his thumb in his brother's direction and asks, "Are you sure we 'kids' should be witness to such open affection?" Wrapping his arms around me, he says, "Congrats Aunt Becky, you're the best!"

When Joe returns to the waiting room, he tells us, "She didn't know I was there, but I held her hand and told her that I loved her."

"That's good," I say. "There's a lot of evidence that supports the importance of human contact with patients even when they are heavily sedated or in a coma. You just never know what they do or don't hear."

Joe nods. "Hope you're right. So," he says, scanning our faces and smiling at the stash of food resting on the coffee table, "what were all of you laughing about?"

"We were kidding Josh about marrying Aunt Becky," answers Jake. For a moment, Joe looks puzzled. Then, it registers that Josh has proposed. Shaking hands with him, Joe says emphatically, "Welcome to the family. We may not be blood related, but make no mistake about it, we are family!"

Josh smiles conspiratorially. "I just hope that the ladies will give me a break and that I meet their expectations. They seem to come as a package deal."

"Oh, give that one up," replies Joe, good-naturedly. "I learned long ago to go with the flow and to stay out of the way when they're having one of their spats. Now," he grins, "I'll have an ally to commiserate with when they plan their antics or do whatever else they do."

"Dad calls them the 'coven' of the sisterhood," interjects Jake.

"Yeah, it's weird," adds Jeremy. "It's like they always know what someone is up to before anyone else."

Amy, Leen and I burst out laughing. "Come on boys," sputters Amy between giggles, "we're not that bad."

"Nobody said anything about bad," answers Jake, with a wide grin. "It's just that a guy doesn't stand a chance against the four of you." He holds up his hands, in a defeated gesture of compliance, and rolls his eyes.

"Yeah," agrees Jeremy. "Just think what Mom and all of you could do if you decided to hold a U.N. peace conference." Using his thumbs and index fingers to make a frame, he peers through it as if it's a camera lens. "I can see it now ... all of you dictating to the world leaders and when things get tense, Aunt Leen, here," he jerks his head in her direction, "drawls out, cut the crap; let's get down to business, shall we?"

We pass the next few hours alternating between bouts of silence, idle chatter, and some discussion about the wedding and when it will take place. Twice I go to the nurse's station only to return with no news. Around six a.m. I return from yet another check with the nurses and report, "Sarah's been taken to recovery. I'm going to find Dr. Stittswell and ask how the surgery went." Lightly touching Joe's shoulder, I promise, "I'll be back as soon as I know something."

☙

Amy

Time passes slowly for our little group as we watch the clock's hands move through the minutes until six thirty. Jake and Jeremy make another quick run to vending machines for more coffee and some danishes. Conversation is limited to comments about how long it's taking Becky to return.

Around seven a.m. Becky returns, accompanied by a tall, broad shouldered man. He has a neatly clipped, copper-coloured beard peppered throughout with grey. Standing close to six feet, five inches he's taller than either Joe or the twins.

"Mr. Calder, how do you do ..." he begins, stopping mid-sentence when Jake blurts out, "How is she?"

"Jake, please!" admonishes Joe. Used to dealing with anxious family members, Dr. Stittswell replies, "Your mother made it through the surgery without any complications. She's in recovery now and will be brought to her room within the next hour. She won't be up to having visitors for any long periods of time, but she'll know that you're here."

Joe's voice is steady, but his shoulders are tense and his face is lined with concern. "What's the prognosis?"

"There may be some aphasia or speech issues and she may have some weakness particularly on her left side. We'll know more over the next few days. Right now she needs time to start the healing process. There are therapists that can help her with the consequences of the aneurism but overall, she will recover."

Jake almost bleats his words. "But she's a lawyer."

All eyes turn to him silently questioning what on earth that has to do with the report of Sarah's surgery.

"She speaks for a living," he sputters. "How will she deal with that?"

"Sweetie," says Leen softly, resting an arm around Jake's shoulders, "Dr. Stittswell didn't say she couldn't or won't talk. He said that she *may* have some speech problems, but there are therapists that can help her. It will just take time to heal."

Stittswell nods in appreciation of Leen's input. "Your mother will need support from everyone as she copes with what has happened to her."

I explain, "As far as your mom is concerned right now, she is still in yesterday's mode. The aneurism left her unconscious and she has been in surgery. When she wakes up, she'll have to deal with what's happened to her. She loves life and you guys way too much to let anything get in the way of her recovery."

Extending his hand, Joe says, "I'm indebted to you, Doctor. Becky's spoken highly of your skill."

"You're welcome, Mr. Calder. And I thank you, Doctor," Stittswell smiles at Becky, "for your vote of confidence." He pauses. "If there are no other questions, I'll leave you all to wait to see Mrs. Calder and then, my advice is for you to go home. You'd be wise to get some rest while you can."

Becky says, "I'm going to go to the recovery room to see how she's doing." Following Dr. Stittswell out of the waiting room, she leaves us to recap what he said and to wait for when Sarah is returned to her room.

⁂

Becky

Entering the recovery room, I head to the nurse's station. A slightly plump, prematurely grey haired head nurse grins with pleasure. "Dr. Sutherland? It's a surprise to see you here."

Recognizing the nurse, I answer, "Hi Angie. It's been a while." Angie had done a three-month stint on the psych ward last year. I had liked her easy manner and composure with patients. "We've missed your sense of humour on the psych ward."

"I just changed the clientele," replies Angie, smiling. "Figured that people in recovery needed some of my magic."

"How is Mrs. Calder?"

"Is she a patient of yours?" asks Angie, conversationally, reaching for the chart.

"One of my best friends. She's like family to me."

Angie glances at the chart. "Well, she's had a tough time of it. I just gave her some morphine about ten minutes ago to ease the headache. We're waiting on the orderlies to take her to her room."

Sarah's head is wrapped in mounds of white gauze and her eyes are blackened as if she has been in a prizefight. The hospital issued blue Johnny gown hangs loosely over one shoulder, allowing the I.V. tubing to snake down her right arm. I reach to take her pulse.

"Steady but weak," murmurs Angie. "I checked her myself before you arrived."

Hot tears swell in my eyes and I try to blink them away before Angie can see them. A large salty droplet trickles down my cheek in spite of my efforts. Angie touches my shoulder and says, "She's fine, Doctor. She's going to be just fine."

Two orderlies arrive. One is chewing a wad of gum, reminiscent of a cow chewing its cud. The other orderly is balding and has the weather-beaten skin of someone who spends a lot of time outdoors. Angling the gurney alongside Sarah's bed, they slide her onto the stretcher. Angie hands Sarah's chart to the bald orderly. Their faces register surprise when I say, "I'll follow along with you."

"This is Dr. Sutherland," says Angie. "And, this lady is a member of her family."

Smacking his gum, the gum chewer jerks his head in acknowledgement. The balding one mutters, "Doctor." Angie follows us to the elevator saying, "She'll be fine, Doctor. You take care of yourself."

Settled back in her room, jarred from the transfer from the stretcher to her bed, Sarah opens her eyes briefly to see anxious faces peering at her. I can tell that she wants to speak but she is either too groggy from the anaesthetic or unable to form the words. Her eyes, wide with fear similar to that of a trapped animal, openly question what has happened to her.

Joe quickly takes her I.V. free hand and leans so that his face is close to hers. I caution, "Easy, Joe. Sound is often magnified after brain surgery. Keep your voice low."

Speaking softly, he says, "You're in the hospital, Sarah. You had an aneurism. You've just come out of surgery."

Sarah's eyes trace his face. I touch Joe's shoulder and murmur, "It'll take time. Just be strong for her."

In turn, each of her visitors touches her. Amy squeezes her toes; Jeremy and Jake lean in to kiss her forehead; Leen gently rubs her leg; and I take out a small penlight to check her pupil responses.

"She needs to rest," I say. Speaking gently, I ask, "Sarah, are you in any pain?"

She nods her head and grimaces with the pain caused by the movement. I check the morphine drip on the I.V. and place the bulb-like attachment into Sarah's hand. "Squeeze this bulb when you feel the pain, Sarah. It's a morphine drip, calibrated so that you can give yourself a dose when you need it." I pin the bell cord onto Sarah's pillow and say, "Pull this cord if you need a nurse."

"What's this?" Jake points to the railing at the side of the bed.

I look at the bag hanging from the railing and tubing running under the coarse white hospital linen sheets. Smiling, I answer, "That's a catheter bag. Your mom won't be able to get out of bed for a day or two. That's there to collect her urine and help the staff measure her output while she is still being closely monitored."

Both boys eye the bag and its half-full contents of urine. Had it not been Sarah lying there, I would have found their reactions comical. "It's standard procedure after surgery. When a patient can't move, it's important to monitor all bodily functions."

Jake takes a deep breath. "Well that settles it. Medicine is off the list as a career choice."

Jeremy nudges him. "Jerk. What about when you have kids? They'll pee too and you'll get to clean that and more."

A weary Joe, sighs, "It's been a long night. Your mom needs her rest, not a discussion about catheter bags."

"Well, piss on that," jokes Jake. Joe shoots him a warning look and he quickly mutters, "Sorry Dad. I was just kidding."

Sarah's eyelids are heavy with fatigue and sedation. Leen, seeing that Sarah is struggling to stay awake, says, "Let's go boys. Time to get some sleep. We can come back."

Signalling appreciation for Leen's observation, I say, "She's right, guys. Your mom needs to get some sleep and the morphine needs time to do its thing. She won't rest if you're here." Throughout our discussion Sarah's eyes have not left the boys. When they lean to kiss her, she blinks, letting them know she understands. Joe pours water from the pitcher resting on the night table, bends the plastic straw, and places it between her lips so that she can sip the water.

"Not too much water," I caution. "The I.V. will help take care of Sarah's need for liquid but she'll need to have sips of water so that her mouth will be less dry. Morphine causes dry mouth and don't forget," I smile at Sarah, who is listening to the exchange, "she's had tubes in her mouth for close to six hours. They have to do that during surgery, Sarah," I explain, patting her blanket-covered knee. "You'll have a bit of a sore throat until the mucous membranes are less raw from the effect of the tubes."

Grinning at Sarah, Amy says, "Scotch or a glass of wine would be better. We'll see what we can do about arranging that for you."

I say, "When you're up to it Sarah, we can celebrate. Until then, it's strictly hospital fare."

The bantering over, Leen and Amy say their good-byes and, after giving the boys a private moment with their mom, Joe and I usher them out of the room. He hugs each boy and says, "Seeing you guys was good for her. Go home and get some rest. I'll let you know if she needs anything."

We return to Sarah's room: Joe to begin his vigil and me to check Sarah's vitals once more before I go home. Already dozing, Sarah is oblivious to her surroundings. I say, "You need some rest too, Joe."

"I'm not leaving, Becky."

I answer firmly, "I know that, Joe, but you still need to try and catch a few winks while Sarah's sleeping. I'll have the nurse bring in a pillow and blanket for you. You can rest right in the chair but please, try to take a nap."

"Thanks," he answers, with a weary smile.

"It's going to take some time."

Acknowledging my comment, with a tired nod, Joe answers, "I know. Thanks for everything, Becky."

"I love her, too."

"Congrats, once again on your engagement," says Joe. "Just wait until Sarah hears she missed all the excitement. You'll have to give her a replay of everything."

Grinning, I reply, "Speaking of Josh, I'd better go and find him. He's been waiting in the visitor's room."

"Thank him for me."

"I will. Don't forget what I said to you about getting some sleep."

࿇

Joe

Only the sound of Sarah's breathing interrupts the quiet in the room. I settle down into the high-backed chair and feel numb as I stare at my sleeping wife. The perky little nurse who had brought the consent papers for surgery enters the room carrying a blanket and pillow and holding a styrofoam cup of tea in her free hand.

"Dr. Sutherland thought you could use a cup of tea," she says in explanation to my quizzical look, "and she wanted me to tell you where the kitchen is."

"Kitchen?"

"We have a small kitchen for patient and visitor use. There's always some instant coffee, tea bags and hot water available. If you want to bring in some special drinks for Mrs. Calder, write her name on them so that someone won't take them by mistake."

She glances at the monitor. "Ring the bell if you need anything. We'll check on her periodically and this," she points to the monitor, "allows us to read her vitals from the main desk."

"Thank you."

Left alone with my thoughts, I sip the tea. When I'm certain that Sarah has fallen into a deep sleep, I rest my head against the pillow and within minutes I start to drift off.

Chapter Eight

Leen

The city section of The Ottawa Citizen prints a half page story detailing yesterday's courthouse drama complete with photos. The first shows a huddle of people with shocked expressions staring as paramedics lift an unconscious Sarah onto a gurney. Janice Kellep, a wiry courthouse reporter well known for her keen sense of getting news *as it happens* had, by pure chance, been in Courtroom 12 when Sarah collapsed. She had quickly gone into action; interviewing and reporting bystander reactions to what had happened.

Judge Hanlon is quoted as saying, "Ms. Calder is a well respected counsellor and I, for one, hope that she will soon be back in my court."

Crown Attorney, Tony Greetly, talks about Sarah's endless enthusiasm and sense of fair play. Ted Baker, the bailiff, says, "Ms. Calder had just started to address the court when she sort of staggered. She looked as if she was going to pass out and tried to reach for the bench. She grabbed her head, groaned, and fell down. It was pandemonium after that."

Another photo from The Ottawa Citizen archives – not as sensational as the first–depicts a beaming Sarah at last year's charity drive, sponsored by the local Bar Association, to raise awareness and funds for victims of domestic abuse. Underneath that photo, Janice devoted two full paragraphs citing Sarah's advocacy for abuse victims and her reputation as being a voice for the underprivileged.

Hospital spokesman, Tony Alder, is quoted as saying, "Ms. Calder is making a full recovery from an aneurism. Thanks to the skill of Doctors' Stittswell, Bennett, and staff, she received emergency treatment in time." His statement is followed by a plug for the hospital's fund drive to purchase another MRI machine.

Having read the article that Jake's now perusing, I'm anticipating some questions. When we returned from the hospital, I borrowed a pair of jogging shorts and a t-shirt from Jake's closet and managed to get a few hours sleep. As I wait to see what his reaction to Janice's article, I freshen my coffee.

"What did you think about the article?" asks Jake. Although I had been expecting it, his question gives me a jolt and I wish that Becky were here. She'd know what to say. I try to sound optimistic.

"Well, that sort of thing is to be expected. After all, your mom had her aneurism in a very public place. The media is bound to put a spin on it."

"Yeah, but she sounds like a heroine or something like that," he says, staring at his mom's photo. "I never realized she did all this stuff." Biting on his lower lip he traces his mother's smiling face with his fingertip and then abruptly taps the photo of her on the gurney. "To me and Jeremy, she's always been just Mom. Sure we know she's a lawyer and all that stuff but ..." in a voice laced with self-recrimination, he adds, "I just never knew, Aunt Leen."

"Don't beat yourself up, Jake. Kids tend to view parents as existing for them and not as people with feelings and needs of their own." I pick up his empty cereal bowl and walk over to the dishwasher. "You couldn't have done anything to stop this thing from happening."

Fortunately, the phone rings and glad for the interruption I pick up the receiver. For the next two hours, the boys and I take turns to answer get well messages from a slew of people who'd read the article about Sarah.

By noon we're ready to return to the hospital and I wait as Jake packs sandwiches into a lunch bag. He explains, "I thought Dad would appreciate some ham sandwiches."

"We can get some Tim's coffee on the way to the hospital," says Jeremy, walking into the kitchen, clean-shaven, and tucking a white, long sleeve shirt into his jeans.

Out of nowhere my chest swells with a gush of pride and love for the boys. Standing side-by-side they look to be identical, but to me there have always been noticeable tell-tale differences. Jeremy tends to smile more frequently than Jake and Jake has just the slightly deeper dimple in his chin. After they started to shave one of the most obvious differences between the twins has been that Jake shows a mid-afternoon shadow whereas Jeremy can shave in the morning and wait until early evening before his stubble shows. Their laughter even sounds similar. Of the two, Jake is more prone to practical jokes. Jeremy favours long sleeved shirts and Jake opts for easy pullover sweaters and shirts. Natural athletes, they enjoy competition but I've never known either brother to resent the other if he scores a goal or has a better track meet. From the time they were sharing crib space it's as if they've had an unspoken pact to be different and yet, compliment one another's strengths.

"You know, you two guys are great! Your mom would be so proud. Your dad will appreciate the sandwiches and coffee." Picking up my purse and car keys, I add, "We also have to talk about contacting the school and when you guys will be back on course."

"School!" Their simultaneous response makes me laugh. "Yes, gentlemen, school. You know that institution where you go on a daily basis and from which you will graduate this year before heading off to universities with the promise of great futures and incomes. Don't forget you're supposed to take care of your parents and long-suffering adopted aunts, in the style to which we will quickly and gladly become accustomed." I sigh with apparent pleasure as I tack on, "We all expect to be well taken care of in our old age."

"Yeah, yeah," Jake quips back, "if you all have your way, Jake and I will be working for the rest of our lives, taking care of all of your interests."

"Ah, what noble young men you both are," I retort with a wide smile. "Let's go. Don't forget to lock up."

I'm opening the car door when my cell phone rings. Recognizing the ring as the one I've assigned to Amy, I say, "Hi Amy, how are you doing?"

"I'm good," answers Amy. "Did you manage to get some sleep?"

"A few hours, but the bit that I did get was the solid sleep of the dead."

"Me too. I got up about two hours ago and started to raid my freezer. Thought I would make some meals for Joe and the boys. When Sarah comes home, I plan on stocking her freezer with casseroles and easy meals."

I smile. Not for the first time, I think it's a shame Amy never had children. She's maternal in the care of her friends and has always lavished attention on Sarah and Joe's boys. Amy's reaction to any crisis necessitates a barrage of prepared food. Cooking is her personal version of yoga.

"What's on the menu for today?"

"Cabbage rolls, penne, and lasagne. I'll put them in storage containers and bring them over late afternoon. Joe and the boys will need some down time together, a good meal, and nothing to worry about but who gets to control the remote for the TV."

"Sounds good," I say, glancing at the front door but the boys were nowhere in sight. "Right now, I'm sitting in my car waiting for the boys so that I can take them to the hospital. I'll pick up some fresh bread on the way back. Some for them and some for us to have at your place." Anxious to get going, I say, with mild irritation, "I wish they'd get their butts moving so we can get out of here."

Chuckling, Amy answers, "What do you want to eat? Penne, lasagne, or cabbage rolls?"

"How about cabbage rolls. It's been a while since I've had some." I sigh with relief as Jake locks the front door. "Got to go. The boys are finally ready to leave." I flip my cell phone shut as Jake climbs into the front seat. Jeremy takes the back seat, his long legs scrunched up against the back of Jake's seat.

"Move your seat, Dufus," complains Jeremy, tapping the back of Jake's head.

"Give me a break," replies Jake, but he eases the seat forward.

Rolling my eyes, I say, "Come on guys, you both have enough room."

"Aunt Leen, the problem is you," replies Jeremy.

"Me? Now how do you figure that?" I start the ignition and back out of the driveway.

"Well, both me and Jake are over six feet so we, naturally, need the leg room. You're tall so you push your seat back. Aunt Amy is shorter. We have more leg room in her car."

"So now my height is a problem in my own car?" I shake my head and suggest, "You could always walk to the hospital if my car is too cramped for your comfort."

Jake wheedles, "Ah now, Aunt Leen. No need to get touchy. We're just having fun with you." He bestows a charming smile. "You could always consider letting one of us drive this baby of yours." Running his right hand over the black leather dashboard and console, he adds reverently, "This is one sweet machine!"

Feigning resignation, I pull to the curb on Woodroffe Avenue. When safe, I open up the driver's door and walk to the passenger's side of the car. Grinning ear-to-ear, Jake bounds out from his seat as I hand over the keys. Once he's settled in the driver's seat, I pretend to be stern. "Jeremy drives home. Agreed?"

"Agreed." Jake glances over his shoulder and winking at Jeremy baits, "I'll show you how to drive, Jeremy, so we can have a safe drive home."

"Ha, ha. You're so funny. Just keep your eyes on the road, Dufus!"

"Guys!" I fasten my seatbelt and half-warn, half-joke, "Enough with the competition and the rising testosterone."

Flicking my hand and affecting a pseudo British accent, I command, "Forward Jeeves. You really must learn your place if you intend to serve as my driver."

Jake takes the Queensway on ramp and accelerates as he merges onto the 417. I smile at his set jaw and self-satisfied grin as he shifts the gears to accommodate the increase in speed.

Jeremy asks, "Was that Dad you were talking to on the cell phone when we came out?"

"That was Aunt Amy. She called to say that she was preparing some meals for you guys."

"Hope she's making lasagne," says Jake. "She's the best cook around."

I retort, "Remember whose car you're driving, mister. I'll be sure to tell your mom and Aunt Becky what you said. Can't tell you how much we all appreciate your enthusiasm for our cooking. What is it with you guys today? Keep it up and by the time we get to the hospital I'll throw you both into one of Aunt Becky's counselling sessions." Loud guffaws follow my warning.

"Come on Aunt Leen, you know we love you too." Jeremy reaches over the back of the seat to pat my shoulder. "It's just that Aunt Amy has cooking down to a fine art, but when it comes to cars and techie stuff, you're the best."

"Keep feeding me back-handed compliments like that one and you might just stay in my will."

Undeterred, Jake replies, "Dibs on the BMW!" He pulls into the parking lot and stops to take a parking ticket from the automated machine before winding the car through the maze of concrete floors in the parking garage.

At the hospital's florist shop we purchase orange and blue orchids along with a vase. The first thing that strikes us like a hard punch when we enter Sarah's room is her black eyes; followed closely by the realization that her face is so swollen it's hard to tell where her nose is. She looks like a punched in pumpkin head. The boys stand quietly at the foot of her bed, trying not to gawk at their mother's appearance.

Holding two fingers up to his lips to make a soft shushing sound, Joe gets up from his chair to embrace his sons.

"Dad?" Jake's eyes are round and his expression is anxious.

"It's okay, son," says Joe, resting one arm around Jake's shoulder and using the other to pull Jeremy close. "Doctors' Bennett and Stittswell said that swelling is to be expected in the first forty-eight hours. All patients who've had this type of surgery look like they've been in a prizefight. If you think about it," he grins, "she did fight for her life. She might look battered, but she did win!"

Jake hands over the brown sandwich bag to his father. "Brought you some sandwiches."

Making a face at his brother, Jeremy adds, "Yeah, we were going to stop at Tim's and get some coffee but someone insisted on driving Aunt Leen's BMW."

Joe raises one eyebrow sceptically at me. It's no secret that my BMW is my "baby". He realizes that letting the boys drive my car has been an attempt to give them some respite from worrying about their mother. "So, Leen," says Joe, "they're taking over your car, now?"

I teasingly complain, "I think they have plans for me to have car keys cut for them on the way home."

"Dad," says Jeremy, "there's a Mocha Bean kiosk near the cafeteria. Want me to get you some coffee? He smirks with boyish charm. "Name what you want, Aunt Leen. I want to keep you in a good mood so that I get to drive it on the way back. Your wish is my command."

"A medium cappuccino would be nice," I reply.

Joe reaches into a jean pocket for his wallet. "No, Dad," says Jake, "this one is on us. We have to keep the lady with the keys happy, don't we?"

In spite of his fatigue, the boys' have succeeded in lifting Joe's spirits. He shoos them away, saying, "Go, before you wake your mother. I'll visit with Leen and," he shakes the sandwich bag, "eat my sandwiches."

As soon as the boys are out of earshot, Joe asks, "How're they doing?"

I answer frankly. "You would have been proud of them. They have their parents combined strength. They'll be fine."

I can see the visible relaxation of his shoulders. "Good. I was worried." He lifts the newspaper from the windowsill. "When I went downstairs earlier to get some toast and a coffee, I picked up the morning paper. Did you see the article about Sarah?"

"Yes," I answer truthfully. "So did the boys."

Joe frowns. "How'd they take it?"

"From what was said I get the impression that they both feel somewhat guilty for not being there to help her or noticing if she was ill."

"That's ridiculous," interrupts Joe gruffly.

"We know that," I reply, "but it'll take them a while to realize it. On a positive note, I think they were surprised by the number of phone calls from neighbours, colleagues, and friends. I don't think they knew their mother is so highly regarded."

"She's going to feel a little embarrassed about all the excitement she's caused. But it's nice to know that so many people are in her corner and wishing her well." He takes a deep breath and exhales slowly. "Right now, all I want is for her to get better."

Resting my hand on his shoulder, I say, "We all do and she will." I peer at Sarah's sleeping form, fervently hoping that she won't be in too much pain when she wakes up.

As if hearing my thoughts, Joe says, "She's got a lot of morphine in her. Dr. Stittswell said they want to keep her sedated for the next day or so to help her start to heal."

A nurse with short curly red hair enters the room carrying ice bags wrapped in towels. She addresses her comments to Joe. "Dr. Stittswell wants us to pack ice around the sides of her head and to have cold packs over the bridge of her nose. They'll help reduce the swelling." After positioning the bags she reaches to take Sarah's pulse just as Becky walks in the room.

"How's the patient?" asks Becky, as her eyes follow the steady waves on the heart monitor attached by leads to Sarah's chest.

The nurse removes the stethoscope from her ears. "Pressure and vitals are good, Dr. Sutherland. We've just started with the ice."

"Good," answers Becky. "I stopped at the station and read the orders left by Dr. Stittswell. Has Dr. Bennett been back in?"

"Not yet," answers the nurse, placing the blood pressure cuff on the side table. "He does rounds with the residents on Mondays, Wednesdays, and Fridays. Tuesdays and Thursdays, he holds clinic hours. We don't usually see him until around three or four in the afternoon." She moves towards the door. "Ring if you need anything."

"Thank you," replies Becky with a quick smile. Fixing her attention on the dark circles underneath Joe's eyes, she asks, "So how are you holding up?"

"I'm good, Becky. The boys brought me some sandwiches. The pillow and blanket you had the nurse bring came in handy. I managed to doze off for a while. Jeremy and Jake just went down to get some coffee. If I'd known you'd be here, we would have got you some too."

"No problem. I was getting off the elevator as they were getting on. I placed my order for mocha."

"So Becky," I ask, speaking softly so as not to disturb Sarah but making no attempt to hide my curiosity, "what does the chart say?"

"She's in good shape, but," Becky responds cautiously, "the surgery was more intense than they originally thought it would be. Dr. Stittswell caught another weak vessel while he was in there so he snipped it before it had time to burst." She looks at us somberly. "She's lucky to be alive. She'll have a tough time and have to do some rehab, but she is going to make it through this."

When Jeremy and Jake return with the coffee Becky suggests, "Let's go out in the hallway, Leen. We can chat without disturbing Sarah and the boys can have some time with Joe and their mother."

Outside Sarah's room, Becky leans against the wall, sips her mocha and checks her watch. "I have about twenty minutes to spare before I collect my residents and start rounds. So, how are you holding up?"

"Like you, I'm worried, but I've got to tell you …." I stop mid-sentence and peer at Becky, thinking about what I want to say before continuing, "all these years we've known one another and I've never seen you in a hospital setting. You're good, Becky, really good!" I give her right shoulder a playful tap. "Quite the little professional. I'm impressed."

Flushing slightly, Becky answers, "There's no reason for you to have ever seen me at work. But," she grins, "from what you've said about some of your co-workers, I sometimes think I should open up a clinic at Scenes. That way, I'd never have to worry about a shortage of patients."

I snort. "Don would be the first on your list."

Becky just laughs. "There you go; no shortage of patients."

"How much time do you spend at the hospital doing rounds?" I jerk my thumb towards the nursing station. "This isn't a psych ward and yet, the nurses seem to know you quite well."

"Clinical supervision of residents accounts for about 25 percent of my practice," she answers, "but the bulk of my practice takes place at the out-patient clinic or counselling sessions at my office. This floor is a neurological ward and most of the staff knows me because I'm often called in for a consult in neuro-pysch evaluations." Modestly she adds, "I'm just glad that I was able to offer some help last night."

"Last night you were hurting, just like we were, but you were able to maintain a clinical perspective. I'm not sure that I could have done that. You really helped us to hang in there."

Becky shrugs off my compliment. "I'll expect the same professional courtesy if I ever need someone to design a campaign for me or," she slips in, "if my husband-to-be needs help to promote his restaurant."

I laugh. "Done deal, pro bono marketing advice but seriously, it really made a difference having you here for Sarah."

"We're family," responds Becky simply.

I shift my position against the mustard coloured wall. "Amy's kicked into cooking mode."

"I heard," replies Becky. "It's her coping mechanism. She called earlier to invite me to join the two of you at her place but I'm having dinner with Josh."

My lips curl into a suggestive leer, "Making up for last night's loss of romance?"

Becky giggles softly. "Can you believe that? He picks a hospital waiting room to propose? We were all too worried about Sarah last night for it to really register. Now," she teases, "I'll have to decide what type of bridesmaid dresses the three of you should wear. Maybe I should give Jess Owen a call and ask her advice."

I grunt derisively. A few years ago a mutual friend of ours had her bridesmaids wearing what could only be described as hideous dresses. "Oh, yeah, you be sure to do that! With Jess advising you, we'll be decked out in pink, puffy fru fru's like she had for her wedding." We laugh out loud as images of me, Sarah, and Amy come to mind in vivid colour. A nurse walks by and gives us a stern look. Recognizing Becky, she nods curtly and says, "Doctor." Becky beams a polite smile but it's obvious she's struggling to control her laughter. Like two admonished schoolgirls, we lower our voices as we make a few more cracks about Jess's choice of bridesmaid gowns.

We chat for a few more minutes before Becky leaves for her rounds. As she steps into the elevator, I say, "Call me tomorrow. I'll be expecting a full update on the "Josh scenario".

Grinning, Becky pushes the button to close the elevator doors. "Count on it."

When I return to Sarah's room I suggest to Joe that he consider going home with the boys. "She's out of it right now. Go home, Joe. Take a shower, shave, and spend some time with the boys before coming back for the night shift. I'll stay with her for a while."

Joe declines. "I want to stay for a while longer. I'll follow in an hour or so."

"I'll stay with Dad," offers Jake. Looking at his brother he adds, "You go with Aunt Leen and have your turn driving the BMW."

I reach into my purse and take out my car keys. Handing them to Jeremy, I say dramatically, "My driver and I go forth to triumph over the perils and dangers of the traffic that awaits us, as we battle our way forth to purchase fresh bread for supper."

Jake elbows Jeremy. "She's seen you drive."

With a weary but sympathetic smile, Joe says, "You're brave Leen. Letting them drive your car is one step away from them taking ownership."

I throw my hands up in defeat. "A moment's weakness and now, I'm going to lose my car?"

"Next, we'll go after Aunt Amy's Nissan," says Jake.

"How about Aunt Becky's Mercedes sports coupe?" suggests Jeremy.

Grunting, I say, "Oh won't they just love the two of you!" Tugging on Jeremy's shirtsleeve, I say, "Speaking of Amy, we'd better get going. She'll have our heads on a platter if we're not there to open the door when she arrives laden with *vittles* to wet your manly appetites."

"Vittles?" Jake looks puzzled. "Making up words now, Aunt Leen?"

"Prerogative of the media and advertising world, my dear innocent one. Besides, it's slang for food."

"Yeah," interjects Jeremy. "I'm already drooling." He taunts his brother, "One of us understands the English language." Looking at Joe he says, "You see, Dad. I was right. There's much to be said for having an older and wiser son."

Jake snorts. "Ten minutes, that's nothing."

"Ten *very* important minutes," retorts Jeremy, pleased that his taunt has hit its intended mark. "Still makes me number one son and you *are* number two."

"Go." Joe waves his hand dismissively.

I give him a quick peck on the cheek and say, "Call me if she wakes up or if you guys need anything."

We stop at DeGracia's Bakery for a loaf of crusty Italian and pick up some cold cuts for sandwiches. By the time we pull into Sarah's driveway I'm feeling warning pangs in my gut and comment to Jeremy that I'm getting hungry.

We're in the kitchen when Amy arrives with two thermal bags. "Jeremy," she asks, "would you be a sweetheart and help me get the rest from the car?" I put the kettle on to heat water for tea and make it to the front door in time to take a large platter covered with two shopping bags taped together.

"You've brought enough food for an army."

"This gives them the option of freezing what they don't want to eat tonight," answers Amy, plunking the bags onto the kitchen table.

I sniff at the aroma wafting in the kitchen. "Everything smells so good. I'm starving."

"It's for the boys and Joe so don't get any ideas," she warns, pulling out containers of potato salad, coleslaw, and fresh cut vegetables. "These items are to help out with sandwiches and cold meals. The only question I have is *what do you want* for dinner tonight, Jeremy?"

"I'm in for the lasagne," says Jeremy, lifting her off her feet with a bear hug.

Swatting his shoulder playfully, she orders, "Put me down!"

"Enough already!" I say with feigned annoyance directed at Amy. "The boys have been telling me on and off, all day long, how you are the best cook."

"Aw, Aunt Leen," cajoles Jeremy, squeezing my right shoulder affectionately, "you know we love you too. Aunt Amy is a great cook, but *you drive* a beautiful car."

Smiling, I whisk his hand from my shoulder. "Careful what you say about my cooking or the closest you'll get to that BMW will be to wash it."

Pleased with Jeremy's compliments, Amy says, "Every chef appreciates a loyal and true patron." She asks gently, "How's your mom?"

Immediately, his expression becomes sombre. "She has a face like a punched in melon."

"Punched in melon?" Amy looks to me for clarification.

"He's not exaggerating." I reply. Seeing the concern on Amy's face, I add quickly, "But, Becky and Dr.Stittswell say that sort of swelling is to be expected after neurosurgery. They're using ice packs to reduce it and she is heavily sedated to control the pain."

The phone rings and Jeremy hurries to answer it. He lowers his voice and walks with the portable phone to the other side of the kitchen. We eavesdrop with amused grins, letting him know we're aware that the caller is a girl. Smiling, sheepishly, he waves a jaunty good-bye and heads upstairs to the privacy of his room.

"What tells me that call is from a girl?"

"You think?" Amy answers, with a knowing smirk. "They all grow up, don't they?"

While we organize the freezer to make room for the food, prepare a fresh salad, and cut slices of the crusty bread, I talk about Becky's excitement and relate the nurse's reaction to our spontaneous laughter. Before leaving, I write a note for Jeremy telling him to call if he wants anything. Amy pens a teasing postscript saying, "Can't wait to meet the girl who has you talking low and laughing. Do you realize you've been on the phone for over an hour? Reheat the lasagne at 325 for forty minutes or until warm."

Just as we're pulling our cars out of the driveway, Joe and Jake pull in. We put our cars into park and get out to greet them.

"How's Sarah?" asks Amy.

Jake answers, "She woke up for a little while, but she was in a lot of pain and has a lot of trouble talking."

"Dr. Stittswell came in to check on her," fills in Joe. "He said the trouble with her speech is called aphasia and that it sometimes happens while the brain is in recovering mode." He pauses. "She may continue to have speech problems for a long time." He moves his hands in a helpless gesture, as if throwing Sarah's fate to the gods of the universe and adds, "Or, she may continue to have speech problems for the rest of her life."

"Well," I answer cautiously, "we knew last night that it might be an issue." I glance at my godson. Jake's visibly shaken by Sarah's speech impediment. I feel for him but I want to keep things positive so I say, "Concentrate on the fact that your mom's alive and starting to recuperate. Just imagine how awful all of us felt yesterday, not knowing how things would play out. Yet, here we are today talking about her recovery."

"Yeah, you're right, Aunt Leen," admits Jake, grudgingly, "but it's still hard to believe."

Joe changes the topic. "What's for dinner? Jake, here," he jerks his thumb, "was saying how glad he was that we weren't going to have to fend for ourselves tonight. We're all so tired that the idea of thawing a steak or chops is almost mind boggling."

"Pizza's good in a pinch," grins Jake, "but Aunt Amy's lasagne is the best."

"Then, you're going to be one happy camper," jokes Amy. "Jeremy opted to freeze the cabbage rolls and have the lasagne today. As long as the two of you keep those compliments coming, I'll feed you anytime." She plants a kiss on his cheek and addressing me, says, "We'd best leave these guys to their food."

Winking, I say to Jake, "We're having cabbage rolls tonight and I'm starving."

My fingers tap on the steering wheel as I wait for Amy to stop giving needless instructions. "Come on, Amy," I call out, "Joe knows how to warm up food." For effect, I beep the car horn.

Climbing into her car, she calls out, "Don't forget, there's some fresh grated romano in the fridge."

With a wave Joe answers, "I'll call if I get any more news about Sarah."

Chapter Nine

Amy

Leen is adding lemon slices to the iced tea when the doorbell rings. Removing my oven mitts, I close the oven door and wonder out loud, "Who can that be?" Within moments, I return to the kitchen with Anna.

"Hi Anna," says Leen, genuinely pleased to see her. "We were just going to have some iced tea. Want some?"

"That would be lovely," answers Anna. Carrying the drinks over to the table Leen sits down to join Anna and me.

"As I was saying to Amy at the door," says Anna, in that direct manner and tone we've come to expect, "I read the newspaper article about Sarah. I was wondering if there's anything I can do to help out?"

"Right now we're all in a holding pattern," answers Leen. "Amy has made a mountain of food for Joe and the boys. I stayed with the boys last night while Joe slept at the hospital to be near Sarah. Becky's monitoring the medical end of things. In fact," she says with a grin, "we just got in from Joe and Sarah's house where, as I speak, Joe and the boys are enjoying homemade lasagne."

"I cook when I'm nervous or stressed out," I explain with an apologetic smile.

Impulsively Leen asks, "Want to stay for supper, Anna? Amy's cabbage rolls are awesome."

"Thank you but no," Anna answers, "I've already eaten." Her blue eyes twinkle as she comments, "Perhaps, Becky can provide some counselling that would result in less caloric intake to deal with anxiety."

Feigning shock and holding her hand over her heart, Leen retorts, "Are you kidding me? If she dares to do that, she'll be facing the wrath of two disgruntled gourmets."

"People react differently to stress," Anna sympathizes. "Me, I tend to make tea and putter around my house looking for things to move from place to place."

"Thank you," I say, pleased that she understands my need to keep busy. I poke Leen's shoulder. "See, Leen."

"Come on, Amy," grins Leen, "you know we love your cooking. If you weren't so good at it, we wouldn't tease you about gaining weight."

"Yeah, yeah," I answer, waving her off, "you're just trying to get on my good side."

"Well, there's that too," replies Leen.

"How *is* Sarah?" asks Anna.

I answer truthfully. "It'll be a long haul."

"I don't want to intrude," says Anna, softly, "but you ladies have been so kind to me. If there's anything I can do for Sarah, just let me know."

"Actually, right now we can only wait," says Leen, "but, when she gets strong enough to come home, she'll need company. Sarah is not going to react well to being off work for a while."

"Then, there's the question of her speech." In response to Anna's quizzical expression, I explain, "The doctors are saying that she might experience problems. Both the boys are obviously upset with that consequence of her aneurism and have already pointed out that Sarah earns her living by talking. That's going to hit her hard."

"I imagine she'll have speech therapy," says Anna.

"Sure, but that won't stop her from feeling like she's less than adequate," responds Leen. "Sarah's like a little battery; she just keeps running and running. It's going to be really hard for her to slow down and take the time to re-charge."

I get up to refill our glasses. Pouring the tart sweet liquid, I ask, "Would you reconsider about dinner, Anna?"

Leen agrees readily. "And, if you don't want to eat; how about just joining us as we eat? We'd love your company."

"I don't want to impose," protests Anna. "Both of you look exhausted."

"It's not an imposition," I reassure her. "There's plenty and we'd like it if you did."

Anna takes a second to reconsider my offer. "Okay, but tell you what," she says, "I have some fresh apple pie next door. How about I go and get it?"

"Sounds good to me," says Leen rising to set the table. "We're ready to eat when you are."

Anna returns with the pie just as I'm setting the cabbage rolls, thick slices of crusty bread and salad on the table. Admiring the piecrust's light, golden colour I compliment Anna.

"My mother could make the flakiest crusts of anyone I've ever known,' replies Anna whimsically. "To this day, whenever I make one, I can hear her saying, "You have to mix the dough lightly and then, when it's just about ready to come out of the oven, brush milk over the crust to make it a light brown."

"Well, here's to mothers!" toasts Leen, handing Anna a glass of wine.

As we eat, Anna and I exchange thoughts about the therapeutic value of cooking. "Those cabbage rolls are some of the best that I have ever tasted," says Anna. She rubs her stomach lightly. "But I have to admit that I've over-eaten."

"Oh that'll pass," promises Leen flippantly. "We'll just wait a few minutes to digest and then have the apple pie. In the meantime, I'll make some tea."

"It never fails to amaze me," I remark, in a conspiratorial tone directed at Anna, "that Leen is as fit as her name implies and yet, she eats with the gusto of an Olympian in training."

"It would appear that she has an excellent metabolism," replies Anna.

Although the jokes have been at her expense, Leen's laughter is genuine. "I'm simply going to ignore you both," she says.

As we start in on dessert, the phone rings. Hanging up, I say, "Well, I guess you could tell that was Joe. Sarah's awake and still experiencing a lot of pain, but he says that she's very aware of where she is and understands what has happened to her."

"Did he say anything about her speech?" asks Leen abruptly.

"He said she started to cry when she realized she couldn't speak properly. One of the nurses tried to explain to her that this was common and she shouldn't get too anxious, but Sarah didn't accept that explanation. According to Joe, she was frustrated to the point where the nurse called the doctor to issue an order for something to relax her."

"It might be *common* for the nurse," replies Leen, with a hint of annoyance, "but for Sarah, it's a major shock and a tranquillizer won't make that go away!"

"She will need time to adjust," reasons Anna. "The nurse wasn't dismissing her concerns. The request for the tranquilizer was to get something to help blunt the shock of all that has happened. I certainly don't know Sarah as well as either of you but in my short acquaintance, I've found her to be a strong person." She takes time to choose her words. "I think her tenacity for life will help her through this." A few seconds pass as Leen and I silently mull over Anna's astute observation.

"Joe said he was going home to get some sleep," I say, filling in the silence that followed Anna's remark. "The boys will go back to school tomorrow. Now, that the crisis is over, he wants to return some normalcy to their lives."

With dry humour, Leen comments, "Oh, I'm sure that'll please the twins since they are so *fond* of school." Both Anna and I smile.

Continuing with her train of thought, Leen says, "We all have to get back on track. Sarah would be the first one to kick ass if any of us fall short of meeting our obligations." Leen's expression is gentle as she adds, "You know Sarah. She has a plan for every waking moment of her life."

We begin to regale Anna with stories about Sarah's antics over the years. She listens, knowing that it's our way of releasing the stress of having come so close to losing her.

෴

Anna

I sit with Leen and Amy for another hour, listening to their stories. It occurs to me that over the last few months I've become very comfortable with and fond of my four new friends. On numerous occasions I've satisfied my growing interest in their lives with questions and they've talked openly about their friendship and careers. Tonight is no different. When there's a lull in the conversation, I steer the talk to Amy's work at the university and ask Leen for an update on her search for Claire Holowitz.

"Well, you've made progress in your quest," I observe, carefully. "From what you've said, you've organized your campaign effectively and managed to get Holowitz's endorsement."

"I've worked my butt off," frowns Leen. "But no matter what I do, I can't shake the feeling that she's out there somewhere – watching me and interested in what I'm doing."

"Her lawyer would've contacted you if he thought anything was wrong," says Amy with characteristic pragmatism. "After all, isn't that what he did when you first started this whole business? Out of nowhere, came the magnificent Marc Andre Aumount." Her humour does little to improve Leen's mood.

"I never said he was magnificent," responds Leen, defensively.

"Come on Leen," counters Amy. "It was no secret that you found him attractive." Seeking confirmation from me, she says, "I think we've all heard her denials before."

Amused, I say, "Amy does make a valid point, Leen. From everything I've heard, it is clear that you find him attractive as well as interesting."

"Oh, both of you give it a rest!" says Leen, clearly exasperated. "Besides, I haven't heard from him since that first meeting." Eying us suspiciously, she asks, "Since when have the two of you become co-conspirators with Kathy? Sometimes I think she's an escapee from a Harlequin Romance. She might as well be, seeing as she's so busy plotting my love life."

"I've always liked Kathy," answers Amy, smiling, "and I think she shows marked common sense." To me, she explains, "Kathy is Leen's administrative assistant. You'd like her."

I laugh. "Oh, I see, your master plan is for the three of us to organize Leen's love life." Keeping a straight face, I suggest, "Maybe we should ask Becky to help us. After all, she is a psychiatrist. Her input as to how we should address this *attraction* might be helpful."

Leen groans, "Cut it out, Amy."

Amy flashes a saccharine sweet smile. "You're the one who said that he had removed roadblocks. If there wasn't *some* sort of attraction, would he have been so accommodating?"

"Give it a rest," warns Leen, but I can tell she's not truly annoyed with Amy's teasing. "Aumount's just acting for Holowitz. It's Holowitz that I want to meet. She's the focus of this Gala."

"What would you do if you met her?"

For a moment I think she won't answer. Amy and I exchange quizzical glances. We wait for her to respond but she takes her time to consider the answer. When she does, she speaks with slow deliberation.

"I'd try to get to know her. It's gone past my wanting to profile her for the campaign." Speaking with more intensity than I've ever heard her use, she continues, "The more I learn about Claire Holowitz, the more I want to know her! In fact," she emphasizes, "I wouldn't even tell Don that I'd met her. I need her to realize that I am not out to market her per se. Sure, I'm marketing her works but more than that, I am celebrating her life."

I reply tersely, "I don't think Don will take kindly to being cut out of the loop."

Leen doesn't reject my assessment. "I don't care. Like I said, I wouldn't tell him."

"But you know realistically he'd find out somehow, some way. And if he knew you concealed her whereabouts, he'd probably want you fired."

Biting her lower lip, Leen considers my comment. "This isn't about *what* Don wants. It's about *what* I need to do. He'd turn her life into a media circus. She deserves better than that." Pushing her hand through her wheaten hair, she says plaintively, "My God, doesn't anyone get it? I don't want to intrude upon her life with media frenzy and expose her to stupid questions asked by word crunching reporters."

Amy tries to reason with Leen, saying, "Holowitz wants her privacy and not intrusion from anyone for any reason. Including you." Speaking firmly, in spite of the glint in Leen's eyes indicating that she might explode in anger, she adds, "She *doesn't* know that your motives are altruistic. She *doesn't* have any reason to trust you." Unperturbed, Amy sits calmly, not wavering under Leen's glare.

Redirecting the conversation to the actual project, I ask, "So where did your trip to Toronto lead you in your quest?"

Leen's demeanour and tone make it clear that as far as she's concerned, Amy has been deliberately obtuse and she doesn't appreciate her playing the devil's advocate. "I met with Taylor Jones. He's directed three Holowitz plays.

"Did you get anything useful?" asks Amy getting up from the table and taking some nachos and salsa from the cupboard. A crease of amusement crosses my face as I observe how Amy, not at all fazed by Leen's frustration, is trying to make light conversation. They have the inexplicable comfort that only true friends can share – the freedom to become annoyed and yet, move on as if nothing has happened.

Leen, having spent her anger, is now moving towards becoming conciliatory. "Actually, he's a very interesting man," she answers, her brow furrowing in concentration. "He's somewhat eccentric what with his hair askew, sandals, and seeming laissez-faire attitude about life. He personifies the stereotype of a sixty-five year old man trying to recapture his youth. Having said that, he's terribly articulate and passionate as to what he believes should or should not be in theatre."

Placing the tray of nachos on the table, Amy comments, "Taylor Jones has an impressive list of credits to his name. One of my PhD candidates wants to centre her thesis on his contribution to theatre. Among some circles, he's considered a genius."

"I don't know about genius," muses Leen, "but I'd definitely agree that he comes across as a renegade and trail blazer." She looks at me and asks, "How about you Anna? You know a lot about theatre. Have you come across any of Taylor Jones' works?"

"I have seen a few Holowitz plays that he's directed. I recall having read or heard that he's 'consumed' with the need to create in theatre a venue for the written word that the silver screen, with all of its imagery, will never be able to capture."

"Consumed would be a good descriptor," replies Leen. "He talked, almost with reverence, about the brilliance of Holowitz's works. He claims that despite her phobic aversions to the media," Leen makes finger quotation gestures, "he's always found her to be compliant, via her lawyers, for any of his directorial adaptations to her plays."

"Will you be able to use any of his comments?" asks Amy, spooning salsa onto a nacho chip.

"Most definitely," answers Leen, quickly. "He's agreed to be one of the guest speakers at the Gala and is providing original marquees of the Holowitz plays he's directed."

I ask, "Did you come up with anything else from this visit?"

"Taylor gave me the name of a bookstore owner in British Columbia," replies Leen reaching for a nacho. "Her name is Edna Windstrom. She owns a quaint little shop in New Westminster's Quay market area. Taylor's story is that Windstrom was struggling to make ends meet about five years ago to support herself and a teenage son when, out of the blue, Holowitz decided to launch *Hollow Dreams* from Edna's shop. The publicity resulted in Edna's little shop becoming a venue for other authors to launch their novels." She shrugs. "And, as we all know, good publicity makes for good profit."

Amy's interest is piqued. "Did Edna meet Holowitz?"

"That's the funny part," answers Leen, getting up to get a glass of water. "Does anyone want some water?"

"I'd love a glass, please," I answer.

Shaking her head no, Amy pursues the topic of Edna, "So did she meet Claire?"

"Apparently she did, but wasn't aware of it. Edna's story is another classic example of how Claire moves about in the public eye without being recognized."

Leen sucks air between her teeth and thinks for a moment. "Claire must have altered her looks somehow. So many people claim to have benefitted from her generosity and or their erstwhile association with her works and yet, few can claim to actually have met her. And the ones who have are keeping silent."

"Not necessarily," I interject. "It could just be that she's gotten forty years older since she isolated herself. Age alter features. She'd be different now from the last photograph taken of her when her husband and daughter died."

"You'd think someone would recognize her," replies Leen, her brow creasing in thought. "It's all so very aggravating."

Curious, Amy prods, "Okay, so finish the story about Edna."

"According to Taylor, Edna was contacted by Claire's lawyer," resumes Leen, her tone tinged with scepticism.

"Ah hah," cries Amy, a triumphant knowing smile lighting across her face. "Let me guess, one Marc Andre Aumount."

"You got it!" says Leen. "Unannounced, Aumount made an appearance at Edna's 'Timely Books' and said that he was representing Claire Holowitz who had selected Edna's store to launch her novel."

Enthralled with the unfolding story, Amy says, "She must have been flabbergasted."

"Who wouldn't be shocked?" answers Leen. "I mean there she is one day a virtual unknown shopkeeper and, out of the blue, Holowitz picks her store to launch her latest book. There's no rhyme or reason to the stories that I'm hearing about Holowitz and her motives for what she does."

"But *does* there have to be a reason?" I ask.

Leen considers my question. "Everyone has a reason for their actions."

"Just the same," I say, quietly, "whatever her reasons – Holowitz is under no obligation to make them public." A flicker of annoyance flashes in Leen's eyes but she doesn't answer.

"So what did Edna do when she realized that her shop was about to receive a lot of free and very needed publicity?" asks Amy.

Leen flips aside a fallen strand of hair. "Taylor said that she asked the obvious question. Why her store?"

"And?" persists Amy, getting tired of the story being dragged out. "What was Aumount's explanation?"

Leen stares at Amy, bewilderment evident on her face. "Taylor says that Aumount told Edna that Claire had been in the store when some other customers were there. Apparently Edna had asked her if there was anything she could help her with. One thing led to another and it seems that they had a discussion about various authors and Edna's love of books. That led to Edna telling her about buying the store and hoping to make it work in terms of providing financial security for her and her son."

"Wouldn't Edna be able to recall this encounter and identify Holowitz?" An avid fan of mystery novels, Amy adds excitedly, "At least provide a description of her."

"You would think so," answers Leen, "but according to Taylor, Edna chats with a lot of customers and can't recall exactly what the woman looked like. She does remember having a lengthy discussion with an older woman about her love of Holowitz's works, but since that took place five years ago …" she sighs audibly, "she can't remember what she looked like. What she does recall is that the woman was older and her knowledge about Holowitz and literary works in general was impressive."

Talking more to herself than to either of us, Amy reflects, "So, to recap, Edna met Holowitz, but didn't realize it. And, Holowitz, for reasons only known to her, decided to launch her novel from this struggling bookshop." Brow furrowed, she asks, "How'd Holowitz launch her book if she wasn't there?"

Grimacing, Leen answers, "The same way she's done in the past. She sent someone to represent her. In this case, she sent Aumount and the publicity people took care of the rest."

"What does Taylor think of Edna's story?" I ask.

"According to him, it was typical Claire Holowitz: she moves in and out of literary circles with anonymity. Edna credits that launch as the beginning of a turnaround for her little store. Since then, she has had other authors come by, sign autographs for customers and a few, like Lynch and Bretton, have even done publicity sales from her store."

Amy asks, "Are you going to meet with Edna?"

Without hesitation, Leen answers, "Yes, I think so. I haven't planned it out yet, because I'd only heard about it and then Amy called with the news about Sarah, so I came home. Now that things are settling down with her, I think I'll go out to Vancouver as soon as I take care of a few things at work. Maybe meeting Edna will give me better insight as to what motivates Holowitz to take interest in the most unlikely of people or places."

I stifle a yawn. Apologetically, I say, "I guess I'm a little tired."

Concern washes over Amy's face. "We've kept you too long with our chatter."

"Oh but I've enjoyed the evening and your company," I reply, pushing back my chair and rising. "The problem lies with me, not the conversation. I just can't keep the hours that I used to." Recalling the original purpose of my visit, I say, "I'd appreciate if you would keep me informed on Sarah's progress and let me know when it might be a good time to visit her. Perhaps she'd like some of my apple pie or I could make a casserole." I smile at Amy and add, "Not that I can compete with your legendary skills."

"Sarah will appreciate anything that you do, Anna," replies Amy. "And, it's not a competition of cooking skills. Leen's made it sound like cooking is all that I do."

Amused, Leen retorts, "If the pie you brought over tonight is a sample of your cooking, then Amy here has finally found a soul-mate."

Leen and Amy see me to the front door and, cutting across our adjoining lawns, I make my way back home.

Amy

After helping me place the remaining dishes and cups in the dishwasher, Leen gets ready to head home. Slipping on her coat, she says, "The more I think about it, the more I like the idea of going out to Vancouver. I'll call the hospital tomorrow to see how Sarah's doing, swing by my office and tidy up some files that need attention, and make the flight arrangements."

"Will you be gone long?"

"Three days. Two for travel and one will be to meet Edna." Leen flicks the button on her remote key chain and the BMW's headlights come on and the doors softly unlock. She climbs into her car, waves goodbye, and pulls away from the curb.

Before returning inside, I glance at Anna's house. The lights are out except for one room at the front on the second floor. Blinds block the view of the room, but given the fact that the rest of the house is covered in darkness, I surmise that it must be her bedroom. I make my way upstairs to my own bedroom and, as I turn down the bed covers, the thought occurs to me that despite our age differences Anna fits in well with the four of us. In a strange sort of way, it's almost as if we've been friends for a long time. I think about how she impressed Leen from their first meeting and how Leen has drawn Anna into her circle of advisors in her search for Claire Holowitz. And, with these thoughts on my mind, I fall asleep.

Chapter Ten

Claire

Leaning back into the Adirondack chair, I welcome the warmth of the late afternoon sun as I gather my thoughts. I have always loved this time of day. Tonight there will be a full moon. I love the clarity of a moonbeam almost as much as I relish basking in the sun. I exhale slowly before opening my eyes, to address the matter at hand. My gaze settles on the deep red colours of the maple trees, interspersed with bursts of burnt orange and rust. Fall has always been one of my favourite seasons and I make no apologics for jealously guarding the time that I can spend soaking in the splendour of its colour.

Today's meeting is necessary, but I'd insisted that we take advantage of the good weather and that is why we are still sitting outside instead of around the kitchen table. There is a slight chill in the air; enough to signal that fall will soon be a memory. Pulling the throw over my knees, I break the comfortable silence and speak aloud my idle thoughts. "The long hot summer is over, leading to a fall of uncertainty and to a winter of despair."

"I've always liked that line," comments Marc Andre.

Allowing myself the luxury of this whimsical moment, I reply, "I used it in *The Fallen Mother* ... I remember how proud I was when I came up with that line. I was so young; so full of life." I chuckle at the memory. "When I started to write, owning an electronic typewriter was a big deal. Word processing has made my life much easier when it comes to making revisions."

"So many stories, so many years," replies Marc Andre in that soft, understanding voice he reserves for when we're having one of my more revealing conversations. It's as if he has always known intuitively that idle chatter or brash responses would halt my trip down memory lane and that I would put away the memory tidily in a corner of my brain and resume discussing the more practical matters at hand. He lets me take my time. Once I'd asked him how he'd become so insightful regarding my need to talk about seemingly insignificant matters and then suddenly, when least expected, address the topic of concern. He'd smiled that smile – the one that has always charmed me – and replied that it was his considered opinion that was my way of 'processing things'.

At first, I'd rejected the notion that I use a convoluted process to make decisions but it wasn't long before I realized that Marc Andre knew my soul in some ways better than I. Somehow the process of veering off into tangents of reminiscent experiences helps to congeal my thoughts so that when I finally speak or act upon a decisive matter, it is as if I am striking with the clarity and swiftness of a highly honed rapier. As is his practice and our custom, Marc Andre is content to sit beside me in companionable silence while I sort the cobwebs of my mind.

These days though I think he must think my age is showing. I see it sometimes in the flicker of his eyes, a quickness to assist me to rise from a chair and the gentle touch to my elbow when we walk. He's not said it but I know that he has had to develop newfound patience for me to complete tasks that a few years ago would have been done quickly. In these things as with all our dealings, Marc Andre is tolerant of my eccentricities.

༺༻

Marc Andre

I glance sideways and hope that she hasn't spotted me. She still possesses much of the youthful vigour and enthusiasm that has always characterized our discussions from as far back as I can remember. But there are changes now – too obvious for me to deny. Slender, graceful hands that once were steady occasionally shake. She has aged gracefully. To my mind's eye, she is still beautiful.

When I was a child, she would tell me stories, comfort me when I was upset, and allow me to tag along when she set off – Nikon in hand–looking for photo opportunities. Always, she was strong. She was integral to my life. She was as much a part of who I was and who I would become as my parents. As I grew, so too did our relationship.

As a teenager I went with her to Rome. There we walked the streets looking for photo opportunities. After a few hours I began to grumble about my aching feet and the fact that she had not yet taken one photo. She commiserated about my feet and promised to take me to the restaurant of my choice, if only I could be patient a little longer.

"But, Aunt Claire, a photo is a photo. The coliseum won't change," I'd sullenly replied.

"That, my dear Marc Andre is where you're wrong," she had patiently answered before launching into an explanation of how lighting at different times of the day can alter the message of the photo. I have never forgotten her look of satisfaction – as she held the camera for me to peer through its lens – her blue eyes so intent and a soft smile on her face. Even now, as I wait for her to tell me what the purpose of today's meeting is, I can hear her voice in the echoes of my mind. "Ah, Marc Andre, many people will never see the streets of Rome or the Coliseum. It's up to us – you and me – to explore how we'll capture the essence, the people, and the history of this ancient city." She had stretched her arms expansively and whirled about, delighted at the thought of capturing Rome on film. "When people look at the photo, it will be as if they are actually there. The same applies when you speak or write, Marc," she had added excitedly. "You must use words so that what you *want* to convey is alive and real to the listener or reader."

At the time, I'd been too young to fully comprehend the import of what she was sharing but the wisdom of her words have come to mind on many occasions in my legal career. I think of Aunt Claire's patient tutelage in the use of what I call her 'mystical vocabulary' and how she taught me to use words cleverly.

Without preamble, Aunt Claire says, "I'm tired, Marc Andre; so very tired."

I don't argue or offer false platitudes. She would not tolerate pity. I nod that I understand and looking at her, I feel a sense of impending loss. She has become so thin and her movements lack her former agility. Certainly the medication has contributed to that, but there's something else happening—a sense of letting go, as if she doesn't have the strength to hold on.

"The drugs contribute to the tiredness, Aunt Claire. Remember," I tease, "you're not as young as you used to be. It's to be expected that you will tire more easily."

"True enough," she replies. "But just the same, there's a bone weary fatigue about me that I just can't seem to shake. Enough," she says suddenly, "there is no point in belabouring the obvious!" Giving physical expression to her words she gives her body a small shake as if by doing so she can shake off her fatigue. "Thank you for letting an old woman air her thoughts. I know that you're busy and yet, I've been sitting here just allowing my thoughts to wander."

"Aunt Claire, I'm glad to be here." I rest my hand over hers. "Tell me, what would you like me to do?"

I see a spark in her eyes and a jut to her chin, reminiscent of the Aunt Claire of my youth. In that instant, I know that she has another agenda for our meeting.

༄

Claire

Instead of answering Marc Andre's question, I reply, "So what is your impression of *Ms Adrienne MacLeen?*"

His seemingly nonchalant attitude about Leen, whenever her name comes up, hasn't fooled me one bit. Before I decide what I want Marc Andre to do, I need to know what his feelings and impressions are of the woman seeking me.

Brushing imaginary lint from his golf shirt, he stares at the maple trees and hedges. "Next weekend, I'll cover the shrubs with burlap," he states. "The fall chill is starting to settle and they need to be protected for the winter."

"Uh, huh," I murmur. "It's that time of year."

I know that look on his face. He's trying to avoid answering my question and that speaks volumes. Marc Andre has never been a good liar which makes it all the more ironic that he became a lawyer. But usually he can maintain a good poker face. There's no doubt from his silence that Leen has gotten to him. *Interesting,"* I think, *well, we'll have to see where this goes.*

We've always been close but the spring that he stayed with me for three weeks, while his parents were on a cruise to celebrate their fifteenth anniversary, forged a new bond between us. He had been embarrassed that he still needed to have adult supervision and was going through that awkward teenage phase – crossing the threshold of childhood into early manhood. I had managed a delicate balance between enforcing his parents' rules and curfews while playing my godmother role of allowing for some liberties. I'd chosen to ignore the fact that he would answer the phone and leave the room with it when the caller was a girl. I looked the other way when walking past his bedroom door and saw that his clothes, instead of being properly hung up, had found various resting places on the floor. They were small oversights, but ones that at the time signalled that I was aware of his new need for adult privacy.

I can tell that he knows I'm prying, wanting to know his personal reaction to Leen as opposed to seeking his opinion about her professionalism. I know him well enough to reason that he'll tell me but on his own terms.

Finally ready to answer, he ticks off the facts as he sees them. "She's bright, witty, driven to excel. She can also be defensive, obstinate and singularly strong-willed."

My godson's tactics to avoid personalizing his response amuses me. I push. "And?"

His sigh is barely audible but I know that he's searching for a way to circumvent my digging for information that he's not yet ready to deal with or to share. To me, it's as obvious as the nose on his face but I want to hear him say it. Sooner or later, he's going to have to deal with his reactions to Leen and, from where I sit, I want it to be sooner. Attempting to appease me, he says, "I believe that she truly wants to represent you in the best possible manner."

"That much I have gathered." Deciding that bluntness is called for, I say, "You know very well what I'm asking. What do *you* think of her?"

His puzzled expression betrays his quandary as to how he can best answer. I take the position that I have all the time in the world to wait for his response. I pour iced tea into a tall glass and hand it to him. He takes a long swallow.

I tease, "One would think that iced tea is bourbon the way you're using it to calm yourself. Speaking of which, would you like some?"

"No, I'm good, "he answers, "maybe later."

"Come on now, Marc Andre," I prod, gently, "tell me. I need to know."

He frowns, nods his head slowly, and lets out a long, deep breath.

༄

Marc Andre

Were it anyone else demanding that I expose my personal reaction to Leen, I would tell them exactly what they could do with themselves. Aunt Claire has always been able to extract information from me in such a way that while I know she is interfering; I don't object. Shifting my position in the chair, I ask, "Don't you think I'm a little too old to be cross-examined about how I may or may not view a woman?"

"Don't take the upper hand with me, Marc," she retorts, "you know I have always had your best interests at heart." It pleases me to hear her deep, belly laugh. Lately, she's not done much of that. When she touches my shoulder, I rest my fingertips on her hand letting her know that she has hit her mark.

"I know," I concede, "but to be honest, Aunt Claire, well ..." I pause, thinking about my meeting with Leen and her reaction to my probing questions. I remember how she eventually relaxed and that I had found myself enjoying her company and liking how her face lights up when she smiles. When she dropped me off at the airport, I'd deliberately walked away without looking back, knowing that what I wanted to do was to go back and spend the night with her.

Speaking with candour, I say, "She unnerved me. There's something intriguing about her and I get the feeling that only a fool would try to rush her into anything. Besides" I add drily, "there's the little matter that I represent you and that could cause a conflict of interest."

Aunt Claire scoffs. "You sound so much like your father. For Emile, there was always an issue that had to be resolved ethically. This is a simple matter Marc .... you either like the girl or not."

"I like her."

"Ah, good," remarks Aunt Claire. "Now, we're getting somewhere. One of your mother's favourite maxims was that when it comes to matters of the heart, it's important to just 'spit it out'. Genevieve was a firm believer that only then could a person deal with the reality of feelings versus pushing them aside." She slyly slips in, "Smart woman, your mother."

I tease, "If she were alive, the two of you would be teaming up – doing your utmost to ferret out my love life and play match makers." Too late, I realize that I've slipped up and revealed more than simply liking Leen.

Practically cackling with delight, she taps the chair's armrest and remarks, "Who would have thought? A woman has finally caught your interest. Genevieve would have loved this. She used to say that she feared you'd end up being a hopeless bachelor."

I groan. "Don't play the innocent! You, who insisted that I fly back immediately from New York to discuss Scenes' spearheading the Holowitz Gala. You who said, 'Marc Andre, I need you to handle this one personally.' Wagging my finger, I add, "You old plotter! You knew exactly what you were doing! And, as for my mother's opinion that I would be a hopeless bachelor ... my marital status or lack thereof, is solely my business. Besides ..." I grin, "if memory serves me well both of you used to tell me to take my time."

"There's a big difference in taking one's time when one is in college and avoiding the chance to love when one is a grown man with a successful career," snaps Aunt Claire. "Two very different scenarios."

Rising, I say, "Think I'll fix myself that bourbon now. Your futile attempts at match making are duly noted."

"Caught in the act. What can I say?" She dismisses her meddling in my personal life with a wave of her hand. "Your family has been as my own for over forty-five years. Your father has been one of my closest friends and confidants since Drew and Emily died. Your mother was like a sister to me and I have missed her terribly these last seven years. I still say she'd be enjoying this moment very much." Her expression softens. "You have done well following in your father's footsteps. He's very proud of you." She pauses and then, adds softly, "I'm sure that wherever your mother is, she is smiling down on you. Rightly so."

I don't know what to say to her last comment. I lightly touch her shoulder with my fingertips and ask, "Can I get you something?"

"No thank you, dear. You go get yourself that bourbon. We have much to talk about."

༄

As I fix my drink, I think about Aunt Claire's reference to my mother. I miss her. The only family I have left is my father and Aunt Claire. My father's health has become a concern and despite his protests, it's clear that he is becoming frail. Three years ago, following his heart attack, he relinquished the management of his firm to me. Increasing bouts of angina have necessitated that he avoid the stressful demands associated with the daily practice of law. Although he still consults when it comes to Aunt Claire's legal matters, he has been content to lead a quiet life. My thoughts turn to Aunt Claire. She's been a second mother to me for as long as I can remember. The last few times we've gotten together I've noticed that she too is becoming frailer and her pain is becoming more obvious.

Returning to the patio, I see that Aunt Claire has dozed off. Lately, she's been doing a lot of that. I quietly return to my chair and sip my bourbon. She'll tell me what's on her mind when she's ready.

To be truthful, I'm glad for the quiet and hope that when she wakes Aunt Claire won't resume her inquisition of my feelings for Leen. From the first, Leen has had an appeal for me but like it or not, the fact remains that I am not at this time in a position to do anything about that interest. There is the matter of the business at hand. I know enough about Leen MacLeen to know that when she finds out everything that is going on behind the scenes, she will react with feelings of anger and betrayal. The thought of being part of the cause for that anger doesn't please me. At best, I can hope that in time she will have enough perspective to objectively analyze the motives and recognize the need for the subterfuge.

When Aunt Claire opens her eyes, I let a few minutes pass before I venture the question that has been niggling at the back of my mind. "Aunt Claire, I need to ask this as your lawyer."

"Go ahead." She sighs softly, already resigned to the fact that my question is bound to be a zinger.

"Leen's going to find out sooner or later. She's one sharp lady. What are you going to do when that happens?"

"She hasn't realized it yet?" answers Aunt Claire, casting a sideways glance and pursing her lips as she thinks about what I've said.

"She's smart and intuitive, Aunt Claire. She's relentless in digging up old photos and articles about you. She's pushing to meet you. Taylor told me that when he met her in Toronto, he had the distinct impression that she suspects more people actually know you than the general public is aware of."

Chuckling Aunt Claire says, "Taylor has always had a flare for the dramatic; that's one of the reasons I love having him direct my plays. He makes my words come to life on stage."

Aunt Claire not only has a soft spot for Taylor but she trusts him. They've been friends for many years and shared a lot of history. Their friendship started shortly after she'd written her first play. He had been a young aspiring director and Aunt Claire had just published her first novel when they met at a mutual friend's house party. It had been a meeting of like minds and neither of them ever looked back nor regretted the friendship they forged. Occasionally Aunt Claire would ask him to read a draft manuscript before sending it to her editor or publisher and he, in turn, never hesitated to seek her opinion on how to bring about the visualization of characters to the stage.

Frowning, I say, "Taylor's penchant for dramatics aside; he may be right. It could be an issue when dealing with Leen."

Aunt Claire's brow furrows. "I should do something but I really don't want to. I feel as if I am learning not only about her, but as if a part of me is coming alive again. Do you know I'm actually thinking of writing a play?"

This bit of news surprises me. "A play? That's wonderful! What brought that about?"

She smiles gently as if she were recounting a chance encounter with an old friend. "I'm not entirely certain," she replies with candour. "I had thought last year that my days of muse were over and yet, the idea just seemed to pop into my head and I found it to be welcome and comforting." Her face lights up with excitement. "The other day I took out my Nikon and played with the lenses. I'd forgotten how good it feels to hold a camera." She lifts her hands from her lap and slowly examines them, as if seeing them for the first time. Resting them back on her lap, she says, "It was like revisiting an old friend."

I look at her outstretched hands. They are long hands with thin fingers and the veins are prominent. Once they had been slender and graceful. And, yet, her voice and demeanour reflects a vitality I've not seen for several months.

She seems to know what I'm thinking. "These hands may look old but they still work; they will know how to use the camera when the time comes." She laughs softly. "Let's hope my eyes hold out so that I can focus properly."

"Since when has your vision become a problem?

"There's nothing wrong with my vision. I was just thinking aloud. So much has happened to me in my lifetime; I've gained and lost so much. Now, dealing with the leukaemia and all the complications of my immune system, I take nothing for granted. I'm counting on my sight to hold out. She pats my hand. "I may have to take more time than I did when I was younger but that is to be expected at my age. But to not see," she pauses reflectively, as if measuring what any deity may or may not have in store for her, "that would be unbearable." She bites her lower lip and in a voice close to a whisper, says, "There's no way that God would do that to me."

I can't help but smile at her blatant self-confidence and for lack of a better word, pigheadedness. "Anyone ever tell you that you're one stubborn woman? Not even St. Peter would tamper with you once you've made up your mind."

She snorts derisively. I go back to my questions. I need to know how she wants me to proceed. "What do you want to do about Leen?"

She taps her temple. "I have a plan."

Now it's my turn to snort and I do so enthusiastically. When she's satisfied that I've had my moment of humour, she begins to outline her plan. I listen carefully, interjecting only when I have a question. When she finishes, I'm amazed at the thought and effort she has put into all of this. I let out a slow, long whistle. "I hope that your assessment is right. It could backfire."

"Let's hope it works out for everybody." Aunt Claire stifles a yawn, rises, and folds the blanket that had covered her knees. "There's a chill in the air. Shall we go inside?"

I carry in the empty glasses and pitcher. As I shut the dishwasher door, I ask, "Can I pick up anything for you at the grocery store before I leave?"

"Leave? Since when do you come to my house and I don't feed you? How about you take me for a ride in that nice new Mercedes of yours to the grocery store? We'll get some steaks, potatoes and salad. You can barbecue them and we'll just talk about everything and anything. Just like we used to do when you were a boy?"

I think of the files waiting for me but I don't want to pass up the opportunity of this time with her. "Okay, but when was the last time you watched a video?" Slipping on my jacket, I add, "Unless you're too tired ... we could have dinner another time."

"It's a done deal," she answers quickly. She brushes my cheek with her lips. "I'd like the company. I can sleep whenever I want to."

"Why do I feel like I'm twelve years old again?"

Her smile is broad. "Because the only way I can get what I want with you is to pull out the 'I'm your godmother card' and guilt you into relenting." She opens the front door and practically marches out to my car.

Around eight o'clock, I lean over to kiss her cheek saying, "The steak was great, but that movie was definitely a woman's movie."

The corners of her eyes crinkle upwards. "You said it was *my* pick tonight. Next time, I'll endure one of those action movies that you're so fond of."

"I'll hold you to it," I reply. She watches from the front door as I open the car door. I call out, "Get some rest."

Three hours later, I finally turn off my laptop. As per her instructions I've drawn up the necessary documents and organized my notes. Restless, I flick on the television, do some channel surfing and settle on a late night talk show. By midnight I'm finally ready to make my way to bed. I think of how I would have liked to have known Aunt Claire before tragedy changed her life. I think of the stories my father has shared about her younger days – the days when her career was looming before her and she was a young wife and mother. The days when she didn't seclude herself from the fame that her writing and photos brought. The days when according to my father, she laughed freely and had a smile that could light up a room. Recalling the few photos I've seen of that part of her life, I reflect that neither age nor tragedy has managed to erase a natural beauty. I reach to switch off the bed lamp and wonder aloud, "Will I ever know a woman as passionate and insightful as you?"

A final thought occurs to me just before I fall asleep. *You have my work cut out for me, Aunt Claire. I hope you never stop viewing life as a play. This world needs you and so do I.*

Chapter Eleven

Amy

Engrossed in my work, I swallow the last dregs of coffee. It is long-since gone cold but it's liquid. I reach into the desk drawer and withdraw a stick of gum. The peppermint flavour erases the sour taste of the coffee as I reread the last paragraph. Things are not going as well as I would like but I'm making progress. With each page written, I continue to build the framework for what can later be revised, embellished or deleted. Probably, based on my recent edits, I'll delete most of today's work but having written it, I am closer to finding out how to develop the flow of what I really want to say.

I've just made it through two more paragraphs when the doorbell rings. At first, I hope that whoever it is will be satisfied with one ring that no one is home and go away. I ignore the second. Exasperated, I push the bangs off my forehead and glance back at the laptop's screen. Rings three and four jar me into action. Annoyed, I hit the save command and reluctantly get up to answer the door.

I'm surprised to see that the bell-ringing offender is Anna. She hands over a large brown paper bag filled with fresh tomatoes, saying, "Some of the vendors at the Byward Market have started to harvest their field tomatoes – albeit hothouse versions." She grins. "I thought you might enjoy having some."

Sniffing the tomatoes, I answer, "I love fresh tomatoes." Opening the door wider, I motion for her to come in. "Tonight I'll make a toasted bacon and tomato sandwich – it's one of my favourite comfort foods."

She hesitates. "I don't want to disturb you."

Feeling guilty for having made her stand – arms full with a bag of tomatoes bought for me, I apologize, "Sorry about not answering the doorbell sooner. I was working and thought it was one of those door-to-door salespersons. If I'd known you were going to drop over, I never would have made you wait."

"I admit to being guilty of the same," replies Anna. "I rarely answer my doorbell unless I'm expecting company. How is the writing coming along?"

"I could use a break and in answer to your question..." I grimace, "not as well as I would like. Would you like a cup of tea?"

"Only if you want to take a break," answers Anna. "I can visit another time."

I lead the way into the kitchen, put the kettle on to boil and place some fig cookies on a plate. "I've been drinking a new type of tea called white tea."

"White tea? I don't think I've had it before," says Anna.

"Supposedly it's chock full of good things for the body. I have some regular tea and one or two types of herbal. Do you have a preference?"

"I'll try the white tea," answers Anna, slipping off her red cardigan and tossing it on the back of the chair. Pushing up her shirtsleeves, she asks, "How's Sarah?"

"Joe says that she's starting to get cabin fever."

"That's to be expected when anyone, especially someone as active as Sarah, has to take things easy," remarks Anna, "but overall is she improving?"

I drop two teabags into the teapot. "Joe doesn't say much but I can tell he's concerned about her growing frustration with her speech problems. When I visited the other day it was obvious that she is choosing to listen rather than trying to talk." Frowning, I add, "If you knew her better, you'd know that is simply *not* Sarah. It's not her style to shy away from conversation."

Compassion evident, Anna says, "It's only been a month since her aneurism. She has had to make some harsh adjustments. Being robbed of her means of communicating has to be threatening to her." Propping an elbow on the table, she rests her chin in the palm of her hand and considers her next statement. "Hopefully she'll regain all of her former abilities. I'm certain she realizes that she's fortunate to be alive but she'd be less than human if she did not mourn the loss of her former self."

I place the teapot on the table alongside the plate of cookies.

Pointing at the teapot, Anna comments, "I used to own a Brown Betty. Did you pick it up on one of your trips to England?"

"No, it was given to me years ago by a good friend of my mother's. Margaret was from England. She always maintained that the best way to make tea was to steep it in a Brown Betty."

"I know that Sarah has been through a lot," I say, returning the conversation to her recovery, "and I agree that a certain amount of depression is natural, but I'm worried that without something to grab her interest, it will consume her and drag her down." I pass Anna a teacup. "Frankly, I'm at a loss as to what I should be doing."

"Right now, you do nothing," answers Anna, adding milk to her tea.

"Nothing?" Surprised by her response, I feel the need to justify my concern. "I wouldn't be much of a friend if I sit back and do nothing."

Anna replies gently. "That's exactly how you can be a good friend Amy. Before I can argue the point, she continues, "I know that you care deeply but Sarah is coping with issues that only she can deal with. She needs time to find herself: to learn how to deal with the obstacles ahead of her." Seeing my reluctance to buy into that line of thinking, she qualifies her response. "That doesn't mean you can't be there for her. What it does mean is, regardless of what *you* think Sarah should feel or do, you have to accept where she *is* coming from. Give her the time. *Her* whole life has changed. She's not capable, at this point, of dealing with the expectations of others."

Anna sips her tea as I take a few moments to mull over what she's said. Biting into a cookie, I say, "Becky has said much the same. She says that we all have to learn to deal with Sarah's frustration without letting it become personal."

"Becky's a good friend and a wise psychiatrist," observes Anna. "Once Sarah realizes that she can still practice law, she'll overcome her anxiety about her speech."

"Problem is, she won't go into the office," I counter. "Joe says that she's told her partners and staff to carry on without her. Instead of trying to get engaged in her life, she is withdrawing from it."

"Sometimes what may appear to be withdrawal is really a survival mechanism kicking in. Sarah's been wounded by life." She pauses and then, says, "I'd like to visit her, when she's ready for company."

Without reservation, I answer, "I think she'd really like to see you. Perhaps having someone other than Leen, Becky, or me to talk with will be a good diversion for her. Are you sure that you don't mind?" I smile apologetically. "She can appear quite remote at times."

"I'd be delighted to visit with her and I can talk up a storm when I want to." She chuckles softly. "She won't have to utter a word if she doesn't want to."

"Great." Replenishing our tea, I add, "But don't say I didn't warn you."

Anna ignores my caution. "Can you think of anything that she might like or need?"

I think about that. "Sarah wants for nothing. Joe and the boys do whatever they can for her around the house."

"Okay then," she answers, "how about something she likes? What type of books does she read? Chocolates? Flowers? I'd like to bring some sort of get-well gift."

I can tell that Anna doesn't want to go empty-handed but knowing Sarah the way I do, I know that she wouldn't want any fuss. Then, I have it. Recalling that she has a greenhouse slash solarium attached to her house, I suggest, "How about a few flowers from your greenhouse? She would appreciate the fact that they were from your garden. As far as novels go, Sarah is an avid reader. She leans towards mysteries but generally is eclectic in her choices."

"I'd be delighted. What's a greenhouse for if not to share its bounty with friends? And, I'm certain I can rummage up an assortment of old novels that she may not have read." Smiling she adds, "Come to think of it, would you like some flowers for your kitchen?"

"That would be marvellous." I push the cookie plate towards Anna. "Another cookie?"

"Consider it done," agrees Anna happily. "When we're finished our tea, come on over with me and I'll make up a bouquet for you."

"That would be lovely," I answer, genuinely pleased with the idea of having fresh-cut flowers especially now that we're into the winter season. "According to the weatherman it won't be long before we get hit with a big dump of the ugly white stuff. Flowers will remind me that there is spring to look forward to."

"Not a winter person?" It's more a statement than a question.

I laugh. "I've never been a big winter fan. Aside from Christmas and Winterlude, I can't think of any benefits of snow."

"The snow makes for picturesque greeting cards and there's something to be said for the comforts of a crackling fire, a hot casserole, a bowl of chilli, a pot roast, and an Irish coffee on a winter night." She smiles. "At my age, I take my pleasures when and where I can find them. I enjoy finding ways to offset the dreariness of winter by making my home snug and indulging in comfort foods; especially when opening the front door hits me with a blast of cold reality."

"Cold being the operative word," I rejoin with a grin. "Listen to us, Anna. We're definitely not poster children for the 'winter fun' posters and ads. I vote we get Sarah, Leen and Becky on board for a week of healthy southern States' sun or an all-inclusive Mexican resort next year. It'll break up the monotony of winter and would be fun."

"How about a Caribbean cruise?"

"I'm game for both. It's been a while since I've done any travelling just for the fun of it. Usually, my trips are centred around academic-related symposiums." Energized by the thought of a vacation, I suggest, "Maybe we can talk them into two weeks of vacation. Take one prior to the Christmas Season and one in mid-February before the annual Spring Break Exodus. That way we can take advantage of the lower prices but still have the benefits of being able to get away from the snow and cold."

Anna laughs. "Well, it's something to think about but plans have a way of getting changed."

"So, we can adapt," I say. "We'll have a good time no matter what we do."

"I'm flattered that you would want me to tag along."

Surprised, I answer, "Why wouldn't I want you to come along? I know the others would be thrilled to have your company." Growing serious, I add, "We all love having you join us when we have our evenings together. You listen to our tales of work woes and show humour and patience when Leen lets loose with some of her more colourful language."

She returns the compliment, "You ladies have brought life and laughter into my dull world. Your stories interest and amuse me and, as you say, Leen's vernacular can get quite 'colourful', especially when she's entertaining us with stories about her boss, Don."

Impulsively, I take Anna's hand in mine. "Like it or not, you're stuck with us."

"Thank you, Amy," replies Anna gently. "It means a great deal to me to have all of you as friends."

Withdrawing my hand, I tell her truthfully, "I only wish I'd been able to know my mother the way I've come to know you. I would have loved to have been able to sit and talk with her."

༄

Anna

Touched by Amy's expression of affection, I am filled with a sense of humility. "You honour me. I know from what you've said previously that you were quite young when your mother died. She would have been so proud of you." In spite of my best efforts, my eyes start to shimmer with tears. Embarrassed, I laugh. "Look at me. Enough sentiment!"

Amy smiles. "That's another thing Leen and I have in common."

Unsure as to what she's referring to, I say, "I'm not certain I understand."

Amy explains. "Most of our friends had two parents to celebrate holidays with. But Leen and I only had our fathers." She attempts to smile as if to imply that both she and Leen had dealt with the loss of their mothers, but her expression lacks conviction. "I sometimes think that's one of the reasons we connected so well at university. We both knew what it was like to grow up without a mother."

"A mother-daughter bond is unique," I reply. "I'm glad that you and Leen found one another and were able to somehow bridge that sense of loss."

"Please don't misunderstand," Amy rushes to explain, "we both had caring fathers." Reminiscing, she says, "Our fathers were driven by their work and often were away during our school breaks. Oh for sure, they both managed to be home for Christmas, but Easter, Thanksgiving, and long weekends were up for grabs. One Thanksgiving when we were both on our own we got it into our heads to cook ourselves a turkey. Fortunately," she grins, "we've both learned how to cook considerably better since then."

Commiserating with the pangs of learning how to cook, I say, "The first time I made a lemon meringue pie I didn't realize that the crust had to pre-cook before adding the filling. I created a gooey mess that bubbled much like you'd expect from one of Macbeth's witches' cauldrons." I struggle to overcome the laughter gurgling up in my throat. "It took on a life of its own; as if it was actually breathing. I can still hear it going bloop, bloop."

"You see, Anna. That's what I was talking about. You *fit in* with us and you've got plenty of amusing stories yourself."

"Would you tell me about your mother?"

"She died when I was twelve. In fact," adds Amy, thoughtfully, "the last conversation I had with her was right after I had my first period. She explained the facts of life to me." A soft expression comes over her face as she reminisces.

"Ah, the rites of passage into womanhood," I answer, hoping I don't sound glib. "All women go through it but few have mothers who take the time to make it less awkward. The first sighting of blood on one's underwear can be very unsettling." I grimace sympathetically. "Not to mention the cramps. Men just have no idea of what we go through."

Amy taps the tabletop and says, "Spoken like a true woman!" In a more serious tone, she continues, "Leen's the sister that I never had. We're very different in many ways, but if push comes to shove, despite our disagreements, we're always in one another's corner."

"The two of you are good for each other. In fact,' I add, "all four of you are extremely remarkable women and it's little wonder that you all share a unique friendship." In what I hope is not an intrusive tone, I ask, "What happened to your mother?"

Amy absentmindedly chews on her upper lip. Despite all the years since her death, it's obvious that the memory is still fresh. Fidgeting with the ring she wears on her middle finger – a lovely white gold with amber and orange amethysts surrounded with diamond chips, she says, "This ring was my mother's."

"It's very nice. I've often admired it."

"It reminds me of her." Taking a short breath, steadying the wavering composure that the memory has triggered, she says, "My mother had to go over to a friend's house that day. I can't remember exactly why. I think it was to pick up something she wanted to borrow." She shrugs. "Whatever the reason, she never made it. A truck driver ploughed through a red light hitting her broadside and t-boning her car. The police told my dad that she was pinned underneath the car's steering wheel as it rolled from the impact. They said she died instantly."

"That must have been horrible for you."

Pensive, she answers, "It was."

I simply nod. "I think she would have been proud to see how her daughter turned out."

"I hope so," answers Amy.

Redirecting our conversation to lighter topics, I say, "Tell me about your writing. Were you working on your novel?"

"Has Leen been telling stories again?"

"She mentioned that the novel was progressing."

Amy snorts. "Hah, if only. She probably told you that I was whining about how difficult it is to find the right words to express what I want to say. I always tell my students that 'less is more and more is less' but when it comes to putting my advice into practice as far as my own writing goes ..." she shrugs, "I'm not having too much success."

"What's it about? Do you feel comfortable talking about it?"

Amy

The level of comfort I feel sitting here in my kitchen talking with Anna surprises me. When she asks me about my novel, I realize that I actually want to tell her about it. For whatever reason, Anna's opinion is important to me. Timidly, I offer, "I could show you a few pages if you like?"

Anna replies graciously, "I'd like to very much that is, if you don't mind."

Rising, I go upstairs to the loft to get the pages. When I return, Anna is in the process of making fresh tea.

"I took the liberty of making some more tea," she says, "I hope that you don't mind."

"Not at all," I reply, holding forth the sheets feeling very much as if I'm a student instead of a professor accustomed to evaluating the papers of others. Anna reaches into her handbag and withdraws a pair of glasses.

"You wear reading glasses?"

"It's my well kept secret indulgence to vanity," she answers, perching them on her nose. "My eyes need some extra help to, as the expression goes, 'read the fine print'." She settles back onto her chair and without comment begins to read.

It's a good half hour before Anna breaks the silence. During the time that she's been reading, I've refilled her teacup and busied myself cleaning the kitchen counters; trying not to be obvious as I cast furtive glances and wait for her reaction. Removing her glasses, Anna stares towards the window over the kitchen sink, seemingly lost in a world of her own.

"So, what do you think?"

Anna shifts her gaze to me. "I like how you've created an atmosphere of expectancy for things yet to be revealed."

"But ...?"

"There's no but to it. A reader needs to be able to visualize what the author creates. You've definitely done that. Having said that, your characters need to be developed more fully. Reading is a very personal experience. What I think is good may be totally irrelevant to someone else." She shifts her position on the chair and purses her lips as she thinks about what she wants to say next. "A writer needs to stay true to his or her vision as to how a story should develop. Stylistic alterations are to be expected. After all," she states pragmatically, "that's why authors have editors. But, creativity and the story belong solely to the author." She taps the pages with two fingers. "What do you plan to do with your characters? How will you inter-relate their connections and what exactly is the theme of your story?" She smiles. "It is quite a promising novel."

I'm transfixed by the transformation in Anna as she renders her critique. Sitting across from me is a worthy adjudicator. She has been deliberate in her appraisal, focused on details, and insightful. I now know why Leen is so full of praise when she says that Anna has lent tremendous insight into her evolving understanding of Claire Holowitz's writing.

Grinning ruefully, I say, "I've used the word 'promising' on many occasions with my students. Translated, that means, they have a lot of work to do."

"It *is* promising," replies Anna. "And, yes, you *do* have work to do. Editing and revisions are all part of the process."

"I know I have to work it all out, but do you really think it is any good? Or," I bite down on my lower lip nervously, "are you being kind?"

Anna's brow furrows. "*Like* is a relative term. I'm sure that as a professor of literature you recognize that variety is what makes it possible for people to discern preferences. For the sake of argument, let's say that the term 'like' is used to denote those preferences."

Nodding, I agree but in the back of my mind I think that she is leading up to a way to let me down gently. I've done that myself many times with my students.

"But the question you asked was, do *I like it?* The answer is yes. When I read, I look for the intrigue, the hook to my imagination and if you like to quibble;" says Anna, smiling, "in line with what I've already said, that's what helps me to discern my preferences."

Pleased to the point of childish elation, I think excitedly, *She actually likes what I'm writing!*

"This is my first crack at trying to write a novel." I roll my eyes and admit candidly, "I've spent my academic career interpreting and analysing literature. Writing, however, is much harder than what I ever imagined. Having said that, I truly do enjoy writing."

"I think you should write this book," says Anna with conviction. "Every writer has to start somewhere and," she adds pragmatically, "every book that's written is subject to scrutiny before and after it gets to press. Don't let the reactions of others determine your style or stop you from creating what you want to create." She sips some tea. "You need to accept that not everyone *will* like it. Conversely," she continues, "not everyone *will* dislike it. Variety is the key. Any writer – any artist – is at the mercy of their audience and their preferences."

"I could write the next *Gone With The Wind* but without an agent, I'm not going to get anywhere. It's a very daunting process. Grinning,

I recall a statement made by a visiting author at the university during my undergraduate days. "Layton Taylor once said, 'Doctors think they're gods; lawyers think they speak for the gods; writers think they write the script for the edicts of the gods; but agents convince the publishers to disseminate to the masses what has been written. The masses believe what they are led to believe they need – be it literature, scientific advancement, or garbage control.' His point ..." I say more curtly than intended, "was that having access to a good agent is critical to the success of any author. At times," I add ruefully, "I think I'm defeated before I even start."

"One step at a time," answers Anna. "The world of publishing has changed dramatically in the last decade. Many authors are opting to self-publish or to e-publish. There's no right or wrong way to publish but first, the story has to be written. Publishing a book is only part of the process. There has to be a marketing strategy and you have to be patient. It takes time for people to know that a new author is on the scene."

"What it boils down to," says Anna, her blue eyes twinkling, "is that writing is a very lonely process. Get used to it and the fact that you will have to do more than just write. But first," she taps the table with her knuckles, "outline what you want to happen in your novel. Know your characters and think of them as real people with real emotions! You were right in saying that this type of writing is very different from writing for an academic journal. You're writing for an audience and creating a world for them that takes them away from the pressures of their daily lives. Then you'll revise, edit, and sweat out the changes that you or an agent and editor will demand. All the while, you'll struggle to stay true to your story. If you compromise the drive you have to write in order to simply sell, you'll lose yourself to the glamour of publication and in a sense, forfeit your soul." Anna stops abruptly. "Oh my," she says, "I must sound like a woman on a tirade or worse, eccentric to a fault.

To say the least, I'm stunned. The passionate woman sitting across the table is not the gentle Anna that I've come to know but instead an insightful critic. She speaks with conviction. Her knowledge of publication makes me wonder if I've been guilty of viewing her as a retired and kindly neighbour and not giving her credit for who she truly is. I ask, "Anna, what did you do before you retired?"

Anna answers, "What a strange question. Where did that come from?"

I attempt to sound casual. "It's not that strange of a question. I don't mean to pry but you seem to be so analytical and knowledgeable about writing. I just wondered. That's all."

Anna takes a moment to consider her response. During that time I get the feeling that she is, as Leen observed the first time that she met her, 'taking my measure'. She meets my look with one of her own and says, "By the time a person gets to my age there's been a whole lot of living. I have travelled and met many people. I miss my husband to this day." She lifts her right hand just enough to wave off any further probing questions. Reluctantly, I accept the fact that she has avoided a direct answer. None of us know much about Anna's earlier life. Although she will occasionally share a memory, it is always limited and we've clearly understood that she prefers to keep it that way.

Almost as an afterthought, she throws out a few titbits about her working life. "When I was younger, I wrote in a journal as a means to gather my thoughts. For the first two years of university I washed dishes in a hospital kitchen on weekends. After that, I worked weekends in a department store. After graduating I taught school for a while. You could say I've been a Jack of all trades." Reverting to the familiar kindly neighbour role she states, "Amy, you *can* write. You just have to believe you can finish what you have started." She organizes the pages into a neat stack. "I hope my comments have not persuaded you to disallow me from seeing the additions and changes as you make them. It would be my pleasure to read more." Timidly, she adds, "That is if you want me to."

"Want you to? I'd like that very much but..." I hurry to qualify, "you have to remember that it's a work in progress. I don't want Leen, Becky or Sarah to see it until I have a really good draft. I want them to view my writing as serious and not as a frivolous whim."

"Then, mum's the word," agrees Anna in a conspiratorial tone, "I won't mention anything to them. You can show them your novel when you're good and ready. In the meantime, I look forward to being your silent editor." She grins. "That is until you get a professional one."

After Anna leaves I sit at my kitchen table contemplating her reaction to my novel. It appeared to be genuine and her words of encouragement, sincere. As I wash the teacups I think, 'She must have been one amazing teacher.' Imbued with a rejuvenated incentive to write I boot up my laptop and begin to make revisions; putting aside all thoughts of trying to get an agent, self-publishing or e-publishing.

First, I must write.

Chapter Twelve

Anna

On Thursday morning Amy calls to say that Sarah's up for a visit this afternoon. Pleased, I answer, "I just brewed a fresh pot of coffee. Do you want to pop over and chat a bit about your novel?"

Fifteen minutes later I'm handing her a cup of coffee and settling down to read.

"You want the reader to feel the conflict but not doubt the love," I say, putting down the pages. "The reader needs to feel as if he or she is in the kitchen listening to the argument about Carlee's choice of boyfriends." I angle the page so that Amy can read where I've made a notation. "I've pencilled out this part," I say. "It's too much information at this point. You've got to concentrate on the emotional tension between mother and daughter. For now, less is more."

Amy grimaces. "How do I do that? The relationship between Carlee and Kevin is important."

"You can develop that theme later on."

We pass a good hour exploring options before Amy gets up to go. Collecting her manuscript, she says, "Thanks Anna. Talking with you helps me to define some of the dialogue."

"You're most welcome," I answer, "glad that I was able to help. It's like playing. To be honest it reminds me of when I was a child."

Amy arches an eyebrow and asks, "How so?"

"To pass the time on hot summer nights my sister and I would make up scenarios of what people on the street were doing." I smile. "In my day we had to entertain ourselves. TVs were just starting to come into their own and even at that, only the well-to-do families had one and video games, movie rentals, I-pads, and Internet had yet to be invented. Once a week my mother would take us to the library where we could pick out books." I shrug and grin, "It was a big deal for us."

"You learned to use your imagination," suggests Amy.

"That too," I agree. "Because we didn't have the distractions that kids have today, we learned how to create our own fun and didn't rely on having it provided."

"Well, I'm glad you developed the skills you have," says Amy. "Like I said, talking with you about my book helps."

"Just remember," I caution, "you're the writer. People can make suggestions but you're the one who will choose to weave what you want into your story. It has to be your words and thoughts coming through to the reader. Think of it this way ... you're an observer of their lives and simply recording the information." I tap my temple and wink. "You've got to do what my mother used to tell me and my sister, 'use your noggin'. In other words, let your imagination bring the story to you. The more real it becomes, the more you will hook or engage the reader."

"It all seems to be so natural for you," replies Amy, leaning against the counter. "Did you ever think of writing? I mean, seriously writing ... as a career?"

"Ah well, that's a topic for another day," I answer. "Another favourite adage of my mother's was, 'Everybody has a story but few take the time to write it down.' Life has a way of keeping a person busy and then, one day you find yourself looking back on all that has passed." I grin. "And here I stand in my kitchen – an old woman spouting off about her younger days. My mother was right: the older you get, the more time you have to reminisce and to embellish the past so that some events come out better than what actually took place."

Amy laughs. "You're not old Anna. Quite to the contrary. You've got more energy than most people I know. Listening to you I get the clear impression you would have made a great editor and ..." her eyes flicker with a spark of thought – the kind that ignites brain cells into action – and says, "Why don't you write some of your stories? I could read them and be your editor." Enthused, she continues, "Who knows? Maybe we both could publish a novel."

I shrug off that notion. "Let's concentrate on your writing," I say, "and use my stories to pass time when we've got nothing better to do."

Reaching for her jacket, she asks, "Are you sure you won't let me drive you to Sarah's? You don't need to take a taxi."

"Oh, I'm used to taxis," I say, declining her offer. "I'm going to see if I can tempt Sarah with my apple pie."

"Your apple pie beats mine any day." Mischievously Amy adds, "Leen will be jealous that she didn't get any."

Holding the door open, I ask, "Speaking of Leen, have you heard from her since she came back from Vancouver?"

Uttering a tiny groan, Amy replies, "Damn, I almost forgot to tell you. She wanted me to remind you that she and Becky are coming to my house tomorrow night. We're doing pot luck. Sarah still can't drive so Joe will bring her over and one of us will drive her home but it all depends on how she's feeling."

"I'll bring a cherry pie," I answer.

"Are you sure you'll have time to bake both apple and cherry? After all, you've still got to get ready to go to Sarah's."

"Making one or two is not a big thing," I reply, "but you're right. I'd better get a move on if I'm going to get my baking done before it's time to leave."

As soon as Amy leaves – instead of heading straight for the kitchen to start on my baking – I make a beeline upstairs to the room I use as my personal workspace. Talking with Amy has given me an idea and I want to act on it while it's still fresh. Sitting down on the chair in front of my desk I take a few moments to gather my thoughts before placing a phone call. When I'm done, I'm satisfied with the result of my conversation and convinced that what I'm about to do *has* to be done, I go downstairs to make the pies.

At two o'clock I lock my front door and carry my apple pie to the waiting taxi. Harry, my regular cab driver, greets me with that big smile of his. I gave up driving two years ago when my doctors thought it might be the wise thing to do considering the medications that I've been taking. At first, I used any available cab driver but after a few times driving with Harry I started to request him. I enjoy his company and find the stories he likes to share about his wife Kim and their two daughters, Susan and Kayla, to be interesting.

"Afternoon, Anna," grins Harry. "Where to, today?"

"Afternoon, Harry. Sixteen twenty-two Foxdale Crescent." Sliding onto the back passenger seat I ask, "How's the family?"

"Kayla's received her acceptance to Queen's University," says Harry, grinning with fatherly pride. "Susan's busy with basketball this semester and of course, boys."

"Good for them," I answer. Genuinely pleased about Kayla's acceptance to the university of her choice, I ask, "Has she narrowed down her speciality or is she still thinking about it?"

"Oh that," groans Harry, adjusting the rear view mirror, "is a source of constant chagrin to Kim. "Kayla told me that she wants to study biology with a view to going to medical school."

Perplexed, I reply evenly, "How is that a problem for Kim?"

"Well," snorts Harry, "Just to get her mother going Kayla told her that she's considering making theatre arts her major." Stopping for a red light, Harry glances over his shoulder and says, "Kim has visions of her doing Mime on a street corner to make a living."

I burst out laughing. "From what you've told me about your girls, I don't think either one of them are going to be counting on the generosity of strangers to make a living."

The light changes and Harry starts to drive. "Oh, I know that," he says agreeably, "but Kim seems to think that there's a kernel of truth in Kayla's wanting to study drama. The way I see it," he adds, "Kim's the one with the melodrama and Kayla is milking it for all it's worth."

"Nothing wrong with studying theatre arts if that's what she decides to do," I reply. "Just as long as she realizes that while she's waiting for her *big break*, she'll have to make some sacrifices in order to pay the rent. Too many aspiring actresses and actors are content to live hand-to-mouth rather than actually working long enough at a paying job to have the luxury of pursuing the dream."

"Yeah, I know," agrees Harry, merging into the other lane. "But Kayla's got a good head on her shoulders. She wouldn't be content for too long to doing without and," he adds matter-of-factly, "Kim and I don't have the income to sustain her pursuit of an artistic lifestyle. Medicine will guarantee employment. The Arts, while great for those who actually make it, leave a lot of *wantabees* wondering how to pay the rent."

Taxi driving is Harry's second job. By trade, he's a cabinet maker. A year ago I had him restore the cabinets in my house and his work was extraordinary. His two jobs and his wife's teacher's salary make it possible to help out with the girls' post-secondary education but even with their pooled salaries, it will be a tight squeeze.

"I'm sure things will work out, Harry," I say encouragingly. "Both girls have part-time jobs, they're saving to help with their university expenses, and there's always the chance they'll qualify for scholarships."

"That's the plan," replies Harry, making a left turn onto Sarah's street. Pulling into Sarah's driveway, he says, "There you are Anna. When do you want me to come back?"

"Someone's picking me up," I say, reaching into my purse to withdraw a twenty dollar bill. "It's been good getting caught up. See you soon."

"Sure thing." Harry puts the car in park and gets out to open my door. These days most cab drivers don't offer that courtesy. Extending his hand to help me out of the cab he says, "Thanks for listening Anna. Next time, you do the talking and I'll do the listening."

I smile. "No problem, Harry. I enjoy listening to you. Your life is much more interesting than mine." He refuses cab fare. "Not this time, Anna, this one was on the house."

"What am I going to do with you Harry?" I ask, trying to push the twenty into his hand. "You have to make a living."

Harry grins. "I'll pick up a few extra fares at the airport tonight."

"Thank you," I reply, putting the bill back into my purse. "I've known him long enough to tell when arguing is useless. "Next time, no arguments."

"Done deal," answers Harry, returning to the driver's side of the car.

I make a mental note to look into setting up an endowment for Kayla's tuition fees. It will have to be masked under the guise of an award based on her grades and arranged so that Harry will never suspect me of funding the award. When the time comes, I'll do something for Harry's second daughter, Susan. Pleased that I can help Harry, I wave good-bye and head up to Sarah's front door, wondering what her reaction will be to the question I've come to ask.

Sarah

I'm upstairs putting on a clean sweater when I hear the sound of a car door being shut. I look out my bedroom window and see Anna chatting with the cab driver. Her body language and smile tell me that she is comfortable with him and him with her.

Stepping back from the window, I realize that I'm apprehensive about her visit. I've not seen her since my aneurism and I wonder what she'll think about my awkward and slow speech. Joe says that I'm improving but to my ear I sound like a robot short circuiting. Sentences, phrases, and words pass through my mind but they just don't make it out of my mouth. I look in the mirror. My eyes still resemble a racoon's and my face shows the weight loss. *Not that I didn't have to lose a few pounds,* I think, *but I sure as hell didn't have to do it this way.* Using the banister for balance, I make my way downstairs just as Jake answers the doorbell.

I can hear Jake's voice as I walk to the living room. "Apple pie! I love apple pie. So does Jeremy but he's out now. Tough luck for him."

Anna gives me a big hug. "I see you've met Jake," I say, taking care to articulate. The doctors say that in time I should regain facial control but for now I give Anna what I've come to think of as my lopsided smile. "No doubt, you ... have picked up on the fact that there is no brotherly love when it comes to food."

Jake's big grin is both charming and mischievous. "Every man for himself, Mom. This wonderful lady knows how to touch my heart."

Anna replies lightly, "I'm sure your mother won't mind sharing *her* pie with you." With sly coyness, she adds, "What say you leave your brother a piece so I can win his heart too?"

Anna's ability to engage in good-natured rapport is a characteristic that I've appreciated from our first meeting. As a lawyer, I've learned the value of being able to help people relax but I have to admit that I'm surprised at how quickly Jake has taken to her. Although he is the more outgoing of my sons, he normally doesn't engage in banter with someone he does not know.

Striking a comic pose, Jake says, "Like I said ladies, it's every man for himself."

Throwing a look in my son's direction, I say, "Thank you for the pie, Anna. As you can see, Jake is already drooling."

Ignoring my mock exasperation, Jake winks at Anna. "I'll just take this pie to the kitchen," he offers sweetly. "It's my duty to sample it."

"Jake," I call after him, "remember to leave some for Jeremy. And before you wolf it all down, please bring Anna and I a piece with some tea."

"No problem," replies Jake.

Anna does not appear to notice my slow speech. I've not seen so much as a wince and for that I'm silently and immensely grateful. She picks up the conversation as if I'm the same person I was four weeks ago. I'm grateful for this moment of seeming normalcy. It's not that Joe, the boys, and my friends haven't been good. They've been great. But, now, being with Anna I realize that my aneurism affected all of us. We're all drifting through uncharted territory. They don't know what to say to make me feel better about what has happened to me and I don't know what or how to say anything that can make it any easier for them.

"Are you going to Amy's tomorrow night?"

I sit on the couch and Anna takes the chair facing me. Until now, I hadn't given much thought to going to Amy's house. I've been looking for a way to get out of it without coming across as if I'm not appreciative of my friends. It just seems easier to exclude myself from another reminder of how things have changed. Now, looking at Anna's expectant face, I find myself wanting to go and to be – if only for a few hours – the person I was. The person I want to be again. And so, I answer, "Yes." More tentatively, I add, "It will be my first outing since the hospital. Becky is coming to pick me up."

Jake brings in our pie and tea. His cell phone bleeps and he flips it open. After a few terse 'yeses' and 'I'll see what I can do' he remembers that Anna and I are sitting directly in front of him. His cheeks flush and he flashes an apologetic smile at me and mouths, "Sorry". To the person on the other end, he says, "Just a second, I'll go to my room".

Anna and I exchange knowing glances. "Girlfriend," I say, as he bounds up the stairs.

"Wants his privacy," supplies Anna, her lips curving with amusement.

"Her name is Stacey," I say, glad to be talking just like any normal mother would when explaining her teenage son's sudden flush and need for privacy. "She wants to be a doctor, but with the amount of time those two spend on the phone ..." I breathe out a what-can-I-do sigh,

"I seriously worry about them making the grades necessary to even get into a university."

Anna looks at the clock on the mantle and asks, "Doesn't he have school?"

"Ah, the benefit of the semester system," I reply. "He has a spare period every second day." Grinning I add, "Much to Jeremy's annoyance."

Anna smiles. "Things are very different than when I went to school. Ah well," she says with characteristic pragmatism, "Times change and so do people."

She sips her tea. "So Sarah," she says, without any pussy footing about, "how are you really?"

※

Anna

When I first see Sarah I'm shocked at how much she has changed. The fact that she has dark circles under her eyes and is on the verge of being gaunt does not escape me despite the makeup she has carefully applied. Although Amy warned me about Sarah's speech, I wasn't prepared for the level of difficulty."

She doesn't balk at my question and for that, I'm grateful. Perhaps I should have been less blunt but the Sarah I've come to know would not appreciate me soft pedalling. The Sarah I know has always been direct and forthright – a characteristic which I think must serve her well in her line of work. Oh sure she can put on a lawyer's poker face and play her cards close to her chest but she's a straight shooter and I can think of no other way to broach the purpose of my visit other than that of being direct.

Sarah's expression flickers and for a moment I'm uncertain if she'll answer. Her moment of hesitation passes quickly and I see a trace of the Sarah that I've laughed with at the girls' get-togethers. She answers, "I'm tired, Anna. Very tired. It's hard to talk."

Her mouth works from side to side as she presses her lips together and then, pointing to her forehead, she says, "I understand what is being said but I can't respond as quickly as I'd like to nor do the words always come out the way I want to."

Brow furrowing in frustration, she practically spits, "It was so easy before. I never thought about speaking. I just did. Now, I'm a lawyer who can't talk properly." She lowers her head in an unconscious reflex hoping to hide her anguish and embarrassment. "Don't misunderstand me. I know I'm fortunate but ..." she stares straight at me, as if she's challenging me to deny the rest of what she has to say, "I want it – this speech – to go away. I want my life back."

"It's only been a few weeks since the aneurism," I respond in what I hope is not a patronizing tone. "It will take time."

I'm many things but blind and stupid I'm not. Sarah's normal exuberance has been replaced with an awkward shyness and hesitancy to express herself. Her frustration at not being able to control her aphasia is understandable but I don't want her to think it's a reason to give up. She has to deal with the facts. Facts are what a lawyer deals with. I need to get her to realize that she's 'Sarah' and the 'Sarah' who she was before the aneurism is, and will continue to be, 'Sarah'.

"Yes," I agree, "the aneurism dealt you a cruel blow, physically and emotionally. You've lost a lot of weight and I won't pretend that your face doesn't show your fatigue or the stress you have been under."

Sarah's right hand moves to her short-cropped hair. A few weeks ago it had been thick and resplendent, shimmering with natural highlights and capping her face with softness. Now, her skull bristles with the promise of new growth that will cover the angry scar curving like a large hook from her left temple to the right.

"The hair will grow back," I say, dismissing it with a wave of my hand. "Look at it this way," I add with a grin, "you're in style with the kids of today. Many are purposely shaving their heads. You've just joined the ranks of the 'in crowd'."

~

Sarah

Anna's bluntness makes me laugh. At first I didn't recognize the bubble of laughter springing up through my chest; I was too surprised by her direct approach. But, the look on her face and the way she so easily dismisses my scar is a welcome relief. The few times Joe has taken me out for a drive or to see my doctors, I've remembered to wear one of the head kerchiefs I bought at the hospital gift shop for chemo and neurosurgery patients but, here at home, I don't cover my head. It strikes me as odd that I'd not thought to put one on before Anna came and then, I realize that in the short time I've come to know her – sitting on Amy's deck or at her kitchen table sharing a meal with Anna, Becky and Leen – Anna has become part of our inner circle. Half teasing but with total candour, I rub my still raised and angry scar and say, "It itches."

A sympathetic expression touches Anna's face. "Have you tried any oils?"

"The doctor prescribed something," I answer, "but it still itches and is taking a long time healing."

"Have you tried using Emu oil?"

"Emu oil?"

"Yes," she says, with a smile. "Emu oil works all sorts of wonders. I use it on my joints. My doctor laughs at me but I swear by the stuff. It works on scars too."

I'm not able to hide my scepticism. Anna says, "I'll bring you some but you have to promise me that you'll give it a try. You'll find that the scar will heal more quickly and the itching will stop."

I suggest that we move to my kitchen where we can sit around the table as I make a fresh pot of tea. After a few more hair jokes and Anna's extolling the virtues of Emu oil, she blindsides me with, "Will you be going back to work soon?"

I take my time in answering. "Joe thinks that I should go back soon but I think I need more time. I have some good staff and they are providing updates, but active practice for me, right now, is out of the question."

Nodding, Anna replies, "Take the time you need. You have a partner and I'm sure she understands. Besides, Sarah, you can still do legal work, read briefs, oversee office matters. For the time being, leave the court appearances to others."

"Yes." My answer may be a monosyllable but it speaks volumes. Despite the kind assurances of the people who love me, I know I have a long way to go before I will be confident enough to speak before a judge or jury. Tiredness and anxiety increase my difficulty with speech. Joe likes to joke that I'm like a battery in need of charging. "It's like someone going out to their car and playing the radio without turning on the ignition," he teases, making me laugh at the simplicity of his analogy.

But what he says is true. My brain seems to demand that I take time to re-charge. If I could limit the conversation in court to something easy – like it is talking with Anna – I'd be fine but court isn't like that. Any litigation lawyer worth her salt knows you have to be able to articulate properly and to respond quickly.

Anna says, "I like your kitchen. I'm glad that you suggested we come in here. There's something nice about sitting around a kitchen table with a good friend.

"Thank you Anna." I pour her a cup of tea. "And, you are a good friend."

She smiles and I can tell that she is pleased with my acknowledgement of her. Then, gazing around the kitchen, she says, "I like your use of earth tones and ceramic tiles. The light and openness of this kitchen just begs one to sit down and chat. It's comfortable here."

"We spend a lot of time in here," I answer with an easy smile. "Joe likes to have family dinners." Jokingly, I add, "Between us, he says that's the one sure way he can ferret out what the boys are up to."

A bubble of laughter makes its way up Anna's throat. "My mother used to say that the dinner table was the control centre of the family's comings and goings."

Settling herself comfortably in her chair she takes a deep breath. "Sarah, I have to ask a favour."

There's something different in her voice. I can't put a name to it but I know that whatever she wants to ask is important to her. I become serious and say, "Whatever I can do for you, I will. What is it that you want to ask?"

Anna starts with, "I know that you've said that for now you don't want to return to active practice but ..."

I narrow my eyes but don't comment, preferring to wait to find out what she wants to ask. Anna's expression softens. "I was wondering if you would mind taking on a private client. One who wouldn't demand too much talking, but who could use a good lawyer." From her self-conscious smile, I have no doubt as to the identity of the client.

Wanting to confirm my suspicion, I ask, carefully, "And that client would be?"

"Me."

Taking a deep breath, I think about my answer. "Anna, if there is something I can do for you, I will. You don't have to retain me. I will do it as a friend."

"But I want to retain you," Anna answers firmly. "Business is business. I appreciate your offer to help me out of friendship and I'm touched that you would do so, but what I have to ask of you needs a lawyer's skill and confidence. I want to retain you and have the benefit of lawyer-client privilege."

The resolute expression on Anna's face surprises me. Perplexed by her insistence for lawyer-client privilege, I arch an eyebrow and say, "Go on."

Deliberate and direct, Anna asks, "Will you agree?"

"What could possibly be so important that you need a lawyer rather than simply taking free advice from a friend who happens to be one?" Her expression doesn't change. "Okay," I say, "but if we're talking business then, let's talk about my fee."

Nonplussed by my mention of a retainer, Anna relaxes. "Good. You'll do it! Thank you. Now," she leans forward, peers intently, and asks, "What would you like as a retainer?"

I meet Anna's look with a steadfast one of my own. "I set it as one dollar. You'll have your lawyer-client privilege and I," I say smugly, "will have the knowledge that, in friendship, I did not take advantage of you."

※

Anna

I pretend to consider Sarah's fee but truth be told, I'll pay whatever she asks. She's the lawyer I want. In fact, she is the only lawyer for the task I need. Still, I'm somewhat startled. By setting a symbolic fee of one dollar Sarah, plain and simple, has outsmarted me. From the smug expression on her face I can tell that I must comply with her terms. This is not a battle that I can win and I've come here today with a bigger purpose in mind.

"I'll agree to your terms," I say, taking a dollar coin from my leather change purse. Holding it between my thumb and index finger I pause before passing it over. "Once you accept this, you are my lawyer. Lawyer-client relationship will exist."

Sarah's eyes dart to the proffered coin and then back to me before accepting it. "Now," she says, placing it on the table, "what is so important that you're insisting on having lawyer-client privilege?"

I withdraw a piece of paper from my purse and hand it to her. Curiosity shows on her face as she scans the phone number I've written. There is no name.

"I need you to call this number and speak to the person at the other end," I say, answering her unspoken question. "He will ask to speak to me and when I confirm that you have agreed to be my lawyer, he will want to talk to you again."

Sarah pushes her chair away from the table. "Would you prefer to go to my study? It's more private."

Silently, we cross the living room to the main hallway and turn into the room on the left. This room emanates purpose. The walls are painted in a shade reminiscent of chocolate milk with white trim. The polished oak floor gives the room a feeling of warmth and sunlight streams in from a large bay window. A laptop rests on the desk with a printer and fax machine to the side. Nestled in a corner is a small copy machine. Sarah sits behind her desk and I take one of the two chairs facing her.

Without a word, she dials the phone number. I know what to expect but I watch as she listens to a man's deep rich baritone answer after three rings. Sarah hesitantly explains that she is calling this number as requested by a client.

I can hear the murmur of the voice at the other end of the phone. Looking at me, she answers, "Yes, she is here." She listens for a moment and then passes the phone to me.

"Hello," I say, not taking my eyes off Sarah. I listen to his question and answer, "Yes, she has agreed." Again, I listen. Then, firmly, I answer, "No, I want to do this. Just as I said."

He issues a warning, just as I knew he would, but I'm determined to see this through. Once again, I repeat, "I want to do this." Silently, I hand the phone back to Sarah. What she is about to hear will change our friendship. For the first time since arriving at her house, I have the tingling sensation of doubt. I wonder if she will hate me.

Sarah

I'm perplexed. So far, Anna's air of mystery, verging on cloak and dagger secrecy, has accomplished one thing: I'm not lost in my world of woe-is-me anymore. Instead, I'm sitting behind my desk, thinking like a lawyer and wondering what in hell is going on? It's not that I've not dealt with sensitive issues in my practice. It's not that I'm not used to keeping secrets. Keeping secrets is part and parcel of being a lawyer.

Becky and I have often discussed how similar our two roles are. We have different careers, different training. We are both guardians of secrets. Becky likes to joke that we are society's secular version of priests: people tell us their secrets and their problems. We are bound by ethics to not reveal those secrets unless and only if what we are told would cause great harm to the person or society. Even then, there are legal quagmires to overcome.

I wonder what Becky would make of Anna's strange behaviour? But, Becky isn't the one sitting behind the desk right now. I am. Becky isn't the one who will be asking the questions necessary to unravel the mystery of what is going on in Anna's mind. But, one thing I do know for certain: Anna has a definite plan and nothing will happen until I dial the number.

I introduce myself but the man with the deep baritone at the other end doesn't extend the same courtesy. Instead, he says, "I would appreciate it if you would pass the phone to Mrs. Wright.

I would like to confirm she is present."

A prickle of annoyance at having to engage in this subterfuge surfaces but I keep my tone neutral. "Of course."

From the expression on Anna's face, it is obvious that he is trying to dissuade her from something. At the very least, to reconsider. But, she's insistent. "I want to do this," she says, maintaining a level gaze straight at me. She listens intently and this time, responds with terse formality. "I now authorize you to tell her what is necessary. Make the arrangements to meet."

Despite the oddity of this arrangement, I am amazed at the metamorphosis that is taking place in me internally. Anna's insistence on lawyer-client privilege and this phone call has resulted in my assuming my lawyer skin. This is comfortable territory for me. The alteration from 'sick me' to 'lawyer me' washes away the invisible chains that have tethered and stopped me from returning to work. I feel a perverse pleasure; a sense of relief. I am thinking like a lawyer. I'm no farther ahead in being able to articulate clearly but now, as opposed to the hour before Anna's visit, that no longer seems to be an insurmountable problem. It's simply a matter of finding a way to cope. I am a lawyer and it's good to be acting like one. The bonus is having a trial run, with my new circumstances, in the comfort of my own home.

Face expressionless and body taut, Anna passes the phone back to me. I put it to my ear and state crisply, "You know who I am. Who are you and what is this about?"

This time the voice is more congenial. "Ms Calder, I understand that all of this may seem to be a bit cloak and dagger but I am certain that, in a few minutes, you will understand Mrs. Wright's caution and need for discretion."

"Alright," I answer. "Go on." Anna's expression reveals nothing. Only her eyes reflect nervous anticipation of what my reaction will be to what I'm about to hear.

"My name is Marc Andre Aumount," says the man.

My breath catches in my throat. Involuntarily I flinch, thinking, *Leen's Aumount?*

"You know the woman sitting in front of you as Anna Wright," continues Aumount. "In fact, that is how she chooses to be known."

Wide-eyed, I stare at Anna. Grappling with the knowledge that I'm dealing with 'Leen's Aumount', I say nothing. He asks, "Are you still there?"

I sputter, "I'm listening." I can feel my jaw clench. He has all of my attention.

"Anna Wright has asked me to disclose some information to you. In addition, it is her express wish that we work as joint counsel to represent some of her specific interests. Do you agree to this?"

"I have agreed to represent Anna," I answer, coolly. "I don't know anything about working as joint counsel for her." Anna's reaction to my close scrutiny is to raise her chin slightly. Whether it's in defiance or anxiety that I will refuse, I can't determine. At this point, I don't care. I speak with cautious deliberation. "As her counsel I will listen to what you have to say. After that, I will assess what and how we can or cannot work together."

Aumount cuts to the chase and in an assertive tone, says, "Anna Wright has directed me to disclose that she is, in fact, Claire Holowitz." My fingers clutch the desk's edge. Dumbfounded, I look incredulously at Anna. I speak slowly and deliberately. "The Claire Holowitz?" My thoughts frantically tumble about as tiny spears of anger form. My first instinct is to slam the receiver down in his ear and throw Anna out of my house. This seemingly simple woman, so lacking in pretence and all that one would associate with someone of her fame, sits quietly in her chair. The only concession that Anna makes to any feelings of personal apprehension regarding my response to Aumount's disclosure is a slight movement towards the edge of her seat.

She has the common sense not to smile. Just above a whisper, she says, "It's true."

"I realize that all of this must come as a shock to you," Aumount continues, "but you need to know that Claire, whom you have known as Anna, has not misled you nor has she intended to cause discord with your friends. In fact, it is because of the friendship that she has formed with all of you that she has decided to make herself known to you."

What were tiny spears of anger now pound with thunderous rage. Anna's played Becky, Amy, Leen, and me for fools! How many times has she listened to Leen's grief about her search for Claire Holowitz? How many times has she listened to our discussions about Holowitz's works and given no indication of the truth? My legal mind may be intrigued with the reasons for Anna's duplicity but my reaction to the news as a friend to Leen, Becky, and Amy is one of seething fury.

Aumount's tone infuriates me. He acts as if my cold anger is nothing unexpected. "I would like to meet with you. We can sort this matter out and, hopefully, clarify any questions or concerns you may have."

Making no attempt to restrain my sarcasm, I reply, "I take it that you know where I live?"

Not ruffled by my disdain, he answers, "Yes. I can be there within half an hour."

"Fine, I'll see you then."

I slam the phone down before he can reply. The lawyer in me takes over. I must not allow emotion to determine my actions. I need to think. I don't give a damn that Anna is sitting there, waiting for me to say something. She can wait. I need to mull over the information I have just received. With a harsh snort purposely intended to convey my disgust, I rub my forehead and eyes with the palms of my hands before rising from my chair.

Anna starts to say something but she quickly clamps her mouth shut in response to my upheld hand discouraging any conversation. I walk to the window and, with my back turned to Anna; I stare outside as a multitude of conflicting emotions flood through me.

I speak flatly, fighting to control my anger. "So, you're Claire Holowitz. Have you had a good laugh at our expense? What the hell were you thinking? How could you sit and listen to Leen talk about her search for you? You even took on the job of acting as her consultant." My laughter is harsh and cruel. "No fucking wonder you were so knowledgeable about Claire Holowitz."

"I never laughed," answers Anna.

Spinning around, I confront her. The frustration of not being able to properly form the words I want to hurl at Anna fuels my anger and heightens my sense of impotence. I feel duped – she has deliberately retained my services knowing that in so doing, she has put me in the position of being a partner in her schemes to thwart Leen and the Gala. I force myself to speak, measuring my words, struggling not to confuse them. My head aches with the effort, but I plough ahead trying to give voice to the thoughts raging in my mind. Anna sits motionless, knowing that at this moment it would be pointless for her to speak.

"What about Leen? Did you not once consider her feelings? Here she is running around Canada and the United States, talking to people in Europe, doing all that she can to learn about you and you sit in your home and in Amy's kitchen, leading her on a merry goose chase."

"Ah shit!" Frustrated I rub my eyes and finally, resigning myself to wait for Aumount to arrive before I can get answers, I say, "I'm going to make some more coffee. Would you like some?" The question seems so incongruous and out of sync with the raw emotion I feel. Truth is, I don't give a damn what she wants. The only thing I know right now is that I want out of this room.

Making coffee is just an excuse to busy myself until Aumount arrives.

"Do you want to talk about it?"

I close my eyes, take a few deep breaths, and remind myself that I am trained to expect the unexpected from clients. I know that reacting in anger will accomplish nothing.

I fix my gaze purposefully on Anna. "Aumount will be here within half an hour. Then, we can talk." I feel my eyes narrow as I add bluntly, "For now, if you're smart, you'll stay quiet or keep your comments to a minimum." I cross the room and leave her sitting there.

Unbidden, Anna follows me into the kitchen. I ignore her presence and start to make a pot of coffee.

Jake chooses this moment to come bounding down the stairs and heads straight for the fridge. "Hi ladies," he says, sticking his head inside the fridge to rummage for a snack. Both Anna and I answer with perfunctory hellos. He pulls out an apple, some cheese and a bottle of chocolate milk. He's reaching for a glass when the silence in the kitchen finally strikes him. Surmising quickly that his absence might be a good idea, he says, "You know I think I'll pass on the snack." He replaces the articles in the fridge. "I'm going over to Stacey's for a while. Her mom asked me for supper."

"When will you be home?" My question is automatic but the mere asking of it restores some normalcy to my life.

Jake visibly relaxes. This is a routine he and his brother play out on a regular basis. He teases, "What will you do next year when Jeremy and I are at university?"

I, too, have the routine down pat and deliver my lines with a deadpan face, "Next year is next year. I am your mother. It's my job to worry."

He rewards me with one of his winning smiles. Addressing Anna, he says, "It was nice to have met you, Mrs. Wright. The apple pie was great."

"Good to have met you, too, Jake," answers Anna.

More to fill the dead-air hanging between us than to relieve herself, Anna asks where the bathroom is and excuses herself. I use the opportunity to escape to the privacy of my own bathroom where I can hide from Anna's guarded looks and give myself time to think. I splash cold water on my face and around my neck. Staring at my reflection in the mirror I mutter, "Bring it on Aumount."

The cold water has done its trick. Refreshed, I am determined to see this business with Anna out. From the top drawer, I sort through my array of head kerchiefs and finally settle on the deep blue one. I fix it around my head to cover my scar and decide to change my yellow sweater to a black cashmere v-neck. Satisfied with what I see in the mirror, I decide that a touch of blush will relieve the paleness. I'm just finishing up when the doorbell rings. I take one more glance and, with renewed resolve, make my way downstairs.

My first impression of Marc Andre Aumount is that Leen wasn't kidding about the sheer magnitude of his allure. Dressed in an expensive looking navy blue suit sporting a pristine white shirt and crimson red tie, he radiates success, confidence, and outright sexual magnetism. Flashing a killer smile he says, "Mrs. Calder, it is nice to meet you. I am Marc Andre Aumount. Thank you for receiving me into your home."

I hold the door wider so that he can step into the foyer. "I'm not happy about having been manipulated into this meeting.

"True," he answers, "but I wouldn't be here had you not consented."

Anna rises from her chair when we enter the living room and gently squeezes his broad shoulders as he kisses her cheek. "Thank you for coming Marc Andre."

I wonder at this unusual show of affection between attorney and client, but since this is a day for surprises and secrets being revealed, I check my cynicism and wait until they are finished exchanging their greetings to say, "I've made some coffee. Perhaps we can take it into my study where we can all discuss what it is that Anna …" I pause to rephrase, "Claire wants from me."

He does not comment on my use of both names, but merely glances at Anna with a look suggesting that for the moment it is better not to engage in confrontation.

Wordlessly, we make our way to my study where I pour the coffee and settle into my chair behind the desk.

Stirring sugar into his coffee, Aumount speaks in a conciliatory manner, "I know that all of this appears to be very sudden, but let me reiterate that Claire Holowitz has not intentionally misled you or your friends. In fact, if anything, her decision to reveal her identity is a mark of her trust in you and her respect for your friendship."

Not ready to let go of my simmering anger. I stare at him and wait for him to continue.

Aumount sips his coffee before resting the cup on the edge of my desk. Ignoring my palpable annoyance, he says, "Claire, whom you have known as Anna, has requested this meeting. It is her wish that we work as co-counsel, to represent some of her interests."

His conciliatory tone does not fool me. Coldly and deliberately I reply, "We've already established that fact, counsellor. Please move on

The Search for Claire Holowitz

with the explanation for the subterfuge?" My headache intensifies. My instinct is to call this meeting to an end and I promise myself that if he doesn't get to the point soon, I will do just that.

"As you know," continues Aumount, "Adrienne MacLeen – Leen – is spear-heading the Holowitz Gala to be held in New York. Normally, the doors that have been opened for her are not available to people. Claire," he glances in her direction, "instructed me to facilitate that access. As a result of that directive, I was merely the conduit for the business end of things."

My glance flickers from Aumount to Anna. She sits silent and stone-faced. The only indication of tension is revealed by the rubbing of her thumb against her index finger as her hands rest on her lap.

Returning my gaze to Aumount, I say, "Go on."

His tone is measured as he resumes, "She met you and your friends, quite by accident."

"No accident," I murmur. "She introduced herself the day Amy moved in."

"Semantics," replies Aumount, unruffled by my sarcasm. "She prefers to view Amy's move to the neighbourhood as serendipity. She has lived in that neighbourhood for over thirty years. Everyone who knows her as Anna will tell you that she has always been a friendly neighbour who is welcoming and polite but who never intrudes on anyone's privacy. That same courtesy is extended to her. Her offer to assist you in anyway was the act of a good neighbour. Nothing more, nothing less." He smiles. "She is often seen around the local community and has for years worked as a volunteer: helping senior citizens, kids groups, local play groups, and canvassing for charity drives. She has not 'hidden' per se from the world, but, instead, chose to live in a world that allows her to be the person Claire Holowitz was not permitted to be."

He sips his coffee. A contrived move but one which allows me time to process his line of thinking. "Imagine," he says in a reasonable tone, "how she must have felt when she learned Leen was conducting an active search to find Claire Holowitz: to have her existence as Anna Wright threatened because someone has decided that Claire Holowitz must come out of seclusion for a Gala."

I counter sharply, "Everyone knows that Claire Holowitz withdrew from the public forty years ago and everyone thinks she did that because of her grief when her husband and child died." Inwardly, I feel a twinge of shame as I notice Anna flinch. I console myself with the thought, *This woman has let all of us talk about her as if she didn't exist.* I almost volley my next words. "She duped us!"

Aumount doesn't rise to the bait. Instead, he reaches into his briefcase, withdraws a sheet of paper and passes it to me. "This is a confidentiality agreement which we are going to ask each of your friends to sign. Claire would like them to know who she is but wants to be ensured that her privacy is respected and maintained."

With a scathing glance I look at the proffered agreement. "Why would they have to sign this? Or even want to?" Ignoring Aumount, I address Anna. "What do you think Leen is going to do when she sees this?"

Anna's expression is non-committal but there's the slightest suggestion of a tentative plea as she answers, "I suspect that she will be quite annoyed to begin with ... but I'm hoping that once she learns the whys and wherefores, she will give me the time I need before the public knows who I am."

She looks tired and pale. For a moment I regret that I'm lashing out at this woman who – until a few hours ago – I considered to be a friend. But, I'm not about to let her off easily. She may have tricked me into a lawyer-client relationship but my loyalty is firmly with Leen, Amy and Becky. Sarcasm dripping from my tongue, I demand, "Why is time so important to you, Anna? Or, should I more correctly say Claire? Is Leen getting too close to finding out the truth that you decided to come clean?"

"Mrs. Calder" cuts in Aumount, sharply. Rising, he places a protective hand on Anna's shoulder and openly glares at me. His eyes are cold as flint. Before he can continue, Anna interjects.

"No Marc Andre, she has a right to be angry." Business tone, crisp and direct, she replies, "The world will know my story soon enough." She meets my stare and unblinkingly adds, "I'm dying."

My guard collapses. I don't know what explanation I'd thought she might offer but the one she has just given had definitely not been in the equation. I feel the weight of Aumount's gaze: watching me, waiting for me to react. Instinct and training kick in. Exposed vulnerability is never an asset when engaged in negotiation or litigation. I rein in my emotions and wait for further explanation as my mind races with questions. *Surely, this is not some joke? A ploy to garner my sympathy?*

I consider Anna's slight frame. Like my friends, I had simply assumed that her thinness and occasional fatigue were signs that age was creeping up on her. Looking at her now, I realize that she *is* ill. The dark circles under the eyes, her excuse that the maladies of age were creeping up on her when we questioned her about her health and fatigue, fall into place. All along Anna – or Claire – I'm not certain as to what name I should use, has been progressively more ill. So ill, that she feels it necessary to disclose her identity; risking my anger and the anger of my friends. Seeking further clarification, I say, "Go on."

Glancing protectively at Claire, Aumount, says, "During the course of Leen's information gathering, we have been garnering information about the people with whom she works and *their* motivations for wanting Claire to make a public appearance."

The hint of a frown and impatient flick of his hand silences the questions that pop into my mind. "Our sources have brought to Claire's attention that Leen's boss, Donald Harris, is out to discredit her. For him, the coup of having Claire Holowitz appear at the Gala is a career maker. He doesn't care how he gets to her. What he does care about is who will get the credit when she is ultimately found. To that end, he needs to use Leen to find Claire Holowitz and when that is achieved, he needs to remove Leen from the limelight. Conversely, if Leen should fail to produce Claire at the Gala or to not put together a Gala that truly represents her works then he can point the damning finger at Leen. The other consideration is this..." He glances at Anna and then, levelling a gaze so intense at me that the charcoal grey of his eyes burn like dark orbs, he says, "Once Leen is made aware of what is being disclosed to you today, she will be positioned to make or break her career."

I arch an eyebrow. One of the many attributes I've learned exceedingly well throughout my legal practice is to not give my opponent the upper hand by knowing I'm in a quandary. Aumount is like a cat playing with a trapped mouse. He's ready to pounce and there's no doubt in my mind that what I say and do next is exceedingly important.

I feel as if I've been sucker punched.

Should Leen promise publically to produce Claire Holowitz at the Gala, the hype and publicity surrounding the event will rocket. Should she expose Claire's suburban identity as Anna Wright then, she'll definitely have the coup of being the one to find Claire Holowitz but in so doing, will risk the success of the Gala. Why should anyone attend if the prize has already been revealed? What if Claire decides that the loss of her anonymity and privacy does not necessitate her presence at the Gala? No Claire, no Gala. If, however, Leen does not reveal Claire's identity as Anna but sets the stage for Claire's appearance at the Gala then, she's gambling on Claire's cooperation.

My legal mind hums as I absorb the full import of Aumount's words and the various *what if* scenarios they conjure. I know that there will be considerable angst to deal with when my friends are made privy to this information. I hope I know them well enough to bank on them being able to get over it. They will need to deal with their emotions.

I speak directly to Anna. "I'm not saying that I approve of what you have done. I'm not even going to try to understand it right now. But, this much I promise," I say, automatically speaking in what I think of as my courtroom voice, "I will represent your wishes to Leen, Amy and Becky. What they do and how they will react will be up to them." I pause to make certain that I have her full attention, wanting her to hear and feel the weight of my anger and, if I'm being honest about it, my hurt, "… from this moment on, you are Anna-Claire to me. Agreed?"

Anna pales visibly in response to my ultimatum. I had uttered the moniker with every intention of causing hurt; a double name laced with contempt, born out of hurt and crafted in response to Anna's duplicity. The tension between us is electric.

Aumount asks sharply, "Is that necessary?" I don't answer and I don't relent.

Anna looks at Aumount, her jaw line tight, her lips pursed. Quietly, she says, "A double name for a double identity." Nodding slightly, she nods in assent.

Aumount asks, "Are you certain? You want to do this?"

Anna-Claire's face is awash with sadness akin to grim acceptance of the inevitable. "Agreed."

Aumount's smile is tight and forced but he does not push her to reconsider. Instead, he returns to our legal sparing of final terms for our agreement. The art of negotiation rests in knowing when to concede on one point in order to gain the greater objective. They had manoeuvred me into this position and now, I have done the same to them.

He doesn't pretend to be working towards conciliation. We're hammering out our business arrangement; how we will proceed legally and factually with respect to this whole Anna-Claire business. "Now, that we have agreed on these matters, perhaps we can all work out how to proceed. Anna-Claire ..." he pointedly uses the moniker, "wants to make the others aware of everything as soon as possible. Once done, you and I can address the matter of Donald Harris." In a tone brooking no argument he says, "Leen will have the information and assistance she needs to ensure that the Holowitz Gala is a success. But the timing of when and if *Claire Holowitz* makes a public appearance will depend much on her health and *if* she is even willing to do so. Of course, we realize that once Leen is given this information we risk the possibility of her immediately exposing Claire Holowitz's whereabouts. But," he says with pointed meaning, "should that happen, the active participation of Claire whom you have facetiously dubbed Anna-Claire will cease to exist."

I answer sharply, "Leen won't take well to blackmail."

"This is not blackmail," retorts Aumount, "this is business. Anna-Claire will do nothing to impede the Gala. She will simply reserve her right not to appear or to be involved in any interviews."

Grudgingly I silently admit to the legal sense of his rebuttal. I shrug as if it's neither here nor there to me. "So be it."

Aumount withdraws more papers from his briefcase. "This is where we will begin."

Throughout the afternoon, I take copious notes, asking for clarification and directions as we feverishly hammer out details. Aumount answers all my questions. As we progress, I admit to myself that I would have found him to be a worthy legal adversary, had we not been collaborating.

Anna-Claire provides input and both Aumount and I listen attentively to her instructions. She has thought long and hard about her actions. She is genuine in her intention to protect and help Leen. I no longer doubt that the impetus for her to come forward is from a place of caring for me and my friends. It will be up to me to convince them that – at the very least – they need to hear her side of things.

By the time they leave I'm exhausted but infused with purpose. For the first time since my aneurism, I'm ready and willing to resume my career. Over supper I answer Joe's questions as best I can about my visit with Anna without revealing the actual purpose. I tell him, "Anna's hired me to act as her lawyer."

"Lawyer?" Joe's incredulous. "That's why she visited you?"

"I think that was one of her reasons," I answer, guarding my response. "But, I also believe she came as a friend."

In the back of my mind, I realize that a few hours ago I would not have believed that but now, I don't doubt Anna's sincerity. Having said that, some of the best intentions in life are the most misguided ones. She kept her identity secret from us and now, she is prepared to reveal it but at what cost to our friendship? No matter how I view it – there is the issue of duplicity and the burning question as to how the others will deal with that.

"Are you sure you want to do this?" asks Joe once again, as he lays his watch down on the bedside table.

We've been through this a few times over the course of the evening. Each time Joe wants to know if I'm truly prepared to represent whatever legal matter Anna has retained me for. I know that he's secretly pleased that her request has seemingly pulled me from my reluctance to return to work but he's trying to give support to my previously spoken fears about not being able to resume my career due to my speech problems.

"Yes," I answer as I climb into bed. "Tomorrow is going to be a very interesting day."

Joe turns off the light. Kissing my forehead he whispers, "Whatever Anna has got you doing, I'm glad. She's got you rejoining the world again."

"Hmmm," I murmur, thinking, *If only you knew how complicated all of this is going to get. You may have second thoughts.*

Chapter Thirteen

Leen

Knocking on Amy's door brings no response. I check my watch. We weren't supposed to get together for another hour. Thinking that she must be out doing last minute errands, I decide to let myself in using my spare key. But, when I reach for it, I remember that the last time I used it I had my other purse. Frustrated, I glance over at Anna's house. There's a car in the driveway and I wonder who might be visiting and if she'd mind if I invited myself in while I wait for Amy to return. After all, Anna is coming to Amy's tonight so whoever is visiting will be leaving soon. Having used that logic to intrude on Anna and her company, I cross over the lawn to her house thinking, *I either sit in my car and wait for Amy or I visit Anna.*

Just as I reach out to knock on Anna's front door a man, looking to be in his late sixties, with a salt and pepper fringe around what would otherwise be a bald head, opens the door. Stepping back, I ask, "Is Anna home?"

Staring at me with open curiosity, he answers, "She's in bed. Are you family?"

"No, I'm not," I answer, wondering who he is and how he knows that Anna is in bed. She has never mentioned a boyfriend or companion and I feel a flush of embarrassment thinking I must have interrupted what was supposed to be a private moment. With a flash of insight I register the import of what he's said, thinking, *A male companion wouldn't be so forthright about Anna being in bed. Who is this guy?*

Throwing manners to the wind, I bluntly demand, "Who are you? And, why is Anna in bed?"

"I'm Dr. Anderson." He has an easy manner about him and his eyes twinkle with amusement at my obvious confusion. "I should have thought to introduce myself but I was just on my way out to the car to get something for Anna. Seeing you at the door caught me by surprise."

"Doctor? Is Anna alright?"

"She will have to answer that," he responds cautiously.

"What the hell is going on?" I look over his shoulders, towards the stairs leading to the second floor. I'm about to go around him when he places a firm but gentle hand on my shoulder.

"Ms?" He pauses, waiting for a name.

"MacLeen," I reply curtly, annoyed at his having stopped me. In a voice tolerating no interference, I say, "Anna has no family that I or my friends are aware of. She was to join us for dinner tonight. I arrived early and thought to visit with her for a while." Exasperated, I demand in my most aggressive tone, "Tell me what's wrong!"

"Ah, yes," replies Dr. Anderson, as a smile crosses his face. "She was insisting that she had to go out this evening. Now, that makes sense. But..." he adds soberly, "that's out of the question."

I stare at him. Numbly, I'm registering that whatever has happened to Anna is serious.

"Yes," he answers. "Now I understand what she's been muttering about. Clearly, she intended on being with you tonight. Come in," he says, pocketing his car keys.

Stepping inside, I say, "Doctors don't usually make house calls."

"We're old friends. When she needs me to, I make house calls. It saves her having to come to my office and gives us, on most occasions, an opportunity to chat a little."

"And today?" I watch his expression closely, hoping to detect something that will give me a hint as to the seriousness of Anna's unexplained illness.

Taking his own good time to make a decision, he finally answers, "As I've already said, it is up to Anna as to how much she wishes for you to know."

I force myself to remain calm but I want to shake the answer out of him. "What can you tell me?"

Ignoring my demand to know what's wrong with Anna, Dr. Anderson responds, "I was about to call her nephew, but since you are apparently friends with Anna ..." stopping mid-sentence, he considers his next words before continuing, "is there any way that you could possibly spend the night?"

Without hesitation I answer, "Of course I'll stay but what's wrong?" I think, *What nephew? Clearly, I have to speak with Anna.*

Relenting a bit, he says, "This much I can tell you. She has contracted a virus and called me." He strokes his moustache and I know that he's trying to be kind and informative without compromising Anna's right to privacy, but I'm not about to be deterred in my questioning.

"Should she be hospitalized?"

"Hopefully, by tomorrow, her condition will improve. If not ..." he shrugs, "I may have to reconsider the benefits of leaving her rest at home." A throaty chuckle springs up as he adds, "One thing I know for certain about Anna; she will do anything to avoid being in the hospital."

"I'll stay," I repeat. Inanely, I feel the need to justify my decision saying, "We were going to have dinner."

Touching my elbow in a soothing gesture, he says, "Anna's a strong-willed woman. Now," he adds gently, "Just let me get my bag in the car. We can go upstairs together and tell her that you'll be spending the night."

Anna's awake when we enter the room. She insists, "I'm fine," but her heavy eyelids and strained face contradicts her assurance.

With joviality that I don't feel, I say, "Dr. Anderson tells me that you need a house guest for the night. I've volunteered."

Anna's raspy cough is thunderous. My chest and ribs ache in sympathy. I glance at Dr. Anderson who has just injected a syringe into her thin arm.

Catching her breath, spent from the effort, she takes several moments to regain her strength. "That would be nice, if you don't mind."

"What's wrong, Anna?"

She looks at me thoughtfully and replies, "I'll explain it all later, Leen."

Dr. Anderson says, "I've told your friend that it is up to you to discuss your medical condition."

"It's fine, George," replies Anna.

I can tell that the conversation is tiring her so I say, "We can talk when you're up to it. In the meantime, I want you to rest."

Placing the used syringe and vial in his bag, Dr. Anderson says, "The morphine will help ease the discomfort caused by your chest spasms. With your friend staying overnight, do you want me to call your nephew?"

"No need to bother him, now," answers Anna.

He nods. "Hopefully, you'll feel more like yourself tomorrow."

"Thank you, George. You're a good friend."

He admonishes with affectionate sternness, "For once follow the doctor's orders." He signals me to follow him downstairs.

I wait until we reach the landing before I try to glean more information. "What's wrong with Anna?"

He pulls a pad and pen from his suit jacket's inner pocket and begins to write. "She needs to rest. Here's a prescription for an antibiotic and for a pain reliever." He holds the prescription out. "This needs to be filled."

"No problem," I answer, thinking I'll ask Amy or one of the others to do the pharmacy run. I repeat, "What's wrong with Anna?"

"As I said before, it is up to Anna to disclose that information. I cannot." He withdraws a business card from his wallet and writes on the back. "Here are my home and cell phone numbers. Call me if her condition worsens."

I am on my way back upstairs before he pulls his car out of the driveway.

Returning to Anna's room, I ask, "Would you like a cup of tea or a glass of water?"

The effects of the morphine have begun to settle in, causing Anna's words to sound slurred as she answers, "A tea *wud* be nice."

"Tea it is, then," I say.

Glad to have something to do, I head for the kitchen, thinking *I have to get a hold of Amy and let her know that neither Anna nor I will be joining them for supper. Plus, I have to get one of them to pick up Anna's prescription.* I find the teabags in the cupboard and while the water boils, I pull out my cell and dial. Amy answers on the third ring.

"I saw your car parked in front," Amy says, all chirpy. "Sorry that I wasn't here when you arrived, but I forgot to buy strawberries to go with the angel food cake so I did a quick run to the local grocery mart."

"Amy," I interrupt, "I'm at Anna's."

"I figured that," Amy bubbles back. "Why don't the two of you come on over now? Sarah and Becky will be here soon. We can relax and have some tea while we're waiting or," she laughs, "a glass of wine as a warm up for the meal."

Irritated that Amy's bubbling responses are not letting me get a word in edgewise, I blurt, "Anna's sick."

"Sick?" Immediately, her tone becomes one of concern. "What's wrong?"

Filling her in on the details I end with, "So, I'm spending the night."

"I'll bring over some sweats, a t-shirt and an extra toothbrush. Is there anything else you want or need? Does Anna need anything other than her prescriptions?"

"Thanks, but I don't think she's going to want much of anything. Dr. Anderson has given her a fair amount of sedation along with the morphine. I expect she'll soon be out for the night and if she wakes up, I'm to give her the pain killers. He said that she's had the antibiotic already today and what you'll be picking up is a refill so I can give her that in the morning."

"When I bring over the clothes, I'll pick up the prescription and take it to the Pharmacy.

They're open twenty-four hours." Genuinely concerned, she asks, "Is Anna in a lot of pain?"

"Doctors don't pump morphine into people without a reason," I answer, tersely. Annoyance sparks again as I add, "And no matter how often I tried to find out what was wrong with her, aside from this virus, he wouldn't answer."

"Maybe she'll open up to Becky," Amy replies. "Anna might be more willing to tell a doctor than she is to tell you or me. Becky's good at foraging information from people. Maybe she can get Anna to agree to let her talk to Dr. Anderson so that she can get the full scoop. After all," she adds pragmatically, "doctors tend to speak more freely to colleagues."

"Yeah, maybe," I answer, guardedly. "But I have the impression this is not an isolated incident. If Anna had wanted us to know she was ill, I think she'd have done it before now."

"Well, not really," answers Amy. "After all Becky's a psychiatrist. Anna might have thought there was no reason to ask her about anything medical."

The kettle starts to whistle shrilly so I say good-bye. Anna is already sleeping when I return and the room is filled with a soft wheezing that accompanies her shallow breathing. Putting the tea cup down on the bed stand, I pull up a chair and sit down. Drinking Anna's tea, I rest there for about twenty minutes just watching her sleep and letting my thoughts drift. It bothers me that Anna has not told any of us that she hasn't been feeling well. When the front doorbell rings, Anna stirs slightly but does not wake up.

I take the overnight bag from Amy and refuse her offer to bring over a plate of food later on, saying, "I've lost my appetite. If I get hungry, I'll make some toast later on." I give her Anna's prescription. "Thanks for doing this."

Pocketing the prescription, Amy says, "I'm going to take a quick look in on her. Don't worry," she adds before I can answer, "I have no intention of waking her." She goes upstairs to peek in on Anna and quickly returns saying, "She's out like a light."

I answer. "This is all so strange."

"I'll wait until Sarah and Becky arrive to get the prescription filled," says Amy. "One of us will drop it off and I'll call later on this evening to see how things are going. Call us if you need anything."

After Amy leaves I surf the TV channels but nothing interests me. Feeling restless, I decide to go out to my car and get my briefcase. Returning with it, I head back up to Anna's room and resume my place on the bedside chair. The last of the afternoon's light has faded so I switch on the bedside light, pull out some files, and start to get caught up with my expense account invoices.

When I answer the front doorbell, I come face-to-face with Becky.

"Amy had the prescriptions filled," she says, jiggling a small bag holding two pill bottles. She slings her jacket over the staircase banister. "I've come to look in on Anna and to ask for her permission to call her doctor."

Following Becky up the stairs, I say, "She was still sleeping when I came down."

Anna stirs in response to Becky's fingers resting on her wrist to take a pulse and groggily murmurs, "Hi Becky. How are you?"

"More to the point," Becky smiles back, "how are you?"

"Feeling a little weak and very tired," admits Anna.

"That's the sedation," replies Becky. "Leen told me that Dr. Anderson gave you some. Would you mind if I called him?"

Anna struggles to focus her attention on Becky. "Why?"

Becky doesn't attempt to sugar-coat her response with empty rationale. She states, "Because I'm a doctor and you're my friend. You're obviously ill and I want to know what I can do to help you."

Anna's eyes dart from Becky to me and then back to Becky. I gnaw on my lower lip as the by-play between Becky and Anna unfolds. It's a contest of wills – one wanting information; the other weighing the merits of releasing information. Becky tries one more time, "Please, Anna, we're friends. Let me help."

Anna relaxes. A hint of a smile crosses her face as she says quietly, "Your being here is a help."

Becky moves a few wisps of hair from Anna's brow and says softly, "Anna, please, I need your permission to talk to him."

Anna coughs and her laboured wheeze stops her from answering. I reach for the glass of water on the nightstand. Easing one arm behind Anna's back I help her to lean forward so that she can take a sip of water. Lying back, Anna says, "Too much trouble."

Becky takes a conciliatory tactic. "No trouble at all, Anna. Besides," she jokes, "imagine how difficult Leen and the others will make my life if I don't do the *doctor thing*. You've heard them complain that I'm paid ridiculously exorbitant amounts to sit and listen to people's problems." Grinning mischievously, she adds, "This way I can actually do what they think a doctor does."

Picking up on Becky's teasing tone, I throw in, "Yeah, Anna. Let Becky do the *doctor thing*."

Our teasing earns us a small chuckle from Anna. Widening her eyes, Becky cajoles, "You know what sceptics they are; help me out Anna." Switching to a serious tone, she adds, "We all care for you very much. If there is something that I can do, I'd like to help. Including," she looks from Anna to me, "staying the night if need be."

Anna closes her eyes and I wonder if she's fallen asleep, but she's merely resting. She takes a deep breath and, with an air of resignation, says, "Perhaps it is better this way. George can explain that part of my life to you." Fatigue obvious, she smiles weakly, "Sarah will explain … And Becky," Anna's eyes plead with her, "after you talk with George,

I'd be grateful if you helped the others understand. I'm just too tired; words fail me."

Patting Anna's shoulder reassuringly, Becky soothes, "It's okay, Anna. We'll take care of everything. You're tired. Thank you for your permission to talk to Dr. Anderson. Once I do that, we can talk more."

Looking distressed but resigned, Anna murmurs, "Just remember ..." Fatigue gets the better of her and her thoughts drift off. Within moments, her breathing becomes steadier, yielding to the narcotic.

Not wanting to disturb her, I mouth, "Just remember?"

Becky shrugs and mouths back, "Who knows?" She retakes Anna's pulse, feels her flushed forehead, and whispers, "There's still a fever. I want to talk to this Dr. Anderson. Let's go." She adjusts the blanket to cover Anna's frail arms.

Throwing Becky a sideways glance as we walk down the stairs, I ask, "What's that business about Sarah? And I still don't get the *just remember* bit."

"Your guess is as good as mine," answers Becky. She frowns. "She could just be confused because of the drugs. If not, we'll all find out soon enough." She grabs her coat from the banister and says, "I'll go next door and fill Amy and Sarah in on what's happening. After that I'll call Dr. Anderson. Once I know something, I'll call you. And, Leen," she says, resting her hand on the doorknob, "I don't mind spending the night. It'd give you some company."

"Thanks," I reply, "but I'll be okay. She'll probably be knocked out for the night."

Becky opens the door, "It'll be a good thing if she is, but you'll have to check in on her several times. If she becomes more congested or if her fever increases, call me."

"I know," I answer. "Call me after you talk with Dr. Anderson."

Nodding her assent, Becky leaves and quickly crosses back over to Amy's house.

Feeling pangs of hunger, I wish I hadn't been so quick to refuse Amy's offer to bring over a plate of food. In the kitchen I make myself a cup of tea and cut a few slices of cheese to go with crackers. Carrying my small meal upstairs, I resettle myself by Anna's bedside and resume my work.

About an hour later I'm finished with my files and still have not heard from Becky. Annoyed, I think, *Damn it, Becky, how long does it take to get some information?* I stuff my files back in my briefcase and decide to rummage around the fridge for something more substantial than cheese and crackers to snack on.

It's not that I'm hungry but when I'm nervous, I have the bad habit of picking at food. Looking for something to eat preoccupies me for a few minutes before I settle on a club soda and a TV dinner. Picking up the phone, I dial Amy's number.

"We were just about to call you," says Amy.

"What did Dr. Anderson say?"

"Here, I'll pass the phone to Becky." As I wait for Becky to pick up the receiver I can hear but not make out muffled background conversation.

"Hi Leen," says Becky, her tone suspiciously flat.

I cut to the chase. "Did you talk with Dr. Anderson?"

Becky hesitates. "Look Leen, it's going to be a long night and I have some research I want to do concerning what he said. It's like I've told Sarah and Amy, I want to be sure of what I'm saying before I go completely on record."

Prickles of fear tingle on the back of my neck. I almost shout back my response, "What's wrong, Becky?"

This time, Becky gets right to the point. "Bottom line, Anna is really quite ill."

I go completely numb and sputter, "What the hell are you talking about? How ill? She has a fever. A chest infection."

Becky remains calm. "Yes but that's not the underlying problem," she says, carefully.

"And, does this *problem* have a name?"

"Yes," answers Becky, "and that's what I want to check up on ..."

"Damn it, Becky, just tell me!"

I can hear her intake of breath. "The layman's version is that Anna has a type of cancer that is no longer going to respond to treatment. Leen ..." she pauses, "there's no easy way to put this – Anna is dying."

I hear myself mutter, "Oh my God, no!" but it's as if the voice belongs to someone else. "Are you certain?"

Becky tries to reason with me. "How about I come next door? We could talk about this."

"No," I reply, wanting to shut everybody and everything out. I need time to absorb what I've just heard and no amount of talking is going to change things. I pull myself from my mire of confusion and shock long enough to ask, "How are Sarah and Amy dealing with the news?"

Becky lowers her voice. "About the same as you. It's a lot to absorb." After a moment, she adds gently, "But, in fairness, we've had a bit more time than you to adjust and we have each other to talk to. Are you sure you don't want me or all of us to come over?"

I exhale a breath that I hadn't realized I'd been holding in. "Yeah," I answer, "I'm sure. We might wake Anna."

"True enough," replies Becky. "We thought about coming over right after I'd spoken to Dr. Anderson but we decided that it might be better to wait. As I said earlier, I want to do some research so that we can all understand what she must be feeling and going through."

"What can I do here?"

"Exactly what you're doing. Be there in case she wakes up and needs something. If she's in a lot of pain, breathing with difficulty, or if her fever increases, call Dr. Anderson and then, call me."

I decide it's time to hang up. Talking won't change a damn thing. "I'll go check on Anna and then try to get some sleep. Do you think it's okay to use one of the spare bedrooms? Or should I make a makeshift bed on the floor using a few blankets and some pillows?"

"Use one of the spare bedrooms," answers Becky quickly. "Anna would want you to be comfortable. Leave the bedroom doors open so that you'll hear her if she wakes up."

"Okay."

"Leen, before you hang up there's one more thing …" She puts her hand over the mouthpiece, talks to the others first.

Tired and frustrated, I demand, "What are you not saying?"

"Sorry," answers Becky, "Sarah just wanted me to say something."

"What is it?" I ask, hoping that there's no more bad news.

"She wants to share some information with you about Anna tomorrow morning."

"Tell me now. Why the delay?"

"No delay," replies Becky. "It's just that it's a bit complicated and Sarah wants to talk in person. Is that okay?" There's a pause as she listens to something that's being said in the background. I suspect it's Sarah. She offers again, "We could come over there."

"No," I answer, sticking to my earlier decision that it's best not to have everyone over here and possibly disturbing Anna's sleep. "As long as it has nothing to do with her illness, it can wait. I've had enough news for one night." Then, I think to ask, "It *can* wait, can't it?"

Once again, there's a muffled conference before Becky says, "Sarah says it can wait until morning and I agree. What's important right now is that if Anna wakes up, don't confront her about what we know about her illness."

I know that there's more to Becky's caution than what appears to be on the surface but I decide not to pursue it. "Yeah, okay."

"That's best," replies Becky; relief evident in her voice. "Sarah and I've decided to spend the night at Amy's. That way, if you need us we can be there quickly. Tomorrow we can come up with a group strategy."

Less agitated now that we are beginning to form a plan, I lighten up and tease, "I'm over here and the three of you decide to have a pyjama party!"

"Not quite," answers Becky, but I can hear the welcome bubble of laughter in her voice. "Anna has wine. Why not pour yourself a glass? Last chance, Leen, do you want one of us to come on over and spend the night with you?"

Now that Becky's sounding more like herself, I put aside any suspicions that she's not telling me everything I need to know and reassure her, "No, I'm fine. I'll see you all in the morning."

༄

Becky

"That was hard," I say, putting down the phone and facing Sarah and Amy.

"Do you think she'll be okay?" asks Sarah while Amy uses the delaying tactic of studying the wine in her glass and for extra effect, gives it a light swirl. We're all searching for the right time to tell Leen that not only is Anna terminally ill but she is, also, not who Leen thinks she is.

Folding my arms across my chest, I lean against the kitchen counter. "The news of Anna's being so ill has rattled her. No surprises there." I look at Sarah. "For a moment I thought she'd push to talk to you."

"She needs to know," answers Sarah. "The sooner, the better."

Amy says, "There's no telling what her reaction is going to be." Grimly, she adds, "Leen's temper can be volatile."

There's nothing any of us can say to that. What we all know for certain is that after Sarah tells Leen about Anna's real identity, her reaction to the news is bound to be explosive. Breaking our dismal silence, Amy throws out, "There's going to be hell to pay." Pouring more wine she groans, "Oh my God, tomorrow is going to be one special day!"

"Special is not the word I'd be using," answers Sarah, dryly, "but I get your meaning."

Helping myself to the grapes and cheese, I reply, "There's nothing any of us can do about it tonight." I raise my wine glass. "Here's to us and to each of us, good luck."

୬

Leen

After hanging up, I open a bottle of Merlot and pour myself a glass. I take a few sips but find I don't want to finish the glass. I pour the rest down the sink and cork the bottle. I decide to check in on Anna before making up a bed in one of the spare bedrooms.

Anna doesn't budge. Her forehead is cooler to the touch than it was earlier in the day and I think that the antibiotics must be working. Carrying the bag of clothes that Amy had brought over, I head to the bathroom where I brush my teeth, change into the sweats and go in search of the guest room.

Anna's upper floor is bigger than I had originally thought. The master bedroom has an ensuite attached, there's a bathroom in the hallway and three other rooms which I assume are bedrooms. All the doors are closed. The first room to the left of the hallway bathroom has been converted into a small sitting room with a settee and a TV. I move on to the next room, expecting it to be a spare bedroom. What catches my attention immediately is the soft understated décor. The wall to my left is lined with books resting on what appears to be a very expensive oak bookcase. The front wall facing the street has a large window through which moonlight filters in and shimmers over the massive cherry wood desk resting in front of it. Instead of curtains, there are shutters and I walk across the room to pull them shut before switching on the desk light. A laptop rests on the desk and positioned on the far corner of the desk is a printer and fax machine. The floor is hardwood and there's a small but expensive looking carpet placed where Anna must rest her feet when working on her laptop. But it's the wall to my right that intrigues.

I cross the room to take a closer look and what I see takes me by surprise. Swallowing hard, I try to absorb what I'm actually seeing. I'm staring at original Holowitz photos. A large portrait of a man standing behind a woman seated with a child by her side, dominates the wall. The man is smiling and his handsome features depict a gentle protectiveness and pride. One hand rests on the woman's shoulder and the other on the little girl. The resemblance between he and the little girl is striking. Both hold their chins in the same manner and they share identical deep blue eyes. The woman has long, honey brown hair and is slender with rich body curves suggesting a sensuous nature. Her smile is soft, maternal and yet, suggests she's keeper of a great secret. Her crystal blue eyes denote sharp intelligence. The little girl has wheat coloured hair and is grinning as if in response to some joke. It is as if she has taken the best from both parents and although still young, has the frame and slender build that promises she will grow to be a beautiful woman. My eyebrows pull together as I wonder about the significance of this portrait amidst the other framed photos. I search the woman's face, wondering why I'm drawn to it and then, recognition dawns. There's not a doubt in my mind that this is a photo of Claire and her family. I'm sure of this because I've seen a few photos of what Claire looked like as a young woman. The Claire posing for this photo is a very young and happy Claire Holowitz. Still, there's something about the woman's expression that triggers a sense of déjà vu. Muttering aloud, I ask, "But how the hell did you get this family portrait, Anna?"

It isn't until I wander over to scan the titles on the bookshelves that the proverbial penny drops. Gone are all thoughts of going to sleep. My body and mind tingles with excitement as my eyes take in the fact that the bookshelves are lined with actual Holowitz manuscripts and novels. Amazed, I mutter, "No wonder you know so much about Holowitz, Anna." I turn around, stare at the photo wall, and return my attention to the bookshelf. My mind spins with questions. "Why didn't you ever mention any of this? What's the story here? Why did you not tell me about this collection?"

The magnitude of the wealth that lines these walls strike me like a fist. These first editions, manuscripts, and signed photos are worth a fortune on the open market. Going back to the photo of the woman with the child, I peer closely at the faces. The sparkle in the little girl's eyes resembles Anna's eyes when she laughs. There's no mistaking the resemblance.

Enraged at my stupidity, I swear. I've seen plenty of photographs of the young Claire Holowitz, but despite my friendship with Anna, I had not made the connection. Voicing my anger, I demand, "How can I have been so stupid? You're Claire Holowitz!"

Thoughts rush through my mind as I say to the empty room, "I trusted you! I took you into my confidence! Damn you, Anna, you've listened to me – Amy – all of us talk about Claire Holowitz. You even volunteered thoughts about Claire's need for privacy." Frustrated by Anna's duplicity I want to hit something or someone. I pace the room for a minute and then, make up my mind. Clutching one of the manuscripts, I practically stomp my way back to Anna's room where I park myself by her bed and silently fume with rage while she sleeps.

The fatigue I felt a half hour ago is replaced with an alert, steely determination. I thumb through the manuscript reading penned in notes and revisions. Despite my anger, I'm captivated by the words. I want answers and Anna's going to give them to me.

By the time she wakes, I've calmed down enough to focus on what I need to say. Used to corporate scenarios where the underlying rule is "take no prisoners", I'm determined to have this conversation. Anna's eyes flutter open. Seeing the manuscript resting on my lap she flinches in response to my clenched jaw and smouldering anger. Sighing, she says, "So, now you know?"

"Well at least you have the decency not to deny it," I retort sarcastically. "When did you expect me to find out?" Practically spitting my next question, I demand, "Or, was it your intention to just play me along?"

"I knew that you were going to find out, sooner or later," answers Anna.

I snarl back, "Maybe you should have thought about that?"

"I did think about it," says Anna. "I took steps to help correct any misunderstandings that might arise when you found out."

I snort contemptuously.

Anna doesn't react to my harshness. "Believe what you want to believe, Leen." She eases herself upright and rests against the headboard. "The matter of *when* you found out was taken out my hands. The pain came on quickly. I called George. That's when you arrived …" Her unfinished sentence hangs in the air.

I spit out, "Well, Anna, or should I say *Claire* … what the hell do I call you?"

The first indication of Anna's temper surfaces. "For all that it matters … Sarah's already dubbed me Anna-Claire."

"Sarah? What has she to do with this?" Anger bubbles. "Sarah's recovering from an aneurism." I begin to pace, stop abruptly, and glare. "Are you saying that Sarah knows who you are?"

"I retained her as my co-counsel."

I explode. "Shit! You're fucking kidding me!"

Anna attempts to explain. "She was going to help me explain everything at Amy's dinner. But things happened. You found out this way." Wearily, she shifts her position, trying to get comfortable. Her voice becomes hard and practical. "So now you know Leen. Let's get down to business. You can pick up the phone and call your office and the media. You can say that you have found Claire Holowitz and that will give you momentary glory and fame."

Her biting words and the force at which she is speaking momentarily takes me off-guard. I'm not prepared for this Anna. The Anna I've known has always been friendly – an older lady with mild eccentricities but one with endearing qualities. This woman, despite her obvious frailty, displays no fear. She has a temper and clearly is used to speaking her mind.

I feel the weight of Anna's look knowing that she's hoping for some concession on my part but I'm in no mood to relinquish my anger. "On the other hand, you can do what you've so often said you wanted to do – learn about Claire Holowitz *from* Claire Holowitz. Your choice, Leen. Keep my identity to yourself until such time as it is necessary to reveal it or pick up the phone and tell Don Harris you've found me."

She throws back the bed covers. "I'm going to the bathroom. Do whatever you want to do. I can't stop you."

I watch her cross the room, clad in blue pyjamas, trying to walk with dignity, unable to hide her obvious weakness. Her gait is off and she rests her hand lightly on the doorframe to steady herself. She shuts the ensuite's door firmly, leaving me to stare at it in hard silence.

I hear the toilet flush followed by the sound of running water. I think about Anna's ultimatum and realize that I want to take the 'business deal'. I definitely have the upper hand and can expose her at any time I want. She's offering me a chance to know her as Claire Holowitz. I decide to learn all that I can but I'll be damned if I'll let her play me for a fool again. I want to talk with Becky and find out what she has to say about Anna's medical condition and I sure as hell want Sarah to explain her part in this whole Anna subterfuge.

Opening the door, she leans against the wall, waiting for me to speak. I hurl accusations at her. "Just who do you think you are? You've played me and you've known all along that I was looking for you."

Anna draws in a sharp breath. I can tell that I've hurt her but surely she can't expect me to just slough off her deception and say, "Oh, that's okay, Anna. Let's all be friends."

I know that I'm lashing out at a sick woman and something within me tugs at my heartstrings, but I'm tired, feeling betrayed, and frustrated. I see the grimace of pain and remind myself of the purpose for my being here. I cross the space between us, touch her elbow and guide her back to her bed. I reach for the bottle of pills and water glass. The simple action of walking to the bathroom and back has exhausted Anna. Her breathing is laboured, but her fierce independence demands that she not succumb to the fatigue. Grudgingly, I admit to myself that she's got spunk.

Anna speaks deliberately; determined to say her piece. "Leen," she says, "I wanted to tell you. I didn't count on having you find out this way. That's why I went to see Sarah."

When I don't answer, she continues, "I can get along without you, but I don't want to. You now know who I am, but that shouldn't change your relationship with me. You liked and accepted me as Anna. You wanted to know Claire because you *need* her for your job. When I met the four of you, I had no idea how much my life would change. I have been happy knowing you. Can't you try to see it from my perspective, just for a moment?"

I hunch my shoulders as if I don't care but we both know that's a blatant lie and an attempt to not show my hurt at her deception. "I needed to know that if I allowed you to *find* me that I would be safe – that you wouldn't use me to advance your career. It was not unreasonable to try to determine your motives."

"You lied to me!" I fight back the swell of hot stinging tears. "I trusted you."

Addressing the hurt and not responding to the anger, Anna answers, "I never lied. I never once told you I *wasn't* Claire Holowitz. I answered your questions about Holowitz. I sent Marc Andre to meet you and instructed him to contact the people who would help you and whom you are still interviewing. I purposely told him to watch out for Don Harris and to not let him in any way hurt your career." Voice cracking with emotion, she adds, "You have had more access to *my* private world than anyone outside of my closest confidants." Pausing to catch her breath, Anna fumbles with the bed sheets and nervously gnaws on her lower lip. "Please," she begs softly, "Let's find a way to make it work?" She wipes away her own spill of tears as I shed mine.

Incredulous, I demand, "Make this work? How do you suggest we do that Anna?"

"I won't fight you if you want to expose me although I have the means and the ability to lock you and Scenes up in court for a very long time if I so choose ..." She lifts her hand, warning me not to interrupt. "No, hear me out, Leen. Contrary to what you may think, I am not threatening you. I'm saying that you can do whatever you want and Claire Holowitz will not stop you. But it is me, Anna," she taps her chest and her eyes openly plead for understanding, "that is begging you to know me. What's a name, Leen? Have I not lost enough in my lifetime?" She draws in a deep breath and holding her arm outstretched in the empty space between us, offers her hand. My eyes drop to her hand and then rise to meet her unwavering gaze. I know what she wants but I won't do it. I touch her hand gently with my index and middle fingers but I refuse to let her hold my hand. I'm not ready for that intimacy. I'm afraid that if I do allow it, I will give in and she will have won all.

Anna lowers her arm, slowly nods and then, turns her head to stare at the window. Heavy, awkward silence permeates the room. She stares, I wait. Like two tired warriors we are unsure of what, if anything, is left to be said, prepared to do battle if necessary, neither knowing how to bridge the chasm that exists. The damage has been done. Anna rubs her eyes, blows out a long, tired breath and turns to face me.

Determined, she says, "This isn't just about you, Leen. This is about me, too. For the first time since Emily died, I found myself hoping that maybe you, Sarah, Amy, and Becky might get to know me the way I would have wanted my daughter to know me. Not Claire Holowitz, the writer or photographer! The me who laughs, cries, dreams, and aches. I wanted you to know my life – from my perspectives – and to share it with you. The words I write are creations. The photos I take are images of what exists. But I am me. Is it such a crime to want you to know me for me? Not the public personae?"

She rests her head against the headboard and I'm shocked at how much this outburst has taken out of her. She is pale and has aged visibly in minutes. Voicing raw emotions can do that. You don't know if what you said will be accepted or rejected. I feel a twinge of guilt that I am the reason she has made herself so vulnerable. I know that having said what she wanted to say, there will be no more words; no more pleading. She is shutting down, guarding her emotions, and is done with trying to make herself understood. The pills are starting to take effect and her pain is ebbing, but she fights the sleep that threatens to overtake her body.

As quickly as my anger had risen, it now dissipates. I want and need for the tension to be gone. I know there will be issues to resolve, but I'm simply not ready to walk out of Anna's life or to let Anna leave mine. Now, it's me who extends a hand. An offering, the promise of a truce. Silently, she curls her fingers around mine. Neither of us speaks. We're just content to know that our friendship – what we share with one another – is stronger than what most people ever experience.

Finally, I say, "You're tired, Anna. Try to rest for a while. I'll make us breakfast." I surprise myself by leaning over to gently kiss her forehead. Exhausted, Anna does not resist when I cover her with blankets.

When I reach the door, she asks, "Are you coming back?" She has the look and sound of a small child, unsure of what the night will bring and wanting the security that if "monsters" come, someone will be there to frighten them away.

I have not known the love of a mother for many years. Standing here in Anna's bedroom with her looking so fragile and so hopeful, I think that I am experiencing what many daughters must feel when they realize their mother – the woman to whom they looked to for so long for answers, strength, comfort, refuge and hope – has reached a turning point in life's pendulum where the one who once seemed indestructible and able to conquer the monsters of the night, becomes the one needing protection. Right now, here in this moment, I am the adult. I am the one who must step up to the plate to make the world 'safe'.

"I'm going to make breakfast, just like I said I would and when you wake, we'll talk. Okay?"

"Okay," agrees Anna.

She closes her eyes, letting the drugs do what they are intended to do.

I'm not sure but I think I hear her murmur, "Promise."

I hurry down the stairs.

Chapter Fourteen

Leen

The next few weeks are wrought with a swinging pendulum of conflicting emotions as Becky, Amy, Sarah, and I reconcile and adjust to our new relationship with Anna.

The morning following my overnight stay at Anna's, Sarah explained what she had shared with Becky and Amy the night before. The pieces are falling into place. It has taken some time to adjust to our new relationship with Anna. We've all taken to calling her Anna-Claire and she seems to accept that name as part of the transformation in our relationship.

Becky has filled us in on what she's learned from Dr. Anderson and it's not good. Anna has chronic lymphocytic leukaemia. Raging throughout her body the leukaemia depletes her immune system and weakens her ability to fend off even the smallest of colds. "Putting it in layman's terms," Becky explained, "doctors refer to it as the leukaemia that one dies with".

When asked to elaborate, Becky was blunt and clinical. "The weakened immune system leaves her susceptible to the smallest of infections. She simply can't fight them. She's had the disease for years and been able to maintain her lifestyle, through a series of treatments, drugs and chemotherapy. Now, however, it's advanced to the point that the abnormalities in her blood are affecting her systemically. Dr. Anderson and her oncologist give her a year, at best. She's in the terminal phase now and knows it. She's experiencing excruciating pain in her joints and bones. Her breathing is affected due to the swelling in her liver and spleen which causes extreme distress and pain. There has also been marked enlargement in the lymph nodes in her neck, underarms, stomach and groin."

"The fever, weight loss and lethargy?" asked Sarah. "It's all part of the disease?"

"All side-effects," answered Becky, munching on a peanut butter cookie. "This is a bitch of a disease and it has reached its aggressive stage. It also accounts for the night sweats that she's been experiencing."

"All her jokes about old age affecting her bones and needing her rest ..." murmured Amy, "all cover ups?"

"Exactly," answered Becky. Then, in an uncharacteristic move, she abruptly pushed herself away from the kitchen table and left the room mumbling that she shouldn't drink so much coffee.

Leen

None of this was easy for Becky. Not one of us had bought into her grumbling about a weak bladder. We knew that she needed a few moments to gather her thoughts. Patiently, clinically, and objectively, she had answered our questions – giving us time to deal with the reality of it all. As a doctor she had presented the information but as a friend, she needed some time to deal with it.

Returning to the kitchen, she's back to being the old Becky. Strands of wet hair lie across her forehead and I suspect that she splashed water on her face to deal with the tears she must have shed in the privacy of the bathroom. Matter-of-factly, she says, "Anna didn't want us to know." She waves off Sarah who is about to say something and continues, "I've done a lot of thinking. When we met her, she didn't know us from Adam. Imagine how she must have felt finding out that Leen was commissioned to find Claire Holowitz. We've been caught up in how we felt about her *not* having told us. But, how must she have felt? She manipulated behind the scene to make Leen's search easier ... no, it's true," she insists staring at me, "she did and you know it. Until Anna could be certain that we could accept her as a person – as a friend – as Anna – she couldn't tell us that she was Claire. But when she found out that Don is doing all he can to hurt Leen's career and using Claire Holowitz as the means to do it, Anna went to Sarah and wanted to put things right. Think about that for a while."

With that having been said, she folds her arms across her chest and leans against the counter waiting for all of us to process that mouthful. When none of us respond immediately, Becky takes a deep breath and plunges ahead with what she's determined to say. "She's making peace with her life the best way she can. She wants her dignity. I suspect that is also one of the reasons that she was so protective about her privacy. She doesn't want pity; she wants acceptance for whom she is and the life that she lives."

Becky's right. Despite having affected a truce with Anna, I've still allowed myself the luxury of being righteously angry. I've not truly given thought to the 'bigger picture'. It's time for all of us to move on and to help our friend."

"The fact, ladies …" says Sarah, breaking the lull that has followed Becky's speech, "is whatever her reasons, good or bad, Anna-Claire did not originally feel comfortable enough with us to reveal her identity."

"Sure," I agree, trying – but not succeeding – at keeping the edge from my voice, "I know what you're going to say. She was caught between guarding a private life that she had protected for forty years and dealing with the fact that she wanted to help us." I look at their faces and add, "Or, perhaps, I should say *me* specifically since I'm the one arranging the Gala. But," I point a finger at Amy, "she's sat there and acted as an editor for your novel. She never let on, not once, who she was. I've said it before and I'll repeat it. That's bullshit!"

Becky frowns. "Get over yourself, Leen. She puts some cheese on a cracker. Munching, she adds, "We made the decision to move on. Rehashing the hurt is like giving permission to a boil to fester. The result is the same; it's putrid."

"That's true, Leen," says Sarah. Although her speech has improved, she still speaks in measured and halting words. "You and Anna-Claire have talked a lot over the last few weeks." She looks around our little circle, adding, "We've all spoken with her and all of us have promised to be there for her." She blows out an exasperated breath. "So what if she's Claire Holowitz? The woman we love is Anna *who happens* to be Claire. Do you see the difference? We would never have known Claire but because of Anna, we can know and love both women."

Amy and Becky stare open-mouthed. Becky speaks first. "Sarah, you've nailed it! Talk about clinical accuracy! With that sort of perception, you could sit in my office any day and hang up a shingle. I'm truly impressed." Laughing, she points at Sarah and exclaims good-naturedly, "Ladies, the doctor is in!"

"To Sarah," toasts Amy.

Sarah flushes but from her grin, it is obvious that she's pleased with the praise. Addressing me, she says, "It's time Leen."

She's right. Becky's right and I can tell that Amy agrees. "Okay, Sarah, I give in." I hold my hands up in surrender. "I was just blowing off steam."

Sarah smiles. "Time to use the steam for better things."

"Proves what I've always maintained," says Amy, her expression deadpan. "Leen's nothing but hot air."

I smirk. "Like you can tell the difference between hot air and steam, Ms PhD.?"

Grinning, Amy replies, "Now there's the Leen I know and love."

After they've taken a few more good-natured jabs at me, I raise the next question. "Where do we go from here?" What do we do and what do we say?"

"We do what we do best," says Amy. "We start by going next door and inviting ourselves into her home. We bring her our unconditional acceptance and let her know that we like the person she is. We're *not* the media. We're her friends."

Becky mischievously adds, "We've done an admirable job of coping with Leen's outbursts over the years. We're certainly capable of handling any glitches that may come up with Anna. Unconditional acceptance. That's it," she says, her mouth forming a determined line, "we'll all do what we have to do to help one another."

Springing into action and opening her freezer to dig out a spinach quiche, Amy says, "I say that we bring food and laughter to her." Rummaging her fridge for some fresh fruit to add to Anna's food bag, she looks pointedly over her shoulder at us. "Imagine how she must have felt, listening to us talk about how eccentric and odd it was for Claire Holowitz to recluse herself from the public."

Becky picks up the plate with the cheese and grapes. Heading our little procession, she proclaims, "Anna-Claire, here we come!"

༶

Leen

Anna answers the door with a cautious smile.

"We come bearing gifts," I joke, as she lets us in.

Settling in around Anna's kitchen table we talk about our anger, but reinforce the fact that we understand her need for caution. Eventually Becky gets up to make a pot of tea and places it along with mugs onto the table.

"What is important, now," says Anna, clasping her mug of tea and staring down at it, "is that we can all move forward. As I told, Sarah," she looks up at Sarah and smiles, "when I retained her as my legal counsel, I never intended to mislead you. When I met the four of you, I realized that I genuinely found myself looking forward to your gatherings."

"To be honest, I think a part of me thought that if you knew I really was Claire Holowitz, you would stop thinking of me as Anna. With a saucy smirk, she adds, "I've even come to like the name you've given me. The double name seems to suit our relationships with one another. It works well."

Anna's comment about the name dissipates any sarcasm previously associated with it and cements it as a name used with affection.

"Tell me something, Anna-Claire," I ask, trying to be nonchalant, "did you send Marc Aumount to size me up or did you send him for another reason?"

"Ah, the famous Marc Aumount," interjects Sarah, wriggling her eyebrows.

"Yes, Anna-Claire," says Becky, picking up on the teasing, "what strategy did you have in mind for Aumount and Leen?" Softly, she adds, "You're sure you're good with the dual name?"

Anna laughs. "I'm good, Becky. After all, that is who I am. I won't say it didn't hurt at first but I've had time to think about it. I'm Anna to you and Claire to the world. Two names; just one person."

"Here's to Anna-Claire," says Becky, saluting her with a raised mug of tea. "Now," she says mischievously, "tell us about the plans you have for the dashing Marc Aumount and our highly eligible friend."

I can feel the hot flush creep up my cheeks. At this moment I could gladly throttle Becky but my glare only adds fuel to the fire. Laughing she says, "I so love it when you're speechless."

I grumble, "Give it a rest, Becky."

Anna-Claire's expression becomes thoughtful. "At first, I wanted Marc to get a feel for Leen's motives and the direction of her campaign. But," she looks at me, "when he returned from meeting you, he was uncharacteristically effusive in his assessment of your integrity and intelligence." She smiles. "I knew then that my initial assessment of you wasn't wrong. What I found amusing was that Marc does not impress easily and yet, he was all pro-Adrienne MacLeen." Shrugging, she jokes, "So I thought to myself, let's get the show under way and see what happens. If he was willing to trust you; I was willing to give you a chance."

Narrowing her eyes and casting a "told you so" look at me, Becky observes, "Had Aumount not liked Leen, would you have kyboshed Leen's project?"

"As a matter of fact, yes," Anna-Claire answers candidly. "I couldn't stop the Gala but I didn't have to make it possible for her to be connected with various people."

I don't let her off the hook. "From the beginning you were pulling my strings?"

"No," answers Anna-Claire. "That implies I was manipulating you. I did nothing of the sort. I simply maintained my privacy as Claire Holowitz and made it possible for you, through Marc, to have access to people and information. Listen to me, closely, Leen," says Anna-Claire leaning forward, intent on making her point, "I liked you when I met you. But you met me as Anna. Anna, not Claire, was invited to be a friend."

"What about when we met at the Speckled Rooster? I demand, ignoring Becky's warning glance not to stir things up.

"I was as surprised as you were." A soft chortle escapes as she adds, "You looked so out of place in that suit."

I roll my eyes. "Yeah, I know." To the others, I say, "Talk about being over dressed. That place was your stereotypical roadside, greasy spoon."

"Why were you there, Anna-Claire?" asks Amy.

"I had helped Eleanor's daughter with a paper for her English literature class. As Leen discovered that day, it was about Claire Holowitz." She shakes her head as she adds, "You have no idea how shocked I was when Eleanor started to tell Leen about it." Her eyes seek mine. "I thought for sure that you'd figure it out that day. I just wanted to get out of there without you putting two and two together. When you asked me to become a consultant, I truly didn't know what to say. I couldn't get around the fact that I knew about Holowitz ..." she grins self-consciously, "for obvious reasons and so I opted for the excuse that I had simply helped Eleanor's daughter." To Amy, she adds, "But, in answer to your question, I hadn't been there for about a month and so I decided on an outing to find out from Eleanor how things were going for her daughter and if I could be of any more help."

"How do you know Eleanor?" asks Becky, openly inquisitive.

"We met five years ago at the cancer clinic," answers Anna-Claire. "She was finishing her chemo and we got to talking. One thing led to another and we became friends." Sucking on her upper teeth Anna-Clair becomes pensive. "She's a strong and proud woman. I have a lot of respect for her."

"Does she know you're Claire Holowitz?" asks Amy.

"No," replies Anna-Claire, clearly surprised at Amy's suggestion that she might have revealed her true identity to Eleanor.

"What about her daughter?" persists Amy.

"No," Anna-Claire answers emphatically.

None too tactfully, I ask, "What must you have thought when I offered you a job?"

"Right after that I met with Marc and told him about our chance encounter," answers Anna-Claire truthfully. "It was then I made my decision to tell all of you, but Sarah ..." she glances at her and smiles, "had her aneurism and I decided the timing wasn't right."

"What did Aumount think? asks Becky.

"Like I said, he talked a great deal about Leen and thought I should work with her but he wasn't sure about the wisdom of..." she makes quotation marks with her fingers, "coming clean about my identity." She looks at Sarah. "I waited until you were up to a visit and then, based on Marc Andre's advice, approached you to ask for lawyer-client privilege. I knew that you all had to know who I was but I was banking on you being able to represent my case ..." again she makes quotation marks, "to everyone." Addressing Becky, she says, Marc Andre and I discussed coming to you and asking you to help present the rationale for my decision—my emotional entanglement—but he felt that lawyer-client along with the non-disclosure agreements would be the best way to do it." She shrugs. "He ... I ... we knew you would all be upset and that I was risking everything but we hoped that by presenting a logical and legal argument for my double identity, you would have time to understand my reasoning and accept me." With disgust, she adds, "He doesn't much care for Don."

"You're close to Aumount," I say. "He's very protective of you."

Anna-Claire smiles. "The feeling is mutual. As his father did, he takes care of my legal matters but our relationship, especially since his mother died, is very special. In fact, he is my godson."

I let out a low whistle. "You're kidding?"

"No," she answers, "To Marc, I'm Aunt Claire."

For a few seconds, none of us say anything. We just let that bit of information settle. Amy is the first to recover. "So you were saying that Marc Andre expressed an interest, other than purely business, about Leen?" says Amy, cupping her chin in the palm of her hand.

Ignoring my groan, Amy adds pleasantly, "Details, Anna-Claire, details."

I complain, "We've covered that territory, Amy."

Undeterred, Anna-Claire answers, "Marc Andre is his own man and makes his own decisions about his private life, but there was no doubt in my mind from listening to him talk about Leen and then, hearing Leen's opinion about his ..." she emphasizes, with a mischievous grin, "dove-grey eyes that there was mutual chemistry at work. Guess it's the writer in me, I wanted to see a happy ending."

"Enough said!" I raise my hand, mimicking a traffic cop and snort, "Chemistry? Our first meeting in Don's office bordered on being explosive."

"So you say, now," replies Anna-Claire, drolly, "but from what he told me you were more than capable of defending yourself from anything thrown your way."

When we eventually part for the night, Becky walks me to my car and says quietly, "Leen, don't dismiss Aumount. Maybe Anna-Claire is right about there being some chemistry between the two of you. Look at me and Josh. I thought that my time for finding someone had passed me by. He came into my life in a way that I would never have suspected. All I'm saying," she protests, in response to the automatic stiffening of my shoulders, "is give yourself the freedom to take a chance for love if it comes your way."

Relenting, I promise, "Okay if Aumount does express an interest, I'll leave myself open to the possibility of meeting him in a social setting. But, in the meantime…" I poke her arm gently, "how about if you all drop the topic of my love life or lack thereof?"

"Agreed," answers Becky, giving me a quick hug. "Now go home and get some sleep so that if he shows up at your office, you won't have bags under your eyes." With that having been said, she charges off to her car laughing because she's had the last word.

Chapter Fifteen

Anna-Claire

I'm at loose ends this morning. Nausea from the drugs has made me lose any desire for food. I know I have to eat so I force myself to swallow some yogurt and gulp down two pain pills with a glass of cranberry juice. I need to find the energy to shower. I've always disliked the idea of lounging around all day in pyjamas but some days it just doesn't seem worth the effort to get dressed. I refuse to let the lethargy win. I need to pull myself together. Leen and the others are coming over later today and I don't want them to know that each day is becoming more of a struggle.

I find it to be an odd, bitter irony that it is in facing death that I have once again found life. I've told them about my other life – when I was a wife and a mother – about Drew and Emily. I've answered their questions and they in turn, have told me more about their lives, lost loves, and hopes.

Becky has made a point of 'just happening to drop by' when the others are at work or before our get-togethers. Without being overbearing or clinical, she has helped me talk about my thoughts and feelings. I don't think of her as a psychiatrist. She is my friend who happens to be a psychiatrist. It has to be that way. I won't deal with a psychiatrist but with my friend, I have let down my guards and it eases the pain I've carried for so long in my heart.

This morning, as I putter about my kitchen, my mind is wandering back to the conversation Becky and I had yesterday. "You know, Anna-Claire," said Becky, "everyone needs to talk about things in their lives. That's what gives me a job. You shouldn't feel that you can't. It's all natural."

"I'm starting to have vivid dreams," I'd replied, surprised at my frankness but accepting it as part of our new relationship. "It's as if a flood gate of memories has opened since I started to talk about Drew and Emily. The dreams are coming at a pace I can't control and seem to be not only real but larger than life."

She didn't seem taken aback at my revelation. Instead, in Becky-like manner, she was quick to reassure, "That's a good thing and it's also natural. Your sub-conscious held everything safe for you until you were ready to allow the memories to surface." She made me smile. I knew she was thinking – but was good enough not to say it–it only took you four decades to deal with it."

"I know that on an intellectual level," I freely admitted, "but emotionally, it's strange and sometimes hard to deal with. They are, after all, only dreams. At times, I can almost hear Drew's laughter or feel Emily's silken hair brush against my cheek. In my dreams I'm leaning forward to kiss them both and just before I can, I wake up. If only just once, I could tell them how much I love them."

"I think they knew that," said Becky, her tone comforting and non-judgemental. "The accident was one of life's crueller moments. Neither of them would have wanted you to live a life feeling blame for something you had absolutely nothing to do with."

"Intellectually, I know that what you say is true," I'd answered, "but I have no control over how the night takes over reason. Sometimes, I even wake to the sound of my voice calling out to them and when I realize I'm all alone, the pain is so bad that I don't think I can bear it. It's been forty years and yet, to me, the pain and grief is just as real as it was then."

She had the good grace not to belittle my feelings or spout off platitudes about there being nothing I can say or do that will ever bring Drew and Emily back into my life. I can recreate their existence as many times as I want to – consciously or sub-consciously in my dreams.

But, the reality is, my life with them ended the day they walked out the front door – never to come back. Every day – since then – I have just existed. All the plays and novels I've written; all the photos I've taken; all that I have done since their deaths has been motivated by one driving force. If I stop, they will cease to exist. Marc Andre is the surrogate child of my heart. He and Emily would have been good friends. In my mind, they would have been like brother and sister. Watching him grow into a man and loving him like a son has been my salvation.

༺༻

Becky

Anna has given this visit a valiant effort but I can tell that she is fighting sleep. Being a doctor helps me understand and be alert to subtle changes in demeanour that the others mightn't pick up as readily. It's not unusual for her to drift off for ten, twenty minutes at a time. Today, she rallies and when she opens her eyes she wants to tell me about her dream.

"I'm sorry," apologizes Anna, "I drifted off."

"No need to be sorry," I answer. "You need your rest and the medication is also contributing to your mini-naps. Are you sure that you want to continue? Maybe we should just call it a day?"

"No," Anna replies, "definitely not. I want to tell you about my dream. Usually when I nap, that's all it is – a nap. But, today – just now, everything seemed so real. Just let me tell you about it."

"Okay, Anna," I say, "if you're certain that it won't tire you out, I'm all ears."

She smiles. "I'll tell you it the way I remember. Don't interrupt; I might lose my train of thought."

I motion as if I'm zipping my mouth shut and sit back in my chair. Anna's cheeks are flushed and her eyes are alert. I can tell that whatever she dreamt is important to her and I'm curious.

Anna straightens up in the big black leather recliner. She shuts her eyes saying, "If I close my eyes, I can still see it. The dream... it was that real."

"Keep your eyes closed," I say. "Do what feels right."

She opens her eyes and laughs lightly. "Always the shrink."

"Yep," I answer, smugly.

Once again, she closes her eyes and I can tell from her expression that she's sorting her thoughts; letting the dream flash before her in vivid colour. Like a reader or movie watcher, she starts to describe events leading up to the day Drew and Emily died but, instead of being able to alter it with the stroke of a pen or tapping of letters on a keyboard, she can only recall and watch her life re-play in her mind. My training kicks in and my reaction is instantaneous: I'm fascinated with how she can recall her dream and the process she's using to bring it back to her mind. As a doctor and as her friend, I listen carefully.

༄

Anna-Claire's Dream

I roll over the tossed sheets and ease myself out of the bed. Drew is sleeping and I can hear his slight snore. I stand at the side of the bed, watching his chest move in slow steady rhythm. His tussled hair makes me think of a little boy and I smile as I make my way to the bathroom. Stripping down I turn on the shower, fiddle with the temperature and let the water cascade while I brush my teeth. Stepping into the shower, I ease my fingers up my arm before reaching for the soap, wanting the memory of his touch to linger. I feel the night's sleep fall away with the soap's lather, swirling with the water into the drain.

Drew had come home with a mixed bouquet of red, blue, white and yellow carnations. This was not unusual. I put the flowers in the lead crystal vase Aunt Agnes gave us as a wedding present. Dinner had been an easy affair; meatloaf with fresh asparagus.

༄

Becky

Anna-Claire opened her eyes and smiled.

"Sounds like a good dream," I said, not wanting to disturb the flow with too much chatter. It is important to acknowledge a patient's recall of a significant event or perception of that event without unduly influencing it. This is one of those times between Anna-Claire and myself that I wish I was less of a doctor and more of a friend but I can't help myself. I revert to looking at things clinically and when that happens, I make a conscious effort to separate the two parts of my instinct. The clinical part of me wants to take notes that I can review later on so that we can flesh out the whys and wherefores for the vividness of her dream – to put together the pieces that, like an unsorted puzzle, need piecing together. The friend wants to simply listen; to glean a better insight to help my friend. I'm torn between the professional interest and friendship.

~

Anna-Claire

Becky makes coffee and I'm glad for it. She's been very quiet since I told her my dream. That is not unusual; she is a good listener. I suspect, however, that her silence has more to do with the fact that she knows I don't want her to comment or to have to sit and politely listen to her perspective – I simply need to talk and to share what I've kept so long to myself.

I'm not a fool. I've done my fair share of reading on how grief affects people and their lives. Repressed memories can surface years after a traumatic event. There are a lot of messed up people wandering around and I'd venture to bet that less than ten percent ever seek professional assistance. A lot has to do with the cost as well as the stigma attached to seeking psychiatric help.

Money isn't a factor in my case. It hasn't been for years and for that I'm grateful. I don't have to think about what I'll need to give up in order to spend an hour babbling to a psychiatrist. When you try to share your innermost feelings with friends or family, you walk on treacherous ground. They may tell you that they'll listen and even be sincere in believing that they can be impartial but, inevitably, they will associate what you say to something that is personal and when 'personal' comes into play, feelings can get hurt.

I tried years ago after Drew and Emily died to tell Sadie my best friend at the time to stop bitching about her husband and to appreciate what she had but she didn't understand I was trying to save her from the hurt – the unbearable loneliness that loss of someone whom you love brings. Instead, my ineptness at expressing my fear that she would know the pain of being alone despite her constant claims that she is dissatisfied with her life was interpreted as my being a bitch and ungrateful for her friendship. The result was that I lost her too.

You can't tell friends what hurts you the most.

You can't tell them how you cry in the night or how you ache for the simple comfort of knowing that someone shares your life. It's just too personal. But Becky has the training and she can disassociate herself from my pain and simply listen to what I am saying and what I need to say in order to heal. Now, I know why I never could seek professional help – I wasn't ready to say good-bye to Drew and Emily. Writing and photography were not just my means to escape from the pain of losing them; they shielded me from the emptiness of my life. I convinced myself that I had learned to cope; that I was moving on with the reality of my life.

I did move on, but only in certain ways. I became successful, even famous. Claire Holowitz was my professional persona; insulated, removed from the world; existent only for the purpose of stories and photos. Anna Wright was the persona that lived in the world.

Yes, I had Emile, Marc Andre and some close confidants and friends but I needed something more – a sense of belonging, of purpose and involvement. A psychiatrist may have helped but I doubt it. I needed a friend who knew how to help.

Becky is both friend and psychiatrist and I find comfort in talking with her. Perhaps it all boils down to the simple fact that now I am ready – able to cope with the emotional wounds. My want and need to keep my friendship with Leen, Sarah, Amy, and Becky supersedes my want to separate the lives of Claire Holowitz and Anna Wright.

Ours is a unique friendship – forged as a result of a lot of factors; none of which make sense on the surface. I don't care for the whys and wherefores as to how we got to where we are; I'm just humbly grateful that we are in this place in time. It's been a long time since I've known the comfort of sharing my thoughts and the satisfying intimacy of intellectual acceptance.

Talking will not bring my family back but talking with Becky may help me gain peace and acceptance. It may make my days easier or my nights less lonely. They are gone. I am the one who was left behind. Becky is my friend who *happens* to be a psychiatrist; for me, that is an important distinction. I tell her things that I would be reluctant to share with others.

I sip my coffee and think about what I want to say next. I search my thoughts, wondering how to articulate them so that she will understand. But, it doesn't matter if she understands. What matters is that I give voice to what crowds my brain and, after so many years, is demanding release. What matters is that Becky will not judge me. She will not try to put her own spin on what I say. That is one of her strengths. She knows how to listen and in so doing, she knows how to help heal the hurt of intellectual and emotional pain.

"Ready?" asks Becky.

I look at her and smile. "Yes," I answer. "But, are you sure you don't mind?"

"Just share what you're comfortable sharing," says Becky.

I wet my lips with my tongue and fidget for a moment feigning interest in removing lint from my sweater. Then, I close my eyes and allow the dream to come back to me. It's strong. So real, I can almost smell the scent of Drew's aftershave lotion and lingering scent of baby shampoo in Emily's hair. It doesn't come out in any real order; it just needs to be said.

My momentary pause – hesitancy to give voice to intimate memories – doesn't fool Becky. In that quiet tone she uses, she says, "Just tell your dream the way you want to … the way that it has meaning for you."

Yes, I think, *just tell it.*

This time I don't close my eyes. I look right at Becky and continue with my dream—as if I'm an observer to my life – as if I have gone back in time and I am still in the shower, glowing in the aftermath of my night with Drew.

༄

We had sat quietly watching a fire, snacking on cheese and apple slices, listening to jazz playing in the background. Nothing had suggested that this last night would be extraordinary.

As I rinsed the shampoo from my hair, a sensuous, self-gratifying smile came to my face. Last night – that night – was the stuff that makes movies memorable, novels sensational, and poetry ageless. I felt a sense of satisfaction and fulfilment that had eluded me for the last few months. With the last of the trailers for my latest novel having been complete I was now at ease.

For weeks, I had been edgy; working all hours to meet the publication dates. It was always like that just before a book or play came out. I would work myself into a frenzy of activity, review and second-guess every suggestion or comment my editor or agent made. My work, my writing, was integral to my life. Drew and Emily were my reason for being. My search for perfection was an onus that I put on myself and despite what anyone said or the comfort Drew offered me, I did it every time.

Now that the first reviews were in, I was content that the work had been well done. I was edging towards a best seller. Just the day before I had been told by Arnie, my agent, that Hollywood was looking at putting "Gala Girls" into a movie framework.

Stepping out of the shower, I rubbed my body dry with the soft cotton towel and dried my hair. I was pleased that Drew and I had reconnected. It had been a while since we had been so intimate. Tomorrow we would leave with Emily and take a much needed break from our respective jobs. Drew, a founding partner in Aumount and Henderson, had his own "work devils" and, in his own way, he drove himself and those around him to meet his concepts of what and how things should be achieved. His partner Emile Aumount handled my legal matters.

Drew often joked that he had enough to contend with the "Claire" at home and he had no intention of taking on the Claire "of fame" at the office. "Too much Claire" can be stressful and demanding" he liked to quip to his friends. "I'm only too happy to let Emile handle Claire's legal matters. People would laugh as he added with feigned exasperation, "Believe me, being her husband is enough of a full-time job! Imagine how quickly I would age if I had to handle her legal affairs. If Emile does something to displease her, I can pour a glass of wine and be the sympathetic husband."

When Emily was born, Drew – convinced that she was the most perfect specimen of human life – stood in the hallway outside the nursery forcing every person, nurse, custodian or other visiting parent, to stop and admire her. He was totally smitten.

That morning as I applied blush to my cheekbones, I recalled how Drew would lie for hours on the couch with a small Emily laying on his chest – sometimes they would fall sound asleep and I would cover them with a blanket.

As Emily grew, so did Drew's seemingly limitless energy and passion for cartoons, colouring and story-telling. According to him, Emily's blond hair was like strands of golden wheat and her eyes were sapphires blessed with glints of diamonds. When Emily started kindergarten she was, according to his assessment of her classmates, the most beautiful and intelligent of them all. Now, at age seven, Emily was his weekend companion and enthusiastic, co-conspirator in the planning for our upcoming holiday. The Florida Keys and Disney World were, of course, on the secretly planned agenda.

Drew dubbed Emily the "Official Keeper of Secrets" and "Planning Coordinator". She would bubble with unrestrained excitement when I'd ask, "So what have you two planned? What's so special about this trip?"

Face solemn, eyes twinkling, she would answer, "You'll just have to wait, Mommy. It'll be so special!"

She would wait until Drew came home or, if he was home, rush to tell him that Mommy was trying to find out about the holiday again. It was a game that delighted her and her small chest would puff up with pride that she was a good "Keeper of Secrets".

Drew would enthusiastically compliment her resolve and reaffirm that she was doing a good job of not giving up the surprise. Basking in his praise, Emily would demand, "Tell me again, daddy, what it will be like when I grow up."

Drew would smile, wink, and assume a sombre expression as he replied, "One day, Emily, when you are a partner in my firm, clients will tell you things that you will have to keep to yourself."

"That's called lawyer-client privilege," she would interject seriously and he would nod back just as seriously.

"I'm not going to tell her, Daddy. Truly, I won't!"

In my dream, I can hear Emily's musical giggle escaping as she exclaims, "But wait until she sees what we've done!"

༄

Here, I stop. I need to think about what to say next. How to share what I'm feeling?

"Go on," says Becky. "I'm listening."

I draw a deep breath and plunge onwards; telling Becky my dream as I replay it in my mind.

༄

The Search for Claire Holowitz

  I'm in the kitchen putting the final touches on a salad when I hear her. Playing along with the game, I call out, "Did I hear my name being mentioned?"
  The silence that follows my question erupts with a giggle of laughter from Emily. Drew comes into the kitchen to get the steaks for the barbecue, Emily follows closely behind. Drew winks at Emily and says proudly, "We know how to keep secrets." His lips brush my cheek, his hand slips around my waist and lingers for a moment before he leans around me to pick up the steaks. He and Emily, two co-conspirators, head outside to grill the steaks, whispering about their vacation plans. I call out, "Sooner or later, you'll have to tell me. We're leaving tomorrow, after all."
  Forehead pressed against the patio screen, she says, "You'll just have to wait, Mommy. It's the best surprise and I'm a good keeper of secrets."
  Drew calls out, "Just like her old man."
  I'm not sure which one is the bigger child but I play along with their game of keeping me in the dark. Throughout supper and for the rest of the evening I repeatedly ask Emily for clues but she remains steadfast in her role as 'keeper of the secrets'.
  After we put Emily to bed, I check one last time to ensure that everything we'll need is packed. Drew lines up our tickets and passports. We divvy up the American money and traveller's cheques. Our clothes are set out for the morning and I check in on Emily. She's sound asleep and I smile as I think about her excitement. Climbing into bed, I let my body ease into the stage of easy breathing that comes before sleep. Drew moves his arm around my waist eases his fingers over my shoulder and strokes the nape of my neck. No longer tired, I welcome the warmth of his breath on my flesh.
  I start to speak but he says, "Shh," and kisses my temple, easing his one arm underneath my body and works his hand up to cup my right breast. Almost immediately, my nipples surrender. Wantonly I arch my body, aching for his touch, craving his love. I turn to reach for him, but he holds me there keeping me captive to the endless sensations pulsating through me. He plays with me as if I'm a doll to caress at his will.
  A willing partner, I give in to the movements of his hands, the command of his mouth on mine – gentle, passionate and demanding. He eases me into a climax, holding me with the palm of his hand; my moisture betraying me and letting him know that I'm completely at his mercy. Just when I think that I can take no more, he rolls over onto his back, pulling me close and taking me with him. I straddle his hips and lowering my head I lick his nipples, the scar on his left upper shoulder

from a childhood hockey incident, and caress his abdomen with my fingertips. As he enters me, I feel his need surpass mine. I draw him into me – demanding fulfilment – and being so damned grateful that it is me whom he loves.

We had been too long apart. The recent demands of our careers and schedules had sidetracked us from being able to connect in the way we each needed. It had been simple sex, but for some strange reason, pure magic – beyond anything I had ever experienced and that which within 24 hours, would never again know.

೧൦

I stop. "Enough said for now," I say, feeling the heat of embarrassment at having been so descriptive. I reach for my water glass. "Thank you for listening, but let's just leave that there – between us."

೧൦

Becky

When Anna-Claire takes a break to drink some water, I ask, "Are all your dreams so vivid?"

She smiles and with a shrug, answers, "In Technicolor too."

"Listening to you recall your dream is like listening to one of those recorded stories you play on a road trip or download to an I-pod. It's easy to see why you're a writer."

"Really?" Anna-Claire raises an eyebrow. "How so?"

"Dreams are just another way for imagination to create," I explain. "You describe your dreams like you write. The listener ..." I tap my chest, "in this case, me, gets the feeling of actually being there, with you in that dream, seeing and hearing everything as it happens."

Anna-Claire laughs softly. "You asked me to tell you about my dream ... are you sure you want me to continue?" Timidly, her vulnerability naked, she says, "You may have noticed that I'm leaving nothing out."

"I noticed," I smile back. I lean forward, prop my elbows on my knees, rest my chin in my hands, and tease, "dreaming about sex is also a good thing." Anna-Claire leans back in her chair and belly laughs. I've not seen her do that for a long time and I feel good about it.

Grinning, she says, "You must hear a lot of stories from your patients. Mine must seem pretty tame."

"Oh, I hear a lot of stories," I admit, truthfully, "but hearing your story; the way you tell it, is special."

"Special?" Her expression becomes serious. "You're good for me, Becky. You truly are. But my dreams ..." she looks down at her hands, "I'm not sure I could tell them to the others."

I nod that I understand. She trusts me to listen as a friend but guard her privacy as a doctor. "No problems, Anna-Claire," I say, reaching out to hold her hand for a moment, "what you tell me stays with me."

She takes in a breath and exhales softly. "So," she says, "where was I? Ah, now I remember ..."

༶

The trip to Disney World and the Florida Keys had been Drew's idea. "We need to get away and just be a family. Emile can manage the office and your editors can simply wait." He was right. We were comfortable and secure in our marriage, but becoming complacent, not because we lacked love but, because of our busy careers, our sexual meters and needs for one another were often out of sync.

Drew's rationale for Disney World had been flawless. "It's time Emily meets Mickey Mouse and experiences the Epcot Center," he declared. "Every child should know the magic of Disney." To seal his point he added, "Emily needs some mommy and daddy time."

I teased him. "You're using your daughter as an excuse to visit Disney World."

Not disagreeing, he laughed, saying, "Think what you want, but Emily and I will have planned a great vacation."

Breakfast that morning was fast and simple consisting of coffee, buttered toast and strawberry yogurt. Drew walked into the kitchen and before saying a word, reached for the steaming cup of coffee waiting for him. He looked at me and laughed as my cheeks flushed with the memory of the night we'd shared. I walked over to him and kissed his neck, whispering, "I love you, Drew. I truly do."

"Me too, right back at you," he had said. "So what's up today?"

"I have that interview with Source Magazine," I answered. "You?"

"I have to check out the Linderman file and review some details with Emile in preparation for the labour mediation process starting next week. I'll pick

Emily up from school at noon and then, we'll come home to get our suitcases, have a quick bite to eat and head off to the airport." After all," he grinned devilishly, "we have to be at the airport for our five o'clock flight and she's going to be busting to get there in time."

As if on cue, Emily bounced into the kitchen. Drew made her toast and I poured milk over her cereal. In between mouthfuls she kept reminding me, "Don't forget, we're leaving this afternoon. You can't be late, Mommy. Please hurry up with your interview. You simply have to be ready to go."

Exclaiming with mock incredulity, I replied, "Forget, darling? How could I with all this secrecy and conspiracy you two have going on? Just when are the two of you planning on letting me know what I'm doing on my holidays?"

That earned me an excited giggle and winking at Drew, she answered, "Soon, mommy, very soon."

Drew put his coffee cup in the dish washer, tapped the face of his wristwatch, and pointedly reminded me – largely to fuel Emily's excitement – "Try to wrap up the interview with Source Magazine by one. We need to be at the airport at least two hours in advance. Emily and I want all of us there early and not tempt fate with afternoon traffic."

"I don't expect that to be a problem. Arnie's told them that I'm on a tight schedule. Worst case scenario," I added, "you two can go on ahead and I'll grab a taxi." Placing Emily's empty cereal bowl in the dishwasher and taking time to pour another cup of coffee, I apologized to both Drew and Emily. "I'm really sorry that Emile and Arnie scheduled this interview, but with the legalities associated with the publication and release of "Gala Girls," I had no choice but to agree."

"Don't worry," answered Drew, winking at Emily reassuringly. "Arnie assured me that he personally will see to it that you're on the flight with Emily and me."

"That's right, Daddy," Emily piped up, all serious and speaking in a firm tone. "We have a schedule to follow, Mommy, and first on the list is getting you away from the press". Her chin moved forcefully up and down, as if she was making a profound statement. Unable to contain our amusement, Drew and I burst out in laughter. It was a good moment. One that I often replay in my mind.

Drew finished his business earlier than expected that morning and came home shortly before I had to leave for the interview scheduled to take place at Arnie's office. We had time for a quick coffee before Drew had to leave to pick up Emily. I remember asking, "Did you get out to Walkers' Range?" It was *just the simple sort of conversation spouses have. Sometimes I wonder if either of us had known that it would be one of our last moments together, what we would have talked about and then, I realize that's why we don't see into our futures.*

Pride evident, he replied, "It's right on schedule. Weather conditions going right," he crossed two fingers, "we'll meet all deadlines."

I remember asking, "Do you ever regret leaving the day-to-day management of the sites to other people?"

"No, not really," he answered. "The law has been good to me and to us. Merging the two interests has been challenging at times; but it's not unusual to merge two careers into one. Look at you? You're an established writer and photographer."

Then, and still now, I thought he had done more with his careers than I had with mine. I was just beginning to become known.

"A lot of the business Emile and I pick up comes from the construction industry and the contracts associated with them," said Drew, almost as if he knew I felt that my career was insignificant in light of his success. "Your success comes only from you ..." He held my hand and repeated, "Someday you're going to look back on these days and laugh at the doubts you had."

Drew's father had owned a construction firm and from the time he could safely work at a site, Drew had accompanied his father on weekends and summers. His favourite jobs had been the ones involving carpentry and he never lost his love for working with wood. When his father died, Drew inherited the firm. By then he and Emile were building their legal practice. So, instead of working at the sites full time, he hired a manager and Drew oversaw the legal end of things. That had led to him meeting other construction and trades people and they, in turn, had sent their legal business to Drew and Emile.

"I still like to visit a construction site or have a wood project on the go," continued Drew, thoughtfully. "It's become more of a hobby than a honed skill. When I'm working on a site or building something, I can see the results almost immediately. There's a certain satisfaction in that. The older I get, the more I understand why my father loved working with his hands so much." Helping himself to a ham sandwich I'd prepared for lunch, he asked, "Why all the questions today?"

"Don't know," I answered, truthfully. I remember a slight chill on my neck and a sense of something I've never been able to put words to ... at best, I think of it as some sort of warning but it was faint and I shrugged it off. Maybe if I hadn't; maybe if I had paid attention to what my mother called intuition, I would have done all that I could to stop he and Emily from leaving for the

airport. I remember my answer. I said, "It's just that I get so involved in my writing and various projects. Sometimes, I wonder if you're happy too."

"I'm happy Claire." At that moment, I knew I'd never again know a love like the one I shared with Drew.

As he got ready to leave, Drew asked, "What does Arnie think about the Hollywood lead?"

"About the same as Emile," I answered. "Apparently it's going to happen."

He spun me around in circle. "That'll be your second book that has made it from the written page to the silver screen".

"Who would have thought it," I'd answered, thrilled that my news pleased him. I had wanted to tell him when we were in Florida but the moment seemed right to tell him then. I've always been grateful that I didn't wait. He never would have known and had I not seen his pleasure and pride in my beginning success, I doubt if I would have continued to write.

Every novel, every play, every photo, I've taken since then has been with the memory of telling Drew about it.

I remember excusing myself from the interview to make a quick call to Emily before she and Drew left for the airport. I smiled as I listened to her warning, "Don't be late, Mommy. We've got such a special surprise vacation for you. Promise me, you'll be at the airport."

I promised her with all my heart that I would be there.

"It's okay, Mommy," said Emily. "Daddy explained it all to me on the way home from school. You have to do this interview because they're going to make a movie out of your book." I remember thinking how old she sounded; so much older than her seven years.

"I'll take a taxi just as soon as I'm done with this interview. Here's a secret you can tell," I whispered into the telephone.

"What is it?"

"I love you and daddy very, very much!"

"Oh Mommy," Emily sighed with exasperation, "everybody knows that!"

"Everybody knows what?" asked Drew, hovering in the background.

"That mommy loves us," answered Emily. "She thought she was telling me a secret."

"Ahh," Drew said, "so the secret's out. What will we do now?"

"Just don't be late, Mommy," repeated Emily. And, those were the last words I ever heard my baby girl speak. "Just don't be late, Mommy."

Becky

Anna-Claire stops abruptly. She wipes a tear from the corner of her eye and clears her throat. The colour has drained from her cheeks and I can tell that this has taken a lot out of her.

She's interspersed her dream with editorial comments about how she felt and still does. At points I wanted to ask her to stop but I didn't, knowing that I would interrupt a flow that has been waiting years to be released.

We've passed an entire afternoon and I'm startled to realize that moonlight is filtering through the window. I get up to draw the blinds. "How about a bowl of soup? We've been so busy talking that time has just slipped by. Don't know about you, but I'm hungry."

"Yes," answers Anna-Claire, slowly lifting herself off the chair. I know better than to offer assistance. "I have some excellent smoked gouda that will go well with crackers. There are some cold cuts to make a sandwich to have with the soup."

"Soup and some gouda will be fine," I assure her, heading to the kitchen.

"What are your plans for the rest of the evening?" she asks.

"I thought I'd drop over to see Amy. She'll have seen my car in your driveway and will want to know how you're doing."

"Strange that she didn't call," says Anna-Claire, taking out a pot to warm the soup.

"Not really. We've all agreed that each of us is entitled to some alone time with you." I give her shoulder an affectionate squeeze. "We're being a bit selfish about that." I grin and admit, "I guess we're like a bunch of grown-up kids clamouring for their mom's attention."

My analogy amuses Anna-Claire. "Well," she says with a sly smile, "I like my grown-up kids and I'll look forward to Mother's Day this year."

Her humour and acceptance of each of us in her life touches me. There's great truth in the fact that she has become a part of our lives.

"Don't worry, Becky," she says, setting the soup bowls on the table. "I'll be fine. We'll all be fine. This illness won't … it can't ever change what we are to each other."

There is so much wisdom to what she says. A lump forms in my throat as I remind myself that she is on borrowed time. Then, I realize there was purpose to her opening up the way she did with me this afternoon. Yes, the dream reveals her past but she didn't have to share that with me. It was her way of telling me that she wants all of us to live each day as if we won't have another to share; so that when she does leave ... we will live on, knowing that she knew she was loved and that she knew we loved her.

After finishing our meal, I say goodnight to Anna-Claire and hugging her tightly, I whisper, "Thank you."

"For what?" she asks.

"For this afternoon. For sharing your dream and memories."

Cupping my cheek with her hand, she answers, "No thank you is needed. Now," she winks, "I need to sleep. After all, there are dreams to be recalled so that I can share them with you ... my friend who *happens to be* a psychiatrist, who listens as a friend, and whom I love as a daughter."

I walk over to Amy's feeling drained emotionally. It had been a lot to absorb and yet, I'm not tired. Instead, I'm looking forward to hearing more about Anna-Claire's dreams – to spending time with this woman who has touched my life.

෴

Anna-Claire

It had all been so real! Even as I told Becky about the dreams – it was as if I could see and hear Drew and Emily. The peace I'd felt earlier with Becky eludes me now. My mind is spiralling into another dream but this one is a nightmare. Try as I might to avoid it, sleep draws me deep into my subconscious and once again, I'm trapped in the day that changed my life.

෴

At one thirty I'm interrupted by Arnie's office assistant. Visibly agitated, Cecile says, "Claire I am sorry to interrupt, but there are some reporters in the outer office and ..."

I interrupt her mid-sentence and turning sideways, ask Arnie, "What's this about? I have to leave by two to get to the airport and delays won't stop me." We stare at Cecile with some confusion. She's known for her unshakeable approach to anything. Arnie often jokes that an earthquake wouldn't dare come anywhere near Cecile without first having received permission.

"What is it Cecile?" asks Arnie, a touch impatiently, "We asked not to be disturbed."

"I realize that but..." she gulps a deep breath and blurts, "there are two policemen waiting." She blinks nervously. "They insist on speaking with Claire."

Joan, the interviewer from the magazine and Max, the photographer, immediately are curious as to the commotion in the outer office and sniffing a story, rise to go out and see what is going on. Arnie signals for them to stay put.

"The whole purpose of having the interview at your office was that it's closer to the airport," I say, moving to the door.

"I don't know what this is about anymore than you," says Arnie, following closely on my heels. The second we step into the outer office a flash goes off. Holding his hand to shield his eyes, Arnie growls, "Stop that!" His outburst startles everyone, but he angrily repeats his order, "Stop that now!"

I dimly register that behind the officers are reporters and two camera men. Joan and Max having ignored Arnie's order for them to stay put, crowd behind in the doorway, anxious to see what is going on.

The taller of the two policemen asks if we can speak in private. At that moment, I know something very bad is happening. A chill snakes through me. Apprehensive, I stare at them. Nodding curt assent, Arnie ushers the officers into his office and signals for Joan and Max to leave. I try to catch Cecile's eyes for a hint, but she casts her eyes downwards as I pass through the doorway muttering, "I'm so sorry."

Cecile positions herself in front of the doorway like a human shield, pleading with the reporters as she resolutely shuts the door, "Leave her alone. Just leave her alone!"

I hear one of the reporters shouting, "What the hell is this? Move lady. This is a story."

I stare at Arnie and the sombre faces of the police officers. I freeze, sealing their expressions in time; knowing without having to be told why they are here. The voices behind the door fade and my world starts to spin. Arnie grabs my elbow. He's telling me something but I don't hear his words. The policeman is speaking but all I register is that his mouth is moving. I hear sounds and voices but it is as if they are coming from some distant place and then, I hear a low, escalating scream and one drawn out wail of "Noooooooooooooo".

Then, as suddenly as it had originated, the sound is followed by thundering silence.

༄

As I sit in the hospital's waiting room for the doctors to finish examining Drew, I ask Arnie to tell me again what happened. "Are you sure you want me to do this?" he asks.

Numbly, I answer, "Yes." I've heard the words, know the explanation but hearing is not accepting. I'm not ready to accept this. I can't accept this. My life is crashing down and I'm desperately clinging to anything that helps me understand this horror. He holds my hand and once again, recaps the pandemonium that followed my scream.

"Cecile dealt with the reporters," he says. Apologetically, he murmurs, "They already knew Claire. That's why they were there. You know how they listen to police scanners." He curses, "Damn them. They could have waited."

"Waited?" I find this curious. 'Waited for what' I think. 'There's never a good time for this sort of news but they're in the business of news. That's what reporters do. They go after the story.'

"What did she say?" I ask, hating to listen to this but knowing that I need to. I'm going to have to deal with them – one way or another. It's better that I know now what was said than to be sandbagged later with a question that I know I won't want to answer. At this moment I hate every reporter ever born or to be born. I resent their intrusion into my life.

Arnie's brief. "Cecile told them there had been an accident." He pauses. I stare at him, daring him to say the words he has already said and knowing that each time he does, part of me dies again. Gently, patiently, he says, "She told them that Emily had died and that Drew is in critical condition."

Again he curses but I just sit there, numb and morbidly needing him to fill in the gaps for me. I feel as if I've been swept into a very bad nightmare. Everything seems surreal. I'm me but I'm not me. I am detached and distanced from myself. Someone in the person of my body is sitting in this hospital waiting room – that is who is grieving for my precious Emily. It can't be me. It just can't! I cover my ears as my mind replays her smile and I hear her pleading with me, "Please don't be late, Mommy."

I can hear Emily's excited giggle on the phone and hear myself promising not to be late. Tears flow down my cheeks and I start to shake. My world is crashing and I'm frantically grasping at straws. I don't care that I look like *a wild woman. My nose is dripping, my eyes are red, my hair is mussed, and I'm rocking like a pendulum, keeping rhythm with the march of death. Arnie hands me a Kleenex. I wipe my nose and with tears streaming, I hear my voice say, "Tell me what happened."*

Arnie looks straight at me. I can see the redness in his eyes. He's crying too. "Claire, please," he begs, "this is not doing you any good. You're torturing yourself."

A flicker of my old self – the one who existed before the police arrived – surfaces. I touch his hand and say, "I need to know Arnie. Tell me, again."

He takes a deep, laboured breath. "After you screamed, the reporters burst past Cecile into my office but the police officers quickly halted any movement or conversation. I grabbed your coat and bustled you to the elevator. God, Claire," he says, voice faltering, "I was so scared for you. You were so pale but so determined. I've never seen you so fragile and yet so strong. As soon as we were on the ground floor the policemen put you in a waiting cruiser. They got us here as fast as they could."

"I remember," I say, as the memory slips out of the fog of my brain and becomes sharp. "An officer met us at the entrance of the Civic Hospital. There were reporters and cameras."

My heart pounds. I feel anger. I feel grief. But I can't give in to either emotion now. Drew needs me. I need Drew. I have to be strong. I ask, "How could this happen? We were leaving for a vacation. Emily," I gulp for air, "My beautiful baby girl. She was so excited."

I feel Arnie's embrace and hear him whispering, "I'm here Claire. Hang on to me. I'm here. Cry it out, and, then, go do what you have to do."

A nurse appears at the doorway and tells me that I can go in to see Drew. Nodding that I understand, I release myself from Arnie's protective arms. Using the sleeve of my coat to wipe my eyes, I feel my chest constricting. I greedily suck air into my lungs as I follow the nurse into the room where Drew lies; head bandaged, eyes shut – attached to machines and tubes that keep him breathing. The whiteness of the blanket reminds me of a shroud and I involuntarily gasp. I stand by his bedside; resenting the ominous bleep bleep of the heart monitor and yet, clinging to the sound because that sound means that he is alive. I hold his free hand, glancing at the intravenous tubing taped to the other. Someone pushes over a chair and tells me to sit down. My eyes never leave Drew's face.

"Oh Drew," I whisper to his silent body. "Emily … my God … my baby is gone. Our baby. Our beautiful Emily."

All I know is that I need Drew and I'm hoping against hope that he can somehow hear me and know I'm here. There is a hole so large in me that I'm consumed with grief and the pain that it causes is horrible. I never knew such gut wrenching pain. I cup his chin in my hand, letting my fingers gently rub the stubble that is starting to show. I wonder how many times I have caressed his face and now, as I do so, I'm terrified that he'll leave me too. "Please, Drew," I beg, "Please. I'm so lost. You have to fight Drew. Please, fight. I need you. I love you. I can't lose you too."

Nurses come and go. Time passes and I don't care. With stoic silence I wait. I listen to the neurosurgeon. I listen to the internist who talks about massive haemorrhages and a ruptured spleen. I nod when they ask if I understand. Not once do I move from my vigilant guard. When the machine starts to bleep erratically, sending its shrill warning, someone pulls me away from my perch on the metal chair and, in that God-awful moment, I know that it is over. God has turned his back on me and refused to hear my pleas. There will be no miracle. Agonizing pain seers my soul as tentacles of grief spread throughout every fibre of my being.

Arnie holds me as doctors and nurses lean over Drew's body. He gently pulls my head to his shoulder as they turn off the respirator. The bleep bleep is gone and in its place follows a cruel and desperate silence. Someone tells me that I can have some time with Drew. 'Time,' I think, 'has stopped.' The irony of the wording does not escape me. I sit by his bedside, cover his hand with mind, whisper my thoughts – my final good-byes. I feel Arnie's hand on my shoulder, the slight squeeze telling me it's time to go. I kiss Drew's lips. A child's fairy tale comes to mind, piercing through the numb fog that has settled – clouding all that is real and not real – and with sadness so profound that I can feel the burden of its weight, I realize that my kiss will not wake Drew. Complacent as a small child, I let Arnie lead me by the hand to the doorway. I turn and watch as a nurse pulls the white blanket up over Drew's head.

Cold numbness ebbs throughout me. "Shrouds," I think, "shrouds." My body shakes from within but I say nothing. I don't have the words to express the utter loss and abandonment that grips my soul and locks my mind. My world, as I knew it, has been viciously wrenched from me. The pain is unbearable.

The doctor offers to write a prescription. Arnie nods but I don't answer. I don't care for something to help me sleep. 'Sleep,' I think. 'How can you think I want to sleep?' And then, I think, 'Yes, sleep. I can sleep with Drew and Emily.' But just as the thought takes shape in my mind and I'm reaching for the prescription like an addict for her next fix, I can feel a presence and in my mind and whether it is imagination or not, I hear Drew telling me to walk away, to not do this thing. It would be so easy to take the pills and to sleep like Drew and Emily. I lower my hand and shake my head no.

I murmur, "Thank you Doctor. I know you tried." I walk away.

We take the same elevator that we took only a few hours ago. Reaching the lobby, head bowed and tasting the salty residue of tears on my tongue, I make my way to the main doors. A flash blinds me. Startled, I cover my face. Arnie shouts, "Put that down! Leave her be!"

Reporters. Surrounding me like a pack of wolves. Hospital security personnel appear seemingly out of nowhere, arms outstretched. They force the reporters to stand aside. One of the guards, thinking he can help matters, shouts officiously, "Let Ms Holowitz through!" People in the lobby, who only moments ago had been idly watching the drama unfold, now point and murmur my name. Like a scared cat hanging onto a tree branch, I cling to Arnie's arm as he steers me outside. The reporters follow, surrounding me on the steps.

My anger pops. My sudden halt jars Arnie. Cold resolve floods through my body. I glare at the now silenced reporters. It is as if my body has become a pillar of stone – hard, forbidding and formidable. A police officer steps out of a waiting cruiser to escort me away, but stops mid-stride when Arnie signals him to wait. I take in every moment that is happening. Every stare, every gasp, every breath. The night air has a decided chill. I stand stock still. I welcome the cold. It numbs me. I lick my lips, pursing them slightly. Tears fall in silent streams riveting down my cheeks, trickling onto my neck and chest.

Arnie coaxes, "Please Claire, come."

"No," I answer. "They want their damn interview; I will give it to them."

"Claire please ..." Arnie reaches to touch my elbow but I move away from his grasp.

"I will answer your questions," I say, deriving perverse satisfaction that the reporters have to strain to hear me. "Only today. Never again."

One reporter calls out, "What do you mean, never again?"

"I mean never again." My words crack like a whip slicing into the night air. "Now ask your questions."

The momentary silence that follows my edict is striking. A reporter breaks the silence. "Is it true that your husband and daughter were in an accident?"

I nod.

Another reporter, shocked at the insensitivity of the question, utters, "You know it is, Asshole. That's why you're here!" Looking at me, he has the decency to say, "I'm sorry Ms Holowitz for your loss."

For several seconds I stand there looking at the man. He may have said that he's sorry for my loss but he's here for the story – my grief, my loss, means nothing to him. He has merely said what he thinks is expected – they are rote words, void of empathy. He is the first to break our connection.

"Thank you," *I answer. There is no point in saying anything more.*

Cameras flash. Microphones are held high to record my statements. Trance-like, I answer their questions keeping my responses short.

Arnie whispers, "It's okay, Claire. You can leave now. You've given them what they want. Let's go home."

But, I don't move. I have one more thing left to do. Something I must do. Then, I will be finished.

"I will tell you this and then, I ask to be left alone. Today, my husband and my daughter died. Today, I was not with them because I had gone to give an interview." *I gulp for air and continue,* "I should have been with them; not talking to reporters."

Arnie steadies my trembling shoulder with his hand. "Ms Holowitz is done here," *he announces brusquely.*

Just as I'm leaning into the cruiser, a reporter calls my name. Instinctively I turn. Flashes go off. I squint and speak so softly that only those close to the cruiser can hear. "This is the last public interview I will ever give. I am done."

❦

It's mid-morning by the time that I wake up. I'm glad to see the sunlight. The years have not changed the pain of losing Drew and Emily – I have simply learned to deal with it. Or, so I thought. But, lately, talking with Becky about the dreams, I've come to realize that what I learned was how to hide my pain; to give the pretence of having picked up on my life and moving forward. I also am coming to terms with my dual identity. Yes, I withdrew because of misplaced anger and guilt. I lashed out at the media for having been the reason that I wasn't with Drew and Emily.

I didn't want to be their story and I refused to have them come anywhere near my memories of Drew and Emily. Living as Anna Wright removed me from publicity and as the years passed, it became easier to be Anna Wright.

In the first five years after Drew and Emily died, I moved eight times because I'd been recognized in a store, on the street, at a market. Ironically, my seclusion became the media hype that I had not wanted. The more reclusive I became, the more in demand were my novels and plays.

Emile and Arnie did a spectacular job of representing me at book launches and fund raisers. They hired people to do readings when required and acted as conduits for messages between myself and directors for my plays and eventually, for art gallery managers. We had a system and it worked well. Claire Holowitz was a ghost as far as the media was concerned and the phenomenon of searching for Claire Holowitz became part of the mystery and the lure of anything I did.

But, as Anna Wright, I could be among people. I changed my hair style, altered my taste in clothes, and lost twenty pounds that I didn't need to lose with the result that I was very thin and not at all like the Claire Holowitz people remembered. I moved to a suburb and lived a quiet life as a widow – that part was true. People accepted me as a kindly, perhaps slightly eccentric retiree who busied herself with gardening and who was pleasant to talk with.

As my fame grew, there was a need to maintain an apartment in New York so that I could be near Jacob Symthington, the editor for my publisher. Having an apartment in New York made it easy for me to work closely with him when deadlines were due for one of my plays or novels. Jacob became part of the conspiracy to shield Claire Holowitz from the media. He, Emile, and Arnie eventually convinced me to meet a select few directors and again, our circle conspiracy grew.

In all those years, not one person betrayed my confidence.

My secret was safe.

I went to see my plays performed on stage without anyone realizing that I was among the audience. I had been successful in my dual identity.

As my success grew, I increased my donations and patronage to the Arts. Again, any presentation was done by Emile, Arnie, or Jacob. The media loved the ghost of Claire Holowitz and that love continued to spur public interest in what I wrote and the photos I took. I had never once regretted my dual identity. That is, until I met Leen and her friends.

At first, I was suspicious of Leen's search for me and cautious about what I said around her and her friends. When she pulled up old photos of me from media archives, I worried that she'd see the resemblance.

But, I had become Anna Wright – the power of suggestion is a strong factor when it comes down to how people view you.

I had learned what movie stars learn – how to move among the very public that seeks you. Because you do not wear the make-up, hair styles, or clothes they associate with you, they do not recognize you. I had made friends over the years – some who knew me as Anna and a select few who knew me as Claire. But, with Leen, Amy, Becky and Sarah, I found something that had been missing in all those years.

With the exception of Marc Andre, I had never known what it was to once again feel the protective love of a parent. He kept that part of me alive after Emily died. With Leen and her friends, I grew into the role of surrogate mother without even realizing the transformation had taken place. My talks with Becky have helped me come to terms with this new part of my life. Now, with the days I have remaining, I want to do what is right by them.

Sluggish, I answer the phone.

"Hi Anna-Claire," says Amy. "I'm home early. What do you say to an early supper? I've done some editing on those chapters you read last week. I'd like to hear what you think about the revisions. That is, if you are up to it."

I rub my eyes, shake off the dull lethargic residue of sleep, and check my watch. I say, "I overslept. I spent yesterday with Becky. I guess I was more tired than I realized."

"If you'd prefer, I can just make us an early supper," says Amy.

"No," I answer quickly, "I want to read what you've written and supper sounds good."

"Good. I'm making my spaghetti. We'll review my writing for as long as you can stand it," she says, "and after supper we can watch a video if you feel up to it."

I listen as Amy rattles off the names of actors and films. "You choose the video," I say, feeling good about that. "I love all the actors you're mentioning."

"Okay," says Amy. "Here's the plan. I'll pick you up in an hour and we can go together to the video store and select a movie before we do any work. That way, we'll have it ready for whenever we want to watch it."

I find the thought of watching a video appealing. All the girls are good about including me in activities that don't highlight my need to rest but which do give it consideration.

"Sounds wonderful," I reply. "I have the fixings for salad and cheese bread. Would you like some?"

"I can make that," offers Amy.

"No," I reply, "I'd like to bring something."

After my shower, I spend a quiet half hour sifting through editing notes for a play that I am writing entitled 'Ladies Night'. It is going to be a surprise for Leen, Amy, Becky and Sarah. I want to re-create for the stage some of the laughter and shared moments of our friendship. I need to let them know that they have touched my life. Writing gives me the means to leave something of me – of us – when this disease finally is done with me.

When Amy arrives, we prepare the salad and cheese bread together. When I apologize for not having done it sooner she brushes it off saying, "We have all day, Anna-Claire. Today, we are not run by the clock. Today, we do things as they happen." I'd like to tell her about 'Ladies Night' and for her to know that I've started to write again but that would ruin the surprise. I just hope that my strength will hold up long enough for me to complete the play and to see it performed. I like to imagine the excitement they'll have when they find out I've written a play for them and more importantly, because of them.

Entering Amy's house, after our trip to the video store where I selected a movie featuring one of my favourite actresses, I stop midsentence as the pungent aroma of fried garlic, onions, tomato sauce and sautéed meat waif to my nose. "Oh my God," I say, "that smells delicious."

Placing the garlic bread and salad on the counter Amy lifts the pot lid, sniffs, and answers, "For me, it's comfort food." She adds sweet basil to the sauce. "But I have to be careful not to eat too much of it. As much as I like pasta, pasta likes my hips."

Laughing, I reply. "Weight's not an issue with you, Amy. In fact, it wouldn't hurt to add some meat to your bones." Looking at her slender frame, I ask, "Are you losing weight?"

"I've just been exercising more and it seems to have toned up some loose flab."

"Flab ..." I roll my eyes, "is not a word I'd use to describe your physique."

"Well, thank you," answers Amy, draining the water from the pasta. "What's new and interesting in your life? Grab some plates from the cupboard, will you?"

"I thought we were going to work on your edits," I reply, wishing that I could tell her about my new play.

"We will," answers Amy, "but let's eat and talk first."

I smile at her thoughtfulness. She knows that I'm frequently plagued by nausea, a side-effect of the drugs. To be honest, the smells coming from her kitchen tease my taste buds and it is kind of her to want me to eat when I can as opposed to following a timetable.

"Sounds like a plan," I answer, setting the table.

As we eat my resolve breaks down and I decide to tell Amy that I've begun to sketch out notes for a new play. My logic for this admission is simple: I want her to know that I'm not just lolling around during the day – that I have found a purpose to keep me occupied and distracted from my illness. Besides, it pleases me to know that what I'm writing will be a gift to Amy and the others.

"Any hints?" she asks, reaching for the Parmesan cheese.

"Not yet," I smile in response, "it's a work in progress. It's my practice not to reveal my writing until I am completely comfortable with the characters and setting." Looking at Amy, I rush to add, "I make my notes; play with them in my mind, and then rough the story out. I follow the advice I gave you when you first showed me your drafts – take time to mull over the ideas, let them take shape in my mind, and let the characters become real."

Amy twirls spaghetti onto a fork. "In fact..." she says, holding her fork in mid-air, "I wanted to talk to you about that."

I take a mouthful of salad. "Talk about what?"

"Well," she hesitates before continuing, "I know that I'm not a writer like you."

Resting my fork across my plate, I answer cautiously, "I thought we were going to get past the Claire Holowitz thing?"

"Oh, I'm good with that part of you," answers Amy cheerfully, putting my fears to rest. "It's just that you've made a career of writing but it's all so new to me. I never realized when I set out to write a novel how very hard the process is. And, you were right when you told me that I needed to learn how to make my characters real." She smiles. "At the time I couldn't fathom how you and other writers do that. Intellectually, as a professor of literature I know how to assess writing but to write, I had to re-learn and tap into the imagination I had as a child. It was a completely foreign concept to me and yet, working with you has taught me how to play games in my mind." She laughs. "It will be very interesting next semester when I introduce my students to this idea. No doubt, I will be the target of some criticism for not following the rigid standards of pure academics."

"Not to worry. We will devise a rationale that will satisfy the need for academic credibility but also permit you to, as you so aptly stated, 'Teach students to use their imaginations as opposed to merely reciting what others have written.' Too often, academics stifle the potential of students by their rigid adherence to imposed guidelines. Just think," I say, wanting to make my point, "of what our world would be like without electricity or cars. Edison and Ford had to use their imaginations in order to go beyond the boundaries of what people knew. Imagine a world without books, movies, theatre ... these things and more are products of what can happen when imagination becomes real."

"I'll be sure to point that out to the Dean when he questions the rationale and academic merit of my alterations to the syllabus," replies Amy. "The other day when I was editing, my characters seemed so real that I could hear their conversations in my mind and visualize them. It seems strange to have figments of imagination becoming so real that I actually view them as friends."

"You can't write unless your characters and settings are real to you," I answer, pleased that she has reached that point as an author. "Once you cross that bridge, you don't go back. That is what makes an author. Technique is important but bringing imagination to life through words and imagery is how an author pulls the story together so that the reader can visualize and believe what he is reading."

Amy takes our plates and places them in the dishwasher. Softly, she asks, "What next?"

I answer truthfully. "The next step will be to write, just write. When I first started out, I was given some advice which I've never forgotten. Regardless of whether your friends like or dislike your writing; write what you feel, hear and believe. The format, the appeal, and the selling power of what you've written comes after that. That advice has guided me through some touchy writer's block moments and times when Jacob, my editor, and I have argued about how a scene should play out. Bottom line," I say emphatically, "every author develops a unique style ... that's why there are so many different genres and stories. What you write is your baby, your creation. You must be happy with it before you share it with anyone else."

Over tea and dessert, I listen to Amy's revisions and I'm impressed with the progress she is making. Afterwards, she pours us each a snifter of brandy and moving to the living room, we settle down to enjoy the video. By the time I leave for home, I'm tired but happy.

Climbing into bed, I think, *It won't be long and she'll need to have an agent. I know how hard it was for me when I started out. Very few agents want to take a chance on a newcomer. It's much harder than when I started. Back then, I could send a hard copy to any agent. Now, agents are picky; many won't even bother to read a query.*

Pleased that I am in the position to help Amy, I decide on what I'm going to do. I know she'll work hard to make any revisions an agent may want and I'm confident that her writing can stand up to public scrutiny.

Everyone needs a break, I think, as I turn out the bedside light, *and I'm going to make sure that Amy has hers.*

Chapter Sixteen

Leen

I hurry past stalls filled with fresh vegetables and flowers, making a mental note to return to the vendors after lunch. The scent of grilled steak assails my nostrils as I push open the doors to The Keg. It takes a moment for my eyes to adjust to dim lighting as I scan the room. Amy's seated at a booth towards the bar and I make my way over.

Sliding a menu over for me to look at, Amy says, "I've ordered some water and coffee for both of us. When the waiter returns, we can order."

"Have you been here long?" I ask, laying my coat and purse down on the bench. "Sorry I'm late. I had to take a last minute phone call."

"About ten minutes. No problem, it gave me time to jot down a few notes of things I have to do this week."

The waiter appears with the coffee and water. Amy orders the Caesar salad, Chicago style rib eye and baked potato. I order the garden salad with blue cheese dressing, New York sirloin and baked potato. As is our practice when eating out we share side orders of schezwan beans, steamed asparagus, and portobello mushrooms.

The waiter returns with hot bread and butter. Helping myself to a slice, I murmur, "Mmm, this is so good!"

"It'll be treadmill time tonight with a vengeance," says Amy, buttering a slice of bread. "But for now I have every intention of enjoying this meal."

She sips her water. "You were going to visit with Anna-Claire the other day. How are things coming along for the Gala?"

I wait as the waiter puts down our salads before answering. "I was really pissed off that she hadn't told us about her identity, but as you know," I stop to take a bite of salad, "we've moved beyond that."

"I know what you mean," replies Amy. "My immediate reaction was one of anger, too. It was a shock to think that I actually had Claire Holowitz editing my writing."

"She never meant to hurt any of us. She just needed to know that we, especially me, the media queen, wouldn't hurt her."

"Becky refers to her whole dual identity thing as her survival," says Amy, pushing aside her salad plate to make room for the steaks the waiter has brought."

I eye my steak hungrily. "Ooh, that looks good!"

"Wow," teases Amy, "you're bordering on being predatory about that steak."

I smirk and pretend to plunge my steak knife into the meat.

"Okay," continues Amy, grinning as I make a production of savouring my steak, "now that you're satisfying your ravenous appetite, can we get back to the conversation about Anna-Claire. What have you learned about the real Claire Holowitz?"

I take a moment to think. So much has changed since I first started out searching for Claire. Not only my perspective on how to arrange the Gala but about the woman herself. The process of learning about both of her identities has, also, brought about changes in me. I answer truthfully, "I feel as if I am finding what Claire refers to as my soul. It's weird. I sit there listening to her stories and aspects of her life. I know that she talks to Becky about her dreams but that part of her life is shared between them. With me, she's revealing other aspects and helping me to put a real face ... a voice ... to the Gala. Listening, learning to understand her, has made me think about my own life."

I can see the scepticism in Amy's eyes but realize given my past history of making the media work for whatever project I had underway, she's right to question my claim that working with Anna-Claire has changed me. I try to make her understand. "I've come to appreciate what a leap of faith it was for Anna-Claire to take a chance on getting to know me ... us. She openly acknowledges the role that the media has played in her success as an author and photographer. She couldn't deal with them as Claire Holowitz. That woman had been hurt too much by their insensitive intrusion into her life when Drew and Emily died.

"No, I'm serious," I say to Amy, wanting her to understand what knowing Anna-Claire has done to me on a personal level. "I can't really describe what's happening. All I truly know is that the more I learn about her – the more I learn about myself." I shrug and speculate, "Talking with her is what I like to think it would have been like to talk with my mother, had she lived. Anna-Claire is sharing what it was like for her and what she did and felt when she was my age." I grimace. "I'll miss her."

"I know what you mean," answers Amy, softly. "She has that way about her – she would have been a great mother." She pauses. "Maybe she'll get better. Maybe she'll beat the odds?"

I let her thought settle between us before answering quietly, "Becky says that we have to be realistic and deal with it." Reaching for my water glass, I say, "One thing is for sure; Anna-Claire is a powerhouse of information."

"Has she said anything about attending the Gala or at least, making her identity known?"

"Not yet," I answer, "and, I'm not certain that I'd want her to give up her privacy. The more I go with it, the more I realize that I am changing my outlook on life and what's important."

Amy whistles softly. "That's quite an endorsement."

"I just know that Anna-Claire's story must be told," I say, no longer interested in my steak. Caught up in the moment I clarify, "Not the public Claire but the private Claire. The Anna-Claire we know. The one of indomitable spirit, laughter, and strength. I have no doubt that if there is a heaven, she'll find ways to script the angels into character roles." Not giving in to the swell of emotions I feel, I add with determination, "I would like the world to hear about Claire Holowitz, a.k.a. Anna Wright, the woman."

Amy scrunches her face. "A thought just occurred to me. This arrangement you have with her will help you achieve the Gala's objectives, but have you discussed with her what you just told me?"

"Sure, but she's not said yea or nay."

"Then, write your notes as you work with her," suggests Amy. "Keep the ideas and the memories alive."

I consider Amy's suggestion. "It's going to be difficult. I would have to describe how our lives have been transformed because of her."

"Just write it as it comes," advises Amy. "She likes to say that the characters fall into place as the ideas form but the story takes careful editing. Make it as accurate as you can. She has touched all of us, in different ways."

Amy continues gently, "Leen, she's dying. She wants to do it with dignity and grace. She's sharing with you and with all of us her memories. We've become her family. As such, we must be there for her in any way we can."

I wipe my mouth with a napkin. "We've all signed the confidentiality agreement."

"For now just write it," reiterates Amy with a force of conviction that reminds me how determined she can be when focused on a project.

"What's so funny?" asks Amy when I start to laugh softly.

"I was thinking about something she said recently," I reply. "You know what she's like peering over those reading glasses of hers when she's intent on something?" Amy nods.

"Well a few weeks ago I asked her to define the process of writing. I was expecting the normal sort of responses I've heard from various artists – it's part of responding to a muse; giving words to life events; a discipline; hard work etc. etc. ."

Interested, Amy asks, "What did she say?"

Doing my best to mimic Anna-Claire's voice, tone, and mannerism, I say, "It just comes when you least expect it."

In response to Amy's quizzical expression, I continue to play the role of Anna-Claire. "Descriptors and emotions come into play only after you have the basis for the story."

"Yeah, she's said much the same to me," comments Amy. "She's relentless in her editing techniques. She spares no time for niceties when she's editing." She laughs softly. "I'd love to turn her loose on my students. The other day she asked me how work was coming along and I said that I had to mark some third year student essays. She asked if she could see one. She read a few pages and then, all of a sudden, she whipped out her reading glasses and demanded a red pen. She settled herself down with a cup of tea, muttering as she read, 'No, no, you've got that wrong! Or adding: Now that's the ticket. You're thinking.' It was really funny to watch. She was totally engrossed."

I can easily visualize Anna-Claire reading student papers. "So what'd you do?"

"I did what any smart person would do," grins Amy. "I poured another cup of tea for both of us and for the next three hours we sat at the kitchen table grading papers and talking about the points students either made or missed. It was like being involved in a literary symposium." Her eyes light up with amusement. "It was fun."

The waiter asks if we would care for dessert. "No, just the bill," answers Amy.

While we wait for the bill, I continue our discussion. "There are times she brings me to tears and others when her stories are so comical, I just burst out laughing." Grumbling, I admit truthfully, "I don't know how to write like the novelists do. That's not my trade." Using my fingers to make quotation marks, I emphasize, "I'm used to creating 'hype' for the moment. Since meeting Anna-Claire I have begun to see people for who they are as opposed to whom they represent or what they do."

Signing the bill, Amy says, "She'd call that *characterization*. Don't be too hard on yourself, Leen. Your job necessitates that you deal with the image of people.

"True enough," I say, pulling on my coat. "But there's something to be said for the human element in media promotion."

Amy slides out of the booth. "She often tells me that characterization creates possibilities for changing the outcomes in a story."

As we walk towards the market area I start to chuckle.

"What's so funny?" asks Amy, tucking her chin into the collar of her coat against the bite of the wind.

"The other day she had me trying to visualize Don," I reply. "Her theory is that by being able to characterize him I can lower my angst when I have to deal with him."

"How so?" asks Amy.

Once again, mimicking Anna-Claire, I say, "Leen, Don annoys you and threatens your sense of self. Why? He gets up in the morning just like you do. He has the same basic needs as you do. He has to eat, sweat, sleep, and urinate. Put a *character* on him. Get into his head and his space."

Resuming my own voice, I say, "Her theory is that when I can do that, I won't have to second guess what his motives are. She insists that I'll know how to respond to his stupidity and greed and having figured that out, I'll be in control of any situation involving him."

Amy stops at a store front showcasing large red onions and peppers. We go inside and she selects two onions, pays the young Vietnamese girl, and we continue on our trek to the parking garage.

"Don has been a thorn in your side for a long time. Do you think it could be as easy as learning how to characterize him in order to stop his manipulative behaviours and reduce your toxic work environment?"

"At first I dismissed her suggestion outright but, after giving it some thought, I think I understand what she was trying to get me to realize. In essence, Anna-Claire is telling me to walk away from the destructive characters in my life. She's a great fan of the adage that 'everything is relative' and likes to joke that 'Einstein was not brilliant; he just knew how to characterize the world into relativity.' I never get tired of her saying it."

I spot a booth selling maple sugar cubes, syrup and butter. Amy waits as I choose a small, plastic jug of syrup and a tin of maple butter. I hand the vendor a twenty dollar bill and he returns the change with a grin revealing teeth permanently stained from years of tobacco smoke.

Entering the parking garage, I remark, "She came into my life at a moment when I was lost without even knowing it."

"Hmmm," murmurs Amy. "What will you do when Don demands to have Claire Holowitz present for the Gala?"

"I don't know."

Pushing the elevator button, Amy comments, "You'll have to make that decision soon. Time, as they say, is marching on." There's nothing I can really say to that.

I ask, "I'm on level four. Where are you parked?"

"Level two," answers Amy, with a sideways glance. "What will you do?"

As the elevator jerks into movement, I think about her question. Just before she steps out at her level, I answer, "I don't know what I'm going to do. But, for now, Don and everything else can wait.

The doors close before she can respond. As I make my way to my car, I wonder how I'm going to deal with Don and still make the Gala a success without revealing Claire Holowitz's whereabouts or identity.

Amy's right, time *is* marching on.

Chapter Seventeen

Leen

"Where did *'Dreamer On Ice* come from?' I ask, as Anna-Claire adds a generous dollop of whipped cream to each mug.

Anna-Claire avoids answering immediately by saying, "I really enjoy this café latte machine that Amy gave me." Smiling impishly, she adds, "Part of the secret to making a good latte lies with the amount of whipped cream added."

Peering over my mug's rim I observe how her cheeks have sunk into hollows. Her thin frame looks to be swallowed up by the grey cashmere wool sweater draped over a white turtleneck and despite the use of a belt, her black slacks hang loosely on her hips. In spite of these tell-tale signs that her illness is progressing, I know that she's having a good day. She's relaxed and willing to talk. Lately, these moments have been rare.

Deliberately, I repeat, *'Dreamer On Ice'*.

"Don't quit, do you?' replies Anna-Claire, wiping away a thin cream moustache from her upper lip.

"No," I reply. "Tenacity is necessary in my line of work."

She picks out an apple from the fruit bowl and begins the process of paring it. Accustomed to this particular idiosyncrasy, I am content to wait. It was Amy who first pointed out that Anna-Claire's ritual of paring an apple is her way of occupying her nervous energy and provides the opportunity to gather her thoughts.

Her task complete, Anna-Claire asks, "Want some apple?"

"Well, if you insist," I tease, taking a slice.

This morning her blue eyes are like dark sapphires; thoughtful, unreadable. Her eyes are one of her most identifying features. Every photo that I have seen of Anna-Claire: the public ones taken before Drew and Emily's death, and the private ones she has shared, draw attention to her eyes.

"I can see from your expression that I am going to get no rest unless I answer your question," says Anna-Claire. She smiles lightly and taps the side of her mug. "This is going to take some time. Before we're done, I expect we'll both want another cup."

"Do you want another latte or will regular do?"

"Use the Keurig," she answers. "I've had my quota of rich cream for now. How about we try that new Italian dark robust blend?"

I make the coffees and bring them to the table. A moment passes before she lifts her gaze to meet mine and then, she begins.

"Dreamer On Ice came from Maggie, my sister," says Anna-Claire. "Her real name was Margaret, but I always called her Maggie."

Up until now she's not talked either about her childhood or her sister in any detail. I want to ask a dozen questions that pop into my mind but I know that I can't push her. She has her own method of doing things.

I ask, "How so?"

"We were young and our parents were not all that well to do financially. We didn't have money for frivolous indulgences but we always had the security of being loved." She thinks for a moment and then adds, "Maggie would have been a beauty when she grew up. I mentioned her that time we met up at the Speckled Rooster."

"I remember." Delicately, I ask, "Do you feel comfortable talking about her?"

Anna-Claire answers. "I want you to know about Maggie and since you've asked about *Dreamer on Ice*; now seems to be a good time."

"How did she die?"

The sparkle present in Anna-Claire's eyes a few moments ago fades. "Tuberculosis. Now T.B. is rare ... at least in our country, but that was not always the case. Back then they had other names for it like consumption or lung fever, but the result was the same. People died choking on their own phlegm and blood. T.B. did not spare any segment of society. Rich or poor, families lost their loved ones to it. She contracted it at the parochial school we attended. She was only nine years old."

Not wanting to be intrusive, I answer, "I'm sorry."

"Maggie loved life," continues Anna-Claire, nodding at my expression of sympathy. "I have always thought that I learned how to write because of Maggie's influence. She loved to observe people, places, and events: their clothes, their gestures, the inflections of their voices. You name it and Maggie could give it a life and vitality like a verbal Kodak moment." She says, empathetically, "She would have been a great author!"

"I wish I could have known her."

Smiling appreciation for my sentiment, Anna-Claire answers, "You would have liked Maggie. Everybody did. I was three years older. When she became too sick to leave her bed, she would have me describe everything that I had seen or persons whom I had met; demanding that I put in the details about their clothes, how they smiled, moved, talked etc.. We would pass away the hours creating stories and altering events. That was the beginning of my story telling. Maggie took such delight in creating stories."

"And you don't?" I ask my question, wondering how she can have written so many successful plays and novels and not enjoy the process of creating them.

"Oh, I've grown to love it," answers Anna-Claire, "but I had to work at it. With Maggie, words just came naturally."

Anna-Claire chuckles. "She had one hell of a temper." Blue eyes twinkling with amusement, she says, "In that respect, you remind me of her."

"Who me? Temper?" I shake off the notion. "Whatever gave you that impression?"

"Hmmnn-uh," murmurs Anna-Claire. "Whatever indeed." Not giving me time to protest further, she continues. "I remember an incident that happened as we were walking to school. One of the local bullies decided to put earthworms in Maggie's lunchbox. She was only five years old then ..." she reminisces, "really only a baby. Robbie – that was his name – was in my grade. Well, before I could do anything, Maggie pulled those slimy earthworms right out of her lunchbox and stomped on them so hard the poor things were literally pulverized."

With unrestrained delight at the memory, Anna-Claire struggles amidst guffaws to add, "Without missing a beat or hesitation, she picked up some of that pulverized slime and threw it right back into Robbie's face." Anna-Claire swipes her right arm and hand as if she's the one holding the slimy mess of the worms and heaving it at Robbie's face. Her laughter is infectious and I begin to laugh as much from watching her mime the act of throwing worms as from hearing the story of how Maggie dealt with the bully and the worms.

"What did Robbie do?"

"He was such a stupid bully!" replies Anna-Claire. The pace of her story slows as she allows herself the time to visualize the memory. "He'd done the worm thing to other kids. That was one of his favourite tricks. He'd taunt the younger kids or ones that for whatever reason were not able to protect themselves."

She digresses with the comment. "It wasn't the first time that he'd picked on Maggie but usually it came in the form of verbal taunts. The worm thing was a step up in his victimization." Shrugging, she says, "He was three years older but then that's what schoolyard bullies do. Over the last decade or so, the media has treated it as being endemic in schools but truth be known, it's been practiced in schools for years." She adds sourly, "Most bullies grow up and become adult versions of their younger selves. Few ever change. What they alter are the twisted ways they enact the techniques of humiliating and subordinating people. She throws me a piercing look. "Take your own situation with Don and his posturing. He didn't acquire the traits of meanness and lording it over staff as an adult. They were there from childhood. He's been smart enough to hone his meanness under the cloak of what some people erroneously identify as characteristics essential to good leadership."

I recognize the truth of her observation but I'm not as cynical about all leaders. "Surely you don't believe that all bosses are like Don?" I say, attempting to keep my tone casual.

"Of course not," replies Anna-Claire quickly. "But some of them get to their positions by undermining their colleagues. When bullies grow up, the workplace takes the place of the school yard."

Knowing that a philosophical discussion about workplace bullies won't help me learn more facts that I can use for the Gala, I redirect her back to her childhood reflections. "So what did Robbie do when Maggie fought back?"

Her eyes dance with merriment. "The intent had been to get his jollies by making a little girl scream in front of his peers. His mistake was that he tried to make Maggie his victim. Oh Maggie screamed alright," she softly snorts , "but it was a scream of rage coupled with a fistful of mashed worms landing smack on his face. His stunt backfired. The story flew like wildfire among all the kids at school with the result that the little creep's image as being the tough guy got seriously crushed. Maggie emerged from the whole scenario as the girl who took out Robbie Beammer. For weeks after that he had to put up with kids taunting him with cracks like, 'Hey Robbie, we're going fishing after school. Think you can spare some mashed worms for bait?"

"How'd he handle it?"

"Eventually he resumed his role as the local bully, but he never again picked on Maggie. In fact," she says with a serious expression as she recalls the memory, "when Maggie died a few years later, Robbie came with some of my classmates to the funeral parlour. He brought a single red rose with him. He walked right up to the casket and placed it near her folded hands. I remember how he mumbled to me and my parents, "I'm sorry for your loss." My mother commented later on how well-mannered the young boy with the rose was but back then, I wasn't willing or ready to cut him any slack or even consider that he might have had real remorse. To me ..." she smiles, "he was, using your vernacular, 'an arrogant little prick.' I never told my mother that he was the jerk who had done the worm thing to Maggie."

Curious, I ask, "Why do you think he came? He must have known that you wouldn't want to see him."

When I thought about it, I took it for what it was. In his own way, he respected her for standing up to him and by that time, he had matured enough to want to do right by her." With a slight shrug, she adds, "Unfortunately, it was too late for Maggie to ever know that he was apologizing for being such a little shit."

"How did he treat you?"

Anna-Claire waves her right hand dismissively. "We'd been in the same classes since kindergarten," she says, "but I'd never been one of his targets and, after the incident with Maggie, he gave me even wider berth. Other than the few times we were forced to work together for some class project, we never exchanged any pleasantries or entered into what could be called a conversation. That is," she says, slowly, "until Maggie's wake. After his appearance there, no matter where he was – even if he was with friends, downtown, or at school – he would nod hello to me. And I, for my part, would nod hello to him. That was the nature of our relationship right through elementary and high school."

"Did you ever hear what happened to him?"

"Oddly enough we met years later at a function in Toronto." She helps herself to a doughnut from the box I'd brought. "I was in Toronto to help promote and open a new play. Drew and Emily were still alive. In those days, I was just beginning to be known as an author and playwright. By coincidence he was on the list of invitees attending the V.I.P. reception for opening night. At first it was awkward; meeting face-to-face after so many years but we both performed the civil niceties expected at that sort of function. He had become a very successful lawyer and, from the cut of the suit he was wearing, a rich one."

Sympathizing with how she must have felt, I say, "It must have been hard for you to resist not snubbing him."

Her answer surprises me. "No, I took the high road. That's what Maggie would have wanted me to do. As I said before, we had both matured. I looked him straight in the eyes and said, 'Good evening Robbie.' What else could I do? What had happened years ago had no place for accusations that evening."

"What did he do?"

"I think he was surprised because for a moment he hesitated but then he introduced me to his wife. I could tell that she was curious about me. After all, she'd been at the play and here was the playwright talking to her husband. We shook hands and I asked if she had enjoyed the play. It was small talk but I think Robbie appreciated the gesture. At these functions there's always someone to meet, a photo to pose for, or a hand to shake. I posed with her politely, smile plastered on my face when she asked if she could have a photo. Fortunately, there were a lot of dignitaries present and I was expected to circulate and glad handshake the V.I.P.'s. so I had the perfect excuse to cut the conversation short saying that I was expected to mingle. The next day I received two red roses delivered by the hotel concierge. The card attached was simple. It read, 'One for Maggie; one for you. I'm glad you're successful, Claire.' It was signed, Robbie.

I hadn't seen that coming. Stunned, I ask, "Did you ever call him to thank him for the roses?"

"I called one of the organizers of the function who gave me Robbie's home address and telephone number. I opted for the easier course of writing a thank you note. I told him the gesture had been gratefully appreciated and wished him continued success in all that he did."

"That was it?" I'm incredulous. "It sounds as if Robbie outgrew his bullying behaviour and developed a sense of style."

"You're going to find this odd but it's true. In those days, I attended every opening of a play or a photo exhibit. I was getting a lot of well-paced publicity that really jettisoned my career. When *Dreamer On Ice* opened on Broadway the following year, the stage manager brought back a single red rose with a simple card with the words, "For you. Congratulations". It was signed 'Robbie'. All in all, I have fifteen similar cards from Robbie interspersed over the years. By then I'd become Anna Wright and wasn't attending openings but they still were sent and of course, Emile or Arnie or one of my confidants would bring the rose and card to me. Ottawa, Winnipeg, Vancouver, Toronto, New York, and even London: opening night came with a rose from Robbie."

"You're kidding?" I can't hide my astonishment.

"Don't look so surprised, Leen," she says. "People can and do change. If you check out the top drawer in my desk you'll see that I kept all the cards. They seemed, somehow, to bring Maggie closer to me. With each card, I would laugh at the memory of her stomping down on those worms. I think that was Robbie's way of bringing her back to me. I never responded to any of the cards and I never saw him again."

"That's such an incredible story!" I can't help marvelling at this latest snippet of information. Through her memories I am coming to understand the process Anna-Claire uses when sharing her insights into her life. She starts off on one topic and digresses to another seemingly unrelated discussion. What this story about Robbie the bully has to do with the writing of *Dreamer On Ice* is, at the moment, lost to me. Nonetheless, she answers my question about what was the inspiration for *Dreamer on Ice* by speculating on the irony of how Maggie threw slimy worms at a schoolyard bully. That incident seemingly altered Robbie's heart to the point that years later he would send roses to his victim's older sister.

"Well, yes, it is," remarks Anna-Claire, easing herself off the kitchen chair. "I've never shared that memory with anyone." She ambles over to the cupboard, removes a glass, and says, "I'm thirsty. Would you like a glass of water?"

I shake my head no and wait as she fills her glass. Her vitality seems to be the only thing holding her thin frame up. No matter how much she likes her herbal teas and lattes, water is the only thing that quenches the constant thirst caused from the dry mouth side-effect of her medications. As if reading my thoughts, Anna-Claire says, "Nothing like water."

"As much as I've enjoyed hearing about Robbie and the worms, I'm not certain how it answers my original question. What was the inspiration for *Dreamer on Ice?*"

"Maggie's tenacity and feisty mannerisms were the characteristics I gave to the lead character Paula," replies Anna-Claire. "Those qualities and memories of her laughter and ability to dream provided the frame of reference for Paula's personality." Her expression takes on the look of someone cherishing a private memory. "I don't know if you recall the scene when Paula dreams about skating. In the play Paula becomes consumed with the goal of achieving greatness on ice. Maggie loved to skate. To tell the truth, she was quite good at it. For her, skating was a release of energy; something to be savoured and enjoyed." She laughs lightly. "Creating Paula wasn't a problem. All I had to do was think of Maggie – the things she said and did – and my characterization of Paula took place."

With the skill of a consummate storyteller, she has used her digressions to set the stage for her answer to my question.

"Paula was the waif girl in *Dreamer On Ice*," I say, gently. "Why didn't you call her Maggie?"

"I never said that Paula *was* Maggie," answers Anna-Claire. The corners of her mouth turn upwards into a satisfied grin. "I said I used Maggie's traits to create Paula's character." She pauses, allowing that thought to sink in. "Subtle differences are important to the flow of a play or story."

She sips her water. "In the play Paula wears a red jacket."

Recalling that detail, I nod. Anna-Claire's eyes twinkle. She's in a story telling mood, enjoying the process of whetting my appetite for more; leading me from one story to another.

I ask, "What's the connection of the red jacket to Maggie and Paula?"

"I had been in New York for a meeting with Jacob. His office is located near Radio City Music Hall's big open air rink. I stopped to watch the skaters. There was a little girl learning to skate, clinging to her mother's hand. She wore a scarlet jacket, matching toque and mittens, and was bundled up with heavy blue snow pants. Wisps of blond hair escaped from underneath her toque and she was laughing with such wonderful abandon – the type of laughter that only children seem to have – as she tried to glide across the ice. I was totally absorbed watching her tackle the ice, learning to skate. She was so determined. Something about that moment jarred my memory and I recalled how Maggie loved to skate and how proud she was when she wore her red jacket and matching red hat."

"So the red jacket is the connection," I say, trying to piece together all the snippets she's throwing out; wondering how to use them for the Gala.

"My parents gave a red jacket and hat to Maggie for her fourth birthday. She strutted around the house, refusing to take it off until our mother finally insisted that she had to. Seeing the little girl with her red outfit and watching her learn to skate led me to wonder how Maggie would have turned out had she lived. That was the moment I decided to write what would eventually become *Dreamer On Ice*."

Captivated with Anna-Claire's explanation as to how *Dreamer on Ice* originated, I think how my assumptions of her have altered. Initially I expected someone of Claire's fame to be pretentious and overbearing, surrounded by the trappings of wealth. Her reclusive lifestyle had ironically increased her fame and people grasped for details about Holowitz's seeming eccentricities. Sitting in her kitchen, listening to her reminisce, I realize that my perspective about Claire Holowitz's mysterious absence from the public limelight and her anonymity as Anna Wright is not a testimony to her eccentricity but rather a comment on her basic humility.

Fame has never been a huge deal to Anna-Claire. She likes her quiet and her own space. Long ago she'd taken stock of her life and knew what was important to her. Void of pretence, she possesses an air of confidence that dares anyone or anything to stand in her way.

The Search for Claire Holowitz

Stretching her neck to ease its kinks, "Anna-Claire says, *"In Dreamer On Ice*, Paula grows up to become a sculptor and her work is the catalyst for others in the play to interact and change their lives." She makes a slight depreciatory wave of her hand, saying softly, "The little girl on the rink grew up. Because Maggie didn't, I wanted to create an image of what she might have become."

Engrossed with her logic, I say, "Go on Anna-Claire."

"Remember that moment in the play when the child Paula crafts out a wonderful ice sculpture of a skater? In my mind, it was Maggie – not Paula – who was sculpting. She closes her eyes briefly. "I used Paula as the conduit to build Maggie a monument out of the ice she loved so much." She looks straight at me and says with naked honesty, "I used Paula to create Maggie's dream of being one with the ice."

Moved to the point of tears, I reply, "I'm sure Maggie would have loved how you used childhood memories to write *Dreamer on Ice*.

"In the play Paula starts her sculpting, using ice blocks from the ice wagon that her father drove on hot summer days. To help with Maggie's medical expenses our father took a second job as an ice-man during the weekends. He drove those wagons up and down the streets, never once complaining about how he never had a day off." She smiles fondly. "On hot summer days, he would chip off pieces from a block of ice and give them to Maggie and me. He'd make a game of it, calling out, 'The Ice Man is here. Who wants ice?' She looks down at the table and softly says, "When Maggie lay dying, my father would chip off pieces of ice and put them to her mouth, saying over and over again. 'Who wants ice? Why, my girl Maggie wants ice.' Right to the end, Maggie would smile and whisper, 'I do.'

Caught up in the moment, I say excitedly, *Dreamer On Ice* was a huge success! It ran on Broadway for five straight years and in Toronto for three. The musical score that accompanied scenes made the hit charts and thrilled audiences."

"That's right," answers Anna-Claire, pleased that I remember the scene about the ice blocks. "Resting on Paula's bedside table stood a wooden statue of a little girl stretched out, head held up by her hand, belly down on a block of ice. Underneath it laid a note addressed to Paula's son, Casey. It read 'Never stop dreaming'. The statue and note were the symbolic embodiment of Paula's lifelong struggle to achieve success and love – brought about by her courage and drive – to achieve her dreams."

Excitedly, I exclaim, "For the Gala I'll arrange to have large blocks of ice carved with images from your plays! It'll blow people away! Can't you just see it?"

Anna-Claire jokes, "Better make sure they don't melt before the night's over or you'll have lots of puddles."

Laughing, I reply, "We'll create the effect of a magical wonderland! It'll be amazing!"

"Definitely different," remarks Anna-Claire. A look of fond remembrance lights up her face. "*Dreamer On Ice* was a pleasure to write."

Enthused with new themes I can use for the Gala, I say, "That play had it all! Drama, music, humour, love, anger, tears, and growth of awareness. Critics characterized it as 'human heartstrings' and that while 'smultzy' to the point of being the literal 'tear jerker', it evoked laughter straight from the soul. Several critics of your works have said it was the best of all your plays. All critics agree that the lure of *Dreamer On Ice* was how it evoked imagery and imagination in its portrayal of raw human emotions."

Arching an eyebrow, she says with an amused look, "You've done your homework. Reviews are reviews. They come and go." Wistful, she continues, "Paula was my version of what Maggie may have been like had she lived. Maggie embraced life with zest and exuberance. She would get me to make up stories, persuading me to add details: clothing, wrinkled faces, big feet, smelly bodies, harsh and soft voices … We called our game 'Imaginings' and *imaginings* became our gifts to one another."

"Even then you were writing stories?"

Her laughter is deep and throaty. "I do not remember a time when I have not been weaving stories. Some good and some positively terrible. Maggie insisted that I write them down so that she could read them when I wasn't able to be with her."

"How about your parents? What did they think about your stories?"

Anna-Claire shrugs. "My mother thought it was nice that I was entertaining Maggie. She even read a few of them but you have to remember, she had to work hard and leisure time for reading wasn't an option for her most nights." Expression wistful, she says, "To the day he died, my father called me a hopeless dreamer. He was not in favour of my writing. He never acknowledged my writing, or story-telling, as being of any real worth." At this point, she stops, pinches the bridge of her nose and closes her eyes; lost in a moment of reflection.

I can tell from her expression that this memory is causing her emotional pain. I envision a little girl trying to show her father one of her stories and learning how to harden herself from the pain of being dismissed. I think about how my father would hang my drawings on the refrigerator door as if they were works of art and the pride I felt as he enthused about them. I remember sitting on his lap as he read to me and when I was old enough, reading to him.

"It must have been sad for you to grow up knowing that your father didn't approve of your writing." My admiration for Anna-Claire has increased ten-fold. "Many people would use a parent's rejection of their dreams as an excuse *not* to achieve success. Instead, you built a career proving that what he had dismissed as folly was actually *the means* to your success."

"Don't get me wrong," continues Anna-Claire, briskly. "He was a good man. Life had made it so that he didn't have time to "dream". He lived from pay cheque to pay cheque and what with the bills, and trying to cope with Maggie's death, he viewed life as something to be endured as opposed to being created and loved. The necessities of survival quashed any opportunity for the luxury of imagination. I had youth on my side and the wonder of having had Maggie as my sister. She was my inspiration. After her death I'd pretend that she was there with me, telling me to add more details and colour to my stories. It was my way of keeping her alive."

"As I grew older, I continued to look at the world as one big amusement park from which stories could be created. As a result, a little girl, who could not afford a new dress and who was grateful for hand-me-downs from neighbours or church basement sales, stayed alive in those stories and grew into a writer. The '*Dreamer*' was Maggie."

She looks at me and says, "It's getting late, Leen. Maybe we should call it a day."

The afternoon light has faded into the darkness that early winter nights bring. I've been so captivated by this glimpse into Anna-Claire's childhood I've not realized how time has passed. I get up to turn on the kitchen light. Admiringly, I say, "You wrote an entire Broadway play around the *imagining* games you played with Maggie?"

"I used my memories of Maggie and the images of that little girl skating on the ice to write the play. I know that you would like to hear something more dramatic but the reality is, the basis for my writing comes from having learned early on in life, to see, hear, and touch life and then, above all else," she grasps my hand and adds earnestly, "to not be afraid to know life."

Releasing my hand Anna-Claire asks, in the tone she uses when she wants to change topics, "Are you hungry? I'm famished." Getting up from her chair she goes over to the refrigerator. "How about a cucumber sandwich with that special tartinade you like?"

"You've been entertaining me all afternoon with your stories. How about I order in from that Thai restaurant you're fond of?"

"No thanks, something light will do."

Her answer doesn't surprise me. Anna-Claire eats small amounts at any one time in an attempt to prevent the nausea that heavier meals bring on. "You sit and I'll make the sandwiches."

I stay for another half hour. We chat while we eat. I collect my notes and say good-bye to Anna-Claire. My last thought before falling asleep that night are about how happy she looked when she was talking about Maggie and their game of *Imaginings*.

Chapter Eighteen

Marc Andre

I've never said this to a woman and the fact that I just blurted it out dumbfounds me.

"I don't know what else to tell you," I say. Uncharacteristic and unfamiliar emotions churn in my gut causing me to experience the naked vulnerability that accompanies emotional honesty.

Leen's startled expression tells me loud and clear that she hadn't expected me to say this. I don't push for an answer. My hesitation is rooted more in a fear than in patience. What if the feelings aren't reciprocal? My mind is racing with thoughts of how I got to this point, but the bottom line is that I know what I've said is true. The silence between us is heavy. Leen bites her lower lip lightly. It's a subconscious thing that she does when she is thinking, concentrating hard on something – a gesture that I have come to love and find endearing. I can feel my heart beating as I wait for her to answer. We are in the front hallway, near the door. I've just kissed her goodnight and blurted out that I love her.

After Aunt Claire made her identity known, Leen and I began to work closely together; each for different reasons but both driven by genuine care for Aunt Claire's right to privacy. We'd taken up the practice of going out for dinner on the days that we worked late. That led to my asking her to go out for a meal that wasn't work related.

We went to Roy's Ribs, ordered the house speciality with side orders of fries, onion rings, and salads. While sipping on a draught beer and listening to Leen recount the latest incident with Don – telling it with both humour and justifiable rancour – I fell in love. The realization hit me like a ton of bricks. I've always been a roamer when it comes to women; enjoying romantic liaisons and walking away when the initial attraction fades. Now, without me even realizing that it was happening, Cupid drew his arrow and took aim.

Finally, she answers, "Tell me the truth, not what you think I want to hear."

"I've said it all," I say, my voice sounding strange to my ears. It's husky and low and betrays my want of her as much as my fear that she will reject me. "I love you, Leen. It's as simple as that." My gaze drifts to where her silk shirt opens at the neck, giving hint to the breasts that lay beneath the fabric. My blood quickens and I know that I want to go exploring – to release those breasts, to cup them in my hands, to satiate my naked hunger for her. I can smell the soft, alluring scent of her perfume and my body stirs with the want for her. I desperately want to reach out and pull her to me, to let my hands roam over her soft curves and supple skin. Until now, I've managed to control my need for her but I know that I can't hide it any longer. I don't want to hide it. I need to know if she feels the same way.

Her eyes search mine, looking for any hint that I regret what I've said. Silently, she steps forward. I pull her into my arms, brushing my lips against her neck. She takes a step back and slowly loosens my tie. My blood rushes and stifling a groan I instinctively stand still, giving in to her control of the moment and me. In her eyes I can see the promise of her love.

Her voice is husky with sex as she murmurs, "Well, counsellor, I think this is where your opponent says, "I rest my case." This time I don't try to restrain my passion. I kiss her forcefully, long and deep. She has given me permission to love her and I intend to as if she is the first, last, and only woman alive. I am completely at her mercy and crave her touch with every inch of my body.

Leaning her against the wall, I remove her blouse, watching her eyes and expression as I slide the silk shirt down her arms. She stirs trying to kiss me, but I shake my head no and feel the thrill of hearing her gasp with anticipation of the unknown as I kneel down, my face eyelevel with her mid-waist. I brush her stomach flesh with my nose – lightly, teasing, and deliberately as my hands move to unhook her bra. Her breasts fall loose and I pull her to me, cupping one breast in my hand; using the other to grasp her hips, while beginning to suckle on her breast. I hear her sharp intake of breath as she grips my shoulders and leans downwards to tease my ear and neck with her tongue and kisses.

"Not here," she moans softly. "Let's go to bed. Please, let's go."

I hear her plea but in response, I move my mouth to her other breast and slide my hand slowly up her back and then move it onto her breast, teasing her nipple between my thumb and forefinger with gentle, steady strokes. Her body tenses and she arches her back, thrusting her breasts forward. I want this moment to last forever, to burn it into my mind so that years from now I will feel this passion, intensity, and need.

Leen

I'm impatient to be free from his hold. Feeling the urgency of my body demanding release, I'm almost beyond sensibility as I respond to the command of his touch – a captive of his hands, his caresses, his kisses, and the pure, delicious scent of him. Rising he leads me to the living room couch and stands my semi-clad body in front of him, lightly stroking my arms with his fingertips and letting his eyes roam over me. Stepping back, he removes his shirt and loosens his belt. Breath catches in my throat as my eyes soak in the call of his muscular body. I reach to free him from the confines of his zipper. Seeing his need for release and responding, at a primal level to the seductive lure of his body with my own telltale wetness, between my thighs, warm and waiting for him. I whisper huskily, "Take me, Marc. Take me now. Make me yours."

Certain of his hold on me, he lays down on the couch pulling me to him. I lose myself in his touch, begging him to make me his while I take all that he has to give me and make him one with me. Passion spent, our bodies lay side-by-side, comfortable in their closeness and natural in how we have imprinted each other with our love. We fall asleep.

Waking up to the morning light filtering through the living room windows, we move to my bedroom and make love again. This time we gently explore the wonder of each other. Spent, we lay together lost in our own thoughts, feeling the impact of what has happened between us.

Marc is the first to break the silence. Sitting up, he peers down at me and with a roguish grin, asks, "How did we get from being two determined opponents to lying in your bed?" He lifts the sheet and playfully peeks at my nakedness.

"I believe you said we needed to talk."

He pushes his hand through his hair and smiles, "Who would've figured that we'd end up like this?"

"Anna-Claire."

His nod is almost imperceptible; his smile amused and indulgent. He traces my mouth with his fingertips and I relish the feeling of contentment that surges throughout me.

I say, "From the first, even when I only knew her as Anna, she has been interested in what I thought of you." I laugh. "When I think of the times that sly matchmaker would tell me to cut you some slack, that you were only acting on Claire Holowitz's directions ..." I break midsentence and drawing him close so that I can kiss him, I murmur, "I must remember to thank her.

༄

Marc Andre

Leen rises from the bed and pads her way to the bathroom. Left alone to my thoughts, I stare at the ceiling and recall yesterday's meeting with Don Harris. I had arranged for it at the request of Aunt Claire. She had wanted me to see if Harris would try to undermine Leen. I purposely arrived forty minutes ahead of my appointment with Leen to meet up with Don. True to form, Harris had been ingratiating and whined about Leen's inability to find Claire Holowitz, despite the support she was receiving from the Arts Community.

Harris had not liked my response. Pursing his lips tightly in barely concealed anger at being thwarted, he became petulant. "We all have our jobs to do! Certainly Ms Holowitz knows that for this Gala to be a success, she must come out from her self-imposed seclusion."

"Ms Holowitz is well aware of the Gala's importance. To that end she has facilitated interviews with very established and credible people. People," I added, with a deliberate edge to my voice, "who know the meaning and importance of her privacy."

The bathroom door opens and thoughts about yesterday's meeting fade as I watch Leen bend to pick up her tossed silk shirt with as much decorum as she can muster given her nakedness. My body stirs as I recall the feel of her breath on my neck and the sensual ecstasy of having her cry out my name. Reluctantly I reach for my clothes lying in a heap on the floor. Spotting her silk panties I pick them up and bring them to her. "I believe you may be looking for these."

She snatches the panties and slips them on. "I think this is where I ask if you'd like some coffee or breakfast."

"I think you're beautiful in the morning light." I smile at how different this shy Leen is from the passionate Leen of last night or the cool, composed Scenes' executive. I say, "How about I take a shower and you make some coffee? Then, while you are showering, I'll make you breakfast."

☙

Leen

I can hear the rush of the water and wonder what it would be like to climb in the shower with him. Spooning coffee into the filter and adding water to the machine, I make up my mind. I flip the switch to begin the brew and head straight for the bathroom, hesitating only briefly in front of the frosted shower door. I slip off my panties and shirt and step into the shower. His soap-lathered body visibly reacts. I no longer feel self-conscious. I lay claim to him, letting him know that just as I can comply with his needs, I can also demand. As the water streams down on our flesh, our bodies and mouths melt into one.

Afterwards, we smirk like two children; thrilled to have received the keys to the candy store. I now understand why I've never married. Until Marc, there was no one who could fill my senses with such passion or make me want to let down my guard – to make myself open to his presence in all aspects of my life. Until Marc, I did not know the meaning of love.

Stepping out of the shower, Marc Andre reaches for the fluffy, cream coloured, towel. Handing it to me, he asks, "Where can I find another towel?"

"Hall closet." He returns two minutes later with a towel wrapped around his waist.

"Coffee should be ready." I pad over to my closet and pull out jeans and a sweater.

"Do you have a spare toothbrush?"

I open a drawer and hand him one. "I didn't feel strange a few minutes ago," I say as he stands there grinning at me like the cat that swallowed the canary, "but now, sharing my ensuite with you, I feel self-conscious."

"Would you like me to use the guest bathroom?"

"No, that would be silly. In fact, I don't know why I even mentioned it." I reach for the toothpaste, place some on my toothbrush, and begin to brush my teeth.

The coffee has brewed by the time we make it down to the kitchen. I pour each of us a cup. Completely at ease, making himself at home as if we've done this a hundred times before, Marc Andre scrambles eggs and pan fries bacon slices. Strangely enjoying this domesticity I make the toast. Sitting at the kitchen table we chat about casual things. Neither of us broaches the topic of how our lovemaking has changed things between us. But, the everyday acts of brushing teeth, making breakfast, and reading the morning paper make us a couple.

Chapter Nineteen

Leen

Anna-Claire is resting on her bench swing under the oak tree when I arrive. She's wearing jeans and an old baggy grey sweater over a red flannel shirt. Her dark rimmed eyes emphasize her fatigue but her voice is strong. She motions to the swing. "Leen, come and sit down. What brings you my way?"

I swat at a fly buzzing by my head and climb onto the swing. "I came to see how you are doing." I'd set the date last week but don't comment on the fact that she must have forgotten. The morphine she's taking to help manage the pain has put her into a no man's land. Time passes in ways she can no longer manage.

"Fine thank you. Just fine." Anna-Claire's response lacks conviction.

"I see that you have been gardening."

Her gaze drifts to the bucket, partially filled with the last of the herbs from her garden. "Thought I should do what I can on a good day. These are the last of the herbs now that fall is here." She smiles ruefully. "Some days it seems to be a monumental task to just get out of bed."

Knowing a response is not expected, I merely nod. For a few minutes we sit in silence, listening to the soft, rhythmic creaking of the swing. When Anna-Claire rubs her arms, I climb off the swing.

"Where are you going?"

"To get a throw blanket to put over your shoulders. Or," I peer closely, "would you prefer to go inside?"

"No, I want to sit out here for a while. But to tell the truth I would appreciate the blanket."

I retrieve a red wool blanket from the living room couch and return outside. Draping the blanket over Anna-Claire, I can't help but notice her protruding shoulders. She smiles at me and I watch as her eyes drift off to another place. I'm used to these periods – the after-effects of her pain medications – when it seems as if her mind is wandering aimlessly. When she's ready, she'll talk. Until then, I'm comfortable just gliding on the swing.

"I was thinking of Drew today."

I look at her. Her eyes are clear and she's a sharper version of the Anna-Claire of half an hour ago. "Were you? What about?"

"Usually I talk to Becky. She helps me with my dreams ... the ones about Drew and Emily. But," she smiles mischievously, "you keep asking questions about my life. Since I told you about Maggie, I thought maybe you'd like to hear about Drew."

"Only if you would like to," I answer cautiously. We're entering new territory. "I don't want to intrude."

"The days are getting cooler. I'm glad I got those gladiola bulbs in before the snow. It's going to come soon enough."

I ask again, "Do you want to go inside?"

"No, no, of course not." A flicker of annoyance crosses her face, but she relaxes quickly. "I want to enjoy the last days before the weather becomes too chilly to sit outside. It's all a matter of dressing for it." She fingers the blanket around her shoulders. "I should have thought to bring this out with me."

I know better than to argue with Anna-Claire when her mind is made up. "Well, you've got it now."

"You're patient with me Leen. I know that I tend to digress from one topic to another, but that seems to be what I do best these days."

"Digress away. I enjoy your stories." I clasp her hand in mine. "I wish I had been able to share moments like this with my mother."

Anna-Claire gives my hand a tight squeeze, letting me know that she's heard me. I pull the blanket over her hands. "Keep your hands covered, Anna-Claire. Your fingers are cold."

A full two minutes pass and I wonder if she's forgotten what she had intended to say about Drew, but I should have known better. She was only sorting the thoughts she wants to share and how to begin. Her memories have been sealed in time and to let them out is not easy.

"Andrew James Henderson was the one true love of my life." Resting her head on the back drop of the swing she smiles wistfully. "I loved him beyond any words that I could ever write. He made me complete and he broke my heart when he died."

"Drew was his nickname?"

"I suppose it was. Everyone called him Drew."

"If his last name was Henderson, how did you end up with the surname Holowitz?"

"Holowitz was my grandmother's maiden name. When I started to write it was common practice to use a pseudonym." Grinning, she says, "It was also a good thing to do in case my writing flopped. I didn't want my failure to embarrass Drew."

I let that comment pass. I can't imagine why she ever thought her writing would fail or that she would be the cause of another person's embarrassment. I wait for her to continue. The swing creaks as we move in rhythm and the late fall sun sneaks out from behind the clouds. A cool breeze signals that the evening chill will soon follow.

"Drew had a way with me. He could make me smile at the drop of a pin or cry with the abandonment of a lost child. He was magical. I loved him to distraction."

"He did carpentry as a hobby, didn't he?"

"Yes." Anna-Claire closes her eyes and there's such a sense of tranquillity about her that I think she's drifted off to sleep. Thinking that I should leave, I slow the swing to a halt and step down from it. I don't want to wake her up but I can't leave her outside. Who knows how long she'll sleep? The chill could cause her to catch a cold or pneumonia.

"That man could build and design anything. He had a way with wood that would make the most sophisticated architect envious."

"I thought you'd drifted off."

"No. I was just resting my eyes and thinking about Drew."

Despite my misgivings about her catching a chill, I take my seat like an anxious child waiting for a bedtime story.

With each memory that Anna-Claire recounts, I realize how much I appreciate her. She has lived her life as she saw fit and met it head on. Although she doesn't talk about the fact that she is terminally ill, she does joke about preparing to meet her 'final critic'. Becky has told all of us to accept her dark humour for what it is: her way of coping. With each snippet of her life story shared with us, she is becoming more expansive in what she wants us to know. "It's her way of leaving a legacy of memories," explained Becky when we questioned how we should respond to Anna-Claire's cracks about the *final critic*. "She's telling us about her life so that when she's gone, we can remember who she really was, what mattered to her."

One lesson that has come through loud and clear is: just as the tangible lure of love can fulfil a life, its loss can devastate. She's fond of saying that 'life is to be lived'. While it can be argued that she hid from life as Claire Holowitz, it cannot be denied that she has lived life well as Anna Wright. Also, in defence, of 'living life' – Anna-Claire didn't bury Claire Holowitz with Drew and Emily; she simply withdrew from public life. Claire Holowitz lived. She continued to write, she advanced in her career, and she gave back to society in a hundred different ways through her stories, plays, photos, charitable donations, scholarships – all examples of her 'living life'.

She doesn't fear death, but neither does she wait for it to come calling. Instead, she balks at its rapping at her door, refusing to answer until she's ready, on her terms, to welcome it. Just as she has lived her life with dignity; she will meet death with dignity.

One thing that has surprised me is Anna-Claire's deep, spiritual side. Although she has long since rejected organized religion claiming it to be too artificial and dictated by the whims of people aspiring to power, she believes in cosmic universality. Her homespun spirituality reminds me of the adage, 'there are no atheists in foxholes.'

Becky thinks that Anna-Claire, like a Tibetan monk, chose to isolate herself from the frenzy of the world, media, and petty conflicts. After Drew and Emily's deaths, her writing became prolific. She set a gruelling pace that many thought could not be maintained and yet, with each play, novel, and photo exhibit; she had shown a growing appreciation for life's nuances and a simple humbleness of her role in the cosmic realm of things.

Breaking the silence between us, I say, "Tell me about him."

With a gentle breath drawn inward as if to fortify herself, she exhales slowly. "Drew and I grew up during the days of the construction boom after the war. His father recognized the need soldiers would have, as they returned home from the horrors of war, seeking stability in family life."

"George, that was Drew's father's name, was young, strong, and imbued with the vision to build homes that would last. Everyone seemed anxious to have the house with the proverbial white picket fence. It was as if they were all searching for tangible proof that life could be good and if they built homes to last then nothing, or no one, could ever threaten their little nests of security."

"George built his construction company from the ground up. Having adopted the view that his only son should have a university education, he insisted Drew get a degree. Drew, however, loved working on construction sites and initially he resisted the notion of university. George would have none of that. Maintaining he would need good legal advice from a lawyer who knew the 'ins and outs' of the construction business, he convinced Drew that it was his duty to become a lawyer and to help advise his father. Drew's love of construction stayed with him. That's why even after he and Emile started their law firm, you could often find him at one of the construction sites."

"Children born during the war years and throughout the next decade grew up being indoctrinated with the notion that having a home was a sign of stability and synonymous with a safe refuge. There had been too much pain and suffering witnessed, on both sides of the ocean. People wanted the Sunday barbecues, family picnics, the smell of fresh cut grass, and baked bread. We were a generation healing from the nightmares of war. It was a time of hope and indulgences. Looking back, I sometimes think it was a period when people were intoxicated and obsessed with life. These were the days that laid the foundation for the hippie generation."

Fascinated, I listen to Anna-Claire's digression from one topic to another, knowing that she is weaving the memory the way she wants me to hear it.

"I never thought about the origins for the hippie generation in the way you are suggesting," I say, thinking that there's truth in what she has said. "I always just equated it with the Viet Nam war."

"This is where we could use Becky's perspective on things," answers Anna-Claire. "She might tell me that I am completely mistaken or, she might see the connection between what we as a generation were trying to instil and what our children took and changed as they became adults.

The transgressions of youth are often misguided reactions to their perceptions about what their parents have done wrong."

"Make love, not war," I interject glibly.

Anna-Claire laughs. "Something like that. The Viet Nam War may have been the U.S. versus the East but make no mistake about it, the fall-out was universal. Many of the hippie generation took their resentment to higher levels using marijuana and hallucinogens to check out of reality. Not everyone bought into the *make love* scene but for those who did, it was easier to live the myth that communal living and drug enhanced stupor disenfranchised them from their parents' society. By then we had social assistance and welfare programs and even though the hippies rejected much of their parents' work ethics and acquired signs of affluence; they were only too happy to take the free handouts."

"Becky would love this discussion. I can just imagine her sitting here with clinical poise, soaking it all in and making connections."

"I enjoy Becky," says Anna-Claire. "Drew would have liked discussing things with all of you." Grinning widely, she adds, "He would have given all of you a run for your money."

I ask, "So Drew kept his hand in the construction business after he became a lawyer?"

"He worked his way through law school by working on construction sites during summers for both George and some of his friends. After he graduated he picked up various litigations from the contacts he had made."

"Didn't he continue to work for his father?"

"Oh most certainly!" smiles Anna-Claire. "He met Emile – Marc Andre's father – at law school and the two of them became fast friends. They articled at the same firm and the rest is as you say, *history*. After a few years they had had enough of doing briefs for senior lawyers and were itching to develop their own practice. When Drew's father died of a heart attack they put together their mutual resources – Drew used the construction firm as collateral for the down payment on their first office space and start-up funds. They built their firm up from a one room rented office to the corporate one that Marc Andre now oversees." She smiles at the memory and her pride is evident. Rubbing her hands and arms she says, "It's starting to get chilly."

"Maybe we should think about going inside?"

Frowning, Anna-Claire answers, "Not just this minute. Let me finish my train of thought before we move."

I don't argue though she looks chilled. "Okay, just a few more minutes."

"Drew hired a manager to run the construction firm and dedicated himself to their law practice. He and Emile benefitted from the many contacts gained in the construction industry and as their law practice grew so too did the construction business, with both of them sharing equal say in the finances and profits."

A gentle smile pulls on her lips as she says, "Let me tell you, it was a very proud day for Emile when Marc Andre entered the firm. Drew would have loved that. Both he and Emile used to joke that when they were old they would turn the firm over to Marc Andre and Emily. Their plan was to spend their days on a golf course and evenings heckling Marc Andre and Emily about how they were handling the firm. They had such plans for their children."

Anna-Claire meets my gaze and for a moment neither of us says a word. I wait to see where her thoughts will take us next.

She says mischievously, "Speaking of Marc Andre, I understand from my godson that the two of you have put down your swords and have decided to explore the benefits of a truce."

I bat my eyelashes and put on a southern drawl. "Why, I do declare Anna-Claire, I never would have thought that you'd add matchmaking to your list of credits."

"Harrumph," snorts Anna-Claire and twangs back at me, "I learned long ago that I couldn't make that boy do anything he didn't have a mind to do ..." staring pointedly she drops the twang, "I suspect the same can be said about you Adrienne MacLeen." She sniffs theatrically and wags her index finger. "The fact that I had more sense than either of you from the beginning of this whole Gala affair and could see the writing on the wall is a testament to my superior detecting abilities." Settling back on the bench, she lifts her chin and striking a pose she resumes the twang and remarks, "Well I do declare Leen darlin, that I might have missed my true calling – Anna-Claire: consultant to the love-sick and too foolish to know their hearts."

I let her have her moment of glory before saying, "Enjoy the moment, Anna-Claire."

"Oh, trust me, I am," she answers with a self-satisfied smugness. "Now," she says, removing the blanket that has kept her warm, "let's go have some brandy by the fireplace."

"It's only after four," I comment, "since when did you start having a pre-dinner drink?"

"Since I've got something to celebrate," she replies, taking the hand I offer to help steady her as she climbs down from the swing. "After all, this is a special day. I'm passing time with the woman my godson has fallen in love with." She winks. "Always did say that boy had a good head on his shoulders."

After I've poured our brandy and have the fire crackling, Anna-Claire picks up our earlier conversation, as if it had never been interrupted. "But he never stopped going to the sites—mixing with the men, picking up a hammer or drill, working with a crew."

"I take it you're talking about Drew," I say, folding my legs underneath me on the couch.

Anna-Claire's sitting comfortably in the recliner she favours; leg rest up and holding her brandy glass. "Now where was I? She lets the statement hang in the air between us and stares at me as if she's lost and searching for help.

"You were talking about Drew ..." then, I stop and realize that she's teasing me. "Very funny," I say.

"Just making certain that you're paying attention." Having had her few minutes of levity at my expense, Anna-Claire resumes. "Some men spend countless hours on a golf course or in pubs to manage stress. Drew's release was working at the construction sites. Specifically, working with wood." She sips her brandy, looks at the fire and smiles. "But no matter what he did, Drew always had time for me and Emily."

I lock eyes with Anna-Claire. "You loved him a great deal."

After a moment she says, "I never had to worry about him taking up with some office tramp."

I just about choke on my brandy. "Office tramp? Anna-Claire, I never thought I'd hear that coming out of your mouth."

She arches an eyebrow and with dry humour says, "I didn't get to my age without having heard those words, Leen. My point is that where some women always have to worry about the dear sweet office ..." she pauses, widens her eyes and carefully articulates, 'office tramp', that was not something I had to deal with and God knows, we had our share of disagreements. Lots of men of less character than Drew would have turned to another woman's sympathetic arms. But not my Drew. We loved one another enough to fight openly and settle our differences." She sighs softly. "Sometimes you've got to love enough to fight. It's not all happily ever after like in fairy tales. And there's always an office tramp just waiting in the wings to be the golden voice of comfort to a man who lets his ego control his libido and vice versa."

"I get the distinct impression that you are making a point here that you want me to understand."

She smiles. "I'm just saying that you and Marc Andre have finally come to your senses. Don't ever let anyone or anything get in the way of what you feel for one another. If you have to fight then by God, fight. Never use violence or meanness to control your partner. Drew and I were both young and our careers were starting to take off. That meant that we were often busy doing career things when we rightfully should have been doing man and wife things and after Emily, family things. Plain and simple, we could have been one of those marriages where one of us or eventually both of us would have looked elsewhere for comfort that should come from one another. But early on, both of us swore that we wouldn't let that happen and we didn't."

I think of how Dick the Prick broke Amy's heart and how Becky's first marriage ended badly. "Sarah and Joe have a good marriage. They've raised two fine sons and they still love one another."

"And I'd be willing to bet that Sarah would be the first person to tell you that there have been times when either one of them would gladly have walked out that door and taken up with another person."

She's right. Sarah can be feisty when she chooses to be and Joe can be downright stubborn. Somehow, the two of them have managed to stay in love despite the times when love wasn't in the air.

"Now, take you and Marc Andre," slips in Anna-Claire.

"Me and Marc Andre? How did we get into this discussion?"

She stares at me as if I'm a complete dolt. "The two of you started off as combatants and now look at you. Why you're head over heels with him and I can tell you for certain that you've had that boy eating out of your hand since the day he met you. I'm just saying, when you have love ... don't throw it away."

Anna-Claire takes a moment to sip her brandy. "It still hurts," she says. "I miss Drew and Emily every day of my life."

"But you learned how to survive."

She shrugs. "I had no choice but ..." she looks straight at me and says softly, "I did have the choice to continue on as Claire Holowitz. I kept her alive as far as my writing and photography went but the woman who moved on was Anna Wright. The first few years after they died, I cried my eyes out behind closed doors and lay awake more nights than I can remember. I didn't want to write or even take photos. I survived living off the royalties of a few novels and photos and doing the bare minimum to keep my editors happy."

"When did you start to *really* write again? What about the photography?"

"Like I said, I did the writing that was necessary for the editors and publishers but the real writing – when words demand to be released – that didn't happen for about six years. The same goes for photography. I had a vast collection of photos. The time between when they died and when I started to *actually want* to create, using a camera – that took about seven years. Eventually the pain of their loss became more bearable. I searched for places to live and eventually settled on buying this house." She tilts her chin in a semi-defiant pose as she adds, "It is one of the homes that Drew's construction firm built. I felt I was coming home to him."

"Drew built this house!" This piece of information surprises me.

"He built Amy's too. In fact, a lot of the homes in this neighbourhood were built by his company." Her eyes light up with pride. "That's why they've lasted so long. His craftsmanship and attention to detail was meticulous. Drew was as driven on a construction site as he was in his preparation for a legal brief or courtroom appearance. He had good people working for him. He paid them well and he got the results he wanted."

"Wow," I mumble, taking in the room and thinking about the layouts of Anna-Claire's and Amy's homes. "I didn't know."

"No reason you would have known. I don't exactly go around announcing that the builder of these homes was my husband." She smiles. "That wouldn't do much for my privacy, now would it? People knew me as Anna Wright. Had I used my married name, someone would have made the connection to Claire Holowitz. As I've said before, I used my grandmother's maiden name for my literary purposes but it wasn't a secret that my married name was Henderson.

"I've read what the critics said about your work during that period. You wrote *Whispering Hope* and had that photo exhibit in London called ..." I stop for a second as I try to recall the name and then, remembering, I say, *"Hollow Dreams.* The critics characterized them as "Holowitz's Return."

Scowling, Anna-Claire answers, "It wasn't a return. It was a period of survival. I did what I knew how to do. I buried myself into the work and drove myself to the point of exhaustion. I couldn't escape the hurt and so I did my best to outrun it the only way I knew how ... work. It was a period of relentless discipline. But," she sighs, "there was no passion. It was just work. Funny thing, though," she pauses, "ironically, the critics ate it up. They talked about my new and raw emotions. The more I withdrew, the more they raved about what I produced. I remember how I held their reviews in contempt. On occasion, Emile would try to convince me to meet with the media. Until the day he died of a heart attack, Ernie spent more hours than I can count begging me to grant just one interview. Nothing either of them said or did could persuade me to change my mind." Her eyes take on a steely blue shade and her expression is one of proud defiance as she adds, "And, I've never broken that resolve or even considered it – until I met all of you."

Throwing caution to the wind, I blurt out, "Are you thinking of meeting with the media?"

"I don't want to but if I have too, I will." Anna-Claire sits perfectly still, letting the impact of her statement settle. There is no sense of defeat, no anger; just resignation to what she thinks might be inevitable.

"I wouldn't ask that of you, Anna-Claire. You don't have to do anything you don't want to." I get up from the couch and stand before her, making her look directly at me. "Listen to me. No one is going to find out who you are. No one. I promise you. No one."

"Times and things change, Leen," answers Anna-Claire. "It may turn out that I will choose to attend the Gala or grant an interview. Who knows?"

"I love you, Anna-Claire." The words come out of nowhere and I'm surprised at the force with which I've uttered them. They were impulsive, instinctive and needed to be said.

Anna-Claire straightens her shoulders. Looking at me with gentleness, she answers, "I love you, too, Leen. Don't ever forget that."

I start to say something but Anna-Claire holds up a hand and says softly, "There's no need to say anything else, Leen. I know and what's important is that you know I will do whatever I must to protect you." Then, with a smile, she says, "Let me finish what I started out to tell you."

"About a year after they died, I was spending some time with Marc Andre. He was only a little fellow – about three or four. We had come inside from a walk in the park and his little hands were cold. I went to rub them between my hands and he just reached out, with the simple trust of a child to hug me. I'll never forget that moment – I think it was then – that moment – when my soul started to heal. I must have been returning the hug too tightly because his little voice piped up, saying, "Aunt Claire, not so tight. I won't go away. I won't move." She smiles fondly. "His simple trust; open, unconditional love reaching out to me – assuring me that he wasn't going to go away – was the 'watershed' moment when I began to let go some of the pain I had locked in my heart."

She clears her throat. "That night, I cried long and hard. To this day I remember the bitter acid in my stomach as I wretched with convulsive sobs. I had cried so much before that day; it seemed beyond any scope of my imagination that I could shed more tears. But cry, I did. I felt the anguish of dealing not only with their deaths, but with the need to 'bury' them in my mind. I kept alive their memories but emotionally, I could finally accept their deaths. I reached down deep inside of myself and allowed the passion, the love of writing, my sense of freedom with a camera, to be unleashed from the crypt of grief in which I had buried them. Those burning tears washed over me, purging me of such deep grief that I had no words to describe." She pauses to think and then, softly admits, "I still don't.

I think of all she has revealed; trying to absorb the magnitude of Anna-Claire's sense of loss and the courage it has taken to give voice to her grief.

As if she has not spoken with such candour and expressed such raw emotion, Anna-Claire surprises me by bluntly asking, "So, you and Marc?"

I have to laugh at the way she has switched the focus back to me. It's pointless to evade her question. "Oh, Anna-Claire," I say, knowing that I must sound like a giddy school girl, "he's the one." Embarrassed, I look away.

"The *one* is he? Well, well ..." Anna-Claire smiles affectionately."

"I sound like a star struck teenager, don't I? Who would have thought meeting you would change my life? No," I say, stopping Anna-Claire from interrupting, "it's true. If someone had told me a year ago that I would be sitting here, in the kitchen of Anna Wright, who *is* really Claire Holowitz, I would have scoffed. If someone had told me that Claire Holowitz's godson and lawyer, Marc Andre Aumount, would be the one to take my heart to a place I never knew existed – at least, not for me – I would have downright laughed."

"Cupid's arrow has hit you hard, has it?" asks, Anna-Claire. I can't miss her smugness as she says, "He's fallen hard too. Just love him, Leen. Let him love you."

Pushing herself upwards to get out of her chair, she says, "Now, if you don't mind this old lady suddenly feels very tired."

I walk Anna-Claire up to her bedroom and after ensuring that she is comfortable, I let myself out, locking the front door behind me. She's given me a lot to think about. Not just background information on Claire Holowitz but the strength of love.

It's been forty years and Drew and Emily are still present in her mind and her heart. I want to believe that Marc Andre and I will be strong enough to not just *be* together in thirty or forty years – I've seen too many marriages where both spouses co-exist in a world that negates the whole purpose of marriage. They live together; silently resenting one another but remain that way because either or both don't have the guts or inclination to do something about it. In some cases it boils down to simple finances. It's cheaper to stay married than to divorce.

Strangers in the same house with shared history.

But the rare ones ... they actually love one another, at least on some level.

Then, there are the truly, unique marriages. The ones where they are partners in every sense of the word. They have intimacy of thought and emotions. They are the ones who truly know what it means when they say, 'I love you'.

I want and need to know Marc Andre's love not just now in the beginning ... I want and need his love until I draw my last breath. I don't want to fall into the pattern of assuming that he will always be there for me. I don't want stony silences and nights and days spent living my life alone even though I have a spouse to drag out for social events or holidays when family and friends gather. I want the real deal. I want my love to last and to count. Whether or not that's too much to hope for, I don't know. But, one thing I do know is that I'm going to do my best to learn from the lessons Anna-Claire shares and to not be afraid to love. I need to know that when I say 'I love you', I mean it and I'll go to hell and back to prove it.

Chapter Twenty

Becky

"Is that your famous cherry glaze I smell?" I wrap my arms around Joshua's waist and nuzzle against his back. Through his shirt I can feel beads of sticky sweat that have trickled down his spine. Using his shirtsleeve he wipes his brow as he stirs the glaze for the torte.

Peering around his shoulder, I sniff the sweet smell. "Hmmm, smells delicious!"

"Careful, I'm working with a very hot sauce." Josh angles his head to meet mine and quickly kisses my forehead. "What brings you here this early in the day?"

"My last patient cancelled. I thought I'd drop by to see my favourite chef." Stepping away from Josh, I spot some éclairs sitting on the far counter. "Are all those éclairs spoken for?"

"Give me a minute and I'll join you. Tim," he calls out to one of the waiters, "can you please get some coffee for us and set it at table four?"

"Sure thing, Josh." Grinning, he says, "Afternoon Dr. Sutherland."

"Hi Tim, how's the studying coming along for the mid-terms?"

"Hectic but manageable," he answers. "I'll be glad to have them over. I need a life."

I joke, "Don't we all." Pointing to the éclairs, I smile sweetly. "Will you steal me two of those sumptuous éclairs? It would seem as if my cavalier chef is determined to offer me only coffee. Winking, I add, "Do you think he's afraid that I won't fit into my wedding dress?"

Tim picks up some tongs. "Already on it Dr. Sutherland." He grins. "From where I'm standing, you have nothing to worry about in the weight department."

"Okay, Tim, that's enough." Josh wipes his hands and good-naturedly scowls. "Just what are you doing assessing my fiancée's waistline?"

Immediately I admonish playfully, "Don't you dare give that wonderfully perceptive and highly intelligent young man any grief, Josh! Come on Tim, I'll carry the éclairs and you bring the coffee. We'll go into the dining area and you can tell me all about how I can well afford to eat whatever my little heart desires."

"Right behind you Doctor." Tim scurries past Josh calling over his shoulder, "I think this is where the knight in shining armour comes in."

"Ha, Ha, very funny." Josh groans, "Now, I'm getting advice on love from my waiter."

"We can all learn from those younger than ourselves," I answer, taking a seat at the table.

Smiling at Tim, I say, "Don't pay him any mind. I think you're wonderful and you're going to make a good psychologist someday."

"Gee, thanks, Dr. Sutherland. Graduate work has a life of its own. Some days I just don't think I'll get through."

"Have you applied for the internship programme at the hospital's outpatient clinic?"

"I took you up on your offer," answers Tim with a shy smile. "I listed you as one of my references."

"Good." I reach for an éclair. "Let me know if I can do anything to help out."

"Sure will and thanks again," grins Tim. Looking at Josh with mock seriousness, he says, "Guess I'd better get back to work so I can afford to pay for all those books I need."

Josh answers with a grin. "Sounds like a better idea than making time with my chocolate éclair friend."

"Hmmm, but this is sooooo good!" I say, wiping my mouth with a napkin and reaching for my coffee cup.

"So, tell me, what really brings you down my way?"

"Am I that transparent?" Secretly, I'm pleased that he's intuitive enough to read my signals. "Ever think about turning in your ladle and taking up psychology?"

Ignoring my attempt at levity, he answers, "Not transparent, just slightly obvious. You're very structured in your routine at the hospital. You rarely leave before the end of the day. What's up?"

I gnaw at my lower lip while I try to think of a way to describe the churning of emotions that I feel. Josh takes my hand. "Come on Becky, what's upsetting you?"

"It's not that I'm upset …" I begin, "…it's just that I've been wondering about some things." I fiddle with my coffee spoon and ask, "What makes you think I'm upset?"

"Because you are biting your lower lip," he says.

"A lot of people bite their lips."

"I'm not marrying those people," answers Josh. He cocks his head at an angle. "When you gnaw at your lower lip, you've got something on your mind."

I hear the concern in his voice and once again I think to myself how fortunate I am to have this amazingly creative and sensitive man in my life. Sighing, I say, "I was talking with Leen earlier today."

"Did the two of you have a fight?"

"Oh no, nothing like that!" Chuckling, I say, "Trust me, you'll know when we decide to spar. It's a war zone and we take no prisoners."

"Promise to give me lots of warning if the two of you decide to do battle."

Placing my hand over my heart I say, "I swear."

"Good," says Josh. "Now tell me what has Leen said or done that is making you gnaw your lip?"

"She wants me to check in on Anna-Claire today but I'm supposed to make it look as if the visit is purely spur of the moment. But the real thing is that she wants me to assess her. She thinks that Anna-Claire is getting too weak and she's worried."

"I don't see the problem." Josh's face is an open question. "You may be a psychiatrist but as you are fond of saying, you are a doctor, first. What's the issue?"

I try to explain. "It's different, Josh. Anna-Claire's my friend; she's special to me. She's dying and we all know it. Her way of dealing with it is to ignore it. I know, on an intellectual level, that's the way she copes, but I'm finding it difficult to disassociate myself from the reality of my affection for her."

"I love you, Becky."

Disconcerted that Josh seems to be ignoring my concern, I reply, "Where did that come from? I was talking about Anna-Claire."

Ignoring my flash of peevishness, Josh says, "Most of the time you present yourself as some sort of strong woman – capable of taking on the world and having all the answers. Other times, like today, I am reminded that beneath that exterior of your *'I can handle anything'* persona lies the gentle soul of a woman who struggles to make things better for the ones she loves." He pauses long enough for his words to sink in and then adds gently, "You can't change Anna-Claire's fate, but if you can help her – as a doctor, friend, or confidant then do it."

"I know what you are saying is true and I accept that," I answer. "It's just that…" I reach for his hand, "on my way to her house I found myself turning the car around and heading here. I needed to tell you that I love you. You're so much a part of my life; I don't know what I would do if you weren't."

I squeeze his hand. "On the drive here I thought about what Anna-Claire has gone through in her life. Drew and Emily's deaths could have been emotionally crippling but instead she built a whole new life. I don't know if I'd have her strength. Now, death is knocking at her door again and it's so unfair!"

"I'm not going anywhere, Becky," answers Josh. "I promise." Grinning he says, "I'll remind you when we're old and I'm annoying you because I keep forgetting where I put my false teeth that you once drove to my restaurant in a panic so that you could tell me you wanted me."

His teasing makes me laugh. "Yeah, well, you'd better not leave your false teeth where you can't find them or you'll be gumming it a lot."

Before he can answer, I impulsively say, "Marry me, Josh."

Surprised at the intensity of my words, Josh tries to joke. "But, I am going to marry you. We're engaged or is someone else wearing my ring on her finger?"

"No, I mean, as soon as we can arrange it. I don't want to wait. I want the world to know that I love you. I want to be your wife. I want our marriage to be blessed with the kind of breathless, all-consuming love Anna-Claire had and I don't want to wait for it."

Josh smiles. "Tell you what. You pick the date. I'll close the restaurant and we'll hold a small celebration right here. We won't even bother looking for a hall. We will get the minister and set the date."

Happy, salty, tears cascade down my cheek. I practically gush. "Oh, Josh, I know I'm being so silly about all of this. It's like something out of one of those smultzy romance novels but I don't care. I want to marry you. How soon can we do this?"

"Well, we'll have to get the license and it would be good to let our friends have a few weeks to get their schedules organized. How about Christmas Eve? We'll make it small and intimate. There'll be red and white everywhere." He stands up and looks around his restaurant, exclaiming, "It'll be perfect!" His sudden unrestrained laughter draws glances from some of the customers.

"What's so funny?"

"Red and white? Not only will it be a Christmas Eve wedding, it'll be so Canadian in colours we'll look like poster ads for national identity."

His comment strikes me as hilarious. In between guffaws, I manage to choke out, "As long as the place settings aren't adorned with maple leaves."

Draping one arm over my shoulder, Josh theatrically announces to the customers watching our little side show with amused interest, "Ladies and gentlemen, we're getting married. This wonderful woman standing beside me is my bride to be. Meet Becky." He kisses me with such passion that no one can doubt his willingness to be led to the altar. Customers shout congratulations and clap.

Josh happily jokes, "At least we know who will be the head chef in our marriage." His comment is greeted with ripples of laughter.

I quip, "I'm only too happy to let a man do what he's good at." My retort evokes more laughter and brings a blush to Josh's cheeks.

"She's a keeper, Josh," a customer yells, "my ex spent all her time telling me *what* to do. Yours is going to be happy *letting you do it.*"

Laughing, Josh holds up his hand to get their attention and with the graciousness of one accustomed to dealing with the public says, "Please join in our celebration by having a glass of wine, on the house. Waiters will be by in a few minutes to serve you and of course, if wine is not your pleasure, then please have coffee, tea, or pop. In honour of our engagement, we'll be serving slices of glazed cherry cheese torte which," he smiles broadly, "happily falls into the colour scheme for our Christmas Eve wedding, red and white."

Tim and a few of the waiters who have been standing by the kitchen doors listening to Josh's announcement burst forth in a frenzy of activity, taking orders for wine, coffee, tea, cool drinks, and torte. We mingle with the patrons, shaking hands, and accepting congratulations.

Josh soon excuses himself from our spur-of-the-moment celebrations thanking everyone but reminding them that he needs to get back to the kitchen and start preparations for the next meals. I remain talking with the customers and receiving their congratulations for another half hour before I take my leave, telling Josh, "Wait until Anna-Claire and the others hear about our Christmas Eve wedding plans."

Grinning as he adds seasoning to the mixture in the bowl, Josh said, "Go forth and convene the ladies. Plan to your hearts delight, but remember the colours are going to be red and white. Sure you don't want to wait until Canada Day?"

"Very funny," I reply, pulling on my jacket and wrapping my scarf around my neck.

Wiping his hands on a towel, Josh walks me to the door. He whispers into my ear, "Don't come home too tired from all your planning. I'll have a few appetizers waiting."

I giggle like a schoolgirl. "Oh Josh, you're incorrigible!" Kissing him quickly on the cheek I head out the door, already anticipating what the reaction of my friends will be when I announce that we've moved the wedding date up to Christmas Eve.

Chapter Twenty-one

Leen

I yank my beige silk shirt from the hanger and toss it on the bed. Stepping back into the walk-in closet, I survey my wardrobe. Today I want something that screeches 'power'. Eying my tailored blue pin stripe suit I make my decision and quickly choose a pair of blue heels to compliment it. Snippets from my conversation with Kathy replay in my mind, refuelling the anger I felt last night.

I had left Ottawa at six in the morning and returned on the red-eye from New York. Exhausted from my hectic trip, I had barely walked into my condo after midnight when the phone started to ring. I had made the trip to take care of some logistic issues for the Gala ranging from the positioning of Claire's photos and manuscripts throughout the hall to ensuring that the caterers had a variety of hors d'oeuvres and cocktail snacks for the expected five hundred guests. While there, I'd commissioned three local artists to design sketches for the ice sculptures. Wanting the luxury of a hot bath, a good glass of wine, and some much needed sleep; I had been in no mood to hear Kathy's tale of Don having used my absence to call an emergency meeting of the Board so that he could rant about my handling of the Gala and woeful inability to locate Claire Holowitz.

"...And there was Don," Kathy spat into the phone, winding down her spiel, "bustling about as if he was the commander-in-chief."

Sleep had done nothing to improve my fury at his attempt to discredit and undermine me. Still too annoyed to make a decision about what jewellery I want to complement my *power* outfit, I stomp into the bathroom to brush my teeth, thinking about Kathy's warning. "Honestly, Leen," she said, making no attempt to conceal her righteous indignation, "he's up to something and from the smirk he was wearing when the Board members left, I'd say it's no good."

Livid that a Board meeting had been called behind my back, I absentmindedly squeeze the toothpaste tube with such force that it spurts onto the counter. Grabbing a tissue to wipe up the mess, I swear, "That son of a bitch is up to something alright!" I brush my teeth with anger mounting. Slipping off my bathrobe I step into the shower and let the water cascade over my tense shoulders.

What's really ticking me off is that I had spoken to that devious shit twice yesterday, answering his shotgun questions and dealing with his pompous manner. Annoyed that I'd not located the whereabouts of Claire Holowitz, he had made insidious and snide comments asking me exactly what the coup would be for the Gala. Towelling myself dry I frown as I recall his snippy tone. "Honestly, Leen, one would think that with the money and resources you've had at your disposal you would have been able to, at the very least, garner an interview with the woman. What have you been doing?"

As I blow dry my hair, I mentally rehearse all the things that I dearly would like to tell him prefacing my righteous tirade with what a supreme ass he is, thinking, *I've not only garnered an interview – I've had supper with her, laughed with her and seen her original notes.*

Sighing, I quickly dress and apply make-up. I take one last sidelong view of myself, smiling with satisfaction at the results of my carefully crafted business-like appearance. Grabbing my London Fog coat, I slip on black, leather gloves, gather up my keys, and set off. By the time the elevator reaches the parking garage, I'm focused on my morning's agenda and set to put Don in his place.

Greeting me with a sour expression Kathy jerks her thumb in the direction of my office. "Don's waiting for you."

I lower my voice and answer, "Good. It saves me the trouble of going to see him."

Striding into my office, I deliberately take my time to remove my coat and gloves. Placing my briefcase alongside my desk, I smile and ask, "To what do I owe the pleasure of your company at," I glance at my watch, "seven thirty-five in the morning?"

His lips curve into a sneer. Obviously under the delusion that I have no idea as to what he's being doing behind my back, he answers arrogantly, "I like to work early in the mornings, Leen. You know that. As a leader it's important to know the workings and the idiosyncrasies of one's subordinates."

Seething inwardly, I think, *'Since when, you bastard?'* With deliberate control over the distain I feel for the odious scumbag, I sit behind my desk and calmly answer, "Now that we've discussed your *leadership* style, I'll be sure to set my alarm so that I can follow your example."

Not fooled by my sarcasm, Don says, "I'll get right to the heart of the matter."

"Please do."

"The Board members are anxious to know what, if any, progress you've made with respect to locating Claire Holowitz."

I think, *You pompous, pretentious, asshole!* My outward response is calm. "You knew from the start that she's a recluse who disseminates information through her lawyers. No one in forty years has managed to interview her. I have told you repetitively that it's been an erroneous misrepresentation of our firm to insinuate to anyone that we would be able to one, locate Claire Holowitz and two, convince her to attend the Gala."

"Your reputation is that of one who knows how to get the job done," he snipes, spitting saliva. "This account has brought in a couple million in clear profit. If she shows up, we'll corner the market on all major exposes and accounts. You knew my expectations when I *permitted* you to be in charge of the Gala and now, the Board members want those expectations fulfilled."

"Well, you've said it right there," I retort. "They were *your* expectations, Don. And, for the record," I add, not concealing my contempt, "you didn't *permit* me to be in charge of the Gala. Claire Holowitz *chose* me, not you! You've just not been able to suck that one up since that first day when Aumount dismissed you."

His icy glare leaves no mistake in my mind – Don will do anything he can to destroy me. He will twist Claire's not attending the Gala as being proof of my incompetence and use it to have me fired and my credibility destroyed. Wanting to rid myself of him, I ask without any show of deference, "Is there anything else, Don? I have work to do."

Rising, the glint in his eyes is lethal as his mouth curves into a venomous sneer. Even though I knew what an underhanded, power-seeker he was, the hate on his face and malevolence of his tone is disturbing. In a low, threatening voice, he replies, "You would do well to remember that you answer to me and I report to the Board." His glance travels contemptuously from my toes to my face as he adds, "They will be very disappointed in their *so-called star* of the company." He crosses my office, throws open the door, and speaking so that Kathy will hear, orders, "Find her!"

As soon as the elevator doors shut, Kathy bustles into my office, indignantly pronouncing him to be a supreme idiot. Softening her tone, she asks, "Are you okay?"

I smile wearily. "Yes, of course I am. He's in one of his more bitter moods today and determined that he'll have my head served on a silver platter to the Board members." I blow out a long, frustrated breath and say, "He wants Claire Holowitz at the Gala and he's convinced the Board members that because of my ineptitude she won't be there."

Kathy bristles. "But Holowitz was never part of the plan. He's known that from the start. What's up his butt?"

"The coup of finding Claire Holowitz and getting her to come out of seclusion would in his sick little mind prove to the Board of Governors and the media world that he, Don Harris, is a great and powerful director who knows how to achieve the impossible."

"A legend in his own mind!" The full weight of my answer dawns on her. Kathy sputters, "You mean he's going to try to have you fired?"

Knowing I can trust her, I reluctantly admit, "It would seem so."

"But that's nonsense," Kathy protests. "Why not try again with Aumount? Ask him if he can get Claire Holowitz to reconsider."

Before I can answer, a voice says, "Reconsider what?" Startled, we look to the doorway.

Entering my office Marc Andre nods hello to Kathy, saying, "No one was out there so I thought I'd take a peek inside and see if this is where I'd find you." Quickly discerning the strain on my face and Kathy's agitation, he attempts to diffuse the tension. "Well," he says patiently, "I couldn't help overhearing the name Holowitz and the *'ask her*' part. Are either of you willing to tell me – her legal counsel – what exactly you wish to ask Claire Holowitz?"

Ignoring my warning glance, Kathy squares her shoulders, juts her chin defiantly, and spouts, "Don Harris is demanding that Leen find and produce Ms Holowitz for the Gala. If she doesn't, he's plotting to have her fired. I was just asking Leen why she just doesn't ask you to convince Ms Holowitz to grant Leen an interview – one maybe that can be taped. That way she wouldn't have to actually come to the Gala but it would prove that Leen did find her and that she convinced her to do what no one in the media world has been able to do for forty years – give an interview."

"Kathy, please," I plead for her to stop. "It's not going to happen."

Marc Andre narrows his eyes and from the tightening of his jaw, both Kathy and I are aware of his annoyance. "Claire Holowitz has made her feelings known about not wanting to be interviewed or to make an appearance."

"We know that, Marc," I quickly interject. "It's Don's doing. He wants to use her lack of appearance as an indication that I am not competent." I slip onto my chair. The frustration caused by Don and his antics take their toll. I feel weak, nauseous, and I can feel my body starting to tremble.

Realizing that his anger has been misunderstood as being directed at me and Kathy, Marc Andre rushes to explain. "I'm not annoyed with either of you," he says gently, "but that man infuriates me. I have a good mind to go up there and set him straight on a few things."

Relief spreads across Kathy's face and I can tell she's ready to cheer him on but I, however, can easily visualize what Don's reaction will be to a confrontation with Aumount. Panic clutching at my throat, I gasp, "No!"

"And why not?" asks Marc Andre, narrowing his grey eyes so that I'm reminded of hard flint. I know he is controlling his anger, but his look tells me that what I say next must not only be the truth but that I have to find a way to make him see my reason.

"Yeah, why not?" chirps in Kathy, who has regained her earlier bravado and clearly relishing images of Don's quick corporate demise when Marc Andre is through cutting his career to shreds.

I try to explain so that they can understand and accept my reluctance to do battle with Don. "To do that would be to play right into his hands. He would think that I called you and worse yet, see it as me trying to undermine his authority. For Don, the projection and pretence of authority verging on omnipotence is imperative. I just have to hope that all the preparations I have done along with Kathy and the others," I glance sideways at Kathy, "will convince the Board that the Gala will be such a success that it will be talked about for a long time yet to come."

"What will you do?" asks Marc Andre. It is hard for me to reconcile this intense, fierce looking man with the gentle lover I have come to know. I want desperately to go to him – to feel his protective arms shielding me from harm but I can't. He is a warrior, ready to do battle and I must do the same.

I meet his gaze and truthfully answer, "Right now, I'm not sure. I need time to think." I let out a long slow breath and say, "He's on the attack and has the Board members thinking that I'm failing in my job. I wouldn't be surprised if he's on the phone now, doing what he can to undermine my credibility." I walk to the window and stare down at the street several floors below. Everything looks so small; I feel so distanced from what is right and good in my life.

Turning to face Kathy and Marc Andre, I say, "For now, I just have to deal with it. I've a lot of work to do so I'd best get to it before Don has something else to use as leverage against me."

I can tell that Marc Andre is not happy but I smile and reassure him, "I've been dealing with Don and his underhanded ways for a long time. I'll be fine. It'll blow over."

"And that is supposed to reassure me that everything is going to be alright? You're going to wave some magic wand and poof, everything will be fine?"

"If only," pipes in Kathy, her expression worried. "He's going to come at you with all he's got. You can't ignore it, Leen. Not this time."

"I agree with Kathy," says Marc Andre, but seeing that I'm about to put up an argument he doesn't push the matter any further. "So be it. As you wish." Pushing up his shirtsleeve he glances at his watch. "I have to be at a meeting for ten. I dropped by this morning hoping to get an update on the progress of the Gala but," he says with charming wit, "I've heard enough from this brief interlude to know that you have a lot left to do this morning. What say I let you get back to work and come back around one? We could go to lunch and you can bring me up-to-date then."

Grateful that he's not going to charge upstairs to confront Don, I answer, "Lunch is good. In between now and then I have plenty to keep me occupied."

"Good," replies Aumount, allowing his eyes to linger a little longer than necessary. I hope that Kathy has not picked up on that tell tale intimacy.

Turning to Kathy, he says smoothly, "It occurs to me that you've had a stressful morning too. Would you care to join us? If Don asks why you and Leen are going out to lunch, you can lay the blame on me saying that I asked you to come along to take notes." Taking her wide grin as a clear indication that she's pleased with his suggestion, he oozes charm saying, "Leen speaks highly of you. I may just try to steal you away to work in my office. What do you say, Kathy?"

Grateful to him for including Kathy, I say, "That's a good idea. We both need a break from him and the sentinel but squash any thoughts of luring Kathy away."

It's almost comical the way Marc Andre has charmed Kathy. The image of a smitten schoolgirl comes to mind as I listen to her demure response. "I'd like that very much, Mr. Aumount. Thank you."

Smiling warmly, he says, "My friends call me Marc or Marc Andre. Please feel free to do the same."

I can't resist teasing, "Always the charmer, Marc?"

Eyes twinkling, he answers, "It's a simple matter of wanting to work with two beautiful and intelligent ladies in a congenial environment. We are, after all," he adds, assuming an innocent expression, "joined in a common project."

Before I can come back with a witty retort, Kathy snaps out of her smitten state and, sounding more like the Kathy I know well, states, "I'll be going back to my work." She smiles smugly. "I need to call Erma …" she smiles at Marc Andre, "a.k.a. the sentinel, and let her know that you've requested my presence with yours and Leen's business lunch and that neither of us will be in the office for the remainder of the day. That's bound to put another burr in both their butts." She laughs. "That's what I call killing two vultures with one stone!" Imbued with a new mission she turns on her heels and practically marches to her desk, ready to sound the trumpet and begin the battle.

Marc Andre and I burst out laughing. He calls out after her, "Enjoy the moment, Kathy."

"Thank you," shouts Kathy from her desk. Laughing she adds, "My only regret is that I won't be able to see her expression. Second thought," she calls out, "maybe I should go upstairs to tell her in person."

"You're having way too much fun with this, Kathy," I answer.

Softly, so that only I can hear, Marc Andre says, "All either of you have to do is give the word."

I look at his face; the face of the man I love. My anger at Don disappeared the moment Marc Andre walked through my office door. He was like a knight on a white charger, set to rescue his damsel in distress from an evil overlord. Silently I admire how his grey suit shapes to his body and accents the colour of his eyes.

"What's so funny?" asks Marc Andre. "For someone who is about to lose her job, you've got quite a smirk on your face."

"Oh, nothing," I answer, walking to the door and closing it. Returning to where he stands, I lean up towards him and kiss him fully on the mouth." When we break from our embrace, he says with a teasing leer, "If this is the response I get for offering to take you and Kathy out for lunch, what will I get if I throw in dinner for just the two of us?"

Slowly letting my fingers drift down his arm, I answer, "You'll just have to wait and see, Mr. Aumount. Now, if you don't mind, I have a considerable amount of work to get done before my luncheon date with my knight in shining armour."

"Knight? Armour?" He's momentarily puzzled but then bows as if paying homage to the Queen, and gallantly says, "Your every wish is my command, my lady. I shall return promptly at one to free my damsel from her chains." Picking up his coat and briefcase, he winks good-bye. I can hear Kathy openly laughing in response to his comment, "Tell Erma that I send my regards."

Chapter Twenty-two

Leen

Dressed and bundled up to ward off a chill, Anna-Claire accompanies us to the Rideau Centre. Amy is driving Joe's van so that we can all travel in one vehicle. We're all busily chatting about what has to be done for the Christmas Eve wedding.

"Red velvet will be nice," comments Amy, turning off Nicholas and heading towards the parking garage adjacent to the mall and convention centre.

"Wow, check out those lights," interjects Sarah, cutting off any discussion about bridal gowns and drawing our attention to the decorations adorning the street and canal lamps. She has only recently started driving again, but since this is her first trip to the city centre, Amy volunteered to drive saying, "Until you get used to the busy traffic, best to limit your driving to your neighbourhood." Although her speech still tends to be hesitant, the return of her driving privileges has been a major boost to her morale, signalling that the worst is behind her.

Admiring the display of seasonal lighting Anna-Claire comments, "They've gone out of their way this year. Almost as if they know you'll be celebrating your marriage, Becky."

I tease, "All this for Becky!"

Easing the van into a space on the third floor, Amy turns off the ignition. "Okay, Becky, this will be the eighth mall we've visited in two days. You liked the red velvet the first time you saw it and nothing since has compared. Hopefully this time, you'll be convinced that red velvet is the way to go."

Becky laughs. "Okay, okay, but you have to admit, it's been fun even if a bit tiring."

"Speaking for myself," says Anna-Claire, leaning against Becky's proffered arm as we walk towards the elevator, "I haven't had this much fun and excitement in a long time."

"How are you holding up?" asks Becky, casually. She, like the rest of us, is trying not to show concern for Anna-Claire's apparent fatigue, knowing that she would resent what she refers to as mollycoddling. Our shopping expeditions have taken longer than they would have normally but we've been using the excuse to make frequent stops for coffee breaks saying that we need time to discuss the pros and cons of the dresses we're inspecting.

"I'm doing fine," smiles Anna-Claire. "You don't have to worry about me. Besides, I'm travelling with my own in-house doctor."

"That you are," chuckles Becky.

As we enter the store, the clerk bustles over. "You're back. Would you like to see the red velvet dresses again?"

"Yes, please," answers Becky, throwing a quick glance at us and adding, "and these ladies would like to try them on again."

"Oh, you've got to be kidding!" groans Amy. "This will be the fourth time today I've had to climb out of my boots, jacket and jeans. The dress fit the last time I tried it on. I doubt if I've gained weight in twenty-four hours."

Unperturbed, Becky replies, "Consider it training for when you can have me do the same for you."

"I'll just wait over there," says Anna-Claire, pointing to one of the chairs set aside for customers to sit on while people try on outfits.

"We won't be long," says Amy.

"Take your time," answers Anna Claire. "I'm quite comfortable."

*

Anna-Claire

Glad to have a few moments of rest, I glance around the store. There are a few other customers being attended to by other clerks and it's quite clear that management has made it a policy to cater to their clientele. The head clerk, the one who is looking after Becky and crew, is named Adele. She's pleasant but not overbearing. I smile at her as she approaches.

"Would you care for some herbal tea while you're waiting?" asks Adele.

I decline with a smile. "I'm fine thank you."

"Are you the mother-of-the-bride?"

The question startles me momentarily until I realize that given my age, it is a natural leap to conclude that I might well be the mother-of-the-bride. Add to that, Becky and the others have been solicitous in watching out for my comfort and deferential when asking my opinion about the dresses. I'm about to answer when Becky emerges from the dressing room. Dressed in red velvet, trimmed with white fur, she is simply stunning in spite of wearing no make-up.

"Yes," answers Becky, who has overheard Adele's question, "she is." Winking at Adele, she asks, "Would you bring out the suit that I had put aside yesterday?"

"Certainly." Adele smiles graciously and heads off to retrieve the lay away suit.

"Yesterday?" I'm puzzled as to what Becky's talking about. "You didn't put aside a suit yesterday. Are you thinking of changing from the dress to a suit?"

Becky lightly touches my shoulder. "Just wait and see," she says, as the other three parade out dressed in vibrant red velvet with red trimming around their hoods and sleeves. Mesmerized by their collective beauty, I murmur, "You all look so beautiful."

Placing her hands over mine, Becky smiles. "I came back here last night, after I'd dropped all of you off. As you know, my mother died ten years ago. My father has long been gone with his mistress for the last twenty years of my life. My family, as I know it to be, is in this room. I would be so privileged if you would consider standing in as mother-of-the-bride."

My breath catches in my throat and my eyes begin to water. "Mother-of-the-bride," I say, liking the sound of it. "I would be so honoured."

"Good, then, it's settled," says Becky, leaning over to give me a quick hug and whispering into my ear, "I am the one who is honoured."

Adele returns with a beautifully tailored ankle-length skirt and fitted jacket, the colour of rich cream. "It's beautiful, Becky," I say, genuinely pleased with her choice.

"I thought you might like it." Beaming, she asks, "Adele, do you have the shirt?"

"Susan's bringing it over," replies Adele. "I thought it'd be nice to give your mother a chance to see the suit first."

"Your turn, Anna-Claire," says Leen, jerking her thumb at the change rooms.

Smiling at me, Adele remarks, "Your daughter has your smile."

Not missing a beat, I answer proudly, "Yes she does, doesn't she?"

Susan arrives with a red, silk shirt and hands it to Adele. I follow Adele, listening to her prattle on about the importance of selecting the proper clothes for a wedding.

Five minutes later I make my grand entrance feeling like Cinderella; transformed from rags to riches. "Admittedly, the stockings have to go," I say with a small laugh.

"Do you like the suit," asks Becky.

"Like it? I love it," I answer, slowly turning around so they can see how it fits.

"To the manor born," says Sarah. "That suit looks like it was made for you."

"Yes, it does," remarks Adele, crouching to adjust the hem. "We'll have to make a few alterations but she looks quite elegant in it." Susan reappears with a small box of straight pins and she and Adele discuss the length of the hem and the jacket's cuffs, asking for input from Becky and the girls before placing the pins.

Amy points to my stocking feet. "Next, we have to find the proper shoes for our wedding outfits."

"Shoes? Today?" My reaction makes them laugh.

"Well, of course, shoes," answers Becky. "We can't go to my wedding barefooted."

"Before we do the shoe shopping expedition," says Amy, "I want to eat." Glancing at me for support, she asks, "How about you Anna-Claire? Are you ready for some lunch?"

"That's a good idea," I agree.

"Then, let's get out of these dresses and head off to the food court," says Sarah.

Leen grimaces. "I'm not sure that I want fast food. Let's find a restaurant and sit down for a proper lunch."

"There's that bistro on the first floor," suggests Amy. "It provides a full smorgasbord and they bake their bread in a stone oven right on site."

Twenty minutes later we're headed down the escalator and manage to get in before the lunch crowd arrives.

"Thank God, you didn't hold out for purple taffeta or something equally ridiculous," says Leen.

"Well," teases Becky, "I had entertained the idea of letting you think I would pick out something hideous but Anna-Claire persuaded me not to."

"Thank you, Anna-Claire," says Leen, deferring to me. "Nice to know you provided the voice of reason."

Changing topics, Becky asks, "So what's new and exciting with Marc Andre?"

"Speaking of whom," I answer, "I have to give him a call and tell him that I'll be late. Shoe shopping is taking priority."

Sarah teases, "And to think that I was beginning to give up all hope of seeing a day when good old Leen here would actually factor in any man's schedule to hers. Oh, how the times they are a' changing."

"No kidding," agrees Amy, "Lately, everything is Marc Andre this and Marc Andre that."

Anna-Claire jokes, "If I didn't know better, I'd say all of you were school girls instead of accomplished professionals. If I could capture your antics onto paper, I'd have a Broadway hit."

"Really?" Amused, Amy comments, "Leen could provide the comic relief."

"Enough from the peanut gallery," retorts Leen, poking Amy with her elbow.

We wander about the room, making selections from various tables and return with heaped plates. Eying the brownies on the dessert table, I say, "I'll be back."

Lunch is a fun affair. We chatter about Becky's wedding plans and what type of shoes will go best with our outfits. Drinking bottled water,

Leen pats her stomach and says with satisfaction, "Eating at the bistro was a good idea. I got to sample pizza, roast beef, ribs, and two types of salad. How often does one get that combination in a restaurant?"

"I don't know how you pack away so much food and still stay so fit," remarks Amy.

"Genetic make-up. I take after my mother's side of the family. Grinning, Leen adds, "I hate to admit it but every once in a while, a meal out and total abandonment with respect to calories is like good sex. It leaves a pleasant aftermath."

Immediately there's a chorus of 'what?' followed by our laughter.

"Leen," guffaws Amy, "is there any place where we can count on you not to equate the pleasures in life with sex?"

"If you must be so blatant about it ..." sniggers Sarah, "could you lower your voice?"

In a pouting voice and affecting an injured expression, Leen appeals to me. "See what I put up with Anna-Claire? Constant criticism. What's wrong with speaking openly and honestly?"

I wipe my lips with my napkin, using it to hide my own smirk. Picking up on the mirth around our table, I teasingly admonish as if they are schoolchildren. "Ladies, and I do emphasize the word, ladies ... it's important to govern one's self with decorum especially when in public." Winking at Leen, I add in hushed tones, "In answer to your question, it's been so many years since I've had any *good sex*, as you so colourfully put it – I'll just have to live vicariously through my palate and enjoy the experience."

Sarah laughs with such gusto that she attracts attention to our table from other customers.

"Oh, Anna-Claire," enthuses Leen, as we leave the Bistro, "you are absolutely priceless."

Smiling, I reply, "I do my best, my dear."

Leen links her arm through mine and I'm grateful for her humour, support and, feeling very much like a mother, thrilled to be with my 'girls'. Shoe shopping proves to be a much faster expedition than was dress shopping. It takes exactly one hour to find the shoes we want to match our respective outfits. "They had to be stylish but comfortable," reiterates Becky, as we drive back to Amy's house.

"My tender tootsies appreciate your consideration," comments Sarah, looking out the passenger window at the snowflakes falling in clusters. "If this weather keeps up, you'll definitely have a white wedding."

"You're going to be a beautiful bride, Becky," I say, meaning every word. "I've had so much fun over the last few days."

Amy squeezes my shoulder. "And, we've had fun too."

Amy offers to make me a cup of tea before I go home, but I decline saying, "I'll take a rain-check but for now, I really need to get some rest. After all," she joked, "Becky can't have an exhausted looking mother-of-the-bride."

All four walk me to my house and come in to make sure that I am safely settled for the night, clucking over me like a gaggle of mother hens. I'm quick to reassure them that I've been putting myself to bed for several years and that there's no need for them to fuss.

"We're not fussing," protests Becky, handing me a glass of water and my medications. "We're just making sure you're okay. After all," she adds, "we've kept you to a busy schedule for the last two days. I'm a doctor, I should know better."

"Oh, but you do," I answer, patting her cheek. "The four of you have been the perfect medicine for me and done way more to make me feel young and alive than these darned pills." I smile at their concerned expressions and add, "I've loved every minute of our shopping sprees. But now …" I glance at Becky, "I will follow the good doctor's advice and head off to bed."

When Leen offers to turn down my bed, I joke, "I think I can handle sleeping without supervision."

"You go on up," says Becky. "We'll turn out the lights and lock up."

I hear the click of the lock as Amy uses her key to lock the front door. In the quiet solitude of my room, I'm quite content to follow their advice and to allow exhaustion to take over.

༄

Amy

I put the kettle on to boil for tea and comment, "I'm glad that she had a good time but I hope we didn't tire her out too much."

"Me too," answers Leen. Looking at Becky, she says, "I think you blew her away when you asked her to fill in as mother-of-the-bride."

Becky smiles. "I'm glad she accepted."

"Hey, where are you going?" asks Sarah.

Becky and I stare at Leen. Curious that she hasn't bothered to remove her leather bomber jacket and not sat down at the kitchen table, Becky asks, "Why do you still have your jacket on?" She pushes her big toe against the leg of a kitchen chair so that the chair slides towards Leen. "Sit down. I thought we were all going to have a post-shopping gab fest with Amy before we went home."

Leen grins mischievously. "Marc's waiting."

"How does he even know you're here?" I ask.

"I called him before we left the mall and told him that we were heading back."

"Whoops Sarah," I joke. "We're slipping. Becky's got us so wrapped up in her wedding plans that we're not up to our usual standard of sniffing out Leen's covert operations. How did we miss her calling Marc Andre to give him an update?"

Sarah laughs. "Good thing you picked up on that flaw. If we're not on top of things, Leen will be off getting married to Marc Andre and we'll have missed the announcement."

Becky joins in. "Do I hear wedding bells in the not too distant future?"

"Cut it out," replies Leen, letting out an exasperated sigh, but her expression is a dead giveaway. She's not upset with our teasing – she's embarrassed that we're on to the fact that she's more serious about Marc Andre than she's been letting on. "We're just beginning to explore our relationship. I'm nowhere near ready to take that long trip down the aisle."

Becky arches a sceptical eyebrow. "Long is it? Want to know what I think when my patients get all prickly about answering truthfully?" Her eyes flicker with alert interest up and down Leen and not waiting for a response, she says, "I think, to paraphrase the great Bard, you're protesting too loudly for there not to be a kernel of truth beneath the denial."

"I'm not one of your patients," counters Leen.

"Getting a little prickly are we?" drawls Sarah.

"Oh, how the mighty have fallen," I joke while Sarah hums a few bars from the wedding march.

Not ready to let Leen off the hook, Becky plays innocent and says, "Refresh my memory Leen. Wasn't it you who equated a good meal with satisfying sex …?" She winks at me. "Do you remember something along those lines being said?"

"Well …" I assume a thinking expression, "… now that you mention it …" but Sarah who is clearly enjoying the banter at Leen's expense, cuts me off.

"Lunch wasn't enough. Now, she wants dessert."

"Different type of appetite," mumbles Leen.

"Ah, come on Leen," soothes Becky, "we're just teasing you."

"If it were one of us, you'd do the same," justifies Sarah, her expression absent of remorse for the embarrassed flush creeping up Leen's cheeks.

Leen throws her hands up in surrender. "Okay, so you've all had your fun for the night. I can see that I'm fighting a losing battle." With a jaunty wave, she heads for the front door calling out, "Loved the lunch and now I'm off to get dessert."

Laughing, I retort, "After dessert, find out if he has a twin brother or equally charming and handsome friend for me."

After Leen's gone, I comment wryly, "I seem to be the only one of the four of us without someone to hold me and whisper sweet nothings."

"You're time will come," says Sarah, slipping an arm around my shoulder. "Wait and see. I'm right about that."

"Oh sure," I answer, "and pigs are about to fly."

"Joke as much as you want, Professor, but I am absolutely right. You have way too much love in your heart not to share it with someone special. We're just going to have to find him."

Becky agrees. "Sarah's right. It's going to happen. You just don't know when."

Unconvinced, I answer, "Sometimes, I get lonely." I shrug. "It's not that I'm unhappy. For the most part I like my life. What's not to like? I have a great job. I have you three as my best friends and now I've got Anna-Claire as a surrogate mother and mentor. But, honestly, it's no fun being the odd person out all the time at social events or even if we go out to dinner. Let's face it … we live in a couples' world and when you're minus that companion for a show or dinner out with friends etc. it becomes clear that life without love or having someone to care about you is pretty damn lonely."

"We care," reassures Becky.

"A lot," adds Sarah.

"I know," I answer. "But surely you can see my point too? I don't doubt that I'll always have you guys, but I sure as hell do doubt that I'll ever have what all of you have – a companion, lover and friend. Phew," I say, blowing out a breath, "there, I've bared my soul." Trying to lessen my sombre truth, I tease them saying, "I trust that in both your cases, I've just entered into lawyer/doctor/client privilege?"

"No worries," answers Becky, as Sarah nods agreement. "We like to tease but we're good at respecting one another's opinions."

"Come on, let's have some tea, talk about life, and share our thoughts about love and," she glances at me, "being open to love when it comes knocking on your door." She giggles. "Josh is working late tonight and I'm in one of my expansive, philosophical moods."

"I've unleashed a monster."

"Just couldn't keep your mouth shut, could you?" laughs Sarah, as we lessen the seriousness of a few moments ago. "Now, we're going to have to listen to Becky wax eloquent."

"It could be worse," I answer, with a sly smile, "we could be listening to Leen's capsule version of *good sex*."

"Now you're talking," Becky quips. "And, to think people pay good money for the wisdom I willingly impart to my friends."

The next hour passes quickly as we exchange jokes, banter, and comment on life, love, politics, and anything that enters our minds. By the time Sarah and Becky leave, I'm no longer feeling badly about my non-existent love life.

As I settle down for the night, I think, *All in all, I do have a good life.* But, as I pull the blanket over me, I do something very uncharacteristic and revert to a childhood practice of saying a silent prayer with the hope that if there is a God, He is listening. *I don't want to die alone, God, please, don't let me die alone. Let me find love again and this time, please let it last.*

Chapter Twenty-three

Sarah

Joe hollers, "Jeremy, Jake, get a move on. We're going to be late!" He pulls on his black tuxedo jacket and taps an impatient foot as I slip on the red velvet cape with hood to accompany my dress.

"Your eyes are the colour of sapphires," smiles Joe. "All these years and you can still take my breath away." His eyes travel to the dip in my dress hinting at the cleavage and he lets his gaze linger long enough to cause me to blush. Wickedly, I think how nice it would be to simply nip off to our bedroom. All it takes is one look like the one he has now to make my body ache for his embrace and touch.

"Joe Calder!" I admonish. "You stop that!"

"Stop what?"

"Don't play innocent with me," I tease, adjusting his bow tie. I rest my hands on his chest and kiss his lips. "The way you're looking at me, Becky is going to be left standing at the altar minus one bridesmaid and Josh missing his best man."

He clasps one hand over mine and breathes out a husky breath. "I love you, Sarah."

"I love you, too," I answer, "and, as I said, we have a wedding to get to. So, if you don't mind, keep your looks and hands to yourself." He cracks a wide smile as I step out of his embrace and whisper, "That is, until later. Remember to save the last dance for me."

Laughing, Joe turns back to the staircase and shouts, "Come on guys, get a move on before your amazingly beautiful mother makes me forget all about Aunt Becky's wedding." Turning to me he says, "I'll start the car and if they're not down in two minutes, I'm going to start honking the horn just like I used to do when they were kids."

Jeremy bounds down the stairs with Jake following on his heels. "How do I look?" asks Jeremy, pulling down the cuff of his suit jacket.

"Let's see," I answer, motioning for my sons to stand ready for my motherly inspection. "Well I have to admit that you boys clean up very nicely," I tease, secretly awed at how grown up they look. Both have chiselled chins like Joe but less angular, more refined. They look so handsome in their blue suits, white shirts, and red ties.

"It's hard to believe that you are my sons. The very same ones that make t-shirts, open long-sleeved shirts, and jeans look like a fashion statement. Where did the two of you come from?"

"Thanks, Mom. We love you too." Jake slips on his overcoat and tosses Jeremy his.

"You look beautiful, Mom." Three sharp beeps sound out from the driveway.

Jeremy laughs. "What's Dad beeping for? We're not even going in the same car."

"You know him," I answer. "He wants to make sure that we are all on time." I hand over my car keys to Jake and locking the front door, say, "I'm quite proud of my three men tonight."

Jeremy holds the car door open for me and Joe leans over to say, "No dallying guys. Pick up your dates and get to the restaurant."

"Drive safely," I warn, "no speeding."

"Ah Mom," groans Jeremy. "We don't speed and there's plenty of time."

"Just the same," I answer, "it's snowing."

"Don't worry, Mom," says Jeremy, opening the door to my Porsche.

"I'm a mother. Worry is my middle name. Besides, it's part of the job description."

Joe backs the Mercedes out of the driveway. It's rare that he drives the Mercedes, preferring to use his work van but since this is a dress-up occasion, we're using the car.

"I love these seat warmers." I say, wiggling my bum on the soft leather. "They make the cold night more bearable."

"Know what you mean," answers Joe, slipping the clutch into third gear and turning the corner. "How are you doing? Not too tired?"

"Tired? The night hasn't even started."

"Yeah, but you had the rehearsal last night, the hair dresser this morning, and you and Becky have talked at least a dozen times today."

"I'm having fun," I answer. "Becky is excited and I am happy for her."

Pulling up to a light, Joe's brow creases in thought. "I'm not given to fanciful moments as a rule, but I can't help thinking how much we have to celebrate this Christmas. You have recovered from your aneurism. You rarely hesitate or confuse your words and one of your best friends is getting married." The light changes and he eases the car into gear.

"It's hard to believe a full year has passed and so much has happened. I'm so happy to be celebrating with everyone – Becky's marriage is the icing on my cake."

Joe reaches to squeeze my hand. "What do you think of Stacey and have you met Jake's new interest? What's her name?"

"Stacey's really quite nice. She's been over a few times to watch videos with Jake and get this," I add, barely able to keep a straight face, "once they were actually studying for a biology test."

Joe rolls his eyes. "This is supposed to give me comfort? Jake and his girlfriend studying for a biology test, together."

I giggle. "That struck me funny too, but they were actually studying." Glancing at him, I add, "But, just in case, either of them decided to take the biology to a more personal level, I made coffee, served up some munchies, and had them use the kitchen table using the excuse that the desk in Jake's room wasn't large enough to spread out their papers."

"Devious," remarks Joe, grinning widely. "How did Jake take to your little ploy?"

"He didn't put up any argument. Mind you, though," I answer mischievously, "they got their work done in record time and then Jake said they were going out for a quick pizza before he had to take Stacey home."

"How'd he do on the test?"

"I waited a week to ask and asked in what I thought was a very casual manner but Jake's nobody's fool. He proudly produced a test paper with a big *I know what you're thinking look*. He got ninety-three percent. There wasn't much I could say about that. Stacey got a ninety-five. I think he threw in the later titbit for my benefit – his way of letting me know that they had actually been studying." I grin. "He's got your sense of humour."

Joe chuckles. "He's growing up. A year ago, he would have raged at you about not trusting him. Now, he's just toying with you and having a good laugh."

"I'm not naïve, Joe." I try to sound slightly miffed, but I know he's right. When it comes down to anything having to do with either of the boys, I'm downright fiercely protective.

"How about Jeremy's girl? What's her name?"

"I begin to tick off what I know. Her name's Alicia and she wants to be a teacher. Pretty, petite, has brown eyes, and according to Jeremy she is an awesome soccer player. So good that she's hoping to be offered a scholarship to an American university. Full tuition, accommodation, and some expenses if she keeps up her grades and agrees to play on the varsity team. Jeremy's smitten." I pause. "So smitten that he's started to make noises about going to the States to take his bachelor of science."

Joe clears his throat. "And just how does Mister plan on paying for the American tuition?"

I had wanted to avoid this conversation during the holidays, preferring to wait for a time when we could sit with both of the boys and calmly discuss their post-secondary plans. I limit my answer to bare facts. "Yesterday, Jeremy announced that his coach thinks he stands a good chance of getting a football scholarship to a few U.S. universities – Princeton, UCLA, and Duke being three of them. Apparently, they had scouts at a few of the games who expressed an interest in his post-secondary plans. The coach encouraged Jeremy to apply to their universities. At first, he had been undecided because he's always wanted to go to Simon Fraser or University of Toronto. But, when Alicia announced she was hoping for a soccer scholarship to an American university, he decided to send in his applications."

"Doesn't he have to write the SATS for entrance to American universities?"

I sigh softly. "He already has."

"Without telling us?"

"Without so much as a peep," I answer. I can tell from his clipped tone that Joe is not sure which way he's going to swing on this one. On one hand, it's awesome that Jeremy had the initiative to write the SATS and to send in the applications and yet, on the other hand, I'm not thrilled that he hadn't bothered to let us in on his revised plans for university. Nervous, I bite on my lower lip wondering how I'm going to answer what I know his next question will be. Right on cue, Joe asks it.

"What about Jake?"

"Monkey see, monkey do. But," I quickly add, "Jake's still interested in Queens. His rationale for applying was that he wants to explore his options and the coach told him he has a good chance of getting a hockey scholarship. In fact," I add, proudly, "both boys do."

Joe blinks. "But I thought you said football."

"Well big guy," I answer, using one of my pet names for Joe, "seems the boys have your athletic prowess. Jake said that the coach thinks that both boys should try out for both sports and that way they'll stand a good chance of being accepted." I glance sideways. "Listen to us. You'd think they were failing the way we're carrying on. Most parents would be overjoyed. After all," I laugh softly, "there are worse things in the world than getting a sports scholarship to an American Ivy League university."

"Damn," Joe thumps the steering wheel. "You'd think one of those two would have bothered to let us into the change of plans. Just the same ..." he grins, unable to keep the pride out of his tone, "not too shabby." He glances at me. "You seem to be taking all of this rather calmly."

"Not really," I answer, "but I've had twenty-four hours to think about it. I was upset yesterday – not that they hope to get sports' scholarships or that they want to attend an American university. My issue was, and still is, adjusting to the fact that they're growing up and making decisions without consulting either of us." I stare out the windshield at the falling snow and don't even try to hide the sadness in my voice. "It's the beginning of the end for us, Joe. When they go off to university – wherever it is – they're going on to whole new lives which we can only hope they will share. They're becoming men and we're entering the empty nest years."

"And?"

"And what?" I ask, knowing perfectly well that he's sniffing out that I have something else on my mind.

"Spit it out, Sarah. What else is bothering you other than the fact that your little chicks are about to leave the coup."

I speak so softly that Joe turns off the stereo. "There are a lot of stats that some parents – especially mothers – have so much difficulty adjusting to losing their mother role that husbands think they've lost interest and begin to look elsewhere for female companionship." Working myself up, I add, "Just because I'm having difficulty with the idea of relinquishing my role as being their primary care giver doesn't mean that I don't love you. I can't bear the thought of you leaving me for another woman just because you can't understand that I'm going through a grieving period that many mothers experience when their children leave home."

Joe's shoulders stiffen. I can tell that I have hurt him and find the silence that permeates the car to be stifling. I have loved him from the first moment I set eyes on him; I always will. I know my husband; reason will soon replace his hurt. "Joe," I ask, my voice barely a whisper, "what are you thinking?"

"What makes you think that I won't love you after the boys leave home?"

"Like I said, there are statistics proving that many of the marriage breakdowns following children leaving home are due to the misunderstanding on the part of one of the spouses – usually the husband – that the wife no longer loves him when, in reality, what the wife is going through is a grieving process." I frown. "And out of that misunderstanding, the silences and distance between the spouses grow until what they have left is a chasm of emotional pain caused by two people who have forgotten how to talk with one another, to forgive, and to understand one another."

"Well, that won't happen in our case," answers Joe. "Why didn't you tell me earlier about their new plans? Didn't you think I'd like to know about them applying for scholarships to American universities? And how about Jake wanting to attend the same university as his girlfriend and Jeremy following suit, just because his twin is doing it?"

"If you remember ..." I answer, keeping my tone reasonable, "last night there was no opportunity. We had the rehearsal party. I told the boys that as soon as we have a quiet moment we would have to discuss their plans. With everything that had to be done today for Becky's wedding, there just wasn't a good time to talk to you about it."

"A full scholarship to the States wouldn't be a bad thing," comments Joe, smiling with fatherly pride. "Maybe the boys will get into different universities."

"Well, that could be a good thing. Maybe it's time they have a chance to cultivate new friends without being known as the twins."

"Those two will never be separated. They could be three thousand miles apart and still be together."

I smile, knowing he's right. Jeremy and Jake are too close to allow distance to separate them on matters that count. "Agreed, but I still think that it might be good for them to attend different universities."

Pulling into the parking lot, Joe finds a place to park and turns off the ignition. "Wait here," he says, opening his door. "There's ice on the ground. I'll help you."

Leaning on his arm as we walk into the restaurant, I say, "We can be really proud of them, Joe. They're good boys."

"I know it." The pride in his voice is evident.

"There you are!" Amy rushes over to meet us as we enter. "Can you believe this?" she says, swinging her arm in an expansive arc. "Josh has transformed the restaurant into a shimmering winter palace.

The transformation is spectacular. The main lighting has been turned off, replaced by Christmas lights hung from the oak beams in the ceiling, creating the effect of twinkling stars. The entire room is decorated with taste and elegance. A red aisle carpet stretches down the centre of the room from Josh's private office to where the large field stone fireplace stands. Tables have been set with starched white linen, each with a centrepiece of red roses. Cutlery and crystal glasses glimmer under twinkling lights and from candles placed on each table. To the left of the bar is the expansive side room which Josh, after purchasing the restaurant, had gutted and transformed into The Friar's Getaway Bar. Tuxedoed waiters and waitresses circulate with champagne and hors d'oeuvres and for those guests who prefer something stronger, two more waiters are mixing drinks and serving wine and beer at the bar and in the Friar's Getaway.

"How's it going back there at wedding central?" asks Joe, looking in the direction of Josh's office and the room to the side normally reserved for private parties but, for tonight it has been designated as the room where the bride and her attendants will be closeted until the ceremony.

Amy grins. "Becky's back there pacing. You can't see her because Josh's put up lace curtains to block anyone from seeing her until the wedding."

"Pacing? Becky?" I return her smile. "Is Leen back there with her?"

Linking her arm with mine, she laughs. "The clinical wonder we all love and admire for her ability to analyze with cool objectivity is a total mess. Leen's trying to reassure her that she looks absolutely beautiful and is not making a mistake."

Amused, I say to Joe, "You'd best go and check in on the groom."

"Speaking of whom," says Joe, "where exactly is the man of the hour?"

"Last time I saw him, he was heading in the direction of the bar," answers Amy, tugging on my arm. "Come on Sarah, we've got to go."

෴

Joe

I exchange greetings with some of the guests and head off to look for Josh. Will, the senior bartender, waves me over to the bar. He's in his late twenties, works out three times a week and his wife is expecting their first child. He's young to be a senior bartender especially in one of the most prestigious restaurants in the city but Josh, adamant that he wanted Will to work for him, had lured him away from his previous employer with a very attractive salary and benefits package. "Josh said that if I saw you before he did to pour you some of his private stock," grins Will, reaching underneath the dark oak counter to withdraw a bottle of twenty-year-old scotch. "He said you like it on the rocks."

"I do indeed." Seating on a stool, I ask, "How's life treating you?"

"Can't complain," answers Will, placing a cocktail napkin under the glass before passing me my drink. "The wife just got back from her mother's and I had two weeks to myself to watch all the sports I wanted, eat when I wanted, and to leave my socks on the floor." He smiles conspiratorially. "I won't say it to her, but I was getting tired of being able to switch the remote control without complaints from the sidelines."

"Know what you mean, Will," I say, sipping my drink. "Women just don't get the need we men have to use a remote control. Speaking of the trials we husbands put up with in the name of love, where is the groom hiding out?"

"Last time I saw him, he was in the kitchen issuing orders about the appetizers." Referring to one of the waiters, Will says, "Dan said on his last pass through the kitchen he thought Marco was about to pop Josh with a rolling pin." Will shakes his head. "The guy's getting married and he's worried about appetizers. Go figure."

I chuckle. "Do you remember the day you were married?"

"Sure do," laughs Will. "I washed my car an hour before I had to be at the church. My mother was having a fit."

"Guess I had better go and see if I can persuade the groom to leave the appetizers to others and make sure that his tie is in place."

"Good luck." He glances at my glass. "Would you like me to freshen up your drink?"

"I'll leave it the way it is now," I answer, "but if the groom's as nervous as what you say, I'm going to need a stiff drink as soon as we get him married off."

Dressed in his tuxedo, Josh is at the far end of the kitchen engaged in a heated discussion with Marco, the sous chef. Marc Andre greets me with a sardonic grin and juts his thumb in Josh's direction. "The groom is venting. Seems one of Marco's sauces isn't to his liking."

Smiling, I answer, "More like he's got a case of nerves before the wedding." Observing the look of frustration and flush on Marco's face, I ask, "Should we rescue Marco?"

"Probably," replies Marc Andre, "but it's been fun watching. Marco's more than capable of handling the groom's nervous outbursts."

Counters are covered with platters of appetizers and the waiters are picking them up to take out into the main restaurant. One of the waiters crosses over to where we're standing. "This is Tim," says Marc Andre.

Lowering his voice, Tim asks, "Do either of you think you could get the groom out of here so we can go about doing our jobs?"

"Getting that bad, is it?" Marc Andre casts an amused glance in Josh's direction. Josh is taking off his tux jacket, giving the impression that he's about to take over the kitchen's operations.

I pat Tim on the shoulder. "We'll see what we can do."

"Josh," calls out Marc Andre, getting his attention as we approach, "what in the hell are you doing now?" I exchange glances with Marco. His dark eyes plead with me to get Josh out of his way.

"I'm going to show Marco how to make the sauce for the glaze on one of the desserts."

"Not now, you're not," answers Marc Andre, touching Josh's elbow. "You're coming with us. You can leave Marco and all the others to take care of anything connected to food."

For a moment it looks like Josh isn't about to come peacefully. Sheepish, he relents. "Sorry about that Marco. Guess my nerves are getting the better of me. Your sauce is fine."

"It's okay, Josh," answers Marco. The mirth in his eyes show he understands Josh is experiencing pre-wedding jitters, but his expression is one of relief at having been rescued.

Paul, the headwaiter, enters the kitchen to announce the arrival of the minister and his wife. Addressing Marc Andre, he says, "Ms MacLeen is asking that you join her, Sir. To Josh he says, "Your brother said to tell you that he'd like you to join him in your office."

Marc Andre and I make a show of grabbing Josh by the arms and step marching him out of the kitchen. We clown it up to the laughter of the kitchen workers and sing an enthusiastic but off-key rendition of 'he's getting married in the evening ... ding dong the bells are going to chime ... we're getting Josh out of the kitchen and getting him to his bride on time ...'

Sam, Josh's younger brother, grins as we bring in our captive and I say, "Reporting as ordered Sir. The prisoner was found in the kitchen harassing the sous chef."

"You're staying put until the ceremony," orders Sam. "Marco knows perfectly well how to cook without your micro-managing."

Both brothers have fair colouring, but that is where the physical similarities end. Josh is tall and lanky but well muscled; Sam is broad shouldered, about an inch shorter, and sports a well-clipped beard. Like Josh, Sam has a keen wit and enjoys a good joke. Sam, his wife Kate, their two sons and daughter flew in yesterday from Vancouver in time for the rehearsal party. Eric and Nathan are in first and third year university. Following in his father's footsteps, Eric is studying to be a civil engineer whereas Nathan is in third year law. Jamie, their daughter, has just started her surgical residency in Vancouver. Last night, I spent a good hour talking with Sam about our mutual interest in construction projects. He and his family will be staying in Ottawa until the day after Boxing Day and I have promised to take him on a tour of the thirty-floor business complex that my company is building downtown.

"Come on big brother," Sam teases, "settle down. You're marrying the girl of your dreams. Isn't that what you told me several times last night?" Addressing us, he says, "We had several nightcaps last night and by the time lover boy lay his head down, he was declaring to the world that Becky is the most marvellous woman ever to draw breath. And," Sam laughs heartily, "he kept telling me that if he knew getting married was such a rush, he would have done it years ago. Kate's never going to let me live it down that she had to steer the two of us to our beds last night."

Smiling at Josh, I tease, "What would you have done without Becky?"

Playfully punching Josh's shoulder, Sam replies, "He'd have told you that he would have found Becky even if ..." he pauses to roll his eyes with theatrical flair, "he'd had to search the four corners of the earth."

Throwing a sympathetic glance at Sam and me, Marc Andre says, "Make sure the groom stays put." He taps Josh on the shoulder, "I'm off to greet the minister and find out what the ladies are up to."

Sitting down on a comfortable leather chair, I say, "Long years of marriage have taught me to stay out of Sarah's way when she's on a mission." Throwing a knowing glance at Josh and then winking at Marc Andre, I say with wisdom gained from experience, "You guys have no idea the force you are dealing with when those four get wrapped up in something. It's every man for himself when that happens."

༄

Marc Andre

I leave Sam and Joe to supervise Josh and make my way through the dining room. Reverend Robert Jones and his wife Ada are patrons of the restaurant and long-time friends of Josh. Bob, a thin man with a salt and pepper captain's beard, stands just over six feet tall and has the erect bearing that twenty years of service as a naval chaplain brings.

Ada, the more outgoing of the two, is just shy of five feet, three inches. Bob greets me with a warm smile and handshake saying, "We heard that you were trying to get the groom settled down."

I grin. "Talking to Tim were you?"

"Yes," smiles Ada. "According to him, you and Joe rescued the kitchen staff from Josh's interference."

I answer, "Pre-wedding jitters. You must get to see a lot of that in your line of work."

Bob laughs. "True enough, but I must admit I'm surprised at Josh. He's normally so calm about things."

"Bob," says Ada, smiling at her husband, "there's a big difference between making an award winning soufflé and taking the leap into marriage."

Tim, accompanied by Paul, approaches with appetizers and flutes of champagne. I select a small sausage roll and pop it in my mouth. Ada accepts a flute of champagne but Bob refuses, saying, "Some water would be great for right now."

"Certainly, Sir," answers Paul. "Will Perrier suffice?"

"Thank you," answers Bob.

Tim says, "Please let me know if there is anything else you or Mrs. Jones require."

"Thanks Tim," replies Bob, with a wide grin. "Right after the ceremony, I'll be more than happy to avail myself of the good stuff."

Joe approaches to welcome Bob and Ada. Seeing his sons enter the restaurant with their dates he beckons to them to come over.

I exchange a few more pleasantries with Bob and Ada before excusing myself to make my way to the back room where Becky and her attendants wait. I knock hard on the door before turning the knob and call out loudly, "Man in the room."

"Quick, close the door," hisses Sarah. "No one can see the bride before the ceremony."

Laughing at how the ladies are staring at me as if I've committed a serious mistake, I obligingly shut the door and tease, "No harm done, ladies. The groom is being closely supervised by the groomsmen." I try to maintain a straight face as I casually throw out, "But, don't worry, I'll personally ensure that they are sobered up in time for the ceremony."

Immediately, a hush falls over the room and then I hear Leen's infectious giggle. "Marc, stop being such a tease."

Momentary pre-wedding panic resolved, all activity is resumed as the ladies put last minute touches to hair and make-up. I walk to where Aunt Claire sits, kiss her forehead, and say, "You look beautiful. Truly beautiful."

She kisses my cheek and whispers, "They are all so excited, Marc." She pats my hand playfully and says, "For just a second there, they almost bought into your fib about having to sober up Josh."

"Who says it's a fib?" I reply, making a quick X on my tux's breast pocket with two fingers. "Cross my heart, it's true Aunt Claire."

Her answering laugh is light and relaxed. I'm pleased. Her involvement with Becky's wedding has been an excellent distraction from the worries associated with her illness.

"Having a good time?" I ask.

"Better than a good time," answers Aunt Claire. Her eyes are soft with thought and happiness as she adds, "I am so pleased that Becky asked me to fill in as mother-of-the bride."

Hearing the catch in her voice, I answer, "They all love you very much. But, don't get too comfortable being mother-of-the-bride as your crowning delight." I take her hands in mine and look straight into her beautiful blue eyes. "I have a secret Aunt Claire. Do you think you can keep a secret?"

She huffs good-naturedly. "I won't even dignify that with a response."

"Okay, then," I reply, releasing her hands, "Since you won't answer my question, I guess it's better not to take a chance on telling you my secret."

"You were always a precocious and obstinate boy," replies Aunt Claire, taking a deep breath and blowing it out with exaggerated exasperation. "Fine, if that's what it takes," she says, making an imaginary big X across her chest, "I promise. Cross my heart."

"Want to really seal the promise?" I ask.

She arches an eyebrow. "What do you have in mind?"

"Let's spit on it," I answer. Pretending to spit on my palm, I hold out my hand and wait for her to do the same.

She does the same and as we shake, she says, "You're lucky I didn't really spit."

"You too," I answer, with a grin. "It'll be our concession to good manners on Becky and Josh's wedding day."

"Enough of this tom foolery," says Aunt Claire, grasping my elbow as if I'm an errant schoolboy. "You've definitely piqued my interest.

What's so important that we had to go through elaborate top secret negotiations?"

I whisper in Aunt Claire's ear. "Think of Becky's wedding as a prelude ... training if you will ... for the role you'll have to play when Leen and I get married."

The tingling, pleasing, thrill I get seeing her shocked expression puts a goofy grin on my face but I'm so happy right now, I don't care how goofy I may or may not look.

Aunt Claire peers across the room at Leen with constrained excitement. "Does she know yet? Or ..." she whispers, "is this one of your take charge plans?"

"I plan on asking her tonight."

Aunt Claire clasps my hands. "I am so happy for you Marc. She's perfect."

"I gathered you'd say that," I answer, pleased with her approval. "After all, you're the one who had it planned from the outset."

"Not from the outset," she retorts with sly humour, "but perhaps within the first few days."

"Not from what outset?" asks Leen, slipping her arms around my waist. "What are you two conspiring about now?"

"What makes you think we're conspiring," answers Aunt Claire. "I'm just sharing thoughts with my godson about how exciting all of this is."

"Hi Marc." Becky, Sarah, and Amy wave at me.

I reply, "You ladies look absolutely beautiful tonight."

"Tonight? Only tonight?" jokes Sarah, posing with one hand placed provocatively on her hip. "You've got to get your lines straight, Marc Andre. Tonight, the bride is truly *beautiful and radiant*. It's her moment, but we all gratefully accept your praise and remind you that our beauty is not limited to one night."

I drily respond, "I stand corrected, counsellor." Bowing, I rephrase, "Becky is beautiful and radiant. All of you ladies are breathtaking in your amazing beauty."

"Much better," laughs Sarah and to Leen she calls out, "That man of yours is a quick study. Easy to see why he does so well in court."

"Once a lawyer, always a lawyer, counsellor?"

"More or less," agrees Sarah, blithely.

I can't help but wonder how my relationship with Sarah has altered since the day of her righteous indignation when Aunt Claire decided to reveal her true identity. It's hard to believe that we began our friendship under such tense circumstances but over the last few months of working together we have developed an easy rapport and healthy respect for one another's legal skills.

Tapping her gold watch, Leen cuts in. "Marc, we need to get the guys ready. Are the musicians ready? Can you make sure that the guests are seated?"

"No problem," I answer, smiling at how she is rattling off orders. "Is that all you wanted to see me for?"

"No, I wanted to tell you that I love you." My heart skips a beat as her eyes meet mine. Aunt Claire tugs on my sleeve and beaming, says, "Marc Andre, the wedding."

"I'd better go and get the groom," I answer, breaking eye contact with Leen. I kiss her on the cheek, saying, "I love you."

Aunt Claire pipes up, "Marc Andre, you will have enough time for all of that later but right now, get going." Glancing at Leen she adds with amusement, "Even as a boy, he had to be reminded to be on time."

"Enough with the memories," I tease, kissing the top of her head. "I'll be back in a few minutes to walk the mother-of-the bride down the aisle."

I'm amazed at how the main room has been transformed for the wedding ceremony. The tables have been moved to align the walls and rows of chairs have been placed on both sides of the long red carpet, creating a dramatic aisle for Becky and her attendants to walk down. Near the field stone fireplace stands a canopied arch decorated with seasonal colours of red and white garland, interspersed with red and white roses. Combined with the star lighting from above and the soft candlelight, the effect is magical. Soft music filters throughout the room as the instrumental quartet hired for the evening creates an atmosphere of expectation, culture, and refined taste.

"Well, gentlemen," I say, entering Josh's office, "I've been instructed by the ladies to inform you that your presence is requested. I believe the good doctor wants to get married."

Sam pats the breast pocket of his tux. "Let's see, do I have the ring?"

Josh casts a bewildered glance at his brother. "You didn't lose it, did you Sam?"

"Josh, you've got to settle down," warns Sam. "It's right here."

Together we walk out to take our places in front of the canopy. There are expectant murmurs throughout the room as the guests, knowing that the formal ceremony is about to begin, straighten up in their seats. Nudging Josh with my elbow, I say, "There's still time to back out."

"Just go," grins Josh.

"Entirely my pleasure. I'll be right back."

Seeing that I'm leaving to get the ladies for their grand entrance, the musicians end the Vivaldi selection and begin to play Streisand's famous song. Kim, a surgeon friend of Becky's, sings in a clear, alto voice, "Like a rose ..."

The door to the back room opens and Aunt Claire, looking elegant, takes my extended arm. Everyone stands and we make our way down to the front row where I settle Aunt Claire in her chair and leave to take my place alongside the other groomsmen. Next comes Leen, followed by Amy and Sarah; all looking resplendent in their gowns as the room's soft lighting casts gentle glows on their beaming faces. Just as Kim ends the song, Becky makes her appearance. For a dramatic moment she waits in the doorway for the quartet to begin the processional music. Stunning in her red velvet gown and accompanying cape and hood trimmed with white fur, her hair falls in wisps around her face and she *is* positively radiant. Her poise is in complete contrast to the excited woman I'd seen only a few minutes ago. Reverend Jones waits at the front of the canopy and in response to his nod; Josh steps forward to wait for his bride. Becky seems to float up the aisle unaware of the guests as she heads straight in the direction of Josh's waiting gaze. As she draws near, Josh reaches for her hand and standing alongside her, faces the minister.

"Dearly beloved," begins Reverend Jones and the ceremony is underway.

Sarah

The dinner is excellent. Roast beef, Yorkshire pudding, roasted potatoes, asparagus, green beans, and carrots followed by lemon and lime sherbets, tortes with sweet glaze sauces, and fruits. Joe is finishing his torte with relish. Sam and Kate, are engaged in an animated discussion with Leen, Anna-Claire, and Marc Andre. Turning my attention to the table in the middle of the room, I watch proudly as my sons laugh with their girlfriends.

"Sarah," says Joe, "you look lost in your own world."

"Not lost," I answer. "Just thinking how much I'm enjoying this wedding."

"Thanks for standing up with me," grins Josh, who is seated alongside Joe, "and for getting me out of the kitchen before I started a revolt among the staff."

Joe laughs. "Yeah, things were starting to get a little tense, but they all knew you were working out your jitters."

"No jitters; I wanted everything to be perfect."

"Well, you expended a lot of worry for naught," answers Joe. "Your problem, Buddy, will be coming up with something next Christmas Eve to match tonight's splendour."

Josh has a satisfied grin as he looks around his restaurant. Waiters are busily clearing up the tables and everyone is clearly enjoying the evening. Marc Andre rises from his chair and walks over to the musicians' area. Attentive to their needs, Josh had made certain that they had their own table near their sound equipment. Lifting the microphone from its stand, Marc Andre addresses the guests, saying, "We hope you have all enjoyed your dinner. The bar's open for anyone wanting to refresh their drinks. Sandwiches, hors d'oeuvres, and salads will be brought out around ten."

Nudging Josh, Joe says, "I see that the ladies are re-convening and helping Becky to the back room. Probably to admire once again the wedding band you gave her."

"I'm off," I say to my husband, rising to follow Becky and the others. I overhear Josh saying to Joe, "Let's get a scotch before we start with the speeches and dancing."

"Now you're talking," replies Joe. "Not a husband for a day and already you're like me, watching and waiting for the ladies to do their thing." Grinning, he adds, "It's good to finally have some male company when those four get together."

I roll my eyes at Joe and say, "Very funny."

Sam takes the microphone from Marc Andre and announces, "There will be a fifteen minute interval to give the waiters time to finish cleaning up and to move tables to the side of the room in order to create a dance area. Thank you all for helping to celebrate Josh and Becky's wedding and they sincerely hope that all of you will enjoy the rest of the evening."

By ten o'clock, Joe has admitted to Jeremy and Jake that their girlfriends are indeed charming and keepers. Having had the chance to talk with the girls, Joe has satisfied his curiosity and is relieved to know that for the immediate future nothing is going to steer them off their educational course. I have to suppress my laughter listening to Joe explain quietly to the boys that he was simply trying to get information to allay my fears about their romances interfering with their postsecondary education.

Jake laughs with outright amusement at his Dad's sorry cover-up, saying, "Give it up, Dad. Mom's already told us that you know about our applications to some American universities and that we should reassure you that we're not going to do anything foolish."

"Yeah," pipes up Jeremy, picking up a coke, "like getting married before we're out of university." His eyes twinkle mischievously at having exposed Joe's worries above and beyond any that I may have had.

Joe is spared further teasing by the approach of Stacey and Alicia who are back from a washroom break. He uses the opportunity to suggest that we join Leen and Marc Andre who are sitting with Anna-Claire.

"They make good looking couples," remarks Marc Andre as Jeremy and Jake lead Stacey and Alicia to the dance floor.

"Yeah, they do,' admits Joe, watching the boys dance with their dates. "Hard to believe my sons are grown men. The bright side is that their girlfriends seem to have good heads on their shoulders."

Leen comments, "They're young. Neither of them is going to rush out and get married." Leen's perceptive observation brings forth amused glances from the rest of us.

"What's so funny?" asks Josh, as he and Becky arrive with their basket containing wrapped pieces of wedding cake. They've been making the rounds, personally thanking their guests and ensuring that everyone is having a good time.

"Joe's acting like a mother hen," teases Leen.

Momentarily perplexed, Becky says, "Mother hen?"

Smiling, I answer, "The twins and their girlfriends."

Becky and Josh glance at the dance floor. "Had to happen sooner or later," says Becky.

"Later would have been better," replies Joe. Placing his drink on the table, he says, "I think it's time that I dance with my wife."

༄

Becky

After the formal ceremony, I float through the rest of the evening feeling every inch like a princess. Surrounded by my closest friends and new family from Josh's side, Josh and I mingle, laugh, and exchange Christmas greetings with our guests. By the time that we're standing at the door saying our final good-byes, we're looking forward to beginning our new life as husband and wife.

"Well, that's it," grins Josh, with unabashed lust, closing the door behind the last guest. Looking at his watch, he says, "It's just past midnight. Merry Christmas, Mrs. Sinclair." Taking me into his arms, he kisses me passionately. "I've been wanting to do that all night."

I wrap my arms around his waist and nestle my cheek against his chest. "Let's go home, Josh. When will Alex be here?"

"He should be back soon from driving Amy and Anna-Claire home." Marc Andre had arranged for Alex, Emile's chauffer, to drive not only Emile and Anna-Claire but also to take us home. Alex has been with the Aumount family for over forty years and although he could have retired comfortably long ago, he preferred to stay on and be with Emile. Over the years they've become good friends and both Marc Andre and Emile consider him to be a family member.

A knock on the door interrupts our embrace. Josh lets Alex in, saying, "We really appreciate this, Alex. We'll just get our coats and be right out."

"Pleased to do it," answers Alex. "I'll wait outside."

Josh helps me with my cape as I climb into the limo. Resting his arm around my shoulders, he asks, "So Mrs. Sinclair, how do you like being married?"

I rest my head on his shoulder. "I like it just fine, Mr. Sinclair. Now, let's go home and see if you're not too tired to perform husbandly duties."

Pulling me close to him, Josh taps the window separating us from the front seat and laughingly says to Alex, "It seems the lady wants to go home."

"Right away," replies Alex, easing into drive. "On her wedding day, a bride should get exactly what she wants."

Chapter Twenty-four

Marc Andre

Stirring, I roll over on my side and reach out to touch Leen's warm body. Returning to Leen's condo after the wedding, we had fallen into bed completely exhausted. Leen had been so worn out that she refused a nightcap and went straight to bed. It had been my plan to ask her to marry me but as I crawled in beside her and she snuggled against me, I was content to listen to her breathing as she fell into sleep. With the early morning light streaming in from the skylight and six hours of sleep behind me, I feel the need to be with Leen and I'm renewed with my intent to propose. I'm startled that all I can feel is the empty space on her pillow and the blankets that have been thrown aside.

Wide-awake, I shoot up in bed and survey Leen's bedroom. Spacious and elegant are the words that come to mind. Like so much about her, this room echoes her penchant for organization and yet, indicates underlying gentleness and passion. The colours are muted and soft. The wood floor's hue is a deep oak colouring and the curtains are a rich brown with hints of gold. Not a man's room. A woman's room.

The sound of the shower being turned on tells me where Leen is. I lie back down, thinking about the day ahead. The plan is to spend the morning quietly together and then, mid-afternoon go over to Aunt Claire's to share in the Christmas Day activities and meal. My father and Alex will be joining us for the turkey and all the trimmings. Aunt Claire insisted that she host Christmas Day this year and despite our concern that she would tire herself, she had been adamant. Leen and I finally gave in to her wishes after she protested, "Marc Andre, I am not dead. I want and need to do this."

My eyes burn with tears as I recall how she held my hands and said, "Marc Andre, this may well be my last Christmas and I want it to be special. I want to celebrate life, my new family, and to laugh. Can't you help me with that? You and Leen can come early to help prepare the meal and make sure that everyone has enough to drink and eat. Your father is coming with Alex and the three of us will laugh over old times and share memories. We'll make a party of it. Sarah and Joe will come and the boys will bring their girlfriends. Amy is bringing two types of desserts. Josh and Becky will come since they don't leave on their honeymoon until the day after Boxing Day when Sam and family return home. I invited Sam and his family but they're spending the day with Kate's sister, Sonia and her family in Gatineau. There will be presents under the tree, mistletoe and carols playing in the background. By the time I'm finished, Hallmark will want to put our celebration on their cards."

"Ah, there you are, sleepy-head," says Leen, emerging from the bathroom with her bathrobe tied loosely around her waist, breaking into my reverie. I smile as she climbs onto the bed with her towel-dried hair falling in unruly tendrils. Inching over to my side, she says, "A penny for your thoughts."

Pulling her face down to meet mine, I crush her lips with a kiss.

Catching her breath, Leen stares closely and drawls, "If I didn't know better, I'd swear that you've got one very serious licentious grin on your face." Her eyes drift to the sheet covering my lap. She smiles. "And if I'm not mistaken, I'd be willing to bet that we're going to be having a late breakfast."

I pat the bed and say, "Not only are you beautiful but you possess amazing intelligence and perception."

"You are completely shameless, Aumount," teases Leen. Straightening, she pretends to be distraught. "If we don't hurry, we'll miss Christmas Mass." She starts to squirm off the bed but I grab her by the waist and pull her back down.

"Reverend Bob told me last night's wedding ceremony doubled as Christmas Service," I answer, busily untying her robe's sash.

"Did he now?" answers Leen, her full lips curving into an alluring smile. "And did he also explain how an Anglican Service could substitute for a Roman Catholic Mass especially on Christmas Day?"

"Got that one covered, too," I reply, slipping her robe off her shoulders. "The way I see it," I murmur, as I tease her earlobe with the tip of my tongue, "Anglicans and Roman Catholics are kind of like kissing cousins; both can trace their origins back to the first pope."

"Ah," says Leen, tracing my chest with her fingers, "and this conclusion of yours is based on sound theological doctrine?"

I cup one of her breasts. "Yep and as for your comment about me being shameless, you have no idea how shameless I can be."

"Oh, I think I have a good idea," responds Leen, resting one long leg over mine.

I whisper, "As for doctrine, isn't it written somewhere in the bible that we are supposed to love one another?"

"Definitely have heard that somewhere," murmurs Leen.

And with that, I push aside all other thoughts and lose myself completely in the sheer wonder and ecstasy of her body.

༄

Sarah

Joe and I are preparing our traditional Christmas morning breakfast of scrambled eggs, bacon, toast, orange juice and coffee. Earlier, we'd opened our presents and now Jake is upstairs taking a shower and Jeremy is occupied with setting up his new laptop. Neither of us have bothered to get out of our pyjamas and I'm turning the bacon over in the pan when the phone rings.

Happily, Joe says, "Merry Christmas" to the caller.

I mouth, "Who is it?"

Joe holds up a finger, signalling for me to wait. Then he says, "You can't stay there. Get in a taxi. Breakfast will be ready when you get here."

Placing the receiver in its cradle, Joe announces, "Seems we're going to have company today."

"Really, who?" I place the bacon onto paper towels to drain off excess fat before placing it on a hot dish to keep warm.

"Mike Andrews. He's the architect I met last fall when I went out to check on the progress of the shopping mall we're building in Winnipeg."

I think for a moment and then remember Joe having mentioned him. "So what's he doing in Ottawa?"

"Seems he was en-route from Halifax where he'd been to oversee a housing development that his architectural firm designed. His connecting flight got delayed in Ottawa due to the ice on the runway. No sooner are they ready to take off when the flight gets cancelled until further notice due to weather in Winnipeg. The west is getting hit with a mother lode of snow. Nothing's moving in or out of Winnipeg." Leaning against the refrigerator, he pushes his hand through his hair, and says, "I know it's Christmas, but I had told him that should he ever be in town, to give us a call."

"That must be terrible for him trying to get home for Christmas and having to sit in an airport. I'm glad you asked him to join us. I'll fix up the spare room for him."

"He said he was going to try to book a hotel room."

"Nonsense. The hotels will be glutted with stranded passengers and the ones that can't get rooms will be sleeping on every available seat and floor space at the airport. He'll stay here with us."

"Well, he doesn't have a family," answers Joe, "so that part is okay, but he said he had been planning on being back in Winnipeg in time to join a friend and his family for Christmas dinner."

"No family?" I scoop the eggs onto a platter. "Divorced?"

"Never married," answers Joe. "He's a nice guy and I enjoyed doing business with his firm. In fact, we talked about getting together in late January to discuss a possible joint venture." He pours coffee into our mugs. "Looks like we might discuss some business today."

"Not today, you won't! In case it's slipped your mind, today is Christmas – a day families and friends celebrate. There'll be no talk of business today."

Joe wraps his arms around my waist. "Sarah, I'm not talking about drawing up contracts. I'm simply saying that we might discuss some possibilities; the same as we'll undoubtedly discuss sports. I'm not completely insensitive."

"No one said you're insensitive," I reply firmly. "In fact," I continue, as I walk my fingers up his chest, "if this morning's wakeup call was an indication of your sensitivity to my needs, I'd say you're scoring in the high numbers."

Joe's still guffawing when Jake and Jeremy take their usual places at the table. "What's so funny, Dad?" asks Jake, unfolding a napkin.

"Nothing," replies Joe, carrying over the plates with bacon and eggs. "Your mother just made me laugh at something she said … an inside joke."

"More information than we need to know," grins Jake, helping himself to a slice of toast.

I roll my eyes. "Okay, guys, enough jock humour at my expense."

Winking at the boys, Joe says, "You heard her boys—the commander-in-chief has spoken."

"Jeremy, pass the ketchup, will you?" asks Jake as he heaps bacon onto his plate.

"Leave some for me, will you?"

"Guys, it's Christmas. Play nicely." The boys humour me with looks of contrition and make a comic production of passing the plates of food with an excessive amount of pleases and thank you's.

"And just last night you were saying how *grown up* our sons have become," comments Joe.

"So what time will your friend be arriving?" I ask, returning the focus to our unexpected Christmas guest.

"I would think he'll be here within the hour, provided he could get a cab right away."

"Who's coming?" Jake swallows a forkful of eggs and reaches for another slice of toast.

"Mike Andrews, a friend of mine. His connecting flight in Ottawa got delayed due to weather conditions in Winnipeg," explains Joe, sipping his coffee. "I'd ask him over anytime, but definitely on a day like today, he shouldn't have to sit in an airport lounge eating stale peanuts."

"Neat," says Jeremy. "Kind of like something you'd see in a Christmas movie or read in a novel. A stranger coming to share Christmas."

I smile at my son. "Sometimes, you completely surprise me with your sensitivity."

He shrugs. "Whatever …"

"I'm going to Stacey's," announces Jake. I don't miss the fact that the timing of his comment is perfect in that it draws attention away from his brother's embarrassment about my saying that he was 'sensitive'. "Remember Mom? I asked you last night and you said it was okay. Her mom's making an early meal."

He's right. He did ask me last night. I had agreed only after securing his promise that he and Stacey would save some room to sample Anna-Claire's meal.

"How about you, Jeremy? What are your plans?" asks Joe.

"Alicia's mom is serving her turkey dinner at noon. I promised Alicia that I would be there. She wants me to meet her aunt and uncle from Port Dover and her grandparents who were arriving today from Halifax. They probably came in on the same plane as Dad's friend this morning." Smiling, he says, "But don't worry, Mom, I'll be at Mrs. Wright's for supper."

Resigned to the fact that this is not going to be an intimate family Christmas by any stretch of the imagination, I say to Joe, "Well that's it, then, our sons are grown. Now, girlfriends and their families take precedence over my pumpkin pie and stuffing."

"But we're eating at Mrs. Wright's," reasons Jeremy.

"I prepared the stuffing two days ago, froze it, and had your father drop it off at Anna-Claire's yesterday morning before we all got wrapped up in the wedding preparations. She and Aunt Leen are using it today. As for the pumpkin pies ... Aunt Amy and I made them the other day when we did our Christmas baking blitz."

Jake puts his empty plate in the dishwasher. "Don't worry, Mom. We love your stuffing and pies. No one can cook as well as you."

"Wait till Aunt Amy hears that one," I answer, but pleased with the compliment. "She was bragging to me last night that she'd made those macaroon and coconut cookies that you guys like to devour."

"Well," answers Jake, the soul of diplomacy, "we'll make the sacrifice and eat them. After all, *it is* Christmas and we wouldn't want to hurt Aunt Amy's feelings, would we Jeremy?"

Jeremy obliges. "No way."

"Ah, Joe. See how noble our sons are."

"I noticed," laughs Joe.

The doorbell interrupts any further teasing. Jumping up from my chair, I say, "Damn! I'm still in my pyjamas. You guys clean up. I need to take a shower and change."

"Sarah," calls out Joe as I dash upstairs, "relax. Mike knows that he called us at the last minute." I don't' answer.

When I return downstairs, freshly showered, wearing jeans, and a red cashmere sweater, Joe introduces me to a tall, good-looking man with puppy dog eyes. I say, "Merry Christmas. Welcome to our home."

"Merry Christmas, Sarah, and thank you for allowing me to intrude on your family today." His smile is both charming and rueful as he adds, "Air travel has its benefits but on days like today, there are definite drawbacks."

Motioning to the boys, he says, "I've just been getting to know your sons. When I first met Joe, he bragged about his twin sons but he didn't mention how identical they really are."

"The ugly looking one is Jeremy," jokes Jake.

"Jake! Mr. Andrews doesn't' even know you and you're already making wise-cracks."

Laughing, Mike looks at Jeremy and says, "Your brother seems to be confused because the two of you are mirror images of one another."

Jeremy shrugs. "Jake just can't get over the fact that I have better features then he does; so he likes to have people compare him to me. That helps him feel better about his ugly face."

"Jeremy!" I exclaim, laughing outright.

Joe laughs. "Guys, give Mike a chance to acclimatize to our home, before you start in on one another. Let him think that you know the meaning of *brotherly* love." Turning to Mike, he says, "We set aside some breakfast warming in the oven. Come on and sit down."

I can't help but notice that Mike's angular features are striking when he smiles. "This is really nice of you," says Mike, nodding thanks to Jake as he passes over the plate heaped with food.

"We're glad to have you here to celebrate Christmas with our family and friends. You'll be meeting some of them this afternoon. In fact, I'll just go and give Amy and Leen a call to let them know there will be one more for dinner. I know you, Joe Calder," I grin at my husband, "as soon as I'm gone, you're going to shift the conversation to business. Just remember, this is Christmas Day and I want it to be without any wheeling and dealing."

When I return, Mike and Joe are sitting comfortably in the living room, sipping coffee, and talking about site locations. The boys have gone to get ready to go to their girlfriends.

"Gentlemen," I begin, shooting Joe a warning look, but the expression on his face breaks my resolve and I start to laugh. He looks as if he is a little boy caught with his hand in the cookie jar.

"We're just talking in generalities, Sarah," explains Joe, with a winning smile.

Relenting, I say, "I have to get over to Anna-Claire's to help prepare the meal. Take advantage of that time to discuss whatever it is that you both are so intent on." To emphasize my point, I turn up the stereo system and leave them listening to 'I Saw Mommy Kissing Santa Claus.'

Joe

"She's quite a woman," remarks Mike, after Sarah leaves to do whatever she needs to do before going to Anna-Claire's.

"She's been through a lot this last year, but looking at her now, you wouldn't know it."

"When we talked in the fall, you said that her speech had been impacted by the aneurism," comments Mike. "I came here expecting that, but it seems that her speech has improved."

"She worked hard on that one," I answer, feeling a surge of pride. "It's more obvious when she's very tired or excited but, for the most part, she is biting at the bit to get back full-time to her law firm and resume, as she puts it, her life."

"It can't have been easy for any of you," replies Mike, resting his legs on the ottoman.

I take a moment to consider his comment. "No, it wasn't. She set the pace and tone for her recovery. It was hard to watch her struggling for words, but she's a survivor and she went at it like a pit bull."

"Proof to the cliché that bad things either make a person stronger or they fall with it." Mike reaches for a slice of Christmas cake. "M'mm, this is really good!"

"That's Amy's homemade Christmas cake. Actually, it's her grandmother's recipe and," I add, helping myself to another slice, "I wouldn't tell Sarah this, but no one can cook like Amy."

Mike raises a quizzical eyebrow. "Amy?"

"You'll meet her this afternoon. She's one of Sarah's closest friends. In fact, you'll get to meet her two other best friends, Leen and Becky. The four of them have been together since university."

Amused Mike answers, "I've never been married, but even I know that it's never in a man's best interests to tell his wife that another woman is a better cook."

"I'm not saying that Sarah isn't a good cook," I answer, feeling only marginally guilty about my comment, "but, Amy raises cooking to a level that would give some chefs cause to worry." Grinning, I add, "In fact, you'll meet Josh, a real chef this afternoon. The reason we were all lounging about so late this morning is because we were at his and Becky's wedding last night. He and Becky are leaving for their honeymoon in the Caribbean the day after Boxing Day."

"A wedding on Christmas Eve?"

I shrug. "A bit unusual and we had a good time but I will admit I'm in no particular hurry to do more than lounge about until we have to gear up for the Christmas festivities."

Mike laughs. "So I noticed."

Still wearing my pyjamas and bathrobe, I joke, "Sooner or later, I'll remember my manners and go upstairs to shower and change."

"Stay comfortable," answers Mike. "Look at me. I hadn't planned on a flight delay and all the clothes I've got to wear are presently on my back. I've got an overnight bag with pyjamas and basic toiletries."

"I can lend you a fresh shirt and sweater," I offer. "We're close to the same size."

"Thanks. I'd like to meet your friends not looking too dishevelled."

"You'll like the people you'll meet," I say, relaxing in my chair. "And, like I said, whenever Amy is doing any of the cooking, it's bound to be worth the visit."

"Her family must enjoy the benefits."

"Amy's not married." Then, without rhyme or reason, I throw in, "She's a professor at the university and divorced."

"Career woman who likes to cook," replies Mike, grinning. "Makes for an interesting combination."

I lower my voice, glance at the stairway to make certain Sarah is nowhere within hearing distance, and say, "I like to tease Sarah that she and her friends are like a coven."

Mike's face registers surprise. "Coven?"

"Yeah, she, Becky, Leen, and Amy."

Mike smiles. "Sounds like they are all pretty close."

"Close doesn't begin to describe it," I answer, getting up to refill our coffee mugs. Making quotation marks with my fingers, I reiterate, "Definitely a coven."

"I heard that," says Sarah, entering the living room. Wagging a warning finger at me, she says, "You'd best be careful about what you say Joe Calder. One of these days, we might just cast a spell on you and then you'll find yourself croaking like a frog."

Laughing, Mike teases, "Talk about getting caught in the act."

I raise my hands in surrender. "See what I have to put up with, Mike. She's threatening to turn me into a frog."

"Leave me out of this one," protests Mike. "I have no intention of joining you at a swamp croaking out Christmas carols."

"Now there's a man who knows how to keep his own counsel," says Sarah.

Jeremy and Jake came bounding down the stairs to say their good-byes, both clutching neatly wrapped packages. Not about to let that go by, I remark, "Those packages look professionally done. When did you guys learn how to do that?" I point to the blue bow on Jeremy's package. "Bow and all! For me, you shouldn't have."

"We didn't," grins Jake. "There's a kiosk at the mall where people wrap gifts."

"Sarah," I ask, all innocence, "were our gifts packaged as nicely?"

"Dad!" hisses Jeremy, kissing Sarah on the cheek. "Mom doesn't need fancy wrapped packages to impress her."

"Yeah," echoes Jake, "she's already impressed that she has two such amazingly handsome sons."

"I am, am I?" Poking my arm, Sarah says, "Leave them alone, Joe. My two handsome sons are off to impress their ladies." Addressing the boys, she warns, "Don't forget. You have to be at Anna's by four."

"No problem," answers Jake.

As they go out the door, toting their wrapped packages, Jeremy is letting Jake have it—the way siblings do when wanting to register displeasure —"Tell me again, Dufus, why do you get to have the car?"

"I'm a better poker player," comes the reply as the door shuts.

"Never a dull moment," observes Sarah.

"Brothers," says Mike. He smiles. "But you can tell they're close."

"Yeah," I agree. "Just last night, Sarah and I were saying that they're going to miss one another's company when they head off to separate universities next fall."

"Well, I'll be off too," says Sarah. She can be very comical when she wants to be and right now, she's doing a great impression between wifely caution and motherly advice. "Mike, I'm putting you in charge of Joe. Make sure that he doesn't eat too many shortbreads and leave no room for turkey. And you," she gives me a once over with a glance, "I trust you'll change?"

"Gee, do I have to? I kind of like lounging around in my pyjamas."

"Lounge all you want," replies Sarah with a saucy look, "just show up at Anna Claire's wearing something other than pyjamas and bathrobe."

As soon as she's out the door, I say, "Make yourself at home. I'm going to shower and get changed."

"I'll use the time to make a few calls," answers Mike, removing his cell from a pocket. "Get the Christmas greetings out of the way to my brother in Seattle and sister in Dublin."

"Dublin?"

"Janie did her fellowship there after graduating from med school," explains Mike. "Fell in love with a surgeon, the people, and country. I go there every few years and she visits Winnipeg and Seattle when she can. Then, there's Skype and Face-time. Distance is no longer what it used to be."

"Use Sarah's laptop in her study. You can make your calls on Skype and save your cell time."

"That'd be great," answers Mike.

I take thirty minutes to shower, shave and change. Mike is talking with his brother when I poke my head through the doorway, toting fresh shirt and sweater for him to wear. He motions for me to come over, saying, "Tom, this is Joe."

The family resemblance is strong. "Hi Joe," grins Tom. "Mike was telling me how you and your wife are putting him up during his overlay in Ottawa. Nice of you to do."

"Glad to," I answer. "Merry Christmas."

We exchange a few more pleasantries before I excuse myself to raid Sarah's supply of shortbreads. I've just returned to the living room with a stocked plate when Mike enters, saying, "Thanks. It was good to talk with Tom."

"Were you able to talk to your sister?"

"No. She and her family must be out visiting his family or friends. There's five hours difference so I'll give her a try later on."

Looking at my watch, I say, "We have a couple of hours before we have to go."

"I don't have the specs with me," says Mike, "but I can give you a general breakdown on the site for the project we were going to talk about in January."

"Sounds good to me."

"Just let me change into this shirt and sweater," answers Mike, "and then, we can talk."

We spend a good hour talking about the merits of a joint venture and I'm intrigued with his plans. Using paper purloined from Sarah's printer, Mike's roughs out some sketches for me to look at. I know that this is going to be a project that I'm going to enjoy working on.

Stretching, I say, "Feel like a game of pool?"

"Lead the way," replies Mike.

"Grab a bottle of eggnog from the fridge," I say, "while I get the rum to add flavour. We'll take our drinks downstairs."

Seeing the wide screen plasma TV mounted on the finished basement's wall, Mike whistles softly. "Very nice, Joe." Fixing a glance at the pool table at the far side of the room, the built in walled wet bar, and the dartboard, he comments, "Do you think we can fit in a game of darts too before we have to leave?"

I flick the wall switch and the gas fireplace pops into action as Mike breaks the balls. Picking up my cue stick, I grin and ask, "Loser buys first round after we break ground for our joint project."

"Done deal," smiles Mike. "Hope you like paying for fifteen year old single malt."

Chapter Twenty-five

Anna-Claire

The lingering scent of fresh spruce competes with whiffs of roasting turkey. These are the smells I associate with my childhood Christmases. Pleased with how Leen and I've set up the dining room, I take a few moments to inspect the tall Christmas tree laden with twinkling lights and the gifts underneath, waiting to be opened. Places have been set at the table and I check to ensure that I've not forgotten anything. I light the mulled wine scented candle atop the fireplace's oak mantle. Background Christmas music floats softly through the air – loud enough to create an atmosphere but not so much as to drown out conversation.

I'm dressed in grey wool slacks, a red sweater on top of a white cowl neck shirt, and I'm sporting the funny elf socks Leen bought for me to wear on Christmas Day. For years, I've joined the Aumounts on special occasions, but other than my annual New Year's Day dinner which I host in return for Emile and his family, I've not set a Christmas Day table since Drew and Emily were alive. My heart twitches with the memory of Emily's pleasure on Christmas morning and Drew's laughter as she squealed her delight with her gifts. This Christmas, unlike any other in between, I can feel their presence so strongly that I almost expect to turn around and see them. I feel a sense of comfort knowing that Drew and Emily would be happy for me.

Marc Andre walks into the room and says, "Everything okay, Aunt Claire?"

"Yes," I answer. "I just came in here to make certain that I've forgotten nothing. I want it to be nice and festive."

"It is," he answers. "Right out of a Dickens's novel."

"How are things coming along in the kitchen?"

"Leen and Sarah have organized it like a command post," jokes Marc Andre. "They've had Dad and Emile peeling potatoes and me dicing carrots. Josh and Becky will bring an assortment of cheeses, crackers, and appetizers and Amy's bringing the desserts. He rests an arm around my shoulders. "I don't think a single thing has been forgotten. I was thinking that maybe you and I could sit and have a drink before everyone arrives? What's your pleasure?"

"I should go back to help Leen."

"No," replies Marc Andre. "I'm under strict instructions from Leen and Sarah to make certain that you have a few quiet moments before everyone gets here and you get wrapped up in the excitement of the day."

"What about them? Everything is under control. Perhaps they would like to have a drink before the others arrive?"

"They'll join us in a while," answers Marc Andre, "but right now Dad and Emile are too busy entertaining Leen with stories of my youth and Sarah's busy storing up titbits of nostalgic information to tease me about."

"How's Leen enjoying that?"

"Oh, she's soaking it all in. As for me, I had to get out of there. When I left, Dad was regaling them about when I broke my arm." He pauses. "Dad's taken quite a shine to Leen. How about that drink?"

"A brandy would be lovely, Dear. And, of course your father is delighted with Leen. How could he not be? She's an impressive woman."

"That's an understatement," grins Marc Andre, reaching for the bottles of brandy and scotch from the sideboard. "If I'm not careful, Dad's going to propose to her before I do."

Chuckling, I reply, "Speaking of which?" My question hangs in the air as Marc Andre hands me my brandy.

Taking a chair, he replies, "We were both so tired last night I put off planning to ask her. This morning we got caught up in the rush to get over here to help out with the meal preparations. Amy, Sarah, and Leen have been coordinating their cooking times all day. Between telephone calls and my father's stories, I've not had the chance to ask her." Looking at his watch, he says, "In fact, I expect Amy will be ringing the doorbell any minute. Maybe I'll get a chance tonight."

"No time like the present," I answer, taking a sip of brandy. I say in a no-nonsense voice, "You walk right out to that kitchen and send your father, Alex, and Sarah out to join me. With them out of the way, the coast will be clear. And, don't you dare come back until you've proposed."

"Now?"

"Yes, now. Before the others arrive." Waving a dismissive hand, I say, "You have something to do, my boy. I suggest you take my advice and do it."

He hesitates before resting his glass down on the sideboard. "What if she says no?"

"Don't be ridiculous. She's not going to say no. Leen is in love with you. Now, go and ask her to marry you." I make the pretence of rising from my chair. "Really, Marc Andre, must I do everything myself? I'll go and ask her for you. Then, we can be done with your infernal procrastinating."

"You will not," answers Marc Andre, laughing at my charade.

"Well, then, go and do it. I'm an old woman and can't stand waiting for you to muster your courage. Go!"

He kisses my cheek. "Going to try to use that excuse of being old again, eh." Wagging his index finger playfully, he says, "That's wearing very thin!"

"Works for me," I answer, shooing him away. "Now get going!"

"I love you, Aunt Claire."

"I have no doubts about that but before your father insists on dragging out the family albums, go and ask Leen to marry you."

When Emile, Alex, and Sarah join me, Emile asks, "What was so all-fired important you needed us to come in here?"

"Fix yourselves a drink and sit with me before all our company comes. Trust me, there's going to be a lot of excitement today. A few quiet moments won't hurt any of us."

Still annoyed that I'd insisted they join me instead of letting them monopolize Leen's time in the kitchen, Emile complains, "Why couldn't you and Marc Andre just come and join us in the kitchen?"

"Because, Emile," I reply, ignoring the pique in his voice, "Marc Andre needs to ask Leen a question."

Sarah looks sharply and from the widening of her eyes and grin, I can tell that she has caught on that Marc Andre has gone to pop the question. She gasps, "Oh my God, this is fantastic!"

Emile demands, "What's fantastic? What sort of question?"

I shake my head from side-to-side. "You know for a smart man, you can be incredibly obtuse at times. Think for a moment. What sort of question does a man need to ask without an audience?"

He sputters, "Obtuse ..." and then, breaks into a smile. "You're kidding?" He leans back in his chair and mutters, "I'll be damned."

I raise my glass.

Returning the toast, he says, "I'd given up on his ever getting married."

Before I can respond, Marc Andre yells out from the kitchen, "She said yes!"

Beaming, I remark, "Well, we have our answer."

Grinning like two teenagers, Leen and Marc come into the sitting room. She gushes, "Can you believe it?" Proudly she holds out her left hand for our inspection. Her ring finger is adorned with a beautiful gold band imbedded with rubies and diamonds."

"What a beautiful ring!" I exclaim. Emile and Alex are on their feet, clapping Marc Andre's back and enthusiastically shaking his hand.

Hugging Leen, Sarah says, "Becky and Amy are going to be sorry they weren't here for this. Congratulations, Leen."

Emile clasps Leen's hands and in a voice rarely given to choked emotion, says, "Marry that boy of mine and make me a proud and happy man."

"Will it be a short or long engagement?" asks Alex.

Laughing at our enthusiastic endorsement, Marc Andre replies, "Short. We'll get married as soon as the Gala is over."

"What's the Gala got to do with your wedding?" asks Sarah.

"We don't want that ass Harris claiming Leen was too busy planning her wedding to me – Claire Holowitz's lawyer – to find Claire and convince her to come to the Gala. It's no secret that as Claire's lawyer, I know her identity and location. He'll use our marriage as a means to discredit Leen. We want to avoid that complication."

Visibly agitated, I retort, "Nonsense. You don't set *your* wedding plans according to what Don Harris may do or not do. That man is trouble, no matter what." My body snaps with irritation at the thought of them having to postpone their happiness based on the fear of reprisals from Harris. "That's ludicrous!"

"It's only a few months," says Leen.

"Preposterous," mutters Emile. Turning to Alex, he asks, "What do you think."

"I think they should do what's best for them." He frowns. "Who is this guy Harris and what hold does he have on Leen or," he looks at me, "you?"

"Leen's boss at Scenes," explains Marc Andre. "He's determined to force Aunt Claire out of her seclusion so that he can claim the coup of finding Claire Holowitz." With a grim expression, he adds, "What would really please Harris is to get Leen fired for incompetence."

Sarah clarifies, "Harris assigned Leen the job of finding Claire."

"Now, I understand," says Alex. Turning to Emile, he asks, "Surely, you have enough legal tricks stored up that sleeve of yours to stop this asshole in his tracks?"

I suggest, "Why not have a quiet ceremony? Pick your date and don't disclose your marriage to the public until after the Gala?"

Leen says, "We don't want to do anything that might jeopardize the success of the Gala or bring Harris closer to finding you."

"Nonsense," I snort. "That fool couldn't find me with the resources of Interpol at his disposal." Glancing around our little circle, I say proudly, "I have a battery of lawyers and agents who will stop him at every turn."

Sarah says, "She's right. Pick a date and have only your close friends in attendance.

The doorbell rings and we hear Amy calling out from the entrance, "Merry Christmas."

"Marc Andre replies, "We're in the sitting room. Come and join us."

"Give me a minute," she answers. "I have to bring some items to the kitchen."

"Do you want help?" calls out Leen.

"No, I'm good," answers Amy. "Be there in a minute."

Walking into the sitting room with an armful of wrapped presents, Amy places her parcels underneath the Christmas tree, exclaiming, "It's like a Christmas Wonderland in here!"

Handing Amy a glass of wine with her left hand, Leen attempts to look casual but can't hide the smirk on her face. The rest of us watch with amused interest.

"Thanks," says Amy taking the glass. "What has you grinning like a Cheshire cat?"

Leen wiggles her ring finger. Amy grabs Leen's left hand and exclaims, "You're engaged!" The rest of us double with laughter as she does a little happy dance. Marc Andre grins. "I take it that we have your approval?"

"Details," demands Amy, her voice cracking with excitement. "When did this happen? You weren't wearing that ring last night."

"About fifteen minutes ago," answers Marc Andre. "Aunt Claire sent me into the kitchen to extradite my father and Alex from their perches; monopolizing Leen's time. I had to move quickly because the way my father was enjoying her company, I was afraid that he might ask her to marry him, himself."

Emile snorts, "It's a good thing that you decided to make your move. I had given up on you ever giving me grandchildren."

"Hold on there," laughs Leen, "we have to set a date to get married before we start talking about the possibility of children."

Wrapping his arm around Leen's waist, Marc Andre asks, "Can I refresh anyone's drink?"

When the doorbell rings, Marc Andre gets up to answer it. Muffled voices can be heard as he hangs up their coats. Within a few minutes, he returns with Joe and Joe's friend, Mike Andrews.

"After introductions are made and greetings exchanged, Sarah says pointedly to Leen, "Why don't you offer Joe and Mike a drink?"

"Yes, do!" encourages Amy, ignoring Joe's quizzical expression at the urgency for Leen to get the drinks."

Heading for the sideboard, Leen asks, "What would you gentleman like?"

"Scotch would be good," answers Joe.

"I'll have the same," adds Mike. Addressing me, he says, "You have a lovely home Mrs. Wright."

"Please call me Anna-Claire."

"Here are your drinks," says Leen, handing Mike and Joe their glasses.

Joe looks suspiciously at Sarah who blurts, "Don't you think Leen looks especially nice today?"

"Yes," agrees Amy. "Positively blushing."

"Okay," says Joe, "what's going on? You ladies clearly want me to know something."

"Take a close look at Leen," orders Sarah.

Obediently Joe glances at Leen who raises her left hand for his inspection.

Joe's response is immediate. "You're engaged!"

"Ha," laughs Amy, "that's what I said."

Once again the room resounds with congratulations. We don't have to wait for long for the newlyweds to arrive and following the same procedure as we have done with the others, we wait, watch, and delight in the surprised reactions to Leen's and Marc Andre's engagement. By the time the twins arrive with their dates, the mood is jovial and the conversation full of exciting plans.

An hour later, between mouthfuls of turkey Jake asks, "What's the date for the wedding?"

Because the boys and Mike Andrews don't know that I'm Claire Holowitz, Marc Andre tactfully avoids mentioning the Gala and instead, expresses the wish to make their wedding a small, family and close friends' affair.

"Why not New Year's Eve," suggests Jeremy. "It's a night for celebration."

"Impossible!" exclaims Becky. "Josh and I'll be in the Caribbean."

"Way too fast," agrees Leen. "We need some time to plan. And, besides I want Aunt Becky to be there."

"Okay then," answers Jake. "How about the weekend after Aunt Becky and Josh get back from their honeymoon."

"That's a great idea," says Josh. "We can use the restaurant and I'll cater."

"What do you think, Leen?" asks Marc Andre. "Will four weeks be enough time to plan a wedding?"

Silence descends on the room and all eyes focus on Leen.

"Are you sure you'd be okay with that?" asks Leen.

Works for me," answers Marc Andre.

"Then it's settled," says Josh, "the week after Becky and I get back from our honeymoon, we host your wedding."

I hear my voice before I realize what's coming out of my mouth. "I want the wedding to be here."

"Well, why not," I argue, a touch petulant because they are looking at me as if I have grown two heads. "Marc Andre is my godson."

"He's my son," interrupts Emile, his tone taking on a huffy edge. "It'll be at my house."

"Be practical Emile," I say, dismissing his suggestion, "you don't know the first thing about planning a wedding."

Miffed, he retorts, "I was married."

"And tell me," I answer, "what exactly did you do to plan for your wedding? Ah yes," I smile thinly, "you showed up for it. Besides," I argue with what I think is the persuasive point, "I will have four perfectly capable assistants." The frown on his face tightens. Firmly, I seal my position. "She'll be married from my home."

Positioned like two combatants – oblivious to the stares we are drawing from everyone else–I stare him straight in the eye and say, "There will be no negotiating."

Amy clears her throat with deliberate intent. "Excuse me folks," she says pleasantly, "but it seems to me that the obvious choice for the wedding celebrations is *my* house."

My jaw slackens with surprise. "Your house," I stammer. "And, why is that?"

"Leen and I have been best friends for over twenty years," replies Amy. I don't say anything and care not a whit that my silence speaks eloquently of what I think of her plan.

"We can compromise," she adds, with smooth calmness.

"What exactly do you suggest?" demands Emile, his tone curt and lawyer like.

"It's absolutely perfect," answers Amy, pleased with what she views as a diplomatic solution. "It's traditional for a bride to spend her last night with her mother before marriage. Since Anna-Claire is fulfilling the role of mother-of-the-bride, Leen can dress from here. A son usually spends the night prior to his wedding with his family." She glances at Marc Andre and Emile, smiles, and slams home her point, "So he should spend the night before with you and Alex. My house is next door so

Leen can be kept away from the guests and the bridesmaids can all dress here without running into guests before the ceremony. Besides," she grins at me, "that way you won't have to deal with the clean-up the next day. Seems to me that I've provided the perfect solution."

Becky throws in her opinion. "I agree with Amy." Her eyes drift to Leen who, like Marc Andre, has remained quiet throughout the entire exchange. "What do the two of you think?"

"I like it," answers Leen. "It'll be a family wedding in so many ways and if you're all good with it, I'm for it." She looks at Marc Andre. "What about you?"

"I like it too," he answers. Facing Emile and Alex, he teases, "I'm not certain I'll want to play poker with the two of you the whole night before my wedding but if you're willing to lose some money, I'll gladly take the winnings for my honeymoon."

"Hah!" snorts Emile. "What say you Alex? Should we teach this son of mine a lesson or two about his lack of poker skills?"

Alex eyes Marc Andre carefully, and with characteristic dry humour, says, "A man should know his limits." Eyes twinkling, he adds, "You may be an excellent lawyer, Marc Andre, but your father is right, you're not a very good poker player." He shrugs. "It'll be a shame to take your money the night before you get married but perhaps Emile and I will ease the pain of your loss with some decent scotch."

"I'll still cater the wedding," says Josh. "I'll have my waiters come to Amy's and we can all pitch in beforehand with decorations."

Emile snorts with amusement. "Got you there, old girl! What Amy suggests makes perfect sense to me."

Recognizing the merits of Amy's suggestion, I concede, "I know when I'm outnumbered." I peer at Marc Andre. "After the rehearsal, don't even think about visiting on some pretext the night before the wedding. You can wait to see your bride. The only visitors to this house will be the bridesmaids and between Amy's house and mine, all the women can have bedrooms. As for you men – resign yourselves to being bachelors the night before the wedding."

"That so?" grouses Emile, not to be outdone. "Well, I've got plenty of rooms at my house too and that's where I'll be hosting the groom and his attendants." He nods at Alex and says, "We'll turn our poker game into a bachelor party while the ladies are having their sleep-over."

"Emile," I warn, "don't you and Alex get carried away. We will expect all of you men to be wide-awake and definitely not hung-over the next day."

"That's what Aspirin is for," teases Alex, his craggy face breaking into a wide grin.

After dinner, we settle in the living room listening to Christmas carols playing softly in the background, and begin the merriment that the exchange of presents brings.

Leen says, "Let's begin with you." She hands me a small package and when I open it, I gasp. Lying atop white velvet is a beautiful gold locket with the engraving, "With love". Opening the clasp, I see that left side of the locket holds a picture of Leen and Amy and the right, a picture of Becky and Sarah. Lifting the locket to my chest, I ask in a voice, tight with emotion, "Would one of you please be so kind as to help me put on this beautiful locket?" All four jump up to help but Amy is the closest and taking the locket, she gently fastens the chain around my neck. Fingering the locket, I look at their beautiful faces and murmur, "Thank you."

Marc Andre sensing the mood in the room has the potential to erupt into feminine expressions of love and tears, passes out gifts to Jeremy and Jake. "These are for you," he says, grinning. "Leen and I thought long and hard about what to give you and we settled on these *twin* gifts."

Watching their reactions of pleasure as they open their presents, Leen says, "A little bird told me that you guys have been eying those watches for the last year."

"This is just great!" exclaims Jake, putting the pilot styled watch on his wrist. "Look, Mom, check it out!"

"Mine too," echoes, Jeremy. "This is awesome."

"Speaking of gifts," says Sarah, lifting two slim packages from underneath the tree, "Joe and I brought something for Stacey and Alicia."

Surprised, the girls open their presents and are genuinely thrilled to find gold pens engraved with their names.

Sarah smiles. "We wanted both of you to have something to take to university. We're glad that you like them."

Stacey says, "I don't know what to say, Mrs. Calder except that it's a beautiful pen and I will keep it as memory of a wonderful Christmas."

"I feel the same," says Alicia, passing her pen over for Jeremy to admire.

Emile pulls out his pocket watch. "It's getting on," he announces to no one in particular.

I glance at my old friend indulgently. "Emile, don't act like an old man. The evening is still young. Just sit back and relax."

Handing a gift to Emile, Marc Andre says, "This is from Leen and me."

Emile mutters gruffly, "I have received a gift already. You had the common sense to ask this girl to marry you."

Amused, I think, 'In typical Emile fashion, he has given his son a compliment—the backhanded way.

Opening his present, Emile withdraws a gold tie clasp and matching cufflinks. Fingering the tie clasp that he's wearing, he says to Marc Andre, "This one has been my favourite for over forty years. Your mother gave it to me on our wedding day. Now, I have another favourite; to remind me of the day my son got engaged."

Leen says, "Look at the engraving on the back of the tie clasp."

The corners of his mouth twitch as he reads the inscription. Passing the clasp for me to see, he says to Stacey and Alicia who, like the rest of us are watching his reaction, "Looks like I, too, will have a memento of this Christmas."

"This is lovely, Emile. Leen, Marc Andre—what a wonderful gift!" I read aloud the engraving, "With love."

Emile clears his throat. "Enough," he says, "let's move on. Time for someone else to be in the spotlight." His bluster draws a laugh from everyone as we resume the exchange of presents, complimenting one another on the gift choices.

Leen's gift from Jeremy and Jake starts with a joke one. It's a model BMW with their names stencilled on the front doors. "I think they're trying to tell me something," she remarks, passing the model around for everyone to see. "No way, guys, the BMW is mine."

"No harm in trying, "grins Jake. "Jeremy and I just wanted to thank you for letting us drive your BMW when Mom was in the hospital."

"And for the times since then," interrupts Jeremy, "when we've borrowed your car to take out Stacey and Alicia."

"This is the real gift," says Jeremy, handing her a rectangular box. Leen smiles as she pulls out an ivory white v-neck sweater. Slipping it on over her silk shirt, she lets her fingers glide down one sleeve. "Cashmere, guys? Having girlfriends definitely has taught you how to treat a woman."

Jake grins. "Yeah, well ... Alicia and Stacey helped with the choice of gifts but we are the ones who thought about them."

Joe laughs. "Give it up while you're ahead, son. Just accept the compliment."

Jake hands a box to Sarah, as Jeremy passes out boxes to Becky and Amy.

Sarah asks, "What this? You guys gave me my present this morning."

"The bath oils and perfume were for Christmas morning," answers Jake. "We saved this for you to open here."

Unwrapping hers, Becky exclaims, "I love it!" Sarah's and Amy's reactions are the same as they unwrap their cashmere sweaters.

"Looks like we all have the same sweaters. Same colour, even," says Leen.

"Dad's always saying how the four of you are like knights on white chargers ..."

"Or members of your own coven," interjects Jake.

"Yeah ... so, we thought you should have matching, symbolic sweaters."

Joe bursts out laughing. "Couldn't have said it better," he comments.

Leen, Becky, Sarah and Amy parade around the room, modelling their matching sweaters. Posing in front of the Christmas tree, Sarah jokes, "Get a good photo of us, Joe. We're going to have it blown up and call it the "Coven".

Everyone guffaws when Joe replies, "So, you finally admit it. I've been saying that for years." Looking at Josh and at Marc Andre he makes a comic face. "What did I tell you guys, they're dangerous together."

Pointing at his wedding ring, Josh says, "It's too late for me, Marc Andre, but you can still bale."

Marc Andre plays along. "I'd be afraid of what they'd do to me if I did."

Rising from my chair, I say, "I could do with a snack right about now. Does anybody else want dessert?"

"No, you rest," smiles Leen. "The coven will get it."

Leen

Once in the kitchen, we slice pieces of fruitcake and place an assortment of Christmas cookies on a serving tray. Filling cups with coffee and adding the creamer and sugar bowl onto a platter, I remark, "Anna-Claire and Emile are holding up well."

"It's been a long and exciting day," replies Becky, placing shortbreads on the tray. "And with the lateness of last night, they have to be tired. I know I am."

"You're tired not because of the wedding," jokes Amy, nudging her elbow. "Did you get any sleep?"

Blushing, Becky answers, "Let's just say, I saw the sun rise."

"Okay," I say, picking up the tray, "let's agree to have an early evening. Anna-Claire and Emile are looking happy but tired. And you," I smile at Becky, "have to be at the airport bright and early."

"Just don't elope while we're gone on our honeymoon," warns Becky.

Returning to the sitting room we find the men engaged in animated discussion about the Stanley Cup playoffs, arguing whether or not the Senators will make the playoffs, and Anna-Claire is listening to Stacey's and Alicia's plans for university.

Rolling my eyes, I mouth, "Hockey."

"Figures," answers Sarah. "They live and breathe it." She shrugs with an air of resignation. "What can I say? I can't leave them alone for a minute."

We pass around the snacks. The mood is festive and there's lots of laughter. Becky is the first to make the move to end the evening, saying to Josh, "If you're through trashing the short-comings of the NHL we have to think about leaving. Five o'clock will come fast and I still have to throw some things into my suitcases."

Taking the signal, Josh places his coffee cup on the table. "It's been a wonderful Christmas everyone."

After helping with the clean up of dishes, Jeremy and Jake thank everyone again for their gifts and leave with Stacey and Alicia. Alex and Emile remain for another half hour before calling it a night. The rest of us sit down in the living room to share a nightcap. Marc Andre stokes the embers in the fireplace and adds another log. Soon, the fire is crackling and throwing its glow out into the room.

"So, Mike," says Joe, "you've managed to survive the whole gang, got Jeremy and Jake to discuss their university plans and ..." he adds with a glance at Sarah, "you've been a good sport about the coven."

"Joe!" exclaims Sarah, poking him lightly in the ribs, "enough with the coven jokes."

"Admit it, Sarah, you like it when I tease about the coven," laughs Joe.

Grinning, she retorts, "One of these days I'll find a broomstick and hit you over the head with it."

"If I were you, Joe, I'd be careful," teases Mike. "Earlier today she threatened to turn you into a frog."

"Now that I'd like to see," I joke.

After the laughter dies down, Mike says, "I can't thank you all enough for letting me share your Christmas Day with you."

"It has been great having you here," replies Joe. "It's too bad you have to return tomorrow. Can you arrange to take a few more days? Sarah's ban on business talk will be lifted tomorrow and we can discuss our plans for that joint project."

Immediately Sarah agrees. "We'd love to have you stay with us for a few more days, Mike, if your schedule permits it. And," she looks at Joe, "despite what Joe says, I'm not entirely opposed to business discussions. I just didn't want them on Christmas Day."

Mike considers the suggestion and grins. "Well, I could manage a few more days as long my staying doesn't inconvenience you."

Observing Amy's reaction to Mike's decision to remain, I can tell that she's trying to look uninterested but I know her well enough to realize that Mike Andrews has captured her attention. What I had taken to be casual exchanges between her and Mike throughout the day takes on new significance. Mike confirms my suspicions when he looks at Amy and suggests with a tentative smile, "Perhaps, while I'm here you could find time in your schedule to show me those museums you were mentioning earlier today."

Deliberately ignoring my pointed look, Amy flushes as she answers with a warm smile, "My pleasure. The university is out of session for the holiday season so my schedule is my own."

"Our firm reserves a box for the hockey season," says Marc Andre. "I can get us all tickets for the Senators' game on the twenty-seventh."

"Count me out," says Anna-Claire. "I'll be quite happy to sit here at home, enjoy a warm fire, and watch television."

The idea of attending an NHL game appeals to the rest of us and it's quickly agreed that Sarah, Joe, Mike and Amy will join Marc Andre and me for the game. Nightcaps finished, we decide to call it a night. After commenting on the wonderful day we have enjoyed, the rest of us wave good-bye to Anna-Claire and Amy and make our way back to our homes.

Amy

I insist on making Anna-Claire a cup of tea to have at her bedside saying, "You go on upstairs, Anna-Claire. I'll bring the tea up when it's steeped and to say good night."

By the time I get upstairs with the tea, Anna-Claire has turned down the covers and has changed into her pyjamas.

"Are you sure you're not too tired from the day?" I ask, placing the teacup on the bedside table. "You've had two busy days in a row."

"I'm pleasantly tired," replies Anna-Claire, stifling a yawn. Sitting on the bed, she takes a sip of her tea and says, "I know I should be exhausted, but strangely I am not. And you," she asks with a mischievous glint in her eyes, "have you had a good day?"

"Yes, but I admit you put me to shame. I'm exhausted."

"Joe's friend Mike seems to be a very nice man. It was nice of you to agree to act as a tourist guide while he's here."

I know what she's getting at but I want to avoid this discussion. I'm not certain how I feel about Mike but I do know that I found him to be interesting and I'd like to get to know him better. I answer, "It would have been rude to say no to him."

"Yes, indeed," remarks Anna-Claire, but she's not fooling me with her casual response.

"There's nothing more to it," I say.

"To what dear?"

"To my showing him the museums and around Ottawa."

"I never said there was," answers Anna-Claire. She smiles. "It's been a wonderful day and it's time that we both get some sleep."

I kiss her forehead. "You take care, Anna-Claire. I'll be by tomorrow morning to empty the dishwasher. Don't forget we're having left-overs tomorrow so I hope you like cold turkey sandwiches and re-heated stuffing."

"I'm looking forward to it."

As I get to the front door, Anna-Claire calls out, "Why don't you ask that nice Mike Andrews to join us for left-overs? It seemed to me that he was interested in more than museums."

Holding onto the banister, I call back, "What is that supposed to mean?"

"Nothing, dear, nothing at all," answers Anna-Claire but I can hear her soft laughter. "Just trying to be friendly to Sarah and Joe's houseguest."

I sigh and can't help but laugh as I repeat, "Good night Anna-Claire."

Walking back to my house, I'm surprised at the tingle of excitement I feel as I think about my day and having met Mike. Flipping on the hall lights, I decide an Irish coffee would be nice. I make myself one and take it with me to the living room where I can sit in front of the gas fireplace and reflect on my reaction to Mike Andrews. Glad for the solitude after a busy day, I sit with only the glow of the fireplace. It's nice. It's peaceful. By the time I finish my drink, I'm ready to admit – at least to myself – that I'm looking forward to knowing Mike Andrews better.

On my way upstairs to bed I tell myself Mike is only going to be here for a few days and nothing will come of it. I tell myself not to be foolish. But as I brush my teeth, I can't help but wonder what – if anything – did Mike think about me?

Chapter Twenty-six

Anna-Claire

The week between Christmas and New Year's is an uneventful one for me. Despite my protests to the contrary, I was exhausted and the aftermath following Becky's wedding and the Christmas Day festivities found me having to face the reality that I needed to rest. I spent my days working on my new play and reviewing the information I had gained about Don Harris. I turned down invitations to accompany Amy as she played tourist guide for Mike and refused to succumb to Leen's pleas to take advantage of the Boxing Day sales. I outright refused any invitations for New Year's Eve celebrations other than that which I had been doing for four decades – spending a quiet evening with Emile.

In the old days, when Marc Andre's mother was alive and he was young, we would pass the evening eating snacks, playing board games, and watching the ball drop in New York City's Times Square. Now, it's just Emile, Alex and me. There's something to be said for the quiet traditions one has in life and for me, New Year's Eve has always been a time to reflect on the year that has passed and to wish my close friends the best of health and happiness for the year to come.

Emile agreed to attend the hockey game, but sided with me about New Year's Eve, saying that it was our tradition to spend it together watching the celebrations televised from Times Square. When Marc

Andre asked him, Alex, and me to reconsider our plans for New Year's Eve, Emile told him in true Emile form that he was content to sit in the comfort of his own living room, sipping drinks with Alex and me.

I said much the same to Sarah and Amy when they questioned me about my plans for New Year's Eve. "Alex, Emile, and I will be quite fine as we pass the evening away playing poker and rummy," I had told them sincerely. "And, if memory serves me right," I added with justified smugness, "I took them both for close to forty dollars last year. This year, I plan to bluff my way to a hundred."

As planned, Mike and Joe began on Boxing Day to draw up tentative plans for their joint venture. Mike has been eying a property on the outskirts of Winnipeg for over a year and wants to build a large shopping mall.

Sarah tells me that Amy and Mike seem to be getting along so well that from an observer's point of view it is as if they have known each other for years. I asked if she sensed a budding romance in the air but Sarah laughed at the idea saying that Amy is too sensible and set in her ways to fall for someone she has just met. "True enough," I replied, "but I thought they were making a connection on Christmas Day."

"You're just being a matchmaker," teased Sarah. "You've got Becky married off and now Lean is getting married. Since when have you started writing romance novels?"

"Hah," I snorted. "You don't have to be a romance writer to pick up on nuances.

Besides," I purposely added, "every writer knows that if you want to be successful, it's important to pay attention to what's happening in the world that surrounds you. That's where the kernels of all novels originate."

"Ah, Anna-Claire," replied Sarah, "Amy's being nice to a friend of Mike's and because the introduction came that way – through friends – she's relaxed her normal reserve with the result that the two of them are enjoying one another's company. There are a lot of miles between Ottawa and Winnipeg. The possibility of their friendship going beyond anything more is remote. You just want to play match maker."

Deciding to leave the matter of Amy's love life to private speculation, I joked about her reference to 'match making' saying, "Who knows, maybe I will try my hand at writing a romance novel and use all of your lives as the plot line."

Amused, Sarah answered, "You wouldn't dare ..."

"Never dare an old woman," I smiled, "and certainly not one who is an author. What was it that Shakespeare wrote? Ah let me see," I said stroking my chin thoughtfully, "I believe it was something about the pen being mightier than the sword."

෴

Joe

Pushing aside the papers and draft plans for our proposed business venture, I ask, "So, what does Amy have planned for you today?"

Rubbing his neck, Mike answers, "She mentioned something about going to see an old jailhouse."

I smile. "She's probably talking of the Nicholas Street jail. It's where Patrick James Whalen was hanged. Nowadays, it's a hostel and does well as a tourist site for visitors to the city."

"Patrick Whalen?"

"Yeah, think back to your grade 8 or 9 history lessons. He was accused of killing Thomas D'Arcy Mc Gee back in 1869." I shrug. "Legend has it that to the very end Whalen protested his innocence and that his ghost haunts the jail."

"And I'd be interested in seeing that because...?"

"Because it's a tourist site and you get to see the architecture of one of the oldest buildings in Ottawa," I answer, smiling. "Hey, you're the one who asked a university professor to come up with some interesting sites to see."

"You're right," he agrees. "After the jail house, she says we'll do a tour of the Parliament buildings specifically to see the library, have dinner at a restaurant in the Market area, and then, a must see are the Christmas lights on Sparks Street and Parliament Hill."

Laughing, I say, "Before you know it, she'll have you rhyming off stats about Ottawa's tourist sites like a pro."

Looking at his watch, he says, "I have just enough time to shower and shave before I have to leave. Seems strange having a woman pick me up. I should have rented a car."

"Hard to do over the Christmas season," I answer. "Besides if you want to use one of ours or a company van or truck, you know you're welcome to. But," I can't resist adding, "I think Amy likes playing the role of tourist guide."

Mike rises. "Why don't you and Sarah join us for dinner? The least I can do for your hospitality is take the both of you out."

"Give us a call after the jail house tour," I answer, sorting the papers on my desk. "I'm not sure what Sarah's got planned for today but if we don't do dinner tonight, let's try to do it before you leave. It would be nice."

"I know I've already said this, but I really appreciate how you and Sarah have opened up your home to me. And, I'm pleased that my flight problems ended up with our making what I think will result in a profitable outcome."

"Do you mean our business deal or," I smirk, "are you referring to the fact that you seem to be getting along well with our hitherto academic recluse?"

Mike's face colours at my jibe but he answers, "I have to admit, Amy has been a pleasant surprise. When you told me that I would be meeting a university professor, I conjured up images of a grey haired, stern, old maid stereotype."

I answer truthfully, "She's one of the most beautiful women I've ever known – inside and out – but don't tell Sarah I said that."

"Don't tell Sarah what?"

Startled, we spin around. Openly smirking at my having been caught saying not to tell her something, she says smoothly, "Joe, I would be a rotten friend if I didn't have the honesty to admit that Amy is gorgeous."

Gallantly, Mike says, "If you weren't married to this guy here…" he jerks his thumb in my direction, "I would persuade you to take me as a suitor but he's made it perfectly clear that he's a one-woman man." He lowers his voice, winks at Sarah, and says with theatrical flair, "I hate to be the one to have to tell you this but if your husband has a flaw, it's that he's a liar."

"A liar! What the hell are you talking about?"

Sarah plays along and enjoying my discomfort and Mike's harmless flirting, asks sweetly, "Whatever do you mean, Mike?"

"Well," drawls Mike, "when I worked with Joe last fall he told me he had a great wife and two wonderful sons. What he left out was how stunning you are when you smile and how beautiful you are in person."

Having had enough of their teasing at my expense, I drape my arm protectively over Sarah's shoulders. "That's enough from the two of you." Playing the role of an aggrieved husband I glare at Mike. "Didn't you say that you needed to shave and shower before Amy gets here? I'm sure Sarah can suggest some cream for those wrinkles under your eyes. And," I say, letting my gaze drift to his waist, "don't forget to suck in that mid-waist flab before Amy arrives. Admit it man, your age is showing."

Poking me in the waist, Sarah asks, "Are you saying I have wrinkles?"

Mike laughs heartily. "Stepped right into that one, Joe."

Pretending to be sympathetic, Sarah says, "Don't worry, dear, I still love you."

"Are the two of you finished having a good time bashing me around?"

"Oh, I think so," replies Sarah. "At least for the moment."

"I'll leave the two of you alone to reconcile your differences," grins Mike, "while I go upstairs and try to do something about my gut and my wrinkles."

After he leaves, Sarah asks, "Do you think he likes her?"

Switching off the desk lamp, I answer, "It's hard to say if he likes her in the way you're hinting at. I don't think either one of us should play the role of matchmaker."

Her disgusted grunt tells me that she has absolutely no intention of following my advice. Knowing that she expects more of an answer, I say, "He's a nice guy. She could do a lot worse." Wanting to change the topic, I ask, "What's for lunch?"

"Left-overs," answers Sarah. "Cold turkey sandwiches with cranberry and stuffing on the side and for dessert, pumpkin pie."

"Mike suggested that we join him and Amy for dinner downtown tonight."

"Really?" Dutifully, I follow Sarah into the kitchen, knowing that her silence means her mind is racing. Handing me the butter and pointing to the bread, she says, "You get started on the sandwiches while I cut the meat and warm up the stuffing."

"Dinner? Tonight?" I reach inside the refrigerator for the mustard.

"I think Mike might just be the answer."

Suspecting where this conversation is headed, I decide to play dumb. "The answer to what?"

"There's more to life than academia. It's time that Amy allows herself the chance to have someone special in her life. Dick the Prick was a first class jerk but everything said and done, she loved him. She's never gotten over his shabby treatment of her." She frowns thoughtfully. "Sometimes I think that her love of literature has been a drawback for her, emotionally."

Completely stumped, I stop buttering the bread and stare. "What? I'm confused. What has Amy's ex got to do with whether or not we join Mike and her for dinner?"

"Just thinking out loud," answers Sarah. "Besides, there's truth in what I'm saying. Even Becky told her that she's read so many novels where the heroine and hero end up together that she – on some level – is looking for that romantic ending in her life."

Used to how my wife and her friends have a no-holds barred relationship when it comes to analysing the ups and downs of their lives, I know better than to try to figure out what direction Sarah is going with this conversation. I decide to let her break it down for me.

"Come on Sarah," I say, "you know I can't follow the logic you and your friends use to examine one another's lives. Give me the simple version and would you please also let me know if you'd like to join them for dinner." Deliberately, I heave a loud sigh, wanting her to know that I'm getting frustrated. Adding mustard to the bread slices, I ask, "Has anyone ever told you that you're like a pit bull gnawing on a bone when you get something in that head of yours?"

She shrugs. "You may have mentioned that once or twice in our many years of marriage. I'm simply saying that I hope Amy and Mike get to know one another better."

I groan, "And you and Becky say she's the one who reads too much romance." Deciding to direct her attention to our life, I say, "The boys are off to Mont Tremblant to ski with Stacey and Alicia and some of their friends and Mike will be out all day with Amy."

"Meaning?"

"Meaning ... we have the house to ourselves."

Placing turkey on the bread she says, "Don't eat too much, Joe. Turkey makes you sleepy. It'd be a shame if you fell asleep especially since ..." she smiles coyly, "we have, as you pointed out, the whole house to ourselves this afternoon."

"Don't you worry about me sleeping," I answer, sweeping my gaze over her.

Sarah bites into her sandwich. "Well, we'll see about that won't we?" She wipes mustard off her upper lip with a napkin.

Reaching for a pickle, I let myself take a satisfying crunch and with the comfort of friendship and love nurtured over our years together, I say, "When I said Amy was beautiful, I didn't mean you weren't."

"Oh," smiles Sarah, in that way she has which is both inviting and teasing, "I've no problem with you telling Mike that Amy's beautiful; I just want to be certain that in your eyes, I'm the one who holds your attention."

Impulsively I take her hand in mine. "Sarah, I love you more than you'll ever know. You do know that, don't you?"

Her eyes scan my face and then with a slow, easy, mischievous smile, she says, "I know but it's nice to hear it every once in a while."

I help myself to an extra scoop of hot stuffing. "About dinner?"

"Sure, let's join them. Besides, that'll give me more time to spy on them. Leen is going to want a full report." She looks up from her meal and adds with deliberate emphasis, "And so will Becky when she gets back from her honeymoon."

"Ah yes, the coven will need to know. After all, you ladies may want to conjure up a love spell." Pretending to sprinkle fairy dust at her, I say, "Heaven forbid that Amy and Mike simply have a good time just as friends."

Sarah taps my shin with the toe of her foot. "Stop with the coven jokes, Joe, or I may just put a spell on you."

I grin. "Too late, Sarah. You did that years ago."

Picking up our plates to put in the dishwasher, she adds smugly, "As I like to say in court, I rest my case."

Chapter Twenty-seven

Marc Andre

Furious, I slam my hand down on the conference table. "What the hell is that supposed to mean?"

Unruffled by my verbal explosion, Bill James answers, "It means a Board of Directors' meeting will be convened tonight. At that meeting, Don Harris will be asking for a vote of non-confidence in Adrienne MacLeen."

Cold anger rages through me. "On what grounds?"

"He's claiming that your relationship with Leen is more than a working one. That – coupled with the fact that you're Claire's legal counsel – is a clear case of conflict of interest."

Clenching my fist and wishing that Harris were at the receiving end, I growl, "Fuck him! When I'm done with him he's going to seriously regret pissing me off."

"For you to get involved at this point would be disastrous. You'd be playing right into his hands," answers Bill. "You have to get control of yourself and listen long enough to hear my plan."

"Are you certain that's what this meeting is about?"

"Yes, absolutely. Ed Blaine is a good friend of mine. He called this morning, wanting to know if the rumour was true."

"What rumour?"

"That you and Leen are an item."

"What does it matter? Has that idiot never heard of lawyer-client privilege? Who the fuck does he think he is!"

Bill continues in a reasonable tone, "Ed has no love for Harris but he did say that Harris has garnered some support from a few of the Board members that because Leen and you are involved, it makes sense that she would know where to find Claire Holowitz. The fact that she's not done so is, according to Harris, proof that she's allowing her personal life to interfere with her responsibilities to Scenes." He pauses and waits for me to finish a new string of expletives before continuing. "To put it bluntly… according to Harris, if Leen were not so busy screwing you and vice versa, she would use her relationship with you to convince Claire to appear at the Gala – with the result that Scenes would achieve a major coup in the media industry."

"Who I screw," I retort facetiously, "is not the concern of anyone on that Board and certainly, not Harris's."

"Be that as it may," replies Bill, "Harris is a smooth enough talker to twist anything and come out smelling like a rose."

Bill's sigh leaves no doubt that he's becoming exasperated with my uncharacteristic lack of objectivity. I stare out the window at the cars below, wishing I could squash Harris like a bug. When he's certain that I'm calm enough to continue our discussion, he asks, "What exactly is your relationship with Leen?"

I turn to face him and answer, "I'm going to marry her."

Bill whistles softly. "Okay then," he says. "Harris is on the right track. The two of you are involved. And does Leen know where Claire is?"

Ten years younger than my father, Bill joined the firm fresh out of law school and has been both friend and business partner to my father for over thirty years. He is well aware of Claire's identity as Anna Wright and has, on more than one occasion, met with her.

I take a chair opposite to him and say, "Bill, I didn't mean to fall in love. It just happened and as for Leen knowing where Claire is and her other identity … I wasn't the one to tell her that."

He arches a bushy eyebrow. "So how did she find out?"

I take a deep breath and start to talk. I explain how she met Claire and how she, Becky, Amy and Sarah came to be friends with her. I talk about when Aunt Claire retained Sarah and her reasons for doing so. When I finish, Bill says with characteristic dryness, "More reason than ever for you not to meet with Harris and the Board members. No," he says, holding his hand up for me to stop in mid-protest, "I'm representing the firm at that meeting. I've already told Ed that I will be there to answer any questions they may have with regard to Claire's continued refusal to attend the Gala or to permit her whereabouts to be known."

Having vented my initial rage, I'm now thinking clearly. "Make it clear to your friend and other members of the Board that my relationship with Leen is none of their business. Any suggestion or innuendo from Harris that Leen has compromised her work ethic will result in a major civil suit. They'll end up paying for damages beyond anyone's wildest nightmare."

Bill tenses but his voice is calm as he answers, "I think I have enough legal experience to know how to deal with the Board members."

"I'm sorry, I didn't mean ..."

"It's fine," interrupts Bill. "no offence taken." Leaning back in his chair, he asks, "So when are you getting married?"

"The end of the month." Smiling, I add, "Actually, you're on the guest list. Leen and I want it to be a private wedding with only family and our closest friends. Claire insisted that we not wait until after the Gala to get married. Harris can go to hell."

"And that is exactly why you are not attending that meeting even though you are Claire's primary counsel."

"What?"

"You can't walk in there and tell Harris to go to hell. You're too involved." He thinks for a moment and in a lighter tone, says, "You're in a difficult position, Marc. This is clearly a case where the axiom suits."

"What axiom."

"A lawyer who represents himself is a fool." Amused at my snort of derision, he adds, "You're many things, but a fool is not an adjective that I would apply to you."

"They can't dismiss Leen because she's engaged to me," I answer. "Nor can they say that Claire Holowitz has ever agreed to make a public appearance. From the outset, her compliance with *Scenes'* for the Gala research was based on the sole premise that her identity, whereabouts, and privacy would never be compromised."

Bill swallows the last of his coffee. "I have every intention of making that point tonight."

A voice from the doorway to the conference room interrupts, "You'll have company."

Turning in our chairs, we watch as my father walks in. He has the look of a seasoned litigator ready to do battle – dressed in a grey business suit, pristine white shirt, and deep red tie. His features are set and his eyes snap with anger.

"Dad, what are you doing here?" I get up to pull out a chair for him.

"Bill called me this morning and filled me in. He knew that you'd want to take on Harris and I knew that he'd need help in controlling your reaction." Unbuttoning his suit jacket, my father relaxes in his chair and looking at Bill, asks, "So," was I right?"

"Right down to wanting to stomp over to *Scenes* and punch out Harris," answers Bill, with a wide grin. "Although I've known him since he was a kid, I have to admit this is the first time, the words "temper tantrum" come to mind."

"Love can do strange things to a man," chortles my father, enjoying their repartee at my expense. Pouring a glass of water from the pitcher resting on the table, he adds, "It can make a man crazy and cause him to lose his objectivity."

Feeling embarrassed for having lost control earlier, I remark, "If the two of you are through taking digs at me, would you explain what you intend to gain by going there together?" Addressing my father, I say, "You talk about me needing to be reasonable. What about you? The doctor said you were not to do anything to raise your blood pressure and besides, you've not been directly involved in any legal matters for over two years."

Dismissing me with a flick of his hand, he responds, "I am the most senior partner in this firm and it is a moot point whether or not I have done litigation in two years, two days, or within the last two minutes. What matters," he says, firmly, "is that I choose to be involved. Furthermore," he scowls, "I want to see the man who thinks he can malign my future daughter-in-law and get away with it."

"And you say you're objective?"

"I'm making no such claim. That's why Bill will do most of the talking, but as the long-time legal counsel of Claire Holowitz, my presence is going to make a statement."

"And that would be?"

He leans forward, eyes snapping with determination and says, "Don't mess with Claire Holowitz, this firm, or imply the actions of my son and his future wife have been less than discreet and completely appropriate. Your engagement is not the business of the Scenes' board members. Sometimes all an opposing force needs to know and see is the presence of firm resolve." Leaning back in his chair, he takes a long hard look at me. "My being there will indicate the gravity of Harris's allegations and give the Board members cause to think about the wrath of litigation that will descend on them if they so much as say anything other than congratulations to either you or Leen."

"Marc," interjects Bill, "Leen is going to be asked by the Board to attend the meeting. I've asked her to come here this morning to prepare her for the inquisition that she will have to face tonight. In fact," he glances at his wristwatch, "she should be here anytime now."

As if in response to his words, the intercom on the table buzzes. Pushing the button, my father says, "Yes Eleanor?"

"Ms MacLeen has arrived, Sir."

Eleanor has been with the firm for forty years and is due to retire in June. Her primary focus and loyalty has always been to Dad. He had hired her fresh out of secretarial college and my father has always had great respect for her intelligence and discretion. Many times over the years he offered to fund her law degree, guaranteeing her a place in the firm upon graduation, but she steadfastly refused saying that a lawyer's hours would interfere with the time she wanted to spend with her husband and children. My father is fond of saying, "Law or no law degree, Eleanor's one of best backroom lawyers I've ever met."

"Send her in, please." My father throws me a cautionary glance. "You need to remain calm. If Leen thinks you're upset, she'll not be able to deal with Harris. Anger only clouds the ability to react with logic. In the absence of logic, confusion reigns and you'll lose your case before you even begin."

Half listening to his caution I watch as Leen enters the room. She's pale but I can tell from the jut of her chin that she's determined. She's dressed in a tailored blue skirt, vest, jacket and white shirt which despite its formality, does not hide the curves of her slender body. The addition of a gold chain and earrings accents unrestrained femininity. I can see the approval in my father's and Bill's eyes and I smile as my gaze travels over her. I pull out a chair for her saying, "So you've heard about Harris?"

"Bill called me this morning." Looking at him, she says calmly, "I wasn't at work five minutes before Harris summoned me to his office to tell me about the Board meeting."

"Well you seem to be quite calm about the whole thing. I would have thought that you would be upset."

Her deep blue eyes rest on me thoughtfully and her smile is soft and yet so sad that I want to take her in my arms and tell her that everything is going to be okay but I know this is not what she would want. Not now. Now, she's here to do business with my father and Bill. She replies, half in jest, "Oh, I was initially furious with Don and had he made the mistake of being anywhere within my presence when I got Bill's call, I probably would be under arrest now for having crushed his skull with the first object that I could lay my hands on."

Her blunt, honest answer makes all of us smile at the thought of her bludgeoning Harris and relaxes the tension in the air. "But," she adds, "this isn't about me and my reaction to his lies and manipulations. This is about business. I need to remain calm and think with objectivity."

Grinning his approval, my father slaps his hand down on the table. "I told you this woman's a keeper. If you don't marry her, I will. She knows how to approach a situation even when the stakes are personal."

"Enough with your avowals to marry Leen. She's marrying me."

"Thank you, Emile," says Leen, favouring him with a fond smile. "It's nice to know that I've got at least one Aumount man who doesn't doubt my ability to take on a lion in his own den."

"Lion!" I snort derisively. "When I'm through with Harris, he'll be more like the snake he really is."

Picking up one of the legal pads resting at the end of the conference table Bill comments, "Now that we've gotten over the initial discussion of Harris's inadequacies, can we please have a discussion with Leen about the meeting for tonight?"

"One moment," says my father, pushing the intercom button. "I want Eleanor in on this meeting." Looking at Leen, he says, "She has a knack for words and is a great strategist."

For the next two hours we review and grill Leen about all her actions and correspondence since first learning that Scenes was to handle the

Holowitz Gala. Calmly and succinctly she answers our questions, helping us to create a timeline of chronological events that clearly demonstrate her diligence and attention to the tasks. By the time we're finished, Bill and my father are smiling with satisfaction at the poise and professionalism she demonstrates.

"Answer that way tonight and the Board will want to endorse you for Prime Minister," says my father, returning his fountain pen to his suit's breast pocket. "What do you think Eleanor? Have we missed anything?"

"No, I don't think so," replies Eleanor. "As long as Leen answers the way she did for the two of you, she'll be fine." Her thoughtful hazel eyes rest on Leen. "Remember Leen, you may have been in tough Board room conferences before but this one is different. This one is set with a hidden agenda." She pauses and says, firmly, "Your blood."

Leen takes a deep breath and exhales slowly. "I know."

"Then, you'll be fine," smiles Eleanor. "It's only when you don't recognize the enemy or anticipate his attack that you make a mistake. A good general plans for all contingencies and a wise lawyer schools his client in how to answer without necessarily giving away more than what is necessary to respond to any given question." Lips pursed, she studies Leen through narrowed eyes. "Wear something suitably business-like but not so much so that it hides your femininity. Let them fear your intelligence and appreciate the attraction. In other words, use every weapon in your arsenal to take them out."

My father says, "Eleanor always provides good advice. For years, she's been my secret weapon and all the time opposing counsel thought she was merely taking notes. Hah," he scoffs with delight, "another good example of how people make inaccurate assumptions."

"Enough Emile," says Eleanor, blushing at his praise. "Leen needs to get ready for tonight and you need to go home and rest so that you can be there for her."

Had I or anyone else suggested that my father was exhausting himself, he would have been loud in his denial. But Eleanor, with the comfort gained of years of working with him and weathering his cranky and abrupt moments, has a way of getting him to do exactly what he should be doing.

Putting a spin on it, as if it is his idea, my father says, "I think that I'll go home and have an early supper. Alex will bring me to the meeting and wait for me." He looks at Bill. "The only thing left to discuss is the timing of our arrivals."

Leen looks confused but she attempts to joke. "You make it sound like a military operation."

"Timing is an important part of the overall strategy," answers Eleanor. "What we want to do is strike a balance between your compliance with the Board's directive to be there and send a subtle message that you're not unduly worried." She explains further. "They're expecting Bill so he won't be a surprise but Emile will be. For him to ..." she wriggles two fingers in the air to punctuate her point, "come out of retirement will send notice that while they have their agenda, Claire Holowitz's legal representatives have theirs. Couple that silent message with the fact that you – the primary target of the meeting–are not there waiting like an errant student outside the principal's office to be chastised will undoubtedly fluster Harris. We're banking on him thinking you've been outflanked. Having two senior partners in attendance before your arrival sends the message that you will not be without protection."

"I plan on being there by six forty-five," answers Bill, snapping his briefcase shut. "Emile will arrive five minutes later." Peering at Leen over his reading glasses, he says, "I want you to arrange to arrive a few minutes before seven o'clock. That gives Harris no time to try to undermine your confidence. When you enter the board room, simply take your seat and smile as if it is the most natural thing in the world for you to be there."

I feel a surge of pride as Leen nods her understanding. She is more focused and intense than when she arrived for this briefing. Although outwardly calm, she had still been wrestling with her fear. Like me, she had been insulted and enraged by Harris' claim that she had been duped by sex and not done her job with due diligence and attention to details. As we hammered out the strategy for tonight's meeting she answered all questions openly and when Bill asked if she regretted having signed the confidentiality agreement not to reveal Aunt Claire's identity or whereabouts, she answered without hesitation, "No."

Leen claimed that the months of knowing Anna-Claire had been some of the most rewarding of her life. She looked Bill straight in the eye and said that her search for Claire had led to a close friendship with her and our engagement. Grimly, she smiled her assent to Bill's plans, listened to my father's counsel, and paid attention to Eleanor's suggestions. One thing was clear – she was resolute in her determination to protect Aunt Claire's privacy at all costs.

My father crooks his arm for Leen to take and says, "Now my dear, allow me to escort you to your car. You are not to worry about anything. Bill and I have a few tricks up our sleeves that you need not know about." He smiles reassuringly, "When we're done with Harris tonight, he'll seriously regret causing you any grief."

"Shouldn't I know them?" asks, Leen.

Bill answers, "No, you shouldn't. Your job is to go home and get some rest before tonight."

"Nothing to worry about," says my father.

"What about Sarah?" asks Leen.

"What about her?" I ask.

"Aren't the two of you supposed to be working together?" answers Leen. "Earlier today Bill asked me about the confidentiality agreement. I meant to ask then but got sidetracked. Does she know about the meeting?"

"I spoke with her this morning," says Bill. "While we've been meeting with you, she has been working with Claire."

Leen's face clouds with worry. "I don't want Anna-Claire upset."

My father laughs. "Don't worry. I know her better than you do and I can assure you that the Claire I know will send her response to Harris and the Board in a very dramatic manner."

"But ..." Leen begins to protest.

"No buts,' answers my father. "Now what are you going to do until you have to be at the Board meeting?"

"I was thinking of going back to my office," answers Leen, "but, I could do with some downtime." She winks at me and asks, "And will you be joining me for supper?"

Reaching for my coat, I say, "I have to make a stop at the grocery store first."

"I have food," answers Leen. "I'll make us something."

"Not tonight," I reply. "Tonight I'm going to cook you an athlete's meal before you go to do battle and when we return home, we'll open a good bottle of wine and toast your triumph over that bastard."

"Listen to him, Bill," chortles my father as we collectively make our way to the elevator. "First he wanted to punch out Harris and now, he thinks he's a chef going to cook the supper of champions!" We laugh when he grumbles, "Someone would do well to remind my son that he's a lawyer!"

Chapter Twenty-eight

Anna-Claire

As Leen is being coached by Emile, Bill, and Marc Andre, I've been discussing my intent to put an end to Don Harris' manipulations and lies by appearing in person at the Board meeting. Not for the first time, I say, "He has no right to expect me to forfeit my privacy or to accuse Leen of not having done her job properly."

Providing the voice of reason, Sarah counsels, "Be reasonable Anna-Claire. Harris will use your appearance as proof of Leen deliberately withholding that information because of her relationship with Marc Andre."

"This is ridiculous," I argue. "The man has to be stopped."

"And that is exactly the message your legal team will deliver tonight." For the second time in the last twenty minutes, she says, "You know very well what Harris will do when he finds out that Marc Andre is your godson and, make no mistake about it, he will find out. He'll tell the Board members that her involvement with Marc Andre is proof that she has placed personal pleasure and self-gratification over corporate priorities."

"And, how exactly, will he do that?" I demand, not caring that my tone is clipped.

Sarah lifts her eyes from her notes and reiterates calmly, "He'll claim that since she won't divulge your whereabouts, it's necessary for him to take over the search – all for Scenes to achieve what no other media has managed to do for forty years. He'll feign disappointment in Leen's lack of loyalty to Scenes and, after receiving the Board's grateful thanks for his executive leadership and self-sacrifice, he'll position himself as a humble hero." She taps her pen on her notes and says grimly, "In short, he'll use the work that Leen and her team have painstakingly done for his own self-aggrandizement."

Digesting Sarah's rationale, I ask for the third time, "Are you truly satisfied with the wording of the statement we've put together for them? Do you really think it will be enough to stop Harris?"

"Yes," answers Sarah. Patiently she asks, "Would you care to re-read it?"

I slip on my reading glasses. Essentially, the document states that in addition to legal representation from Emile's firm, Sarah has been retained as independent counsel and that without Leen's active involvement, I will withdraw any endorsement of the Gala and prevent cooperation from all sources. It's a blatant ultimatum to the Board that *Scenes* stands to lose not only the initial retainer for the Gala but also, if they pursue Harris' folly of discrediting Leen as a ploy to force me out of my seclusion, they will rue the day they tangled with me and my legal team. What isn't said in the document, but nonetheless is the end message, is that if I withdraw my endorsement, Scenes will be effectively blackballed within the media community. Well pleased with Sarah's wording and smiling at the thought of Sarah showing up at the Board meeting, unannounced and unscheduled, I say, "You're bound to create quite a stir tonight. My only regret is that I won't be there to watch you in action."

"He's going to sputter protests that I have no right to interrupt a closed Board meeting but once I identify myself as your independent counsel they will have no choice but to listen to what I have to say."

"What does Leen say about all this?"

Sarah hedges for a few seconds and then, says, "She doesn't know about the plan for me to be there."

"What? You can't be serious!"

"We thought it best to keep Leen and Marc Andre out of the loop on this part of our strategy," answers Sarah.

Unrepentant, she says, "Anna-Claire, you hired me to represent and protect you. As your legal counsel, I have discussed strategy with your other counsel of record. You're just going to have to trust Bill's, Emile's, and my judgment on how to best play out this scenario." She rests two fingers lightly on my hand. "We don't tell you how to write a play or take a photo. One of the oldest legal tricks is the effective use of the element of surprise. Please, let us do our jobs."

"I retained you to work with Marc Andre," I answer.

"Marc Andre works for the firm that represents you," answers Sarah. "Emile and Bill are full partners and have authority to act on your behalf. When you retained me to work with Marc Andre, you also retained me to work with the firm that represents your interests." She softens her tone. "You know as well as I do that Marc Andre is not objective when it comes to Leen. He's a great lawyer but he's also a man in love. Think about it. You know I'm right."

Stumped for words, I begin to pace. Finally, I stop, turn around, and stare at Sarah. "I don't know whether to be furious or to laugh at how the three of you are using legal-ease to bamboozle me into complying with this deception."

Sarah's lips crease into a smile as she replies, "You are our client. We represent you and as such you – the client – have been informed of everything. We are not obliged to divulge strategy to anyone else."

"Marc Andre is going to be livid."

Relieved that I'm coming around to their logic, Sarah allows herself to laugh. "Actually, that's what I told Bill and Emile when they decided to nix Marc Andre's attendance at the Board meeting." She lifts her hands and then returns them to the table, "Marc Andre is a member of their firm and it's up to them as to whether or not he acts on the firm's behalf. I had no part of that decision."

"But you didn't disagree."

"I never disagree with common sense or good legal strategy. The legal system is adversarial by design. The objective is to represent the client and to win."

In spite of my previous annoyance, I have to laugh. Sitting back down, I say, "I'm glad you're on my side, Sarah. You would have made one hell of a general."

I turn my attention to the dramatic improvement in Sarah's speech and confidence. She's come a long way since her aneurism. "You're biting at the bit to get into the legal arena and deal Don Harris a blow and I have no doubts that you're going to do just that. In fact, I relish the thought of you crushing that man." I reach across the table and rest my hand over hers. "Leen and all of you are like daughters to me. For the first time in years, I am prepared to come out of my seclusion; just for the sheer satisfaction and pleasure of telling him what I think of him."

"Vengeance can be a short lived gratification," replies Sarah. "This is not the time for you to make a public appearance and knowing Leen, she wouldn't want you to do it."

"She's paying a big price for my privacy."

Sarah purses her lips and lets out a soft sigh. "We've covered this ground, Anna-Claire. Leen's a big girl and she knows the stakes. She chose not to tell them about you because she *cares* for you." Smiling warmly, she says, "If anything, Leen wants you concentrating on her wedding plans. Once again, you'll be filling in as mother-of-the-bride. Focus on the positives and let your legal team take care of the negatives."

Her diversionary tactic works. Smugly, I answer, "I knew from the outset that they were meant for each other."

Sarah laughs. "Leen says that you must have been a matchmaker in another life." She gathers her notes, puts them in her briefcase, and says, "It's time for me to leave. I'll have just enough time to go home, shower, choose what business suit to wear, and organize my thoughts for this evening." Grinning, she adds, "Talk about coming out of seclusion. Look at me. This is my first appearance as a *lawyer* since my aneurism ... I want to make a formidable impression."

"Oh I have no doubt they won't forget you easily, my dear." I look her directly in the eye and ask, "Do you regret taking only a Looney for your services?"

Sarah laughs. "To be honest, it's the best retainer I've ever accepted. The rewards have been beyond monetary value. You knew what you were doing when you came to my house that day. You hired me because you knew that I was embarrassed by my speech and feeling lost about my future. Your strategy to retain me as your lawyer gave me time to reacquaint myself with the practice of law in a safe and unthreatening environment."

Dismissing Sarah's compliment, I reply, "I retained you because I knew that you would be emotionally invested and because I knew that you would represent and protect Leen as a friend and as a lawyer. I could tell that Marc Andre was falling in love with her and despite his claims to the contrary, I could foresee the time when he would have to step away from his representation of me in order to safeguard his relationship with Leen."

Sarah raises an eyebrow and says, "Did you hear what you just admitted?"

Momentarily perplexed, I rethink my words and then I start to laugh. A deep, belly laugh. "I just admitted to the same logic you three have employed in having Marc Andre not involved with tonight's board meeting." I wag a finger. "Do you do that in court?"

Sarah smiles. "Trick of the trade."

I walk her to the front hallway where she retrieves her jacket from the closet. Kissing me on the forehead, she says, "Don't worry about anything. I'll make you proud tonight. Everything is going to be taken care of."

Opening the front door, she adds, "Now, try and rest. I'll call you later and let you know how things played out."

Chapter Twenty-nine

Emile

Alex pulls up in front of Scenes' corporate building, turns around to look at me and asks, "You okay?" I adjust my grey cashmere scarf around my neck and slip on my black leather gloves.

With a grim smile and quick nod, I reply, "I am going to enjoy destroying this man."

"Just say the word and I'll find a reason to meet him in a back alley." His gruff reply and reference to using street tactics makes me grunt with laughter.

"Since when did you become a street fighter?"

"Since today when you brought me up to speed as to what is going on," grins Alex. "Besides, when I was in the army, I was on the boxing team. I'd be willing to bet Harris doesn't know how to make a fist let alone avoid a punch." He makes a fist and smacks the palm of his other hand. "Just say the word."

"While the idea of punching the lights out on that insufferable man is pleasing," I reply, opening the car door, "the thought of watching him squirm and fear the power he is tampering with is much more satisfying than one punch." Stepping out of the car and lowering my chin into my collar against the wind's bite, I add, "This much I promise you, Harris is about to experience a knock out."

"I'll be waiting in the lower parking garage," answers Alex. "Good luck."

I take the elevator up to the sixteenth floor and when the doors open, I see Bill waiting for me in the reception area. Dressed in corporate black he projects the image of a man who resents having to be here instead of sitting by the comfort of a warm fire enjoying the company of family and friends on a bitter cold winter night.

"Evening Emile," he says politely, his eyes darting towards the closed doors of the Boardroom.

Since we're alone, I remark with undisguised amusement, "I can see you're pitching that 'I'd rather be elsewhere' trick of yours."

Bill smiles. "At least three people have come by to gawk at me. Thought I'd let them stew about my feelings about having to be here." He makes a face and strikes a pose. "Do I look sufficiently corporate and annoyed?"

"Let's see if they're smart enough to take the warning, but if they want to play hard ball then I'm more than willing to hit them with all we've got."

The elevator doors open and Leen steps out. Outwardly she appears to be calm but the flicker in her eyes as she greets us betrays her anxiety. I let my hand rest for a moment on her shoulder and say softly, "Stay focused, my dear. Remember what we talked about and you will do just fine."

Leen answers, quietly, "Thank you Emile." Glancing at Bill she adds, "And you, too, Bill. I would prefer not to be doing this tonight but if I have to, I'm glad that the two of you are here."

"If things work out the way I hope they will," says Bill, "you may not even have to answer any questions."

Before Leen can ask why she might not have to answer questions, I ask, "Where exactly is my son hiding out?"

Her soft laughter is warm and rich. "Downstairs in the lobby. When I left him, he was still complaining that you're treating him like a little boy rather than admitting that he's a good lawyer and able to take Harris on."

Amused with her description, I reply, "As long as he wants to come in here and punch out Harris' lights, he *is* acting like a little boy. Speaking of which," I say, pulling out my cell phone, "I'll ask Alex to baby-sit while the grownups are busy."

Her spontaneous giggle pleases me that my little joke about baby-sitting has helped to ease her tension. Looking at her approvingly, I say, "Can't say as I blame him. You're worth fighting for."

Removing her coat and draping it over her arm, she asks, "How do I look? Do you think Eleanor would approve?"

"Outstanding," says Bill. "Eleanor will be pleased you took her advice."

Her lithe figure is clothed in a tailored black jacket and skirt. Her choice of a rose coloured silk shirt adds a touch of soft femininity. Knee high leather boots fit fashionably underneath the mid-calf length skirt. Her makeup is subtle and the simple elegance of her jewellery infers quiet, good taste.

"I see that Marc Andre gave you the earrings," I say, smiling with pleasure. "That boy never could keep a gift a secret."

Leen touches her left earring and positively beams. "He said that he'd wanted them to be a wedding present, but given what's happened, he insisted on my wearing them tonight."

"Quite the romantic," observes Bill.

"You look stunning, my dear," I say, meaning every word. "When you get in there, remember you have nothing to fear."

The big doors to the Boardroom swing open. If Don Harris is surprised to see me there, he doesn't react.

With curt politeness, Bill says, "I don't believe you've met. This is Mr. Emile Aumount, co-founder and senior partner of the firm. After hearing about this meeting, he was kind enough to agree to come this evening."

There's a slight twitch to Harris' upper lip and a narrowing of his eyes. Whether it's due to annoyance or fear is a matter of speculation. I'm hoping it's fear. Barely acknowledging my presence, Harris addresses Leen. "We're ready for you."

Leen walks briskly past Harris as if he's of no consequence and I take great satisfaction in knowing she's not about to let anyone steam roll her. Bill and I nod grimly at one another and as we enter the Boardroom, he says in a low voice meant only for me to hear, "And so it begins."

Leen

My stomach does a leap as I walk into the room and see the expressions on the Board members' faces. Not wanting to give Don the satisfaction of seeing any momentary trepidation on my part, I smile pleasantly at Shirley Lawson, the Board's oldest member and place my briefcase down to the side of my chair.

Water glasses have been placed around the table and I reach for mine. My mouth has gone dry and, doing my best to present a calm and somewhat bored demeanour, I take a sip and lean back in my chair as if I have nothing better to do than wait for the meeting to convene. The Chairperson, Garrett Jameson, clears his throat and suggests that the minutes from the last meeting be read.

The business of the minutes is handled quickly and the members move to the present matter. Harry Coleson, Treasurer for Scenes, following a glance from Jameson, rises to introduce Emile and Bill. Formalities done, Coleson moves to the agenda for tonight's meeting beginning with the request for Don to update the Board members with respect to the progress and revenues generated since the initial retainer for the Gala. As instructed earlier today, I strike a pose of passive interest as Don names the corporate sponsors that have come on board and the revenues to be gained from their involvement. There is no mention of the fact that had Claire Holowitz not endorsed the Gala, there would be no additional revenues from corporate sponsors. From my peripheral vision, I notice Bill discreetly lifting his cuff to look at his watch and wonder if he's timing Don.

The screen on the far wall flashes charts as Don provides a dry analysis of the debits and credits. He's in the process of claiming that had I used the resources available to me, in a duly diligent manner, the projections for increased revenue would have exceeded any expectations when a firm rap at the door interrupts him. Coleson gets up to answer it and I can feel my jaw slacken as Sarah walks into the room. Emile, who is sitting on my left side, murmurs, "Right on time." Bill, seated on my right side, allows a satisfied smile to crease his face and leans close enough to say in my ear, "Stay calm. We've been expecting her."

Commotion breaks out at the interruption. Having recovered from my initial shock at Sarah's entrance I now suppress the urge to laugh.

Sarah is all business. Garrett Jameson clamours to his feet, irritably demanding Sarah explain who she is and her purpose for this intrusion.

With great pride I watch as she calmly walks to the head of the table and positions herself directly beside Garrett. Having caught the attention of everyone, Sarah is thoroughly enjoying every minute of the pandemonium she has caused. Nodding to Emile and Bill, she says sweetly, "Gentlemen. I realize that my presence here tonight is unexpected, but as you know I, too, represent Claire Holowitz."

Playing along with her little dramatic scene, Bill affirms solemnly, "Quite right."

Emile rises to his feet and says, "May I present Sarah Calder who, as she has already stated, acts as additional counsel for Claire Holowitz."

"What is the meaning of this intrusion?" demands Don. "I was unaware of any additional counsel being present tonight other than Mr. James and he…" Don's eyes narrow as he adds in an icy tone, "was invited by Ed Blaine."

Garret Jameson calls for order and addresses Sarah. "Ms Calder, please state your purpose."

Sarah surveys the faces of the Board members and with perfect timing, honed from her years of addressing juries and judges, she says, "Claire Holowitz has asked for me to be here to act as additional legal counsel." With all due deference to Garrett's position as Chairperson, she continues, "I am here to provide you and members of the Board with Ms Holowitz's response to the purpose of this meeting."

"How would you know the purpose of this meeting," sputters Don, agitated that Sarah had stolen his thunder and intuitively aware that her purpose is to destroy his chance to discredit Leen. Pointing a finger at me, he practically shouts, "She's one of Leen's closest friends. This is a complete farce!"

"Obviously, Mr. Harris," responds Sarah using a frigid tone, "you have underestimated Ms. Holowitz's communication with her legal advisors. Mr. James and Mr. Aumount advised my client this morning that this meeting was being convened and that the purpose of the meeting was to have Ms. MacLeen answer questions pertaining to her not having located the whereabouts of Claire Holowitz. Further, it has come to my client's attention that you are responsible for the slanderous allegation that Ms. MacLeen and Marc Andre Aumount have compromised the success of the Holowitz Gala due to their romantic involvement. And yes..." she glares at him with undisguised contempt, "you are quite correct in saying that I am fortunate enough to call Leen MacLeen a good friend."

Ed Blaine, sitting at the far end of the table, covers his mouth as he tries to suppress his amusement. I can see approval in his eyes for the way that Sarah is taking Don down. He's not looked at me other than to acknowledge my entrance. I promise myself that when everything is said and done, I'll thank him personally. He's not alone in his amusement. From the expressions on several Board members, it's clear that they too are enjoying how Sarah is dealing with Don.

My eyes travel to Sandra Snowden. At sixty-five, she's one of the wealthiest real estate developers in Eastern Ontario. She's watching Sarah with avid interest and it's obvious from her expression that Sarah is scoring points with her. Snowden is known for being cutthroat in business dealings, but completely above suspicion. As merciless as she can be with respect to accruing wealth, she likes to play a fair game. Sitting erect and acutely attentive I can tell that she scents underhandedness in play and from the squint of her eyes and glances in Harris' direction; she's doing little to conceal her growing contempt for him.

Sarah snaps open her briefcase and withdraws a file folder. Opening it, she takes a moment to scan the contents and addressing Garrett says, "I would like to share with you Ms Holowitz's statement."

Garrett nods curt assent to her polite request without acknowledging that it was a command.

Pulling out reading glasses, purely for effect, and with just a flicker of a glance at me, she begins to read aloud. *"This is to confirm that I, Claire Holowitz, have retained Sarah Calder to represent me at a Board of Directors meeting for Scenes. This in no way implies that I am dismissing my trusted legal counsel and wish it to be further known that Emile Aumount and William James act on my behalf, as does Marc Andre Aumount. My legal counsel has my full endorsement and trust.*

I wish it to be known that I have from the outset of the Gala's preparations been impressed with Ms MacLeen's ethics, diligence, and intent to represent my works fairly and without compromise for the terms agreed upon. I have complied and made available to Scenes original manuscripts, photos, and access to persons who honour me by sponsoring and presenting my works. I wish further to reiterate that my agreement to cooperate with the proposed Gala has always been based on the condition that my personal privacy not be violated. For any person, or for any member of Scenes' Board of Directors, to assume that I would permit disclosure of my identity and whereabouts was at best erroneous and in violation of any agreement into which I had entered, in good faith."

Sarah pauses to slowly let her gaze travel to each Board member, letting Claire's words of condemnation settle in their minds. Most have the good grace to sit with their eyes downcast; realizing that any attempt to violate Claire Holowitz's privacy will be dealt with swiftly. Satisfied that she has their full attention, Sarah continues, *"It has been brought to my attention that the relationship between my godson Marc Andre Aumount and Adrienne MacLeen has come under the scrutiny of Scenes' Board of Directors. I wish it to be known that any further suggestion that either Marc Andre or Adrienne have engaged in a relationship intended to circumvent directives from this Board of Directors will be taken with grave consequences. As of this moment, their relationship is not of any concern to Scenes. Further, I wish it to be known that Adrienne MacLeen has conducted herself with propriety, ethics, and discretion. She has honoured the initial agreement at great cost to her personal tranquillity and, for that demonstration of professionalism and personal ethics, I will continue to co-operate with the Gala preparations. Adrienne MacLeen has my full endorsement, respect, and support. Should the Board decide to listen to any allegations that she has not represented Scenes with due diligence then I, Claire Holowitz, will see to it that she be properly compensated for the slander against her professionalism. Her compensation will come from the pecuniary damages that I will receive as a result of litigation taken against Scenes Inc. and each member of its Board. In addition, I will immediately withdraw my cooperation and make public my reasons for doing so.*

I state here and now, categorically, that my personal life is of no interest to this Board and that any further transgression upon it will meet with the full force of legal entitlements. I instruct William James and Emile Aumount to demand a formal apology to Ms MacLeen and to insist that Donald Harris be withdrawn from any control with respect to Ms MacLeen's governance of the Gala's preparations."

Sarah pauses, slides the paper in front of Garrett, removes her glasses, and calmly takes the chair that Bill has pushed over for her to sit on. "You will see that the statement is duly notarized and that Claire Holowitz has affixed her signature to it."

Jameson reads it and, passing it to the member on his left, says, "I am sure Ms. Calder that I speak for the other members when I thank you for coming here tonight and for presenting Ms Holowitz's position. I believe I can assure you that her wishes will be complied with."

Harris starts to speak but a cold, furious look from Jameson checks him. Looking at Emile and Bill, Jameson says, "Mr. Aumount, I would assume as senior partner of your firm and long standing representation of Ms Holowitz that, based on what Ms Calder has read, you have something to say."

I catch my breath. Poised and yet tense, Emile reminds me of a lion stalking his prey. There is a feral glint to his eyes and for a moment I imagine him swiping an arm as if he's swatting with a massive paw.

Emile rises, slides his hand down his tie, and measuring his words and speaking in a voice so modulated that neither his authority nor controlled anger is in question, he states, "We are pleased with Ms Calder's statement and fully support her representation of Claire Holowitz. We demand an apology on behalf of my son, Marc Andre Aumount and Adrienne MacLeen. Further," he adds, with calculated deliberation, "we have brought statements to be signed by the Board members that no action will be taken against Ms MacLeen. She should be commended for her professionalism and ethics. Despite pressure to do so, she has safeguarded Ms Holowitz's privacy and honoured the agreement of Scenes to not violate that privacy. Further, as compensation, we ask the members of this Board to confirm Ms MacLeen's tenure as Vice-President of Scenes with full salary and benefits, as befitting the position. This," he says in calculated tones pausing for effectiveness, "is to become effective immediately. The conditions for Claire Holowitz's compliance with the Gala will remain under the seal of privacy and will be considered small compensation for the aggravation caused to Leen MacLeen, as a result of the suggestion that she has compromised her professional and personal ethics."

Don slams his hand down on the table with such force that several Board members jump while others react with startled exclamations. Shocked by Emile's demands, I tense. Emile and Bill sit calmly as if it's the most natural thing in the world to expect total and unrestricted compliance.

The silence is deafening.

Don starts to protest but Garrett orders him to be quiet.

Ed Blaine rises and waits for Garrett to acknowledge him. "I believe this Board owes Ms MacLeen an apology," says Ed, addressing Emile and then letting his gaze include Bill and Sarah. Returning to Emile, he adds, "We would appreciate it if you would convey the same to your son, Marc Andre."

Sandra Snowden's ripple of laughter breaks the tension in the room. "Well, I'll be damned!" she exclaims. "I for one will sign it and strongly suggest that we all do." She raps the conference table with her knuckles. "This is not how we do business, people. Please," she says to Bill and Emile, "hand me the agreement you wish for me to sign."

Pulling individual statements out of his briefcase, Bill passes one to each Board member. Once signed, he collects them. Addressing Garrett, in a friendly tone, he says, "I believe that our purpose at this meeting is now completed. Since we have no interest in deterring the Board members from attending to other matters we will, at this time, take our departure." He allows himself the luxury of scanning the faces of the Board members, before concluding, "We will report to Ms Holowitz that the meeting has gone very satisfactorily."

Relief evident that they and Sarah will soon depart, Garrett thanks them perfunctorily. Addressing me, he apologizes for my having had to attend the meeting and congratulates me on my engagement and promotion."

Don rises to leave but Sandra Snowden's strident voice cuts across the room. "We have a few questions, Mr. Harris."

Sarah snaps her briefcase shut, shakes Garrett's hand, and winks at me as she exits. Emile waits for me to rise. Numb from the events that have taken place, I manage to thank the Board members and follow Emile and Bill out of the room. Getting into the elevator, Emile puts two fingers to his lips and whispers, "Wait, until we're far away from any chance of being heard."

When the doors open to the parking garage Marc Andre rushes forward to sweep me into his arms. We walk over to where Alex is leaning against the car trunk. He lights a cigarette, inhales, and blows out a long, blue ring.

A quizzical expression crosses Emile's face. "I thought you gave that up five years ago."

"I did," replies Alex, flicking an ash, "but it was either have a smoke tonight or a drink. Didn't think you'd want me to drink and drive."

"The least you could have done was bring me one of those port-tipped cigars that I like to indulge in every once in a while."

Alex reaches into his jacket pocket, fishes out a slender cigar, and wickedly drawls, "Oh ye of little faith."

Ignoring Marc Andre's groan and my surprise at his little secret, Emile takes the cigar and says, "When I get home, I plan to have a very stiff drink and smoke this baby." Turning to Bill, he asks, "What about you? What do you plan to do to celebrate?"

"I'm going to follow your example," answers Bill. "Go home and pour myself a strong nightcap." Glancing at Sarah, he asks, "And you counsellor?"

"I had planned on calling Anna-Claire if the meeting dragged out," replies Sarah, "but seeing as it went without any argument, I'm going to swing by Anna-Claire's house. If her lights are still on, I'm going to stop in and give her a replay of tonight's events. Then, I'm going to do what the two of you are doing – go home and pour myself a decent drink."

"How about you Leen?" asks Bill.

Wired with excitement and yet exhausted from the toll that this evening's strain has caused, I can't think of what I'm going to do in the next five minutes. "I'll need to think about it," I reply, evading a direct answer.

Bill extends his hand. "Go home, get some sleep Leen. Emile said you'd carry tonight off like a professional, but only a fool would not have been unsettled by that sea of faces when you walked in." Admiringly, he says, "You didn't flinch once."

"I didn't do anything. You spent the better part of the day drilling me with questions and then, no one asked me anything. I just sat there."

"We were hoping that it would work out that way but just in case, we wanted you prepared." He smiles. "A wise lawyer always prepares his client and plans his legal strategy anticipating all contingencies."

Emile says, "You didn't have to say a word. Your whole stance spoke volumes. And you, Sarah," he adds with a dip of his chin, "were remarkable. I'll gladly work with you any time."

Sarah returns the compliment saying, "Anna-Claire's going to enjoy hearing how the two of you steam-rolled them into promoting Leen." She laughs heartily. "When did you come up with the Vice-President demand? I don't remember any discussion of that."

Bill slaps Emile on the back. "That little bit was thrown in by Emile. I was as surprised as you when he issued that ultimatum."

Proud of himself, Emile says, "That was easy. The two of you did the groundwork. I could tell they were nervous at the thought of the litigation the three of us would rain down on them if they didn't capitulate to our demands so I moved in for the kill. Old courtroom trick – push the defendant to admit guilt and nine times out of ten they'll want to make a deal."

"Whatever," laughs Sarah, "Anna-Claire is going to love how this story turned out."

"She'll probably express regret at not having thought of it," jokes Marc Andre.

"Who says she didn't," answers Emile. In response to our startled reactions to his statement, he shrugs. "She simply said that Leen should be promoted. I put that suggestion in the back of my mind and decided if the opportunity arose, I'd go for it."

Marc Andre and I walk hand-in-hand to where he parked his car and wave at the procession of their cars as they drive by. "And you, Leen," asks Marc Andre, as we adjust our seatbelts, "what would you like to do to celebrate?"

"Oh Marc, your father and Bill were wonderful. And, Sarah," I say proudly, "was sharp, detached, and powerful. The whole time that she was reading Anna-Claire's letter, I had the impression that she was really enjoying messing with Don's twisted brain."

Marc Andre drives the car towards the exit. "Damn, if I regret one thing about tonight, it's not having been there to watch Don's fall from grace."

"More like a plummet."

"Splat," says Marc Andre.

"Splat?" I look at him. "What does that mean?"

"The sound of Harris's career doing a nose-dive into the ground," replies Marc Andre.

Wiping the tears from my eyes, from my spontaneous laughter at the imagery he's conjured, I say, "In a strange way, I almost feel sorry for him. Pathetic little creature that he is."

"Don't you even dare," interrupts Marc Andre. "Don't you even dare."

Chapter Thirty

Amy

The doorbell rings just as I'm finishing my cup of tea. Looking quickly at Anna-Claire, I say, "That will be Sarah." I get up to go and let her in.

For the last hour, Anna-Claire has been anxiously watching the kitchen clock. She calls out after me "Well, now we'll have our answer."

Seeing Sarah's look of jubilation and thumbs up, Anna-Claire visibly relaxes and says, "I take it that my legal representation went well."

"Better than well," answers Sarah.

Casting a glance at our teacups, Sarah says, "I made a quick stop at home long enough to pack an overnight bag, a change of clothes for the morning, and give Joe an abbreviated version of tonight's success. I told him I'd be bunking at Amy's house because I have every intention of enjoying a stiff drink as I fill Anna-Claire in on all the details."

"My casa is your casa," I reply.

"The alcohol's where it always is," says Anna-Claire. "Choose what you want to drink."

"How about one of your killer dry martinis?" suggests Sarah.

"Coming right up," I answer, opening the sideboard and taking out a bottle of white vermouth and vodka. "How about you Anna-Claire? Do you feel up to a drink?"

"The olives are in the fridge," says Anna-Claire. "If you're going to be drinking dry martinis, don't forget the olives."

"What would you like?"

Anna-Claire thinks for a moment. "I'll have a small brandy."

Tugging off her coat, Sarah drapes it over the back of the chair and says, with a triumphant grin. "It went exactly as you said it would."

As I make the martinis, Sarah describes how the evening went from the time of her arrival. By the time I've made us a second martini, Sarah and I are getting a pleasant glow. She says, "Leen played her part to perfection. Not once did she give in to any semblance of nerves or upset. In fact, as I read Claire's statement, I glanced to observe the reaction of some of the Board members. They were stealing glances trying to gauge her reaction, but she sat there stoically – never once wavering. It was so perfect," crows Sarah, "as if it had been scripted."

Delighted, Anna-Claire claps her hands with the enthusiasm of a child. "In a way, it was. Bill and Emile are outstanding negotiators and sly as foxes. And, Harris," she asks, her eyes narrowing with annoyance at the thought of him, "how did he react?"

Sarah practically cackles. "You should have seen his face when Garrett Jameson more or less told him to shut-up. It was priceless!"

"I would have given anything to have been in that room," says Anna-Claire.

Amused, Sarah replies, "Had you been, Amy and I would be raising bail money. You would have assaulted Harris."

"Imagine what that would have done to your privacy," I joke.

Anna-Claire shrugs and with a wry smile, says, "Ah well, for the satisfaction of punching him, I would have come out from my seclusion." She clenches her fist and thrusts it forward at Don's imaginary nose making a pop noise. "Just thinking about it gives me satisfaction."

Sipping her drink, Sarah says, "After tonight, the Board members are going to keep Harris on a very tight leash. They're going to be standing on their heads to save their asses if anything is done to interfere with your privacy or Leen's career."

I ask, "Why didn't you push for Harris' dismissal? Why let him stay on?"

"Oh we talked about getting him sacked but Emile and Bill persuaded me that it's better to keep him within our radar – at least for now. If we cut him loose now, he'd stir up trouble and spin his firing as if it was a result of Leen being involved with Marc Andre as opposed to his incompetence."

"Now that they know Marc Andre is Anna-Claire's godson as well as her legal counsel," explains Sarah, "they'll want to keep her happy. Up until the Gala, we're not going to give Harris a chance to make trouble. We've got him exactly where we want him."

"When the Gala is done with," says Anna-Claire, her eyes glinting with fierce determination, "we'll hang him out to dry."

We finish our drinks and wait until Anna-Claire has climbed upstairs to her bedroom before letting ourselves out. As we walk to my house, I ask, "Do you think Harris will still cause trouble?"

Sarah's smile fades. "Oh, he'll try but when he does, we'll be waiting."

"And you?" I ask. "How did it feel to be practicing law again?"

"Awesome," answers Sarah. "Simply awesome."

Chapter Thirty-one

Amy

Looking outside my office window at last night's fresh dump of snow, I watch as students scurry across the courtyard, heads bent to ward off the wind, clutching books, and dressed in varying layers of thick winter clothes. A pile of marked second year essays dealing with the social commentaries of Charles Dickens is stacked on my desk. Wearily, I knead at the kink in my neck and think about an essay that caught my interest. It had been well written with an unusual twist. I pull it out from the stack and quickly scan the notes I've written in the margin on different pages.

The student, Arthur Colson, had taken the position that Scrooge had been a good man whose name had been seriously maligned. His points had been well-made and once again I admire how he's presented his case. According to Colson, Scrooge had paid his taxes albeit with some reluctance but like many people – myself included – resented the government's heavy taxation and the frequent and seemingly endless barrage of a multitude of agencies seeking donations from the salaries of people who earn them. Ruefully, I think that tax time will quickly approach and my salary will be gouged by the burden of heavy government taxes, leaving me a little over half of my earned annual income.

"Maybe Scrooge had a better handle on all of this," I say to the empty room. "Can't say as I blame him for questioning what the government actually does with the revenue it garners from heavy taxation – mostly on the shoulders of the middle class while the big corporations get one tax break after another. After all, it wasn't that Scrooge didn't pay his taxes – he simply didn't appreciate that others expected him to give more of his wealth away simply because he had money while big businesses get government funding on top of tax breaks."

Arthur's other convincing point was that even though Dickens wrote that Scrooge lived out his days being loved and doing social good, no one seemed to remember that aspect of him. Instead, Scrooge's name had become synonymous with expressions used to depict the selfish, greedy and miserly actions of people. The entire essay had been written with genuine creativity.

Picking up my pen, I write a note on the cover page complimenting Arthur for having used his essay to act as a medium to voice his own perspectives and interpretation of Dickens' work, while adhering to the process of academic writing. Smiling, I put the paper aside and decide to show it to Norah Stinson who teaches creative writing. Each semester she hand picks a dozen students for her extra credit writing class. I think Arthur will flourish in his writing if Norah will agree to take him on and act as his mentor.

I pick up the empty Styrofoam cup that four hours ago held hot coffee and toss it into the garbage pail. Tomorrow's lectures have been outlined and I'm looking forward to the final few weeks of the semester. This is the part of the academic term where I like to push their comfort zones. Colson's paper has given me an idea. For the next half hour I draft out additional notes that I hope will spur my students to think outside of the box. It will be my position that Dickens was the Victorian equivalent to a present-day fiction or romance novelist. Like them, he wrote for his audience and made money. Yet, he was viewed as a great writer. Choosing names of very successful novelists, I take pleasure in writing out thought provoking questions like, "Will authors like John Grisham, Catherine Dunne, Maeve Binchy, Margaret Atwood, Norah Roberts, Stephen King, and Danielle Steele be considered to be great, within the next century?" These discussion sessions always generate heated exchanges among my students and help to hone their critical thinking skills while having a good time. This term, thanks to Colson's paper, I can add to my repertoire of topics.

When I first introduced my plan to devote the last quarter of the semester to 'think tank' discussions and incorporated that unorthodox approach to my syllabus, the Dean questioned the academic merit. Five years later, my course is one of the most popular in the Arts and Humanities departments and it exists with the full endorsement of the Dean. He enjoys making his annual report to the Board of Governors and pointing out that my second year English Literature classes have extensive waiting lists, thereby generating a healthy income for the university.

I put away my notes, grab my jacket and I'm about to lock my office door when my cell phone rings. Reaching inside my jacket pocket, I flip open my cell and say, "Dr. Keiffers."

"My aren't we formal?" laughs Becky.

Holding the cell with one hand close to my ear and using my other hand to lock the office door, I say, "Sorry, Becky. I was just about to leave and you caught me still in professor mode." Walking down the hallway to the elevator, I say, "Look I'm waiting for the elevator and will probably lose the signal in a minute. Can I call you back?"

"No need," replies Becky. "We all know how you get lost in your work. As promised, I'm calling to remind you that the rehearsal is tonight." I can visualize her grin as she adds, "And, in case you forgot, it *is* at your house."

I smile at her little dig. Time has a way of alluding me when I'm at the university. Fortunately, I had agreed to Anna-Claire's suggestion to hire professional party planners to transform my home to a welcoming environment for both the rehearsal and wedding. Everything that could be done before tonight's rehearsal had been taken care this morning before I nipped out to put in a few necessary hours at the university. Thanks to Josh catering the majority of the food and the fact that he'll have staff present to serve, I have relatively little to do other than show up. A quick glance at my watch reassures me if I hurry there will be just enough time to shower and freshen up before tonight's rehearsal. Stepping into the elevator I say, "I'll meet you at my house in half an hour."

Becky

"Is she on her way?" asks Josh, fumbling with his tie.

I reach over to help with the knot. "She's leaving the university now."

"Does she know that Mike is already here?" asks Josh, following me into the kitchen.

"No," I reply, reaching in the fridge for two bottles of water. I pass him one and twist the lid on mine. "She was expecting to pick him up at the airport tomorrow morning. According to Sarah, he wanted to surprise her by arriving in time for the rehearsal."

I take a healthy swig of water and lean against the fridge. "What's on your mind?"

He tilts my chin upwards and kisses me on the bridge of my nose. "They seem to like one another."

"Who?"

Smiling, he answers, "You know very well *who*. Sarah and Mike. They only met at Christmas and yet, here he is flying back from Winnipeg a few weeks later to be Amy's date for the wedding."

I poke his stomach with two fingers and tease, "I have no idea what you're talking about."

"Hah," replies Josh. "I'll bet you don't. Plane tickets cost money."

"Really?" I blink my eyelashes and feign surprise. "I had no idea." Turning serious, I ask, "What's your point?"

"My point," replies Josh, pulling me into his embrace, "is that a man doesn't fly across the country for a simple date."

Cuddling against his muscular chest, I answer, "I admit it seems very sudden, but they've been talking on the phone and sending e-mails back and forth since the holidays. I think Amy finds him interesting and I add gleefully, "he finds her interesting."

"Interesting, is an adjective that I can well understand." Josh kisses my mouth and I feel the warm rush that signals I'm about to fall prey to his charms.

Sidestepping out of his arms, I answer playfully, "Well, this is one person who has to be a little less *interesting* right now. I still have to get changed for the rehearsal and get over to Amy's or she'll take pleasure in pointing out that I'm the one who is late."

Josh's laughter follows me as I run upstairs to change my clothes.

Joe

Handing Mike a cup of tea, I say, "Who would have thought it?"

"Yeah, I know," replies Mike, rubbing his neck. "I've never met a woman that made me feel like settling down, but ..." he looks seriously at me, "I think I may have found her."

"Does she know you feel this way?"

"Oh, she knows alright," says Sarah, leaning against the wall that opens to the kitchen. Surprised, Mike and I stare. Hands on her hips, she says, "Don't you ever again tell me that my friends and I gossip, Joe Calder." Taking great pleasure in having overheard Mike's feelings about Amy, she adds, "The two of you sound like school kids planning your next date."

"How much did you hear?" I ask, smiling at my wife. Wagging my finger, I add, "And since when have you become an eavesdropper?"

"I haven't become anything," replies Sarah, evenly. "Last time I checked this was my kitchen and I didn't notice any no trespass or men's conference in session signs."

"She's got us there," laughs Mike. "Okay, Sarah, join us and give us the lowdown. How am I doing on Amy's Richter scale?"

"Now see, Joe Calder," says Sarah, teasingly, "here's a man from whom you could learn a thing or two. He obviously appreciates my input and is man enough to admit that he needs it."

I groan and, for good measure, playfully make a face.

She grumbles. "See what I have to put up with, Mike? It's a wonder the boys have any maturity at all."

"I know I'm mature but I have my doubts about Jake," says Jeremy, entering the kitchen in time to overhear Sarah's comment. Heading directly to the refrigerator, he asks, "Any cold cuts left?"

"Bottom shelf in the bin," answers Sarah.

"Thanks," replies Jeremy, pulling out mustard, margarine, ham, and salami.

Watching as he creates a mammoth three-layered sandwich, I ask, "So you think you're mature?"

"I know it," answers Jeremy, returning to the fridge to get cheddar slices for his sandwich. "But, Jake, well, that's another story."

"Here we go again," grumbles Jake, entering the kitchen with his jacket still on and un-zipped. "Did you make me one?"

Jeremy bites into his sandwich. "What do I look like? Your maid?"

Jake rolls his eyes at his brother and says, "Mom, I'm going to make a sandwich. Would anyone like one?"

Sarah, Mike, and I answer in unison, "No thanks."

Poking Jeremy in the ribs with the handle of his butter knife, Jake says, "You may think you're mature, but you sure aren't considerate. Did you think of offering anyone any food or were you just too busy filling your own ugly mug?"

Amused by their banter, Mike asks, "Have they always argued like that?"

Before I can answer, Jeremy replies, "No. Sometimes we actually mean our insults and that's when those two," he waves a hand at Sarah and me, "get involved." He takes a bite of his sandwich, swallows and then, looking at me, says, "When I came in, I caught the tale-end of a conversation about Aunt Amy. What's up with her?"

Mike silently appeals to me with a comic roll of his eyes. Grinning, I say, "Welcome to the Calder family circus where secrets are a myth."

Sarah props an elbow on the table and rests her chin in her hand. "Yes, do tell. I'm very interested in hearing what you and Mike have to say about Amy."

Mike clears his throat and tries to sound casual as he replies, "Just before you guys arrived, I asked your mother what your aunt thinks of me."

"So what's the deal, Mom?" asks, Jake, pouring a glass of milk.

Jeremy looks at Mike with new interest. "So you like Aunt Amy?"

"Yes," answers Mike. Red creeps up his neck as he asks, "You guys okay with that?"

"I'm good," says Jeremy.

"Me too ..." agrees Jake, "as long as Aunt Amy's good with it."

Enjoying Mike's discomfort at being grilled by two teenage boys chomping down on mammoth sandwiches, Sarah says, "See what happens when you've got more than yourself to answer to. Are you sure you don't want to continue living the quiet life?"

I slide in the comment, "Give it up man. When she's got a bee in her bonnet, you might as well save your strength for winning the big arguments."

Sparing Mike, Sarah says to the boys, "Let's just say guys that you're going to have to compete with Mike for Aunt Amy's lasagne."

Jake looks at Mike with newfound interest. "No way would Aunt Amy cut us off from her meals."

Mike looks to Sarah and me for help but we're too busy laughing to be of any help.

"Don't sweat it Jake. We've still got the back-up plan," interjects Jeremy.

"What back-up plan?"

"Think about it bro. Aunt Becky married Josh."

Jake leans back in his chair, makes a production of patting his muscled stomach, and smiles, "Good thinking. We can go and beg at the restaurant."

"My sons," I comment wryly, "always the entrepreneurs when it coming to finding sources of food."

Tapping her watch, Sarah says, "Speaking of Becky and Josh, we'd better get a move on. Amy ..." he grins at Mike, "the object of this discussion is expecting us to be there for the rehearsal. Marc and Leen said they'd pick up Anna-Claire and Alex is bringing Emile."

"Is there going to be food?" asks Jeremy.

"What do you think?"

He flashes a smile. "Feel free to bring back doggy bags for your starving sons."

"Starving, my ass," I answer. Pointing to the countertop, I add, "Be sure you guys clean up."

"Joe, get the salads out of the fridge, will you?" asks Sarah. "I need to change my sweater before we go. And, please don't forget the containers of dressing."

Reaching into the fridge, I say to Mike, "One thing you're going to enjoy about the coven is their ability to cook and to eat well."

"Yeah," agrees Jake with a devilish smirk, "just look hungry. They're naturals for wanting to feed their men."

"Got it down to a fine art, have you?" laughs Mike.

"Oh we had that down pat by the time we were five," replies Jake. "But what we've developed into an art is our ability to convince each one of them that they're the best."

"Yeah," agrees Jeremy, with a knowing smile, "just pick out something special that you really enjoy from each one of them and tell them that it's the best in the world. That way, you'll always be assured of getting their best cooking."

"Your boys have good senses of humour," says Mike, as we collect our coats from the hall closet and head out to the car.

"I'd like to think they get their humour from me," I answer, pushing the button to unlock the car, "but there's a lot of Sarah in them, too." Mike places his hand on the handle of the back door but I stop him saying, "Sit in the front. Sarah's got shorter legs than you. She won't mind."

"You sure?"

"Absolutely." I turn on the car's heater and push the defrost button. "But, if I don't get this car warmed up, we'll both hear about that."

"You're a lucky man, Joe," says Mike. "You've got a wife who loves you and two great sons."

Normally, I'd say thank you and think nothing more of it but from the expression on his face, I can tell there's something else he wants to say. "What's on your mind, Mike?"

"I plan on asking Amy to marry me."

Sarah opens the car door just as I'm sputtering, "You're kidding? You're going to ask her to marry you?"

"I knew the moment I met her that I was falling hard."

Speechless, I stare out the windshield. Overhearing Mike's admission as she slides onto the back seat, Sarah grasps the backrest of my seat, leans forward, and says, "Are you saying what I think I just heard you say?"

Turning in his seat to face her, Mike answers, "I know it seems sudden but ..."

"Well, I'll be damned!" sputters Sarah, taking the words right out of my mouth.

She grabs Mike's shoulder, narrows her eyes, and says, "If this is a joke, I'm not laughing."

"No joke," says Mike. "I want to marry her."

I put the car in reverse and pull out of the driveway. I'm wondering what Sarah's going to say next when she starts to laugh. "Never a dull moment," she says. "Tonight is going to be interesting in more than one way."

"Not one word, Sarah," I warn. "Give the guy a chance to ask her before you spill the beans to Leen and Becky. Think of what you've heard as client privilege."

"I didn't take a retainer," she answers. "I'm not bound in any way."

"Here you go," says Mike, reaching into his wallet and passing a twenty dollar bill between the seats, "consider yourself retained."

"Keep your money," says Sarah. This time her voice is serious as she adds, "Just promise to ask her soon and if she agrees, you be good to her."

"I will be," answers Mike.

"And you're going to ask her tonight?"

"That's the plan."

"Holy shit," murmurs Sarah. "I can't believe this is happening."

"It hasn't happened yet," I say. "Amy still has to agree."

"Oh, she'll agree," answers Sarah, her mind already spinning with wedding plans.

Echoing Sarah's sentiments of a few minutes ago, I say, "Never a dull moment."

Chapter Thirty-two

Sarah

Marc Andre grins as he opens the door. "You're just in time to rescue Leen." Jerking a thumb in the direction of Leen, Emile and Alex, he says, "She's got to be bored out of her mind."

Smiling, I say, "She doesn't look too upset to me."

"Looks like she's enjoying the conversation," adds Joe, removing his coat and waiting for me to do the same.

"What they're talking about is the problem," answers Marc Andre, mixed exasperation and humour evident in his tone and expression.

"What could be so bad?" asks Mike, as he hangs up his coat.

Anna-Claire's approach and soft chuckle interrupts his response. "I'm glad you are here," she says, giving me a quick hug. "This one..." she lightly touches Marc Andre's upper arm, "has been skittish ever since Emile and Alex arrived.

"They're dredging up stories from when I was a kid," says Marc Andre. "So far she finds me interesting and I'd like to keep it that way. Next thing, they'll be telling her about when I started shaving or peed the first time in the toilet like ...," he makes quotation marks with two fingers in the air, "a big boy."

We all laugh at the image he's conjured and Anna-Claire, with an amused but indulgent look, says, "One would think he was the first groom ever to have to contend with pre-wedding jitters."

Marc Andre protests, "I don't have jitters."

"Then, why do you persist in not seeing the humour of those two old fools practically standing on their heads to entertain Leen?"

"What humour?"

Her eyes twinkle mischievously, "Their stories are harmless and touching memories. Now I, on the other hand, have experience at spinning a story. Perhaps, I should go over there and give Leen my version of some of your youthful antics? Better yet…" she adds with a wink at me, "enlighten her about your misspent romantic encounters over the years."

Marc Andre lets out an exasperated sigh. "See what I've been having to put up with? If it's not those two," he jerks a thumb in Emile and Alex's direction, "it's Aunt Claire offering to throw in her two bits worth."

"Not to worry," I answer. "The cavalry has arrived."

Mike asks, "Where's Amy?"

"In the kitchen with Josh," replies Becky who has been waiting for a break in the conversation so she can get a word in edgewise. "Why don't you go and let her know you are here."

"Anna-Claire's right," I say, lightly pushing the small of his back with my hand, "go say hi to Amy while the rest of us go and distract Leen."

"I'll give you a hand after I say hi to Amy," answers Mike.

With interest, Anna-Claire watches him as he strides to the kitchen. "He's looks happy to be here."

Linking my arm with hers, I lower my voice and whisper, "You have no idea."

"Really?" She glances sideways.

Becky asks, "How happy?"

"Sarah…" Joe's smile is friendly but his eyes flash warning.

"I'm just saying that Mike is looking forward to seeing Amy," I answer, avoiding his look. "What's wrong with that?"

Leen's enthusiastic greeting stops Joe from answering and wanting to avoid any further warning from him, I ask, "So how's the bride?"

Flushed with excitement and eyes glistening with approval, Leen says, "Isn't it marvellous what Amy and Anna-Claire have done to the house?"

A squeal of delight comes from the kitchen. Emile says, "What's going on in the kitchen?"

"I think it's safe to say that Amy's pleased Mike is here," answers Anna-Claire.

Emile and Alex look perplexed. I explain, "She wasn't expecting him until tomorrow morning."

"Ahhhh," says Emile.

Arms wrapped around each other's waist, Amy and Mike enter the living room. "You knew," says Amy. "And none of you told me?"

"I wanted it to be a surprise," says Mike, before I can answer.

Positively beaming, she says, "Well, you definitely succeeded."

"I could always return tomorrow," teases Mike.

Tightening her hold on his waist, Amy says, "Don't you dare leave."

"Life is full of surprises," I say.

Sliding an arm around my shoulders, Joe uses his hand to give me a playful but warning squeeze. "We were just admiring what you've done with your house," he says.

"I just said ..."

"I know what you said," answers Joe, whispering as the others look on to his light kiss on my ear. "It's what you want to say that worries me."

Becky, always astute to innuendo and body language, skilfully changes the focus of attention away from me by asking, "What do you think about the decorations?"

Glad for her intervention, I look around the living room. Cleared of Amy's furniture, the room now hosts elegantly set circular tables with accompanying chairs. Flickering candles rest on each tabletop and the ceiling's dimmer light has been set to low. Near the French doors leading to the sunroom stands a canopied archway decorated in silver and white and beyond that are four more tables which Amy explains will be cleared away after the wedding dinner to make room for dancing.

Impressed, I say, "This is amazing! How did you do it?"

Pleased, Amy answers, "Simple." She smiles at Anna-Claire. "Anna-Claire called in a favour from a friend who knows a wedding planner. All we had to do was tell him what we wanted. And poof..." she snaps her fingers, "like magic, it was done."

"What did you do with your furniture?" asks Joe, accepting the glass of scotch Marc Andre offers.

"It's part of the service. Gerald – that's the wedding planner's name – arranged to have it picked up and stored, at no extra cost. It'll be returned the day after the wedding when they come to remove their tables and decorations." She makes an expansive sweep of the room with her arm. "He's worth every penny."

"It really was quite amazing," comments Anna-Claire. "They came in, worked like bees and the result is this."

"And what's really good," adds Amy, "is that they'll be back tomorrow morning to clean up from tonight and make sure all is ready for the wedding reception. Josh and his staff are catering everything. Anna-Claire and I don't have anything to do.' She dry wipes her hands and jokes, "No fuss, no muss. Like magic."

୦୰

Leen

When Pastor Aikens and his wife, Carole, arrive we get down to the business of the rehearsal. Earlier in the day, Marc Andre cleared a path from Anna-Claire's house to Amy's so that my wedding party and I can enter by her back patio entrance and wait in the kitchen for the ceremony to begin. At the right moment, Josh will open the door leading from the kitchen to the hallway. We'll wait near the French doors leading to the living room for the musical cue to start our procession. Tapping into her list of acquaintances Anna-Claire, on the recommendation of a friend, has hired a stringed quartet for the ceremony and the evening. But, for tonight, Mike, Joe and Josh are gamely humming our entrance cues for our walk from the kitchen to the living room and then, for the wedding procession. Amid laughter and good-natured banter about their lack of musical talent, they continue with their loud and off-key key renditions of the music.

Originally, we had planned on a church wedding but when Amy suggested we hold everything – ceremony, meal, and celebration at her home – it made sense. Our marriage and wedding celebrations will be an intimate, private affair. Now, as Pastor Aikens walks us through the rehearsal, I'm glad that he's the one officiating. He and his wife Carole, long-standing friends of Anna-Claire's and privy to her identity, have been extremely accommodating with our wedding plans.

Tonight, on the eve of my wedding, I'm filled with admiration and love for my friends and marvelling how fortunate I am to have them in my life. I can't help but think that my whirlwind engagement and marriage is like something out of a fairy-tale. I have a collection of fairies waving their magic wands – all making certain that Marc Andre's and my wedding lacks for nothing. Every detail has been worked out.

Within forty minutes, Pastor Aikens winds up the rehearsal and jokingly tells Marc Andre and me that the only thing the two of us have to worry about is being on time. "Everyone here will do their parts," he says, "and it's up to the two of you to do yours."

"When do I say, 'I do'?" asks Marc Andre.

"What time do we have to be here?" I pipe in.

We know our kidding is juvenile but the mood is festive and if the rehearsal is any indication of the laughter, goodwill, and friendship that will take place tomorrow; our wedding will be memorable in all ways. Marc Andre and Josh have just freshened everyone's drinks when the doorbell chimes. "That'll be my people," says Josh.

Followed by four waiters, each pushing a trolley laden with food covered with lids, Josh leads the way to the living room. Sheila and Harry, maître d's for his restaurant, stop long enough to exchange greetings and assure us that we have nothing to worry about. "Tonight will only be a small sampling of the menu Josh has planned for your wedding," says Harry, to Marc Andre. "Your wedding meal will be almost as memorable as your beautiful bride."

Marc Andre whistles with appreciation as Harry lifts one of the lids, releasing a pleasing aroma. I throw my arms around Becky, hugging her tightly and gushing my thanks. Smiling, she answers, "Josh is so happy to do this. Wait until tomorrow's meal. Harry wasn't kidding–Josh wants it to be perfect."

Pulling out a white chef's apron from underneath one of the trolleys, Josh slides it over his sweater and slacks and ties it behind his back. Bowing gallantly he extends his hand to me saying, "And for the soon-to-be newlyweds, Chef Joshua Sinclair is proud to serve."

Taking my hand, he leads me to the first tray and with a dramatic flourish lifts the lid on the first platter, releasing the scent of lobster marinating in butter. His staff does the same for the other trays and within minutes everyone is lining up to fill their plates with lobster, roast beef, potatoes, salads, and an assortment of cheeses and hors d'oeuvres. The room soon fills with expressions of delight and hearty endorsements about the tantalizing scents and tastes of the food.

Wiping my mouth with a napkin, I say, "Josh, you've outdone yourself! How do you expect me to fit into my wedding gown?"

His eyes twinkle. "I don't hear Marc Andre complaining."

Patting my stomach, I grouse, "Becky, blame your husband if you and Amy have to stuff me into my wedding gown?"

"Why do you think I've taken out a membership at the gym? Since marrying Josh, I've put on five pounds." Linking her arm around his, she says, "Come on Josh, leave the chef routine to your excellent staff. Harry and Sheila are doing a wonderful job of supervising. You've done your part. Now it's time for you to mingle."

By ten o'clock, everyone is getting ready to call it a night. Pastor Aikens and his wife's departure are followed closely by Emile and Alex, with Marc Andre promising to join them after he walks Anna-Claire home. Holding the care packages Josh asked Harry and Sheila to have prepared for the twins, Sarah says, "Jake and Jeremy are going to love you for this."

Becky smiles warmly, "Can't let my nephews starve, can I?"

"I'll catch a taxi back," says Mike, when Joe goes to pass him his coat from the hall closet.

Looking at Amy, he says, "If it's okay with you, I'll stay a while longer."

"Here, take my key," says Sarah, digging into her purse. "Come on Becky and Leen, Anna-Claire needs to get some rest. Time to go." The way she's herding us to the door is almost comical but I know her well enough to suspect that she has something on her mind. "Why are you going home?" I ask. "Aren't we spending the night at Anna-Claire's?"

Change of plans," announces Sarah, briskly. "Anna-Claire and I were talking earlier and decided that a good night's rest is what we all need. Don't worry," she says, squeezing my elbow, "we'll be at Anna-Claire's early in the morning."

Becky looks momentarily startled at this announcement but quickly agrees, "Yes, that's right. Josh asked me tonight to help with some last minute preparations for the catering."

Arching an eyebrow, Josh says, "I did?"

"Yes," answers Becky, opening the door. "You did."

"But you dropped off your overnight bags and dresses at Anna-Claire's." Disappointed I say, "I was looking forward to our little sleep-over."

Sensing that he's disturbing some pre-set plans, Mike says to Amy, "I can leave now and catch up with you tomorrow."

"No," answers Amy, impulsively resting a hand on his arm. Flushing, she quickly adds, "Stay for a few minutes longer."

I could slap myself for being so obtuse. Lost in the excitement of tonight, I'd not given any thought to the fact that Mike and Amy might want some time alone. Smiling, I say, "Not to worry, Mike. Originally, we'd talked about having a quiet girl's night but the evening went on longer than we thought it would. Now, Anna-Claire and I are simply going to find our beds and fall asleep."

Anna-Claire pats my shoulder. "Everyone's tired, dear. Speaking for myself, it's clearly a case of the mind being willing but the body being weak. It's time I get myself to bed so that I can enjoy tomorrow."

Twinges of guilt surface. "I'm sorry, Anna-Claire," I say. "You're right, we need to make sure you're well-rested. Tomorrow's going to be a hectic day."

She smiles. "I wouldn't object to a brandy before bed."

"That's the spirit," approves Sarah. "You and Leen go and have a quiet nightcap. Becky and I will be here early in the morning." Practically pushing Joe out the door, she says, "Let's go Joe."

Groaning, Joe says to Josh, "Looks like we're being given our marching orders."

Josh plants a hearty clap on Marc Andre's back and teases, "The minute you say 'I do', you'll be subject to a life of saying 'yes dear' and being told what to do."

"Enough," laughs Becky. "You don't look too hard done by to me."

"Didn't say I was," answers Josh. "I was just merely pointing out to Marc Andre what to expect."

"I can't say you guys didn't try to warn me," jokes Marc Andre, "but I think I'll take my chances." Addressing Anna-Claire, he says, "I'll see you ladies safely home."

"Humpf," snorts Anna-Claire. "You're not tricking me, my boy. Don't be thinking I'll be inviting you in for a nightcap."

Marc Andre's lips twitch as he offers Anna-Claire his arm to lean on. "What? No offer of a nightcap?"

The look Anna-Claire gives him says it all. Laughing, Marc Andre says, "Ah, Aunt Claire, it was worth a try."

Silhouetted in the doorway with Mike resting one hand on Amy's shoulder and she leaning against his muscular chest, Amy and Mike make an attractive couple. Glancing over her shoulder, Anna-Claire makes the comment, "Mike seems like a good man. I think he and Amy care for one another."

"Ah, Aunt Claire," murmurs Marc Andre, "you're a hopeless romantic. Don't be getting any match-making ideas into that head of yours."

"Don't have to," answers Anna-Claire, opening her front door. "They're doing that all by themselves."

༄

Amy

Closing the door, Mike takes me into his arms and nestling his lips on my neck, murmurs, "I've wanted to do that all night."

"I was hoping that you'd want to stay a while," I reply, relishing the warmth of his body pressing against mine. He cups my chin and tilts my head so that he can tease my lips open with his tongue. Slowly and without any thought to what we are doing, we melt into one another's passion. Mike is the first to break away.

Somewhat bemused by his expression, I joke, "If you keep kissing me like that, I won't be getting any sleep tonight."

Taking my hand, he says, "Come with me." He leads me to where the bridal arch stands and stepping back; he rests his hands on my shoulders and silently appraises me.

"What are you doing?"

"I wanted to see what you'd look like underneath a bridal arch," he answers. He kisses the tip of my nose. "You look beautiful."

"Thank you," I murmur, feeling a touch awkward about standing beneath the bridal arch and trying to ignore the butterflies in my stomach.

Mike reaches into his jeans' pocket and pulls out a deep purple velvet box. I gasp as he flips open the lid. "Marry me, Amy."

Stunned, I stare wide-eyed at a ring with three large rectangular diamonds set in white gold. I hear my voice blurting excitedly, but it's as if I've been jettisoned to a surreal world. "Yes, oh yes, I'll marry you!"

Mike slides the ring onto my finger. It's a perfect fit. "I love you Amy Keiffers. I've loved you from the first night we met and I'll love you until the day I die and if it's possible, even after that."

I lean against his chest, gently crying, and holding onto the warmth of his body. "I would never have believed this," I whisper. "I never imagined me getting married again. I never thought it was possible."

"It's possible and it's right. I'll be a good husband to you and I'll show you what marriage can and should be for the right couple. I only wish I had met you years ago. Now," he squeezes me tightly, "I'll simply have to make up for lost time."

Kissing me deeply he says, "I told the taxi driver to be here by one thirty."

"Cancel it." Laying one hand on his chest and tracing the cleft in his chin that I've grown to love, I say, "Stay the night."

"Glad to," answers Mike, pulling out his cell to cancel the taxi. "I knew I wanted to ask you to marry me and I was pretty sure you would say yes but just in case, I wanted to be able to make a quick exit if you rejected me."

"Never," I answer, pressing my lips against his mouth.

Taking my hand, he says, "Don't you think we should get some sleep? Tomorrow's going to be a big day."

"Oh most definitely," I grin, feeling wickedly sensual as I lead him by the hand upstairs. "But suddenly, I'm not very tired. I'm hoping that you might have a suggestion or two to help me fall asleep."

Sweeping me off my feet, he cradles me against his chest as he pushes the door open with the toe of his shoe. "Oh I think I have a few," says Mike, his voice husky with the promise of his intention.

Giggling as he lays me down on my bed, I say, "What's Sarah going to think when she realizes you didn't spend the night at her house?"

He lifts his head to meet my gaze and while his fingers loosen the buttons on my shirt, he answers, "She'll think that you said yes."

Chapter Thirty-three

Anna-Claire

A light snowfall has dusted the ground and the afternoon sun glimmers out from behind billowing, puffy white clouds. *A writer's setting*, I think as I look out the window. I watch as Jeremy and Jake, braving the chill, make their way to my front door. Dressed in black tuxedos, pristine white shirts, and red cummerbunds around their waists, they are looking quite dapper. I smile as they approach, thinking how proud Sarah and Joe must be of their grown sons. I open the door to let them in and wiping his shoes on the mat, Jeremy says, "We've been sent to escort you ladies to Aunt Amy's."

Jake grins. "Dad said to make sure no one slips on the way over."

Jeremy whistles in appreciation as Sarah descends the stairs. "Talk about making a grand entrance," says Jeremy. "You look beautiful, Mom."

"Thank you," says Sarah, "and may I say the same about the two of you?" Smiling at me, she says, "Who would have thought they would clean up so well?"

"Take a picture," jokes Jake, "because tomorrow it's back to jeans."

"And you, Mrs. Wright," says Jeremy, appraising me, "you are gorgeous."

Ridiculously pleased with his compliment, I answer, "Why thank you, Jeremy. Don't you think it's time that you and Jake call me Anna?"

Old habits and training die hard, I think, as they glance at Sarah for her say so.

Sarah answers, "If Anna-Claire is good with it, I'm good with it."

"Let me repeat what Jeremy said," says Jake. "You look gorgeous, Anna."

Pleased, I kiss each of them on the cheek and say, "Has your mother told you how positively charming you both are?"

"A few hundred times," grins Jake. With a wink that reminds me of his father, he adds, "That is when she's not complaining about Jeremy here being such a slob."

"Here we go," laughs Sarah, playfully tapping the back of Jake's head, "I knew it was too good to last."

We're laughing as Becky makes her way down the stairs and once again the boys launch into appreciating whistles. "Aunt Becky, you're stunning," says Jeremy.

"No kidding," says Jake.

"Why thank you boys," replies Becky. "And from the look of the two of you, I'd say that Alicia and Stacey are having similar thoughts about you."

"How are they today?" asks Sarah.

"Beautiful and pleased to be here," answers Jake.

"Alicia was saying that the only time she and Stacey see us dressed up is for weddings," says Jeremy.

"Well then," says Amy, descending the stairs, "they'll enjoy the next wedding in the family."

"Take a look at Aunt Amy's ring finger," says Sarah, nudging Jake forward.

"Holy shit," exclaims Jeremy. "Is that for real?"

"Jeremy!" admonishes Sarah, but her laughter dismisses any real objection to his language.

"For real," says Amy, walking forward, wiggling her ring finger. "I'm getting married."

"To whom?" asks Jake.

"Mike, dufus," says Jeremy. "Who do you think?"

"He didn't say anything this morning," argues Jake.

"He wanted Aunt Amy to be the one to tell you," Sarah says, intervening in their brotherly kibitzing.

"Wow," murmurs Jake. "That was fast."

Amy's laughter bubbles as she replies, "So you won't mind getting dressed up in tuxes for one more wedding."

"No problem," grins Jake. "Especially if you throw in some lasagne to seal the deal."

Sarah quips, "My sons ... always thinking of their next meal."

Becky calls upstairs, "Everybody's here, Leen. Time to go."

"Wait a minute," says Jake, already bounding up the stairs. "She should do this right."

Jeremy takes two steps at a time and quickly joins his brother. We wait as they rap at Leen's bedroom door and hear murmurs of approval when she opens it. Standing at the top of the stairs, erect and proud, Jake announces, "Ladies, I have the honour of presenting to you my positively stunning Aunt Leen."

"That boy should consider a career in acting," I say to Sarah. "He knows how to carry off a line."

"They're like their father," smiles Sarah. "They know how to charm."

Emerging at the top of the staircase, with Leen holding onto the crook of his arm, Jeremy pauses for a second to give full effect to her look and then, with ease, escorts her down the stairs.

She's looking positively sultry and innocent, at one and the same time. A long white cape trimmed in white fur covers her gown and the hood falls gently on her hair.

The boys escort us one-by-one across the path to the back of Amy's house where Emile waits with Alex to open the door. Gathering in the warm kitchen, our nostrils are filled with the scents of Josh's culinary magic. Sheila and Harry stop supervising long enough to exclaim over our dresses and tell the bride how beautiful she looks.

"I guess I'd better go and tell them that you are all here," says Jake.

With a wink, Jeremy says, "I'll go with you."

"Don't forget to say hello to Stacey and Alicia for me," teases Sarah.

I repress the grin that threatens to pull on my lips as red creeps up into Jeremy's cheeks and he murmurs, "Ah Mom ..."

"Go," she says, waving him off. "I'm just teasing."

"Have you seen Marc Andre?" Leen asks Emile.

Chortling, he replies, "Seen him? Why, Alex and I personally saw to it that he arrived here safely. Reminded me of the day his mother took him to kindergarten. He balked when we checked to see if his shoes were shined but other than that, your groom is in good spirits."

"Joe has him stowed away upstairs in Amy's room," says Alex. "I'm supposed to get him when everybody's ready for the ceremony to start. When I left him, he was checking his watch every two minutes."

"Alex," I say, resting my hand on his arm and speaking softly, "A few of the guests here don't know I'm Claire Holowitz so you have to be careful not to let that slip."

"Don't worry," he answers, "Emile explained everything to me at Christmas. "Your secret is safe with me."

Jake pops his head around the kitchen door. "Pastor Aikens said to tell you that he's ready when you are."

"Well then," says Emile, puffing out his chest with pride and authority. "Let's get Leen and Marc Andre married."

"Yes, indeed," I grin. "You and Alex go and take your seats. Jeremy and Jake will be our escorts into the living room."

"I'll get Jeremy," says Jake.

"Tell the musicians to be ready," says Sarah.

"Already have, Mom," answers Jake.

Five minutes later Jeremy escorts me into the living room filled with Leen's and Marc Andre's closest friends. Marc Andre and Joe stand to the side of Pastor Aikens who waits for the wedding party in front of the canopy. Taking my seat beside Emile, I mouth to Marc Andre, "I love you. She's here!"

His deep grey eyes smile with happiness as he mouths back, "I love you too."

The soloist, a colleague of Amy's, accompanied by the quartet, fills the room with a voice that is so powerful and with such perfect pitch that I think she could have made it as a professional singer had she not chosen to be a university professor. Marc Andre directs his gaze to the French doors and from the moment we rise to our feet to receive the wedding procession his gaze remains steadfast. Solemn looking, Jeremy and Jake take turns escorting Sarah, Amy and Becky to the front of the room, opposite to where Marc Andre stands with Joe and Josh.

With Leen in the middle, the twins walk her down the makeshift aisle between the rows of chairs. The music ends just as they reach the row where Emile, Alex and I sit. With a graceful nod, Leen says, "I love you."

Touched beyond words, my eyes glisten with tears as Emile answers her with gruff affection, "Go, marry that man. He's waiting."

Laughter ripples in the room as Leen winks at him and says, "That's exactly what I plan on doing."

Welcoming the congregation of friends, Pastor Aikens moves briskly through the ceremony. "Dearly beloved, family, and friends we are gathered here today to witness the marriage of Marc Andre and Adrienne."

Discreetly wiping a tear from my cheek, I murmur to Emile, "They're like two halves coming together as one." His obvious pride in his son and acceptance for his new daughter-in-law touches my heart. Emile and I have seen a lifetime together and together we have buried our respective spouses, wept, and cried. But today we sit side-by-side, celebrating the love of Marc Andre and Leen and the beginning of their life together. As if aware of my thoughts, Emile gently squeezes my hand and whispers, "They'll do just fine."

When the formal part of the ceremony ends, Leen and Marc greet their guests and graciously receive their wishes for happiness. Emile and I chat with Kathy and her husband Tom. She is positively gloating that Leen has finally tied the knot and according to her version, she knew from the first day that Leen and Marc Andre would end up together. The photographer–recommended by a close friend of mine, has taken several pictures before and during the ceremony but as agreed to when the arrangements were made, we're to go to his studio for the formal photos. Emile has arranged for four limos to take us to the studio and we all pile into them with Sarah reminding the twins that in our absence they are to act as hosts.

By the time we return Jeremy and Jake have settled their girlfriends at their table with their name cards and are enjoying their roles as hosts. Sheila and Harry are discreetly supervising the waiters as they serve hors d'oeuvres and refresh drinks. The mood is festive and the fifty guests are comfortably seated or milling about Amy's living and sun rooms. Marc Andre and Leen walk to the head table amidst applause and the wedding party takes their seats at the head table.

Leaning over to Amy, Sarah admires her ring once again saying, "The way weddings are happening around here, we'll soon be having a repeat with you and Mike."

Blushing, Amy answers, "I didn't see this coming."

I interrupt their conversation saying dryly, "Tomorrow, we'll start planning your wedding."

Sarah laughs. "You're getting to be a pro at planning weddings, Anna-Claire."

"Looks like Jake and Jeremy are totally smitten," observes Amy. We follow her gaze to where they sit, laughing with their girlfriends about something one of them has said.

Sarah smiles. "Smitten is all they can afford to be right now."

"Relax, Sarah, the marriage bug won't hit them for a while," laughs Becky. "But you have to admit they're terribly handsome in those tuxes and the girls are crazy about them. It's all part of growing up, *Mom*."

Sighing, Sarah agrees with Becky but just the same, she adds, "You're right, I know you are but I want to see them graduated from university and starting on their careers before either one decides to get married."

"Most young couples live together for a while before getting married," says Amy.

"You really needed to tell her that?" kids Becky.

"Great, just great," grouses Sarah.

Becky pats her shoulder and commiserates, "All part of the process. Trust me, you'll survive."

"Thanks Doc," groans Sarah. "Just what I needed to hear."

"She looks beautiful, doesn't she?" Switching her attention to Leen, Becky admires how Leen radiates happiness. Reaching for her wine glass, she asks, "Did you ever think she would get married?"

"To tell the truth, I thought Leen would eventually get around to it but I was surprised when she fell as hard as she did," answers Amy. "She's been married to her career for so many years but when Marc Andre walked in her office, things started to change for her."

"Anna-Claire," teases Becky, "you've been a catalyst for a lot of changes in our lives."

A friend of Marc Andre's tinkles his wine glass with a spoon and soon the entire room is demanding that the bride and groom oblige them with a kiss. Marc extends a hand to Leen and helps her to her feet.

Cupping her chin, he leans down and kisses her gently on the lips much to the amused satisfaction of all the guests.

After the main course has been served, Joe rises to make his speech. Beginning with a welcome to everyone he observes humorously, "Today is one day we're all going to remember because it's the day that legendary bachelor, Marc Andre, and career woman, Leen, have joined forces." Grinning broadly, he jokes, "And God help us all!" Everyone laughs as he laces his speech with little stories about the bride and her three best friends, ending with his toast. "Marc Andre, today you joined the "brotherhood" of the survivors of the coven."

To the amusement of the guests, Josh pipes up with, "Give in now Marc Andre or you'll make the rest of us look bad."

Rising, Marc Andre gallantly replies, "I gather there is no appeal court for the brotherhood so I bow in graceful admission." Raising his wine glass he says, "Gentlemen, to my beautiful bride and the ladies in our lives."

When Emile rises to give a toast as father-of-the-groom and to welcome Leen to the family, I can't help thinking how – despite his age – my dear old friend is still strikingly handsome. Voice quavering slightly as he attempts to control his emotion and pride, he says, "To Leen, my son's wife and my daughter-in-law. May all your days together be as wondrous as your beginnings, and may you always experience the inexplicable comfort of unconditional love. Welcome Leen, you are the daughter I have always longed for." Raising his wine glass he says with sombre emotion, "To Leen."

Tears of affection run down Leen's cheeks as she reaches for the handkerchief tucked in the sleeve of her gown and Marc Andre touchingly kisses her on the cheek.

Calling upon me, as the mother-of-the-bride to make a toast, Joe says, "And now we'll hear from Anna Wright who has honoured us by calling us family."

Raising my glass, I say, "To Leen, one of four daughters whom I have grown to love and to admire. You all have filled my days with your kindness and your unbridled enthusiasm for life." Smiling, I add, "Leen, you and my godson Marc Andre have made me very proud and happy. I wish you both all the happiness that life can bring. And fulfilling my duties as mother-of-the-bride let me give you both what I hope you will consider to be good advice; may you never let one day go by without telling one another how much you love each other and may you never stop appreciating how much you need each other. The complexities and challenges of life are surmountable when and where there is love. I am blessed to have you both in my life. To the guests I say, "Ladies and Gentlemen, please rise and join me as I toast Leen and her marriage to Marc Andre … May they have a long life filled with happiness."

As the toasts wind down, servers appear to whisk away dinner plates and soon our tables are covered with desserts of caramelized butter cream soufflés, laden with strawberries and whipped cream, along with coffee and tea. The room is filled with laughter, conversation, and well-being. Finally, Joe announces, "Marc Andre and Leen invite everyone to take advantage of the bar set up in the sunroom while the tables are cleared. Tables in the sunroom will be removed shortly so that there will be room for dancing."

The first dance is led by Marc Andre and Leen, followed by Marc Andre dancing with me and Emile paired with Leen. Soon all the guests are either on the dance floor or mingling and enjoying conversations or lining up to take advantage of the open bar. Leen and Marc Andre make the rounds from table-to-table expressing their thanks to the guests and accepting wishes for happiness. Pastor Aikens and his wife mingle gladly with the guests and surprise the twins by actually joining them for a while at their table.

At ten, waiters bring out pastries, cheeses and fruits. At eleven o'clock, Marc Andre announces, "Leen and I have an early flight to catch and as much as we would like to stay with the party, it's necessary to take my bride away."

Everyone follows the bridal couple out to the waiting limousine and laughs merrily as Marc Andre, helps Leen with her wrap and announces for all to hear, "This is the best day of my life and with Leen by my side, each day will be better." He swallows a hard breath as he struggles to control the swell of emotions he is experiencing. "Ladies and gentlemen, friends and family, my wife and I are grateful to all of you for this moment …. And now, I must take the lady home." Winking, he gets the reaction he's looking for and the guests start to good-naturedly tease him about the need to be well rested before they leave for their flight to St. Lucia.

Emile and I wanted to give them something special for their wedding so we offered to fund their honeymoon. Initially Leen didn't feel she could spare time away from Scenes and the Gala's preparations, but we insisted a four-day honeymoon at an all-inclusive resort was exactly what both Leen and Marc Andre needed. What it boiled to in the end was my absolute insistence on their having a honeymoon. Leen was to tell Scenes personnel that she was spending a few days of research and conducting interviews with people who would help make the Gala a success. It wasn't a lie. I arranged for a few more of my friends to meet with her and to provide insight to my career. The fact that those interviews took place before her wedding was to my way of thinking a moot point. She still needed time to consolidate the information learned from those interviews and as Emile was quick to point out, a few days of quiet in the sun, being able to rest on a beach away from the hectic pace of her corporate life, was exactly the 'ticket'.

By midnight, Amy's house is emptied of guests except for me, Emile, Alex, Mike, Josh, Sarah, Becky, and Joe. The twins having said their goodbyes packed their girlfriends into the car, along with *care packages* from the wedding.

After pouring a small brandy for me, Josh helps Joe mix cocktails for our little group before sitting down wearily at one of the tables. "This was a beautiful wedding," he says, taking a healthy swallow of his drink.

"Amy, the house looked wonderful," comments Sarah, casting a glance at the wedding arch. "Everything was done to perfection."

"Thank you," replies Amy, turning to compliment Josh. "The food was amazing and your waiters were absolutely excellent. Everything just seemed to flow so effortlessly."

"Glad you liked it," answers Josh, slipping one arm around Becky's waist. "And now," he smiles winsomely at Amy, "we'll have to plan for your wedding."

Mike who is sitting with a scotch in one hand and his other arm draped over the back of Amy's chair, grins broadly. "The sooner the better. I don't want to give her any time to reconsider."

"It will have to be after the Gala," says Amy.

If only she had said she wanted to wait until the summer break at the university but once said, there was no turning back.

Confused by her statement, Mike says, "The Gala? What Gala? And why would a Gala of any sort interfere with our wedding plans?"

Trying to smooth over her slip of the tongue, Amy replies, "Leen is overseeing the preparations and media for a Gala that is to be held in New York, honouring the works of Claire Holowitz. I'm not certain she'll be able to give her attention to anything else until it's over."

"I see," answers Mike, but it's clear that he doesn't.

"True enough," agrees Becky, attempting to support Amy's nebulous explanation for wanting to delay setting a date until after the Gala. "Getting Leen to agree to take four days off for her honeymoon was a major feat. She'll be making up for lost time as soon as she returns."

"Yes," interjects Sarah, reiterating what has already been said, but trying gamely to put a light tone back into the conversation. "She'll be working around the clock to complete all the finishing details for the Gala."

Josh and Joe are conspicuously silent. Mike, alert to the dynamics in the room, says, "Is there something I'm missing in this discussion?" He thinks for a moment and then starts to shoot questions in rapid succession. "Did you say Claire Holowitz? Are you talking about the author? She's a recluse. How can Leen be planning a Gala without her cooperation?" Jaw clenching, but keeping a tight control on his rising annoyance, Mike, adds, "I don't see how anything to do with Claire Holowitz would or should interfere with our plans to get married."

"Sarah," I say, resting my hands on my lap and intertwining my fingers so that my nervousness will not show, "perhaps you should be the one to explain Amy's conundrum and the concern we all have pertaining to the Gala."

Sarah takes a deep breath and leaning back into her chair, she says, "Mike, I'm going to explain a few things to you that we…" she motions with her hand, "all of us, are involved with. Things," she says, meeting his intense look, "that are highly confidential. To that end, I need to ask if you will be willing to sign a confidentiality agreement."

"What?" Mike removes his arm from around Amy's shoulders and straightens. His voice is controlled but his eyes snap with annoyance. "Why would I sign a confidentiality agreement and what has that to do with my wanting to marry Amy?" Frustrated, he pushes a hand through his hair. "I think somebody needs to give me some answers." Rising to his feet, he stares at Amy and waits for her response.

420

Sarah rises from her chair and walks to where Mike stands. Facing him, she says, "If you'll let me explain ..." and with that she summarizes Leen's involvement with the Gala – discreetly leaving out my identity – but covering some of the problems that have occurred because of Leen's involvement with the Gala. Summing up, she says, "So, as you can see, Leen will be under intense pressure to make certain that the Gala is a success. Because of that, she might not be able to fully participate in the plans for Amy's and your wedding." Attempting to mollify his frustration, she adds, "As Joe has already told you, the four of us are extremely close. None of us would want to be left out of helping one another especially for something as important as a wedding."

"I'd love to have a late spring wedding," says Amy. "I'll be finished with my spring session at the university and will have the whole summer off." Grabbing hold of Mike's hand, she says, "Think how nice it will be to have flowers in bloom, no snow to trudge over—we can plan to go anywhere on our honeymoon and not have to worry about the Gala." Ramrod straight, Mike looks at her clearly weighing his response. Squeezing his hand, Amy adds, "Our wedding will be perfect."

The tension in his shoulders ease. Relieved that he's coming around to the idea of a late spring wedding, I glance at Sarah and Becky who both visibly relax. Sarah returns to her chair and handing Joe her glass, she says, "I think I could do with a refill."

"Anyone else," asks Joe.

"Me too," says Becky, passing her glass to Josh.

"If you want a late spring wedding then that's what we'll have," answers Mike. "But, you've got to admit," he says, for all our benefits, "using the excuse of a Gala for Claire Holowitz to delay our wedding took me by surprise." Looking at Joe and Josh, he says, "I know you warned me about how our ladies march to their own agendas, but what I'm really wondering..." he stares meaningfully, "is why the two of you haven't been throwing in your usual comments about learning to follow their lead, staying out of the way ... making jokes about the coven." He peers closely and sucks some air between his teeth before adding, "What is it that you guys aren't telling me?"

Passing Becky her drink, Josh grins, "We're leading by example. Stay quiet and let them work out the plans."

"Then, like dutiful husbands, we follow," jokes Joe, attempting to make light of their conspicuous silence.

The Search for Claire Holowitz

Touching Mike's cheek with two fingers and tilting his head just enough so that she can look at him straight in the eye; Amy interrupts any further exchange between the men saying, "I want to marry you. I just meant that with so much happening right now, it would be good to have the time to enjoy planning for the wedding and to make our day as special as it can be."

Softening, Mike answers, "If that's what you want then that's what we'll do." Returning his attention to Joe and Josh, he jokes, "Looks like I'm the next man to fall prey to their planning."

"Well," laughs Josh, "one thing I'll say for you. You're a quick study."

"Actually," says Mike, after the laughter dies down, "I own two Holowitz photos. And while I'm thinking about it, I still don't understand from what Sarah explained about the Gala and Leen's idiot boss, why you would want me to sign a confidentiality agreement."

This bombshell brings the group to quick attention. Mike only proposed last night. None of us have had time to discuss when we should tell him who I really am and why the Gala is of such importance. Sarah glances at Amy silently warning her not to say anything. Keen to know about his collection but not wanting to appear so, she asks conversationally, "Which ones?"

"One is called *Fall Splendour*," he answers. "It's a panorama of fall coloured leaves reflecting in the water. The strange thing about the photo is that no matter which way you turn it, you can't really tell what is real and what is the illusion of real."

Becky remarks, "I've seen prints of that one. It's one of her most reproduced images."

"Mine is the original. I paid close to three thousand for it at an auction about fifteen years ago and its value today is way beyond that."

Serendipity, I think. *What were the odds of Mike owning two of my photos?* Casually, I say, "You said you owned two. What's the other one?"

Distracted for the moment from the topic of a confidentiality agreement and warming to the topic of my photos, Mike answers. "It's a black and white of a playground entitled *Lost Innocence*. The photo captures a swing in mid-air but there's no child on it – just the empty swing with leaves swirling around. In the background there are trees with the hint of sun peaking through them." He stops to sip his drink before continuing, "When I saw it, I was drawn to the unspoken message of sadness that there was no child there; as if the momentum of time had come and gone and although everything looked normal, all things had changed." He shrugs. "I bought it on a whim and I've never regretted it."

Moved by his insight, I reply, "I wonder how many people have seen reprints of that photo and not understood the message of it."

Curious, Sarah asks, "When was it taken?"

"It looks like a fall scene," answers Mike.

"I think she means the year?" says Amy, speaking softly.

"I can't say for sure," answers Mike, "but the auctioneer said it was done shortly after she reclused herself from the public." Looking at Amy he adds, "I think you'll like it when you see it."

Joe clears his throat and rises to stretch. Addressing Sarah, he says, "It's late. We should be thinking about hitting the road."

Not about to be sidetracked from his question, Mike addresses Sarah, "I've yet to hear why you want me to sign a confidentiality agreement."

Sarah looks at me and I slowly nod. "Mike," she says, "I think you need to sit down and listen to what I have to say."

"Yes, Mike," I say, "there's something that you need to know."

Perplexed, he sits down. Sarah wets her lips, looks back at me, and takes a moment to gather her thoughts. Josh and Joe shrug and sit back down, accepting the fact that this evening is not yet over. A moment passes before Sarah says, "Everything I told you about Leen's involvement with the Gala for Claire Holowitz was true ..."

"But?" interrupts Mike. "What did you leave out? What is it that I need to know?"

Half an hour later, Sarah has filled in the gaps for Mike. Throughout her explanation, he has not interrupted once. It's clear that the news of my identity was not something that he could have expected to hear. After all, he knows me as Anna Wright and only a short while ago he sat in this very room proudly announcing that he owned two of my photos. "Well," he says, "first things first. Where's that confidentiality agreement you want me to sign? Second," he walks over to where I sit and extends his hand, "I've long been an admirer of your work."

"Thank you for that," I answer. "More importantly, thank you for your understanding. I know we've given you a lot to think about."

His eyes twinkle and his lips curve upwards, as he answers, "I'll sign the agreement, but in exchange, can I also ask a favour?"

Everyone is watching me, waiting to hear what Mike wants and how I will respond. "Ask your favour," I answer. "If I can grant it, I will."

"Can I impose on you to take a photo of Amy and me for our wedding?"

Relief floods through me and all the tension of a moment ago fades. "Delighted," I answer.

Joe pushes back his chair and tapping Sarah on the shoulder, says, "Now that everything's settled, I think I'd like to call it a night." Holding out his hand for her to take, he says, "What do you say?"

Josh says, "We'll see Anna-Claire home and be on our way too."

Joe slaps Mike playfully on the back shoulder blade and asks, "Does this mean we're not to expect you to be sleeping at our house tonight?"

Rolling her eyes, Sarah asks, "Was that crack really necessary?"

"Yes," laughs Joe, "it was." Looking at Josh for support, he says with a straight face, "Seemed like a perfectly reasonable question to me."

"Perfectly reasonable," answers Josh, earning a reproving but amused glance from Becky.

We follow their lead and depart at the same time. With Becky holding one elbow and Josh holding the other to steady my walk through the freshly fallen snow, Becky asks, "You okay, Anna-Claire?"

"I'm fine," I answer, "but I will admit to being shocked that Mike owns two of my photos. I never expected that."

"He was quite proud of it," says Josh, as I turn the key in the lock. "To be honest, I wasn't sure how he would take the news about you being Claire Holowitz. All in all, I'd say he handled it well."

"I hope he and Amy will be happy," says Becky. "She deserves to be happy."

"He loves her," I answer. "That much is clear."

I wave good-bye. Exhausted from the day's events I make my way upstairs, glad to put aside any more thoughts other than simply going to sleep.

༄

Amy

Closing the door, I turn into Mike's embrace. "So, Dr. Keiffers'," he says, "it's been an exciting day and may I say that you looked ravishing today."

Nestling against his chest, I answer, "You were quite dashing yourself, Mr. Andrews."

Stepping back, he holds onto my shoulders and peers closely. "I love you Amy and I always will."

Despite my fatigue, I feel myself responding. I want nothing more than to feel the comfort of his arms around me and quickly dismiss any fleeting thoughts about tidying up the room before we go to bed. "We can finish any clean-up tomorrow morning after Gerald and his people remove the tables and return my furniture. Right now, all I want is to lie in your arms. Would that be okay?"

Smiling, he replies, "It's more than okay."

Entering my bedroom, I switch on the gas fireplace and wordlessly slip one of my favourite CD's into the player, adjusting the volume to low. I move to where Mike stands watching me and I silently remove his tie and unbutton his shirt. Intuitively, he lets me take the initiative. I drop my hand down to loosen his belt. Mike reaches behind my back and unzips my gown. Moving to the bed, we make love alternating between gentleness and passion; exploring and satiating our need for one another. Afterwards, as we lie in the glow cast from the fireplace, we drift off to sleep content in knowing that we are becoming one in mind, body and spirit.

Chapter Thirty-four

Leen

Groggy, I open my eyes and indulge my morning laziness by looking through the bedroom window at the falling big white puffs of snowflakes, wondering if the snow will delay our flight. Time has flown quickly since our return from our honeymoon and it's hard to believe that after so many months of preparation, we're now on the eve of the Gala. Reaching for the bedside phone, I dial Air Canada and listen to the voice recording of flight schedules for the day. With the exception of a flight coming in from Vancouver, there are no delays.

Marc Andre comes into the bedroom wiping his freshly shaven face with a hand towel. "We have to leave in an hour for the airport, Leen. Ready for today?"

I spring from the comfort of my warm bed and head to the walk-in clothes closet where I select the slacks, turtle neck and suede jacket I'd set aside last night. "I don't know Marc," I answer truthfully, as I lay my clothes down on the bed. "Kathy and I have gone over every detail for the Gala but ..." I frown, "although Don has been careful not be overt about it ever since the Board meeting; I know he's still sniffing around, hoping for something that he can use to discredit me." I make my way to the bathroom grousing, "He's such an asshole."

Since our wedding, I've started calling Marc Andre, Marc. If he objects to the abbreviation, he's not said. Leaning against the doorframe as I slip off my nightie, step into the shower stall, and fiddle with the nozzle to change it to pulse mode, he says, "You're going to be fine and don't forget I'll be there as Claire Holowitz's lawyer and representative. It'll be a very public endorsement of her cooperation with the Gala and her personal support for your efforts."

Closing my eyes to avoid the shampoo from stinging them, I lean against the wall and let the water's warm, pulsating motion ease the tension from my shoulders. "I know that," I answer, "but Don will strut about the hall, looking for any opportunity to imply by innuendo that you're not only protecting Claire's privacy but covering for me."

Marc hands me a large white towel as I emerge from the stall. Kissing the top of my wet hair, his hand drifts to one nipple and begins to tease it with his fingers. I place my hand over his and warn, "If you continue with this, we'll miss our flight."

He draws in a breath and with a roguish grin, says, "If you insist."

Laughing, I say, "You make it hard for a girl to refuse."

He smiles. "I hope the bed is comfortable in the hotel you've reserved. I plan to make good use of it. Now, hurry up and get ready. We'll have just enough time to grab a bite to eat before we leave."

By the time I come downstairs, I'm feeling the tingles of energy that I usually experience whenever setting out to finalize a project. I'm slipping into a focused mode and shedding my apprehensions. Nothing I do will change Don's hatred of me and at this point, I can only focus on the Gala. I look at Marc's broad shoulders as he stands with his back to me, buttering our toast. "What did I ever do so right to have you in my life?" I ask, pouring a cup of coffee.

He pours himself a cup and sits down opposite me. "I could say that the gods of good fortune smiled down on you," he answers, with a glint in his eyes, "but in the interest of our busy schedule this morning, I'll give you the abbreviated version."

"Really? And what exactly is the abbreviated version?"

"You searched for Claire Holowitz and found me as the prize," replies Marc, smugly.

Marc does one final walk through the house making sure the lights are off, appliances unplugged, and carries our suitcases out to the car while I re-check my purse for the flight tickets, passports, and pick up my briefcase and laptop. Pulling on my London Fog coat and heeled leather boots, I set the house alarm and go out to the car. As we drive out of the driveway, Marc says, "Don't worry, Leen. It's going to be fine."

"I hope you're right," I mutter, before plunging into a discussion about the day's schedule. Twenty minutes later I'm just summing up details as Marc takes the exit for the Macdonald Cartier airport. "Kathy will meet us at the airport. Among other things, she's bringing the contact details of the set-up crew in New York. She'll have everything and everyone marching to her tune." Grinning I add, "I wonder if New York is ready for her?"

Marc chuckles as he eases the car towards the ramp for the parking garage. "She really is a self-propelled dynamo, isn't she?"

"You have no idea," I respond, admiration evident in my tone. "She keeps my schedule and organizes everyone and everything around me. I don't know what I would do without her."

"I've got a treat for her when she gets to New York," announces Marc, casually.

"Really?" Curiosity aroused, I arch an expectant eyebrow.

Marc manages to find a parking space near the elevator door. Turning off the ignition, he says, "You remember how she said at our wedding reception that she has always wanted to take in a Broadway play?"

Nodding agreement, I step out of the car. "Yes, but she's going there on a working trip."

"True enough," answers Marc, opening the trunk to remove our suitcases, "but I purchased tickets for the night after the Gala. Tom's going to fly down tomorrow for the Gala and then stay at a suite I've reserved for them for the following two days."

I stop walking. Surprised at this news, I say, "But she's my assistant, Marc. Don't you think you could have told me about your surprise?"

"I thought you'd be pleased," he answers.

"I am," I reply, "but I would have liked to have been consulted. Did you think I wouldn't approve?"

"Thought never crossed my mind," answers Marc, "I didn't mean to hurt your feelings."

Realizing that I sound churlish, I apologize, "I'm not hurt, Marc. I just would have liked to have been part of the surprise." Walking towards the ticket counter, I say, "I think it's nice of you to do something special for her."

"Duly noted," says Marc, handing his ticket to the agent.

"I'm just jumpy about the Gala," I say, as the agent stamps Marc's boarding pass. "What you did was really very nice."

"Tell you what," grins Marc as we head to the boarding gate, "You can be the one to tell her about the special treat."

"No," I answer, "you tell her. I'm glad that you did this for her and I'll have fun watching her reaction."

"So we're good?" asks Marc, placing his wallet, overcoat, and shoes in the bin to go through the conveyor scan.

"We're good," I answer, standing aside so that he can walk through the scanner and I wait for my turn to go through.

As we make our way down to the waiting area for our flight, Marc says, "As long as I'm being totally open, maybe I should tell you about Becky."

I think for a moment. "Go on."

Sliding into a seat beside me in the waiting area, Marc continues, "Well, Becky suggested that it might be nice for all of us to take in a play while we were in New York as a way of celebrating the culmination of more than a year and a half of preparations."

It hits me that he's talking as if Becky and the others are going to attend the Gala. Assuming that I've misunderstood, I ask, "Did I mishear you? I thought you said that Amy, Becky, and Sarah are coming for the Gala along with Mike, Josh and Joe?"

Looking sheepish about not being able to keep the secret, he answers, "That's the truth, Leen and I've learned a lesson."

Smiling at his boyish charm, I ask, "What lesson?"

"I should have listened to Joe. A married man can't keep a secret from his wife. One way or another, she'll get to the bottom of it."

"What other tips did Joe, the male guru, have to share?"

"He said that I'd better learn quickly that no matter how hard any of the husbands tried – you, Sarah, Becky, and Amy will always ferret out our deepest secrets and that if we want any peace we should never even try to keep a secret."

Laughing, I answer, "That sounds like Joe. He's never been able to outsmart Sarah. She keeps him on his toes."

"Looks like she's not the only one," mutters Marc, as we follow the flight attendant to our seats. Kathy, who had already boarded before us, waves as we make our way down the aisle.

The flight to New York is a short one and once settled with the coffees and danishes the flight attendant brings, Kathy and I have just enough time to review the agenda for the day before we fasten our seatbelts in preparation for the landing. "The limousine driver should be waiting to pick us up," chirps Kathy, efficiently, "and the hotel is approximately forty minutes from the airport. We'll have just enough time to freshen up before we have to leave for the twelve-thirty meeting at the Rockefeller Centre with the New York people to go over any last minute details." Glancing at her notes, she adds, "Ted Jakes has promised to be there to assist with anything that we may have overlooked."

I nod approvingly. "Ted's a good person." Addressing Marc, I say, "You'll like him. He's been a wealth of information and he's an avowed Holowitz fan."

"Actually," responds Marc with an easy grin, "I've met Ted already."

Kathy blurts out the question on both of our minds. "When?"

"Let's see," says Marc, fingering his lips as if he needs time to think but in truth, enjoying being a step ahead of us in planning. "It would have been last July; right after you told me that you had confirmed the use of the Rockefeller Centre for the Gala." He continues without giving notice to our surprised looks. "After all, Leen," he says reasonably, "I'm Claire Holowitz's lawyer and as such she wanted to know what arrangements were being made and who the New York contact person was."

To be honest, I'm not surprised. It is just like Anna-Claire to want to know every minute detail about the Gala highlighting her life. "What did you think of him?" I ask, realizing there's no point in grilling him about why he's not mentioned this detail before. He will just answer that he's been operating under lawyer-client privilege and could not have spoken about the meeting without Claire's permission.

Taking a moment to think about my question, Marc replies, "His knowledge of Claire Holowitz was impressive. I've no doubt that he'll have everyone jumping to his tune. You'll have little if anything to worry about from his end of things."

I smile, thinking that even six months ago the notion of Claire Holowitz working in the background and following all of my movements would have had me miffed. I would have attributed any background interference from Anna-Claire to be an indication that she didn't fully credit me with the ability to represent her interests properly. But now, I know her intervention with Jakes has been just one more example of her silent caring and protection for those she loves. I squeeze Marc's hand. "She really is some woman, isn't she?"

Tightening his fingers around mine, Marc answers, "That she is, Leen. That she is."

By the end of the day as we sit at a small Italian restaurant in Lower Manhattan, Kathy and I are exhausted. Marc has kept busy meeting with colleagues from his firm's New York office and addressing some legal issues surrounding the Gala. Ordering a bottle of Chianti, we dip warm bread into olive oil and balsamic vinegar as we wait for our pasta dishes to be brought to the table.

"Tonight ladies," he says, as we sip Chianti, "there will be no more planning and detail revisions. You've both done what you can for tomorrow. Just sit back and enjoy the meal before I take you back to the hotel for a good night's sleep."

I hold up my glass in a toast, doing my best to act demure. "Yes, Mr. Aumount," I answer, "we are but lowly maids here to do your bidding."

Kathy laughs as Marc, without missing a beat in the conversation, pours more wine into our glasses saying with a straight face, "Now that's a good wife, wouldn't you agree Kathy?"

Marc's antics and easy conversation throughout dinner work like magic. He chats with Kathy about New York's often-visited tourist destinations but advises walking alone through Battery Park is never a good idea. By the time we take the elevator up to our rooms, Marc has convinced her of the merit of doing tourist activities on the day following the Gala while he and I wrap up details for the legal end of the event and payments of accounts for personnel hired.

Seeing her concern that she would be leaving the tidying up to me, I quickly insist that she do as Marc suggests saying, "That is a marvellous idea, Kathy."

Not needing further encouragement, Kathy happily agrees to the plan. As we make our way towards our room, I tell Marc, "She'll be on her laptop tomorrow, in between all the running around and have her day off planned to the hilt. You can bet on it."

Opening the door to our suite, he steers me to the bedroom. "Now, Mrs. Aumount, as much as I would like to make love with you tonight, we're both going to get some sleep."

As I settle down between the soft sheets and start to doze off, feeling the warm comfort of his body lying close to mine, he whispers playfully, "Having been such a thoughtful gentleman tonight and realizing your need for sleep, I will expect to be rewarded with mountains of gratitude tomorrow night after the success of the Gala."

I shift my body into a curl, fitting neatly into his. Drawing his hand close to my breast, I snuggle down, and reply, "Oh you can count on it, Marc. You'll need your sleep too because I have plans for you also."

As I drift off to sleep, I hear his soft whisper, "I love you Leen so very much."

Chapter Thirty-five

Sarah

I wake to the harsh sound of the phone ringing. I glance at the alarm clock radio noting that it's only seven a.m.. Joe, an early riser, has long since risen from bed, had breakfast, and by now is at his office. He claims that arriving before his staff gives him time to work quietly on the necessary paperwork, leaving the day open to visit construction sites and to meet with contractors and architects. Speaking into the receiver, I say, "Hello."

"Did I wake you?" asks Anna-Claire, surprisingly cheerful for this time of the morning. Somewhat surprised at the early morning call I, nonetheless, smile.

"It's time I got up anyway," I murmur, rubbing the sleep from my eyes. Since taking her on as a client, I have managed my time between working with Marc Andre to represent her interests with respect to the Gala and resuming part-time work at my firm.

"Should I call back later?"

"This is fine. What's up with you at seven a.m.?"

"Only seven?" responds Anna-Claire, momentarily stumped with the timing of her call. "Oh, I am so sorry, dear," she says, contritely. "Sometimes, I just lose sight of the time." I can hear her soft sigh as she adds, "It's just that I was up early this morning and have some things that I need to talk with you about. Do you think you could come by around nine?"

Already moving towards the bathroom, I answer, "I'll shower and come on over. Is there anything particular you want to discuss?"

"Yes, actually there is," answers Anna-Claire. "Normally I would discuss it on the phone, but I think it's going to take some time to work things out. I want your input on something both as a friend and legal advisor." She pauses. "Are you certain you don't mind coming over?"

Curiosity piqued, I reply, "No problem. I'll see you in a little while."

I rush through my shower and quickly pull on jeans and a sweater. Throwing a notepad into my briefcase, I grab my small microphone. Since my aneurism I have found it to be useful when taking notes. Anna-Claire has cheerfully complied with these taped sessions, teasing, "Next, we'll have you writing a book. That's what all authors tend to do. They find a system of remembering details so that they can be quickly retrieved later on."

Pulling up into Anna-Claire's driveway, I'm surprised to see Becky's car already parked. Knocking on Anna-Claire's door, I walk in calling out, "I'm here."

"We're in the kitchen, dear," replies Anna-Claire. "Coffee's waiting."

Tossing my coat on the hallway bench, I walk to the kitchen and ask, "What's going on?"

"You know as much as we do," smiles Becky. "I just arrived before you did and Amy walked in with me. Anna-Claire said that when you arrived, she would tell us all at once what this meeting is about."

Expectantly, we look to Anna-Claire who sits calmly at the kitchen table with her coffee mug resting between her hands. Staring directly at us, she says, "Leen and Marc left this morning for New York."

"And?" I prod for an answer. "We already know this."

"The three of you are flying there tomorrow to join them?"

"Correct," replies Becky. I hear the exasperation in her voice but also the warmth. "Josh and Joe are flying with us and Mike will be flying in from Calgary. What's this about?"

Propping an elbow on the table, she cups her chin in her palm and says, "I got to thinking about everything that has happened over this last year. Amy moved in; I met all of you; Leen started her search for Claire Holowitz; Marc Andre and Leen fell in love; I retained Sarah as additional counsel; Josh and Becky got married; Marc Andre and Leen got married; Mike's flight gets delayed and he comes to spend Christmas with Sarah and Joe; and now, Amy and Mike are getting married ..." She shrugs, draws in a breath, and says, "With all that has happened, it just seems right that I join all of you at the Gala."

Not even Becky, the practical one of our group, professionally trained to unravel people's thoughts and emotions, has an immediate response.

"I can see you're all surprised at my decision," says Anna-Claire, the corners of her lips turning upwards.

Unable to bite my tongue, I stammer, "But your privacy ..."

"True enough," answers Anna-Claire, "but don't I also have the right to change my mind?"

"What brought this about?" asks Becky, her eyes searching Anna-Claire's expression for an indication as to her actual state of mind and comfort level.

"Well," answers Anna-Claire, tone pragmatic, "we all know that I'm too weak to travel alone and my physician won't even countenance a trip. But..." she stares at Becky purposefully, "since you are a doctor, George can't very well argue that I won't be in good hands."

"I'm a psychiatrist," mumbles Becky.

"This too is true," agrees Anna-Claire, enjoying how her announcement has taken all of us by surprise, "and maybe before I'm done with the Gala I will need your professional services to help me get through this, but you are *still* a doctor and I trust your medical opinion."

"Assuming that I agree to this plan, why now Anna-Claire?"

"I think you all know," replies Anna-Claire, determined not to pull any punches. "We all know that I'm on borrowed time. No, no," she waves her hand as we start to protest. "It's true." Her blue eyes lock on Becky with seriousness that is both sad and, at the same time, resigned. "Becky, you've talked with my physician. You know I'm not exaggerating."

Nodding assent to Anna-Claire's calm acceptance of her fate and respecting her for the matter-of-fact manner in which she is speaking, Becky states, "You're doing this for Leen. Isn't that right, Claire?"

"Yes," replies Anna-Claire. We wait as she gathers her thoughts. "All of you have become like daughters to me. Right now, one of my daughters needs me and I need all of you to help get me to her. So," she demands, searching our faces for our responses, "Will you or will you not help me?"

Amy is the first to respond, rattling off a series of questions. "Are you sure you can make the trip? What about the public exposure? Are you ready for that?"

Becky sighs, leans back in her chair, and says, "It's goes against my better judgment, but I can see that you're determined to go." She rises, walks to the kitchen counter, and stares out the window. With her back to us, she asks, "Is this your way of making peace with yourself? What Amy says is true." She turns to face Anna-Claire and says softly, "You'll be directly in the public eye. Are you ready for that exposure?"

I begin to tick off the legal steps and precautions that will guarantee Anna-Claire the least amount of intrusion on her life. "Timing will be key to Anna-Claire's arrival and departure. We'll have to have a prepared statement..." I stop mid-sentence, startled by Becky's expression. "What's wrong?"

"Nothing," replies Becky, "but will you listen to yourself? You're talking about issuing statements and timing. We have first to find out what Anna-Claire's plans are before we plot out a course of action and I have to contact Dr. Anderson." She looks at Anna-Claire and says firmly, "He's bound to have concerns about your travelling." Returning her attention to me, she says, "One step at a time, Sarah."

Picking up on Becky's tone and seeing that I'm primed to start arguing with her, Amy says, "Both of you have valid points, but aren't we all forgetting something?"

In response to our looks of confusion, Amy folds her arms across her chest and says to Anna-Claire, "Tell us what you have planned and how we can best help you."

"Thank you, dear," answers Anna-Claire, clearly grateful for Amy's intervention in our bickering. "As I said earlier, I want to fly with all of you to New York. I need Becky to be my physician and to help with any medical concerns and additional medications George may want to prescribe to help me cope with the trip. I want Sarah to join with Marc – as already planned – to represent my legal concerns. I want you, Amy, to be my companion because the other two are going to be very busy taking care of my other interests. I *don't* want Leen to know that I am coming because then the element of surprise and underpinning anything that Don Harris may have up his perverted and corrupted little sleeve will be lost. Marc Andre already has a video tape which he helped me to make and of which Leen knows nothing."

"A video tape?" The lawyer in me kicks into full gear. "Exactly what type of video tape?"

"Oh it's just a three minute video which we made upstairs in my study," answers Anna-Claire, waving a hand to dismiss the concern that must be blatant on my face. "Nowhere in the video tape do I divulge where I live and, unless someone I don't know about has been in my study, there is no visual indication of where I live. I am surrounded by my books, photos, and manuscripts. Marc and you as my lawyers can and will easily attest to *my very real existence.* On the video, I simply state that after much soul-searching I have decided to make this public appearance to acknowledge the honour people are bestowing on my career and to publicly state that Leen has at all times respected my need and wish for privacy." With a shrug of her shoulders, she says pointedly, "It's all very brief and to the point."

The three of us sit absolutely still, processing what she has said. I look carefully at her, not missing the fact that her blue eyes are sharp but rimmed with dark circles. Aware of our close scrutiny and reacting to the silence in the room, Anna-Claire shifts in her chair and smiles tentatively.

"So Leen knows nothing of the tape?" I mumble, repeating the obvious.

"No. Marc Andre is keeping it until he speaks to the guests."

"Why," Becky asks, "did you make the video and then keep its existence from Leen?"

"Because..." answers Anna-Claire, drawing a breath and taking time to slowly exhale before continuing, "I want Marc to observe what Don Harris says and does at the Gala – how he uses innuendos to discredit Leen and tell people that she has failed to produce me." She grins weakly and I can tell that although she has given careful consideration to her plan, she is exhausted from the energy she has expended. "It's all about timing when dealing with the media. Leen would be the first to acknowledge that I'm right in this. I want to give Harris enough rope to hang himself before Marc reveals the tape."

"But if Marc has the tape, why put yourself through the stress of travelling and the exhaustion that you'll bring upon yourself?" Amy reaches over and touches the top of Anna-Claire's hand. "Leen wouldn't want you to give up your privacy or to risk your health." She looks around the table at our faces and adds, "None of us do."

"I've thought carefully about this," responds Anna-Claire, her jaw set in a determined jut.

"What did Marc say about your making the trip?" asks Becky, her forehead creased in concern. Despite her best effort to control it, her tone indicates the beginnings of anger rooted in suspicion. "Did Marc Andre suggest that you make this trip and risk the possibility of full public exposure to save Leen?"

"He was dead set against it – like all of you," answers Anna-Claire. "In fact, that's why he eventually compromised and agreed to help me."

"Why now?" persists Becky. "After all these years and in your medical condition, why on earth do you want to do this?" Slumping against the back of her chair, she asks, "What do you think Marc Andre is going to say when we show up with you in tow?"

Her answer is simple and direct. "Because now is the time. I've spent forty years of my life reclused from the public or more specifically, from the media." With weary patience she tries to defend her decision. "For forty years I blamed myself for not being with Drew and Emily when they died." She stares at Becky. "You, better than most, should understand how guilt ate at me because I wasn't with my family when they needed me. No ..." she raises her hand like a traffic cop, "that's the truth or at least the truth as I've seen it to be for all these years. I swore that day that I would never again risk losing anyone I loved because I was dealing with the media or the glorification of my career."

"But ..." I try to interject but Anna-Claire simply smiles at me and asks gently, "Just let me finish what I am saying, please."

Biting back my protests, I nod and wait for her to continue.

"This morning I awoke with the realization that a member of my family needs me now..." she taps the table top with two fingers to accentuate her point, "today and tomorrow at the Gala. What I plan to do is the reverse of what I did when Emily and Drew died. It's time for me to meet the media and..." she pauses, taking time to ensure that we are listening, "we all know that there is no better time to do this than on the occasion of the Gala. After that, any benefit of my going public will not help Leen and would be anti-climatic ..."

Paying close attention to our reactions, her eyes show concern for us as well as her need to make us understand the motivation for her decision. "We all know that I'm too ill to think about doing it at any other time. I want to do this because *it will help* Leen. There is no point in my reclusion from the public anymore. It's not enough to have Marc Andre play a video of an old woman sitting in her study. I want to knock Don Harris flat on his lying, sneaky ass. I can't hide the fact that I'm ill from people but I'm counting on their basic compassion that in coming forth to support Leen and to publically thank everyone for the honour they have given to my years of work that they'll not harass me nor interfere with my personal privacy." She lifts her hands, half in surrender and half in admitting that she knows what she is about to bring upon herself. "It's the best that I can hope for."

Becky fingers the cuffs of her white long-sleeved shirt and twists the band of the gold watch around her wrist. I can tell that she's wrestling with thoughts of the many occasions when she's been privy to the thoughts of patients dealing with their own mortality. The process of helping patients to make wise decisions is integral to her line of work; but Anna-Claire is not a patient. She is as much a part of Becky's life as Becky is of Anna-Claire's. Eyes glistening she stands behind Anna-Claire's chair and rests her hand gently on her shoulder. Anna-Claire covers Becky's hand with her own and for a moment they share the unspoken intimacy that exists when love says all.

Anna-Claire is the first to break their silent communication and she does so with a half-turn to face Becky and says simply, "Promise me."

Understanding what is being asked, Becky nods. "I'll do what I can, I promise."

"Then, let's not worry about what cannot be changed and instead, concentrate on what we can do to make the present better." Her gaze travels to Amy and then to me. Slowly we nod our agreement.

Recovering her clinical self, Becky returns to her chair and assumes a matter-of-fact manner. "In a clinical environment, I would try to pursue your line of thinking and determine what your state of mind is." Smiling at Anna-Claire's raised eyebrow and dry smile, she adds, "But this is not my office – this is your kitchen and I can't help but be involved emotionally. All of us," she moves her hand to indicate Amy and me, "have grown to love you. There comes a time in every person's life when decisions are made that others may not understand or even support, but those decisions must be respected. We're just going to have to make sure that the trip doesn't compromise your health. And, you," she wags a finger, "will have to listen to me when I tell you to lie down or to rest. You'll have to remember that I am travelling not only as your friend but also as your physician. Do I have your word on that?"

"And you'll have to let us buffer the crowds for you," says Amy, aligning with Becky's conditions for our compliance.

"The words, 'no comment' will mean exactly that, Anna-Claire," I say firmly, throwing in my support.

The sigh of relief that escapes from Anna-Claire is enormous. Tapping the tabletop with her knuckles, she says, "In the spirit of my new found compliance at letting myself be *bossed* around, which one of you is going to make my travel arrangements?"

Rolling my eyes, I say, "I will." Dryly, I add, "I'm surprised you haven't already done that."

Grinning, she answers, "I would have, but I couldn't remember whether you were leaving on the seven or nine-thirty-five morning flights to New York. Besides," she shrugs her shoulders, "I need to have your flight confirmations so that I can upgrade all of us to first-class."

"What?" exclaims Amy. "You can't be serious?"

"Perfectly serious," answers Anna-Claire, assuming an air of total innocence and glancing at Becky. "Unless I misunderstood all of you – in particular my travelling physician – insist that I do all that I can to conserve my energy and to be well rested. The way I see it ... first-class is the way to travel."

Caught between her own conditions for Anna-Claire's travel and seeing the humour in how she has manipulated us into doing exactly what she had planned, Becky says, "Why do I get the feeling that we've just been played?"

"Not played, dear," answers Anna-Claire, clearly enjoying her moment of levity. "What's wrong with travelling in comfort?"

"Nothing's wrong with it," says Amy, "but we'll pay for our own upgrades."

"Nonsense," answers Anna-Claire. "Let this be my little gift to all of you, Josh and Joe included. I haven't travelled in a few years. It's time that I indulged in a little self-pampering." Glancing at Amy, she says, "I'm sorry."

"About what?" asks Amy, clearly confused at Anna-Claire's apology.

"Without Mike's reservation and confirmation numbers, I can't upgrade his flight from Calgary."

Amy laughs as Becky and I exchange amused glances. "Don't worry about Mike. He'll be just fine."

"Well then, it's settled," says Anna-Claire. "Sarah, I put my passport in my purse. You'll need it to make the flight arrangements to the States." She fixes a pointed stare and adds, "I really mean it when I say that I want to upgrade the flights as my way of saying thank you to all of you for going along with my plans and besides it's only reasonable …"

"What's reasonable?" interrupts Amy.

Anna-Claire stands, makes a half-bow and says tongue-in-cheek, "Shouldn't the object of the Gala arrive in New York in style? After all, I do have to make an appearance …" she thrusts one hand through her hair and feigns hauteur, "in what I trust will be seen as graceful and befitting an author of my stature."

She is so comical in the delivery of her reasoning that we have no choice but to laugh at her antics.

Excited that we have capitulated so quickly to her plans, Anna-Claire lightly claps her hands and says, "Marc Andre and Leen wanted to stay at the hotel but we can stay at my apartment. Unless …" she pauses, "you'd prefer the hotel?"

"Your apartment?" Becky looks at me. "She has an apartment?"

"Of course I do," answers Anna-Claire. "It's a three bedroom one located near Central Park. I bought it years ago to use when I needed to be in New York."

"Do you ever rent it out?" asks Amy.

"No," replies Anna-Claire. "I pay the superintendent, Eric, and his wife, Millie, a monthly fee to look after it for me. Once a month there is a maid service which goes in to air it out and keep the dust at bay. Whenever Marc Andre wants to use it for business trips, I call the maid service and they have people go in to freshen it up. Millie stocks the refrigerator and whatever else is needed before Marc Andre or I arrive."

Sarah asks, " Where do you think you'll be most comfortable?"

Anna-Claire doesn't miss a beat. "The apartment." She smiles. "Now, if you all will be so kind, perhaps we can check out my wardrobe and decide what I should wear."

Standing up, Becky says, "I'm going to call Dr. Anderson and ask him to fax Anna-Claire's file for easy reference, in the event we need medical assistance while in New York." Brow furrowed, she says, "Just to review ... I make all medical decisions, Sarah helps Marc Andre with any legal issues and Amy," she angles her thumb in her direction, "is in charge of talking common sense into you if you ignore Sarah and me."

Lips pursed, Anna-Claire considers Becky's ultimatum. "Done," she says, moving towards the stairway with quick strides.

Becky calls out, "I want complete verbal confirmation."

"Yes, yes," agrees Anna-Claire, already climbing the stairs, "you make medical decisions, Sarah looks after legal matters, and Amy is officially in charge of baby-sitting me. Now, if we're done with setting the rules, I need help with my wardrobe."

We follow her upstairs while Becky makes the call to Dr. Anderson. Seeing that Amy has good control on packing for Anna-Claire, I say, "I'm going home to draft a statement. There's bound to be a lot of demands on Anna-Claire and I want to be ready for that."

Anna-Claire lays a hand on my arm and says, "I would appreciate it, dear, if you'd stay for a few more moments. There is another legal matter on which I would like to have your input."

Puzzled, I wait for her to elaborate. "Just a few minutes," says Anna-Claire, selecting a red cardigan and placing it in her suitcase. "I just want to make sure that I have what I need."

Amy comments under her breath, "It's a good thing that I'm just a simple professor; my job is the easiest because I just get to supervise."

"You think so, do you?" chuckles Anna-Claire "Yours will be a very difficult job, Amy."

Clearly enjoying her moment, Anna-Claire speaks with quiet pleasure. "Tomorrow morning, there will be a news release in the Arts and Literary sections of all major North American papers that Claire Holowitz who has been in seclusion for forty years wishes to acknowledge that Professor Amy Keiffers is her protégé and expects that the same Amy Keiffers is going to be a major player in the field of writing."

Amy flops down on the bed. Stunned by Anna-Claire's announcement, she isn't certain how to respond. For my part, I'm already envisioning the legal blitz Marc Andre and I will have to deal with when the media finds out that Anna-Claire not only will make her presence known at the Gala but that she is publically endorsing a new author.

Amy finally finds her tongue. "But you never even told me what you thought of the last chapters I gave you to read. I thought you didn't like them."

"Really?" Surprise registers on Anna-Claire's face. "What on earth made you think that?"

"I know from reading students' papers and teaching that sometimes in order to help a student revise his or her work, I need some time to think about my approach and how to criticize constructively. I thought you were taking your time to tell me what was wrong with my work."

Anna-Claire stands in front of Amy and says, "What with everything that has been going on, we just haven't had the time to actually sit and talk about your book. But, I did read your chapters. I went over all of it, not as your friend but as an author. I decided to look at your work as if I were writing a critique. I wanted to do that because you are at a stage in your writing where you are moving into ..." she stops, smiles, and rewording her sentence says, "No, what I should be saying is that you have moved past working to be a writer. You have become one. That is what became apparent to me when I put all the chapters together and could see how the story was woven. It's good, Amy ... really good. I sent it to my agent and asked him to have it reviewed by some of his editors. He answered me yesterday. They plan on publishing it; that is, if you agree to the terms." Winking at me, she adds, "That's where you come in."

For a moment, Amy continues to sit dumbfounded by Anna-Claire's announcement. Anna-Claire sits down beside her. "So, that's my announcement. Looks like there will be more than one author 'coming out' at the Gala. Think about it..." she says, excitement in her voice, "the Gala coinciding with my public endorsement of you as an author is a wonderful way to launch a new author."

Within seconds the bedroom is transformed into bedlam with Amy and I jumping up like fools. Shouting over our laughter, Anna-Claire says, "You're going to need a lawyer to represent your interests. I could recommend one that has handled some of my affairs and whom I find to be very ethical. That is unless a certain lawyer thinks that the management of two best-selling novelists might be too demanding."

Smiling broadly, I take a moment to catch my breath and answer, "I need a Loonie to ensure that I'm retained."

"I thought you might say that," answered Anna-Claire, reaching into her pocket and pulling out a Loonie. "Here Amy, use this to retain Sarah."

Taking the Loonie Amy passes it over to me. "Consider yourself retained."

"Done and noted. Wait until Leen hears this one. She's going to be all over the marketing of your book. Oh, Amy," I grab her shoulders, "I am so damned proud of you!"

"So I take it that you'll agree to handle Amy's legal affairs?" remarks Anna-Claire.

"Beyond a doubt."

Standing in the doorway, Becky demands, "What gives with all of the hullabaloo?"

Between spurts of explanation and interruptions from Amy and me, Becky soon understands the reason for our excitement and this time, all four of us are hugging and laughing. Clasping Amy's hands tightly, Anna-Claire says, "You've earned this, my dear, you did it all by yourself. Enjoy the moment."

"Well, I don't know about anyone else," interrupts Becky, smiling at Anna-Claire, "but if we don't' soon get a move on; none of us will be going to New York." Clapping her hands together as if summoning a servant, she says to me, "Enough with the celebrating. Let's go and take care of the arrangements."

Clicking my heels together and snapping a smart salute, I joke, "Always the practical one."

Waving her hand in affectionate dismissal, Anna-Claire says, "You girls go and do what you need to do." Throwing a glance at Amy, she asks, "Are we done here?"

"Just a few more items," answers Amy, heading to the bathroom. "Toothbrush, toothpaste ..."

I tell Amy, "I'll be home within half-an-hour and expecting your phone call. I'll need your flight reservation and confirmation numbers to make the changes to first-class."

Anna-Claire says, "Don't you need my credit card or will a cheque do?" Seeing that I'm about to protest, she says firmly, "Our agreement was that I would listen to you girls: Becky for medical, you for legal and Amy for ..." she laughs, "common sense" but the upgrade to first-class was my treat. An agreement is an agreement. You as a lawyer should know that."

Relenting, I answer, "I'll let you know the costs and you can write a cheque."

"Done," she answers, happily.

As we leave we overhear Amy asking Anna-Claire, "Don't you want to wear something a little more formal tomorrow night." We laugh softly as we hear Anna-Claire respond, "One lesson you're going to learn, once your book becomes the success I know it will become, is that you get to choose what you want to wear and everyone accepts it. I want to be comfortable and besides, they're not expecting me to be there. I can't wait to see Don's reaction when he hears that some old woman in an expensive black pant suit is trying to get into the Gala."

"Sly like a fox," murmurs Becky as we head downstairs. "She's counting on him being upset."

I laugh. "One thing is for sure, she's going to make tomorrow very interesting."

Chapter Thirty-six

Leen

The maid knocks lightly on the door to our suite. Padding across the sitting area in trousers, bare feet, and half-buttoned shirt, Marc opens the door. Pulling in the trolley stacked with items to make-up the room the maid, whose nametag reads Estelle, smiles in response to his greeting.

With a soft accent, she says, "Housekeeping, Sir. I can come back."

"No need," answers Marc. "We'll be leaving shortly. You can start in here."

Pausing to take one more glance in the mirror, I sweep an errant bang to the side of my forehead. Picking up my purse, I walk to the door and wait for Marc who has finished dressing and from my perspective looks fantastic in his new charcoal gray suit. Holding my coat for me, he asks, "Ready?"

"As ready as I'm ever going to be," I answer, slipping on my black leather gloves. "Kathy texted. She says things are moving along as they should be." I check my watch. "She's already been there two hours."

Amused, Marc answers, "That dynamo is probably ordering everyone around as we speak."

"I felt badly about her going in so early," I reply, "but she insisted, saying I should use my time to re-check my notes and the schedule of events." Glancing at him, I add, "Personally, I think she didn't want me underfoot."

"I must say I've enjoyed getting to know Kathy a little better over the last few days," he says as we walk out to the waiting limousine . "She has one heck of a sense of humour and knows how to organize with the finesse of a general commanding troops."

Amused, I say, "She sure can be one determined lady but that is what makes her so good at what she does and, what makes it wonderful for me is that she's my assistant and not Don's."

Opening the limousine door for us Hank, the driver, says, "Good day Ms MacLeen, Mr. Aumount."

Sliding into the back seat of the sleek black Cadillac, Marc whispers, "Mrs. Aumount".

I pat his hand, answering, "We've had this discussion. Professionally, I will continue to use MacLeen; personally, I'll use the hyphenated version of MacLeen-Aumount."

Climbing into the driver's seat, Hank hands us two newspapers and asks if we would care for bottled water or a soft drink from the small fridge that rests behind the front seats.

Answering, "No thanks" for both of us, Marc frowns as he scans the headline in the Arts section of his newspaper. Practically growling, he says, "Looks like Don has made the first move."

I read aloud, "Elusive Claire Holowitz Remains A Mystery". Anger percolating, I say, "That prick has coated his thrust at me by saying that Scenes has done all that it can to bring Claire Holowitz out of seclusion and although she has adamantly refused to attend; Scenes is proud to be affiliated with the celebration of her contribution to the Arts."

Marc folds the paper and places it in his briefcase. Pulling his cell from his suit jacket's pocket, he places a call. Speaking tersely into the receiver, he says, "This is Marc Andre Aumount. Please connect me with Rob Berkenstein." Listening for a moment to the response at the other end, he spits out, "I don't care if he's in a meeting. Interrupt him and tell him I'm holding for his response." Speaking to me, Marc says, "Don is going to hate meeting Rob."

Before I have a chance to ask who Rob Berkenstein is, Marc growls into the receiver. "Did you see the article in the newspaper this morning regarding the Holowitz Gala?"

Scowling, Marc listens to Rob's response. I watch as he bites his lower lip, narrows his eyes, and furrow his brow. Nodding in response to what's being said, Marc smiles. "Sounds good. Do it." Listening again, he answers, "Thanks Rob. I'll wait for your call. I appreciate your being on top of this for me."

Flipping shut his cell phone, Marc explains, "Rob saw the article this morning. He said that he almost choked on his morning coffee and knew that I'd be calling as soon as I saw it." With grim satisfaction, he murmurs, "Harris is about to meet with one of the meanest attorney's in New York or, for that matter, anywhere. He's about to be informed in explicit terms that any further reference to 'significant persons' from Scenes having been unable to convince Claire Holowitz to come out from her seclusion will be viewed as, and I quote, "... causing undue stress to Claire Holowitz's right for privacy and will result in a slander suit for defamation of character."

Frowning, I say, "Nothing that was printed in the paper can be construed as slander."

"Maybe not to you," replies Marc, "but to a lawyer, anything that can possibly harm a client's image is fodder for an argument supporting a suit for slander. Besides," he adds with a devious smile, "it'll make Harris stop and think about his actions. He was warned by Sarah at the Board meeting that Claire Holowitz did not want anything to interfere with her privacy." As far as Rob and I are concerned, Harris' statement is a breach of the agreement reached that night." He puts his arm over my shoulder and gives me a gentle hug. "When Sarah finds out about this she'll attack the article with the ferocity of a shark drawn to blood."

Sighing, I say with a half-hearted attempt at being philosophical, "I've way too much to deal with today. In eight hours the guests will be arriving. In the meantime, Kathy and I have to ensure every last detail is taken care of. I simply can't deal with Harris's underhandedness. Regardless of whether or not you, Rob, and Sarah can throw a wrench into Harris's plans to discredit me, I want this Gala to be a success."

Hank lowers the window partition. "We'll be there in two minutes."

"Thank you," replies Marc. Leaning forward, he reaches into his jacket pocket, takes out a business card, and hands it to Hank. "After we drop off my wife, I'll need you to drive me to this address." Turning to me, he says, "I need to take care of a few things at our New York office."

"No problem, Sir," answers Hank, steering the limousine to the curb. A valet steps out from the entrance and approaches to assist me from the car.

Marc leans out of the car window, causing me to turn back. His voice is gentle as he says, "Do what you have to do today, Leen. It'll be great and I'll be back soon to be with you. In the meantime," he lowers his voice to a cautionary tone, "if you see Harris, don't let him get to you. I promise you, he's about to be hit with a barrage of legal manoeuvring that'll give him nightmares." He waves good-bye as Hank steers the limousine back into traffic. I walk briskly through the front entrance, already focusing on what I have to do.

༄

Kathy

I look up from the clipboard I'm scanning. "Good, you're here."
"Everything okay?"
I can tell from Leen's expression that she is bracing herself for a myriad of problems.
"All-in-all, things are going smoothly," I reply. "Alex, one of the caterers, called to say they will be substituting another type of pastry from the one we originally ordered because there's been a problem with some of the cream fillings." I roll my eyes and gripe, "His big question was how many different types of fruit filling would we like? Like I really care whether it's strawberry, blueberry, or raspberry filling!"
"Lemon's always good," answers Leen.
I snort. "Sure, whatever. Just get them here."
"Has Aisling arrived?"
I pass the clipboard and wait while she glances at it. Satisfied with my checklist, Leen scans the room and asks, "Have you spoken with Aisling yet?"
"Aisling's been in and out all morning," I answer. "It was a good move to put her in charge of all the caterers. She's one Irish fireball." Admiringly, I add, "That girl can charm the crustiest chef and still bark out orders like a general on a battlefield."
"Glad to hear it," answers Leen. "Good find on your part."

Aisling O'Shaughnessy, the delightful owner of "Aisling's Trifles and Canapés" had charmed us with her light lilt and dark Celtic features the minute we met her. She had come highly recommended but neither Leen nor I had been prepared for her youth. Despite being only thirty-three she has become a 'must have' at New York social events. After being told that the Gala was being held in honour of Claire Holowitz, Aisling dropped her professional reserve and said, "I think I've seen every photo she has ever done! And my mother loves her plays." Bordering on gushing, she surprised us saying, "The first Holowitz play I ever saw was "Broken Dreams". My mother bought tickets for my sixteenth birthday."

"Did you enjoy it?" asked Leen, genuinely warmed by Aisling's bubbling enthusiasm.

"Very much so," answered Aisling. "Will Claire Holowitz be attending?"

"No," Leen replied. "She does not attend public functions."

"Do you think she would object to a sampling package of the pastries that will be served this evening? Perhaps someone could give it to her as my way of saying 'thank you' for years of pleasure received from her work?"

Seeing her sincerity, Leen replied that she would arrange for Ms Holowitz to receive Aisling's gift after the Gala.

Now, as we survey the preparations for the Gala, Leen says, "I'm looking forward to seeing Aisling again and tasting more of her canapés."

Turning her attention back to the clipboard, she asks, "Sound technicians?"

"They left about twenty minutes ago saying they needed to get more equipment. I expect them back any minute."

"What about the ice sculptures? Where are they? Have you spoken yet with Jake?"

"See those pedestals," I answer, pointing to workers positioning them throughout the hall. "The guys setting them up are part of Jake's crew. He was here earlier," I say, referring to Jake Aubrey the sculptor hired by Leen, "but he had to leave." I roll my eyes, "Nice guy and friendly enough but when he tried to explain the process he uses to make sure the sculptures won't melt down into puddles of water during the Gala, I told him to 'just do it.' He left these photos for you." Handing them to Leen, I add, "I think everyone will be impressed."

Looking at the photos of the five sculptures she commissioned Jake to create for tonight, Leen says, "He's done a great job. I look forward to hearing the reactions of the guests when they see these sculptures." Handing them back to me, she says, "Hang onto those, please. We can give them to Claire as mementos of tonight. I think she'll be pleased to see how he's sculpted characters from her plays into works of art."

"How about the musicians?" asks Leen. "Everything okay on that front?"

"No problems," I reply, looking at my watch. "I've arranged for a place to store their instruments and expect them within the half hour to arrive for a rehearsal and sound check with the technicians."

"Be sure to remind them that the sound level is to compliment the evening – not control it. I don't want people having to shout over one another to be heard."

"I've already covered that with Phil," I reply, referring to the leader of the band. "He assured me that they're used to playing for this type of event and that we've nothing to worry about."

Gnawing on her lower lip, Leen thinks about what I've said and then, says, "Sorry, I don't mean to be second-guessing everything."

"Not to worry," I answer, "you've got a lot on your plate. It's good to check and re-check things. Who knows?" I say with a shrug. "It's possible that I might overlook something."

"That'll be the day," answers Leen.

Supervising the setup of the hall takes the rest of the morning. Workmen set up the tables to hold trays of meats, fish, salads, and pastries while technicians place cables for sound and lighting. The sound of drills, hammers, and electric saws echo throughout the hall as carpenters erect a stage and other workmen scale ladders to hang large posters of playbills for Claire's plays, photos, and novels. Original photos, placed on stands identical to those found in art galleries, are strategically placed so that guests can enjoy them. Four bar locations are set up and stocked. Lighting and sound systems are checked and re-checked. By the time we're finished, it's hard to believe the transformation. The hall has been turned into something beyond our expectations. Satisfied with the result, Leen says, "If everything else goes according to plan, this Gala will be the talk of New York for a long time."

I have to agree. The hall is magnificent. "Impressive," I say. "Truly impressive. You should be proud Leen. Not one detail has been overlooked."

Drawing in a deep breath she exhales slowly. "We'll have to be sure to get photos of all of this for Claire. I want her to see what's been done in her honour. I hope she'll be pleased."

I touch her elbow and answer, "She will be. Trust me." Glancing at my watch, I say, "Is there time enough left for us to sit in the back office and avail ourselves of a well deserved cup of tea before heading back to the hotel to get cleaned up?"

Rubbing the back of her neck, Leen answers, "Good idea, but we can't take long." She glances at her still-to-do list and adds, "We still have to check in with the various speakers but we can't do that until they have all arrived and ..." she looks up at me, "the security hired for tonight should be here. Where are they? I don't want this hall left unguarded."

In addition to the security regularly attached to the hall, Leen had hired a private firm to protect the many valuable Holowitz mementos, scripts, photos, and collectors' items. She had not wanted to take a chance on anything being accidentally damaged, misplaced, or to leave them unguarded after the guests had left. The publicity for the Gala has been immense and the negative side of that exposure automatically invites possibilities for break and enters.

I point to the group of men and women entering the door. "Right on time. I'll go over and talk with them. Any special instructions?"

Leen smiles. "Review the fact that I want them dressed as if they are guests and not to alert anyone to the fact that they are security."

Laughing, I answer, "Got it. I'll tell them to hide their guns and handcuffs."

"Hah hah," answers Leen. "Now you're a comic?"

"Moonlighting," I reply. Glancing at the stage, I add, "Maybe, I'll do my routine for the guests tonight."

After I'm done talking with security we head to the office for tea with me complaining along the way, "My feet ache. These new shoes are biting at my toes."

Leen laughs. "I thought you liked your new shoes."

"Liking them has nothing to do with them being properly broken in so that I can live in comfort. No wonder people walk around New

York carrying dress shoes in a bag while they go from place to place in runners. Don't know how I'll get my tender tootsies into my heels tonight."

"When we get back to the hotel, a hot bath will help and you'll feel better." Signalling one of the waiters Leen asks him to bring two cups of tea along with a small plate of cheese and crackers. Plunking down onto the brown, leather couch, I remove my offending shoes and begin to massage my toes. Sitting down on the matching armchair, Leen closes her eyes, rests her head back on the headrest, and heaves an exhausted sigh. The waiter arrives with our tray and leaves us to our solitude.

Opening her eyes, Leen reaches for the food. "Eat. You don't know if you'll get a chance to eat much of anything until tonight is over."

Scoffing, I answer, "With all the food that will be available tonight, do you really think either of us will go hungry?"

"Just warning you," says Leen, pouring our tea. "We're going to be busy."

"Not too busy to pop a canapé into my mouth," I retort, helping myself to a cracker and small square of cheddar cheese. "Never never that busy."

Leen is sipping her tea when we hear Marc Andre's voice. "The hall looks amazing!" Entering the room, he presents each of us with a long-stemmed rose. "For my ladies," he says gallantly, "two roses who have bloomed in spite of the thorns that have been in your way."

I blow him a kiss. "You're a thwarted poet, Marc Andre." Breathing in the scent of my rose, I say, "Maybe you could give Tom a few lessons in how to win a woman's heart."

Marc Andre grins. "I don't think he needs any lessons in that department. Seems to me that he's pretty darned proud of you and those kids of yours."

"Oh I'm not denying that, but a rose once in a while would be a nice surprise."

"What would be a nice surprise?" All three of us look up to see who has opened the door. At first I don't believe my eyes. Recovering from my surprise, I jump up from the couch and throw myself into Tom's embrace.

Leen's face is plastered with a big wide grin as she exclaims, "This is a first! Kathy's speechless!"

Shaking hands with Tom, Marc says, "Glad you made it, Tom. You had no problems finding us?"

"None," answers Tom. "One of the security guards stopped me and asked for identification. When I gave him my name, he told me where to find you."

Still reeling with excitement, I ask, "How, when, did you get here?"

"About two hours ago. Marc's driver, Hank, picked me up at the airport, took me to the hotel to drop off my luggage in your room and, after taking a shower to freshen up, I came here." Releasing his arm from my grasp, he asks, "What do you think of your flowers?"

"Flowers?" I step back and realize that all along he's been holding a bouquet in his other hand. Feeling the weight of Marc Andre and Leen's amusement, I widen my eyes and murmur with theatrical flair, "Enough already".

Marc Andre asks, "What do you say Leen? Do they look like flowers to you?"

Using her thumb and index finger to pull on the corners of her mouth, she pretends to consider her answer. "Yep, definitely flowers."

Ignoring their comic sidelines, I say to Tom, "I was so excited about your being here that I didn't even notice them." I bend my head to sniff. "They're beautiful."

Tom answers with a self-conscious shrug and a glance at Leen and Marc. "And I had a bouquet delivered to your suite. To thank you for helping to arrange this for me."

Smiling, Leen replies, "It's our pleasure but I can't take the credit. Marc did all the planning." Wrapping her arm around Marc Andre's waist, she adds, "He filled me in after it was all said and done."

"Thanks, Marc," says Tom, with embarrassed gruffness to his tone.

I'm not so demure. I kiss Marc soundly on the cheek, reaffirming my conviction, "Leen is so lucky to have you!"

Leen grins. "Here's the best part, Kathy. Tomorrow you and Tom will begin two days of New York sightseeing and have a mini-vacation together. You know," she adds mischievously, "for a little of that romance you were referring to just before Tom arrived."

I have the decency to blush at her reminder of my earlier complaints – good-natured but nonetheless complaints – about having Marc Andre instruct Tom in how to reignite romance in our relationship.

"Well, ladies," interrupts Marc Andre, "you have to start thinking about returning to the hotel to get ready for tonight. I suggest you do one last sweep of the place and deal with any last-minute questions or issues before we leave."

His words work like an injection of epinephrine, jettisoning Leen and I into a flurry of action. As we bustle out of the office, Marc Andre and Tom laugh when Leen begins to snap out orders to the workmen.

༄

Marc Andre

Following Leen and Kathy out into the main hall, I point Tom in the direction of one of the bars. "What say we have a drink before we escort them back to the hotel. There's nothing that either of us can do so it's probably a good idea to make ourselves scarce."

"Sounds like a plan to me," replies Tom, as we walk towards the bar. "Do you think they have a good single malt scotch?"

I grin. "I think I'll join you. Never have enjoyed those champagne cocktails they tend to serve at this sort of thing."

I'm leaning against the bar discussing the latest hockey stats with Tom when Don Harris makes his appearance. Spotting us, he briskly brushes the shoulder of his black cashmere sweater and walks towards us with a snarl on his face. He barely approaches before he snaps at me, "What the hell do you think you're doing?"

My peripheral vision takes in the fact that Tom has straightened to his full height and has visibly tensed. Looking at Harris, I casually sip my scotch as I let my eyes rest on him with a deliberate, depreciatory glance. "I have no idea what you're referring to, Harris. My friend and I were enjoying a quiet moment and a good scotch." I jiggle the glass. "That is, until your arrival."

Barely concealing his rage, Harris responds, "You know very well. Sending Berkenstein to see me with some crap about slander and possible defamation not to mention breach of contract." Looking at Tom, Harris demands rudely, "And just who the hell are you?"

From the easy smile on his face, it's obvious that Tom has been enjoying the verbal thrusts between Harris and me and the fact that his presence, as an observer to our exchange, annoys Harris. His earlier combatant stance has relaxed to one of amusement. Taking his time to answer, he finally says, "Tom Burnett."

"Burnett?" Harris's face takes on a quizzical expression. "I don't remember a Burnett being on the guest list."

"Tom's Kathy's husband," I say. "He's here as a guest and at my request for him to be so." I pause long enough to let that fact drill through Harris' anger and add, "One would think that after all the years Kathy has been working at Scenes, the two of you would have met."

"No reason to meet the clerical staff's spouses," retorts Harris, nastily. I notice Tom's hold on his glass tightening and hope that he'll stay calm.

"Who gave you the authority to invite someone without my authorization?" demands Harris.

"Claire Holowitz," I answer, enjoying the clout of Aunt Claire's name. "You know the woman whom you alluded to in this morning's article as being elusive and, if innuendo serves correctly, whose absence threatens to spoil the success of a Gala being held to honour her work."

Done toying with Harris, I place my glass on the counter and square my shoulders; making it clear that his presence is an annoyance.

Furious at my obvious dismissal, Harris spits out contemptuously, "I have more important things to do then be baited by you Aumount." His lips twist into a snarl as his eyes dart from me to Tom and back to me. "Like supervise your wives to make sure that everything is done properly." Neither Tom nor I bother to answer. Turning on his heel, Harris storms off in Leen's direction calling out her name.

Tom remarks, "Kathy says that he's a real ass."

"Your wife," I answer with a sardonic grin, "is a good judge of character." Immediately, my mood changes as I recognize the tall, greyhaired man coming through the doors. "Come on," I say, "Taylor Jones has just walked in. You'll like him."

"Who's he?" asks Tom as we walk across the hall to greet Jones.

"A long-time and very good friend of Aunt Claire's. He's directed several of her plays and is one of the guest speakers tonight." We get there just as Kathy has finished greeting him. Shaking his hand warmly, I say, "Good to see you again Taylor."

Taylor returns my handshake with a firm and friendly one of his own. "Marc Andre, how very nice to see you again; you're doing well?"

"Doing very well," I answer, as Leen approaches. Smiling, I say, "I believe you've met my wife and this gentleman," I nod towards Tom, "is Tom Burnett, Kathy's husband."

Taylor's eyes widen at the mention of Leen being my wife but he absorbs the news with characteristic aplomb and extends his congratulations before shaking hands with Tom.

Taylor says, "I came, my dear, to see if there were any last minute changes to the programme for tonight."

Since meeting him in Toronto, Leen has mentioned on several occasions how much she genuinely enjoys Taylor's comments and wit. I'm not at all surprised when she smiles fondly and answers, "Taylor, I'm so pleased to see you and thrilled that you agreed to speak tonight."

Seemingly out of nowhere, a waiter approaches with a glass of champagne. Taking it, Taylor says, "Thank you my good man. Just what I needed." He sips, looks at me and says, "Nothing like a good glass of champagne. You should try it."

"Tom and I have just come from the bar," I smile. "And how did the waiter know that you'd like champagne."

Taylor looks at me and with a comical expression answers, "My dear Marc Andre, after knowing me all these years, do you really think I don't know how to order a glass of champagne?" Smug, he raises the fluted glass and adds, "I told the security officer that if a bar was set up, a glass of the champagne would go down well."

"By the time this night is over," grins Leen, "I'll need something a bit stiffer. Kathy has the updated programme and the sound techs are here so if you want to speak with them, that would be great."

Kathy directs her gaze to the flurry of activity happening at the entrance. More waiters are arriving and Aisling O'Shaughnessy is busy issuing orders.

When reviewing the details for the Gala, Leen had explained Aisling's plan to have the waiters and chefs arrive in ample time to, as she had delightfully put it, "Rehearse, yet again, how to serve; how to charm; and how to ensure that all guests will be well fed, watered; and catered to." When Leen questioned her plans for a rehearsal Aisling had merely chuckled, saying, "I can see that you're not acquainted with the preparations necessary in my world. An actor rehearses; a doctor reviews before surgery; and a chef ..." she had winked, "a good one that is, oversees all things having to do with her or his kitchen."

Addressing Taylor, Kathy says, "It was a pleasure to finally meet you but if you will excuse me, I need to speak to the sound techs. I can hear the warning signs of feedback coming from one of the speakers." Casting a glance at Leen, she adds, "We have to leave in ten minutes, Leen. Any later and we won't be able to make it back here in time to greet the guests."

"Pleasure was all mine," Taylor responds warmly. "I hope to chat with you again before the evening is over."

"We'll be ready," calls out Leen, as Kathy walks away.

Ten minutes later, Tom and I are herding our wives and Taylor towards the door. "Just one more thing…" says Leen but I kibosh her protest saying, "Hank is waiting to take us back to the hotel and then to whisk us back here." Winking over the top of her head at Tom who is gently pushing Kathy out the door, I joke, "They're about to become our Cinderellas dressed for the ball."

"I'm going to have to take lessons," Tom remarks. "Where do you get these lines?"

Nodding to the valet to signal for a taxi, Taylor says, "I'm off." Leaning forward to kiss Leen's cheek, he reassures her, "It'll be a wonderful evening, Leen. And while you and Kathy are mingling tonight, I'll keep an eye on your husband and lend a hand in helping Tom, here, develop a repertoire of lines."

"Don't let my husband lead you astray tonight," jests Leen.

I walk Taylor to his taxi. Resting his hand on the door handle, he asks, "Is everything alright Marc?"

"Never could hide anything from you, could I, Taylor?"

Tightening his scarf around his throat, he says, "A good director misses nothing about the actors in a scene. Now," he lets his piercing grey eyes rest on my face, "tell me is there anything I can do?"

"Keep an eye out for Leen tonight," I answer, truthfully. "She's put a lot into this Gala." I look down the street at the passing cars. "Harris is still griping about Aunt Claire not making an appearance."

Taylor lets out a groan of disgust. "Yes, I read that article this morning and figured that was his doing." Tapping me on the shoulder, he says, "Not to worry, Marc. Leen has made many friends throughout her search for Claire and not one of us would ever let that odious man hurt her." Climbing into the taxi, he waves a jaunty goodbye and calls out to Leen and the others waiting by the limousine. "Off to work my own miracle. Tom, do you think there's an equivalent of the Cinderella effect for men?" Laughing at his humour, he rolls up his window as the cab drives into traffic.

Throughout the entire drive back to the hotel, Kathy and Leen work in comfortable synchronization of thoughts. As we step out of the limo and make our way to the elevator, Tom says in a low voice, "They work well together, don't they?"

"Like pieces of well-oiled machinery," I agree.

Chapter Thirty-seven

Marc Andre

Looking resplendent, Leen stands in the receiving line, greeting people warmly as they enter the hall.

Not missing my silent appraisal of my wife, Taylor comments, "Classic black dress adorned simply with tasteful gold jewellery." Glancing her way, he says with frank appreciation, "She looks smashing. Well done, Marc!" Slightly nudging my elbow, he teases, "I must admit I was surprised today to find out that you and Leen were married. Considering how long I have known you; I would have thought that I'd be informed of that development."

I grin. "It just sort of happened Taylor. As you so bluntly informed me after meeting her in Toronto, she is a dynamo. Before I knew it, I was happily marching down the aisle." Turning to face him, I add, "You were out of the country at the time of the wedding and couldn't be reached."

Eyes dancing with merriment, Taylor answers, "Who would have thought a perpetual bachelor like you would fall fast and hard?" Casting a glance in Tom's direction, Taylor asks, "Was it a long engagement?"

Enjoying Taylor's jovial taunts, Tom plays along. "It happened so fast, I barely had time to iron my dress shirt." His answer earns him a hearty laugh of approval.

Murmuring softly, Taylor says, "Claire must have loved this!"

I shrug. "You know Aunt Claire. She's taking the credit for introducing Leen and me."

Helping himself to a canapé of smoked salmon and dill cream, Taylor's smile borders on being a leer as his gaze appreciatively follows the waitress as she walks towards another group. "Looks like there's quite a crowd here tonight," he comments, biting into the canapé. "Is that Trevor Hinton arriving?" He squints and, without any attempt to conceal his curiosity, asks, "Who is that delightful morsel clinging to his arm?"

I follow his gaze to where a tall, robustly built man is entering the hall accompanied by a woman half his age. It's easy to see why she has grabbed Taylor's attention. She has a model figure and is dressed to accent all her physical qualities.

"No idea," I answer, grinning, "but knowing you, you're about to find out."

"That is exactly the plan, my dear Marc Andre," Taylor murmurs. "I think I'll mosey on over there and compliment Trevor on the long-running of his new play." Winking, he says, "Personally, I found it to be rather dull at points but since I can't think of another way to get an introduction, I'll put on my best theatrical face." He sighs deeply. "All in the interests of pursuing the fairer sex."

I laugh. "You don't think he'll see through your ploy to meet his companion?"

Placing his hand on his chest and feigning hurt at my suggestion, Taylor answers, "Well, she obviously likes talent because she's with Trevor and as everyone knows, he plays in the big leagues as far as theatre goes. I'm going to give her a chance to meet theatre's royalty."

Dutifully, I bow my head. "Good-luck, Your Majesty."

He teases, "Humility suits you Marc Andre – you should try it out more often."

Tom and I are still smiling at Taylor's hasty retreat when a woman addresses us. "Mr. Aumount," she begins as she approaches. "My name is Stacey Dinardo and I'm with The New York Times."

Cautiously, I extend my hand in greeting. She, like many of the women here tonight, is dressed in a black dress but has added a small red jacket to cover her shoulders. Her smile is genuine and her eyes – the colour of sapphires with flecks of grey – are bright and alert.

Overall, my first impression is that she is a woman confident in her looks but has the good sense not to flaunt them in tasteless exposure.

"Ms Dinardo, this is Mr. Burnett." Stacey extends a hand to Tom and says, softly, "A pleasure to meet you, "Mr. Burnett."

Social pleasantries over, I put my question to her as straightforwardly as possible. "What can I do for you Ms Dinardo?" I knew the press was bound to be at the Gala but I had expected them to be circulating the room looking for the rich and famous, angling for exclusive interviews.

My bluntness does not cause her to lose her composure. Smoothly she replies, "Rumours are abounding throughout the hall that you and Adrienne MacLeen are married." Her grey eyes narrow slightly, giving her the effect of a shrewd observer.

"They're not rumours, Ms Dinardo."

She flashes a brilliant smile. "Congratulations. Would you care to comment as to whether or not Ms MacLeen has met Claire Holowitz?"

Tom bristles at the thrust of Stacey Dinardo's line of questioning. Calmly, I reach for an hors d'ouevre on the tray presented by a passing waiter. Biting into a shrimp roll, I take my time to savour the flavour. Wiping my mouth with a napkin, I answer, "No comment."

Trying to appease what is quickly turning out to be an awkward situation, Tom interrupts. "Marc, I believe you said you wanted to have some time to greet guests before the speeches take place." Making a pretence of looking at his watch, he says, "If you start now, you'll have just enough time before the formal part of this evening's programme."

Astute enough to realize that she's being dismissed, Dinardo smiles. "Gentlemen, I am not the enemy."

Keeping my voice level but knowing that the tone is coldly polite, I answer, "No one suggested you were, Ms Dinardo. Mr. Burnett is simply reminding me that as one of Claire Holowitz's representatives here tonight I must not be remiss in my duties."

"Please, Mr. Aumount," presses Dinardo when we begin to walk away. "You have to listen me."

I stop, turn, and ask abruptly, "And why exactly do I have to listen to you?"

Her cheeks colour and her eyes snap but she answers, "I wanted to inform you that Mr. Harris has asked the press here tonight to meet with him after the Gala. He states that it will be an 'off the record' session."

"And why would you want to make that any of my business?" I answer, inwardly steaming and already planning how I'm personally going to take care of Harris.

Her answer surprises me. "Because Don Harris has always been a rude, pompous man." She hesitates and then says, "And, because my mother used to tell me stories about Claire Holowitz."

Her answer arrests my anger long enough for me to seriously wonder what her real agenda is for talking to me. Seeing that she has my attention, she says, "All I am asking is for five more minutes of your time." Her eyes sweep the hall. "Somewhere where we can talk more privately."

Tom and I stare at her for a long moment but she doesn't flinch. "Fine," I finally agree, "but Mr. Burnett will remain. I want this conversation to be witnessed just in case you have second thoughts about what you're going to say to me."

Dinardo gaze flickers over Tom. "I have no objection. All I ask is that you listen to what I have to say and then, respect the fact that should either of you disclose my information, I might never work again in New York. Or," she adds meaningfully, "with any newspaper."

Scowling, I answer, "That begs the question as to why you would jeopardize your future to divulge information to me." My years of cross-examining witnesses intuitively lead me to believe that despite my reservations, she is a reliable and highly credible source. Grudgingly, I admit to myself that if nothing else, she has spunk.

Moving to the closest bar, we choose three stools away from where other guests have gathered. To any onlooker, it will look at if we are merely enjoying a sociable moment together. Conversations and laughter mix with the music in the air as guests take advantage of refreshments, admire the ice sculptures, and strategically placed Holowitz photos and exhibits.

Sipping her Merlot, Dinardo says, "My mother has told me many stories about Claire Holowitz but the most important one is how Claire Holowitz personally helped her."

I wait for her to continue but when she doesn't, I say, "I don't recall the name Dinardo ever entering into any conversation I've had with Claire Holowitz."

"Perhaps the name Ruby Myles will ring a bell?" answers Dinardo.

Intrigued with how she is leading into her story, I reply, "Ruby Myles, the lead actress in Claire's first play?"

"She's my mother."

"What?"

"I said she's my mother."

"I know what you said," I answer. "Why did you not say so before?"

She laughs softly. "I wanted you to take me seriously – as a reporter – not a name dropper."

"Consider it done," I answer, placing my glass down on the counter. "Now, tell me why Stacey Dinardo, Ruby Myles daughter, is willing to risk her journalism career."

"My mother never forgot how Claire Holowitz sat in on her audition and how – because of Claire's insistence – she got the part of Allie. They've remained friends throughout the years and yes, Mr. Aumount as you know, Ruby Myles is well aware of Claire Holowitz's identity."

Responding to the truth of her statement and the sincerity in her tone I can't sense any deception. Yet, a question burns in the back of my mind. Well aware of Aunt Claire's affection for Ruby and, having met Ruby on more than one occasion at Aunt Claire's home, I say, "If you've known all along about Claire Holowitz's private identity, why have you not divulged it to your newspaper?"

Dinardo reaches into her purse and withdraws an envelope. Taking it from her, I open it and pull out a recent photo of Ruby and Aunt Claire taken in Aunt Claire's living room.

Reaching again into her purse, Dinardo takes out her cell and holds it in her hand. "Mother was unable to come tonight, Mr. Aumount. As you know she has been battling lung cancer. She asked me to tell you personally that she sends her best wishes to Ms Holowitz. That was my original plan – to simply convey her best wishes for the Gala's success.

"But ..." interrupts Tom.

Dinardo bites on her lower lip and then, addressing both of us, she says, "When Don Harris informed the media that an off-the-record interview would be granted after the Gala – one in which you and Ms MacLeen would be excluded – I called my mother and asked her what she thought I should do. She thought, as I did, that Harris' little backroom politics with the media sounded ominous and she directed me to convince you to speak with her." She taps out a phone number and hands me her cell. "She's waiting to hear from you."

Taking her cell phone, I say, "I'm going to the office for a minute. Take care of the lady, will you Tom?"

༶

Tom

I'm the first to speak. "That was a gutsy move, Ms Dinardo. He could just have easily asked security to have you removed."

Grimacing, she says, "Why would he do that? Mother said he has a reputation for being sharp and that I could convince him I was the real thing."

Eying a waiter with a fresh tray of canapés, I signal for him to come over. Stacey has just ordered us fresh drink and I'm finishing my third stuffed Portabello mushroom when Marc Andre returns.

Smiling warmly, Marc returns her cell. "Your mother sends her greetings."

"Thank you," she replies, slipping the cell back into her purse. "I don't know if the meeting Harris has called is of any importance but to exclude two of the principal persons charged with Holowitz's endorsement for this evening alerted what my mother has always referred to as my 'nosy sense'. Something about it just smelled to me."

"I appreciate your 'nosy sense', Ms Dinardo," replies Marc Andre, his tone sincere and sombre. "And, I'm certain so will Claire Holowitz."

Dinardo smiles. "Well, it looks like my mission has been accomplished. Now," she says, looking out at the crowd, "I'd better try to mingle and get some titbits for my newspaper's Arts and Literary Events spread they're planning on running with the morning edition."

I stick out my hand. "It's been a pleasure to meet you."

"And mine, to meet you," replies Dinardo. Looking at Marc Andre, she says, "Perhaps when you or Ms MacLeen are willing to give an exclusive interview, you will consider letting me report it?"

Marc Andre responds, "You have my word, Ms Dinardo."

"Please," she answers as she starts to leave, "call me Stacey."

"Only if you call me Marc."

"Well good-bye Marc. I'll tell mother that you are definitely as sharp as she said you were." With just the tiniest sound of what I think is a giggle, she moves away and strikes up a conversation with a group of well-known actors.

"That was interesting," I comment, as soon as she's left.

"Very," answers Marc Andre. "Nice girl. Her mother said to take care of her."

"What's that supposed to mean?" I ask, as we walk across the room.

"She took a chance on giving us the heads up tonight," replies Marc, smiling hello to people as we walk by. "If Harris finds out that she forewarned us, he'll try to get her fired. At the very least, he'll put out the word that she's not to be trusted. It could destroy her career and reduce her to working for rag magazines. One thing I can definitely make happen," he adds, "is make certain she gets an exclusive interview from me when this night is over."

"Aumount, damn it's good to see you!"

Marc Andre turns to see who is calling to him and a genuine smile lights his face as he recognizes the voice's owner. Shaking hands with a tall man who looks like he could have had a career as a professional quarter back, Marc Andre makes the introductions. "Tom, meet Gale Thomas. Gale, this is a good friend, Tom Burnett."

Gale pumps my hand. "Anyone who is a friend of Marc Andre's is a friend of mine." Addressing Marc, he says with genuine pleasure, "The photos I sent over from the gallery look spectacular. Your charming wife has created an ambiance that does Claire proud – the right combination of mystery and illusion."

"She told me that you were a great help, Gale."

"She was easy to work with," replies Gale, dismissing Marc Andre's praise. He motions with his hand, "Judging by how the photos have been displayed with the proper attention to lighting and positioning, it looks like she and her assistant paid attention to my advice."

Marc says, "Tom is Kathy's husband."

Regarding me with new interest, Gale remarks with humour, "Your wife must keep you on your toes. We had our differences but I'll work with her anytime." I suppress a smile as I recall Kathy complaining about having to work with a big, blustering blow-hard. "She can be a tough task master," continues Gale. Sniffing with amusement, he says,

"She actually argued with me about how to display Claire's Whispering Hope. Funny thing," he adds with good humour, "after I got over her audacity, I actually liked her idea."

After promising to meet up later, Gale moves on to chat with some people he recognizes and I relate to Marc Kathy's initial complaints and play on Gale's name.

Amused, Marc says, "Yeah, I can see how those two would have locked horns. He's a great guy but can be pretty passionate about his work. He and Aunt Claire have been friends for years."

Leen is chatting with a petite woman with hints of what must have once been sandy blond hair in her grey hair. Smiling at Marc, Leen says, "Edna and I were just talking about how the two of you met." Indicating me, she says, "Edna, you've met my assistant Kathy. This is Tom, her husband. Tom, Edna's from New Westminster, British Columbia. Claire used Edna's bookstore to launch one of her novels."

Soft-spoken, Edna's eyes dance with genuine pleasure as she says, "It's good to see you again, Marc Andre." Acknowledging me, she says, "I've had many enjoyable discussions with your wife over the last year in preparation for tonight's Gala."

"I hear your bookstore is doing well," says Marc Andre.

Edna beams with pleasure. "Excellently, thank you." Looking at me, she says, "Ms Holowitz helped my store to get some recognition and well-needed help."

Marc Andre interjects, "She was glad to do it and let's not forget that it was you who impressed Claire when she came into your store."

Edna laughs. "I have been asked so many times what meeting Claire Holowitz was like and people are always surprised when they hear that although she launched a novel from my store, I've never actually met her."

"You're not alone in that," I reply. "Most of the people here tonight know her by reputation or through representation by Marc or someone else close to her.

Leen says, "Edna's one of our speakers tonight. Her story will help to reinforce not only Claire's literary and photographic genius but her celebration of life and people."

"She's always been an advocate for the 'giving back' philosophy," says Marc Andre, with quiet pride.

470

From the corner of my eye, I can see Kathy locked in a discussion with two sound technicians. From her intense expression and the movement of her hands, I gather that she's making a point. Marc Andre notices it too and says to Leen, "I think we'll go over to see what Kathy's being so intense about."

Leen looks to where Kathy is positioned near the stage. "She's probably prepping them for the speeches," remarks Leen, shrewdly. But, just in case it's more than that, I'd appreciate it if the two of you check things out." Smiling at me, she adds, "Your job is to smooth any ruffled feathers she might have."

"Life-long job," I joke.

Excusing ourselves from Edna, we make our way to the stage. On the way, Marc Andre comments, "Edna's a good person. Aunt Claire was genuinely impressed with her."

"And she never caught on that she was talking with her?" I give my head a small shake. "I wonder how many people here tonight have had similar experiences with Claire and not realized it at the time."

"Quite a few," answers Marc Andre, truthfully. "Seclusion might have been her way to deal with the media but as far as life goes, she has always been out in the forefront enjoying every minute."

"Everything alright?" asks Marc Andre, as we approach.

"We're just going over the timing for the musicians to stop playing," answers Kathy, "and the changes to be made to the lighting and sound for the speeches." Addressing the sound technician with the cleanly-shaven head, she motions to Marc and says, "Tim, if you have any questions, this is the man to ask."

Facing Marc Andre, Tim says, "The audiovisual crew will drop the screens from the ceiling and fill them with the digital images we've been given." He checks with his clipboard notes. "Who will be cuing us for when you want the transitions between images to happen?"

"That'll be me," says Kathy. To Marc Andre, she says, "Leen and I have reviewed the order of the photos but Tony and Eric..." she points to two of the technicians, "are responsible for the use of any effects in their display."

Marc Andre begins to discuss with Tony and Eric their ideas for the synchronization and display of the photos but the conversation is interrupted when his cell phone rings. Flipping it's cover, Marc listens carefully. Thinking his intense expression is due to having to listen over the background noise in the room, I listen as Kathy picks up where Marc Andre left off and reviews the details with Tony.

Returning his cell phone to his pocket, Marc Andre informs us, "That was Sarah. She and the others have been held up in traffic but she says to go ahead as planned at eight and they'll sneak their way in."

Leen who has just joined us, rolls her eyes. "Sarah had better never tell me again that I'm the one who is always late." Addressing Kathy, she says, "We'll start as planned but make a few adjustments to the order of the speakers. Don will open with a welcome from Scenes, followed by me. I'll introduce Edna who will introduce Taylor who will introduce Gale. She works her way down the list summing up with, "That should give them the time they need to get here. Then Marc can make the speech on behalf of Claire Holowitz. What do you think?"

Kathy nods, already writing in the changes to the agenda. Tony and Eric leave to make last-minute checks on their equipment. Under her breath, Kathy groans. "His lordship is on his way over. He's all yours," she says tersely.

Dressed in a black tuxedo, Harris is the image of a successful Director of a multi-million dollar advertising firm. In spite of myself, I have to admit that he carries out his role with marked finesse. He's moving his way through the room with ingratiating smoothness as he accepts congratulations for the evening. The smile on his face fades as he says to Leen, "It would seem that everyone appreciates all the hard work we've done for the Gala."

From where I'm standing, I have a good view of what Kathy calls 'Leen's professional mask'. Anyone watching would never suspect the animosity she has for Don and the trouble he has caused. As for him, his words may be innocuous but the look he gives Leen reminds me of one of Kathy's favourite nicknames for him; snake eyes.

Leen answers Harris, "I was just about to have Cheryl give the musicians and technicians a five minute cue. Kathy has already spoken to the speakers and they'll be ready."

"Fine," says Harris, smoothing his jacket with a hand, "I'll be waiting over there."

Leen signals to Cheryl, a senior staffer from Scenes' offices in Toronto, who was asked to assist with the Gala.

"Have you been able to convince her to transfer to Ottawa?" asks Kathy.

"Not yet, but I'm working on it," answers Leen, as Cheryl approaches. "Cheryl, would you please inform the musicians that we're about to start the formal part of the programme. You'll need to cue them when to play their last song and then again, after the speeches are finished, to resume. We'll need all sound and video technicians ready to go on cue."

Turning to Kathy, Leen says, "Time to get the speakers over here."

Speaking into a microphone attached to the lapel of her jacket, Cheryl says, "Five minutes and on cue." Smiling at Leen and Kathy, she says, "I'll be over there with Tony and Eric. Don't worry, everything's under control."

As planned, the drummer taps out a drum roll as eight screens drop down from the ceiling, hanging at various points throughout the room with one becoming a focal point on the stage. The lighting in the room changes and the screens are lit with images of Holowitz photos. There's an immediate and audible gasp of appreciation from the guests.

Chest puffed, Harris steps up to the podium. "Ladies and gentlemen," he begins with a wide smile, "it is my marked privilege to welcome you here tonight on behalf of the consortium of Arts communities from New York, Toronto, London, and Ottawa. These people spearheaded this Gala in honour of Claire Holowitz's contributions to the Arts. I would like to take a few moments to acknowledge some of the key contributors and initial visionaries for the Gala." Guests applaud as he rattles off names.

I overhear Leen remarking to Marc Andre, "I hope that Sarah, Becky and Amy get here soon. I'd love for them to see Don in action."

Harris's speech lasts fifteen minutes – five minutes over the time allotted. His introduction of Leen notably excludes any recognition of her title and job description at Scenes. "Now, I will turn you over to Adrienne MacLeen whom, under my direction, has ensured this evening is a success."

Not giving any indication of his slight, Leen walks up to the podium and smiles. Marc Andre and I grin at one another as the hall breaks out in thunderous applause. The hearty reception of her leaves no doubt that Leen has earned the respect of the guests, speakers, and contributors to this evening and that they have a genuine liking for her. Shading her eyes from the spotlight, Leen says, "Welcome to all of you." She lowers her hand as Tony makes an adjustment to the positioning of the light's beam and continues smoothly, "Before I go any further, I would like to reiterate Don's appreciation to the consortium for their initiative in helping to highlight the career of Claire Holowitz." With perfect timing, she lowers her voice just a hint and says, "Over the last year, I have been asked many times about my search for Claire Holowitz and tonight I would like to talk about the woman whom everyone here tonight has come to honour."

"What's she doing?" snipes Harris at Marc Andre. "She's not supposed to be talking about a search for which there was no fruition."

Pointedly ignoring him, Marc Andre concentrates on Leen as she continues. "Claire Holowitz has consistently exercised her right to privacy but in the course of learning about her, I have had the opportunity and privilege to meet some amazing people with equally amazing stories of her kindness, philanthropy, and love of life. The search for Claire Holowitz and the people whom I have met as a result of that search have enriched my life." Applause breaks out throughout the room. Proud, Marc watches as his wife works her way through her speech with aplomb.

༄

Sarah

Standing at the curb, I wait for Anna-Claire. The taxi had been Anna-Claire's idea. Her plan was simple – to arrive unannounced. Originally, Marc Andre had arranged for us to be picked up by his New York driver – someone named Hank – but Anna-Claire had nixed that idea saying, "A limousine invites attention whereas a taxi does not." Extending my hand I help Anna-Claire steady herself as she clamours out from the taxi. Joe props one hand underneath her elbow, allowing her time to steady herself.

Anna-Claire's blue eyes dart to the group of five photographers standing at the front doors. Smiling with satisfaction, she says in an undertone, "Notice how not one of them is lifting a camera. Told you, a taxi was the right move. They all think that an old woman is just coming to be part of the festivities." Becky, Josh, Mike, and Amy join us and we start to make our little procession to the entrance.

"I thought that was what you wanted," says Becky. "To enter without being seen or photographed."

"Exactly what I wanted," answers Anna-Claire. One of two women photographers squints at Anna-Claire and for a moment I think she might try to take a photo or ask a question but her gaze is quickly averted when one of the other photographers says something.

"See how simple that was," remarks Anna-Claire, as we enter the main foyer. "They're looking for a photo op of a celebrity, not Anna Wright." Smug, she says, "That's always been the secret to my successful seclusion. I was often present at affairs but never recognized due to how I changed my looks, dress, and timed my entrances. Of course," she admits with a tiny shrug, "aging helped. For the first few years, I had to be very cautious but age and its alteration to how one looks greatly assisted in my ability to be incognito. The media were always looking for the old Claire Holowitz – the one associated with fame. So I did what wasn't expected; I made myself obvious but so *normal* in dress and appearance that I wasn't worthy of being a target for a journalist or photographer's notice."

Becky remarks dryly, "Anna-Claire, you continue to amaze me. On one hand, you are an extremely complex woman and yet, on the other hand, you are incredibly down-to-earth and unpretentious. Just when I think I understand how *you think*, you throw in a comment or do something that has me right back where I started."

"And that would be?" asks Anna-Claire.

"That would be not knowing what to expect from you," I fill in.

"Are you ready, Anna-Claire?" asks Becky as we near the Gala's reception area.

Smiling softly, gaze fixed on the door to the hall, Anna-Claire answers, "You advised Marc that I was here?"

"Yes," I answer. "He promised to say nothing to Leen. When I called, Harris was just wrapping up his speech."

Mike says, "I can't believe I'm actually going to be watching history in the making." Squeezing Amy's hand he remarks, "Who would have thought that being snowed in at the Ottawa airport on Christmas would bring me the privilege of escorting Claire Holowitz to her first public appearance in over forty years? By the way," he winks at Anna-Claire, "I'm still counting on your agreement to take Amy's and my formal wedding portrait."

His comment, spoken with such sincerity, releases any tension any of us may feel about Anna-Claire's plans for her appearance at the Gala.

She looks at him and answers, "Anything for any of my girls." Glancing at the rest of us, she straightens her shoulders, draws in a breath and says, "Show time. I expect that an unannounced guest whose name is absent from the guest list will cause a commotion with the security people."

I catch Becky's worried glance at Amy. Smiling tightly, Amy silently acknowledges Becky's unspoken fears. We are about to cause an upheaval in an evening that is supposed to be a pinnacle achievement in Leen's career. But, as we enter, Joe is already waiting with a man dressed in a grey suit and they discreetly lead us to where we can stand without drawing attention to our presence. The security officer says, "Mr. Aumount asked that I assist you in any way possible."

We stand at the back of the room, unnoticed by other security personnel who, thinking that everyone on the guest list is present, have riveted their attention to the video Anna-Claire made and which is now being aired for everyone.

Along with everyone else in the hall, I watch as Anna-Claire, sitting in the comfort of her high-backed easy chair, is thanking the consortium for this honour and acknowledging various individuals including Taylor Jones and Gale Thomas for their support throughout the years. She is just in the middle of saying, "I understand that there has been some controversy about my decision to remain secluded from public life ..." when one of the ushers nudges a passing waiter who in turn signals to another waiter before pointing to where we stand. Their actions attract the attention of people standing nearby and I tense as heads turn to actively stare at us. In rapid motion, heads turn back to the video and bob back to recheck what they've seen. Before I know it's happening, I hear someone shout, "She's here!" The video on the screen is quickly forgotten as all attention in the hall rivets on Anna-Claire.

Harris gapes in Leen's direction but Leen is already down off the stage and briskly striding towards us. Marc Andre signals for the audio-visual techs to stop the video and walks up to the vacated podium. Speaking into the microphone over the hubbub of excited whispers and exclamations, he announces proudly, "Ladies and Gentlemen, it is my immense pleasure to present Claire Holowitz."

Josh and Joe position themselves at Anna-Claire's side while Mike and the security officer lead our little procession towards the stage. The crowd parts almost as if she's Moses crossing the Red Sea. Leen meets us halfway. Josh and Joe step aside to make room for Leen who takes Anna-Claire's elbow and resumes the escort of her to the stage. Marc Andre meets them at the top of the steps and bends to kiss Anna-Claire on the cheek, saying, "Your timing is impeccable." All eyes in the room follow him as he assists her to the podium.

The second she stands in front of the podium, the hall becomes so silent I think *A pin could drop and it would sound like an echo*. Hands resting on either side of the podium, Anna-Claire looks out at the audience. Becky and I exchange nervous glances, wondering if she will have the strength to continue. With a wary smile, Anna-Claire bows her head just enough to acknowledge everyone in the room. Facing the crowd directly, her expression reveals how overwhelmed she is. Eyes glistening, she speaks into the microphone. "I do not have the words to express my sincere appreciation for the honour you have bestowed upon me. Anyone involved in the Arts knows that achievement and success is largely dependent upon the acceptance and approval of one's audience. It is I who should be honouring all of you because you have made it possible – throughout the years – for me to, in my own small way, contribute to a world of imagination and creativity. It has been because of your love for the written word and the transfer of the images of the life that surrounds us through the medium of photography that I have been able to achieve some measured success." She pauses to take a breath and wait for the applause to die down.

"As I look throughout this hall, I see so many familiar faces and know that my life has been enriched because of your multiple talents. Some very dear and old friends are here who have, for forty years, worked diligently to protect what some refer to as my 'seclusion' from the world."

My chest swells with pride as I listen to the words she speaks and admire the poise and grace she presents as she talks to the audience.

"She's really something, isn't she?" murmurs Becky.

"No kidding," I answer, returning my attention to Anna-Claire.

"Before I continue," smiles Anna-Claire, "I would be remiss if I did not publically thank Taylor Jones, Gale Thomas, my godson and nephew Marc Andre Aumount, and two other persons very close to my heart, Marc Andre's father Emile and my dear friend Ruby Myles."

Anna-Claire waits for the loud applause to die down as members of the media push to the front and photographers – who have until now refrained from taking photos – begin to snap photos.

"Who's Ruby Myles?" asks Amy, looking at Becky and me.

"An old friend of Aunt Claire's," replies Marc Andre who standing beside Amy has overheard her question. He puts a warning finger to his mouth and says, "I'll explain more later on. In particular, how she has helped out tonight."

Curious but knowing that we're not going to learn anything more until later, I say to Marc Andre, "She's holding her own but we might want to make certain that the media doesn't' tire her too much."

Nodding agreement, Marc quickly makes his way back to the stage. Photographers ready their cameras for a shot of him and Anna-Claire standing together. He moves to step in front of the microphone but Anna-Claire rests a hand on his forearm, stopping him from taking control. Looking out at the reporters and photographers she says, "I can see that you want my picture and have questions. Please, I ask you to refrain for the moment." Flashing a winning smile, she adds, "I promise that when I am through with what I have to say, I will grant you an interview. But for now, let an old woman speak."

Her reference to her age earns her good-natured laughter from the guests and one-by-one cameras and microphones are lowered.

"That's Stacey Dinardo," murmurs Tom in my ear. I move my gaze to where he points and observe a beautiful young woman, standing among the group of reporters.

"Who's she?"

"Remember Claire's reference to Ruby Myles," answers Tom. "She's the daughter."

"Really?" I narrow my eyes and consider Stacey carefully. "Interesting," I murmur.

"You have no idea *how* interesting," Tom answers, piquing my interest. But when I ask him to elaborate, he shushes me.

Spotting Stacey, Anna-Claire inclines her head gently. I watch as Stacey demurely returns the nod. There's no doubt in my mind from observing their fleeting but meaningful silent exchange that whoever this Stacey is, she is of import to Anna-Claire.

Having the room's full attention, Anna-Claire's tone loses some of its former gentleness. She pulls her thin frame into a steady stance, bracing herself for strength, and begins in a calm but direct approach. "I realize that many of you have wondered why I have chosen to remain silent and withdrawn from public scrutiny." The tiniest of smiles creases her face as she acknowledges expressions of open curiosity and expectations. Continuing, she says, "As everyone knows forty years ago I lost my husband and daughter. At the time I was spared dying in that collision because I had remained at home to give an interview. When they died, I made the decision to live my life away from the public eye." She takes a deep breath, thinks for a moment and then says, "Over the years there has been much speculation as to why I chose to seclude myself and I'm not here tonight to weigh the pros and cons of that decision. However, there is something that I would like to clarify. Contrary to much speculation, I did not withdraw from life – I withdrew from public life to cope with the grief I experienced in losing my husband Drew and daughter Emily. But," she says with quiet emphasis, "not once during my self-imposed seclusion did I ever stop appreciating life and doing all that I could, through my writing and photography, to express my admiration for how we communicate with one another and the importance for all of us to give dignity and appreciation for the life we enjoy."

Once again, guests enthusiastically clap. Anna-Claire's shoulders start to tremble and Marc Andre quickly moves to stand behind her. Placing a protective hand on her shoulder he signals that she need not continue. Briefly touching his hand and forgetting that she is within earshot of the microphone, she says, "No, Marc Andre. These people have a right to know. Thank you, my dear, but I must continue." Immediately, an expectant hush falls over the room. Glances are exchanged and people openly wait for what is going to happen next.

Marc Andre silently steps to Anna-Claire's side. Becky, noticing Anna-Claire's stress, says "She's going to overdo it. She has to quit now."

Josh puts out his hand, stopping her in midstep. "Let her speak, Becky. She needs to do this."

"For all these years, I have lived my life very simply," Anna-Claire says, looking straight at her audience. The atmosphere in the room is filled with an air of expectancy. "It was not until the consortium decided to hold this Gala that I had any reason to believe that I would not finish my days – as I have spent them for forty years – quietly and without recognition." With a slight smile, showing her awareness of the ironies in life, she continues, "One would think that an author or playwright would have seen all the earmarks of a new chapter or scene in what can be called the 'play' of life. To paraphrase an old saying, when one is too close to what is actually happening, one fails to see the events."

Motioning with a hand in the direction of Leen, Anna-Claire says, "When I first met Adrienne MacLeen she was helping a friend move into the house next door to where I live. She had no idea that I was Claire Holowitz and I ..." she pauses, "...had no idea that her life and the lives of her three closest friends would become so intertwined with mine." Her gaze sweeps the audience and she says, "Now I realize that by saying this, it won't take much for an astute reporter to find out where I do in fact live." With a winning smile, she says, "And I'm counting on all of you to respect that my private life – the lives of my neighbours and friends – will not become the focus of any media attention." She waits as murmurs of agreement filter through the audience and then, with a nod of appreciation, she says, "Thank you for your understanding."

Looking straight at where Leen, Amy, Becky, and I stand, Anna-Claire says, "These four remarkable women have brought laughter, wonder and life to me. I have come to view each of them as my own and fully appreciate life's irony in that these four women in becoming my family have helped to ease the pain and loss of my Emily." Raising her hand, she folds her thumb into the palm so that she is displaying four fingers. "One decade for each woman; each decade represents the cleansing of having lost so much forty years ago only to reclaim the gift of love, now, at this stage in my life." People strain to hear her next words, "Ladies and gentlemen, I present you my four daughters: Leen, Becky, Amy and Sarah. I ask that they join me here on this stage with their husbands so that I can share with you my joy and privilege of having them in my life."

Softly someone starts to clap. One-by-one, hands join to create an applause that practically reverberates against the walls and ceiling of the hall. We move in unison towards the stage as Anna-Claire waits for us to surround her in a semi-circle. When she resumes there is no smile, no hint of anything other than marked determination. Picking up on this new stance, the guests quieten and wait for her to say what she has come to say.

"I know that there has been much controversy concerning Adrienne MacLeen's not having been able to convince me to attend this Gala but ..." says Anna-Claire, motioning with a fluid hand movement to include her body, "as you can see, I am here."

Dulcey Griffin, Academy Award recipient for her lead in film version of *When Angels Weep* shouts, "And I for one am glad of that!" Within seconds, her endorsement is quickly followed with similar ones throughout the room.

Anna-Claire stands erect, quietly acknowledging their praise. When the applause and shouting dies down, she continues. "I came here today to set the record straight – to let you all know that Adrienne MacLeen has conducted herself honourably. She did not, as some may have implied," and here she casts a barely perceptible glance to where Don Harris stands trying without success to look innocent of her implied condemnation, "hide me from Scenes magazine personnel and Board of Directors." With quiet but emphatic articulation she says, "Leen – as Adrienne is known by her family, friends, and colleagues – honoured Scenes' original agreement to protect and to preserve my privacy." With a winning grin, she adds in a softer tone, Now, I don't know about all of you, but I do know that if I were choosing an agent to represent my interests in the media world I would want someone with the principles demonstrated by Adrienne MacLeen. She reached the goals of the consortium as is obvious tonight by the presence of all of you and in my humble opinion," she touches her chest lightly, "exceeded all expectations. I wish to make it perfectly clear that I have come here not out of inducement for the self-aggrandizement of any person working with Scenes, but because of her integrity." Leen's face flushes with embarrassment at the praise and the subsequent applause that it causes.

Taking a deep breath, Anna-Claire speaks so softy that people strain to hear her next words. "These women who stand at my side *are* my family. They stand with their husbands and I stand proudly with them. From this moment on, I want it to be known that my estate – such as it is aside from personal bequests – will be left to their care and in trust that my work with the Arts will continue long after I am gone. They will ensure that young artists, authors, actors, playwrights, and directors have a resource to which they can turn for support in the development of their careers and dreams. These four ladies – each representing one decade of my seclusion from public life – are the daughters of my heart and as such, I name them as my beneficiaries."

I gasp. Having had no knowledge of this twist of events, I'm completely overwhelmed by what Anna-Claire has announced. Becky, whose clinical training has ostensibly taught her to remain objective, gapes openly and Amy wears the expression of one who is completely dumbfounded.

Leen casts a glance at Marc Andre who mouths, "I didn't know."

Without losing momentum, Anna-Claire chuckles, "As you all see, this announcement is not what anyone of them expected." Laughter ripples throughout the hall.

"There are a few more things I wish to say," says Anna-Claire, "and then, I promise to stop talking and to let you all return to enjoying the evening, food, and company of one another. "There is a saying in the Arts that 'you must never forget the help you have received along the way and when life affords you the opportunity to help another artist, it is your duty to do so.' I would go so far as to say, it is a sacred duty. If we wish for the Arts to be our legacy to the generations who will follow us, we must nurture and safeguard it."

"Well-said," calls out Taylor. His endorsement is quickly echoed by several others.

Reaching for Amy's hand, Anna-Claire brings her to stand by the podium. "Some of you may have read in today's Arts and Entertainment sections of leading newspapers that Amy Keiffers is a new and exciting author. "It is my pleasure to introduce her." Smiling, Anna-Claire adds, "All of us in this room had to start our careers somewhere. All of us have received help along the way. No one person here tonight has achieved success without the belief of another person that they could do so. I believe in Amy Keiffers."

Red-faced, Amy smiles as photographers snap photos of her and Anna-Claire.

Moving away from the podium, Anna-Claire embraces each of us in turn and pausing in front of Marc Andre, she whispers, "Do you think Don Harris is getting the message that he – not Leen – is about to leave Scenes?"

"Loud and clear, Aunt Claire. You would have made a hell of a lawyer. You made a great summary to the jury of his peers." Winking, he adds, "Talk about *slam and dunk*."

Returning to the podium, Anna-Claire says, "There is one more thing I wish to address tonight and that has to do with my request to all of you. As Dr. Sutherland will verify," she nods towards Becky, "I need to have rest and quiet. I would ask that if any of you want to contact me that you do so through my lawyers, Marc Andre Aumount and Sarah Calder. Leen MacLeen will continue to represent me with respect to any media publications and she, along with Sarah Calder, Marc Andre Aumount, Dr. Amy Keiffers, and Dr. Becky Sutherland, will manage not only my personal estate but also that of what is to be called the Holowitz Foundation."

Taking a step backwards, Anna-Claire acknowledges the audience with a graceful nod and says, "Now, ladies and gentlemen, I will answer any questions you may have but please let me come down from this podium and mingle with you – my friends – and let us all celebrate what we *all* have achieved throughout our years together." Mischievously, she adds, "This old lady would welcome a drink." As Marc Andre and Joe help Anna-Claire step down from the stage, she leans her body close to them to help hide her fatigue.

Glancing quickly at Marc, Joe mouths, "She needs to rest." Immediately, they're surrounded by reporters and well-wishers. Becky steps up to her side and says, "Anna-Claire, you need to rest." She reaches for Anna-Claire's elbow, but stops as Anna-Claire says, "Becky, I need to answer their questions. I promised I would and I will do that before I leave tonight, but..." Anna-Claire smiles at the reporters and well-wishers crowding around her, "if everyone is agreeable I would like to sit down, have that drink I mentioned, and talk quietly amongst old friends. I think that will make my doctor happy and after a while, hopefully everyone will understand that I need to do as she has pointed out – rest."

Mike points to a nearby table. "How about sitting over there?" Signalling to a waiter he says, "Let's get you that drink and some hors d'oeuvres."

With an impish grin, Anna-Claire asks, "Do you think they'll have some cold shrimp with spicy sauce?"

Marc Andre leans close to Anna-Claire's ear and begins to whisper. Whatever he is saying has her full attention. I detect a hint of annoyance in her expression but she quickly recovers. Marc Andre says something else and Anna-Claire's eyes sweep the crowd gathering near here. For the next hour, despite Becky's occasional scowls, Anna-Claire satisfies the curiosity of reporters and poses for photos.

"So what you're saying Ms Holowitz," says a voice rising above the others, "is that you didn't isolate yourself from life but chose, instead, to live life and to write from that experience as opposed to using your fame to experience it." His face shows signs of a beard's shadow but there's no denying the keen glint in his eyes and the earnest appeal in his tone catches Anna-Claire's attention.

"What is your name?"

Young enough to show his eagerness to get a story but seasoned enough to have an air of confidence about him, he answers, "Tom Cleary, New York Times."

"Well, Tom Cleary, from the New York Times," answers Anna-Claire, "I think you could say that. I never was one to let life pass me by and fame, as you so aptly put it, does have a way of stopping one from just simply experiencing day-to-day pleasures."

"For example?" His question is asked impulsively before he has time to think about how abrupt or intrusive it might sound but it does not ruffle Anna-Claire's calmness.

Looking directly at Stacey Dinardo, Anna-Claire asks, "Stacey, do you know Mr. Cleary?"

Stacey who has been standing quietly at the edge of the crowd gathered around Anna-Claire smiles in response to Anna-Claire's acknowledgement. "Yes, Ms Holowitz, I do. He's a colleague."

"Well, then, let's not stand on formality," replies Anna-Claire, grinning openly at Ruby's daughter. Conversationally she says, "You're Ruby Myles daughter and, as everyone knows from my little speech, Ruby and I have been friends for many years. You could answer your friend's question as well as I can, with respect to whether or not I have been enjoying life. I have appreciated your tact and discretion over the years since you started your career in reporting. Never once have you done anything to compromise my solitude or impose on me for an interview despite my friendship with your mother."

Reporters rivet their attention on Stacey who stands silent and red-faced. One of the reporters blurts out, "You knew where she was?"

Anna-Claire reaches for Stacey's hand, "My dear, it is good to see you again. Your mother has kept me informed over the years of your growth but I think the last time I actually saw you, you still had braces on your teeth." Speaking to the other reporters, Anna-Claire says, "Yes, she knew where I was but she honoured her mother's and my friendship." With a winsome smile she adds, "Isn't that a mark of a good journalist; knowing when to be discreet."

It's subtle but I can see from the way Marc Andre lightly squeezes Anna-Claire's shoulder that he's pleased by her recognition of Stacey Dinardo. *Ah,* I think, *whatever he was whispering, it had to do with Stacey.* I can't help smiling at Anna-Claire's finesse. In one fell swoop, she is making a point of helping to establish Stacey's career as an ethical journalist.

On Becky's signal, Marc Andre steps forward and rests his arm around Anna-Claire's shoulders. "It's time for you to leave, Aunt Claire." With a glance brooking no opposition from the reporters and people gathered around he says, "It's been a big night for you."

This time, Anna-Claire puts up no argument and I can tell that she is grateful for his support as he helps her walk towards the exit. The rest of us follow in her wake, pausing here- and-there as she shakes hands and allows for photographers to quickly snap more photos.

Don Harris, realizing that he has no option other than to pretend that he is comfortable with the turn in the evening's events, ventures a smile in Anna-Claire's direction. Seeing Anna-Claire visibly tense, Amy quickly glances at Leen wondering what Anna-Claire's reaction will be. Realizing the potential for a full-scale confrontation, I ease my way to Anna-Claire's side and whisper, "Not here, Anna-Claire. He knows he's done. Everyone in this room knows he's finished."

For one, brief intense moment Anna-Claire lets her gaze settle on Harris. He flinches. Satisfied, Anna-Claire murmurs to me, "Very well."

Becky, Amy, and I leave as we came–with Anna-Claire. Joe, Mike, and Josh return with Leen and Marc Andre to help bring a good closure to the Gala.

Leen

"Well, that was quite the evening!" says Marc, as we wearily climb into the limousine.

"Did you know that she was coming?" I ask, wiping away strands of fallen hair.

Marc reaches for my hand. "I thought the video would be enough to thwart Harris' attempts to discredit you." With a tired sigh, he adds, "When Sarah called and said that she was insisting on coming, I counselled against it. But, as you've come to learn, Aunt Claire has a mind of her own and she decided that she would be the one to finally put to rest Harris's sniping comments about you not bringing her to the Gala."

I grimace. "He's going to be looking for my head on a platter tomorrow and is probably thinking right now, as I speak, about how to hold my execution."

"If I'm any judge of character," answers Marc Andre, "I'd place my money on his trying to devise a way to salvage his own career. Aunt Claire made it obvious that she supports you. He'll be lucky to find a job in the industry posting notices for the Want Ads sections." His comment brings a grin to my face.

"She really did a grand sweep of the hall with her exclusion of him in her speech. And, not once did she say anything directly about him."

As Hank pulls up to the hotel, the doorman steps forward to open the door. Putting his arm around my waist, Marc says, "She has always had a way of making her point and doing it with a flare."

As we walk across the lobby to the elevator, he adds, "It's been a long day, Leen, and tomorrow the papers will be heralding in the new queen of media and toasting the return of Claire Holowitz. I'd say the end result was even more then the consortium could have hoped for."

Chapter Thirty-eight

Leen

The two weeks following the Gala leaves me, Marc, and Sarah dealing with the Scenes' Board members, various reporters, and responding to queries for Claire Holowitz to appear on talk shows. All requests for a personal appearance are refused politely and firmly with us reaffirming Anna-Claire's request that she be left alone to deal with health matters. The Board members asked for Don Harris' letter of resignation and packed him off with a reasonable settlement from Scenes, which according to Sarah's account of the meeting, was more than he deserved. Marc agrees with her but recognizes the advantage of settling in order to not drag out Anna-Claire's involvement with as she refers to him, *that odious man."*

Anna-Claire settles into her life and now exposed identity with more tranquillity than any of us could have expected. With Amy at her side, she continues to take short daily walks and stops to chat with neighbours whom she'd known for years. As if by tacit agreement they in turn, after expressing their pleasure at having read her novels or seen her plays or photo exhibits, carry on as if Claire Holowitz is merely a pseudonym for the woman whom they know as Anna.

By the end of the month, Anna-Claire's continued weight loss and increasing tiredness force her to stay inside and rest. Sitting at the kitchen table, she and I continue to discuss her stories and the events of our lives; recalling moments of pain and desperation and celebrating moments of ecstasy and joy. Like mother and daughter, friends and confidants, mentor and student we pass our time together.

On one of those occasions, I sip my coffee and casually ask, "Anna-Claire, why did you do it?"

"Do what?" she asks, resting her mug on the table. "I'm not sure I understand what you mean."

"Of course you do," I answer. "Why, after knowing that none of us would break our confidentiality agreements, did you risk coming to the Gala?"

"It wasn't a risk," answers Anna-Claire. "It was a decision. Once made, I was comfortable with doing what was necessary."

"You didn't have to," I say, not for the first time. "It took so much out of you physically."

Anna-Claire chortles with smug satisfaction. "It was worth it to see the look on that pompous man's face. In fact, it helped me to demonstrate something that I've always firmly believed in."

Curious, I ask, "And, that is?"

"Life has a way of throwing curveballs just when you think you've got things figured out," replies Anna-Claire. "It can be a simple moment, a catastrophic event, or serendipity, but in a split second, one's whole life can be altered. It can be cruel and relentless – lashing one as if no amount of penance can undo the sin that has provoked such pain and loss. It can be kind – beyond our wildest expectations, acting like a teasing supplicant and enticing us to risk again."

Sighing softly, she says, "Defining moments. Everyone experiences them – but everyone deals with them in various ways." She pauses, and then adds earnestly, "Remember this, Leen. No matter what life throws at you – you and you alone, have the ability to let it make or break you."

I let her phrase settle in my mind and practice the sound of it as I say, "A defining moment." I nod, understanding what she is telling me.

"I gave because that was all I had to give," says Anna-Claire, referring to the endowments and charities she has sponsored over the years. "The giving helped to ease the pain of loss. Like a narcotic, it soothed me and provided a false sense of comfort, but Leen …" she takes my hand and holds it between hers, "it was not life. There was no courage in hiding. It was survival. You and the others have helped me to find life again and in so doing, celebrate it." She shrugs and with a gentle smile, says, "You could say that meeting all of you was one of my defining moments."

༄

Amy

As winter gives way to spring, snow begins to melt and tiny buds start to venture forth in tentative spurts as if testing the capricious tendencies of mother nature. Anna-Claire and I are spending our morning revising my notes and discussing the newfound pressures of my life in dealing with an agent and publisher's expectations and schedules.

Looking out the window, Anna-Claire says, "I have always loved spring. It is a time of hope, renewal and new life."

"You'll soon be talking about getting flowers planted," I answer. "I think this year I'll follow your example and plant a small garden. Have a few tomatoes, peppers, herbs."

"There's something to be said for getting one's hands dirty, caked with soil and watching one's own garden bloom."

"You like gardening," I answer. "Plus, you're good at it. This will be my first attempt."

"Oh you'll like it fine enough, too," Anna-Claire assures me. "It's a license for an adult to play in the mud, just as we did when we were children."

Laughing I reply, "Well, then, if I'm a failure as a hobby farmer I can at least take comfort in that I can make mud pies without looking as if I've gone senile."

"I've often thought that senility is just God's way of reminding us that children shall lead the way to happiness," answers Anna-Claire. "That is, until they lose their innocent acceptance of all things and people."

I let the statement hang in the space between us as I process the thought. Finally, I ask, "Are you suggesting that senility is a good thing?"

"It's neither good nor bad," answers Anna-Claire. "It just is." Looking at me she says, "Think about it Amy. When a person is senile or has dementia; they aren't aware of the moment. They just enjoy the happening of the moment. A child doesn't stop to think about what others may think about his or her actions – a child simply acts."

"But acting without thought to consequences can be dangerous," I counter. "A child may want to play with fire but that doesn't mean we let him or her do it."

"Exactly," responds Anna-Claire. "That's why we have care-givers for children, for people with dementia, the old, and the infirm – to protect them. But stopping someone from doing something harmful doesn't preclude the fact that they can experience happiness in the moment. A child is free to enjoy, to relish, and to experience the wonders of sensations – the taste of fruit, the sense of achievement in taking that first step and going beyond boundaries." Her eyes light up with sheer fascination as her imagination brings images to her mind. "The possibilities for what we can do if only we believe in ourselves," she says, "are endless."

She stops abruptly and briefly closes her eyes. I think that she is thinking of more examples but when I see the grimace of pain, I move quickly from my chair. "Anna-Claire," I demand, "what's wrong?"

Breathing laboured, she says, "Please call Becky and Dr. Anderson." She takes a breath. "Leen, Sarah, and Marc Andre."

Fighting my impulse to panic, I speed dial Becky's office and without preamble with Joan, I say, "This is Amy Keiffers, I need to talk with Becky right now. It's urgent." Becky came on the phone almost immediately.

"Amy, what's wrong?"

"It's Anna-Claire." I try to sound calm but know that my voice betrays my rising anxiety. "She's sitting at the kitchen table and asked me to call you and Dr. Anderson. Becky," I lower my voice, "she doesn't look good. All the colour has drained from her face."

"Call Dr. Anderson," orders Becky, "and help get her to the couch. If she's too weak, lie her down on the kitchen floor and get her a pillow and blanket. George can get there before I can but I'll call 911 and arrange for an ambulance. Stay calm, Amy. She can't know that you're upset. Don't worry about calling Leen and Sarah. I'll get a hold of them."

༄

Becky

I rush out of the office, calling over my shoulder to Joan to cancel all of my appointments and to notify the hospital that I won't be there for my rounds. Dialling 911 emergency on my cell I give the operator Anna-Claire's address and urge them to dispatch immediately. Climbing into my car, I call Josh and tell him what's happening and get him to call Leen and Sarah. I force myself to concentrate, bitterly resenting the traffic.

By the time I arrive at Anna-Claire's, Dr. Anderson and the paramedics are there. Anna-Claire has already been transferred to a gurney with her eyes closed and face drained of colour. Amy collapses into my arms, her face wet from tears. "She's barely holding on," she stammers.

Finishing up with the paramedics, Dr. Anderson motions them to wait and addresses me. "As I was saying to Amy," he says, "Claire is barely holding on. I've given her morphine to ease the pain but she's been refusing to go to the hospital; insisting that she wants to wait for her family."

Nodding my understanding that Anna-Claire is in her final hours, I reply. "If it's her choice to remain here and if you think that nothing further can be done at the hospital then we'll make her comfortable in her own bed and give her around-the-clock assistance."

Physician to physician we meet one another's gaze. He sighs deeply, makes a decision and says, "I'll write a prescription for more morphine and if she needs more than that you can call me or order what you think she needs." He lowers his voice, "She's fading in and out of consciousness. Some of it is the drug ..." He pauses and then delivers the words no physician likes to utter, "It's time for her family to make their peace with this and to let her go with dignity."

Amy's muffled sobs fill the room. Speaking softly to her, I say, "Amy, Dr. Anderson is right. It's time. We all knew this day would come. Right now, we have to be strong for her and not let her see us crying. She wants and deserves her family around her. She's waiting to say goodbye to all of us. There is nothing more any of us can do other than to make her comfortable. Do you understand what I'm saying to you?"

Eyes brimming with tears, Amy answers, "I know that Becky. It's just so damn hard. I know what we have to do and I held it together until she fell asleep but just knowing that she's going to die is tearing me apart."

Cradling Amy almost as if she's a child, I check my own grief and look over her head at Dr. Anderson. Both of us have seen our fair share of dying throughout our careers, but neither of us wants to deal with this loss – the loss of our friend.

Speaking softly, George reminds Amy, "You have to remember that although she looks like she's sleeping, she may just be resting and she'll hear you. Claire would not want you to be upset."

"You've known her many years," chokes out Amy, "how can you just stand there and be so clinical?"

Expression compassionate, George answers carefully. "I am clinical. Right now, as her physician and friend, that's what I must be and all that I can do for her. We've had many discussions about this day and Claire always said that she wanted me to be both a friend and doctor. I'm not without emotion but I know that she deserves to have her wishes respected and she knows that I'll do my grieving – in my own way – after I have done what I can for her."

"Amy," I say, "we're not without feelings. We're trained to deal with death as part of life and to give it the dignity that it deserves. Anna-Claire has said many times that she wants us to send her out smiling because then the angels will receive her in good humour."

My reference to Anna-Claire's joke about angels brings a weak smile to Amy's face. Pulling herself together, she wipes her tears with the palm of her hand and lips trembling, admits, "You're right, Becky. She did say that." She attempts to smile. "Along with wanting an Irish wake and a stiff glass of scotch."

Our heads turn as Joe, Marc Andre, Leen, and Sarah rush in. Marc Andre goes directly to the gurney and lifts Anna-Claire's hand into his. Looking down at her, he remains there for a few minutes as we silently watch him grieve. Leen rests her hand on his shoulder and he slowly moves back.

Dr. Anderson tells the paramedics to take Anna-Claire up to her bedroom and Sarah rushes up the stairs to ready her bed. When she's placed on her bed, Anna-Claire's eyes flutter open, her gaze falling on Marc Andre. Struggling, she says, "You are the son I would have loved to have had. I am proud of you."

Swallowing hard, Marc Andre replies softly, "I love you Aunt Claire."

"It's time. I've had a good life." She takes a deep breath. "Where's Emile?"

"On his way," answers Marc Andre. "Josh too."

"Good," Anna-Claire speaks so softly, that we strain to hear her words. "Your father was never very good at being on time." Her words amuse her and she coughs as she gently chuckles at her own joke.

Eyes glistening, Marc Andre grins. "Remember how my mother loved to tell the story of how he was late for their wedding and how he missed arriving at the hospital in time when she went into labour. She always said that time meant nothing to him."

Anna-Claire smiles weakly. "I must say that this scene would be quite the thing for one of my plays." Her gaze drifts to Amy. "Work it into one of your novels." She draws in a breath and slowly exhales. "It'll be like I've helped you to edit a scene."

Leen adjusts the pillows, asking, "Would you like another blanket or pillow?" The doctor part of me thinks, *How many times have I heard people ask or say something completely meaningless when facing death? Something so ordinary; as if by doing so the shock and impending finality of death can be held at bay. Anna-Claire is dying and an extra pillow or blanket won't stop that but in having something to do – the action of doing – Leen is struggling to cope with the reality of the moment.*

Gathering her breath, Anna-Claire barely sips of water from the glass that Sarah holds for her. "No, I'm good." Again, I think, *The action of doing. Wanting to help but not being able to ...*

Anna-Claire closes her eyelids. No one speaks. The wheezing of her lungs punctuates the silence that fills the room – broken only when Josh and Emile enter.

"Claire," Emile's voice sounds gruff as he chokes back his rising emotions. "I'm here, just like I said I'd be." His shoulders rise and lower with the weight of immeasurable loss and human fragility as he says, "But you promised me you wouldn't leave me alone."

Anna-Claire slowly blinks. Pulling upon something from deep within, she finds the strength to answer, "I'm not leaving you alone, Emile. You have my family here with you." Faint traces of the teasing voice she always used to irk Emile are evident. "It's all about timing."

Emile practically sinks down onto the chair Marc Andre places for him beside the bed. Resigned, he grasps her hand. "Rest old girl, we're all here. Just like you wanted."

Dr. Anderson listens to her chest with his stethoscope and feels for a radial pulse. Moving his fingertips to her carotid artery he purses his mouth and shakes his head slowly at me.

Facing the others I say softly, "Let her know that you love her."

Stepping back from Anna-Claire's bedside I watch as Leen bends to kiss Anna-Claire's forehead and stroke her hair. Amy and Sarah do the same. She's now beyond hearing. Tears streaming down, Marc Andre stands beside his father who has not let go of Anna-Claire's hand.

The unmistakable death rattle fills the room with its guttural sound. *Agonal respiration*, I think. NO ... I inwardly scream; rejecting my clinical training. But, it is time. I've heard it said that the last breath is held to give to God as a person surrenders his or soul but those thoughts belong to the religious. I am a doctor, trained to save lives when I can and to accept death as a natural process. One is born and one dies. Such is life. "God, if you exist," I whisper, "treat Anna-Claire kindly."

Dr. Anderson places his stethoscope on her chest and raises it once more to her neck. Pulling the earpieces away from his ears, his shoulders start to shake as the physician gives way to the friend allowing himself to grieve.

Chapter Thirty-nine

Leen

The funeral for Claire Holowitz is huge. Personages from all around the world travel to attend or send their condolences. Famous and not famous attend. The eulogy is given in part by those who knew her professionally and those who have known her as Anna Wright.

Marc, Josh, Mike, Joe, and the twins are pallbearers. Sarah, Becky, Amy, and I walk solemnly behind her casket helping Emile to his seat in the pew. Each of us silently reliving memories of how Anna-Claire touched our lives.

We listen as the rabbi, joined by the priest, speak the words and give the blessings necessary to commend one's soul to God.

We watch as her casket is carried to the waiting hearse and stand vigil at the curb side as it drives away – lost in the moment of trying to say goodbye; wanting to hang on to the view of the slow moving vehicle as if, by some miracle, we can bring her back to us.

"What do we do now?" Amy looks at Sarah.

Still watching the diminishing hearse, Sarah answers, "First, we follow her to her resting place and then, we hold that Irish wake for Anna-Claire. We celebrate life as she wanted us to."

Linking my arm through Sarah's and Amy's with Becky adding hers to Amy's we form a human chain. "Tomorrow we'll all wake up with terrible hangovers."

"That we will," agrees Becky. "But we'll know we did as she asked."

I smile as a quiet peace falls over me. I know it is a trick of mind but I almost feel as if Anna-Claire is here with us.

In silence, we walk away from the curb and climb into the waiting limousines. We're going to follow her casket to the graveyard. As per the instructions left in her will, there will be no tombstone erected until one year has passed. Such had been her wish.

In one year, we will once again gather – and then, it will be to formally say 'good-bye' and honour her legacy.

Epilogue

Leen

Clasping my pearl necklace around my neck, I reflect on the last twelve months.

Amy and Mike got married in July and she has started on her first round of book tours. Just last week her novel, 'Jake's Laundry' topped the best sellers list. Still retaining her post at the university, she has reduced her academic commitment to part-time and she uses the new-found freedom from the academic world to work on the drafts for her second novel.

Shortly after Anna-Claire's death, Becky and Josh began the process of adoption and are now expecting to become parents before the month ends. Anxious to become parents they willingly agreed, when asked by Children's Services, to take twin girls who have been in foster homes since three months old and are now turning five years old.

Last fall, with considerable pride and many tears, Sarah sent her grown sons off to American universities – Josh is in California and Jake is in Boston. She now heralds in every holiday as an excuse to bring them home and send them back with enough food to feed their dorm mates. She and Marc continue to manage the legal aspects of the Holowitz Foundation.

Marc Andre and I continue to grow in our love with each passing day. We have our ups and our downs but we always have the knowledge that nothing will ever cause either one of us to fail one another. I often think of Anna-Claire's advice to me on the night before my wedding. As she helped clasp the pearls she had given me as a wedding gift, she said, "Love is not easy. Love is not fair. Love can be so strong that it hurts to love because you risk losing your inner self. Trust in one another. Have the courage to tell one another when and why you are upset. Mean it when you say you will love forever and mean it when you say you can tell me anything. Know the beauty of a smile and cherish the gentleness of a touch. Be strong enough to forgive and to allow for human frailty. Speak the truth and hear the tears of words unspoken when a heart is breaking. You mightn't be able to put all the pieces back together but if you are blessed with true love, you will find a way to move forward. When you love – truly love – you must love forever."

I continue to work at Scenes and without Don there to make my days impossible, I look forward to each morning and each new challenge. In my capacity as CEO of the Claire Holowitz Foundation, I have added three new endowments for the Arts in the forms of bursaries and scholarships.

The Board, which consists of Sarah, Amy, and Becky as full voting members, have established the funds for a new wing to the Ottawa General Hospital for Alzheimer patients, a wing for the Children's hospital and one for a new cancer clinic. These are things that Anna-Claire would have wanted to see done.

"Ready?" Marc's voice interrupts my thoughts.

Turning to face my husband, I answer, "It's time."

Moving towards the door, I say, "There's something that we all need to say today, Marc."

He raises a curious eyebrow.

"It's not good-bye."

Settling himself into the driver's seat of our car, he turns sideways and waits for me to finish the thought I'd started at the door. "What do you want to say …" he asks, "if not good-bye?"

Smiling, I answer, "I want to say thank you." I pause. "Do you think she'll know?"

Backing the car out of the driveway, Marc reaches to touch my hand. "You can count on it, Leen. She always knew what we were thinking."

Afterword

Thank you for allowing me to share the lives of Claire, Anna, Leen, Amy, Becky, and Sarah with you.

I hope that Leen's 'Search for Claire Holowitz' has been credible enough to intrigue you and that – as you read the novel – you were able to relate to their characterizations, the events and life's happenings they shared, their dialogue, and those moments in life that are serendipity – when you are meant to know someone and your life changes for the better.

Those of us who have known what it is to be loved, to lost love, and to risk loving again, know the importance of friendship.

Wherever you are ... may you always have the comfort of friendship.

Helen Hansen

CPSIA information can be obtained at www.ICGtesting.com
Printed in the USA
LVOW012244270213